# MAN'S BOOK

# THE SAVAGE SKY
Richard Townshend Bickers

★

# THE MANTRACKERS
William Mulvihill

★

# THE CLYDESIDERS
Hugh Munro

★

also
INCIDENT AT PROJECT FOUR
a story by
Michael Barrett

ODHAMS PRESS LIMITED
LONG ACRE, LONDON

S.1162.SB.
MADE AND PRINTED IN
GREAT BRITAIN BY ODHAMS (WATFORD) LTD.
WATFORD, HERTS.

# CONTENTS

# THE SAVAGE SKY

## Richard Townshend Bickers

*"The Savage Sky" is published by
Robert Hale Ltd.*

## The Author

Richard Townshend Bickers was born in Assam and educated in England at Monkton Coombe and St. Paul's. He has lived in India, Italy, Hong Kong and Malaya and has travelled in many other countries. He served as a regular officer in the R.A.F. from the outbreak of war until 1957, but his chief interest has always been writing. He has so far produced about one hundred short stories, many radio plays and features, some television plays and twenty-six novels. The first two dozen were paper-backs; *The Guns Boom Far* and *The Savage Sky* are published in hard covers.

He is also a distinguished athlete, having been in the R.A.F. Pentathlon team, the events in which contest are riding, shooting, fencing, swimming and running; and represented various R.A.F. formations at boxing, tennis, rugger and athletics.

He admires courage, enterprise and self-respecting independence; and thinks the world needs more people with genuine good manners. His own deepest concern is a compassion for all fellow creatures, especially the afflicted and the frightened.

*To*
MIDGE

# CHAPTER ONE

THE young woman looked up from the chickens she was feeding and watched a white-camouflaged Wellington fly over the cliff on which her cottage stood.

Eight hundred feet above, its pilot rocked the aircraft's wings twice and she waved in the thin January sunlight.

A four-year-old boy came running from the kitchen door, looking after the Wellington and waving both arms. "I wish daddy'd do dives on the house, like Uncle Nig does in the Seafire."

"Daddy'll dive on *you* when he comes home, if he looks down and sees you in the garden instead of at your lessons."

"How many eggs today, mummy?"

"Six. So I'm going to take two to Aunty Melanie, for her and Uncle Nig. If you hurry up with your sums, you can come with me. . . ."

"You never leave me alone in the house, anyway. . . ." He scampered away, laughing at her mock-ferocious dart.

Cynthia Gretton watched him for a moment, smiling. When she looked again for the Wellington, it was a small cross with upper wing surfaces reflecting the light as it banked far out over the estuary and turned for the open sea. The smile went from her face until she reminded herself that at least Paul, her husband, was only on stand-by today; he was not putting himself on ops. again till tomorrow. Unless one of the day's operational aircraft became unserviceable, he would be home to supper. With four extra unrationed eggs in her larder, she felt almost dizzy at the numerous culinary choices before them. She began humming as she scattered the last of the corn among her hens.

Walking back to the cottage she looked across the meadows and treetops towards a squat, grey stone building a mile away, wondering whether some situation was brewing in there which would snatch the stand-by aircraft out to hunt U-boats in the Atlantic that night, after all.

\*      \*      \*

11

From the old farmhouse the Operations Room staff could watch the airfield.

For two hundred years the same Cornish family had built and lived in it: close to their pastures and well above the flood level in bad winters. In January 1944, it was the co-ordinating centre for R.A.F. Tawmouth, whose three Wellington squadrons flew from the aerodrome on the estuary's western shore: because it was far enough from the station to be safe in an air raid, yet close enough to keep intimate, even visual contact with it.

The men and women who worked in the old house now went often to the windows or to stand in the open front door, for a moment, in the midst of their unending busy-ness. Not to survey the farmland, but to scan the sky; looking at the clouds; seeking the aircraft that flew home from ten-hour patrols over the Bay of Biscay. To watch white Wellingtons take off from the black runways slashed across the floor of the green valley; to focus binoculars on their identification letters as the machines stood among the three green-brown-and-black camouflaged hangars with fitters and riggers working on them.

Along the southern boundary of the aerodrome, in sand-bagged bays, a score of smaller aeroplanes caught the sun on the perspex of their cockpit canopies: Seafires, belonging to the Fleet Air Arm Operational Training Flight; the sailors were clannish, and touchy about their fighters which flew sorties of a mere hour or so. In the bar of the Officers' Mess they wrangled fairly amiably with some of the youngest R.A.F. pilots; when both parties drank too much, there was horse-play in the wooden-hutted bedrooms which the Navy irritatingly insisted on calling "cabins"; and the Navy's internecine disaffection, which sprang from the fact that their Commanding Officer was a regular lieutenant, but their best instructor and most experienced operational pilot, a Volunteer Reserve lieutenant, was incomprehensible to the democratic Air Force.

In the Operations Room itself, which gave its name to the whole organization contained in the farm building, Flying Officer Gillam looked up from the navigation chart on which he was pencilling a new set of patrol lines. He saw the shadow of Wing Commander Gretton's aircraft flit over the field on the other side of the lane in front of the Ops. Room. A few seconds later there was a roar as another Wellington swept low over the roof.

"Missed again," Gillam said casually.

Squadron Leader Stevenson grunted, grimaced, but did not

reply. Rising quickly from his chair on the controller's dais at one end of the long room, he strode to the window. Then he grumbled "B Baker" and turned to look at the blackboard, beside Gillam's table, on which were written the details of crews and aircraft on operations and stand-by.

"I'm always telling Trevor Walford he'll take our chimneys off one day." Stevenson tugged his moustache, annoyed.

Gillam smiled. "You brief him to fly at five hundred feet. He says there's no point in climbing even that high till he's on his patrol line."

Stevenson returned to *The Times* on his desk. His navigator persisted: "Trevor's bloody keen, sir; that's the first air test of the day. . . ."

"His squadron commander's was the first, Charles."

"Oh, Wingco. Gretton doesn't count; he's . . . he's . . . setting a good example," Gillam ended lamely. What else could he say without incurring a snub? Stevenson was only a wartime officer, like himself, who revelled in the good-fellowship of being called "Steve" by his juniors, off duty; but he appreciated a fairly frequent "sir" on duty and would certainly rub his rank in if a flying officer criticized a wing commander. Yet Gillam had faltered as much from indecision as from prudence; for he was not sure what he did think of 1111 Squadron's Commanding Officer. He admired and respected him, but resented his stiffness; and suspected that he lacked a sense of humour. They were near enough the same age to have been friends in normal times, but their disparity in rank and duties made him feel almost ignorant and ineffectual by comparison with the other man.

He took off his glasses and sat for a minute with his hands cupped over his eyes, resting them from the strain of close work by artificial light. The Ops. Room navigator's table was in a dark corner and the small window in the house's thick wall opposite was inadequate.

Charles Gillam would not have noticed his eyes growing tired if he had been allowed to work over his charts at the navigator's place in a Wellington—or any other aeroplane. He would not have been aware of eye strain if he was allowed to sit in a gun turret or operate a Morse key or the radar. For the first three years, after joining the R.A.F. on the day before war was declared, he had made no application for a commission, believing that his chances of passing for air crew were greater while he remained in the ranks. At last rejection for flying even under the newly relaxed visual standards for some air crew categories, he had learned to live with his disappointment. He put on his glasses, rubbed the flattened bridge of his nose, thought how glad he was that he could at least look back on three years' undefeated middle-weight boxing for Oxford, wished he could have two minutes in the ring with a German U-boat captain, and resumed his work.

Stevenson, who was fond of his navigator and knew why he had leaped to the defence of the cheerful young Walford, who certainly needed none, turned to the fat sergeant lounging against the wall with his chair tilted back, next to him. "Why haven't we had any tea, Sergeant Murch?"

Murch reluctantly let *The Daily Mirror* drop a few inches. "I don't know, sir." His Lancashire flatness was high-pitched and hopeless. "It's the Waafs, like...."

"Go and chase them, then. You're supposed to be a senior N.C.O." From his loathing of Murch, Stevenson added: "At least, for the time being...."

The sergeant scraped his chair noisily on the dais's boards, provoking a glower and moustache-tug from the controller. He rolled towards the door sucking his teeth furiously. Gillam marvelled at his ability to express dumb insolence by the mere slouch of his back and unwillingness of his gait.

An instant later there was the sound of remonstrance, answered by the yap of an indignant W.A.A.F.

"He found a scapegoat in the hall, it seems, Steve." (They were alone.)

"Useless character. One of the Group's throw-outs. I'll swear he only got his third tape through a slip of the pen at Records."

"You're Chief Controller; why let him come on your watch?"

"It only happens when one of the other assistants is on leave. Thank God."

The door swung open, struck the corner of the dais and re-bounded. Sergeant Murch sidled round it, carrying a dented metal tray on which were three cups filled to the brim with dark tea.

Stevenson rustled his *Times*. "Why didn't you tell a W.A.A.F. or an airman to bring it in, Sergeant?"

"You know what they are, sir. Quicker to do it meself."

"It's not your job. Your job is to see that the erks *do* do theirs...."

"Sir." Resignation was added to implied insolence.

Gillam involuntarily sympathized with the oppressed. Not

because the latter deserved it, but because he was so pathetic and unworthy an object for the squadron leader's lash.

The sergeant balanced the tray on the edge of the long ledge which formed the desk he shared with the controller. It needed only a feather weight to tip it to the floor. He put a cup on the clean chart with which the navigator was working. Though the latter snatched it up as quickly as he could without slopping its contents, it left a spreading ring of tea on the white paper.

"Look out, Sergeant Murch. Damn! You've ruined half an hour's work and I probably won't have time to make it up before Group come panicking through with the ops. orders. . . . ."

Murch's piggy eyes gleamed, downcast. "Very sorry, sir. . . ."

"Leave it alone!" Gillam was just in time to sweep aside the handkerchief with which damage was about to be spread.

Squadron Leader Stevenson folded his *Times*, stood up, stretched, tucked his stomach in consciously, puffed his chest, and put his hands on his hips. "Have you got the total number of serviceable aircraft from 1111 yet, Sergeant?"

"No, sir. Not yet, sir. The squadron said they'd phone it through at ten-thirty."

This was routine and Stevenson knew it, but the tone in which he said "Oh!" would have drawn invective from a Trappist. Gillam felt himself flush.

All three of them knew that the implied contempt and lack of confidence in a subordinate were unfair; angry with himself, the controller snapped: "Don't clutter the line now. I want to talk to 1111 myself."

The navigator awarded him ten out of ten for neat extrication from an awkward situation of his own making, and carried his tea into the room next door. This, the Intelligence Office, combined for him the fascination of a chamber of horrors with the mystery of an esoteric cult.

From the ceiling hung models of German aircraft which attacked the Wellingtons over the Atlantic and the Bay of Biscay; long-endurance Kuriers, and fighters based on Brest and St Nazaire. There were photographs on the walls, of each type of U-boat, E-boat, flak-ship and merchantman; of destroyers and cruisers and battleships. There were maps of enemy fighter dispositions and of flak belts. There was, in fact, exhibited, every sort of lethal discouragement to the Coastal Command aviator.

Besides this display of hazards, there were the "valuable and attractive items" which provoked any right-thinking person's cupidity. High-powered binoculars for issue to crews before a sortie; iron rations packed in plastic boxes and flaunting their unknown lures—pemmican and benzedrine, water-purifying tablets and malted milk pills; maps printed on silk scarves, compasses concealed in items of apparel. And a demijohn of rum, ostensibly to warm the cockles of chilled and weary air crews being de-briefed, but not unknown as a solace for the duty Intelligence Officer on a winter night-watch; and for the duty controller and navigator if they were his friends.

Most alluring of all was the miasma of portentous secrecy which (quite rightly) enveloped the Intelligence Room and those who worked there. Gillam said that if you went in to ask what was showing at the camp cinema, you got the wrong answer—in case the true one should reach the ears of a Nazi agent and do irreparable damage to the war effort!

Voices speaking into telephones were hushed. Feet trod quietly. Sentences were left unfinished and communication was by allusion and the swift picking up of threads, which left the uninitiated bereft and bemused.

Gillam had only got as far as the first exchange of banter which was customary between "The Spies" and the rest of the station, when he heard boots hurrying to the door of the Ops. Room and returned quickly. Hasty feet from upstairs always meant an urgent signal.

A runner from the Signals Traffic Office flung open the door and thrust a signal form at the controller.

The navigator and the controller's assistant watched impatiently while Stevenson read the message twice, tugged his moustache and frowned. Gillam's outstretched hand was imploring. At last the controller gave him the signal.

A Sunderland flying boat from neighbouring St Trewin had reported its attack on a U-boat. But an unsuccessful attack. The U-boat was still on the surface.

Stevenson, Gillam, even Sergeant Murch, knew and could visualize the implications of the brief message. The big U-boat, insolently confident of its armour plating and heavy guns, refusing to dive in the face of the big, slow flying-boat's depth charges and .303 machine guns. Shooting back with 37 mm. and 20 mm. cannon and heavy machine guns; at least two of each, on the bridge and either for'ard or aft of it also. The Sunderland reported damage to its starboard outer engine and casualties among the crew.

Gillam indicated this short battle by sticking a small, red sub-marine-shaped symbol in the place where it had been fought, on the map which covered the end wall opposite the controller's dais. In the three minutes' action which he thus recorded, 3,000 lb of depth charges, costing about as much in sterling, had been dropped. Two German sailors had been killed and four wounded by the Sunderland's guns. The flying boat had been hit in one engine and forced to fly on only three. One of its air gunners had been killed and its navigator and second pilot mortally hurt. Yet, by the time the repercussions were felt and acknowledged in the Operations Room at R.A.F. Tawmouth, all this tragedy, terror and courage, this story of violent widowing and orphaning, was reduced to a small metal plaque mass-produced at fourpence a time.

The U-boat had been identified by its attackers as U 306, which Intelligence knew was bound for its base in Lorient.

Sergeant Murch had barely taken away the empty cups and started to write down, by telephone, the aircraft states of the three squadrons stationed at Tawmouth, when the Signals runner came tumbling downstairs again.

Gillam put down his pencil and ruler, took the signal after Stevenson had read it, and swore.

The crippled Sunderland, having lumbered up to three thousand feet to hide in cloud, had been intercepted by a Focke-Wulf Kurier; a huge, four-engined aircraft whose black fuselage emerging from the empty sky was all the more terrifying for its hideous shape and astonishing endurance. These enemy aircraft gave the impression of being inescapable and inexorable, so far did they fly from their bases. British crews, seeing one approach from seaward when they themselves were six hours from land, felt their morale sag.

The message that Gillam held in his hand read "Emergency Air Attack".

*　　*　　*

In the grey sky above the grey sea, five hundred miles south-west of Land's End, the Sunderland, with both starboard engines stopped now and the wing on that side afire, staggered into a wisp of cloud.

Above and behind it, closing the range fast, the Kurier's guns hammered at the port inner engine. The three hundred yards between the two machines were laced with tracer. In the hull of the Sunderland a gunner reeled back screaming with his entrails uncoiling about his feet.

The flying boat fell out of cloud. The Kurier pulled away momentarily when the British rear gunner found his mark on its cockpit, and, amid shattered instruments, the German first pilot collapsed over his control column, decapitated by a burst of machine-gun bullets.

The Sunderland slumped into a sideslip, the altitude falling off so fast that its crew were lifted off their feet. Its captain saw the line of his wings level off as he and his dying second pilot flung their combined weight on the controls. The bow slammed into the water, the captain cut his switches and the Kurier banked in ugly triumph, raking the wallowing hull with fire. It came too low and the turrets of the flying boat blasted back, driving it finally away.

Five minutes later, when the six survivors were in their dinghy, still made fast to the port wing root, the wet, rounded deck of U 306 slithered to the surface in a millrace of white foam and her bows turned towards the bobbing yellow rubber boat. The wireless operator scrambled back to send one more message.

\*       \*       \*

The Signals Section was on the upper floor of the Operations Room building.

Once, on its uneven board floor, cumbersome wardrobes and dressing tables, washstands and bulky beds had stood in the same places for a generation or two before anyone thought of moving or replacing them.

Now, wireless receivers and Morse transmitting keys, teleprinters and de-coding machines whistled and buzzed and clattered and clanked all day and all night.

There were other noises too; confidential whisperings, an occasional giggle, quick laughter. The monastic world of down-stairs gave way, up here, to feminine influence. An unwarranted invasion, grumbled the veteran regulars; but even they, weathered by arid years in Iraq and on the North-West Frontier, toughened by recruit days of spartan living, soon accepted the cheerful, hard-working W.A.A.F. The oldest bachelor flight-sergeant no longer looked askance when a pretty girl, wriggling in concentration on Morse at twenty words a minute, showed an inch of soft white thigh above her stockings. Not always lisle, as the regula-tions laid down; and none of the male N.C.O.'s objected to the silk that hardly-come-by clothing coupons sometimes allowed.

Some of the bigger rooms had been divided by fibre board partitions. Every corner of the Signals Section was pervaded by the Service smells of boot leather, floor polish, hot metal, machine oil, carbon paper and serge; to which were added Californian Poppy, violet talcum powder and eau de cologne.

One small room was set apart from the rest and locked when empty. This was the Code and Cypher Office where two machines turned plain language into cyphers and de-cyphered incoming signals into more or less comprehensive English. It was the cell in which the Ops. building's Queen Bee, the duty "cypherine", served her King and country; received calls from bored or hopeful male officers (on a long night watch the plainest, brusquest W.A.A.F. officer was transmogrified into a creature of charm and beauty); wrote letters to her admirers (so they claimed—mostly it was to mum and dad and brother Jim); and slept fitfully on an ancient leather couch.

When the flying crews came rushing up from the station to attend briefing, those young women who could spare a few minutes from their Morse keys, headphones and teleprinters, found urgent tasks downstairs; which gratifyingly coincided with the entry of dashing young men in Irvine jackets and flying boots, who filled the hall and passage. Then followed a lot of bumping and squeaking and squeals of surprised recognition; of dating and name-swapping and healthy normality.

The signals that were received here told, every few days, of crises and sudden death; when one came from an aircraft in which a member of the crew was known to any of the W.A.A.F. or airmen on duty, it gave them a sense of personal involvement; but none of them had an accurate idea of what these cryptic messages portended or of the horrors which, seeming almost apocryphal while they remained unencountered, awaited the men who flew every day and night to hunt enemy submarines.

Squadron Leader Stevenson stuck his chest out. Gillam, who had his back to the door, knew that a woman must have appeared. Then he heard Section Officer McEwan say: "I've got a cypher here which you'll want to digest before briefing, sir." She glanced at the map. "Oh! I see there's been a sighting." She gave Stevenson the secret signal and walked across to look up at the aircraft state board on which Sergeant Murch had just finished deftly chalking; his lettering belied his sloth and appearance and had the even, handsome stamp of a trained signwriter.

Gillam pushed his glasses on to his forehead and knuckled his eyes. "The Sunderland that made the attack was shot down, Morag."

"Oh, no! From St Trewin?"

"Yes. 2233 Squadron."

"You don't know who it was, yet?"

He shook his head. They both knew that Trevor Walford's brother was a Sunderland pilot of 2233 Squadron, at St Trewin. Gillam knew Morag McEwan's feeling for Trevor.

The duty controller carried his secret signal into the Intelligence Office, where Section Officer McEwan had already delivered a copy. Gillam heard him say: "What do the spies know about this, for crissakes?" But did not ask any questions. He would learn what was in the signal when Steve briefed the crews.

Stevenson was touchy about several things. All this touchiness arose from one grand rankle—his inability to qualify for flying duties . . . his "bare left breast" as he called it masochistically. When he had a few beers too many he could be a bore about it. But a sincere bore. His low medical category was obscurely connected with his feet. Gillam theorized that the Senior Controller either walked on rudimentary stumps and filled out his size ten shoes with newspaper, or was blessed with six toes—webbed, at that. The truth was that Stevenson had been partly paralysed in the legs as a boy and still suffered much pain, which he concealed. He habitually walked absurdly fast and played cricket and golf with skill and vigour.

The tie-line telephone to the Group Operations Room rang. Stevenson came striding back from the Intelligence Office to snatch it from Murch who was already wheezing and rasping into it. Gillam winked at Morag. The controller was being very crisp and Steve-like. "Sir . . . sir . . . very good, sir . . . right . . . roger . . . got it, sir. . . ."

He put the telephone down with his special air of firm efficiency. "Hammer Two. First E.T.D. 1400. Briefing . . ." he paused, looking at the clock. ". . . in one hour."

"Kee-ee-rist . . . shy-rrrimps!" said Gillam softly as Morag, pink about the ears, scuttled for the door. "I laid off the last of Hammer Two about five minutes ago." He looked at the chart on which he had had drawn the new patrol lines. "I'd better check them."

Stevenson descended smartly from his dais. "I'll check them for you, Charles."

Sergeant Murch had been galvanized. He had a list in front of him, ticking off each person he must notify that Group had issued orders for the station to fly patrols "Hammer Two", with the first take-off at 2 p.m. Within a few minutes he would have informed and activated the adjutant for the Station Commander; Wing Commander Flying; the three squadron commanders; the Flying Control tower; the Meteorological Office; the Officers' and Sergeants' Messes; and Operations Canteen, which provided those irregular meals with which the messes could not cope.

Flying Officer Gillam went to the wall map to move the vari-coloured, many-shaped symbols of Allied shipping, both merchant and naval, to the positions they would occupy at noon. There was a big convoy slogging out its last three hundred miles to South-ampton, and this was undoubtedly the prey U 306 hoped to attack on its way home to Lorient. It was the target for at least six other German submarines as well.

The little coloured symbols crawling across the map were the reason for "Hammer Two", and for the tense activity in what had once been a peaceful farmhouse.

But so far the real professionals had not appeared on the scene.

Although the Operations Room was an essential part of the squadron's effectiveness, and its staff was linked inseparably with the crews, by radio, over hundreds of miles of ocean and sky; although every decision and action they took had some effect on the men in the aeroplanes seeking the enemy, they were only fighting R.A.F. Tawmouth's battles indirectly.

The directly active men, the professionals, would be along soon; at briefing time.


CHAPTER TWO

FLIGHT LIEUTENANT WALFORD, who half an hour earlier had pro-voked Stevenson's annoyance at his low flight over the Ops. Room, and Gillam's swift defence, came out of the crew room and stood on the tarmac. Behind him, the long wooden hut which housed the amenities and services for 1111 Squadron throbbed with noise. Two wireless sets—both providentially tuned to the same pro-gramme—provided music. Few listened to the wireless but every-one heard it. If a set was switched off there was instant loud pro-tests. The radio in the crew room was almost at full volume. In the wireless workshop a small home-made set without a cabinet played more quietly. The strains which floated down to the office windows of the Squadron Adjutant, Signals Officer and C.O. were muted so that they sounded mercifully agreeable. The Orderly Room clerks appreciated them too. Everybody seemed to work contentedly to the appropriate amount of background noise.

Walford strolled towards "B for Baker", his aircraft for the day's operation. He was a pink, fair young man of twenty-four who was at the end of his second year of articles in his father's office, learning to be a chartered accountant, when the war started. If anybody had asked Trevor Walford his views on high-sounding principles such as duty, he would have replied indifferently that there was something mean about the phrase "when I was called up". He would have felt uncomfortable living in a freedom for which he had only fought when he had to: so he went directly to the local police station to enquire for a recruiting depot, on hearing the Prime Minister's announcement that Britain was at war.

He enjoyed flying, but looked forward to returning to accountancy. Five years at a small but ancient west country public school had left him with a comfortable set of prejudices; some in favour of physical exercise and against ostentation. He admired intellectual and athletic achievements but had no ambition to excel. If he had thought about his rules of conduct he would have realized that he lived still by the Boy Scout oath he had taken at the age of eleven: he had promised on his honour (in which he still believed) to do his best (this was still important) to God (a stern but generously rewarding super-father) and the King (a benevolent but vague hyper-Headmaster), to help other people at all times (it was caddish not to) and to obey the Scout Law (which supplemented the Ten Commandments). Four years of war had not changed these.

His chief characteristic was a persistent cheerfulness; and because he combined it with a centre three-quarter's dash, an admirable capacity for drinking beer and a forthright certainty in expressing his opinions of operational flying, he made a good captain.

In and around his Wellington worked fitters, riggers and armourers, a flight mechanic, a wireless mechanic and a radar mechanic. They were loading six five-hundred-pound depth charges; filling the fuel tanks from a bowser alongside, with the help of general duties aircraft-hands who earned two shillings a day and were slightingly called non-tradesmen; giving the R/T set and the wireless equipment their daily inspection; adjusting the radar scope; checking the guns; looking for an oil leak in the port engine; altogether making sure that when he took "B" to the down-wind end of the runway in use to run-up the engines finally before take-off, he would find no fault and that none would bring him back to base prematurely once he was airborne. For ten hours a heavy call would be made on every component, most of which had seen a lot of flying time already.

A nervous young ACH/GD gave him a sloppy salute. He tugged a hand from his trousers pocket to acknowledge it. Standing at the foot of the ladder under the open hatch in the aircraft's belly, he called up: "Cubie? Stan?"

There was an answer from the latter, followed by Flight Sergeant Glover's sharp, dark face. "Any gen, skipper?"

"Ops. on. Briefing twelve-thirty."

"Bags of flap up at Ops., eh?" Stan Glover thought of Jean. She was on watch till one; he'd see her for a moment when they went up for briefing.

"No panic for us, anyway. We're last off. Tell that bloody Yank to pull his finger out and come down here. What's he doing this time?"

Glover grinned. "He's got a theory about the A.S.V. . . . sorry, radar. Reckons he can work it better than what I can. He's telling the mech. how to improve it, too—nearly driving him barmy."

"Tell him not to get in the way. I want him. . . ."

Flight Sergeant Glover disappeared, laughing. Walford waited till his navigator's broad, pallid face appeared in the opening, framed in the fur collar of an Irvine jacket. "Hi, Trev. Say, whadda you know: I've figured out that this goddam A.S.V. . . . I mean radar . . . belongs to the navigator. D'you know that?" Talking fast, not looking where he was going, Flying Officer "Cubie" Meddings came down the ladder like a sailor. He dumped his compact body on the tarmac and stood with his nose level with the top button of Walford's tunic; he had not stopped talking and now was well into his third strong reason for being allowed to take charge of the Air-to-Surface-Vessel set which was newly called "radar".

Walford cut across his words. "Briefing at eleven-thirty."

"Yippee. Roll on tour-ex. Only another seventeen to go. . . ."

"If we get off tonight before the weather clamps. . . ."

"Say, I've got a theory about that. I been thinking about this Cornish weather and I figure. . . ."

"Tell the met. man. Or Nig—he reckons to know more about met. than anyone."

Glover, who had been waiting his chance, got his word in. "Naafi's up."

They went back to the crew room to fetch their mugs for tea. When Meddings sniffed his he made his ritual grimace and utterance: "Jeeze, this *is* total war!"

Pete Brodie, the Canadian second pilot, lying back in a canvas chair, held out his hand for the mug brought him by Lofty Duckett, one of the wireless operator/air gunners. "Thanks, Lofty. My turn tomorrow."

"Yeah. And don't forget it."

Duckett, hatched-faced and stringy, with the same tall height as Brodie, was but three stone lighter. He talked with a rasping Australian accent and managed to get a lot done while appearing to move lethargically. In this also he differed from the Canadian. Flying Officer Pete Brodie concealed a vast indolence under an alert stare.

Walford looked around the crowded, noisy room for the sixth member of his crew, the third wireless operator-air gunner.

"Where's Snowy?"

Lofty Duckett lowered his outsize mug. "He's gone to put on another pullover. Says Trinidad was never like this!"

Stan Glover was pushing his way to the stove. "Lemme put this mug near the stove, you lot; want to keep pore ol' Snowy's char warm, don't we?"

A dozen derisive voices told what to do with pore ol' Snowy's char and he told them they were being very rude. Not at all the old 1111 spirit, said Flight Sergeant Glover.

Then Sergeant Galahad Pomeroy, "Snowy," stamped in. bundled into flying boots, two pullovers, a scarf and greatcoat. He said he was keeping his Irvine jacket aside, otherwise he would have nothing to put on when the winter really set in. His round face shone like a black cherry and he gratefully took the mug that Glover passed to him. "Thanks, Stan. You're a pal." He saw Walford. "Gen, skipper?"

"Half-twelve briefing."

"Panic job!"

"May be."

Someone burst in at the door that opened from the passage leading to the offices. "There's been a sighting!"

He was immediately surrounded by clamour and bodies. "All I know is it was a Sunderland from 2233."

Walford looked up quickly. "Any more grif?"

His own crew glanced at him with instant understanding. He stood up and shouldered towards the man who had brought the news. "Did the boss tell you?"

"Adj says boss is still up at Flying Control. That's all the gen: a sighting. . . ."

Walford pushed on to the door. His crew exchanged glances. He had what the Service called an "operational twitch"; an involuntary tic of the right eye, a shrugging of that shoulder and a sideways jerk of the head. The rest of the station knew that it was caused by one completed tour of operations over the North Sea and a half-completed current one. Nobody paid much attention to it; there were at least half a dozen well advanced twitches at Tawmouth. But his crew wondered how much of Trevor Walford's nervous tension was due to the knowledge that his younger brother was nearing the end of a first tour of ops. from nearby St Trewin.

Snowy's yellow eyeballs seemed as big as ping-pong balls in his black face. He huddled his scrawny body into its many warm layers of wrapping and shuddered. "Man, I bet it's co-o-old out there."

They all shared the same thought but nobody did more than hint at it. For the past few weeks U-boats had stayed on the surface to fight it out with sighting aircraft, instead of hastily diving. They carried 20 mm. and 37 mm. anti-aircraft cannon both on the conning tower and on deck nowadays, in addition to their heavy machine guns. It was a fair assumption that the submarine reported by the Sunderland had defended itself; and that it carried the fire power to do lethal damage—especially to a big, slow target. From there the logical step was to assume ditching. . . .

Pete Brodie pulled his cap over his eyes and lay back. "The Sunderbus'll make it back to base, all right. They always do. At the worst they'll drive it back on the water—and cook a three-course meal while they come!"

The Sunderland's galley was an envied feature of its equipment. And master Brodie was an embittered pilot. Coastal Command flying was almost at the opposite extreme from his desire; only instructing or communications ranked lower with him. He had gone through his training burning to go on to fighters. But he was a clumsy aerobat and could not even be relied on to land smoothly every time; in a dogfight with the Germans his naive, slow manoeuvres would have cost him his life at the first encounter, and no Spitfire would have stood up to many of his ham-fisted touch-downs. Since joining the squadron he had applied for a transfer to Beaufighters—now that he was twin-engined qualified he scorned Spitfires—which his C.O. had been bound to pass on; but with his own discouraging endorsement. Brodie lived in the futile hope that his posting would come soon. In the meanwhile, when he met his friends in London and they, from the imaginedly greater dangers of fighter or bomber flying, asked him when he was going on ops., he could only blush and swear and raise a fist. His red, beefy face looked disgruntled now as he contemplated, without pleasure, the dull ten-hour patrol ahead during which he would actually handle the Wellington for perhaps four—and then with the help of the automatic pilot.

Cubie Meddings lit a cigar. From whichever angle you looked at him, he appeared to have the same dimension in all directions: cubical; hence "Cubie". In another few weeks he would be out of R.A.F. blue and into the U.S. Army Air Corps' khaki, under new regulations which gave to the American forces all those citizens who had volunteered for the British forces before their own coun-try came into the war. He would be glad to have the greatly increased pay; and a miniature R.A.F. navigator's wing on his right breast would remain as a tangible attachment to his old loyalty. He would be allowed to stay on the squadron, as a lieutenant, until his tour was finished. He would be sorry to lose the position he held now: he was almost a mascot; a pet, if one could have applied such a term to so rugged a person. He smoked —and chewed—cigars, chewed gum, told tall stories and generally delighted the squadron, and his crew in particular, with his fulfil-ment of their uninformed ideas of American-ness. Walford had taken him home on leave twice, to show him off with as much pride as if he were personally responsible for Cubie's exoticism. Meddings, who had driven a bootlegger's high-powered launch between Canada and the United States, been to sea with a whal-ing fleet, boxed as a preliminary boy up and down the Coast, lumberjacked, and done a hitch in the Marines, was by ten years the oldest of the crew; and reckoned, compared with what had gone before, that he was having it nice and quiet since he had walked into the war. Its outbreak had found him in England, steward in an airline; he had stayed. This was his second operational tour and he had one as an instructor.

With his cigar going richly, Meddings took a pack of cards from a pocket of his battle-blouse. "O.K., Lofty?" He held the cards up and riffled them.

Lofty Duckett pulled his chair closer. "Good on yer, Cubie. Hi! Snowy... Stan... the game's on."

The two other wireless op/air gunners moved in. Brodie stirred, murmured: "Poker?" and sat up.

Snowy Pomeroy muttered once more: "Man ... I don't fancy a ditching in this weather...."

\* \* \*

U 306 had her machine guns trained on the circular rubber dinghy. The wireless operator, in answer to his captain's order, jumped back from the Sunderland's hull. He had sent out his signal twice: "U-boat U 306 surfaced and approaching". But he knew that at sea level his transmission would be so weak that the chance of its being heard was small.

From overhead a sudden throb of sound came to the men in the dinghy and to those in the submarine, as the latter's engine slowed. Eyes searched the sky and the airmen cheered when they recognized the low-flying, white shape of a Wellington coming near.

The U-boat came closer, until it rocked in the short swell with its side scraping the flying boat's tail.

The Wellington flew straight at them. The British stopped cheering: if depth charges were dropped now, they would be blown up along with the Germans. They knew why the enemy had come right up to them: when the crew of the Wellington saw the survivors they would hold their machine gun fire for fear of hitting them. But nobody could expect the Wellington to hold its depth charges: an attack could not be forfeited to merciful scruples. The six survivors might die, but who could count the lives of sailors saved by destroying the U-boat?

The heavy machine guns and the cannon on the submarine began firing together. The Wellington banked steeply away. It circled cautiously. Rose to a thousand feet. Circled once more.

Before it flew away the Germans took their prisoners aboard and dived into the Bay of Biscay.

\* \* \*

Flight Sergeant Glover found it hard to keep his mind on the cards. He was looking forward to the trip. The crews were keen

to fly for two chief reasons. First, since it was the way they had
chosen to fight the war, they felt that they should get on with it;
it was what they were there for. Then there was the important
fact that each completed operation was one nearer to the thirty on
attaining which they would be "tour-expired". They liked flying,
but they preferred the idea of finishing a tour.

Taunts at the safe uneventfulness of Coastal flying were unjustified. Apart from the risk of attack by enemy fighters, by Ju. 88's
flying further out to sea and by the terrible Kuriers, or of heavy
defence by U-boats, there were the hazards of long, low flights
over water. An engine failure could put an aeroplane down before
its pilot had time to increase power on the sound engine enough
to keep airborne. Errors of navigation, faults in compasses, loss
of wireless communication, could send it off course; at night it
could crash into unseen land and at any time it might be forced
to ditch, short of fuel.

Stan Glover knew that his job was not safe, and no Service duty
could ever be dull for him. He had spent his youth in Married
Quarters on R.A.F. camps all over England and the Middle East.
At sixteen, he had entered boys' service. When the war began, he
was a twenty-year-old leading aircraftman Electrician I. It had
taken him two years, by when he was a corporal, to persuade his
way out of a top-group ground trade into air crew. He was not
merely a good wireless op/air gunner—he was dedicated and
superb. He could take down his guns, find a fault and reassemble
them, wearing gloves and with his eyes bandaged. He could trace
faults in the radio and do temporary repairs, when run-of-the-mill
operators would have despaired. He knew about, and gave a hand
in, arming, fuelling and radar adjustment. From Cubie he had
learned something of navigation. He knew that, in an emergency,
he could land a Wellington safely. In his spare time he studied
under the station education officer so that he could apply for pilot
training.

He wished that Pete Brodie would do what a conscientious
second pilot would have done, and go out to the aircraft instead
of lounging here playing poker. He also wished that Walford
would return. There was no point in the skipper worrying about
his young brother: far better to take his mind off things with a
hand of cards; or Cubie would have helped, understandingly, with
one of his theories or a pungent tale of how he had evaded the
Customs with a fortune in bathtub gin aboard. . . .

Walford was in the squadron adjutant's office, awaiting the

C.O.'s return. He bit in the stem of a pipe which he had filled but found difficult to keep alight.

They heard the C.O.'s door close. A moment later he opened the communicating one. "I'm back, Adj. Hello, Trevor. Come in."

"Thanks, sir. I believe 2233 have had a sighting?"

"Yes, signals have been pouring into Ops. The Sunderland was shot down; the U-boat damaged it, then a Kurier did the rest."

He paused, noticing Walford's twitch. He had suffered from one himself on his first tour, on a torpedo squadron.

"I see, sir."

"It's not a complete write-off, Trevor. The wop. did damn well, getting signals off. The second dickie, the nav. and two gunners were killed, but the rest are O.K."

Walford smiled faintly in relieved reaction. His brother had newly been promoted to captain.

"Then a Wimpey from Chivenor, that Group diverted to the sighting but which had already dropped it's d.c.'s—the area seems lousy with U-boats today!—saw the U-boat take the crew aboard."

Walford jerked his pipe out of his mouth and reddened. "God! Prisoners in a U-boat that Group will keep hunting now with everything they can spare."

"It's one U-boat no one will be sorry to hear has slipped through; but of course the hunt's on. The Wellington from Chivenor made a kill, by the way, so Group are concentrating on the one the Sunderland attacked."

"Do we know its number, sir?"

"They do up at Ops. I haven't seen the signals—I just got the form by telephone."

"Well, thanks sir."

"Hang on, Trevor; I'm coming to the Crew Room."

Walford followed the C.O., wondering if the Ops. Room would know the name of the Sunderland captain, as well as the number of the U-boat in which he was trapped.

The roomful of men began heaving themselves out of their chairs. Gretton moved towards the centre, feeling in his pockets for his pipe and tobacco pouch.

"Sit down, chaps. Before the transport comes, I thought you'd like to know what's going on so that you can appreciate the briefing a bit better."

The crews became silent and the nearest man switched off the wireless. All attention was on the boss.

Paul Gretton took an air of authority everywhere which had

nothing to do with the three rings on his cuff. Other men recognized his quality from his bearing and way of speaking. He wore no decoration, although he was on his third tour of operations. If he survived this one he would surely get a D.S.O. He led his squadron with courage and believed in its excellence. His popularity was not of the life-and-soul-of-the-party kind but owed something to his integrity and more to his kindness.

He knew all about nearly everyone on his crews: who could hold his drink and who needed to get drunk now and again; whom to restrain and whom to prod. He was twenty-seven years old and looked five years more. Each of his last four birthdays had come as a surprise to him: he had not expected to make it. A tough man with a hard face and a quiet voice, nine years earlier he had led the best public school rugger pack of its decade. He was, like Charles Gillam if only given the chance, the best military material: strong and quick, born with guts and stubborn loyalty; and he had the special qualities of a commander—strength, unobtrusive authority and tact.

"First of all, there's definitely some trade in the Bay. A Sunderland made a sighting just now. . . ."

An excited gabble broke and died quickly while he lit his pipe.

"And a Wimpey got a kill this morning. You'll hear all this again up at Ops.; but just to scotch lavatory rumours I thought I'd tell you the facts. There are also six other U-boats out in a pack. . . . As you've all been binding about things being quiet, I hope you'll all realize how lucky you are not to be on leave just now!"

This time the laughter was loud. Gretton stayed awhile, pulling at his pipe and answering questions.

Meanwhile U 306 had travelled about four miles from the point at which it took its prisoners. And Walford's crew had advanced thirty minutes towards the moment in time for which, perhaps, they had been born.


# CHAPTER THREE

EVERYTHING that happened in the Tawmouth Operations Room from now, every emotion felt and decision made by the people who worked there and by those who influenced the station's operations from other offices, was an extension of that morning's events in the Bay of Biscay.

The most powerful local human agency of fate was the Station Commander. Group Captain Laraway had been speaking to Ops. since the briefing message came. He asked a lot of questions in his mild, dry voice then replaced the telephone with characteristic neatness. He came as near to being a fussy little man as is possible for a distinguished senior officer. Lighting a cigarette, he leaned his elbows on his desk, stared at a wall map and concentrated on the problems of finding a U-boat in ten thousand square miles of ocean. The details, the whole conception of a submarine hunt fascinated him: but as a mathematical exercise rather than as a matter of life and death, gunfire, a call to bravery, or a triumph of training and character over human weakness and fatigue.

At this date, many of his Cranwell contemporaries had acquired a notoriety which, without envy, he privately thought in bad taste. He had won the Air Force Cross, as an earnest young flight lieutenant, for five hundred hours of test flying. Now, it was almost a matter for apology, dimmed by the effulgence of D.S.O.'s and D.F.C.'s, of bars, and of foreign decorations studded with palms and suspended from indecently wide ribbons, often of garish colour. These were the rewards for forays against the enemy. They recalled machine-gun and anti-aircraft fire; aircraft in flames; windscreens drenched in glycol; bombs falling on hotly defended targets; bombers plunging through a web of flak; torpedo aircraft holding steady under the guns of a fleet; outnumbered fighters whirling crazily in dogfights.

Group Captain Laraway's surviving friends were cheery, beery, blood-and-guts commanders of stations or wings in Fighter or Bomber Command, or in Coastal Command's anti-shipping strike force which carried torpedoes, rockets and bombs. His powers of logical objective reasoning, however, had brought him to authority in resolving the complexities of tracking down U-boats which could hide under the ocean for 19 hours out of every 24; and, since the introduction of the Schnorkel breathing apparatus the year before, for days and nights at a stretch.

His shy scholarliness misled most people into a wrong appreciation of his character. He was imbued with every principle that professional training could inculcate, and would not tolerate a lowering of the Service's high standards in any circumstances. Many of the war-time officers, particularly those from Commonwealth countries, were antagonized by his insistence on conduct according to his rigid code; but there was nothing they could do but accept it. Only that morning he had interviewed a young pilot officer wop./A.G. who was unable to pay his month's mess bill.

"What time is it?"

"Nine-o'clock, sir."

"That looks a good watch: you should get a couple of pounds on it in a pawn shop. How many pairs of shoes have you got?"

"Two, sir."

"You only need one. You've got civilian clothes, of course?"

"Oh, yes, sir. Three suits."

"There's a second hand clothes shop in Tawmouth. You're suspended from flying for forty-eight hours; you've got just that long to raise the money: sell everything you possess if you have to."

Group Captain Laraway neatly extinguished his cigarette, put his gold oak-leafed cap squarely on his head and went out to his car. He noticed that the pennant on its bonnet was snapping in a fresh breeze and at once raised his eyes to the sky. Clouds were forming on the horizon. He drove off quickly, hearing a loud familiar exhaust note on the far side of the administrative site, approaching: he wanted to reach the Operations Room before his ebullient Wing Commander Flying, Nig Dunford. If he could. . . .

\*          \*          \*

In the Ops. Room, Squadron Leader Stevenson was making Gillam and Sergeant Murch uncomfortable by tugging his moustache and looking as though he must leap from his chair at any second and help them both. As each of them was well up to his work, even under stress and shortness of time, Stevenson's uneasiness annoyed them and could lead to mistakes they would not otherwise make. His faintly bloodshot eyes looked baleful and Gillam wished crossly that Morag McEwan—or any personable woman—would come along and take them off himself; and Murch, for whom he could not help feeling sorry.

There was another reason for haste. Gillam had an awful memory of another day similar to this one for urgency, when Nig Dunford had burst in at his usual premature moment and "helped" him to "straighten out the shipping situation" on the wall map.

Nig was so called because as a diminutive for Nigel the name fitted his raven hair and swarthy complexion.

He had just left his bewildered airman clerk with the shouted words: "I'm going up to Ops. for briefing. I'll stop at Flying

Control for five minutes, on the way." And rushed out of his office, leaving the grey-haired clerk to collect the papers his whirlwind passage had scattered. The latter creaked around, repairing the damage, and muttering to himself: "'Strewth! 'E don' know what five minutes is. 'E'll take over in Flying Control, 'andle a couple o' take-offs and landings, tell 'em 'ow to run the show and booger off on 'is way to Ops. in five seconds flat." But there was considerable admiration in his grumbling observation.

Sergeant Murch was the first to hear Dunford's skidding stop in the lane and the final, revved-up blast of his shattering exhaust. The controller's assistant had been plotting the patrol lines on the general situation map, with wool of different colours for the various squadrons. He shambled crabwise back to his chair, looking over his shoulder, checking that all was correct. He, too, plethoric man though he was, had been tormented to the brink of hysteria more than once by the Wing Commander Flying's well meant interference.

Gillam finished writing the last of the eighteen slips for the crews, which gave their patrol turning points and times on and off.

Nig Dunford hurtled in, his eyes darting from the map to the state board and on to the special chart on which sightings were recorded.

"Whacko! So we're going to clobber the bastards today, Steve old horse."

Stevenson whinnied with proper appreciation for a wing commander's pleasantry.

Dunford bounded across to the navigator. "How's the navigational nark this morning?"

"Overworked and underpaid, sir."

"Christ! Aren't we all? Got permission to fly on ops., yet?"

"Should be through any day, sir."

"Goodo. I'll take you next time I do a trip. What wind are you using?"

"020/10, sir."

"O.K. Changing?"

"045/25 after midnight, sir."

"That's right." Wing Commander Flying gave the impression that the navigator's wind directions and speeds only confirmed his own expert opinion; although they had been worked by a well qualified specialist who consulted his fellow meteorological officers at Group before committing himself.

Dunford had sincerely exulted when he heard of the intensity of the station's effort for the coming twenty-four hours. He thought that all aircrew were as bloodthirsty as himself.

He had started his first tour of operations on Bristol Blenheim bombers at the outbreak of war, as a pilot officer. A year later, as a flight lieutenant filling the shoes of several successively dead flight commanders, he had covered the evacuation from Dunkirk. In those days he would have pushed himself forward for a special operation, even if it meant displacing someone already detailed. He had started his second tour, on a Bristol Beaufort torpedo squadron, as a flight commander and finished as C.O. At that period he would have ordered someone else off the roster to make room for himself. On his third tour, which was supposed to be less dangerous and more restful, commanding a Wellington anti-submarine squadron, he would have put himself down for first take-off.

He knew that he had been disliked for grabbing more than his share of the opportunities to win medals (nobody took into account the risks); and he knew that other crews resented the delays he created in their own tour completions.

But the medals were won and he could relax. With a D.S.O. and two D.F.C.'s, he kept strictly to his place on the flying roster during this fourth tour and was popular on the station.

He stood in front of the map. "What speed are you taking for this convoy?"

Gillam, instead of answering, held out the signal for him on which details of the convoy were given. Dunford grabbed it. "Fifteen knots? Bet they're doing twenty: they'll bust their boilers in an effort to get home when they're on the last lap."

He made for the Intelligence Office, talking over his shoulder. "I'd better see that the spies haven't got any duff gen. . . ."

Stevenson shrugged hopelessly at Gillam, who laughed. Sergeant Murch was wetting his lips and nervously tearing a piece of paper to shreds.

Outside, a grating gear-change meant the approach of the group captain's car. The Operations Room staff stood up as he came quietly through the door.

"Don't get up . . . 'morning, Steve."

"Good morning, sir." Stevenson came lightly to attention, then relaxed with his fists on his hip bones and his chest straining at the buttons of his tunic. The heavy brass buckle on its belt fell with a clink against the lowest button when he pulled in his stomach.

Group Captain Laraway mounted the dais, put his cap on the desk, passed a hand over his greying hair and looked long and carefully at the situation map. Gillam watched him, awaiting the inevitable questions; but the station commander asked them of the controller.

"That convoy, Steve. What speed do the nautics say it's travelling at?"

"Fifteen knots, sir. But of course when they're on the home straight they put the pressure on: twenty knots is more like it."

"Quite."

Gillam, who was always fascinated by Stevenson's slickness at picking up points to turn in his favour, thought that with a little more of this sort of thing his Senior Controller should get an O.B.E. out of the Old Man; at least a Mention. "Home straight" was good, too. Groupie was known to be a keen point-to-point man and something of a G.R. Steve had never been on a race course, let alone to a hunt meeting; before the war he had travelled in toys: and earned more at it than the group captain did now.

Group Captain Laraway ambled to the centre of the floor, among the forms and chairs which a couple of airmen were setting out under Murch's surly directions. He read the state board, turned again to the map and remarked: "One of the last three aircraft should intercept this U-boat about twenty miles from the convoy."

Gillam, who had come to the same conclusion with the aid of his chart and instruments, respected the station commander's mental computation but said nothing.

Stevenson pulled at his moustache. "That's what we make of it, sir." He lifted an enquiring eyebrow at his navigator, who nodded stonily.

"I don't like the look of the weather; it may turn dirty at about midnight.'"

"No, it's not too promising, sir." Stevenson was keeping his end up well.

The group captain nodded and turned back to the dais. "Get me the Group controller, will you?"

Squadron Leader Stevenson picked up the green scrambler telephone and, after a few words, handed it to the Station Commander. Gillam heard the latter's contribution to the ensuing conversation.

"Laraway, here . . . Oh, hello Johnnie . . . yes, looks pretty promising . . . yes, bad show about the Sunderland . . . Oh, was it?" He paused, looking worried. "Yes, I'll hold on . . . 'morning, sir . . . yes, very pleased, but we can offer you three more from each squadron, sir, as you know . . . very good, sir . . . sporting chance, sir . . . more so if we could get our other nine aircraft on . . . yes, I'll take threes about it, sir . . . all right . . . goodbye, sir. . . ."

He gave the telephone to Stevenson to replace for him. "The A.O.C. was in Group Ops. He gave me three to one against a Tawmouth aircraft making the first contact."

"I heard you drop a hint about getting more of ours on the job, sir," said Stevenson, looking keen.

"Yes. He wouldn't wear it. I suppose there's more trade in the offing tomorrow."

Group Captain Laraway's small, pointed features betrayed nothing of the uncomfortable information he had just had about the Sunderland that was shot down. He had better tell his Wing Commander Flying. Before he could start on his way to the Intelligence Office, Wing Commander Dunford leaped up the step between the two rooms. Seeing the Station Commander, he swept his hand up in the aborted naval salute which he thought appropriate to Coastal Command, and knocked from a table a brass shell case which served as ashtray.

Sergeant Murch jumped at the crash. Stevenson winced and pulled his moustache. Gillam smiled privately: he was thinking that, despite Nig's seeming insensitiveness, there was no doubt that, if there was no other ammunition left, Birdman Dunford would think nothing of leaning out of his cockpit and slinging ashtrays at the enemy! Gillam admired and respected Nig Dunford against his own reason and with a reluctance of which he was ashamed. The Birdman evoked an innocent admiration in the most sophisticated, educated or intellectual mind by his sheer blatantly heroic dash. There was an innocence about his thrust and apparent lack of feeling.

The group captain took him to a corner where a chart was kept on which special U-boat hunts were plotted in detail. "I'd like a word with you, Nigel."

"Sir?"

R.A.F. Tawmouth's two most senior officers talked in lowered voices.

"Nigel, I've just been talking to Group. That Sunderland that was shot down this morning: the captain was Walford's brother."

"Oh, God! Poor little sod. Does Trevor know?"

"No. Group haven't allowed the name to leak out; but of course they can't delay notifying the parents."

"Will you tell him, sir? I ought not to take him off today's ops."

"I haven't made up my mind whether it will come best from me or from someone he knows better: Paul perhaps ought to tell him."

"Yes, sir. I won't take him off ops., though: his chances of finding that particular U-boat are slim; especially with a whole pack out. And he'll be glad to have something to occupy his mind."

"Quite. Besides, with the odds favouring the U-boats in this needle-in-a-haystack game, the chances are U 306 will slip through to Lorient and deliver its prisoners."

"Yes. All alive-o. Better to spend the next few months in a P.O.W. camp than shaking hands with St Peter and trying a halo on for size."

"Quite. Even if it's considerably more than a few months, Nigel."

"Oh, come on, sir! Second Front and all that . . . this party's going to wind up next summer. . . ."

Squadron Leader Stevenson wondered what the inaudible conversation was about. He had never seen Nig look so serious.

There was no time for wondering. A coach and a three-ton lorry came grinding up the hill and in a moment the Ops. Room was swarming with pilots, navigators and Wop/A.G.'s. They pushed in with the expectant, excited noise of a football crowd.

"Look at that sighting . . . right where we were two nights ago. . . ."

"That's the same ruddy convoy that was there last week . . . it hasn't moved. . . ."

"What's this . . . Hammer Two . . . ? Never 'eard of it. . . ."

"Bloody fine patrols those . . . bit of wind'll either blow you out into the Atlantic or over ruddy Spain. . . ."

"Look at that! We're first off . . . what a bind. . . ."

"It's all right . . . we'll be back before the pubs close. . . ."

"Ha, ha! I'd rather go after dark, boy, when the 88's and the Kuriers can't see us. . . ."

All their boisterous chatter was a safety valve. Gillam, standing silently behind his table, envied them. He knew the intestinal butterfly-flutter of a boxer waiting in his corner for the opening gong. How much more tense must be the anticipatory reactions of these men. He had applied weeks ago for permission to fly at

least one op. on the grounds that it would help him in his duties;
Stevenson had flown on ops. six or eight times; in Wellingtons,
and standing up behind the pilot of a Coastal Command Beaufighter, on patrol to protect the slow aircraft from enemy fighters
and Ju 88's. Kuriers stayed well beyond Beaufighter range.

Trevor Walford sat at the end of a form and leaned on the
navigator's table. "Wotcher, Charles."

"Hello, Trevor. You nearly took our chimney off again this
morning."

"Damn! Did I miss again?"

Cubie Meddings leaned over and touched a finger to his forehead. "Hi, Charles. When you coming with us, boy? We can
always use a good hand."

"Any day now, Cubie: maybe my permission'll be through by
the time you're on again." Gillam knew a couple of crews on each
squadron well, and Walford's crew best of all. He shared a room
with Cubie and flew with the crew on many of their training
flights and air tests. He had been with them on navigational exercises, practice bombing and fighter affiliation. Walford had
promised to take him on operations when Command let him go.

Pete Brodie, who sat on Medding's other side, lounged forward
and grinned beefily at Gillam. "Save it till I get my posting to
Beaus., Charles: I'll give you a real trip in a real aeroplane."

"Get *him*." Cubie drove an elbow into the Canadian second
pilot's ribs. "Bleriot had nothing on this guy: God's gift to
aviation. Nuts!"

The navigator's taunts could not remove the grin from Pete
Brodie's red face. "G.R. is strictly from hunger, Cubie. And the
Beau. pilots don't get loused up by bad navigation!"

General Reconnaissance may be lacking in the thrills that
Brodie wants, Gillam thought, but it's better than getting a shine
on the seat of my pants in an Ops. Room chair.

Flight Sergeant Glover met his girl friend in the hall. Corporal
Jean Forrow was also a wireless operator and their romance had
started over nothing more promising than a signal he sent giving
the estimated time of return from a patrol. The duty operator at
Group on that frequency had taken it down incorrectly and
claimed that it was badly sent. Corporal Jean Forrow had spoken
up for the unknown sender. Stan Glover, whose Morse was
impeccable at speeds as high as twenty-five words a minute, was
amused rather than annoyed by the query from Group; and
fascinated when he heard that the Tawmouth operator who had

read him correctly was a W.A.A.F. He had gone from de-briefing in the Intelligence Office to talk to her in the Signals Section. She had made him a cup of tea and shared her toast and margarine with him. Their friendship had grown fast to the point where Jean Forrow now wore a minuscule chip of diamond in a thin gold ring on the third finger of her left hand.

She saw Stan Glover's thin, dark face and immaculate patent leather hair and his well pressed battle dress with the pride she always felt in owning an exclusive share of his neat competence and reliability.

He smiled at her. They stood about the same height. "Hello, Jean. Who's minding the nursery while Corporal i/c's down here?" Stan Glover, born, bred and trained in the regular Service atmosphere, had never got over his amusement at the W.A.A.F. It particularly tickled him that his girl was a corporal, in charge of a watch of other young women, and could even be heard saying unfeminine things like "Stand at ease" and "Dismiss"; especially as her fair hair and complexion and gentle way made her essentially feminine.

Jean Forrow spoke with a Cornish burr: her home was only an hour's bus ride from Tawmouth. "Never you mind about my nursery, as you call it. Just you mind your sending today. And tell Flight Lieutenant Walford not to take a diversion; remember mum and dad are expecting us down home tomorrow for tea."

"Oh, I dunno; a diversion to Port Lyautey would just about suit me. Moroccan sunshine an' all that; y'know. It's getting a bit parky round here."

"Don't be soft. Can't you stand a bit of cold?"

He leaned down and whispered wickedly: "Not from you, love," which sent her upstairs again pink with pleasure.

Snowy Pomeroy walked slowly into the Ops. Room. He flicked his glance nervously to the bench on which his captain and the two other officers in the crew were already seated. Then he sidled diffidently in beside Brodie, but leaving a space.

Lofty Duckett twanged: "Slide up, Snowy boy. What's the matter: afraid of a few splinters in yer bum?"

Snowy did not move. He patted the place at his side and Duckett grumblingly shoved past his knees and sat down. "What's the matter with Pete, then? Won't his best friends tell him?"

Gallahad Pomeroy, from Trinidad and conscious of his colour, shook his head and pretended to be absorbed in the situation map. He was not yet sure how he stood with Flying Officer Pete Brodie.

All North Americans were suspect; even Canadians. Cubie Meddings, the genial, came from Alabama. When he found himself
crewed up with what he called "a coloured man", at Operational
Training Unit, he showed his revulsion by disdain. A captain less
decent and friendly than Trevor Walford would have had open
trouble on his hands months ago.

Briefing began.

Squadron Leader Stevenson stood in front of the map, with a
sheaf of papers clipped to a board, in his hand.

"Well, as you can see, we're carrying out new patrols today:
'Hammer Two'. There was a sighting at 1005 this morning, by a
Sunderland from St Trewin, in this position." He bent and tapped
the map. "Group have laid on a hunt in that area, but are leaving
this station to carry on with routine patrols because that U-boat
—identified as U 306—may move into our patrol area and because
there is a pack of at least six out as well."

There was a mutter about the pack.

"The Sunderland reported that U 306 stayed on the surface
and fought. A Kurier joined in and the Sunderland was shot
down."

For a restless half-minute there was a loud conversation among
the crews.

"All patrol times are ten hours. Patrol height five hundred feet;
aircraft with radio altimeter, four hundred and fifty feet."

The crews laughed. Most of them split the difference between a
really safe height and the height at which the airborne radar had
the best range; they flew at seven hundred and fifty feet, which just
gave a pilot time to take effective action if he lost an engine. Five
hundred feet was unpopular and considered foolish, unrealistic.
Four hundred and fifty feet was for people with either no imagination or what half-baked, glossy magazine popular psychologists
called "the death wish"; like racing motorists and bull fighters
and other perfectly normal but outrageously brave men.

"If you're diverted by weather or orders to stay on patrol, your
alternates are Chivenor, Gibraltar and Port Lyautey. Any
questions?"

Nobody asked questions. Gillam went diffidently to the top of
the room. He disliked briefings; he felt self-conscious, telling
others what to expect on an operation on which he was unable
to fly; he did not think that many of the crews paid attention to
what he said.

"As you can see, there are six patrol lines, with three aircraft on each. Other aircraft in the area are: twelve Sunderlands, thirty-six Wellingtons and fifteen Liberators."

Somebody said something aloud about a flock of starlings, and someone else said he'd avoid collision risk by flying at two thousand.

Gillam told them where and when they would fly over the various groups and units of shipping, and walked quietly back to his chair with relief. He noticed that Trevor Walford's twitch was worse than it had been for some weeks.

The duty Intelligence Officer went blandly ahead with his briefing despite the frequent laughs.

"I'll remind you again of the two types of U-boat operating in the area at present. Type Seven, of 750 tons and Type Nine, of 1,000 tons. Those you know. There are also believed to be some of the new Type Twenty-one. A few of all three types are fitted with Schnorkel, but the majority of them will have to surface, as usual, for five hours out of every twenty-four, to charge their batteries. But the important feature about all U-boats today is armament. They all carry 20mm and 37mm ack-ack cannon and heavy machine guns; all three types of weapon are mounted fore and aft of the conning tower as well as on it; many of them are protected by bridge armour and gun shields."

He was forced to stop at last by the loud comments, and the laughter that was fearful anticipation and not amusement.

The list of horrors was not yet exhausted. The I.O. went on to tell of the German Air Force fighter squadrons based on the Brest peninsula, waiting to pick off solitary R.A.F. aircraft which flew too near the French coast. He saved his worst for the end. Dornier 217J night fighters had been posted to Morlaix airfield that week. Hitherto, the R.A.F. had not been attacked in the Western Approaches by night. Now night fighters sought them; Do 217J's with a range of 1,500 miles, a top speed of 325 m.p.h. and an armament of four 20mm cannon and four 7.92mm machine guns.

At this gay news the crews sat up and cheered.

The Meteorological Officer, a Civil Servant dismally metamorphosed into temporary officer, pinned a chart on the wall and clicked his false teeth until the noise subsided. The weather at base would remain good throughout the next twenty-four hours; although there was the possibility of some rain later; and, of course, one must expect local fog patches along the coast. In the operational area, a deterioration would set in soon after midnight; and if the approaching warm front had stronger winds behind it than so far indicated—as could very likely happen—the nearer part of the operational area would be murky by early morning. The weather at Port Lyautey, however, would be excellent; should crews be diverted there. At the end of ten minutes' repetition, qualification and contradiction, the forecaster left his listeners with the muddled impression that they had little to fear from the weather but a rough passage during the end of the homeward trip for the last few aircraft.

Cubie, chewing a cigar, summed it up. "The guy says it's gonna be a hayride, unless mebbe it turns out to be helluva rugged; like he said. . . ."

There only remained the Signals Officer to give them the frequencies on which watch would be kept at Group Headquarters and at the Group stations; to remind them about the importance of sending sighting reports, intentions to divert and estimated times of return; and to mention certain times and codes to which they must keep.

The last speaker had to contend with a rising volume of talk. The signals information was essentially for the senior wireless operator in each crew; the other Wop/A.G.'s could get it from him later; and some of the captains were not interested. Walford, however, leaned forward so as to hear better and called across to Stan Glover to make sure that he had not missed anything. This was a superfluous precaution, he knew; Flight Sergeant Glover wore his usual expression of faintly amused competence and was not ashamed to ask questions if he failed to hear something.

And then there was sudden, utter silence as the Station Commander coughed and moved towards the end of the dais. "There you are. Everything's in our favour for a lot of kills today." He smiled and there was a relieved creaking of benches and grunts of amusement. "I was talking to the A.O.C. a few minutes ago and he was saying how important it is that the convoy you can see coming up to Land's End gets in without being attacked again. It's had a bad voyage across the Atlantic. You may feel out of the picture, and patrolling rather far from the convoy's track, but that's where the U-boats will be on their way to attack it. I hope you all have a good trip."

The three squadron commanders would talk to their own men later; but Wing Commander Flying had a fragrant thought to add.

Nig Dunford jumped down from the dais and still his six-feet-four looked like the Eiffel Tower among the rest of the company. "Well, that's it. All you've got to do now is get cracking and keep your fingers out. Don't make a balls of your signals. And when (no "if" in Nig's outlook) you attack, make a couple of dummy runs to make sure you get a good straddle. You'll have bags of time; you've already been told the helpful sods won't dive and spoil your aim that way!"

There were laughter, cheering and groans. So obliging of the helpful sods to lie on the surface; nothing to those three 37mm and 29mm cannon and heavy machine guns, but encouragement.

"And don't turn back if the weather goes a bit duff. Press on to P.L.E. and lob in at Port Lyautey. Good hunting."

The Met. man, lurking in the hall, heard the sneer at the horrors of stormy weather and nearly swallowed his false teeth with indignation.

Trevor Walford expressed his suspicion about Nig's idea of Prudent Limit of Endurance, to Gillam. "When Nig says P.L.E. I suspect he means staying on patrol by hanging on the props and coming back without enough juice even to make a circuit."

Gillam thought so too. "For Nig it's just Limit of Endurance. No 'Prudent'."

With such a crisp valedictory message the crews were sped on their way. They crushed out of the Ops. Room noisily, and death went with them rattling his bones in their heedless ears.

These were the men about whom deathless words had been written, who had inspired the most glorious poetic imagery; the shambling human race, slouching out into the winter chill; lighting cigarettes, chewing sweets, shoving each other in puerile horse-play, scratching the numbness out of their rumps after the hard benches, exchanging obscenities; making eyes at and lewd comments about the girls whom many of them would never see again.

They were not going to immolate themselves self-consciously on the altar of sacred patriotic duty, like the introspective infantry subalterns of neurotic post-1918 plays and novels. They were on their way—irrevocably, now—to suffocate in floundering fuselages filled with acid fumes, charged with electricity and rank with the stench of burning metal and fabric; to the slow flooding of lungs with sea water; to the frozen weakening of flesh and spirit by exposure to icy seas and cruel winds; to be scorched by flames from exploding petrol tanks, or blown to bits by their own depth charges.

They were the men who would be remembered at the going down of the sun and in the morning; and in many other golden phrases. But as they walked out of the old farmhouse they made crude jokes about the young W.A.A.F.s they met in the hallway, they complained about the weather forecast, and they grossly derided Nig Dunford's allusion to the U-boat's new habit of staying surfaced when aircraft found them.

Group Captain Laraway had looked several times at Trevor Walford during briefing. He was heavy hearted at the knowledge that he must presently share with him. While Nig was adding his encouragement to the general briefing, the Station Commander spoke in an undertone to Wing Commander Gretton. "Paul, Group tell me that the captain of the Sunderland, who was taken prisoner, is Walford's brother."

Gretton pursed his lips and frowned. "Shall *I* tell him, sir?"

"I know you'd rather do it yourself, Paul. But if I can do any good by saying anything after you've told him, by all means bring him to see me."

"I'll see how he takes it, sir. Thanks. We'll take him off ops., anyway."

"Nigel thinks not."

"Oh, God! Sir. Supposing he finds that U-boat?"

"The odds are heavily against it, Paul. And Nigel feels he should be kept busy."

"There are other ways of keeping busy, sir. I don't want him on ops. tonight."

"Speak to Nigel. If you can't agree, let me know."

"Very good, sir." Wing Commander Gretton caught up with Wing Commander Dunford as the latter was climbing into his car. "Nig . . . the stationmaster's just told me about Trevor Walford's brother."

"Bloody awful, isn't it?"

"It'll be bloody awfuller if Trevor's the one who happens to get a sighting on U 306."

"Christ! Don't think I fail to see that. But it would be a mistake to take him off ops. today; he'll only have to fly tomorrow, and U 306 will be at sea for another three days before it reaches Lorient."

"I'm going to tell him about his brother and offer to take him off today's ops. if he wants. Both the stand-by crews are as experienced as his, so the effort won't suffer."

"Well, it's your squadron, Paul. . . ."

"That's right, Nig: it is. And Walford is off ops. today unless he insists on flying. If I thought the strain of worrying about his brother and the possibility of having to attack U 306 would affect his work I wouldn't even give him the option. But he's a very sane pilot. . . ."

"Sane? With that twitch?"

"I know him."

"Well, I can't interfere. You'd better tell him now."

Gretton moved away, searching among the crowd for Walford. He saw Snowy. "Sergeant Pomeroy: find Flight Lieutenant Walford and tell him he's coming down to camp in my car. I want a word with him, alone."

Nig jabbed the self-starter and blipped the throttle. He wondered which part of the station would most benefit from a visit. He decided to call on the Fleet Air Arm Operational Training Unit. He thought that its C.O. would appreciate his help; he would take a couple of the pupil pilots up for battle practice (their own instructors were eminently competent!). He never suspected that he flayed the nerves of these youngsters, with his terrifying dogfight aerobatics and the inverted diving attack that he called "For Jesus". Three years before the war he had been on a Gladiator fighter squadron for some months and was convinced that the sailors had a lot to learn from him. In fact, they dreaded his arrival at dispersals and the instructors always tried to fly the pupils' part themselves.

Looking forward keenly to thirty minutes' frolic at ten thousand feet, Nig Dunford roared down the lane with all the gusto of a competitor in a Grand Prix.

Trevor Walford was delayed in the Ops. Room. First, he talked to the Signals Officer in Stan Glover's presence. "I'm not quite clear about the new procedure for changing frequencies. . . ."

Glover held up the notes he had made. "It's straightforward, skipper. . . ."

But Walford had to hear it again from the Signals Officer. Then he followed Cubie Meddings into the map store. The navigator had asked for a new chart and was plotting their patrol points while Gillam looked on, reading them out for him.

"Has Charles got them right, Cubie?"

"Guess so; within ten miles or so!"

Snowy Pomeroy looked in. "Skipper—boss wants you . . . says you're to ride down in his car."

"Blast!" But as he spoke a cold fear stabbed through Walford; usually Wing Commander Gretton picked up the first three of his squadron whom he encountered outside and took them back from briefing. This specific summons was ominous. Tic'ing violently, Trevor Walford went quickly out.

Morag McEwen met him near the front door. "Hello, Trevor. I see you're on late take-off." She studied his face, longing to put her hand on his cheek to comfort him and still the jerking of his nerves. She was racked with pity and affection.

"Yes, worse luck. Can't leave camp today, and we'll be sleeping it off tomorrow."

"I'll see you at lunch, anyway."

"Yep. Got to go . . . boss wants me. . . ."

Morag felt her face tighten. She, too, guessed why Gretton had sent for him.

Outside, in the pale sunlight, she saw Alison Storey laughing and surrounded by officers. Flight Officer Storey had red-gold hair, sea-green eyes and no discernible moral sense. She was an outstandingly efficient Senior Cypher Officer and Morag McEwen righteously loathed her.

Pete Brodie loomed over Alison, trying to exclude his rivals.

"What about tomorrow, Alison?"

"If you're last take-off, Pete, you won't get to bed till lunchtime tomorrow; then you'll sleep till after dinner!"

"Aw, heck. . . ."

"Besides, I'm going to take a twenty-four-hour pass and slip away to gay Torquay."

"Say, that's a good idea; put it off till day after tomorrow, and I'll come too."

Her eyes danced. "Will you indeed? How d'you know you're wanted, Brodie?"

"Well, let's make a date for two days from now, huh? And I'll see you in the mess at lunch. . . ."

Corporal Jean Forrow walked down the short path to the gate, talking to Glover. "Ring the W.A.A.F. billet after lunch if you can manage an hour, Stan."

"I'll do that, Jeannie. We'll have a ride round the perimeter, anyway; take a look at those curlews. . . ."

She pulled a face. "That'll be romantic!"

Wing Commander Gretton drove Trevor Walford away, aware from the younger man's face that he had already jumped to the right conclusion. He felt that his own anger and actual nausea were unreasonable, unjustified. Why should he feel sick and angry at having to do an everyday job? It was not, thank God, every day that he had to break disastrous news to members of his squadron; but it happened a hundred times a day in squadrons and ships and regiments everywhere. He had done it times without number before; yet his own toughness was no protection against the pain of others.

"Care to come to lunch, Trevor? I'm dashing home for a quick bite."

"It's very good of you, sir. But it's not fair to put Mrs Gretton out. . . ."

"That's all right. I phoned. Besides, keeping chickens, we're almost indecently well-found."

"Thank you very much, then, sir."

Walford felt his misery lift. An invitation to lunch, when he had expected a tragedy. His lips relaxed and he felt the tugging in his right shoulder ease.

"Trevor . . . the Sunderland from 2233 that was shot down this morning by the U-boat . . . your brother wasn't hurt . . . not hurt at all . . . but I'm afraid it was his flying boat; and the Jerries took the crew aboard . . . your brother's a prisoner in that damnable U 306. . . ."

In the silence of the next half-minute Trevor Walford felt the tugging at his shoulder, the jerking in his head and cheek return with fiendishly increased uncontrollability.

"Thanks for telling me, sir. . . ."

"I'm taking you off today's ops. . . ."

"No, sir. It's very good of you, but . . . no . . . I'd rather be in the area, taking part in what goes on, than sitting around here, wondering . . . I wouldn't get any sleep, anyway. . . ."

Gretton did not reply. The Medical Officer would soon fix any insomnia. Walford had the same thought. "And it would be worse if the doc. made me sleep—I'd wake up in hell's panic, wondering what the devil had been going on that I didn't know about . . . I've got to stay on ops, sir, please."

"All right. That's fair enough."

Gretton stopped at the cottage gate and his son came running down the path. Cynthia Gretton stood in the open door, regretting that she had taken those two eggs to Melanie Dunford. The four she had kept would disappear in the omelette their guest was going to share. Paul had telephoned briefly and asked her to do something special for young Trevor Walford. As she watched Paul gather their child in his arms and perch him on his shoulder, and saw the sadness in Walford's face as he thought himself unobserved, she was filled with intense personal animosity for the savage sky that took and took and never gave back.

## CHAPTER FOUR

WING COMMANDER PAUL GRETTON, Commanding No. 1111 Squadron, was a grateful man. He was grateful for holding so high a rank at the age of twenty-seven. He was grateful to his squadron for maintaining an admirable record of efficiency and persistence; grateful that none of his aircraft captains was of the kind who habitually found magneto drops, lack of oil pressure and other faults in their machines within twenty minutes of take-off and only flew one operation in every four for which they were scheduled. Not that he would have hesitated to kick out any such miscreant, for cowardice. "Lack of Moral Fibre" . . . L.M.F. . . . the brand that was mercilessly burned even on the bravest when they cracked.

He was grateful for surviving three attacks by Kuriers and Messerschmitt 109's; for surviving a share in two sightings of U-boats; for surviving four days in a dinghy in the summer of 1941, when an engine failure and electrical fire had forced him to ditch.

Above all he was grateful for his pretty wife and the home she made for them wherever he was posted; and he was grateful for his four-year-old son.

Every morning, after breakfast, he "went to work"; only a couple of miles down the road. He seldom came home to lunch; at supper time, he "came home from work"; although he often returned for short visits to the Ops. Room, or made telephone calls to camp, or went to the mess for a quick one with the boys. But these were on the days when he did not fly on operations. When he flew a patrol, he "missed lunch" or "didn't get home in time for supper".

By preserving this attitude of ordinariness, he tried to obscure the bitter contrast between his domestic tranquillity and the tenor of his hours of absence.

Cynthia Gretton knew much about the risks of flying, because she had heard flying discussed as long as she could remember. Her father, an air commodore now, had made few friends outside the Service. Her husband was a professional airman to his fingertips. Cynthia knew that even a war did not create circumstances which fundamentally altered the main concerns of professional flying men. Their business was with the efficiency of their aircraft and all its equipment; with a respect for routine and regulations. In these matters, a peacetime flight of a hundred miles on a cross-country exercise was no different from a war-time flight of eight hundred miles to bomb Germany, or a thousand miles to hunt a U-boat. It was still the engines and the radio and the weather that occupied the attention of pilots and crews. The fact that angry men with guns were trying to prevent them from completing their flights was, in a way, incidental.

Cynthia well knew the atmosphere in which her husband worked. She understood the hurt he felt when one of his crews did not return from a flight; the horror he had of having to pass on his hurt to the bereaved families to whom he must write. She understood the secret fear that came to him when he thought of facing danger; the fear of death, of the grief to them and the loss he would suffer if he did not live to see his child grow up to fortify his happy relationship with his wife; the fear of disfigurement or crippling injury. She tried to see him as he wanted to see himself; an everyday working family man who came and went at conventional hours and, during his absence, pursued humdrum tasks.

On the telephone, he had only told her that Trevor Walford's brother had been shot down that morning and was unhurt but "poorly placed".

She watched the flight lieutenant walk along the crazy-paved path between lavender bushes and a few stubborn, long-lived but wilting chrysanthemum stalks. His healthy pink face was expressionless but a restless nerve jerked at the corner of his right eye, his cheek twitched every few seconds and he intermittently shrugged a shoulder as though his battledress armhole was too tight. She was, if anything, a few months younger than he, but she felt all the wisdom and compassion and experience of a matriarch and longed to reach out for him and offer him the comfort that she kept in her heart for all suffering humanity.

Instead, she said blithely: "I'm glad you've come, Flight Lieutenant Walford. It's too long since I saw any of the squadron."

"I hope I'm not putting you out, Mrs Gretton; but the boss kidnapped me, very kindly, straight after briefing."

The formality of surnames between Cynthia Gretton and the squadron owed nothing to any aloofness on her part or unfriendliness on theirs. In peacetime, when officers and their wives were together for two or three years, lived as neighbours on a "married patch" and met almost daily, there was a quick intimacy. In wartime, with few married aircrew and fewer wives, and with frequent changes and infrequent contacts, there was no time or opportunity for more than willing comradery.

The child was holding his father's amused attention with a breathless recital of the morning's events. Cynthia took Walford to the drawing-room, while these two lagged behind.

"I expect you'd like a beer?" She knew they never drank anything stronger at mid-day.

"Yes, please." Walford stood at the French window, looking down the garden to the estuary. His eyes, as Cynthia noticed, turned to the south-west; his mind was on a few square miles of choppy, cold, grey water. And, which Cynthia did not know, a narrow black hull, sliding through the darkness beneath the waves, that might at any hour become a tomb for sixty-six German sailors and seven British airmen.

Suddenly four Seafires lanced into view, climbing steeply. The noise of their engines, with the propellers in fully fine pitch, screamed into the little room. In a moment the leader rolled on to his back, pulled through vertically towards the cottage, half-rolled out and shot skyward again in a near-perpendicular.

The child danced and clapped his hands, crowing, "Uncle Nig, Uncle Nig. . . ."

Walford turned and his face reflected his squadron commander's wry tolerance of the Wing Commander Flying's virtuosity.

Gretton unbent to mutter what Walford would have liked to. "Poor bloody webfeet." They wondered which trembling naval pilots were sitting in the other three cockpits.

Cynthia was glad of the diversion. Although bred in the R.A.F.'s custom of ignoring tragedy, her gentleness prompted her to recognize, however tritely, her guest's present grief. Birdman Dunford had, unwittingly, dispelled the awkwardness.

*    *    *

Wing Commander Dunford's wife, Melanie, standing at the telephone with a large pink gin in her hand, also saw the Seafires fly overhead.

Her bungalow was a hundred yards along the lane from the Gretton's, thus Nigel's habitual beat-ups were ostensibly for her. She tightened her wide, thin lips and frowned as the noise drowned the voice on the other end of the wire, in the Officers' Mess.

"Say that again. An aircraft just buzzed the house."

"I said I can't make it for lunch, baby. I gotta work tonight."

"Damn you, darling." She pouted, remembered that Cubie Meddings could not see, and let her mouth relax into its normal predatory line. "Look, I've got a great hunk of venison at a hell of a price; you've got to come and help me eat it."

He knew all about her black market butcher. "Sure, I'll come; tomorrow."

She heard him laugh quietly. Angry at his easy assurance, she flared. "Go to hell. I'll get somebody else."

"You do that, baby. I'll be along tomorrow, like I told you. Today is out. You know I can't leave the station. . . ."

This was true. Crews on the day's operational list were confined to camp.

"All right. I'll forgive you. But don't be surprised if you find someone else here when you do come tomorrow."

"I won't, baby. That's one thing that'd never surprise me, for sure."

They laughed together, then.

*　　*　　*

In the Operations Room the watches were changing over. Squadron Leader Stevenson's watch would come on duty again that evening; the officers after an early dinner, the airmen at midnight, until eight the following morning.

Stevenson still sat in his chair, with the relieving controller leaning over his shoulder, reading the log book. Charles Gillam, handing over to a zealous, newly-commissioned bank clerk, stood before the map. Its buff and blue paint, representing land and sea, was like an idealized illustration in a child's book; insipid and meaningless. The web of coloured wool, and the shipping symbols, mocked him. All this cold simplification stood for ships and men and aircraft; for days and nights of toil and peril; for aching hours of critical alertness, incessant watchfulness. The voice at his side remarked unimaginatively on the size of the Group effort. There seemed no point in inviting further bathos by mentioning the capture of the survivors from the Sunderland.

Sergeant Murch was already at the door, gabbling explanations and instructions to his successor in the controller's assistant's chair. Lowering his voice to a dark rumble, he concluded with a scabrous summary of "yon rutting bastard's carry-on over t'tea and t'squadron states, an' all," nodding in Stevenson's direction. "But I'll get me own back on t'rutter, an' all . . . and it won't be long . . . joost let 'im wait coom night watch. . . ."

The girls were pouring down the stairs from Signals. Their voices, always carefree and full of vitality, came clearly through the open door. Someone asked Corporal Forrow to cycle into Tawmouth and help her spend a few clothing coupons an aunt had sent. "No," said Jean Forrow, "Stan can't go off camp, but we're going to bike round the perimeter if there's time." Whereupon there was giggling, and advice not to let him see she was so keen and then silence as Section Officer Morag McEwen's shiny nose popped round the door of the Ops. Room where she had gone to stare learnedly at the movements board and the maps.

The girls' chatter broke out again as soon as they stepped outside the building and saw Flight Officer Storey leaning against the warm, grey-yellow wall, like a golden panther in the sun; a sun that seemed all the brighter for shining on her, for gathering some of her lustre.

Enviously, Morag McEwan heard the W.A.A.F.s stop and talk to Alison, wishing she had the same universal appeal. Her mind dwelt on Trevor Walford.

Stevenson at last was satisfied that he had left the affairs of the Operations Room adequately covered for the next seven hours. He rose, made a chest, smoothed his moustache and looked distastefully at the relieving navigator; who smirked uncertainly. He hailed Gillam. "Coming, Charles?"

"Aye, aye, sir."

"Now don't you start any bogus naval habits, Charles. This may be Coastal Command, but there are limits."

Gillam thought that was rich, coming from the arch exponent of affectation. But he followed Steve out without retort. He valued his senior controller as a source of entertainment.

On the way down to camp, in the coach, he saw that Morag McEwan looked more withdrawn than he had ever seen her. Usually she smiled readily although she was not given to much talk.

Flight Officer McEwan's level head was a pother of dissatisfaction and doubt which was astonishing in anyone so imbued with John Knoxian principles.

She could not keep her eyes away from Alison Storey, who sat obliquely in front of her, on the other side of the aisle, in a facing seat. Alison's head was turned towards Squadron Leader Stevenson, her neighbour. Stevenson was long-married, forty and the father of three children; but Flight Officer Storey's bright expression and interested eyes were the same as they would have been in conversation with a young bachelor. For the first time, Morag realized that the other girl's studied complaisance was not the shamelessness that her own narrow-minded rectitude condemned, but a compliment to the man who held her attention. Alison Storey liked people. She liked men better than any other sort of people. So, when she gave someone any share of her personality, she did it whole-heartedly. In doing so, she imparted some of her gaiety and innate appeal to him.

Watching Morag McEwan, Gillam was glad to see her pursey mouth soften and the down-drawn creases at each corner of her lips fade. He liked Morag, and he knew that she was worrying about Trevor Walford; he was pleased to notice a sign of easement. For a moment he continued to study her mouth, comparing it with Alison's. He, like nearly every other male on the camp, had a permanent mental image of its generous, soft invitation. Morag's lips were dry and needed more than the dab of almost colourless lipstick she allowed herself when off duty. It was easy to understand Trevor Walford's indifference to her.

The coach stopped at the Officers' Mess. Morag made up her mind to the unprecedented coquetry of darting into the cloakroom and slapping on some powder and lipstick with her usual lack of skill before entering the dining-room. She did not know that Flight Lieutenant Walford had been taken home to lunch by his C.O.

All these emotions, weaknesses and strengths of human nature had their bearing on the ultimate great issue; the converging paths of a predatory U-boat, U 306, and a Wellington anti-submarine aircraft which had not as yet taken off on its mission to find and destroy it.

Wing Commander Dunford came late to the mess for lunch. He took his three Fleet Air Arm victims into the bar to reward them with pints of beer for their tenacity in dog-fighting with him. He never went home to lunch and now it occurred to him that he would be sleeping on camp until the present U-boat alarum subsided. His wife, on the telephone, was beguiling.

"Can't you pop in just for a little minute, honey?" She knew he would not, so she could afford to sound sincere.

"No. The coast's clear; you can have all your boy friends along."

Nig saw his reflection in the glass of the telephone box in the hall
of the mess and thought that his smile could not have been more
convincing if they were talking personally.

"Poppet . . ." Melanie sounded disappointed and reproving and
about as harmless as a tarantula. ". . . this damn little bungalow's
like an ice-box. I do need something to keep me warm. I'm going
to bed early with all the hot water bottles I can find."

"Take a bottle of gin over to the Grettons'. Paul won't be leaving the station and Cynthia'll be fed up too."

"All very well. But what about the trek back in the cold night
air?"

"Enough gin should take care of that. . . ."

He hung up, wondering why he had not insisted on fathering
a child on Melanie. It was what she needed. When they married,
two years ago, he had thought that their sophisticated absorption
in each other would endure and suffice until peace brought them a
better regulated life. She was three years older than he; had been
presented at Court and inherited an independent eight hundred
a year. The handsome, dashing, much decorated young wing commander was like a platinum-and-diamond charm to add to her
bracelet of gold ones; and to outshine the husbands of her friends.
It was chic to own a gonged-up pilot in those days. Already the
lustre was wearing thin. The Thing now was to have an American
who brought hams and silk stockings and canned turkey and
cosmetics from the P.X.

Nig, too busy with flying to give his mind to more than one
subject outside it, loved her.

*　　　*　　　*

In the Sergeants' Mess, Lofty Duckett attacked his victuals with
New South Walesian gusto. Stan Glover, neat and fastidious at
table as at the workbench, was worried about Snowy. The West
Indian had been morose since briefing. Snowy Pomeroy and
Lofty Duckett were bound in the close comradeship of men who
were both in a strange land. Moreover, since Glover was so much
occupied with Jean Forrow, they were thrown much alone in each
other's company. The tall Australian looked after Pomeroy, as he
would look after any living creature he judged feebler than himself. Duckett's big hands were light when they touched a lamb or
an ailing sheep, a horse or a dog. He put Snowy Pomeroy in the
same category.

Stan Glover knew that, when Lofty finished eating, he would, in his own indirect way, tackle the reason for Snowy's obvious misery. But an unhappy member of the crew could not be fully efficient; and this troubled Flight Sergeant Glover.

Snowy ate his tasteless food in silence, his eyes cast down. Only by smothering his mountain of mashed potatoes, watery cabbage and four or five lumps of poor quality beef with sauce could he force the war-time diet into his stomach. And what sauce! Thin tomato ketchup as sour as gall, and another that was brown and pungently unidentifiable. The label on the bottle said it was "Mummy's Favourite" and Sergeant Galahad Pomeroy was not the only airman to reflect that Mummy's taste must have been perverted. Everyone in England had become used to living mainly on potatoes; Snowy had eaten on American air stations, when forced down by bad weather; he was beginning to wish that the West Indies were an American possession.

Lofty Duckett contemplated his leathery portion of treacle tart that was nearly all iron-hard pastry, and sighed. "That old bastard Cubie knew something when he took a transfer to the Yank air corps."

Stan Glover smiled. "I'll say! Though he had no option; it's an order. All Yanks have got to leave the British Services and go into their own."

"Cubie'll be a bloody major in no time—you watch." Lofty shared the common opinion on the rapidity of American promotion.

Snowy seemed to stiffen and come to life. "Cubie's going soon?"

"No, thank Christ, he ain't. He'll be in bloody 'lootenant's' uniform any time now, but he'll stay on the squadron till the crew's tour-ex."

Glover saw Snowy's face fall at Duckett's words. "Don't you get on with Cubie, or something, then, Snowy?" His voice was kind.

"Sure. He just doesn't notice me, so how could we not get on?" Snowy was bitter. "But he knows I'm there, sure enough. Same way he'd register against anyone of a different colour; he knows I'm around, and he doesn't like it."

So this was the root of Pomeroy's discontent. Glover spoke up with false brightness. "You've got old Cubie all wrong, Snowy boy. He's a damn fine navigator, too; lucky for us he is staying with the crew till the end of this tour."

Duckett's long face, usually set in dourness, tried to express cheerful encouragement. "Yeah, Stan's right, Snowy. Cubie don't mean no harm. Hell! He's willing enough to play poker with you, isn't he?"

No reply came from the West Indian.

*          *          *

In the Officers' Mess, a glum Morag McEwan was being wooed.

Flight Lieutenant Donnelly, navigator on a crew in 1111 Squadron which was at present on leave, had stayed behind in the hope of capturing Section Officer McEwan's favours. Waiting for her to come off duty, at a vantage point in the bar, he had pounced as soon as she sat at the dining table. Redolent of bitter beer, his breath played over her while his talkativeness distracted her attention from Stevenson and Gillam. The messing officer had put ham and cold beef on the lunch menu; Morag, a good trencher-woman, allowed that they, with mustard pickle and crisply fried potatoes, mitigated Paddy Donnelly's unwelcome infatuation.

At the other end of the same table, Alison Storey, delectable and shining, weighed Pete Brodie against his most immediate rival. Crude, naive Canadian against suave Englishman. Flying Officer Brodie v. Squadron Leader Rowan; Tommy Rowan's twenty-nine shillings a day in the balance with the Royal Canadian Air Force's unknown but suspectedly bigger pay—even a flying officer's.

Rowan was captain of Paddy Donnelly's crew, now on leave. For him, the attraction to R.A.F. Tawmouth in preference to London night clubs was also concupiscence. Memory of one clandestine escapade with Flight Officer Storey urged him to repeat the experience. Hence her planned visit to Torquay.

Tommy Rowan, dark, quiet and self-assured, sat at Alison's side. Opposite, loomed Pete Brodie; beef-red, noisy and self-assured.

Both Donnelly and Rowan, had they been able to foresee the consequences of their amorous dalliance (sic) on camp, would have lit out for anywhere on the first train.

*          *          *

The hours between lunch and dinner, before a night watch, could be the most arid of their two-day-on-one-day-off duty cycle for the Ops. Room staff.

Stevenson put on civilian clothes and went for a long walk. He strode so fast that nobody would accompany him. Some people

frowsted in the mess ante room, others went to their own rooms
to sleep.

Charles Gillam, boxing Blue and wing forward for the Oxford
University Greyhounds, spent an hour of these afternoons in the
gym.

The sergeant P.T. Instructor had been a leading pre-war con-
tender for the British middleweight title. He and Gillam sparred
regularly, with mutual respect. As the latter, in old flannels and a
yellowing sweater, trotted towards the gym, he heard the heavy
pounding of feet and the stertorous breathing which proclaimed
that a compulsory P.T. class was in progress. He grinned.

Physical Training was scorned by air crews. They said that if
they were fit to pass an air crew medical, they were fit—period!
As a natural corollary to this followed the air crew attitude of
scorn for the ground staff's presumed physical inferiority as well
as for their safer duties. It was healthy and legitimate that young
men following a dangerous avocation should be arrogant and
proud. Gillam, recognizing their justifiable conceit in the knowledge that they shared an exclusive mystique, yet resented their
presumption of all-round superiority. His greatest wish was to
qualify for air crew and he knew that, athletically and scholas-
tically, he could have beaten nine-tenths of them.

He stood in the doorway, watching the clumsy movements of
the podgy and the cadaverous whose bodies were now revealed in
all their pale ugliness; bereft of swashbuckling appurtenances, of
Irvine jackets and brevets and parachute bags, they were sorry
figures. But they were not sorry for themselves and not one of
them recognized himself as a nicotine-saturated, spindle-shanked,
round-shouldered abuse of manly strength and grace. They were
all well satisfied with themselves just as they were. After all, they
passed air crew medical checks at frequent intervals.

One of the corporal P.T.I.'s caught his eye and nodded, winking; muttering: "Only a couple more minutes, sir."

Soon the whistle went and there was a stampede for the changing room, voices croaking for a smoke and trembling hands
groping for packets of cigarettes.

Wing Commander Gretton's navigator, a lout called Tug
Wilson, a flight lieutenant, and God in his own opinion for
weighing fourteen stone and being the squadron's navigation
leader, stared sweatily at Gillam.

"Hello, Gillam. Are the penguins doing P.T. this afternoon?"

"Penguin" was the cruel derogatory term for those outside the air crew clique. The bird that cannot fly. Gillam loathed the term and had found that only the meanest-spirited people used it.

"Don't bloody well call me a penguin; not in that tone, anyway."

Loutish Tug Wilson's stare darkened to a glower. Short-tempered after his distasteful exertions, convinced that his fourteen stones ten pounds made him Herculean, he folded his flabby arms on his big chest and threatened. "You are a rutting penguin, cock. I didn't know they made you people keep fit."

"Nobody has to make me keep fit, Tug. I come down to spar with the sergeant."

"Oh, do you? To spar? I've done a bit of boxing." (The usual claim of all males, who feel that to have no experience of this sport is to admit lack of guts. It usually means a few timid bouts at school.) "We might have a couple of rounds . . . if you think you can last out."

This, overheard, provoked alarm in the conscientious sergeant and glee in the corporals.

The sergeant came forward. "Flight Lieutenant Wilson, sir . . . I don't think . . ."

Wilson cut him off, patronizingly. "O.K., O.K., I know I'm a hell of a lot heftier than he is—but I'll take it easy. What about it, Gillam?"

Wing Commander Gretton appeared in the doorway, uniformed, excused P.T. by virtue of his rank, but there to see that his squadron was not shirking. At his voice, Wilson reddened. "I didn't know you were a bruiser, Tug."

"I can use 'em a bit, sir . . . if Gillam wants exercise, may as well put 'em on . . . if he can see well enough to box, without his specs. . . ."

Gillam turned to the sergeant. "Bring a set, will you, Sergeant?" He winked. "As the fourteen-ounce gloves have gone for repair, we might as well make do with the competition-weight ones."

The sergeant understood.

Wilson had his first premonition when Gillam peeled off his sweater and revealed his big, hard, well defined weight-trainer's muscles. He had his next when the latter began to put on a pair of boxing boots.

He had his third when they climbed into the ring, touched gloves and Gillam glided smoothly away from his looping right. He swung again and Gillam, ducking inside, hit him with a left hook that broke two of his ribs. Recognizing the injury only as an infuriating pain, Wilson charged with both fists flailing. Gillam closed his right eye with a straight left, split his left ear with a right hook, gashed his lips with a left one-two that went on to pulp the flesh and bone of his nose, and knocked him unconscious with a thundering short right to the point of the jaw that laid him out for nearly five minutes. They had been sparring for approximately thirty seconds.

Those of the P.T. class who had not hurriedly left the hated premises as soon as they were dismissed, made loudly wondering conversation.

Wing Commander Gretton looked angry. "Blast you, Gillam. You've wrecked my navigator; if my crew's called out, I'll have to find a substitute."

Savagely, Gillam leaned on the ropes. "If you'd like to change, sir, I'll give you a chance to square it for him."

For many seconds the wing commander held his eyes, and Gillam waited to be rebuked for his insolence. Then Gretton shrugged. "You made your point. I heard what Tug said. . . ."

The sergeant, carrying a set of practice gloves, climbed into the ring. "Look what I found, sir." He and Gillam grinned at each other. The released class settled itself to watch as the two skilled men shaped up to one another.

Wilson, revived, tottered to the ropes. "I'll see you another time, Gillam."

"Rut off!"

Flight Lieutenant Wilson went to Sick Quarters. The knowledge that, by injuring him, Gillam had saved his life, might have comforted him. Unfortunately, there was no way for him to foretell this, and by the time he worked it out in the light of events, a few hours later, his only emotion would be annoyance at having missed an exciting operation . . . albeit a fatal one.

The roar of a Wellington taking off filled the gymnasium. Gillam glanced at the wall clock. That was the third take-off. Hammer Two was well on, now. Already two of the Tawmouth aircraft were out over the sullen water of the Bay. This was the third link in the chain of destructive events which bound them all, the squadrons and the Ops. Room people and everyone else on the station, to a common purpose. His thoughts turned for a moment to U 306.

Meanwhile, the afternoon went forward without obvious signs of the station's participation in the terrors and rigours of air-maritime warfare.

Stevenson, his chest splendidly inflated with ozone, strode along the Cornish lanes towards a farmhouse tea. The night's duty Intelligence Officer dozed in an ante room chair with a copy of "Punch" over his face. Alison Storey, in transparent pyjamas, slept soundly in her bed. Morag McEwan let Paddy Donnelly take her to a cinema and tea in Tawmouth.

Melanie Dunford took her dogs for a stroll towards the airfield perimeter, where she had arranged to meet Cubie Meddings for a few minutes.

Cynthia Gretton and her son went riding across the meadows and through the woods, cantering after rabbits, jumping fallen tree-trunks; she forgetting the war for an hour.

Trevor Walford, shrugging his shoulder, blinking, cheek twitching, went over his aircraft with Stan Glover, from end to end, before they both went to their rooms to rest. Glover to his rendezvous with Jean Forrow, first, and thence to easy sleep. For Walford, uneasy visions of men trapped in a narrow steel hull a hundred feet below the sea's surface, while he tossed and moaned between the sheets.

## CHAPTER FIVE

THEY stood round the palely shining bulk of "B for Baker"; a low-murmuring group of purposeful young men.

An occasional bar of muted amber light escaped from a door when someone went in or out of the crew room, pushing the blackout curtain momentarily aside; the markers along the taxi tracks glowed dimly; overhead swung the bright red and green port and starboard wingtip lights of a Wellington in the circuit, coming in to land from a night navigation exercise.

The diffused yellowness of a taxi track lamp shone on the white aeroplane and cast on it the shadows of its crew. A crew edgy and impatient now, wishing to be free of the ground, to immerse itself in the routine, the problems and anxieties of flight and war.

There was no moon, and storm clouds were forming over the hills. The breeze carried a smell of wet seaweed from the estuary.

Squadron Leader Rowan, Walford's Flight Commander, stood under the port wing, talking to Cubie Meddings.

"Met. say the front's spreading and moving fast. You'll find the winds a bit tricky when you get down to the Bay."

"You can say that again! But I gotta theory about this goddam warm front . . ."

"Stuff your theories, Cubie. Stick to facts for the next ten hours."

Walford joined them. "I thought you were on leave, sir?"

"I am. But I thought I'd stay around camp till tomorrow, and see how the hunt goes."

Pete Brodie, standing beside Walford, grunted. He knew all about the hunt in which Tommy Rowan was really interested. The smooth bastard was staying around so as to take Alison Storey to Torquay for a sticky twenty-four tomorrow. Brodie was in a bad temper: his resentment against having to fly as second pilot, on operations he despised, had been increased by a hint from the squadron's new assistant adjutant that his hope of a posting to fighters was damned. Then there was the weather. All afternoon and evening it had been deteriorating, first in the operational area and later near base. The trip would be bumpy, and visibility probably so bad as to give no chance of a sighting: supposing they did happen on a surfaced U-boat. Walford's authority, his rigid observance of rules and orders, were further aggravations; and his twitch, worse now than it had ever been, robbed Brodie of confidence in such a captain.

Wing Commander Gretton's quiet voice spoke from the darkness. "You might take off a few minutes early, if you're ready, Trevor: the cloud base seems to be coming down rather fast."

Walford moved towards his three N.C.O.'s, who were chatting to the Flight Commander. "All set, Stan?"

"Hold it, skipper; I think this is Wingco. Dunford."

They all turned to look towards the nearest hangar. A car had shot round the corner and was coming noisily towards them, the feeble beam of its masked headlamps dancing as the springs took bumps in the road.

Paul Gretton involuntarily clenched his fists. What the hell was Nig blinding about in the darkness for? Surely not a last-minute insistence on grounding Walford? That argument had been firmly disposed of in the morning.

Nig came to a dead stop from twenty miles an hour and called through the open window. "Another sighting. I've got the position for you." He jumped out and offered a slip of paper which Meddings quickly took. "Quite a party brewing out there. We'll all be in the area before tomorrow's over. You all set, Trevor?"

"All set, sir. As a matter of fact we were going to anticipate E.T.D. by a few minutes."

"Good idea. Looks as though the weather may go clampers; for a while, at least. Got all the gen you want? Anything more I can tell you?"

"No, thank you, sir. Thanks for bringing that last sighting down."

"O.K., cock, good hunting. If Group push out a recall, tell your Wop. to stuff his finger in; but don't say I said so! Have a good trip."

Gretton came forward. "Don't take any chances with the weather, Trevor. I don't want anyone diverted to Gib. or Port Lyautey. I want all my aircraft here tomorrow; there's enough trade in the Bay to keep us busy for days."

"All right, sir. All aboard, chaps."

Cubie Meddings, like a grizzly in his flying clothes, clambered up the ladder and disappeared, singing: "Morphine Bill and Cocaine Sue, were coming down the Aven-oo . . . Honey have a sniff, have a sniff on me, Oh! Honey have a sniff on me. . . ."

Stan Glover followed, as neat and quick as a cat. Lofty Duckett mounted two rungs at a time, butted his head on the edge of the trapdoor, and swore an oath which would have shivered the blue gum trees of his native back blocks.

Snowy Pomeroy, moving like an invisible man, his hands and face being merged with the night, climbed slowly; as though some premonition bade him delay on firm ground as long as possible while he had the chance.

The two pilots lingered for a moment. Brodie to demonstrate his independence, and Walford to take one more long look around the sky, seeing how few were the stars and how threatening the cloud.

Then they, too, were about to break away when the crew room door slammed back against the wall, an airman jerked aside the blackout with such agitation that light flooded on to the tarmac for a few seconds, and a voice called urgently: "Flight Lieutenant Walford!"

Trevor's heart turned over, choking the breath from his throat so that he had to fight for words. He thought at once of his brother, trapped in an enemy submarine; someone had found U 306 and sunk it!

He regained his voice at last. "Yes. Here. What is it?"

"Ops. Room on the phone for you, sir."

"O.K. Coming."

Paul Gretton, filled with the same anticipation that had struck Walford so hard, moved with him. "I'll come, too, Trevor."

Silently, they went at a half trot into the untidy room stinking of old cigarettes and a dying coke fire in the stove. The duty airman held the telephone out to Walford, his eyes full of envy. He would have liked an Irvine jacket and flying boots and a flight lieutenant's pilot's pay.

Walford had control of his voice. "Walford here."

Gretton, standing close, plainly recognized Stevenson's voice in the earpiece. "Hello, Trevor; Steve here."

"What's the trouble, Steve?"

"Nae bother, Trevor; just a final briefing. Me. 410's are operating down here tonight. Keep a lookout for them on your way out. The fighter boys down the road have just shot one down and their Ops. Room has plots on four more. They've slunk in at low level, under the radar, so I expect they're looking for you chaps; the Hun will know that we must be making an all-out effort to cover the Bay, with so many U-boats out, so these Me. 410's must have been sent across to bag as many Coastal aircraft as they can."

"That's nice of 'em. Thanks for the word, Steve."

"Good luck then, Trevor."

Walford replaced the telephone and looked wryly at his squadron commander. The latter shrugged. "I heard, Trevor. Well, forewarned is forearmed, and so on; if you see anything suspicious, nip into cloud as fast as you can."

"You bet!" Walford put the tips of his fingers into his mouth and chewed nervously on his silk flying glove. His shoulder twitched uncontrollably and he blinked rapidly. Gretton felt sickeningly sorry for him, but remained convinced that he was doing right in letting him fly tonight.

They went back to the aircraft. Dunford and Rowan waited in silence; neither of them doubted that the controller had called Walford to the telephone to give him bad news about his brother. Nig had ordered Pete Brodie aboard; this was something best hidden from the crew. Even Rowan had known nothing about the situation until this moment, when Nig Dunford explained it to him. The latter broke the silence, now.

"Troub., Trevor?"

"Not really, sir; it seems there are 410's about. The Beaufighters at Meganporth have just shot one down, and there are four more plotted in the Fighter Ops. Room."

"That's cheerful. I'd better get back to Ops. and have a word with the fighter boys; this gets bigger and better. On your way then, Trevor."

"So long, sir."

With relief, Walford made a gesture of farewell to Gretton and Tommy Rowan and climbed up into the waiting "B for Baker". Now he was in complete command of himself and his crew and their aircraft. He shut the trap door in "B Baker's" floor and eased himself into his seat on the port side. Putting on his helmet, plugging in and switching on the intercom., he told his crew about the intruding Messerschmitt 410's. "So I want you in the astrodome, Stan, when we clear the circuit. Lofty, go into the nose after take-off."

Lofty Duckett made a rude noise. He didn't want to sit in the perspex nose, behind the twin Browning guns, looking for 410's; there was something much more interesting he had hoped to do. A small coastal convoy which Gillam had said, at briefing, should be nearing Land's End by now, would make a convenient check feature for Lofty's A.S.V. radar. Cubie Meddings's chuckle came over the intercom. "I know what's on your mind, Lofty; forget it; I'll check the radar for you." Lofty grunted again, with deeper displeasure. That bastard Cubie was always itching to get his hands on everything.

In the tail turret, Snowy Pomeroy held tightly to the handles with which he traversed and elevated his four machine guns. The silhouette of a Me. 410 flickered across his mind. He made exultant popping noises, in imitation of gunfire; and the imaginary Messerschmitt went down in flames.

Pete Brodie wriggled impatiently in his seat on Walford's right; enormous in the swaddling leather jacket; tall and ungainly in the confined space, sitting hunched and dissatisfied and critical.

For a few seconds Walford sat motionless, collecting his thoughts, quietening his leaping nerves. Presently the familiar smells of dope, petrol, oil, warm rubber and ammunition, that compound the odour of aeroplanes, permeated and saturated his being; filled him with the warm confidence that came from knowing that he was about to do what he had done many hundreds of times before. And done competently.

He put a finger on the starter. There was a whining, a whirring and the port engine stuttered; caught; bellowed. Presently the noise and vibration increased twofold as the starboard engine came in. He selected "fully-fine" on his variable-pitch propellers. His right hand moved gently forward, opening both throttles. The tachometer readings for both engines climbed to a thousand revolutions a minute. He held them at this speed while the oil pressure soared, then steadied, and the oil temperature crept up. He tested both magnetos.

The aircraft trembled throughout its length, from the nose where an empty gun position waited for Lofty Duckett, to the lonely tail where Snowy Pomeroy sat in isolation and discomfort. The great pistons in their cavernous cylinders hammered life into the propellers cutting the cold night air. While it stayed on the ground, now that its engines were running, "B" was an anomaly. A clumsy creature, out of its element, and transmitting only exaggerated noise and vibration to its crew.

Instrument and control panels shimmered and shuddered in their rubber mountings, luminous pointers and figured dials glowed green and hooded lights brought tense faces into silhouette.

Walford eased the throttles further open with his right hand, while his left held the control column and brakes. The noise of the engines rose and thundered through his muffling leather helmet, his safety-belt gripped him to the vibrant aircraft, making his body a part of it and of the din and violence. The noise grew until it seemed as though the engines must protest at the strain; yet they were still not at full power. At two thousand eight hundred revolutions a minute he flicked the magneto switches, watching the gauges carefully; no loss of power. Mag. drop was a fault that often foiled flight after hours of preparation. Letting the revolutions drop to a thousand (no lower, for fear of oiling the plugs), he tested the magnetos again. Satisfied, he let the engines turn over at this speed for another three minutes, until oil temperature and pressure had steadied.

He waved the chocks away. Unseen airmen in the darkness tugged the ropes that removed wooden blocks from in front of the wheels.

Switching on his landing lights, Walford released the brakes and "B for Baker" crept forward, feeling for the runway. Now the pilot was in a two-dimensional world of red, green and yellow lights. He could not see the outlines of hangars or huts; he could forget which way he was facing after a few turns along the winding taxi track; all he had to guide him were the marker lights.

He saw the shiny black of the tarmac, in his lights, against the dull black of the night. He watched the runway lights come up ahead as he accelerated his port engine to follow the right-hand curve of the track. He rumbled on to the down-wind end of the runway and braked with a jolt and a hiss of compressed air, slightly diagonally to his line of take-off.

Gripping the brakes hard against the control column, he pushed the rev.-counter needles up to two thousand eight hundred again; tested the magnetos; eased back to twelve hundred and tested again; dropped to a thousand.

He spoke to Brodie, through the intercom: "All set, Pete?" and saw the second pilot's left hand move forward near the undercarriage lever. "All set," and Brodie sounded surly.

Then: "Captain to crew. Check in."

"Second pilot." Sourly.

"Navigator." Cheerfully.

"Wireless operator." Coolly.

"A.S.V. operator." Reproachfully.

"Rear gunner." With a chatter of teeth. Snowy felt cold.

"Stand by for take-off."

Every man braced himself in his straps. They had all seen aircraft stall on take-off, through loss of an engine; a nose-dive, a burst of flame, an explosion; and not a fragment left of the crew. They had seen a sudden gust of cross-wind fling an aircraft sideways; if that happened here, they would fly into a hillside and be blown to bits.

Walford thumbed his R/T button. "Tawmouth Tower, this is Yeoman two-nine. Request permission for take-off. Over."

"Yeoman two-nine, clear take-off. Wind zero-three-zero, ten knots. Regional pressure setting, a thousand and six. Over."

"Roger."

Walford gunned his starboard engine, swinging from the diagonal to line up along the centre of the runway; slowly opened up to twelve hundred revolutions a minute, letting the brakes go; fifteen hundred, and as soon as he was sure that he was steady and straight, he eased both throttles right forward. His back rest hit him between the shoulder blades. The runway lights moved towards him fast. Faster. Began racing past.

Brodie watched the airspeed indicator mount from zero to fifty knots. Sixty. Eighty. He had to admit that Walford could hold the heavy aircraft absolutely true on the centre line, despite a cross-wind and a full load.

In the tail, Snowy Pomeroy felt his turret lift gently and subside as the rear wheel momentarily left the runway. He felt and heard the thump of the wheel as it hit the tarmac again. He felt the tail lift once more and stay up. The strap round his waist was pulling him away from his guns while the back pressure from the aircraft's forward rush pushed him towards them.

In the darkness of their cubicles, the wireless operator and A.S.V. operator saw nothing; felt a sideways tug at the ribs as the momentum increased; held their flat palms over their earphones to deaden the noise.

The navigator gave a lingering thought to his afternoon rendezvous with Nig Dunford's wife. God! What a mug. How could a guy get to be a wing commander and be too dumb to larrup the bejasus out of a broad like that, instead of letting her give him the runaround that way?

\*     \*     \*

Squadron Leader Stevenson and Charles Gillam stood at the window of the Ops. Room, the blackout curtain pulled aside and the lights out. It was too cold to stand in the open front door without the trouble of putting on greatcoats. They watched the speeding shape of "B for Baker", clearly outlined by the runway lighting, pale against the surrounding darkness. They listened to the deep blast of sound beating against the hillside and filling the valley.

\*     \*     \*

Walford felt the lift of his tail; saw the airspeed indicator at a hundred; eased the stick slightly forward and then, more insistently, back.

The ground fell away. He held the aircraft down, fifteen feet off the runway, ordered "Undercarriage Up", and then climbed again to skim over the boundary fence at a hundred feet before he banked into a slowly climbing turn to port.

Down the intercom came Cubie's assured voice: "Course two-six-five."

\*     \*     \*

Gillam moved restlessly, his forehead touching the cold panes of glass. The runway lights were out and "B for Baker" was only a red starboard light and a yellow tail light now. "That's Trevor on his way," he remarked.

Stevenson looked at his watch. "Ten nineteen. Eleven minutes early on E.T.D."

*        *        *

The noise abated as Walford put his propellers into coarse pitch, throttled back and levelled off at five hundred feet on a westerly heading. Brodie had brought the flaps up. They were on operations.

On the port side, the Drem lighting of the airfield approach made a familiar, homely pattern. On the R/T the crew heard a request for taxi clearance. Looking down, Snowy saw a pencil of light begin to move on a taxi track, towards the main runway. Someone going on a navigation exercise; or practise bombing with four-pound bakelite bombs, on a target submarine in Barnstaple Bay.

They heard another captain warn the tower of his approach, and presently they saw an aircraft flit by on their starboard; one of the Wellingtons which had taken off in the early afternoon, on Hammer Two, and was now returning early due to an oil leak.

Lofty Duckett saw and heard these things from the nose of "B for Baker". He loathed being here, in this perspex nest. It was a lonely place. A place that made him feel vulnerable; as though any bullet aimed at the aircraft could not fail to hit him; it made him feel, also, as though he might fall out. He preferred the substantial darkness of the fuselage and his curtained retreat where he sat at the radar console.

Stan Glover stood on the main spar, resting his elbows against the rim of the big perspex astrodome, scanning the sky for enemy fighters. He rather liked being up here. If they were attacked, he would direct the captain's manoeuvres by maintaining a commentary on the fighter's approach and telling him when to turn, climb or dive. He had practised this many times on fighter affiliation exercises and had no doubt that he was ready for reality. Flight Sergeant Glover had complete faith in the adequacy of Service training.

Walford's crew (all but Cubie Meddings, who was working happily at his navigation table) saw a cascade of sparks from the funnel of a railway engine rattling over the line that followed the coast to Tawmouth. They picked up the glow of another Drem approach, on the starboard beam; the neighbouring fighter aerodrome. A pair of navigation lights circled the field as a Beaufighter came into land. Orange flames stabbed from its exhaust stubs in rhythmic bursts.

"Glad to see the fighter boys working for their living," said Glover.

"I hope there are some of them around where we're going." Duckett sounded doleful, as though he just didn't believe in fighter protection.

Another Beaufighter was taking off and Brodie jabbed a thumb in its direction, looking over his shoulder at Walford. "Jeeze, would I like to be driving that crate."

Walford glanced across at him, unsympathetically. "You've probably got twice as many hours already as that Beau. pilot."

"Hours!" Brodie spat it out. "Hell! Hours aren't everything. That guy's really flying. I'm just piling up flying hours for sitting on my arse, doing nothing; except raise and lower the flaps and undercart."

Walford gave him a second, more intense look. Brodie's dissatisfaction and frustration were almost incandescent; with this attitude, he was no use to the crew.

A figurative kick in the teeth was what he needed; he got it immediately and Walford's voice was uncompromising. "Never mind bellyaching now. Your job's to keep a sharp look out for Me. 410's."

Brodie hunched round to peer through the windscreen and window on his side of the cockpit.

The beginning of any operational flight had a savour of its own. Even the most stolid airman was familiar with the premonitory qualm of parting from the familiar, reassuring earth. "Mother Earth" began to mean something to men who did not know whether they would ever set foot on her again. The routine of taking off, setting course, and testing equipment which no amount of ground checking could prove thoroughly, slowly spread a layer of reassurance over natural uneasiness. There were so many small things to be done, but done quickly, that they imparted a sense of urgency to the crew which raised their actions above the trivial.

Tonight, however, the situation was in some ways different. Only the captain, navigator and rear gunner were doing their familiar jobs. The others had abandoned everything in order to keep watch for enemy fighters.

Below and ahead of them, the blacked-out villages and small towns, the meadows and woodland of Cornwall were an amorphous, dense blackness. Suddenly three broad beams of dazzling light leaped into the sky. Whitely radiant, moving in leisured arcs, they looked solid and tangible. In the side-glow from these searchlights, a hut, a coppice, grazing cattle and a bright-surfaced river flitted into view like objects on a cyclorama.

Every pair of eyes that searched the menacing sky from "B for Baker" followed the searchlight beams as they wavered, huge fan-like antennae, from cloud to cloud and swept the immeasurable heights between.

Flight Sergeant Glover, inherently sceptical of the Army's brains and ability, voiced his mistrust on the intercom. "Those ruddy pongos; wonder what they've picked up on their listening boxes? A courting couple or a herd of cows, most likely."

Lofty Duckett answered him crossly from his unhappy position in the perspex nose. "Might as well give the pongos bows an' arrows; what they want's radar, not ruddy listening contraptions."

"As long as they don't illuminate us . . ." said Walford.

"Any minute now," prophesied Glover, who did not believe that soldiers could do anything correctly.

"Perhaps they're only helping a lost aircraft to find its base," Cubie suggested. "I've got a theory about the use of searchlights as navigation aids. . . ."

Walford replied curtly: "There are no aircraft lights to be seen."

The appearance of the searchlight beams had quickened the pulses of the crew. Their eyes, not yet fully accustomed to the night sky, strove to identify somewhere in the immensity of the threatening darkness the flicker of an exhaust flame or the shadow of a bandit's wing against the background of stars or searchlights.

Snowy Pomeroy leaned back and pressed his head deeply into his fur collar, gazing up. Swinging his head from side to side, he felt the fur brushing his cheeks. He saw a spurt of flame below him, from the corner of his eyes, and sucked in a sharp breath of excitement. Looking down quickly, he recognized the funnel sparks of a train bursting out of a tunnel.

Stan Glover, standing in the astrodome, detected a faint glint of orange. He jerked his head and waited. His eyes began to water and he suspected his imagination. No! A splutter of orange, shot with blue, at three-o'clock, high.

"Skipper, I can see exhaust flames; three-o'clock, high."

Brodie leaned sideways so as to increase his field of upward vision. Walford leaned forward, staring to his right across the second pilot and upward. Snowy Pomeroy twisted his head till his chin rested on his left shoulder, his eyes wide and his teeth bared in a primitive rictus of fear and tension. Cramped and stiff, Lofty Duckett squirmed on to his left elbow and, prone, put his face close to the starboard perspex panel.

Brodie saw it first. His voice was high, quavering. "I've got it! Exhausts, sure enough. No nav. lights."

Walford, one eye blinking helplessly, found his view obscured by his second pilot's hefty shoulder. "Where?"

With calm firmness, Glover cut in. "He's banking towards us, Skipper. Five hundred feet above and quarter-mile on the starboard."

Pomeroy's voice was dry and bass with dread. "I see him. Can't get my guns on him."

Then Walford snapped into command of his crew. This was their first shared crisis; for a moment, with base so near and their own homely countryside only five hundred feet below, he had found it difficult to adjust himself. He was trained for, and his mind had long and often dwelt on, meeting the enemy far from land; once the Scilly Isles or Bishop's Rock lighthouse had been left behind, he was keyed up and ready for emergency; but here, flying over Cornwall, he did not really feel that the operation had begun.

He spoke sharply, with authority. "Hold your fire! May be a Beau. or a Mossie investigating us."

"Like hell!" Brodie murmured.

"He's coming straight in." Lofty Duckett strove to sound cool, but the fine edge of alarm was there.

Five seconds later all doubt was resolved as one of the brilliant cones of lights from the ground caught and held the dark shape which sprang into view around the spangles of exhaust flames. A second beam raced across the sky, crossed the first one and steadied so that the bandit was fixed between them.

A coruscation of scattered eruptions tore up from the gun sites in the fields and woods. Around the Wellington, fireworks blossomed, bursting with noisy splendour on its starboard side and slightly above. Streams of tracer leaped from Bofors guns, converging on the place where all three searchlights now contained the German night fighter as it dived, climbed and twisted.

Next came a bright tracery of fire arching from aircraft to aircraft as the Wellington came under the enemy's guns. In the same shocked instant, Walford gave crisp reassurance. "Stand by for evasive action." The big, white aeroplane was washed by the fringe of a searchlight's beam, and it was a waste of ammunition to fire on a target already engaged by anti-aircraft artillery.

Opening the throttles wide, Walford climbed steeply to port, flung "B for Baker" into a stomach-wrenching dive to starboard, then levelled off.

Glover waited till the aircraft was steady. "Skip., that was no Me. 410; it's a Do. 217 J. . . ."

"Thought so . . ." Walford sounded sure, professional. His sentence was stopped by a burst of tracer bullets which hurtled a few feet above the fuselage, between cockpit and astrodome.

Instinctively, Stan Glover ducked, calling: "Diving turn port."

Walford obeyed instantaneously and they slipped under the belly of the Do. 217 J, rocking in the shattering turbulence of its furious passage.

The winking gun emplacements beneath were suddenly blanked out. The air on the port side shook and heavy shock waves of sound pounded the eardrums of the Wellington's crew. They saw a Beaufighter hurtle across their bows, engines at full bore and cannons blasting with angry yellow gouts of flame. They saw a fresh pattern of tracer as the Dornier's cannons fought back.

The searchlights had the Beaufighter and the Dornier in their beams and the Wellington crew watched with fascination while scintillating fountains of shells and bullets poured from both.

With a red ripple of shell strikes along its port side, the Beaufighter yawed wildly. Two seconds later the Do. 217 J lurched on to its starboard wingtip and sideslipped with plumes of smoke belching from its engine cowlings.

The hostile fighter tumbled and twisted. Walford's crew— Cubie Meddings standing, braced and crouching, in the rear of the pilots' flight deck—watched it roll onto its back a couple of hundred feet under them. They felt and heard the searing blast of an explosion as it slammed into the ground. Burning fragments shot three hundred feet into the air.

There was no awesome, silent contemplation of death and destruction. Instead, every voice clamoured in praise and exultation.

"Boy, oh! Boy." Brodie clapped his hands and rubbed them. "That's really livin'."

"Nice shootin'." Cubie Meddings retreated to his navigation table, glad that he had at least seen the last act of the drama.

Stan Glover was always cautious. "Don't forget there may be another . . . shall I stay up here, Skip?"

Walford, his mind forced from his private worry and his body temporarily released from the nagging misery of an insistent twitch, sounded cheerful. "Get your signal off, first. Then we'll keep a sharp look out till we're a good thirty miles from land. Well done, Stan."

This was praise for Flight Sergeant Glover's quick call for a diving turn to port, under the enemy night fighter's fire.

Lofty Duckett rolled into a less uncomfortable position and complained. "I thought that bloody Beau. bastard was going to shoot our nose off."

Walford's light mood still held. "Stop binding, Lofty; it's only a short way to fall."

Snowy Pomeroy had found his normal voice. He was quivering with excitement, longing now to turn his own guns on an enemy aircraft and see again that exuberance of coloured flashes and the grand slam of the final disintegration. "Wish you'd let me get one squirt at him, Skipper. You never held still."

"Next time," promised Walford.

With the searchlights out, the contrasting blackness was impenetrable by their harassed eyes. But their evasive manoeuvres had scarcely taken them off course, and they could plainly see the line of the incoming tide washing phosphorescently along the coast a few miles to the port beam.

Cubie Meddings remembered to congratulate Walford on his quick, able handling of the Wellington. "Nice flying, Trevor."

Duckett grunted: "Sure. Good work, Skip."

Walford felt his cheeks grow warm at their words. In the first few moments he had silently despised himself for his unawareness of danger; and in that short time they could all have been killed. Even Brodie turned to him now and growled: "Glad *I* didn't have to jink around at this altitude. I'd have pulled into a screaming climb and to hell with corkscrew dives!" He grinned unexpectedly, his big teeth gleaming in the faint light.

Walford managed to smile back, the tic already tugging again at his cheek. "Thanks, Pete. We were lucky that Beau. was around. I hope he was O.K. Didn't like the look of those cannon shells bursting on him."

"He was under control, Trevor; I watched him orbit the wreckage a couple of times. He was O.K."

"Good." But young brother Hugh was not O.K. Hugh was

confined in the maw of U 306, whose course must be aimed at some point on the shipping lanes for which "B for Baker" was now making. Perhaps some other Wellington, Sunderland or Liberator had already seen and attacked U 306; sent young Hugh to his death, crushed by the mighty convulsion of depth charges, or choking and floundering in a cataract of cold, green water.

Stan Glover tapped out a Morse message; swift, vigilant but relaxed. "Enemy air attack." He wondered which of the operators on duty would pick this up at Tawmouth, in the noisy fug of the Ops. Room Signals Section.

\* \* \*

Fifty miles behind "B for Baker", Corporal Jean Forrow bent over a signal pad, writing. The scream of dots and dashes lancing through her headphones made her heart race and a vein throb visibly in her temple.

Like all experienced operators, she recognized individual touches on the transmitter key. Stan sent exactly at the regulation twenty words a minute; smoothly, with a clear break between groups; his hall mark was a certain flourish, an unexpected panache, with which he sent his call sign and with which he signalled "end of message". In these two places he perceptibly lengthened his dashes.

Although the signal coming from "B for Baker" reported enemy air attack, and perhaps there was injury or even death aboard, Corporal Forrow knew that her sweetheart was safe.

Before she had finished scribbling the signal on to its form, the R.A.F. sergeant who was in charge of the whole watch, as she was of the W.A.A.F. members of it, hurried over from the table where he had been checking the traffic log. He was a regular, wind-chapped and kind, middle-aged and now full of concern. "What's the matter, Jean? You went white as my conduct sheet, just now. Feeling all right?"

He leaned over her, smelling of Woodbines and Brasso.

"I'm O.K., Sarge." She could not quite manage a smile.

"Colour's coming back, but you're still a bit pale."

She gave him the message pad. He read, his lips moving, muttered "Blimey" and thrust it at the runner: "At the double", and the youngster ran like the wind, bounding down the stairs two at a time. In the hall he collided with Sergeant Murch.

"Watch where yer bloody going, yer daft booger." Murch

twisted away like an obese chorus boy, raising his battered metal tray with its three cups out of the way.

"Sorry Sarge." The runner was manifestly pleased, and Sergeant Murch glowered after him.

Gillam, with no immediate work to do, was reading C. E. M. Joad's *Guide to Modern Thought*; and yawning. When the war was over, he intended that the University Appointments Board should find him a job in the East; he had read modern languages while he was up; now he was hoping to acquire a general knowledge that would give him something to talk about in the four languages he had learned to speak.

Stevenson was reading Cecil Robert's *Victoria, Four-thirty* which he remembered someone had recommended to him in 1939. He had found it in the mess library, where his process of selection was quite unfathomable. He was not disappointed in his choice.

Neither officer welcomed the startling intrusion of the Signals runner. Gillam knew at once from Steve's vigorous moustache-tug that the message was fearful. He went quickly to the dais.

Stevenson gave him the message form and reached for the Group telephone at the same time. Gillam picked up the other telephone and asked for the adjacent Fighter Operations Room. He soon had confirmation of Flight Sergeant Glover's signal; a Do. 217 J shot down by a Beaufighter; the latter suffering some damage but no injury to pilot or radar observer. Gillam was able to tell the fighter people that all was well with "B Baker" and its crew.

On his way back upstairs, the runner noticed Sergeant Murch. The latter stood with his back to the passage, fumbling in a dark cupboard under the stairs. The runner heard him murmuring to himself. He paused. "What's up, Sarge?"

Murch's head jerked round and his pasty face was suffused with choler. "Nowt t'do wi' you. Root off. I'm moppin' up t'tea yer made me spill."

The runner obediently "rooted off" wondering; he was sure that the sergeant's astonishing agility had saved the tray from a bump.

Murch returned hurriedly to his task. In the dank cupboard reposed rags employed for unspeakable purposes in the cause of hygiene. He took one of these smelly pieces of damp, slimy cloth and hastily squeezed a stream of black liquid from it into the cup destined for the Senior Controller. In the strong, sweet tea the pollution would pass unnoticed: any unusually unpleasant flavour would be attributed to the well-known shortcomings of Sergeant Murch to which Squadron Leader Stevenson so often drew attention. Tasted or not, it gave Murch illimitable satisfaction to make this gesture of defiance and contempt at the man whom he looked on as his tormentor. He was too stupid to foresee the possible consequences; not only to Stevenson, but to those—including flying crews—who were affected by his duties.

Stevenson did not acknowledge the arrival of the tea. Gillam, wondering why more people (Joad included) did not give Dr Johnson's forthright retort to the theory of subjective idealism, instead of arguing prosily about it, said "Thanks, Sergeant". Murch, who would have liked to see all officers' heads stuck outside Station Headquarters on a row of spikes, was sorry he had not fouled the navigator's tea also. La-di-dah young booger, Oxford College an' all, never do a useful stroke of work in his life, likely; and Syd Murch, secondary-schooled till fifteen, owner of three thriving grocery shops, was hard put to it to keep his Alvis running on black market petrol.

Gillam, pausing in his reading while he drank his tea, contemplated the map. There were two ditchings indicated on it. A Wellington and a Liberator, from other stations in the Group, had been shot down; the Liberator, by a Do. 217 J, twenty miles from Land's End; the Wellington by a U-boat, in the Bay of Biscay. He thought of the crews, hindered by heavy clothing, scrambling for the dinghies; some, perhaps, drifting apart from their friends, kept afloat in the cold water by their life belts, dying of exposure. No effective search could begin till daylight.

Stevenson lifted his head as a gust of wind rattled the window. He looked meaningly at his navigator. "If the sea returns grow any worse, there'll be no point in sending an A.S.R. aircraft out, even as a token, till daylight."

Gillam hid a smile. Steve was a great man for sea returns. The expression had just the right hint of technicality about it to suggest a knowledge which, in fact, he did not possess. Sea returns were the echoes from waves, which the radar picked up. Big waves presented a good reflecting surface to a radar transmitter, and the screen soon became covered with responses which obscured those from shipping or other objects on the sea's surface. At night, Air/Sea Rescue aircraft had to rely on their radar; and if sea returns were high, there was no chance of detecting a small object like a rubber boat.

Stevenson drained his cup of tea and grimaced; the vile taste of its dregs smote his palate. Sergeant Murch, watchful, asked if Sir would like another cup. "No. I must smoke a pipe to get rid of the taste of that one." Murch turned away to hide the triumph in his eyes; he pretended to concentrate on a battered copy of *No Orchids for Miss Blandish.*

There was five minutes' silence in the room. Then Morag McEwan came in. She looked fresh and alert and almost brought a tang of heather in her wake. Gillam, glad to put philosophy aside, moved his chair away from the fireplace. "Come on over and have a warm, Morag."

Her eyes were fixed on the situation map and for a moment she did not reply. Then she walked over to the fire and stood with her back to it, her sturdy legs crossed and her shoulder against the chimney piece. "I thought you might be having sandwiches now." Section Officer McEwan had a good appetite.

"Sure. Shall I make some cheese toast?" Cheese toast was Gillam's speciality; he made it, from the night watch's ration, by crouching patiently on the floor and holding the electric fire so that its heat radiated down on bread and cheese laid on the old tray, in the hearth. Stevenson said that only Gillam's excellent muscles and supple joints could have endured so long a crouch; and was proud of his navigator's unique culinary ingenuity. So both the latter and Morag were surprised when Steve stood up abruptly; said with disgust "Cheese toast! " and went rapidly from the room.

Morag looked alarmed. "What's up?"

Gillam didn't know. "Sergeant Murch, have you been putting powdered glass in the squadron leader's tea?"

"No sir. But he did complain it didn't taste very nice, didn't he? Was yours all right, sir?"

"No worse than usual."

Stevenson, with a dull fire glowing in the pit of his stomach and skewers piercing his navel, was being very sick in the lavatory.

Left alone—Murch did not count, and had been sent for bread and cheese anyway—Gillam and Morag talked about the attack on Walford's aircraft. Her face became bright red as she asked: "There's no chance of them turning back, is there? I mean, no damage to the aircraft that they wouldn't find out about at first? They might have been hit without knowing it."

Gillam felt sympathy for her. She was not very attractive and she made herself a little ridiculous with her dogged pursuit of

Trevor Walford; but she was sincere and unselfish. "No, no chance at all."

"What about the weather, Charles? It seems to be blowing up, here. Is it bad in the operational area?"

"Not too bad yet. If Trevor isn't forced to turn back within the next two hours, he'll be O.K. May have to land at Gib. or Port Lyautey, though."

Morag thought back to the early evening, when she had walked into the mess with Paddy Donnelly on their return from Tawmouth. Trevor Walford had come out of his room as they passed the huts, behind the main buildings, where the sleeping quarters were. He had looked, she thought, a trifle hurt. Paddy was being boisterous; he said at once that he had taken Morag to the cinema; implied that they had both had great enjoyment from the outing. Morag would not care if she never saw Donnelly again. Why did Trevor, whom she admired so much, pay so little attention to her? Walford was the sort to shrug and leave her to Donnelly, if that was the way she wanted it.

Gillam, crouching at the fire, intent on perfecting his cheese toasts, looked up suddenly and caught the preoccupied expression on her face. Hell! He thought, someone's got to jolly her out of it. The solution arrived on the instant, with Alison Storey. Flight Officer Storey was sharing the night with Morag, preparatory to sharing the next with Tommy Rowan; clearing away her routine work so as to be free for twenty-four hours. She wore her usual appearance of lacquered beauty and careful dressing.

"Thought I smelt delicious cheese." She went close to Gillam, gently pressing her knees into his back; this gave her an excuse to put a scented hand on his shoulder: "Sorry, Charles; I nearly over-balanced you. I mustn't crowd the fire like this."

"But do. I rather care for it."

She laughed and moved to one side, giving him an intimate, short-range view of her pretty calves.

Alison had immediately taken Morag's mind right off Trevor Walford. For a moment she teetered on the brink of a sarcastic comment; then a bright light shone through the murk of her honest, inexperienced, Presbyterian mind and showed her the cause of her failure to interest him. She looked at the other girl with admiration for the first time; admiration and a resolution to learn and profit.

Stevenson came in slowly, a handkerchief to his mouth. He paused in the doorway, sniffing. "God! Charles, what a stink. I'm going to kip down for half an hour. Sergeant Murch, bring me a cup of Oxo. I'll be in the map store."

Two beds were made in the map store every night, for the controller and navigator to sleep in. During routine operations there were hours when there was no work for them to do. The I.O. interrogated (de-briefed) crews on their return and the Signals Officer handled all but emergency traffic without disturbing the controller.

Sergeant Murch rose willingly. It would be even easier to disguise the flavour of filth in Oxo than in tea.

Alison heard the well-known skid of tyres rounding the corner of the lane, and automatically jerked the edges of her tunic and patted her pretty hair. Nig. dashed in, his greatcoat collar turned up and his forage cap pushed back on his head. He flung his cap on to the controller's desk, swooped on a slice of cheese toast, strode to the map, and announced: "That's wrong", flicking a long forefinger at the symbol for U 306.

Gillam followed him. "According to Group it's correct, sir. And according to the merchantman it sunk only two hours ago!"

"Bloody matelots must have had their fingers in; probably U 308 or something. But not U 306. It's come too far since the attack on the Sunderland this morning."

"Perhaps it's travelling mainly on the surface, sir."

"H'm. Either that or it's one of these new Type 21's we haven't seen yet in the Bay."

"Both, perhaps, sir?"

"I still think they're two different boats. Area's stiff with them, according to the spies." Nig. turned to Alison. "Haven't seen Melanie today, have you? I haven't been home since brekker. Meant to ask you to nip down this afternoon and keep her company."

"No, sir. I slept this afternoon." She looked at him pityingly. She had seen his wife out with Cubie Meddings a dozen times.

Before he could reply, the telephone rang. Gillam looked round, saw that Sergeant Murch was still out making Stevenson's Oxo and more tea for the rest of them, so moved to the telephone. He listened for a few seconds, said "Thank you" and looked at Dunford. "That was the Guard Room, sir. The Station Commander's on his way up here."

\*　　　\*　　　\*

Group Captain Laraway steered cautiously out of the main camp gate, drove a hundred yards and stopped. He could hear aircraft approaching; not one, but at least three; and not at five hundred feet, but about five thousand. Their engines had the unsynchronized beat that he had learned, early in the war, to register as a danger signal.

No navigation lights were visible. He opened the window more and leaned out. Then he cut his engine, switched off his headlights, dim though they were, and waited.

The ground heaved and a tremendous force plucked at the group captain's car, lifted it off all four wheels and hurled it sideways through the barbed wire surrounding his station. A thunderclap rolled through the valley, followed closely by three more. A burst of flames tore the darkness aside, its heat licking around the overturned vehicle. Air raid sirens howled their warning at the station and in the town of Tawmouth. Around the camp perimeter, light anti-aircraft guns—Hispanos and Bofors—sent chains of tracer shell towards the German bombers which were coming in for a second attack.

The group of people in the Ops. Room were shocked, for a moment, into motionless horror.

Tiles slid from the farmhouse roof and crashed on to the road. A window in the map store shattered, bringing Stevenson off his bed with a loud "Damn!"

The whole building trembled and before even Nig's lightning reactions could galvanize him into a rush for the telephone, a second stick of bombs fell.

## CHAPTER SIX

FOUR hundred-odd miles to the south-west of the Scillies, U 306 cruised fast on the surface. She could charge her batteries while under water, because she was fitted with Schnorkel. Therefore there was little need for her to surface; but under the sea her speed was cut to four knots and on it she could make more than twenty; and ahead was a big convoy which she could reach before daylight by risking exposure. And why not take the risk, when you carried so much heavy armament?

However, the weather was starting to shape events; for a freshing wind whipped the wave tops, flinging a cold, solid spray aboard the steel decks.

The weather is, to sailors and airmen, their greatest hazard. The former, at least, travel with their living quarters and ample supplies; their vessels have the range and endurance to avoid or defeat most storms, and if at worst they must call for help they are able mostly to fend for themselves until it arrives. Those who traffic in the savage sky, however, know that they are equipped only to survive there for a few hours; that no replenishment of fuel or food can be given to them in the air; that if their home base is denied them and they can find no other airfield, their setting down on water or even on land will be rough and dangerous; that once they have force landed they may have to await rescue, being unable to help themselves.

The wind which was gathering strength now over the Bay of Biscay was the same which, thirty-six hours ago, had ruffled the fur of polar bears in Greenland and bent the pine trees of southern Iceland. The rapidly moving front of cold air had descended like a cataract on the fringes of Europe. Fierce wind squalls, dense banks of cloud, and heavy rain and hail had followed one another all the way.

Strong up-currents and down-draughts caused bumps and air pockets at all levels where airmen made their way.

Behind the disturbance the polar air flowed, sending temperatures down abruptly and forming cumulus clouds over the sea, owing to the surface heating the lower air.

But so far "B for Baker" was not involved in the bad weather. The aircraft had left cloudy skies behind over Cornwall, and flew now at five hundred feet through a two hundred mile wide area of clear sky.

For half an hour after the German night fighter's attack, Walford had regained the composure with which once he had always flown; on his first operational tour, and during the first three or four trips of the current one. He had recovered some of his old verve, and the misery which had bedevilled him since he heard of his brother's plight had been driven away. But that half hour was over and he felt the hated anxiety and depression overcoming him again.

Cubie announced their arrival at the beginning of their patrol line. "Well, fellas, guess we're in business now."

Walford turned his head towards the second pilot. "Take her, Pete."

Brodie nodded and reached out to adjust the trim as the captain made his way astern. The control column moved gently from side to side and back and forth as the automatic pilot flew the aircraft. Brodie sat with his hands on his thighs, watching the instruments; particularly the altimeter.

Snowy sat with his hands on his guns. After crossing the English coast he had cleared them with a three-second burst; this routine test always delighted him, for he thrilled to see the dancing pattern of his bullets hitting the sea; now he wished another Do. 217 J would pounce on them. Despite his own daily participation in aerial warfare, Pomeroy's conception of it was founded on the comic strips which formed the major part of his reading. Peering out of his tail turret, at the choppy black sea and the sparsely starred black sky, he identified himself with the craggy-jawed heroes depicted in the daily press and children's weeklies. He yearned to "hurl up a red hot curtain of lead from his quadruple Brownings" at a swastika-ed Me. 109 or Do. 217 J. He liked flying because, as a sergeant airgunner, he earned eight and sixpence a day, which was more than he had been paid for clerking in Trinidad; and because he lived more comfortably in the Sergeants' Mess than he had at home; he liked flying most of all because he thought that one day it would bring him the heroism of which he read so avidly. Because, in the strip cartoons and stories, the "good" always triumphed over the "bad", it did not occur to him that he might be smashed to a bloody pulp by German bullets hammering through the perspex of his gun turret.

He looked round and grinned as he felt a hand on his shoulder. Walford's voice spoke close to his ear. "All O.K., Snowy?"

"Fine, Skipper. Wish there was something to see, though."

"We should pass near that hospital ship in about fifteen minutes."

"Good. I'll look out for her."

Everyone welcomed the sight of a ship sailing with all its lights on and portholes unmasked, in this blacked-out war-time world.

Walford went forward along the fuselage, till he reached the Leigh light. This was the big searchlight which was lowered through the floor to illuminate suspected enemy vessels picked up on the radar. He paused and tapped it with his knuckles, in a vague gesture of good luck; as though wishing it well in the task he hoped it would have to perform for them some night; tonight. There were a lot of U-boats out and only one of them held his young brother Hugh.

He moved past and stood by Glover, who was getting a radio fix of their position. He watched Meddings take the slip of paper on which the wireless operator wrote down their latitude and longitude, and peered over the navigator's shoulder as the latter worked with his ruler and pencil. Then he crossed the gangway and put his head round the curtain which shielded the radar screen from light.

Duckett sat with his long, thin body bent close over the perspex mask beneath which green electronic flecks flashed and faded when the radar beam swept over and then past some object on the sea's surface. A scatter of bright pinpricks showed where the water four miles to their starboard was badly disturbed by an errant wind and was giving the sea returns about which Stevenson loved to prate.

Duckett rapped a fingernail on a bunch of six or seven small blobs about which he had made notes at briefing. "That's one of the small convoys we were briefed on." He put his mouth to the microphone and spoke to Meddings, then looked up at Walford and nodded. "It's about where it should be. So are we!"

"Good." Walford breathed deeply.

Duckett pointed out a fleck of light on the edge of the tube. It was fading and they waited for the aerial to sweep in that direction again. This time, nothing showed; but on the third sweep of the beam the response appeared strongly. It was six miles away and forty degrees off their course, to port.

"Something there," Walford said sharply, "better have a look."

He hurried back to the cockpit, and as soon as he was in his seat he spoke into his microphone. "I'll take her, Pete. Now, Lofty, where's the target?"

Duckett answered without hesitation. "One-seven-zero, range six."

Walford banked and turned forty degrees south from their heading; they had been flying south-west, on 210 degrees. When he levelled off, the radar operator spoke again. "Same bearing, range five miles."

This had happened to them before, many times. They had homed on a radar blip, only to find a fishing boat; or some small neutral vessel with a few lights shining faintly; or . . . nothing.

Nevertheless, as soon as the radar operator gave a range and bearing, expectancy gripped the whole crew. It always did. Unless they believed that each unidentified radar contact heralded the presence of the enemy, they might as well stay at home. Flight is compounded of a few basic certainties without which airmen would die violently and soon. The serviceability of engines and airframes; the ground control of the air corridors, ensuring avoidance of collision, and immediate enquiry about aircraft late in arriving; high-percentage accuracy of weather forecasts; these can be relied on. But it is the uncertainties, the imponderables, particularly in wartime, that keep airmen alert.

Walford's crew was faced with an uncertainty now. Duckett gave him the range again: "Four miles," and at the same instant Brodie said disgustedly: "It's lit up like a Christmas tree."

Walford had seen it too. "Cubie, this must be the hospital ship. Are we off course?"

Meddings reply was shocked: "Them's dirty words, Skipper! The ship must be ahead of schedule. You know we only just got a fix."

"O.K., we'll take a quick look."

The ship's lights showed bright and clear now, only a mile or two distant. The red crosses were plain to see as the Wellington circled once. Walford asked the navigator for a course that would take them back to their patrol line at the point where they had left it. Meddings gave it immediately. The captain put his aircraft into a tight turn, banking so steeply that the navigator's pencils and rubber rolled across the table and the rear gunner bumped his head. Brodie glanced questioningly across and saw that Walford was biting his lip in annoyance as he flung them round. Good! thought Brodie; at least he forgets to be a stuffed shirt some of the time. The Canadian perpetually gloomed about his captain's restrained flying technique and his unquestioning exact implementation of orders. He was glad that Walford was needled enough to show some of the dash with which he had taken avoiding action an hour earlier; flying with him was apt to be like sitting next to an automaton.

Walford was absorbed in his work. His diversion, though short, had been made at increased speed. This meant that his engines had used more fuel than if he had remained on his patrol line. For the time being, this would not affect the flight; but it was one of the many events which would accumulate during the next few hours and influence decisions he may have to make towards the end of the trip. He had his fuel gauges and his navigator and his wireless operators to give him facts that were accurate and carefully checked; but he still liked to make rough mental calculations, to file items in his memory as he went along.

Then Meddings gave him his new course and he turned on to the patrol line once more.

They cruised through the darkness at a hundred and fifty miles an hour, as separated from the rest of humanity as though they had come out here alone over the cold Atlantic; yet they knew that around and above them more than a score of other aircraft hunted the same prey.

Brodie shifted restlessly. "How's about a cup of coffee?"

"Good idea."

Duckett, who heard the exchange on the intercom., put in: "Take a look at Rupe. and Dopey, will you, Pete?" The animal-lover in him transcended, for a moment, his concentration on the radar.

The two pilots exchanged smiles. Brodie said: "I get hungry on these ten-hour trips: Rupe. and Dopey are getting temptingly plump."

There was laughter over the intercom. from Snowy, Cubie and Stan Glover.

Brodie eased his bulky person along the narrow way past the radar, navigation and wireless stations. He knelt, near the Leigh light, and ran his fingertips across the wire netting of two wooden bird cages. The sleek pigeons that inhabited them pecked interestedly at his hands and stared up at him with beady bright eyes. The Canadian was always amused by this anachronism of the mid-twentieth century. Coastal Command aircraft were equipped with every modern device that could secure communications, yet they took two carrier pigeons on every maritime flight. And time and again these birds had proved their value by reaching base with messages giving the positions of ditched aircraft.

All the pigeons in the Tawmouth lofts were endowed, by the air crews, with individual traits and personalities. Tonight, "B Baker" carried one which was universally popular: "Randy Rupert," so-called because he was reputedly the most uxorious of male birds; and therefore believed to possess the strongest determination to reach his nest at any cost. The other pigeon, "Dopey", had earned his name by his lethargy and his habitually half-shut eyes. It was a common belief, among the squadrons, that "Dopey", when released on a practice homing flight, descended on the first vessel or vehicle that seemed to be going his way, and rode out his journey in comfortable sleep. Brodie waggled a finger at him. "Wake up, or I'll shoot you full of strong, black coffee and benzedrine." He turned soothingly to Randy Rupert. "Think your

harem's behaving itself while you're away? Sucker!" Rupe.
cocked his head on one side and leered; then darted a peck at
Brodie's fleshy finger.

Brodie was feeling less miserable since the patrol had started.
Once they were far from land and engrossed in the search for
surfaced U-boats, the whole crew became rapt in a smoothly-
working professionalism that left no room for grudges and frustrations. In an emergency, every man's life depended on the
efficiency of his colleagues. Their behaviour under the Do. 217 J's
guns was a well-trained response to the first call ever made on their
co-operation in an emergency; it had been a good start to any
operation and particularly to this one, when there was so much
hidden dissatisfaction among them. As individuals they may not
muster one first-class man among them, but by dint of rehearsal
and usage they fitted together as a first-class crew. Only Walford
and Meddings had much experience, and even they, by comparison with peacetime airmen, were tyros. Walford had seventeen
hundred flying hours in his log book; Meddings nine hundred,
and another five as an airline steward. The civil pilots and navigators reckoned to reach five or six thousand hours before they
counted themselves really well proven.

Brodie put a waxed-paper cup of coffee at the navigator's
elbow.

Cubie Meddings had immense vitality. He was both robust in
body and dynamic in spirit. He had learned to re-energize the
powerful motor which drove him through an average of eighteen
hours a day, by relaxing completely for short periods. He was
resting now for five minutes, his forehead cradled on folded forearms; motionless. But relaxation was elusive tonight. His mind
constantly formed a picture of Melanie Dunford as he had seen
her that afternoon. She had walked her two Alsatians along the
beach bordering one side of the aerodrome. He had ridden over
on his motor-cycle, to meet her; although when she telephoned
to arrange the assignation he was reluctant.

"But, baby, you know I'm strictly the hothouse type. Why can't
we wait till tomorrow, and I'll see you in the 'Galleon'—by a
fire."

Cubie had found a pub, hidden in a fishing village, which was
always accessible to them both; he on his motor-cycle and she in
her car run on black market petrol he provided. It was off the bus
route, therefore unknown and safe. The fire always burned
brightly in the little-used private bar.

"You'll be sorry if you don't," she had threatened. Meddings, product of a matriarchy, had capitulated.

They had spent an uneasy half-hour together. Melanie, who seldom played this rustic role, was nevertheless the genuine "County" article; born to wear expensive tweeds with élan and the poise of a mannequin. Her handsome dogs were merely chic adjuncts to her smart beauty.

She liked to wield power and it pleased her to be mistress of two dangerous-looking animals.

Meddings was tough, but not hardly in the backwoods sense. His was the durability of poor circumstances and city streets; he was fast with a kick to the groin, an elbow in the windpipe; he could sleep on a doorstep in six inches of snow. But set him to carry a fifty-pound rucksack up a mountain and he would have retched after an hour, his legs stiff or trembling. He was embarrassed by the cold, salty breeze that fanned his cigar to burn fiercely; depressed by the empty dunes and coarse grass, the brown water and the wailing seabirds.

Stan Glover and his girl, Jean Forrow, had cycled past. As Cubie saw them, Glover quickly turned his head away.

Thinking about it, with the din of the engines in his ears and the gentle up and down motion of the aircraft cradling him, in warm darkness, he told himself he was a fool. Nig Dunford was a bigger fool, but that was his lookout. He, Meddings, could stop being a fool in this particular way at any time he wanted; and that time had better be now. As soon as he stepped out, Melanie would dig her slim claws into someone else. He would get himself another broad easily enough; the trouble was to shove them off, not to find them. Melanie was starting to get the upper hand, and he didn't like that. She only tried it on because her husband was so casual with her. What she was longing for was to be roughed-up a bit: why the hell couldn't Dunford see that?

He felt a hand on his shoulder and pushed himself back, stretching and yawning.

Brodie steadied the paper cup. "Hey! You nearly spilled your coffee."

"Thanks, Pete. Sure need this; gotta keep awake." He sniffed at the cup's contents. "Jeeze! Coffee, did you say?"

The Canadian grinned. "I know, I know, pal. Don't think it doesn't hurt me as much as it hurts you."

They exchanged a look of North American understanding

that wordlessly expressed their scorn for the travesty of real coffee perpetrated in R.A.F. kitchens.

"Never mind," said Meddings with a sigh, "this war can't go on for ever."

"Can't it? Anyway, you should worry; after this tour you'll be able to fill yourself with all the good Java you want, chum."

"Yeah. Why don't you try for transfer to a Canuck squadron, Pete?"

"Guess I will—when I get on fighters."

"Pardon me; I forgot! Anyways, there aren't many guys around like Wingco Gretton. Me, I'd rather fly for Gretton than any other guy I've worked with."

"Gretton's O.K. The squadron comes first with him, sure enough."

The second pilot moved on with the coffee cups.

The squadron comes first with Gretton, thought Meddings. Flying comes first with Dunford. The difference is that Gretton's got a wife he can trust and enough sense to know what to do about it to keep things that way. The hell with Dunford. Melanie's his worry, not mine. If it wasn't me playing around with her it'd be some other sharp operator. . . .

Glover looked up from his wireless set and tipped a finger to his forehead in a gesture of thanks, when Brodie gave him coffee. He took the hot, flimsy cup gently and drank at once with evident enjoyment. An enjoyment that made the Canadian shudder with disbelief. The latter reached down and moved one earphone out of place, so that the operator could hear him. "What's on the Forces' Programme, Stan? Vera Lynn?"

Glover appreciated this; it was simple, barrack-room humour. "Vera Lynn my aunt Fannie. I'm getting my eardrums punctured trying to pick up a met. forecast from Group. Hell of a lot of static, and the broadcast's due in thirty seconds. Goodbye?" He replaced the earphone, drained his coffee and went on with his work.

Duckett's reception of the second pilot's attention was gloomy and vague. His long, thin face looked dismal even when he was happily drunk; and it was almost impossible to distract him from his radar. Brodie waited with unusual patience, interested also in the still-novel equipment which visually presented evidence found by invisible electronic waves. The A.S.V. was a bit of a mystery, something magical, to most people.

Brodie set the big vacuum flask and the paper cups on the floor and craned over the Australian's shoulder. The bright trace marking the direction of the radar transmissions rotated almost mesmerically, sweeping the face of the tube every ten or twelve seconds. In its wake appeared the evanescent flecks of light which marked steep waves and shipping. Brodie could not resist pointing to a pair which constantly reappeared; close together. "What are those, Lofty?"

"They're all right. We were briefed on them: the merchantman that broke down and is being towed in by a corvette."

"I remember. I bet the corvette's crew are puking blue lights; imagine having to drag your tail at seven knots across that stretch of water! Especially just now, with this whole U-boat pack out. I wouldn't like it to be one of the Asdic operators in the corvette, and that's for sure."

"Hell, those boys haven't got any nerves; they're too used to sitting on top of a blue flash, waiting for it to go up. Worst life of the lot, being at sea. Woof! And down you go in Davy Jones. Asleep in your bunk and Jerry slams a torp. in your ribs and where the hell are you?"

Brodie withdrew. "It must be thoughts like that that keep you looking so happy, Lofty."

He joined Walford in the cockpit. The captain looked round. "Thanks, Pete. It's hot and wet anyway." He sipped some coffee. "Everyone O.K.? How's Snowy doing down at the far end?"

Brodie's eyes did not drop. He said, curtly: "Hell! I forgot to go down there."

Walford was annoyed, because he despised any lack of thoroughness; but he sounded cordial enough as he said dryly: "You'd better take a check list next time. What are you going to do about it now?"

A defiant expression settled on Brodie's plump face. But it was wasted, because his captain was not looking at him but at their instruments. For some weeks now the Canadian had felt himself being influenced by Meddings's southern colour prejudice. At first, unconsciously, he had begun to ignore Snowy Pomeroy; then, consciously, to avoid him. Growing dissatisfaction with the uneventfulness of general reconnaissance flying had prompted an active annoyance with the West Indian who so manifestly enjoyed and was thrilled by it. It was a short step to downright antagonism, aggravated by his vexation with Walford.

After a brief silence, Walford prompted: "Well?"

Brodie was stubborn. "He knows where the rations are kept. I don't want to go all the way down there again."

"Again? 'Take some more tea,' the March Hare said. 'I've had nothing yet,' Alice replied, 'so I can't take any more.' Remember?"

"I don't get you." Brodie sounded sulky.

"And Snowy doesn't get his hot drink. If you're going to do a job—*any* bloody job—in my aircraft, Pete, damned well do it thoroughly." Walford seldom swore and even now he sounded half-jocular; but Brodie stared at him angrily before heaving himself up and trudging down to the tail turret with the flask of coffee and a paper cup.

Walford felt that he had behaved pettily. The issue was a small one and he had enough strength of character to prevail over his second pilot without forcing such a trivial chore on him. Yet Brodie had provoked him and it was best to deal decisively with every situation that arose, instead of allowing it to breed another; perhaps bigger in itself and certainly bigger by being added to the first.

God! He was fed up tonight. What a bloody state of affairs. Prowling through the sky, trying to find your only brother and send him to the bottom of the ocean. And that big-headed, stupid ape Pete Brodie with his self-importance and his imagined grievances.

He heard Duckett on the intercom. "How you doing, Snowy? Still with us?"

"I'm here, Lofty. Not left behind yet."

It was an old joke and, as such, had its special place in their ritual of mutual reassurance. There was not much that they could do to relieve the tension and cramped discomfort of their job. They were all very ordinary men. Some crews were endowed with humorists and musicians, who entertained with patter, songs and even mouth-organs, at appropriate times when amusement did not interfere with work. But most crews were ungifted, uninspired, everyday people, and when they had made a joke they kept it alive and re-used it until it became part of the whole fabric that held them together as a crew.

Duckett said: "This coffee tastes as though it came from the camp laundry, not the cookhouse."

Walford smiled in the faintly lit darkness of the cockpit. "Don't be revolting, Lofty."

Pomeroy sounded injured. "Coffee? What coffee? It's all right for you fellows up front there—in civilization. The Rear Gunners' Union, we have our rights too."

Walford said quickly: "Pete's doing the rounds, Snowy. He's on his way to you."

Duckett growled: "Must've busted his bloody leg, then. He brought me mine a long time ago."

"He's here now." There was little pleasure in Snowy Pomeroy's voice. He sensed that Brodie had come unwillingly. Turning to take the drink, he tilted the cup which the Canadian held awkwardly, spilling much of its contents. He mouthed "thank you" but Brodie backed away without looking in his eyes, expressionless.

Snowy relapsed into a mood of worry. He had met no colour prejudice since he joined the R.A.F., until first Meddings and of late Brodie had slighted him. He had been made to feel inferior, sometimes insulted, on account of his colour, all his life; until he came into the Service. To be badly treated at this stage of his career, when he was so proud of being on an operational squadron, was unimagined cruelty.

He crossed himself and prayed briefly for help. By then, the little coffee he did have was tepid and nasty.

Presently Flight Sergeant Glover spoke on the intercom: "Skipper, I've got a met. report from Group. Wind in the southern part of the area still ten knots. But they think the front will be through to the northern end of the area by the time we're due to come back."

Walford acknowledged this calmly. "O.K., Stan. I'm not going to divert to Gib. or Port Lyautey unless I'm ordered to."

An instant later came Snowy Pomeroy's incredulous, frenzied cry. "Skipper . . . there's a light . . . Leigh light . . . starboard quarter . . . yes, it's a Leigh light for sure. . . ."

Glover wrenched off his headphone and scrambled for the astrodome, slipping and stumbling when the floor raked steeply in the hard turn into which Walford banked at once.

Cubie grabbed for his pencils, rubber and ruler which skittered about the navigation desk.

Duckett's left shoulder thudded hard against the starboard side of the fuselage as he, facing backwards, was thrown against the metal geodetic struts. His radar screen was flooded by the solid brilliance of echoes from the sea as the aerial's beam was tilted down.

Brodie screwed round to look over his right shoulder. Sitting on the starboard side, he was the first to confirm Snowy's report. "Yeah! I got it too. . . ."

Then Glover was wedged into the astrodome, rocking as the Wellington finished its turn and levelled off. He stared directly at the ice-blue radiance of a Leigh light's wide beam. It sped across the surface of the sea, projected a mile ahead of the Wellington whose white nose and wing leading edges it also lit.

This aircraft, they knew, must belong to their own or another station in their Group, patrolling parallel to them.

The same emotion surged through everyone in the crew. They had experienced it before when themselves illuminating radar contacts. Self-preservation being man's dominant instinct, it was fear, in one form or another, that took them by the throat in the first instant of expectation that they were about to engage the enemy.

Walford opened his throttles and the air speed indicator climbed to more than two hundred miles an hour. They were still too far to discern the fore part of the aircraft that had switched on its Leigh light; but at this speed it was only minutes before Walford, Brodie, Glover and Meddings, who had gone for'ard to man the nose guns, saw it together. Walford remarked briefly: "Wimpey."

The surface of the sea directly behind the other aircraft burst into six mountainous columns of spume.

Walford shouted into the intercom.: "On light! Stan," and Glover jumped down from the main spar, hastily lowered the Leigh light while the captain throttled back to cruising speed, and threw the switch. In the harsh light of their own beam, they saw the tall fountain thrown up by the other aircraft's bursting depth charges slowly disintegrate into gouts and droplets which reflected light as brilliantly as crystal.

In the sky ahead, the attacking aircraft was turning tightly, its light cutting a swathe through the darkness. When it had settled on, and held, the patch of sea where it had attacked, Walford ordered Glover to switch off.

In the glare of the one remaining Leigh light, the hummocky sea was in a foaming frenzy. It thrashed and churned, flinging up twelve-foot waves and sending spray to a height of sixty feet. From each centre of eruption, concentric circles of ridged water rippled lustily outward; meeting, mixing with, fighting against each other; pulling and rending the water into steep valleys and hills where foam rushed and slid and swirled in a pattern of chaos and violence.

The attacker had come down to a hundred feet, and Walford's

crew watched it circle slowly. Duckett had taken Glover's place in the astrodome and the latter stood braced between the pilots' seats; everyone had a ringside view. Comments on the intercom. were terse and low-voiced.

"Wreckage!"

"Yes ... and oil. ..."

A sleazy film began to spread, quietening patches of angry sea. Two or three wooden crates, a partly inflated rubber lifeboat, sections of grating; garments; then a body, rolling limply; all these came up from the depths with a rush, were tossed high by the pressure of the air which had burst from the U-boat and flung them up, then tumbled on to the stilling surface where the oil patches widened.

Walford banked his aircraft away: "Well, that's pretty final. Stan, signal him with the Aldis."

Glover climbed back to stand with his shoulders in the astrodome, holding an Aldis lamp. Presently his winking yellow dots and dashes were answered. He spoke the message into the intercom. as he read it. "O for Orange of 172 ... they're Chivenor, aren't they? He's glad to have our corroborative evidence! Going back now; he says the weather's O.K. down south."

From Meddings came a blithe: "Turn onto 180, Skipper, and we'll be back on patrol right where we left it. I've got a theory about tonight; it's our lucky night. Next thing you know, we'll be sinking a U-boat ourselves. Any minute now, fellas. ..."

Walford felt his stomach muscles cramping and a sour taste filled his mouth.

Stan Glover spoke with sudden urgency. "Skipper ... I can't raise base ... I've sent three times, reporting we've seen a successful attack in the position Cubie gave me. No answer ... no ... no ... wait. ..."

He became silent and the chatter that must have followed Meddings's gleeful remark remained unuttered. None of them had known Glover to panic. When he spoke so tautly, it must be for more than the superficial reason that he suspected a fault in his transmitter. They waited uneasily.

When he spoke again he was strained, breathless and plainly controlling himself with difficulty. "Skipper, there's something wrong. They took a long time to answer my call. And there's a strange operator on the key. I know his touch: it's old Emery, the sergeant in charge of the watch. He only comes on the key himself in a ... an emergency, like. Something's wrong back at base, Skipper; I don't know what, but I don't like it. Something must have happened at Tawmouth...."

## CHAPTER SEVEN

THE bomb bursts on the aerodrome and in the field adjacent to the Operations Room lit the night with vivid slashes of crimson and yellow. The echoing boom of each separate explosion was overtaken by its successors until the whole valley shuddered and thundered under the battering of what seemed one drawn-out roar whose intensity mounted in pace with the searing flames which tore the darkness to shreds.

It was a din and a spectacle to stop a man's heart; let alone a woman's; and there were many women, mostly young and all unused to savagery, at R.A.F. Tawmouth.

Group Captain Laraway's car lay on its side in a tangle of barbed wire and uprooted fence posts, the windows shattered. From the nearby Guard Room came running footsteps, steel-shod boots pounding the tarmac heard above young airmen's voices high and taut with alarm.

"Ruttin' 'ell, the Old Man drove out of 'ere not one ruttin' minute ago...."

"I saw him stop, Corp, just past the gate...."

"Can't see no ruttin' lights, mate...."

And then a relieved cry "I've found the car," which quickly turned to a shrill "Gawd! Groupie's inside...."

One of the airmen of the guard paused and picked up a gold oak-leaf Service Dress cap. "Here's the Station Master's hat, Corporal." This forlorn symbol of dignity, lying on the frosty grass, was more frightening in its implication than had been the actual invulnerable, all-powerful figure. To handle an intimate possession of his, to find it crushed and muddy on the roadside, struck at the foundations of the regularity and security of their lives; overthrew the proper and accepted order of things; brutally thrust at them the knowledge that they must act on their own initiative.

As they reached the car the stench of scorched paint choked them sickeningly.

The corporal ran forward and gripped a door handle which felt hot through his thick woollen glove. He wrenched the door open. "Give me a hand, one of you." He leaned in and took the group captain's shoulders, then moved gently back. Another airman reached for Laraway's feet and together they carried the limp, spasmodically groaning figure with its head lolling, towards the Guard Room. Two of their comrades joined hands under the group captain's back, taking some of the weight.

Nig Dunford's telephone call from the Operations Room to the main telephone exchange on camp was interrupted by a skull-splitting detonation close at hand, and a torrent of air which rushed through the building, slamming doors open and shut. He had just told the duty telephonists where he was and asked to be connected with the main Guard Room, when the base of the instrument leaped four inches from the desk and fell, jerking the cord which attached it to the part he held in his hand. There was sudden silence in the earpiece and when he jiggled the rest up and down he could not hear it clicking. "Hell and damnation," he said viciously; and when he looked at the receiver he saw that one of the wires had been pulled from its terminal. He tossed the instrument to Sergeant Murch, who had started yammering to Group before Gillam pushed him away and took the Group telephone. "Fix this, quick!"

Murch, muttering, began to unscrew the base plate with a nail file.

Morag McEwan vanished through the door which had been flung open by the nearby blast and after rebounding twice now quivered half-open.

A confusion of screams and shouts, alarmed and peremptory, came from upstairs.

Alison Storey scampered to the door of the Intelligence Office. Looked in. Called out to ask if the duty I.O. was unhurt. Then followed Morag upstairs after first taking a quick look into each room on the ground floor.

Squadron Leader Stevenson lurched into the Ops. Room, his eyes pouchy and red, his fine moustache limp. Nig brushed past him. "Wotcher, Steve. Spoilt your beauty sleep?" He dashed into the Intelligence Office, with Stevenson trailing him forlornly; and presently Gillam heard him speaking on the I.O.'s telephone to the main Guard Room.

The wing commander put the receiver down. "The Station Commander's car was wrecked by blast. They've got him out and he's unconscious. The Senior M.O.'s on the way to him. No damage to the main runway, but the M.T. garages were hit and . . ." the bell rang and he grabbed the telephone. "Dunford here. . . ." He listened for a minute, said "Thanks," and cradled the instrument.

Dunford was trembling. His lips were compressed and his face had become transformed from its usual full-blooded cheerfulness to a grim pallor. His eyes were fixed on Stevenson, but they looked unfocused, and he did not speak for a good half-minute. Stevenson had never thought to see the Wing Commander Flying numbed. When Nig spoke he was his abrupt self, but his voice quavered.

"A barrack-hut was hit, Steve. There were some poor bloody airmen in bed." Still, he did not stir.

But this misfortune could not be enough to wring such agony from Nig, who had been through and seen so much destruction and death. Stevenson, forty years old and accustomed to making his living by playing on the moods of hard-headed business men and women, had a moment of insight. He tried not to sound solicitous: "You'll be going down to camp, sir? Shall I ring your wife and tell her you're O.K.?"

"There's an air raid wardens' post next to my bungalow, Steve. They just phoned. A bomb fell in the garden; the house was knocked flat."

Stevenson felt his face burning with the rush of colour that was his reaction to the shock of this news. He tried to speak, had to cough to clear his throat, and stammered: "G-good God! How . . . how shocking, sir. I'll go out and see if your car's all right: you'll want to get home as soon as you can."

"No. Never mind Steve. I can't leave camp. If the group captain's had it, I'll have to take command. I'm going down to Sick Quarters, to see how he is."

Then Alison appeared in the doorway, breathless after running downstairs, and pink-cheeked with emotion. She stretched her arms, supporting herself with a hand on each upright of the door frame; with one instep she rubbed the calf of the other leg, in a mannerism of discomfiture. Dunford, who had started to walk out of the room, had to pause with one foot on the step.

She was still breathless, and her words rushed out. "Nig . . . sir . . . the girl in the PBX upstairs told me . . . I'm . . . terribly sorry . . . if you're going down to the bungalow, can I come too? Perhaps I can help?"

"Thanks, Alison. I'm going to Sick Quarters to see the Station Commander. I can't leave camp."

"But Nig!"

He glared at her.

"Well, I'll borrow a bike from one of the girls and go down myself."

"The air raid wardens are already there, Alison."

"I don't care . . . I'm going. . . ."

She turned and ran, scarcely hearing his terse thanks.

Dunford drove like a fury down the steep lane to the main gate; sounded his horn in long blasts for the barrier to be raised while he was still a hundred yards off, braked to ask if everyone in the Guard Room was all right; and flung his car down the road to Station Sick Quarters.

Group Captain Laraway was just conscious. One side of his face was burned and the Senior Medical Officer said that pieces of glass were embedded in his arms and chest.

Hearing Dunford's voice, Laraway struggled on to his elbows and was at once pushed flat on his back again by the S.M.O.'s firm hand. He lay panting and resentful. At last: "Nig . . . I'm staying . . . staying h-here . . ." there was a long pause while he glowered at the doctor and fought for breath and strength. "Doc . . . you've got to patch me up here . . . no hospital . . . that's an order. . . ."

The M.O. smiled and the Station Commander growled immediately: "Don't tell me that medical opinion supercedes orders, Doc. I've got a s-station . . . station to run. Dunford's got a U-boat hunt on his hands . . . if you can't fix me up yourself you're no rutting doctor. . . ."

Lying in the bleak little room, his chest bare and heaving with stress, the group captain tossed out the barrack-room profanity with vehemence. Nobody had ever heard him utter so much as a "blast" before and Nig was impressed.

The M.O. caught the latter's glance, then smiled at Group Captain Laraway. "I don't want a posting to Shaibah, sir."

The lines of pain and anxiety around Laraway's mouth relaxed. His voice was weary: "Shaibah would be paradise compared with where I'd have you posted, m'boy . . ." he closed his eyes.

Dunford's mind was flooded with thoughts of his wife, which he struggled to exclude. All the time he was listening to the group captain and the M.O., chaotic pictures were flickering across his brain. Melanie crushed under tons of rubble. Melanie burnt and broken. Melanie disfigured for life. Melanie crippled. Melanie dying in suffering. Melanie dead. . . .

He was in his car, slamming the door, when a medical orderly shouted from the Sick Quarters entrance. "Sir! Wing Commander Dunford! Telephone. Mrs Dunford, sir."

Nig scrambled out of his seat and covered the ground in long strides that took him barging into the orderly in the darkness. Together they reeled through the blackout curtain.

"Where?"

"In here, sir." The orderly pointed to a small office and shut the door.

The telephone was slippery in Nig's gloved hand. "Damn!" He nearly dropped it. "Dunford here."

"Are you all right, darling?" His wife was her customary serene, languid self.

"Are *you*?"

"Perfectly. Any damage on the station?"

"You're sure, Melanie? You're quite all right? No . . . no trouble?"

"I told you, sweetie. What's happened on the station?"

"Where are you?"

"With Cynthia. I took your advice and brought a bottle round. Only it wasn't gin." She began to laugh. "It was rye. Bless our gallant allies for something." She laughed again, on a higher note.

"Blast you, darling. You had me scared." He laughed too.

"The bungalow has rather had it."

"Yes."

"I'm staying with Cynthia."

"It's either that or the pavement, by the sound of things."

"Yes." She was serious suddenly. "There's plenty to do here. . . ."

"How's young Paul? How's my honorary nephew?"

"The noise woke him up, of course. He's very belligerent; wants to get at the wicked Germans."

"Good boy. You go to bed now."

"Can't. There's a bit of a mess in the village. Cynthia and I are going out to help. The old lady two doors down is coming in to sit in case Paul junior wakes again. Listen: I've asked you twice— how's the station?"

He became serious too. "You'd better see Mrs Laraway. Groupie's been a bit knocked about. Nothing irreparable. The M.O.'s already phoned her. I'm afraid a few lives were lost though . . . I must go and do things, darling."

"All right. When are you coming home? I'll be at Cynthia's."

"For breakfast."

"Fine."

"And Melanie. . . ."

"Yes?"

"Cynthia's spare bed's a double one, isn't it?"

"Yes, sweetie."

"All right. Be seeing you." He went out, smiling. Oh! You beautiful, marvellous little bitch you. Tomorrow morning, my wife; my lovely, tantalizing, don't-give-a-damn wife, I'm going to give you a child.

*     *     *

When Morag left the Ops. Room to run upstairs to the Signals Section she stumbled over a pile of wood, plaster and temporary masonry in a passage that led from the landing.

The old walls of the house had withstood the concussion of the bomb exploding in the adjoining field; but the new structure had suffered in many places.

She heard the high-pitched keening of a hysterical girl, the sharp cries of an airman lying pinned beneath a hundredweight of wireless equipment, the confused calls, weeping and shouted orders of the injured, the frightened and the authoritative.

Corporal Forrow, Jean Forrow, Flight Sergeant Stan Glover's girl, was kneeling on the floor. With her face smudged with dust and flecks of ceiling whitewash; in slacks, her jacket off and the sleeves of her cardigan rolled up, she was only recognizable by her characteristic, brisk diligence. She was digging like a terrier, scooping the debris aside; pausing now and then to brush dust from her eyes and nose.

Section Officer McEwan crouched beside her. A leg was partly revealed under the mound of broken brick and splintered board.

"Who is it, Corporal?"

Jean looked up briefly. "Lacw. Potter, ma'am. She's all right. Nothing broken. Just her legs snagged under all this. . . ."

Morag McEwan plunged her hands into the rubble and together they worked down to the trapped girl's other leg. Then, between them, they heaved at the plank which lay across her thighs; two sturdy country girls, they soon shifted it and stood smiling at each other, dishevelled and triumphant; while Lacw. Potter scrambled to her feet and began brushing the dirt from her clothes. Until, now that she was free, reaction descended on her in a fit of trembling which ended with a gasp as she slithered, in a faint, back onto the floor.

Morag bent, swung the unconscious girl up in a fireman's lift and carried her into the Cypher Office, where she laid her on the couch. "Now then, Corporal Forrow; what about some strong, sweet tea?"

*        *        *

Squadron Leader Stevenson left the Operations Room and explored the bomb damage outside the building.

His stomach was creased with darting pains and his head throbbed. He had confirmed that Gillam had spoken to the Group Controller, and had left the matter there. He felt too wretched to duplicate any action; unheard of in him.

Rumours, which circulate fast in a military establishment at any time, were tonight largely replaced by facts. The telephone operators were eavesdropping on every conversation, and exchanging information. Thus it was quickly known in the Operations building that Wing Commander Dunford's bungalow was destroyed but his wife had escaped injury.

Gillam, frustrated by the necessity to remain in the Ops. Room while everyone else helped in clearing away the mess, sent Sergeant Murch out to find Stevenson and pass this good news on to him. Murch took his time. He loathed being out in the fresh air, but he did not want to be pressed into digging, lifting, shoving and carrying; which was going on all over the house. Eventually he plodded slowly round, in Stevenson's wake; never close enough to find him in the darkness. When he did go in, Stevenson had preceded him and got the word from Gillam. His greeting was not warm.

"Where the hell have you been, Sergeant Murch?"

"Looking for you, sir."

"Why didn't you shout?"

"Didn't know where you was, sir."

"Well, go and give a hand with brewing hot drinks and giving first aid."

So it came about that Stevenson drank yet a third draught of his sergeant's poisonous brew and, an hour later, had to succumb to a fit of vomiting followed by a heavy-headedness that carried him off to sleep at his desk. He fell forward with his head on his forearms, his moustache fluttering under his stertorous breathing.

Gillam looked at him with pity.

*        *        *

When Alison Storey arrived at the village wardens' post on her borrowed bicycle, the first voice she heard was Melanie Dunford's. She experienced a spasm of emotion which sent her heart racing and her stomach fluttering, it was so macabre. Then she discerned Melanie's stance and at once her fear changed to relief and then annoyance. Damn Melanie Dunford and her aristocratic Honourableness! She was a bitch to Nig, who was a clot but a sweetie just the same. She had caused her, Flight Officer Storey with a million better things to do and no end of responsibilities, to come hot-pedalling all this mile and more in the dark along pot-holed lanes. And now she was standing around like a mannequin and—yes, by golly! Exuding the tang of rye whisky!

Alison's voice was sharp. "Melanie! Are you quite all right? Nig's in a fearful flap. . . ."

The slim figure turned—pirouetted . . . "Alison? Darling, what on earth are you doing here? Why is Nig flapping?"

"We heard about the bungalow."

"But, darling, I phoned him. . . ."

"That must have been after I left."

"Oh! Alison I am sorry. You came to see if I was . . ." Melanie broke off and laughed unnaturally, not far from hysteria; she gestured to the ruined little house ". . . in that shambles. But Nig shouldn't have let you. My God! Supposing I *had* been crushed under all that? How nice for you!"

All Alison's anger ebbed. It was impossible to stay angry with Melanie for long, any more than it was with Nig.

Melanie said: "Cynthia's around somewhere. Paul phoned: he's all right."

Cynthia Gretton's voice came from the darkness. "Hello, Alison. Come in and have a drink. You must be frozen; and shaken up."

Alison hesitated. "Now I'm here, there must be something useful I can do? Everything at camp's being well looked after."

"There is," Cynthia answered decisively. "There seem to be at least six children in most of the village families, and with the men away, the mothers are having hell. Melanie and I are just rounding up some of the kids who want pacifying and bedding them down all over the cottage. And there are several old people who need seeing to. The wardens are up to their eyes in work; a whole row of cottages was knocked down. . . ."

"That's where I should be," Melanie said suddenly, "helping with the injured, not nursing healthy kids."

"Come on," said Alison, and they went to start the heavy task that would keep them occupied till dawn. Cynthia called after them: "I'll join you in a few minutes."

Across the Channel, not much more than a hundred miles away—much closer than London to Tawmouth—German flying crews were being briefed for another raid.

## CHAPTER EIGHT

WALFORD's aircraft, "B for Baker", was some five hundred miles from its base at Tawmouth. The weather to the south was fair. To the north, storm clouds were moving across the track Walford and his crew would follow on their return leg. But that was still five or six hours away; they were not due to turn for home for another two hours or so.

They were at the point on their patrol where they felt most distant from the everyday and reassuring world. The world in which people rode on buses, went shopping, visited cinemas and leaned on bars with glasses in their hands.

When they reached the extremity of their patrol, they would know that they were only a few miles from Spain. On some of their patrol lines they flew so near the coast that they saw the lights of Spanish towns. On occasion, they had gone as far south as Portugal before turning for home. It was reassuring to know that land was near. They could easily visualize the life ashore. After all, there were buses and shops and bars in Spain and Portugal, too. When they were almost within sight of peaceful activities, it made them feel an illogical security; for the time being, the dangers of their task were dispelled.

But out here, hundreds of miles from any land, they all knew a quick, surging anxiety when Stan Glover blurted out that something must have gone wrong at Tawmouth.

Their discomfort became worse a few minutes later. Sergeant Emery, the N.C.O. in charge of the watch then on duty in Tawmouth's Signals Section, knew that most of the airborne wireless operators would detect his hand on the Morse key. For their benefit, he transmitted a snatch of information; against the rules, but so briefly lived as to be almost indetectable. Yet it was enough for those whose ears were keenly awaiting some hint of gossip. He sent a three-letter group which meant "Enemy air attack". And he sent it just once, very fast. Not everyone got it; but Stan Glover did, and said urgently into his intercom.

THE SAVAGE SKY 103

microphone: "Old Emery slipped in a quick word, Skipper; there's been an air raid on the station." And then he thought of Jean Forrow.

Flight Sergeant Glover was an airman who had been described as "steady" by every Commanding Officer who had reported on him since he joined the Service. The adjective was used about him even by his mates. The highest praise he himself could give anyone was to call him "a steady type". Yet the realization that danger had befallen his girl while he was too far away to be able to help her, coming so soon on top of the feeling of insecurity engendered by an upset in routine at this point on the patrol, unbalanced even his steadiness. To date, the war had been impersonal. He was paid, as his father had been since he could remember and still was, to fight the King's enemies; whether they were tribesmen in the North West Frontier mountains, desert Arabs, Germans, or Italians. It happened that this time they were Germans. He felt no particular animosity towards them; except that he had the British troops' pitying tolerance of all "natives"; Pathans and Arabs were ignorant and their insurrection puny; but Hitler was a criminal lunatic and the Germans, being white, ought to know better. Hitherto his feelings had run no deeper than that; but now that his home base had been attacked, his own girl perhaps hurt or killed, he was overcome by hatred and anger. And it is anger, impatience to be done with the job, that finally drives fighting men into action; whether they are weary infantry who have slogged for hours over the hills and need one last burst of energy to overrun a strong point; sailors sweating at the ammunition hoists after a day-long running battle; or airmen pressing home an attack through a cauldron of anti-aircraft fire.

Anger was filling the minds of other members of the crew. Walford had an old hatred for the Germans. He hunted their U-boats with a conscious wish to destroy, because he loathed their stealthy destruction of merchant ships and the hideous death they dealt to those ships' crews, the suffering they brought to children and women exposed to the wrath of the sea in open boats and on rafts. He hated them for waging the kind of war that had stretched his nerves until he involuntarily shuddered and blinked; he knew what fun was poked at people who "had a twitch". He would have preferred to know with certainty every time he flew just what was in store and to see his enemy clearly. The bomber pilots had definite targets and knew they would meet flak. The fighter pilots fought their opponents man-to-man; and every time they took off they expected to meet them. But the coastal pilots had only the certainty of incessant vigilance and the hazards lurking in the savage sky and the cruel sea; when they met a U-boat it was only a surprise in the many hours of searching month after month.

Pete Brodie was angry because he didn't want to be there in the first place; because his pride had been hurt by Walford's domination; and because he admitted to himself for the first time that he was frightened; frightened by the thought of being bereft of all help, out here in the blackness of the ocean night. To admit fear to himself was his lowest degradation and his immediate reaction was bitter hatred for the enemy who had caused it.

As yet the situation was not personally threatening enough to engender hatred in Cubie Meddings. He had the confidence that comes from physical strength and mental toughness. If anyone tried to pick a quarrel with Cubie, in bar, barrack-room or street, he would try to ride it good-humouredly. If he failed, he would erupt into ruthless violence with real reluctance and manifest signs of regret; but he would hit or kick savagely and with deadly effect, however great his reluctance. It was the same with the war. Someone else had started it, and so far it had not got at him directly; time enough to brew up when it did. But he was, unknowingly, smouldering already.

Lofty Duckett was slow to anger. He had lived all his days in a small, isolated community in which, if a man did not get on with his fellows, he could not survive. He lived so close to nature and, as he believed, to God, and so unhurriedly, that he was used to examining every situation carefully before allowing his feelings to be aroused. For a few fleeting moments he underwent the same fright as his companions, when they felt cut off from base; but he soon forgot this in concentration on his radar search. Lofty was still a long way from anger.

Galahad Pomeroy, "Snowy", the despised coloured man, was humble and placid. These two qualities, as much as their common loneliness, drew Duckett and him together. Snowy was not angry about anything; he was wretched. When he learned about the temporary loss of touch with base, and the reason for it, he had a sharp stab of terror that quickly gave way to resignation.

And so the patrol dragged on, mile after black mile through the darkness, hour after monotonous hour. From time to time,

Walford handed over the controls to Brodie (the automatic pilot "George" was flying the aircraft, anyway) and did a round of the crew. Now and again Brodie left the second pilot's seat to help Meddings with a 'wind drift' when they dropped a smoke flare down the chute and checked the direction of the smoke with their line of flight; or to take an independent star shot with the sextant, from the astrodome, to check the navigator's. For short periods, Duckett and Glover changed places between the wireless set and the radar. Twice Glover sat in the rear turret, while Snowy took over the wireless watch. When they reached the extremity of their patrol, and had checked the fuel remaining against the time and distance to base, and were set for the homeward run, they ate their sandwiches and hard-boiled eggs and drank coffee. For a while, food and drink made them talkative. The meal was the most important and popular milestone on every sortie. More than a sign that they had, literally, reached a turning point. It was a symbol that the back of their task was broken. For the quarter of an hour that followed this slight relaxation, the intercom. was alive with comment. Then they settled down again for the remaining four hours; during the final thirty or fifty minutes they would be off patrol, approaching or past the English coast.

Walford had been thinking intermittently about his young brother, Hugh. The war was over for him, now. If U 306 returned safely to Lorient, Hugh would be in a prison camp within a few days; better that than being drowned in the U-boat if it was sunk. At least, as a prisoner ashore, he would have a chance to escape. Even though, if U 306 returned safely to port, it meant the sinking of many ships in the future, and although Trevor Walford hated the thought of this, he still prayed that his brother's life would be spared; even at the expense of hundreds of sailors' lives that U 306 would take. He only had one brother, and what were the unknown seamen to him? If U 306 didn't get them, the chances were that another U-boat or a dive-bomber or a mine would. But please God let him have his young brother back from the dead. At any price.

Perhaps it was too late already. . . .

Cubie Meddings gave him something else to think about. "Skipper, we're running into a headwind; about twenty knots."

A quick fuel check, some calculations and Walford opened his throttles. They would use more petrol, but it was imperative to reach the northern end of their patrol before the big U.S.A.–

Britain convoy passed through. It was their job to protect the convoy and they could not do this if he allowed the wind to delay them.

There was a secondary consideration. A comforting one. By putting on speed, they would be past the Brest peninsula before dawn; clear of the German fighter bases that became operational at first light; beyond the reach of the Me. 109 and FW. 190 fighters.

It was at a few minutes after four-o'clock that Stan Glover said sharply: "Message coming for us, Skip.," and began to write.

Walford put out a hand to shake Brodie. "Pete. Go back and see what it is."

Brodie moved stiffly from his cramped position, to stand behind the wireless operator and read over his shoulder. Swiftly, Duckett transcribed the code groups into plain language. Excitement mounted in the second pilot as he read. As soon as the message was written in full he snatched the sheet of paper and hurried back to thrust it at Walford.

"Small tanker lagging behind convoy, sunk by U-boat in position 47.30 N. 7 10 W. Divert and search. No other aircraft in vicinity, due to premature returns on account of weather."

The captain read, nodded, and thumbed his intercom. switch. "Listen, everyone." He read them the message. "Course, Cubie?"

"Right with you, Skipper." Meddings had made a mark on his chart, to show the site of the sinking; drawn a thin line to it from their present position; and was working out, with his course and speed calculator, the course they must fly, with a strong beam wind, to make good the necessary track. It only took him a few seconds. As soon as he had given the course, Walford turned, and opened the throttles until the air speed indicator was up to two hundred miles an hour.

Everyone was wide awake, now. They were on their own, with the weather growing worse and the slower ships of the convoy at the U-boat's mercy. Cracking on speed to finish the long voyage, there must be other old vessels, besides the sunk tanker, that had lost station in the darkness, their tired engines unable to sustain maximum speed any longer.

The aircraft was buckling and plunging in the rough air. Walford had switched off the automatic pilot, and the control column juddered in his hands, the rudder bar kicked gently against his feet. He flexed wrists and ankles against the changing demands of the control surfaces, putting all his skill into maintaining a steady five hundred feet altitude and an exact compass course. Brodie glanced across at him and grimaced under-standingly. Their matched movements were synchronized with the unconscious effort bred of four hundred hours' flying together.

Walford had ordered Meddings into the astrodome, to help with the forward lookout for their quarry; if it was on the surface. Glover, at the wireless, and Snowy, facing the wrong way, chafed at their uselessness. The two pilots and the navigator searched intently, Brodie and Meddings using powerful night glasses; seeking the foaming trail from a periscope (hopeless though, at night), the shape of a conning tower, or perhaps the entire hull outline of a surfaced submarine.

But they all knew that the first contact would come on the radar. None of them was surprised when Lofty Duckett called loudly: "Contact! Bearing 320, range six miles."

Walford responded instantly. Turning onto 320, throttling back to 140 indicated.

Duckett's eyes watered as he stared at the biggest, brightest green maggot on his screen which stood out from the others caused by sea returns. It remained there at each sweep of the aerial, but it was difficult to see and to hold in view. He was working on a small range scale, so as to cover a bigger area with his screen. To ensure accuracy, he would have to change to a large scale; but in the moment of doing so he would lose his radar picture altogether. He held his breath and turned the range selection switch. The face of the tube became blank and then it was covered by responses again; and on the edge was the steadily glowing green maggot which he knew was their target.

"Bearing still 320, range four."

Walford felt icily cold. Time and again he had made a night approach to a target submarine, dropped his 4-lb. practice bombs and pulled away. He had developed good judgment; could make an accurate attack, straddling the target; but those attacks, although against a jinking target, were not made in the face of gun fire. It was time for action stations.

He may need the second pilot's help to fly the aircraft. Perhaps Brodie would have to fly it alone . . . so the navigator must man the front guns. "Cubie."

"Yeah, Skipper?"

"Go down in the nose. And fire another check burst."

"O.K." Cubie sounded happy.

"Stan, lower the light."

"Aye, aye, Skipper."

And Duckett gave the range: "Two and a half miles," as Meddings squeezed between the pilots and crawled into the nose position, behind the twin Browning guns, giving a thumbs-up and grinning.

Walford peered ahead, flying directly towards the surfaced submarine; wondering what number he would see painted on its conning tower. Asking himself by how many yards he could make his depth charges miss if it was U 306. Picturing his brother amid the excitement that would already be prevailing aboard—if, indeed, this was U 306—as the approaching aircraft was heard.

He put the nose down and reduced height to three hundred feet. If he attacked, it would have to be from fifty feet at most, ideally from only thirty.

"Range coming down to one mile, Skipper."

Walford bit his lips. "On light! Stan."

The beam leaped out from the darkness below them, probing ahead with terrible directness and certainty. Its brilliance danced on the wavetops and was mirrored a thousand times in droplets of spray. Walford blinked back tears as his eyes took the shock of sudden transition from darkness to merciless glare.

And then came Brodie's cry, triumphant: "Dead ahead! She's right on the surface . . . the . . . cheeky sod." His hands trembled as he fingered the focusing screw on his binoculars. "I can identify her . . . Damn. She's rollin' . . . wait . . . wait . . . I got her number . . . U . . . U 3 . . . 3 something . . . U 306! That's the bastard that's been causing all the trouble."

Even as Brodie shouted, the first rods of tracer lashed up at them. But the heavy calibre bullets from the machine guns, for'ard and aft of the conning tower and on the bridge itself, raced harmlessly overhead when Walford dived steeply under them and levelled off at thirty feet.

Their height, speed and line of approach would govern the accuracy of the attack. *If* they attacked. Yet Walford's training and instinct had brought him down to thirty feet despite his instant reaction of rebellion when he knew for sure the identity of his target.

The Wellington carried six depth charges. To ensure lethal damage to a submarine, one had to be dropped on each side and very close. Flying fast, it was impossible to judge the moment at which to release them, accurately, and their forward speed might carry all six right over the target. Flying high, there was too much time for the fall and again the depth charges may be thrown beyond the submarine's hull. So the attack must be made low and slowly. And obliquely, because thus the chances were that one depth charge would fall very near and one fairly near, on each side. The combined effect of four well placed depth charges was always lethal. By flying across at right angles, or parallel to the hull, two things could happen. In the first case, only two depth charges could be dropped near the submarine and the remainder would all fall at too great a distance to do real damage. In the second case, it was too much to hope that all six, or even one, would fall very close to the target; it was more likely that all would fall too far off to sink it.

The wet, black hull of the U-boat was a challenging obscenity in the bright beam of the Leigh light. She rocked in the choppy water. Waves, dashing on her weather beam, broke and rushed over her decks, in foaming cascades. Her bow forged through the hillocks of green water, sending sheets of spray arching high over the foredeck. The wind created by her own speed snatched at the bow wave and dragged it back to drench the conning tower.

Walford—and all his crew except Snowy in the tail turret and Lofty Duckett in the radar station—saw the German sailors at the guns as small figures battling with wind and sea to keep a firm footing. They saw men on the bridge in gleaming oilskins, gripping the guard rail and swaying with the motion of the boat.

A rattle of gunfire filled the cockpit and cordite smoke coiled back over the floor. Cubie Meddings was firing his front guns.

Walford felt the nose of his aircraft plunge and then reach up again when an air disturbance eddied across its path. For a second he thought they were going to dive into the U-boat's side. Then, as they flashed over, the port wing tilted with the sudden violence of a see-saw, in the same instant that they heard the crash of splintered metal and the snarl of ripped canvas. Bright flashes of flame pranced dizzily in the corner of Walford's left eye. Then a strong hand seemed to seize the Wellington and shake it by the tail and they heard the back-flung chatter of Snowy Pomeroy's four machine guns. His exultant voice dinned in their headphones: "I gottem . . . I gottem . . . Skipper, I stopped the after gun . . . look at 'em slidin' in the drink. . . ."

But there was only darkness, punctuated by the flames at the muzzles of the U-boat's guns. The Leigh light had raced across her hull and even the afterglow was dimmed. But the beam gave the Germans an aiming mark. Walford snapped at Glover to douse it.

Brodie said loudly, his voice thick: "What happened? We were hit in the port wing."

"She's flying all right. Can't have done much damage. Nice work, Snowy. Sure you knocked out one of their guns?" He had to shout.

"I'm sure, Skipper. The machine-gun on the stern. I hosed right into it. I got one of the men in the big gun crew, too," Snowy yelled back.

"Good show, Snowy." Walford was holding the Wellington in a flat, skidding turn. Lofty Duckett was chanting the changing bearing of the U-boat. At last it was dead ahead again and only a mile away.

Walford ordered Glover to switch the light on. And for the first time since flying over U 306 he thought once more of his brother. On the other side of that black steel plating, Hugh would be waiting for the crump of exploding depth charges which would be the last sound he would ever hear. Walford pictured the tense young face, the sweating hands gripping some nearby projection for steadiness as the boat rolled and bucked. He shared the terror and the mental agony. Yet he knew that his brother must be willing the unknown pilot of the attacking aircraft to succeed. In these troubled moments, with his soul wrenched asunder by the conflict between duty and emotion, he re-lived a succession of occasions when his brother had shown outward indifference to danger. He could imagine Hugh, if he knew the identity of the Wellington's pilot, laughing up at him and urging him to make sure his aim was good. He remembered when Hugh had fallen from a tree and broken his arm; he, Trevor, had almost fainted as he fumbled with the bones; Hugh, white-faced but smiling, had told him what to do. There had been other times. A snowstorm in the Welsh hills, Hugh with a broken ankle, and night coming on. It was at Hugh's insistence that he had left him and gone for help instead of staying to support him while he hobbled. Hugh had defied trouble and mocked at threats, all his life.

As soon as the light came on, the enemy opened fire. Walford had climbed before turning. Now, he came down again to thirty feet. Bullets and shells streaked past, drawing hard lines of tracer across the darkness. A howl came from Cubie: "I hit the bridge ... Jeeze ... like a ruttin' shootin' gallery."

A deafening slam brought a flurry of sparks and flames from the port engine. Walford felt his left arm pierced by a burning shock of red hot pain which coursed from his hand to his shoulder. His ribs seemed to be suddenly exposed to a thousand whip lashes. A roaring wind thrust into the cockpit through a shattered window. He dimly heard Brodie's shout: "All right, Trevor?"

The aircraft heeled over to port and Walford felt himself falling into a chasm, his brain darkened. His face was stiff with cold, paralysed by the rushing wind. His left arm had lost its strength. Then the aircraft rolled abruptly to starboard and everything was an aching medley of fire, multi-coloured; of stenching, choking cordite smoke; and the bark of cannon, the rattle of machine guns and howl of engine. Above and through it all came Brodie's insistent: "Let go, Trevor, I've got her. Let go the stick. . . ."

And then Walford's head cleared and he dashed the blankness from his mind with a shake. Someone was screaming on the inter-com. "I've been hit . . . I've been hit. . . ." He recognized Duckett's voice and managed to mutter an order to Glover through his own pain. "Stan . . . leave the light and see about Lofty . . . Snowy, come up to the light. We won't need your tail guns again: I'm going to attack, next run."

He looked across at Brodie. "O.K., Pete. I'll take her."

"You can't man. You've had it. One arm's gone and your chest's ripped open. Besides, we've had it, too. Not a chance of an attack. They've got too much armament. They can see us. We've lost an engine . . . signal base and tell them to send a Lib. or a Sunder-land."

"Shut up . . . get your bloody hands off the controls . . . or I'll . . . I'll shoot you, Brodie, by God I will. . . ."

"You're crazy. . . ."

"And you're no good . . . don't you know why we're here? To sink this swine. . . ."

Brodie's big fists relaxed their grip on the control column. Moving his left arm stiffly, Walford eased the labouring aircraft round. Glover had shifted Duckett into the aisle and sat now at the radar console, calling the range and bearing.

"On light!"

"O.K., Skipper." Snowy sent the wide swathe scything through the blackness enveloping them. For the third time, U 306 in all her stubborn menace lay across their path.

Walford had learned long ago to drop his depth charges on small, moving shapes that merged with their background. But nobody could reproduce for him the moment of actuality; the crazy world of gunfire, wounded flesh and a shattered engine.

He turned, once and again, until he was approaching at forty-five degrees to the U-boat's track. In his ears he could hear Meddings's incessant, profane muttering while he raked the length of the submarine with his bullets, blasting at each gun to keep it from shooting accurately at the aircraft. He felt Brodie's steadying hands on the dual controls, helping to hold the aircraft level against the dead engine.

Stan Glover had scrambled back to the wireless station to signal base that they were attacking.

Lofty Duckett, lying on his back, his wounded leg roughly bandaged, saw Snowy's face, eyes wide with apprehension, staring down at him. Snowy's lips were moving soundlessly. Duckett groaned as a wave of pain washed through him.

Walford, eyes puckered, flew level at thirty feet. A bullet from a heavy machine gun plugged through the floor near his foot and a cannon shell tore through the wing tip with a bright flash of flame.

His thumb lightly touched the firing button and he watched the target coming up to the line of the leading edges of his wings. When there were only five seconds to go and it looked a mere hand's span away, panic devoured him; over-riding the throbbing agony in his arm and chest, the concentration on his task; it was as though his fixed stare had penetrated the hull and he could see the prisoners the U-boat held. Involuntarily his hands sought to pull the Wellington up and his feet to kick the rudder bar to take it off course, to go zooming harmlessly aside.

Instead, his thumb plunged onto the firing button. The aircraft rocked upwards as though sucked into the heart of an enormous vacuum; lightened by the weight of its depth charges, it leaped a hundred feet even on its one labouring engine. Snowy went skidding and sliding down to the rear turret. His screams of victory came a few seconds later: "We gotter . . . a kill . . . a kill!"

They turned in time to see the whole hull tossed out of the sea on five enormous eruptions which boiled and grew and swelled. Which lifted and flung the submarine onto its side. Which burst a hundred feet above the crushed hull, swallowing it in giant whorls of churning water.

The bow thrust starkly up and the stern was already sucked into the monstrous eddies of the depth charges' aftermath. A few sailors slid and rolled and pitched into the boiling sea. An instant later there was nothing but a vast patch of oil. Every last sign of U 306 and her crew had been engulfed by the titanic turmoil and the whirlpool of her sinking.

With dry sobs tearing at his throat, Walford poured full power onto the starboard engine and then, letting his left arm fall numbly from the stick, tried to hold his aircraft with his one good arm.

He could hear Brodie's shouts and the excited chatter on the intercom. But for the moment he could not even think of Lofty's wound. His eyes blinded by tears, his throat constricted beyond speech, he could not even tell Brodie to fly the aircraft. He dimly heard Cubie Meddings suggest a course for base, and automatically began turning onto it. It was the last thing he did before he fainted. In the moment of losing consciousness, he had the sense to throw his weight back so that he would not collapse over the control column. He would have been astonished had he been able to hear the firmness in Brodie's voice as the second pilot began to give orders to the rest of the crew. More astonished had he detected the note of contentment in it.

"Cubie, get back on your chart and give me an accurate course for base."

"O.K."

"Pomeroy, you get on the key and send the attack signal. I want you up here, Stan; Trevor's in bad shape."

Snowy felt the animosity implied by the use of his surname, even here and in these circumstances. He acknowledged his instructions with a toneless monosyllable.

Meddings, wriggling out of the nose turret, paused and spoke close to Brodie's ear so that his words would not be heard on the intercom. "Did you count the explosions, Pete?"

"No. Six, I suppose."

"Wrong, brother. Dead wrong. I counted. Five. There were just five."

Disbelief showed on Brodie's face and in his voice. "You must've made a mistake. How could you count, with all that going on?"

"I counted. There were five explosions."

"Maybe one didn't go off. . . ."

"Oh, be your age, chum!"

Brodie shouted into his microphone. "Anyone count the depth charges?" Then saw Stan Glover leaning over Walford. He tugged at Glover's jacket. The latter turned and bent over him. "What d'you want?"

"Say, did you count the depth charge detonations?"

"I was in the astrodome, after I fixed Lofty up. Only saw five."

Brodie grimaced and Meddings nodded with compressed lips. The Canadian used the intercom. again. "Hey! Pom . . . Snowy . . . how many depth charges went off?"

"I only saw five."

"O.K.," remarked Brodie to the others, "so we've got a hang-up. And it's armed. Now we know how we stand: I've got to get this goddam crate back somehow. No ditching! Give me that course, Cubie; and make it the shortest, no matter what. No detours to avoid the Brest area; enemy fighters are one chance we *will* have to take! If this engine behaves and the wind doesn't freshen up too much, we should just about scrape through before daylight."

Meddings, from his navigation desk, said: "The wind's blowing us towards France, anyway."

## CHAPTER NINE

Corporal Jean Forrow, W.A.A.F. and wireless operator extra-ordinary, was still giving first aid to the injured when one of the other girls came in a rush of feet and a scream of stop press information. "Jean . . . Jean . . . signal from Stan . . . from your Stan . . . they've sunk a U-boat."

Jean, crouching on the floor, rocked back on her heels, brushed a displaced lock of hair from her cheek, and reddened. "Don't make such a noise!" She got up quickly and took the girl aside. "Now tell me—quietly."

"Well, I thought you'd want to know."

"Don't sulk. Of course I want to know. But those people in there are waiting for an ambulance; they don't want to hear you shouting, do they?"

"I never thought . . . anyway, there's a signal from Stan . . . at least, from his crew—Sarge says it isn't him on the key. . . ."

Jean, her eyes wide now, leaned against the wall. "Not Stan on the key? Oh, my God! He must have been hurt. . . ."

Morag McEwan, who had followed them into the passage, heard. She touched Jean's arm. "It doesn't mean that at all. He's probably doing some other job. Doesn't he operate the Leigh light?"

"Y—yes, ma'am."

"Well then? Be sensible." She turned to the messenger. "You stay here and give me a hand. Go on, Corporal Forrow, go to the

Traffic Office and see what this is about." Morag's own thoughts were a tortured medley of speculation about Trevor Walford. She well knew who was usually the first victim in an aircraft; kill or disable the pilot, and destruction could be most quickly achieved. She watched Jean go with her own face flaming and her hands tightly clenched.

The signal had been carried to the Ops. Room, where Squadron Leader Stevenson still slept with his head cradled on his arms, sprawling over his desk. Gillam read it, then shook the controller awake.

Stevenson blinked, his eyes red-rimmed and his face pale. Automatically he preened his moustache. Gillam read the signal aloud. For a moment, Stevenson did not appear to understand it. Then he tried to speak, but only a meaningless croak emerged. He put his hands over his stomach and looked piteously at his navigator; then heeled his chair back and rushed from the room. They heard him retching on the front steps; the door had been blown off one hinge by the bomb bursts.

Gillam saw Sergeant Murch smirking and rounded on the fat obstructionist in an outburst of irritation. "Wipe that grin off your face, Sergeant. Get out and see if Section Officer McEwan's got anything in the medicine cabinet that might help the squadron leader. See if there's a medical orderly around who can help. Do something, man."

Murch waddled out of the room, his jowls quivering with fright. When Flying Officer Gillam pulled his glasses off and scowled, his face was forbidding; flat nose, eyebrows ridged by scar tissue, big, square chin. His hands were astonishingly big, too; and Murch noticed that they were clenched. Charles Gillam had no more patience left; for the time being.

Stevenson returned, slowly, mounted the dais and sat down. "Oh, God! Charles. My inside feels as though a concrete mixer and a pneumatic drill are at work together."

"You must have food poisoning. I've told Murch to see if there's a medical orderly around, or if Morag's got something in the medicine box. Why don't you go down to Sick Quarters?"

"I'll be all right. I'd like to see that signal again." Gillam put it in his hand and waited. After a pause, the controller asked to see the weather reports that had come in during the past hour. There were eight or nine, from aircraft of various stations. He looked up from them and smiled faintly at his navigator. "Perhaps it was just as well I did pass out, Charles. If I'd read these as they came in, I'd have moved heaven and earth to get Walford diverted; Gib., probably."

Gillam blushed. "You're telling me politely, sir, that I had my finger in. That I should either have woken you or done something about the signals myself."

"It doesn't matter, as things have turned out. We've got a kill."

A W.A.A.F. hurried in with yet another signal. The two officers read it together. It was from "B Baker" and reported that the captain and one wireless operator-air gunner were wounded; that the aircraft was flying on one engine and returning to base by the shortest route. It gave the aircraft's exact position at the time of sending. It added that the U-boat it sunk was positively identified as U 306.

Jean Forrow was in the Signals Traffic Office when this message was received. It swept away her composure at last. She ran back to the room where Morag McEwan was. "Ma'am ... I'm sorry ... I've *got* to get back on duty ... there may be another signal. ..." she had to break off as a sob caught her throat. "S—sorry ... but we've just had one saying one of the Wops is wounded ... I can't bear not being on the key ... I've *got* to find out if it's Stan. ..."

Morag straightened, serious-faced. "Is that all it said?"

"No, ma'am. It said the captain's wounded, too; and they're on one engine."

"I see. Thank you. Thank you, Jean. Of course you must go back on duty. We can manage here now. The ambulance has just taken some of them." She stood motionless, her eyes closed to hold back the tears. Please God, help Trevor! "Wounded" could mean so many things. She quickly wiped her eyes, unobtrusively; then returned briskly to the Cypher Office. The medical orderlies were coping with the injured. There was routine work to be done. But she found it hard to keep her mind on it.

\*     \*     \*

Wing Commander Paul Gretton, O.C. No. 1111 Squadron, had snatched two hours' sleep on a camp bed in his office. He was awake now, and in his squadron crew room, talking to the crews who had returned from patrol; some early, on account of bad weather.

Nig Dunford, highly combustible Wing Commander Flying, acting Station Commander, was in the Operations Canteen. Over bacon and eggs (three) and a huge mug of tea, he simultaneously interrogated crews from all the squadrons and gave them an account of the air raid. By the time they reached the canteen, the crews were relaxed and good-humoured. Nig's story of the air raid, although it omitted none of the tragedy, emphasized the drollery that is inseparable from calamity. In his telling of it, the group captain's injuries were overshadowed by the acrocephalic eighteen-year-old airman surprised in front of a mirror trying on the Station Commander's too-small hat. The collapse of a hut wall, which might have crushed a dozen W.A.A.F.'s if it had fallen inwards, falling outwards became an object of humour; it had imprisoned a W.A.A.F. and an airman who were concluding an evening's courting with an illicit assignation in the adjacent slit-trench.

Dunford was called to the telephone. "Yes?"

"Ops here, sir."

"Yes, Steve?"

"Walford's made a kill."

"Whacko. Whack-bloody-o. Where?"

Stevenson gave him particulars of time and place and added "The U-boat was identified too, sir. It's the one that's been doing most of the dirty work lately."

Dunford's heart skipped. He felt its sudden acceleration in his throat even as he spoke. "They're quite sure they got her number?"

"Positive, sir: U 306. Group have been through already; it's a tremendous feather in our cap . . . in Trevor's. . . ."

Dunford cut in. "Have you told Wing Commander Gretton?"

"I shall as soon as you hang up, sir."

"Well, don't! I'll tell him myself. Where is he?"

"In the squadron crew room."

"All right, Steve. Thanks." He hung up and walked slowly back to his table. The room had fallen silent and everyone watched him keenly. He shuffled like a sleep-walker; then, registering the silence and the attention focused on himself, he brought his head up with a start and stood for a moment looking around at the expectant faces.

"That was Ops. Trevor Walford's got a kill; U 306, the bastard that's been causing most of the grief."

The room came alive with noise. The members of 1111 Squadron jeered at the members of the two other Tawmouth squadrons; the others shouted back that they had driven U 306 to the point where Walford could not possibly miss it. In the midst of the rejoicing, Nig left his food unfinished and went to find Gretton.

The latter, hearing him enter the crew room, glanced over his shoulder and took his pipe from his mouth. "Hello, Nig. I was just thinking of joining you in the canteen."

The other men in the room, stowing their flying gear in their lockers, mumbled incoherently, nodded, or ignored the intruder. Airmen just back from a long, cold flight were not renowned for courtesy.

"Come on, then; but I think we'd better go up to Ops. first. And I'd like a word in your shell-like, on the way."

Portentousness was so unusual in Birdman Dunford, that Gretton stood up at once and knocked his pipe out on the top of the stove. As soon as they were outside, he asked: "Something wrong?"

"Yeah. Stevenson phoned me and I told him to leave it to me to tell you. That poor little sod Walford's just got a kill."

"Christ! I know what you're going to say. . . ."

"Yeah, that's it. U 306. No survivors."

"Oh, rut it!"

"He and one of his wops. got clobbered—no details. They've lost an engine, too."

They dived for their cars, which were standing side by side on the tarmac, and drove away to the Operations Room; Nig leading by a length.

\*     \*     \*

Brodie had climbed to two thousand feet, just below cloud base. The damp air rushing through the shattered window on the port side of the cockpit struck cold on his face and through his trousers. His thighs were growing numb. He blessed the leather and fur jacket and the fleece-lined flying boots that kept the rest of his body warm.

Stan Glover came into the cockpit, carrying a piece of ply-wood on which he clipped briefing notes. He plugged into the intercom., sat down in the first pilot's vacant seat and began to tape the board in place over the hole in the perspex. At once the noise and the coldness diminished.

Brodie switched on his mike. "How are they doing, Stan?"

"Lofty's not too bad. Leg broken just above the ankle, and a five-inch gash. He lost a fair amount of blood, though. But I'm not happy about Trevor; that wound in his upper arm is clean enough; right through, without touching the bone. But the shell splinter that carved his chest . . ." he turned away momentarily from his work and grimaced. "But for the Irvine jacket, it would have sprung his left ribs open. As it is, he's cut to the bone and a lot of skin has been sliced off. Still, it could be worse. He's conscious, but he's hellish badly shocked. Doesn't seem to be feeling much pain, now."

"O.K. You can leave that window—it's good enough. Thanks for fixing it. I'd rather have you on the key; things may get tough later on and I don't think Pomeroy's so hot as a wop. Tell him to go back in the tail turret. Cubie can be nurse; he has time to spare."

Meddings, hearing this, protested: "I got time, but not all that much. You're gonna need navigatin' right back to base, brother."

"I'm flying the course you gave me! You can check it once in a while. Right now, have a look at the patients."

"Yes, sir, Cap'n Bligh; but remember what happened on the 'Bounty'!"

Meddings unwillingly left his desk and went astern of the Leigh light, where both wounded men were lying in blankets.

Walford was shivering, his teeth tight together and his eyes wide and staring. His pallid face looked collapsed, devoid of bone and character. His lips moved over his clenched teeth. Meddings, kneeling, could hear him. "I had to do it . . . I had to . . . couldn't pull out . . . I had to. . . ."

"Sure, sure, Trevor. You did fine. What's to worry about? We made it, didn't we? And we sunk the ruttin' Hun."

"Yes . . . we sunk 'em . . . I had to, Cubie . . ." He turned his head, struggling with something within himself that was far beyond Meddings's ken.

"You did a helluva job, Trevor. Now get some rest."

"You don't know, Cubie . . . you don't know. . . ."

"Quiet, fella. Hurtin' bad?"

"No. No, thanks. Can't feel a damn thing. Pretty numb. Just feel cold."

"I'll bring you some coffee. Just take it easy now."

Meddings moved to kneel beside Lofty Duckett. The Australian's eyes were closed and his face twisted in suffering. Now and again he groaned.

"Hi! Lofty. How're you makin' out?"

"Gawd! Cubie, give me a biff on the jaw, will yer? Be a pal! This pain . . . knock me out, Cubie, knock me out."

"It'll be O.K. in a minute, Lofty. The pain will go."

"No, Cubie, no. Gimme a sock on the chin . . . please. . . ."

"I don't know my own strength, boy! Want me to take your head right off your shoulders? Have some of this coffee." He held a cup to Duckett's lips. When it was empty, he filled another and went back to Walford.

The captain was still talking to himself. But his eyes were closed now. Gently, Meddings held the cup to his mouth and he drained it without opening his eyes.

Trevor Walford closed his eyes to shut out the guilt that filled him as each fresh evidence that he was still alive acted on his senses. After his fratricidal crime, he had no right to life. His mind was achingly alive. His body, though partly numbed, was still responsive to feeling. He had pulled his hands from the blankets, and reached out to touch the side of the fuselage; to watch them moving. Touch, sight, hearing; even the taste of the coffee; all were accusations. Muddled phrases limped through his shocked brain. The quick and the dead. Forgive me, Father, for I well know what I do; but I had to . . . The anguish that assailed him with every fresh thought and reminiscence was unbearable. Until Cubie Meddings's matter-of-fact voice jolted him out of his remorse.

"I'm going to put your Mae West on you, Trevor. Dawn's come up and we're pretty close to the Brest peninsula."

He felt his shoulders being raised, and struggled to support himself on his elbows. Cubie slipped the yellow pneumatic life-jacket over his head and together they laced it up.

Duckett, sitting up, looked round and managed a grin. "Good on yer, Skipper." He saw Walford wince as the Mae West was tightened over his bandaged chest, over the lacerated leather jacket. "Give me a hand, won't you, if we have to get out in a hurry?"

This forced a weak smile from Walford. "I'll give you a hand, Lofty. But we're going to be all right." He turned his head to bring Meddings in view. "What altitude are we?"

"Two thousand. We've left most of the weather to the west, and the clouds are breaking. We'll be able to scramble up another thousand, I guess."

They felt the floor tilt sharply, nose-up, and heard the starboard engine's steady roar build up quickly to a bellow.

Walford fell back against the blanket beneath him. "He must have seen that gap in the clouds."

Meddings muttered abruptly: "I'll go and see," and vanished.

But what Brodie had seen was a pair of Messerschmitt 109's

slanting up at them, the early sunlight glinting on their ugly, long yellow noses. They came from the direction of Brest; and they came fast; at almost three times the speed of which the crippled Wellington was capable.

Thirty seconds later the intercom. crackled with Snowy's warning. "Rear gunner to pilot. Two Me. 109's, three o'clock, below."

Brodie's reply was laced with contempt. "So you *are* awake? They've been there for ruttin' ages. What the hell d'you think I'm climbing for?"

And Meddings, peering from the astrodome, saw them too. He reached for his sextant, hoping to get a shot that would fix their position accurately; for he knew what Brodie's imminent order would be.

The ragged wisps at the edge of a cloud bank reached out for the Wellington in the very instant that the enemy fighters opened fire. And Brodie said curtly: "Stan, signal we're being bounced. Give him a fix, Cubie."

"I got it. Wait one, Stan."

To Stan Glover, the knowledge of enemy attack came without warning in his windowless wireless cabin. He was used to this, but that did not make him like it any better. It was hell, sitting here and twiddling dials, bashing a Morse key, not knowing exactly what was happening outside. It was all right for an ostrich to hide its head when trouble came; but Flight Sergeant Glover liked to weigh things up for himself. Especially with the skipper laid out and only Pete Brodie in "the office". Brodie was, in Stan Glover's book, lazy, self-centred and not really competent. He would have felt a whole lot better if Flight Lieutenant Walford had at least been up there in the cockpit, even if he was unfit to fly the aircraft on his own.

But Stan Glover forgot about these things when he heard the dots and dashes from base acknowledging his signal. Jean! That was all right, then. He could pick out her light touch on the key from a mere three or four letters. It was Jean, he knew; no kidding!

The cloud thinned out and Brodie, staring ahead, saw the two Me. 109's hovering in wait. Before the Wellington had fully emerged, he put on bank and turned back into the cloud.

But not before the Messerschmitts had time for a long burst that sawed into the upper section of the fuselage, just above the heads of the two wounded men.

*　　　*　　　*

On their way to the Operations Room, the two wing commanders called at Sick Quarters. Walford's destruction of a U-boat, his fratricide; these were matters which should be told to the Station Commander. But Laraway was under drugs. The S.M.O. told them that the group captain would not be conscious until nine-o'clock that morning, at the earliest.

"Well," said Nig, "That's that. It's a curse he's knocked out at a time like this; we could use his brain; so could the A.O.C. Have you noticed how many times a day Group come through with personal calls for the stationmaster from the A.O.C."

Paul Gretton had, and said so. Nobody doubted that Group Captain Laraway's promotion to air commodore and a staff appointment were imminent. But, for the time being, the affairs of R.A.F. Tawmouth were in the hands of Nig Dunford; and Gretton was sufficiently prejudiced in favour of his own kind (the unacademic fliers who offered only experience and dash) to believe that they could not be in better care.

He followed the Wing Commander Flying's car up the lane to the Operations Room.

They found Squadron Leader Stevenson restored to his usual robust vigour. Steve's addiction to fresh air and exercise, his long tramp the previous afternoon, had paid dividends. By now, he had vomited out of his system all the noxious filth that Sergeant Murch had secretly introduced into his tea and Oxo. The W.A.A.F.'s had brewed fresh pots of tea and taken mugs of it to everyone in the building. A medical orderly had fetched a sedative from Sick Quarters, and administered it. Steve was even thinking of asking Charles Gillam to make some of his famous cheese toast.

It was first light already, and at this time of the night watch there was always a lot of work to do. Gillam was at his table, calculating the 8 a.m. positions of shipping in the area. Sergeant Murch was making a summary of the past twenty-four hours' flying times. Stevenson was compiling a report on the night's watch, with the aid of a pile of signal forms.

He stood up when he saw Gretton and Dunford come in. The latter beckoned to him to join them as they walked to the far end of the room, where the situation map occupied one wall. Stevenson wondered why neither had said anything about the sinking of U 306, and why both looked so serious.

Nig spoke in an undertone. "You'd better hear this now, Steve. Everyone at Group has strict orders not to let it leak, but they'll have to let it go officially this morning; and then the rumours will start." He stopped and eyed the controller. His voice took on a new sharpness: "You haven't heard anything, have you?"

Stevenson was honestly mystified. "Heard what, sir?"

"That the captain of the Sunderland crew that was aboard U 306 was Walford's brother."

"Oh, God!" Stevenson looked from one tough, expressionless face to the other. There was nothing else to say. His feelings were beyond expression. "Oh, God!"

The fact that there were British prisoners on board U 306 had not been told to many. When Gretton gave Walford the information, as a warning to prepare himself for worse, he had cautioned him not to repeat it. The signal from the Wellington that had seen the U-boat take the Sunderland crew aboard was in code. That Wellington's crew had been forbidden to speak of the event, and their signal had been seen only by duty Cypher Officers and controllers. So far the secret had been well kept.

Charles Gillam knew about it, because a friend of his at Group had whispered it to him by telephone soon after the sinking. It had made him impotently enraged; his face as he sat over his chart was stern and his thoughts were far away; perhaps he could scrape into air crew as a flight engineer? Surely that was a duty that should not demand sharp eyesight.

Dunford said: "You'd better tell your stooge; what's his name ...? Gillam?"

"He's no stooge," Gretton murmured quickly. "I saw him give quite a performance with the gloves on, yesterday afternoon. *Quite* a performance." He turned to look reflectively at the engrossed navigator.

Dunford was impatient. "Yeah, he's a good type. Tell him, Steve. And tell your sergeant, if you think you should. Any responsible person who can quash rumours should be told."

Stevenson looked dour. "I wouldn't tell Sergeant Murch the day of the week."

"I leave it to you."

Stevenson raised his voice and called Gillam. When the latter joined them, he said: "Charles, Wing Commander Dunford has just told me something which he feels all officers should know; there are going to be rumours floating round soon."

Gillam raised his eyebrows. What the hell was Steve waffling about? He waited.

"U 306 shot down a Sunderland this morning, as you know."

So that was it. Play dumb. Don't betray the informant at Group. "I remember."

"The U-boat surfaced and took the survivors aboard as prisoners."

Gillam managed a creditable enough reaction; but it deceived nobody. Stevenson added coldly: "So you knew. Well, that's not all. It was Trevor Walford's brother who captained the crew. He was . . ."

The blood drained from Gillam's face. He snatched the words away from Stevenson: ". . . He was in that bloody U 306 when Trevor sunk it? God Almighty! I suppose Trevor knew?"

"That," Gretton cut in, "is beside the point. The only fact that concerns anyone is that Walford sunk a U-boat in which his own brother was a prisoner. Whether he did so knowingly or in ignorance is quite immaterial. The one fact alone is enough to kick off the biggest imaginable storm of lavatory rumours as soon as the erks get hold of it."

Charles Gillam seethed and something of his resentment showed in his face. Damn you! Wing Commander Gretton; you pompous, authoritative, bloody young autocrat. Who the hell did Gretton think he was, to talk down to everyone junior? The separation of three grades in rank did not warrant the assumption that he, Gillam, B.A. (Oxon.), and a good Second Class, at that, was in all respects inferior.

Gretton recognized the darkening of Gillam's pugilistic face; he instantly regretted his offensiveness; but there was nothing he could do to retract it.

Overhead, there was a loud bump. The four officers looked up, expecting to see plaster fall from the ceiling. They heard a heavy chair being picked up and set hastily on its legs; rapid footfalls; the slam of a door.

"Now, what the hell?" muttered Gillam. "Every time there's a really juicy signal, you'd think a herd of elephants were dancing a schuplattler up there."

"We'll hear a runner tumbling downstairs like a ton of coal, any moment," Stevenson agreed.

It was "B for Baker's" signal that caused the commotion upstairs: "Enemy air attack. Two Me. 109's," and the aircraft's position.

When Jean Forrow heard the staccato message in her head-phones, she began writing with desperate speed. As soon as she had sent the acknowledgement she jumped up to wave the signal form and catch the signal sergeant's attention. It was in doing this that she upset her steel chair.

But it was not the contents of the message that brought her frantically to her feet. She called across the room, with uncharacteristic ebullience: "Stan's safe . . . it's Stan sending. . . ." Only then did she think back to the import of the words she had just scribbled. She sat again, heavily, stricken.

The Signals sergeant, his staff depleted since the air raid, took the signal down to the controller, himself.

\*     \*     \*

Trevor Walford sat up with a jerk that sent pain blazing through his wounded arm and chest. Lofty Duckett, who was already sitting up, supported by his hands, locked his elbows hard and braced himself. Both men cringed involuntarily as bullets ripped through the ribs and fabric above their heads. There was a burst of noise from the rear guns as Snowy Pomeroy snapped off a four-second salvo before the Wellington was hidden once more by cloud.

Walford dragged himself painfully round until he was on hands and knees. Lofty turned.

"Where are you going, Skip?"

Walford did not answer. The agony of movement was demanding all his strength. His despair at being alive, his self-disgust, were gone; swamped by the one thought in his mind; he was still the captain of this aircraft . . . Brodie was a third-rate co-pilot . . . their plight was, essentially, his own fault . . . Brodie had unselfishly chosen the shortest route home out of consideration for the two wounded men, when he should have prudently steered well clear of the Brest peninsula . . . he was needed in the cockpit. . . .

Duckett watched the captain crawl jerkily for'ard. He twisted his own body, groaning and on one knee and both hands, followed slowly; there was a job for him in the nose turret—damn it to hell!

Manoeuvring past the Leigh light and the main spar was almost too much for each man in turn. They both had to pause several times while spasms of torment held them, panting and groaning.

Stan Glover was still sending out signals. Cubie Meddings was laying off a course that would take them out a few miles to the west where the cloud was lower and thicker.

Pete Brodie felt a nudge at his elbow and glanced quickly down.

His jaw sagged when he saw Walford's ashen face. He shouted his protest angrily. "Trevor! What the hell? You aren't fit to be here...."

Walford ignored him, hauling himself into his seat. He found his helmet on the floor, donned it and switched on the microphone, gasping. "I'm O.K., Pete. What were you planning to do?"

"Get the hell out of here! That's what."

"You can't. Look at your fuel gauges."

Brodie looked, and swore. "Ruttin' tank holed, some place."

"Yeah . . . must've been in that pass just now. What was it?"

"Couple of 109's."

"We can't hold this westerly heading for long."

"And we can't climb above cloud; they'll find us, for sure."

Walford made a vast effort, summoning all his strength. "I'll take her, Pete."

Brodie stared across, incredulous and enraged. "You're crazy . . . you can't fly this crate the way you are...."

Walford swallowed, forcing himself not to slur his words. "I've got her, Pete. . . ." He took a firm grasp of the control column with his right hand and began to push against the rudder bar with his left foot, trying to turn.

Brodie relaxed his pressure on the controls and immediately the heavy aircraft dipped its left wing, dragged down by the weight of the dead engine on that side. The right wing reared fiercely and the whole airframe slewed brutally to port under the roaring thrust of the starboard engine.

Meddings and Glover were pitched hard against bulkheads and Duckett was tossed in screaming agony against the frame of the cockpit door.

With a yell, Brodie seized the stick, kicked the rudder bar and snatched the aircraft out of its incipient spin.

Walford, defeated, fell back against the rest. Brodie turned to throw him a look of loathing; obstinate sod! But what he saw; the pallid, determined young face and heaving chest, softened him. He waited till Walford's eyes flickered open, then winked and gave a thumbs-up. Walford nodded.

Brodie returned to his job. "Stan, we're losing fuel; just enough to make base; signal that we may have to ditch. Cubie, guess you don't know where the hell we are?"

"That's right, boy; I don't."

"O.K. Get a fix, Stan." Then he noticed Duckett's long legs, wriggling his prone body into the for'ard gun position. He tried to shout at him, but the Australian could not or would not hear. Brodie told the others: "Trevor's up here with me. Lofty's at the front guns. They're both crazy."

Without warning, they broke cloud. In a brief downward glance they saw the dull sea more than three thousand feet below them. There was a five-mile stretch of clear sky, and beyond it another cloud bank; in the homeward direction.

Brodie opened the throttle as wide as it would go. The aircraft thundered towards the protecting mass of cumulus. Glover, having got a fix, took post in the astrodome.

They had two miles to go when he saw the Messerschmitts diving out of sun and yelled a warning.

Walford shouted to Brodie: "Press on . . . don't turn back. . . ."

Silence fell on the intercom.

Snowy sat licking his lips. He made the sign of the cross and tried to say a prayer. But prayer was an interruption of his concentration. He watched the enemy fighters grow bigger in their three-hundred-mile-an-hour dive.

Cubie had rammed himself into the cockpit, between the two pilots. He was chewing on a ragged, unlit cigar and staring at the air speed indicator and the cloud ahead.

The cloud seemed to have mesmerized Walford, too. But the others all watched the fighters; only Brodie had to keep glancing at his instruments.

Stan Glover yelled a warning of the first attack. Brodie held grimly to his course. He could not afford to lose time in evasive action.

As the 109's came in, Brodie banked hard to starboard, turning into them. They whipped past, baffled, their shots going wide. At last Walford stirred; he smiled at Brodie.

In a few seconds the 109's had turned and one was coming in from above, the other from directly abeam. Snowy sobbed a plea for a chance to get in a burst. Glover called the direction, and Brodie throttled back and stall-turned, losing a precious hundred feet of height.

Came a long burst from the tail turret, a short one from the front, another long one from the tail. Came Snowy's jubilation: "I hit him . . . he's on fire. . . ."

And Glover's "You've done it, Snowy . . . you done it . . . a flamer."

They all saw it; the high-attacking Me. 109 twisting, rolling, cartwheeling; showing its pale blue belly and its brown and green camouflaged upper surfaces alternately; flinging back a trail of dense, oily smoke and long red and yellow flames. No parachute opened.

Duckett howled: "You beaut, Snowy . . . good on yer, sport . . . bonzer . . ." and then broke into a shrill scream that died in an eerie gurgle. Wind hurtled through the shattered perspex of the nose. Brodie was hurled against his back rest by a red hot fury that clutched at his right shoulder and hammered him back with crippling force.

The Wellington nosed down and the air speed indicator leaped to an unbelievable speed. Walford nerved himself to lean all his weight and waning strength on the controls, before the wings were ripped off. Meddings felt a punch in the back and skidded down the slope to the front turret. He pulled Duckett aside and crawled to the guns. Glover, thrown from his stance on the main spar, eased himself on to Brodie's lap, forcing the big Canadian's legs apart to make room. He fought the bucking aircraft with Walford.

The surviving Me. 109 swooped once more and Cubie Meddings, biting right through his cigar, hammered out a burst that sent chips flying from its tail fin. The German pilot pulled away. Still, the Wellington dived.

Together, mostly by Glover's strength, he and Walford got the Wellington level. Brodie thrust Glover from his knees, elbowed him right away, and took the stick in his hands. "Go back and send an S.O.S. Mayday. We're ditching." Shouting and trying to fly at the same time, he tried not to shut his eyes in reaction to the pulsing agony in his right shoulder. The pain stabbed deeply, his torn nerve ends sending merciless shocks of suffering far into his body, probing into his brain; luring him, battering him, to succumb to the warmth and painlessness of oblivion. He fought to keep his senses. He felt blood spurt up, warm on his cheek and chin.

The sea looked hard and leaden grey. Thankfully he noticed that it was only ruffled here by a light breeze. But, from the height of four hundred feet, the size of the waves was deceptive; they looked smaller than they were.

The Messerschmitt attacked again. Once more Brodie flung the Wellington around to give his gunners a view. Once more, Meddings found his mark and screamed exultantly when a chunk of metal plating leaped from the 109's underside and fluttered away, and one undercarriage wheel dropped half-down. The fighter went into a steep, rapid climb.

They hit the sea with a shuddering, rasping impact that

stunned them with its noise and sudden deceleration. They were flung, those who were not strapped in, into a tangle of loose gear and limbs. The wounded groaned and cried out. The air was full of warning cries and imprecations.

And then, somehow, but with an orderliness that even they did not know existed, while they automatically complied with it, they were all in the yellow rubber dinghy. Drenched with cold water, wounds smarting hideously under the sea salt, the brisk surface wind cutting their exposed flesh; fearful, suffering, dazed; they were all, nevertheless, alive.

Cubie Meddings and Snowy, the only ones unhurt, grabbed for the paddles and began to battle with the turbulent sea. Stan Glover, who had been stunned when a shell splinter cut his head, and broke a thumb when the aircraft slammed into a solid wall of water, was struggling to make the three badly wounded men comfortable.

It was Brodie whose howl jerked them all to an outrageous perception of their greatest, most immediate danger.

"Paddle, you buggers! Get cracking! There's a depth charge hung up in that wreck, and it's set to blow when it sinks to thirty feet!"

## CHAPTER TEN

AIDEZ-MOI! The anguished appeal, corrupted to M'aidez and thus "Mayday": the international call for help, the airmen's S.O.S.

When the ugly word struck at Jean Forrow, it was like a physical blow that transcended even the mental shock. Indeed, the immediate frantic rush of images and conjectures through her mind produced a physical reaction: the breath went from her lungs in a wailing gasp, she paled and a pencil fell from her limp fingers.

She had suffered much, during the preceding night; and, though she was a calm and sensible girl, this was not to be borne unemotionally. She had managed to scribble the message before losing control of her fingers. The Signals sergeant tore it off the pad and ran downstairs. Jean covered her face with trembling hands and began to sob.

Morag McEwan, coming in to see if any fresh cypher messages had been received (both runners were hurt in the air raid and so were six of the other watch members), hurried across. As little as a day ago, Section Officer McEwan would have shown no sympathy for feminine weakness, even if she had felt it. Now, standing over the stricken girl, remembering how she had laboured over the injured, remembering that Corporal Forrow was only twenty— six years her junior—she was flooded by compassion. She spoke quietly, sensibly not touching her. "What is it, Jean?"

There was no answer. She repeated her question, gently.

Jean took one hand from her face to grope for a handkerchief. Her answer was muffled. "They've been shot d-down, ma'am."

Morag turned to another girl who stood uncertainly by: "What happened?"

"Well, ma'am, Corporal Forrow was on the key and she took down a Mayday. It was from Stan . . . from Flight Sergeant Glover, ma'am . . ."

"So I gathered: she wouldn't be so upset otherwise . . ."

The sergeant had returned. He said quietly: "A couple of Jerry fighters jumped them, ma'am. They're down in the drink some- where between Brest and here."

"I see, Sergeant." Morag bent over Jean Forrow. "Come and sit in my office, it's quieter."

Jean was blowing her nose, wiping her eyes and repairing her dishevellment. "No thank you, ma'am. I want to stay on the key. They'll have a set in the dinghy: there may be a message."

Morag looked questioningly at the sergeant. He nodded.

"All right, Jean. But Stan must be unharmed, if he sent the message."

"I'm thinking of them all, Miss McEwan. Besides . . ." her voice quavered ". . . he was all right when he sent the Mayday: but ditchings aren't easy; he may n-not be all right now."

"Don't worry. They'll be safe: air-sea rescue will be on its way already."

Downstairs, in the Ops. Room, Stevenson was just putting down the telephone. He looked resignedly at Dunford. "Group can't get anything off for three hours, sir."

Nig exploded. "Why the hell not?"

"They've got other searches on, sir. They daren't divert anyone on ops. to the area, sir."

There was no need to elaborate. When an air-sea rescue aircraft could be sent to look for Walford's crew, it would be given a fighter escort: a Beaufighter or a pair of Spitfires. It would be homicidal to order an operational aircraft off patrol to search in the Brest area, in daylight, unescorted.

Gretton grasped Nig's sleeve and moved him out of earshot. "I'm going."

"You're not. If anyone goes, I will."

"You can't: you're commanding the station. Besides, any crew in my squadron is my personal responsibility; no one else's."

"The group captain's still on the station. I'm only standing in while he's asleep."

"He's not asleep. He's doped and unconscious. You are the Station Commander, Nig. You can't leave camp."

Dunford knew he was right. "In any case, *you* can't do any good by going out."

"I can find them and fix their position. The least you can let me do is ask Group's permission."

"Go ahead." Dunford was confident that it would be refused.

Gretton walked back to the dais, took the telephone and talked to the Group controller. He was asked to wait: Group would call back. He went to the navigator's desk and spoke in an undertone. "Gillam, get on the phone from another room and tell the Squadron I want my aircraft ready for air test immediately."

"Yes, sir." Gillam had not been unobservant of the muttered conversation between the two wing commanders, their manifest disagreement, the low-pitched telephone call. Now this. He made the correct addition of two and two. Looking boldly at Gretton, he asked: "May I come too, sir? After all, an air test's not an op. and I've even got permission to fly three ops. A letter came from Group yesterday afternoon."

Gretton hesitated. Several thoughts passed rapidly through his mind. He owed Gillam something, for past brusqueness. The chap had a right to his self-respect and he knew of the friendship between him and Walford's crew.

Charles Gillam clinched it, with a grin. "After all, sir, I do owe you one navigator! I bent yours a trifle yesterday."

"Can you navigate a Wimpey?" Gretton smiled, despite the strain of what was foremost in his mind.

"You know I can't, sir. But—well, it would square things a bit if I came and . . . and gave a hand."

The wing commander looked at him levelly. His voice was serious. "You really want to?"

"Yes, sir."

"Very good. Go and telephone."

At which moment, Group rang through. It was an air commodore; and he was in a grossly bad humour. "Gretton? No, you bloody well cannot go and do an A.S.R. on your own."

"With respect, sir, it won't help the squadron's morale if I hang around here just waiting for someone else to go out and find one of *my* crews."

"That's not a valid argument, Paul, and you know it. Moreover, the weather isn't going to lift for another three hours: you'd be wasting your time. Your request is refused, Gretton."

"Very good, sir."

"And . . . Paul!"

"Sir?"

"Good luck!"

Gretton replaced the receiver and looked blandly at Dunford. "No."

"That's what I thought." He saw Gillam enter the room and approach hesitantly. "Well, I'm going down to the Met. Office to see if there's any hope of the weather lifting. We may be able to persuade Group to start a search sooner. . . ." Dunford moved towards the door.

Gillam said quietly, to Gretton: "Your aircraft will be fuelled and ready in an hour, sir."

"Thanks."

And then the Messerschmitt 410's hit R.A.F. Tawmouth. They swept in at sea level, below radar coverage. As fast as a fighter, with the hitting power of a medium bomber, and armed with cannon and machine-guns which gave it the fire power of an infantry battalion, the Me. 410 was an elusive scourge.

They came in two waves of four, line abreast and widely spaced. Nig Dunford was at the door of the Ops. Room when they struck. A withering pressure-wave of sound and disturbed air smote the building. Nig darted for the open front door to get the best view. Gretton and Stevenson scrambled for the Ops. Room window. Gillam, crowded out, ran to join Dunford on the doorstep.

The main attack was on the aerodrome, but two of the 410's flew directly at the Operations building. On the other side of the lane, directly opposite the front door, a sandbagged and camouflaged gun post held quadruple Vickers machine-guns, mounted on a Scarfe ring so that they could traverse through a hundred and eighty degrees. The leading Messerschmitt bore down on the gun post, strafing. Gillam saw one of the two airmen flung away from the guns; picked up and knocked off his feet: he folded in a mangled heap in a corner of the sandbagged emplacement and did not move again.

Five seconds later, Gillam was across the road. He vaulted over the parapet and shouted at the surviving young airman, who was transfixed with horror: "I can fire these, if you'll keep loading."

Bullets thudded on the sandbags as the second ME. 410 came in. Gillam fired long bursts, following it, and cursing as he saw that he was falling behind and below the target.

He saw its bombs fall. They were slow, black eggs: mesmeric. The ground trembled underfoot to their explosions: but they were only hundred-pounders. They had missed; the fire from the gun pit had spoiled the Germans' aim.

The second Me. 410 bored in straight and level; and fast. Gillam cocked his machine-guns up, bending his knees and crouching while he traversed. There were tracers in the belts, and he saw that he was aiming in front but too high. He corrected, and to his wild joy and surprise the nose of the attacker was swallowed in a mass of smoke from both engines. His bullets hacked shards of metal off the fuselage and wings, and ripped a big chunk right away from the port engine cowling. Fascinated, Gillam kept firing. He stitched a mass of holes down the length of the fuselage. The aircraft lurched, a wingtip brushed a strand of elm trees, its belly scraped the hedge on the far side of the meadow; and with the rending scream of metal on frost-hardened ground and stones, it ploughed a ragged path through the coarse grass. Then there was sudden silence. For several seconds nobody moved.

Gillam broke the spell with a yell: "Come on! Let's get 'em." He sprinted towards the wreck. While he was fifty yards away, the pilot tumbled out of the cockpit, regained his feet and began to stumble towards him. The space between the two men had diminished to five yards when a scorching detonation flung them both down. A wall of flame shot from the ruined Me. 410. The air pulsed with heat.

Gillam was the first to stand up. He lifted the German pilot and asked: "Your navigator didn't get out?"

"No. He was dead already."

Neither thought it strange that the exchange had been in the German's language. Gillam, indifferent to the fact that he had killed a man, walked beside the survivor towards the Ops. Room, where the airman gunner was almost dancing with excitement and pleasure; and Gretton, Dunford and Stevenson were waiting on the step, while a crowd of airmen and W.A.A.F.s collected around them.

Smoke rose in the air from a fire near the bomb-dump on the airfield. Fire tenders stood near, their asbestos-clad crews working briskly with foam and hoses. The extreme end of one runway had been torn up by a bomb; already it was being inspected and repair trucks were on their way.

The station defence had driven away the Me. 410's and Tawmouth had suffered no disabling damage.

Dunford was in a hurry to get down there. He paused by his car. "Bloody good show, young Gillam. Your boss has got something to tell you." He grinned and was gone, his wheels leaving streaks of rubber on the lane.

The Intelligence Officer took charge of the prisoner. Gillam looked for the youngster who had fed the ammunition belts into the guns for him. The airman had gone; he was in the gun pit, helping one of the Signals airmen to carry the other gunner's body to the roadside while someone else phoned for an ambulance.

Inside, Gretton was speaking on the telephone to his senior flight commander, Squadron Leader Rowan. He ended the conversation as Gillam followed Stevenson into the room. "Good show, Gillam." He smiled at him for the first time. "You'd better fly in the rear turret, when we go on this air test: I don't think I could find a better air gunner!"

Gillam smiled back. "All those boring hours I've spent on compulsory ground defence training seem to be vindicated, sir."

Stevenson stood at his navigator's side with his chest out, full of proprietorial pride. "Wing Commander Dunford's putting you up for a gong, Charles."

"Me, Steve?" Gillam was genuinely astonished. "B-but I only . . ."

"He thinks you deserve an M.C., anyway. Dammit Charles, if you hadn't bagged that 410 he'd have dropped his bombs smack on top of the roof!"

"Good God! I suppose he would have."

Gretton called back from the door: "Get your breakfast quickly, Charles, and come to the crew room."

"We're all going down, in a few minutes," Stevenson told Gillam. "The on-coming watch are being decent and coming up an hour early: they reckon we've probably had enough for one watch!"

*     *     *

The noise of the air raid woke Tommy Rowan, Trevor Walford's flight commander. After seeing Walford's aircraft off, the night before, he had gone to bed, so as to be fresh next day for his coming escapade with the fetching Alison Storey. He woke reluctantly three hours earlier than he had intended; after a night which had already been interrupted by the first bomber attack.

Before he could dress, the telephone beside his bed rang.

"Rowan here." It was his squadron commander, Gretton, telephoning from the Ops. Room. "Good morning, sir."

"Tommy, Trevor got a kill. You can guess, I suppose—U 306."

"Bloody hell. Poor Trevor."

"That's not the half of it. He and another crew are wounded and they were shot down by 109's from Brest, half an hour ago."

"Sod it."

"Group can't lay on an A.S.R. for three hours. They won't let me go, officially: so I've laid on an air test."

There was a pause. "I . . . I see, sir."

"It's got to be a volunteer crew, Tommy. *All* officers. You know the group captain grounded my senior Wop/A.G.—some trouble over his mess bill. And my navigator's in Sick Quarters with a busted nose and ribs. So I want a complete crew from scratch. No—I'll take the Ops. Room Navigator in the tail turret: he wants to come." Rowan tried to interrupt and was silenced. "I can't give you the details now: but he's just shot down one of the Me. 410's that attacked us. Get cracking and roust me out a crew."

"My own navigator's around, sir: he stayed behind from leave, like myself. He's a bit soft on Morag McEwan."

Gretton laughed shortly. "If you hadn't stayed behind to do some leching yourself, Tommy, you'd be well out of this, too. You wasted your time, I'm afraid: Alison's been in the village all night, helping with the air raid victims there. She'll want to sleep the clock round—alone, chum!"

Rowan had the grace to sound rueful. "Just my luck. O.K., I'll see if I can find you a crew before you get down here."

"I'm going to call at the cottage on the way, to see how things are in the village."

Rowan put the telephone down and gloomed about his dressing. Presently he knocked at the door of the neighbouring room. Flight Lieutenant Donnelly, Morag McEwan's swain, opened it. " 'Morning, sir. What a night!"

"We got off lightly, though, Paddy, didn't we?" Rowan told him what had happened to "B Baker". "I'll go as second pilot. We want a navigator and a couple of Wop/A.G.'s."

Donnelly hesitated. "I'm no bloody hero. I think the wingco's stark raving mad."

"So do I, Paddy. But, as flight commander, I haven't any option. Hell—it'll be O.K. There's plenty of cloud to dodge into: and in this weather the Jerry fighters are going to be restricted, just as we are. There's nothing to it, really."

"I wish I could follow your reasoning, sir! I was going out for a day's hunting with the Tawmouth Farmers': seeing that Morag will be sleeping all day."

"It's up to you," Rowan said curtly, closing the door.

"Oh, hell! All right, I'll navigate for the wingco. But don't blame me if I say 'I told you so' when we're all in the drink ourselves."

But Rowan was already on his way to the dining-room, to find two more volunteers; puzzling over Gretton's choice of a "penguin" Ops. Room navigator to man the tail guns.

The whole camp had been roused by the early morning air raid. The mess dining-room was full of potential volunteers; but Rowan felt bound to see them among his own flight, which was also Walford's.

There were half a dozen suitable candidates at one table, and he joined them.

One of them wore a black patch with the letters "U.S.A." embroidered on it in pale blue, on each shoulder. He was another of Cubie Meddings's countrymen who would soon be transferred to the United States Air Corps. Tommy Rowan took the next chair. "What are you doing, breakfasting in mess, Tex? Wife throw you out? Stretching the family rations?"

Tex Latimer, who had nearly completed his second tour of operations, wore a captain's bars, and a D.F.C. under his air gunner's brevet, and often complained that war's greatest hardship was the long interval between filling meals. With so much to fill, this was understandable. "Are you kidding? Stretch the rations! Why, I have to eat two breakfasts, one at home and one here, before I even know I've broken my fast!"

"I think there's a law against that."

"Guess so. No, Tommy, I lep' on my motor-bike and came to the base when the 410's hit; thought maybe we'd all be wanted. Anyway, I was glad of the chance to get away early."

There was a laugh around the table. Rowan was out of it: "What's the joke?"

"Pop" Shapley, sitting on the other side of Tex Latimer, explained. "Tex's mother-in-law has been with them for ten days: she's going home this afternoon, and Tex isn't exactly displeased."

"I'll say I'm not." He had married a London girl, whose mother made the air raids an excuse for frequent inflictions of her sour company on her daughter and son-in-law. Tex dearly loved his wife but would have cheerfully pushed her mother off Westminster Bridge. But for her presence at home just now, he would not have felt obliged to hasten to camp: he had telephoned first, and learned that the damage was not severe.

Shapley leaned across Tex, to look at Rowan. "Any gen on last night's ops., sir?"

Shapley had earned the honorific "Pop" by virtue of his forty-two years, when he re-joined the Royal Canadian Air Force in September 1939. Had he led a less dissolute life, it would not have been conferred on him; but he was grey-haired and his face was seamed with dissipation and he looked over fifty. He was hardy, withal. The outbreak of war was a great opportunity for him. The last steady job he had had was as an observer in the Great War. During the twenty years between, he had lived precariously; due to feckless laziness. From bravado, he had volunteered for flying duties again, confident that his age and physical condition would ground him. He was vexed when accepted for training as a wireless operator air gunner. For three years he had managed to stay in Canada, instructing. It was a blow when at last he came to England. He had been with 1111 Squadron for six months and loathed every operation on which he flew. He consoled himself by playing up his role of "character" with a fund of corny philosophy and bogus bonhomie. It was part of his act to walk on the airfield each morning with a cocker spaniel he had scrounged from the squire. As he suffered from insomnia, it was no hardship to rise early. Thus he could be seen daily, with walking stick and pipe, dog at his heels, strolling on the grass, looking for mushrooms. That way lay disaster: for here he was, confronted with the obligation to add to his own legend by volunteering for a dangerous task.

Squadron Leader Rowan broke the news about Walford's ditching and Wing Commander Gretton's intention to make a search for the dinghy.

As quick as a flash, and sure that one of his younger comrades

would usurp him, Pop Shapley offered his services. Nobody raised
a voice against him. Rowan agreed. "I suppose it is only right to
include a Canadian, Pop, as we're such a lot of odds and sods on
the squadron; especially in Trevor's crew."

"That lets me in," said Latimer. "Meddings is the only other
American."

"Fair enough. That makes up the crew."

Pop Shapley was caught fair and square by his own pretence.
He would have to make the best of it. He suddenly felt very old
and very scared.

*          *          *

Cynthia Gretton was at the kitchen stove and Melanie Dunford
was laying the table in the dining-room, when they heard the
cottage gate.

"They're here," Melanie called. She went to the front door and
was overtaken by a small whirlwind in the shape of Paul Gretton's
son and namesake. "Good morning, Paul. Nig not coming?"

The father picked his child up, the small, firm arms tight about
his neck. "'Morning, Melanie. 'Fraid Nig's acting stationmaster:
he didn't feel he should leave."

He tossed his cap on to a chest in the hall and pushed the door
shut. Melanie looked disappointed. He went through to the
kitchen, set the little boy down on his feet, and his wife came into
his arms.

"You look worn out, darling." He kissed her hair.

"It's been rough for everyone. Nice to have you home, darling."

"Not for long, sweetheart. Lots of work to do."

"Have a good breakfast, anyway. Alison's upstairs, freshening
up. She's been marvellous."

Paul Gretton raised his eyebrows. He doubted stern application
to a dirty job, in Alison Storey. Long hours over cyphers were a
different matter: but amid the carnage of bombing, he could
more readily visualize brisk, plain Morag McEwan.

His wife reiterated: "Yes, really. Ask anyone."

"It's just a job, after all." He was indifferent, at this moment,
to everything but his wife and their child. He sat on a hard chair
with the boy on his knee and they made serious, man-to-man conversation. Covertly watching them, Cynthia felt a great love and
pride. She had many such images in her memory: in wartime,
scenes, and especially faces, stamp themselves more sharply on the
mind. Domestic moments like this, being rare, had a precious

quality that memory retained more readily than if they were everyday routine.

There was movement in the dining-room next door. Cynthia called to Alison, who came in looking glowing and beautiful. "Hallo, sir."

"M'm?" Gretton looked up abstractedly from explaining to his son how the Me. 410 had been brought down. "Oh, hallo! Cynthia tells me you've worked like a Trojan."

"I haven't done any more than she and Melanie. What's been happening?"

He grimaced. "Everything. Trevor Walford's in the drink. Charles Gillam rushed out and grabbed the guns in the gun pit outside Ops., when one of the airmen was killed, and he fetched down a 410 just as it was making its bombing run dead on the Ops. building."

Alison opened her eyes very wide. "Oh, no!"

"Oh, yes. Very much so. Nig's going to put him up for a gong: and I hope he gets a decent one."

Melanie drawled from the serving hatch: "I suppose Nig's revelling in it? He is a gory horror, that husband of mine."

Gretton laughed. "I don't know anyone else who could have coped as he did last night. He seemed to be everywhere at the same time."

"He enjoys it."

"I believe he does. He wouldn't be Nig if he didn't! He does it all without sleep, too."

"That, I don't need to be told!"

Alison, watching her closely, said bluntly that Walford's crew had ditched.

Melanie's expression was transformed from its habitual poise and self-assurance. Cynicism fled. Her eyes blazed with fury and her mouth set in a venomous sneer. "God! How I hate this damned R.A.F. under-statement . . . and bloody nonchalance. 'Trevor Walford's in the drink' is he? My God! Isn't anyone doing anything about it? Isn't anyone *feeling* anything about it?"

Gretton was aghast. "Steady on, Melanie. . . ."

Alison cut across his words. "Of course they're doing everything they can; and of course everyone feels the same as you do about it. But making a song and dance isn't going to improve matters. Isn't that so, Paul?" She turned to Gretton.

"It's bad, Melanie, but it could be worse. Trevor's wounded, and so is one of the air gunners."

Coldly, Alison said: "That means Cubie isn't hurt; so calm down."

Melanie began to laugh shakily. "It is rather damned silly, isn't it? But it's only that . . . well, I know Cubie so well and he's such a dear. The others are strangers to me. Sorry, Paul."

"That's all right. As a matter of fact, they're getting an aircraft ready now and the search for the boys will start very soon."

Cynthia told them that breakfast was ready.

\*     \*     \*

The night watch was over. In the transport that took them back to camp, the airmen and W.A.A.F.'s were singing. All except Corporal Jean Forrow, who was pale and silent, withdrawn and deep in thought. Stevenson looked pensively at Charles Gillam: he was not keen on this "air test". Gillam, haunted by mental pictures of the pulped airman whose place he had taken behind the Vickers guns, and of how near he had come to sharing the same fate, was in a hurry to get to 1111 Squadron's crew room and have something else to think about.

Sergeant Murch was undergoing the frustration of all successful solitary plotters. There was no one in whom he could confide his secret. They all thought it was Walford who deserved the credit for sinking the U-boat. But it was really he, Murch! He had heard Stevenson say that, if he had been awake throughout the night and seen the weather signals, he would have insisted on diverting Walford. And who had laid the controller to sleep? Why, Sergeant Murch, of course! He looked smugly around at his colleagues of the watch, longing to tell at least one of them how he had sunk a U-boat. It would have to wait. He would be going on leave soon. Over a pint of beer, embroidered, bolstered by the air gunner's brevet he illegally stitched on in the toilet of the train, going home, the story would have a good reception from his cronies.

\*     \*     \*

Paul Gretton looked down on the cottage garden; from a hundred feet. From this low altitude, he could see them clearly: Cynthia and their son, on the lawn, waving to him. He pushed aside the dark thought crowding into his mind, and looked away resolutely.

He was in his proper environment, here in the cockpit of a fighting aeroplane. He was a highly-skilled pilot and a born fighter. Faced with the crouching Unknown, on the edge of a dangerous future, he was perfectly equipped to overcome any hazard that could be defeated by courage and training.

Rowan, in the second pilot's seat, was uneasy. He had felt the contrast between flying with this scratch crew, and his own, as soon as they started engines. Without conceit, he knew himself to be a first-class man at his job, as was Gretton. Paddy Donnelly and Tex Latimer were first class, too. Pop Shapley was not in the top category, but he was good. Only Gillam, who had no business to be there at all, was sub-standard. Yet, with all this first-class material, they were only a third-class crew. Rowan was hating the trip.

Shapley sat morosely in the wireless station, cursing his luck. He had really put his foot in it, this time. Nobody was worth volunteering for, when it came to a flight in the very teeth of German fighter bases. Why the hell hadn't one of the young punks on the squadron insisted on taking his place? And the worst of it was that he had been forced to be so damned cheerful: just another chore for old Pop!

Paddy Donnelly worked at the navigation desk, full of disquiet. The weather was dirty, the enemy radar would pick them up, and they would have to hide in cloud: that meant they would be tossed about and he would be air sick.

Tex Latimer, at the radar console, was relaxed and philosophical. He had a poor chance of making contact with the dinghy: the sea was disturbed, and the dinghy was small; but there was no use fretting about anything else. German fighters, U-boats, the sea itself: you could avoid the first two; but the third, and the savage sky with its freakish weather, were always with you. This trip was really no more dangerous than any other. It was just that their chance of running into Me. 109's were higher than usual.

Charles Gillam, in the rear turret, waited to fire a clearing burst. He had learned how to fire the Vickers and the Browning, during hours of "backers up" training: designed to teach everyone how to support the R.A.F. Regiment in station defence. That morning's success had given him zest to try his luck again. He was frightened but confident.

It was a bitterly cold winter morning. A brisk wind blew on the surface. At five hundred feet, there was solid cloud extending far to the west. Further south and eastward, the clouds began to break and scatter; until, in the area where the dinghy was, their base was at a thousand feet.

The dinghy was approximately sixty miles from the English coast and fifty from the French. And the wind was blowing it towards France. A R.A.F. high-speed launch had put to sea, but was forced to turn back after twenty minutes; she had opened a gash in her forefoot, ramming a mass of wreckage from a sunken tanker. Another would sail soon, but valuable time had been lost.

And, meanwhile, a fast German launch was seeking the dinghy also.

## CHAPTER ELEVEN

THEY had been in the dinghy for two hours. Six cold and tired men, four of them wounded.

At first, Meddings and Snowy, paddling vigorously, had let the rubber boat run before the wind. They knew they were going the wrong way, but the supreme consideration was to put a safe distance between themselves and the foundering aircraft. They had managed to cover nearly two hundred yards when the depth charge went off.

First the surface of the sea trembled. Then it began to boil, in the centre of this disturbance. It burst open with a dull boom and a torrent of water leaped high, formed a solid pillar, and seemed to remain motionless, towering and threatening. The tall, thick column fell apart; it opened outwards like a gigantic banana being stripped of its peel. Finally it crashed back on to the sea's surface with a reverberating smack that opened a thousand fissures and forced up a multitude of ridges; sent a countless succession of eddies swirling and pursuing each other until they lapped around the dinghy and raced beyond it.

The six men clung to the sides of their rubber boat and to each other, the stronger holding back the weaker from being flung overboard. Bitingly cold water tumbled over the low gunwale, struck through their clothes, blinded their eyes, acridly filled their mouths, froze their skin and outraged their wounds. Flesh and spirit alike quailed before the monstrous assault of this icy deluge aggravated by a cutting wind.

The boat cavorted and plunged, gyrated and leaped clear out of the water. It seemed that it must overturn, or plunge the gunwale so deep that it filled and sank. But Snowy Pomeroy and Cubie Meddings and Stan Glover baled desperately, saving the few inches of freeboard that kept them all from death.

Trevor Walford lay inert, his head lolling. Pete Brodie's right shoulder and arm were useless; with his left hand he kept a hold on Walford and with his weight he pinned down Lofty Duckett. Duckett had been wounded a second time, in the front turret, when a sliver of perspex slashed his temple: a flap of skin hung over one eye, and the corner of the eye itself was cut.

And Cubie Meddings and Snowy Pomeroy baled, and baled, and baled. Stan Glover, his head aching from concussion, blood trickling from its torn skin, his broken thumb gigantically swollen and throbbing, strove at the same time to bale and to help Brodie keep Walford and Duckett aboard.

At last the terrible upheaval was over. The water became calmer. Glover silently went to work with bandages: binding Duckett's head and his own; putting Brodie's right arm in a sling; staunching the blood which once more flowed freely from Walford.

And now, two hours later, they were struggling to make headway against the wind that bore them towards a hostile coast.

In this extremity of danger, they each had to rely on their spiritual resources for the determination to survive.

Walford, drifting between consciousness and stupor, was comforted by the certainty that God was on their side. A lifetime of lip-service to the refined, middle-class Anglican creed had, at least, provided him with this bulwark. He had conscientiously attended Sunday school as a child, Crusaders as a prep. school boy, and school chapel twice every Sunday at his public school. He had been conscientious about and impressed by his confirmation. At home, he went to church with his parents once or twice a month. Without thinking deeply on the matter, he had absorbed a proper measure of Christian belief. As he was a fundamentally decent person, this was only a half-understood supernatural reinforcement of a standard of conduct that he would have followed anyway. In his moments of consciousness in the bottom of the rolling, pitching dinghy, he was confident that Heaven would send help to them. Above all, he carried the burden and responsibility of leadership: he must stay alive.

Stan Glover had much the same attitude. He had accepted Church of England doctrine in the same way that he had accepted all his Service training. "C. of E." was the religion officially imparted by the R.A.F. Sunday church parade was a routine prescribed by a higher authority whose wisdom he accepted in all matters. He had given himself body and soul to the Royal Air

Force. Part of the curriculum for training a good airman was worship according to the King's Church. So be it. But even more strongly than he believed in providence, Flight Sergeant Glover relied on Service efficiency. He could not imagine that the great organization to which he belonged could let him down; its resources were too numerous and there was a prescribed drill for every situation: carry out the drill, and results were bound to follow. He had sent a Mayday. The aircraft's position was exactly known at base and at Group. It was only a question of time before an aircraft, a launch, or both, found the dinghy. Besides, there was the emergency set between his knees, which automatically transmitted signals by the mere turning of a handle.

Snowy Pomeroy was another man of faith. How much was confusion of Catholic dogma and ritual with atavistic superstition did not matter. He lived by an elaborate ramification of observances which made him feel emancipated and educated beyond others of his colour and status. He was convinced of the validity of indulgences and the exact definition of degrees of goodness and badness. Above all, he was blessed by the simplicity of mind and humility of heart which alone enable man to accept essential truth and ignore casuistry.

Pete Brodie believed in himself and in the essential guts he had inherited from his father and hoped to pass on to many sons. He was determined not to die, because life was so good. He looked forward to long years of abundance and good fellowship. His standards were all materialistic and he was full of the will to live and enjoy what the world had to offer. For him the future was a rosy amalgam of pleasant physical sensations. Adulation for the football and hockey star; complaisant girls; handsome motor cars; a lucrative job; being a regular guy; providing a luxurious home for a doting and beautiful wife; hunting and fishing trips with his sons. He knew what he wanted, and portents were that he would get them. Not for him, extinction by drowning or exposure at the age of twenty-two!

Lofty Duckett was another who had grown up to rely on his own good sense and courage; but in the isolation of the family sheep station, something else had been inculcated: a bleak faith, found between the heavy covers of the family Bible. Lofty was sure that the enemy fought for an unrighteous cause and that his own must prevail; he could best help to achieve this end by remaining alive.

Cubie Meddings was, in many ways, the most serene of them

all. He was one of those very rare people who genuinely do not care a damn. He had been near death a score of times. He lived hard and with conscious enjoyment of every minute. He would take any risk, make any sacrifice, and was the complete pragmatist. He made allowance for human weakness, which would have been called charity by Christians; he would help anyone; and he loved life but did not over-rate it. He quite simply was not going to end his life in this dinghy, if he could help it, because by instinct and experience he was a man who never gave up. But, as he put it: "When the Man says 'go', you gotta go!"

But the first two hours had brought them all to the verge of prostration. Two hours so severe that those who could bale or paddle were stiff and exhausted; and those who were denied the warmth generated by exertion were cramped and frozen.

Stan Glover mumblingly broke the silence. "I reckon old Randy must be back in the loft, by now."

Cubie Meddings bent his head to the wind and forced words between his closed teeth. "Old Dopey too, maybe." He cackled. "Just think of it: all home comforts for those two, and here we are . . ."

Duckett grunted. "Dopey'll never make it. He'll be roosting on some coastal tramp, this minute."

"But not Randy," mumbled Brodie, "Randy's our boy."

"Unless he meets up with a lady seagull on the way," Meddings suggested. He began to shake with silent laughter. After a few seconds he had to stop paddling and fight for breath.

They had released the pigeons, with messages giving the names of the wounded and the extent of their injuries, and the calculated ditching position, before taking to the dinghy. It was the sight of the two pairs of strong, free wings and the assurance of the birds as they circled once and climbed away on a homeward heading, that had kept their morale up in the first terrible minutes.

While they had breath for talking, they had discussed how long it would take a launch or an aircraft to find them. Looking across the vast, formidable desolation of broken water, it seemed presumptuous to suppose that human activity far beyond the horizon would bring succour to them; but it was heartening to talk and calculate. By this time, however, their throats were dry and sore; their lips raw and cracked. To speak was a hurtful effort resulting in a stammering croak.

Glover judged that the time had come to produce his ace-in-the-hole. Old sweat that he was, young in years but oldest of the crew in service, he always kept something up his sleeve. Fumbling painfully under his Irvine jacket and battledress blouse, he drew out a flat half-bottle of rum. The original contents had long been shared between himself and Lofty in their room; but the Equipment warrant officer was an old friend and had replenished the bottle from medical supplies. Stan never flew without it and had, characteristically, never told anyone. He held it first to Walford's lips, then to Duckett's, and then passed it around to the others.

The effect of the rum was immediate, and increased tenfold by their stomachs' comparative emptiness. Walford wriggled on to an elbow and beckoned Brodie closer. The latter bent his head so that the captain could speak into his ear. "Rations . . . share it out . . ." he leaned back, pale and shaking.

There was a new snap in Meddings's voice. "Hey, Snowy; let's go. I'm doing all the work. What's the matter with you?"

Snowy did not reply. He recognized the scorn, the challenge, that he feared. There was no point in protest or retort. He dug his paddle into the sea and settled again into the painful rhythm that had made his arms and shoulders slow with weariness. He felt the strong thrust on the other side of the boat from Meddings, and again the lashing voice: "You ain't tryin', Pomeroy. I gotta do it all?"

Meddings recoiled as Pomeroy twisted towards him, snarling soundlessly, the heavy paddle held aloft in both hands; the edge of its blade poised to crack Meddings's skull. "You crazy black son of a bitch. . . ."

The paddle swung down. Meddings warded off the blow on his thick forearm, invulnerably padded by four layers of clothing.

Duckett fought himself upright against the rioting protests of his wounded leg and head. The rum had strengthened his voice, too. "Lay off him, you bloody swine, Meddings."

And Brodie's big lungs gathered the breath for an effective shout. "You'll have us all over, Pomeroy, you goddam . . ." he broke off and ducked as Snowy, tormented and humiliated beyond endurance, swiped with the paddle blade at his neck.

Brodie sat bolt upright, his spine stiff, bristling with rage and fright. "You're all off your heads . . . the lot of you . . . you, Walford, you're the craziest of 'em all . . . you didn't have to attack . . . you knew we hadn't a chance. . . ."

"But we made it," Glover yelled at him. "And we'd have got back to base except for the 109's. . . ."

"You hold your trap you ruttin' sergeant . . . *I'm* talkin' . . .

Walford! Huh! Too damned scared not to do as you're told . . . and here we are, ruttin' miles from anywhere and not a goddam hope . . ." he broke off, sobbing, his head bowed to his chest; he had collapsed physically; his wide shoulders sagged and his back wilted. Tears coursed down his face.

Walford, ashen-faced, fought for air, fought to force words, effective words, from his arid, aching throat. His wild eyes glared and his lips formed the words he wanted; but no sound came.

There was a feeble cry from Duckett: "Watch it! Snowy . . ."

And from a frozen moment of tragedy they all saw the revolver emerging from under Meddings's leather jacket, and the look of concentrated hatred on his face.

Snowy moved with the smooth speed of a pouncing cat. Although hampered by a glove, his hand produced from, seemingly, nowhere, the knife that was permanently strapped, in its sheath, to his inner forearm. A flick of the arm, to loosen it; a snatch of the fingers, to settle his grip on its haft; a turn of the wrist, and he presented the point of the blade to Meddings's right eye. Leaning towards him, coiled in a threatening attitude of fury, his mouth stretched in a slavering rictus, Snowy's hand shook, an inch from Meddings's face, as Meddings's finger groped for the trigger of his gun.

*     *     *

Flying at five hundred feet, where cloud base permitted, and lower where it did not, Wing Commander Paul Gretton quartered the empty sea. He had called Charles Gillam out of the rear turret, to stand in the astrodome and add his eyes to the others already scanning the surface ahead of them.

In theory, their task seemed an easy one. They knew the position in which "B Baker" had ditched. They knew, roughly, the speed of the surface wind there. Allowing for the fact that this would blow the dinghy towards France, and that the crew would be paddling towards England, they could calculate its probable track. They had all the facts necessary for finding it; yet it remained an elusive yellow dot lost in a heaving wilderness of grey and white. Small waves, only five or six feet high, would create a seascape in which ridges and hollows completely hid the rubber boat from view. There were no signals from the dinghy's emergency transmitter, either: they knew that the survivors must be sending; so the set must be dead.

Squadron Leader Rowan, his eyes watering from the strain of

the incessant scrutiny of every tumbling white crest, was mutely unhappy. They had made the gesture; now it was time to go home. The search was taking them closer to the French coast; Gretton reasoned that the survivors in the dinghy may be too feeble to paddle: in which case, they would merely drift at the mercy of the wind and currents.

Tommy Rowan was regretting the assignation with Alison Storey which had kept him on camp when he could have been away, on leave. He could have gone to London and easily found some other girl, equally desirable and willing.

Pop Shapley squatted in the front turret, hunched and forlorn. This was no place for a middle-aged sybarite. His eyes were not as sharp as they should be, either. He knuckled them hard. He'd go and see the M.O. when they got back, and have his eyes tested: why hadn't he thought of that before? He knew why; he got more pay for flying than he would on the ground. Damn!

Tex Latimer watched the hypnotic sweep of the radar aerial's trace around the darkened tube; the myriad pin-pricks of green-yellow light; the evanescent blip that ever and anon made him think they had an echo from the dinghy. He was happier here than he would have been at home, with ma-in-law yapping her darn head off; cramming a lifetime's worth of unnecessary admonish-ments and exhortations into the few hours remaining before train time. He grinned contentedly to himself.

Paddy Donnelly could not stir from his desk. They were flying a succession of creeping line ahead searches: starting from a datum point and zig-zagging, with turns after every two and ten miles. It was his job to tell the pilot when to turn and on to what heading. He had not looked outside the aircraft once since they were airborne. He only knew they were flying from the din of the engines and the frequent buffets of the stormy air. He would have sacrificed all future promotion to be safe on land; preferably with a hunter between his knees or Morag in his arms. He would see that she rewarded him for his devotion when he got back.

He was disturbed by Pop Shapley, going back to the wireless station to listen for the hourly transmissions from base. Five minutes later, Shapley thumped him on the shoulder and pushed a slip of paper in front of him. It read: "Pigeon returned to loft with signal from 'B Baker' 1111 Squadron. Four wounded, two seriously. Ditching position given 49.15 North, 5.10 West."

The navigator jotted down the figures, nodded his thanks, and the wireless operator shambled to the cockpit to show the signal to the pilots. He paused on his way, to let the radar operator see it.

Gretton read the signal and handed it to Rowan. He asked Donnelly for a course back to the actual ditching position, so that they could start a fresh search line. In the few blank minutes before they resumed the hunt with concentration, he thought about Cynthia and their child. He glanced at his watch: if he did not find the dinghy within the next hour, he would be justified in calling off the patrol. It would be an unexpected bonus, to see his wife and son again.

\* \* \*

The stark tableau in the dinghy held its pose for five seconds too long. Long enough for Walford, charged with galvanic fresh strength by his overmastering sense of responsibility for the two protagonists, to force from his weakened body the action prompted by his fevered brain.

With a titanic effort he called to them, simultaneously straining his back and shoulders away from the dinghy's deck and sides, erect. It was his supreme moment of command. "Drop them! Cubie! Snowy!"

The instantaneous reflex action of both men was to lower their weapons. Ordering them both, Walford had achieved what a shout at one would not have accomplished. It was the shock of hearing his voice, too, so loud and confident, that made them hesitate. In that short moment, Walford won ascendancy. "Give them to me." He held out his hand. Hesitantly, Snowy, with an eye on his adversary, offered his knife, haft first. When Walford had taken it, Cubie Meddings followed suit. Walford tossed both weapons overboard. A fleeting expression of suffering crossed his face as the physical exertion took its toll with convulsions of pain. He forced himself to grin. His voice weakening, he said: "You're the only two of us who can paddle worth a damn. I don't care if you bump each other off: but get us to England, first . . . please!" He slumped, eyes closed; trembling and panting.

Stan Glover and Brodie looked accusingly at the two quarrellers.

Meddings nodded, with a humorous grimace, and shrugged. "You win, skipper. Guess it was a bum way to act, at that. O.K., Snowy, let's go, boy. Keep in time: follow me." He dipped his paddle in the water and the boat moved slowly forward again.

Snowy still looked grim and suspicious. "All right; but remember . . ."

Pete Brodie, who had the sharpest hearing, cocked his head at the clouds and said: "Don't look now, but we're being followed . . ."

And they all saw the two Me. 109's which broke cloud and levelled off, not a mile away.

They watched the German fighters turn and fly towards them, on a course that would bring them within a few hundred yards.

Meddings and Snowy maintained their rhythmical paddling, driving the dinghy surely across the trend of the wind and sea, towards the Cornish coast. They forced themselves not to look for their hunters; but ever and anon they heard the sound of engines.

Brodie was mouthing his despair and hatred, red-rimmed eyes glaring up at the darting, predatory shapes outlined black against the low cloud. He baled, with his one good arm, the water that the waves incessantly tossed inboard.

Duckett followed them with his unbandaged eye; helping Brodie with the baling.

Walford had fallen temporarily into a stupor; and Stan Glover laboured over the radio transmitter, not knowing that it was sending out no signals.

Suddenly, Duckett flung down his baling can impatiently. "Hell, I can do better with a paddle." He picked one up and clumsily set himself to work on Snowy's side of the boat: between them, they about matched Cubie's strength.

It was then that the Messerschmitts turned directly towards them and dived, skimming fifty feet overhead with a rush of wind and noise. They clearly saw the pilots peering down at them.

The fighters climbed two hundred feet in a tight turn and came for them a second time. Walford's eyes flickered open.

The six men in the dinghy tensed themselves for a devil's tattoo of machine-guns and a hail of bullets. They gave themselves not more than twenty seconds to live.


## CHAPTER TWELVE

SQUADRON LEADER STEVENSON had breakfasted, bathed and returned to the Operations Room, As Senior Controller, it was his prerogative to assume duty whenever a crisis demanded. Besides, that way lay an O.B.E.

Another who could not keep away from the building was

Corporal Jean Forrow. She sat in a corner of the Signals Office, silent and pale, watching the airman who operated the set on the frequency being used by Wing Commander Gretton.

There were two more tired but restless members of the previous night's watch who knew they would be unable to sleep and had therefore returned to the Cypher Office. Alison Storey and Morag McEwan. To Alison's surprise, Morag looked less of a frump than she had ever seen her; let alone after a night watch, which usually ended with Morag looking as though she had walked straight from John O' Groat's without stopping to comb her hair. This morning, Section Officer McEwan looked trim; and almost pretty, with the aid of lipstick and powder.

The truth about the sinking of U 306 was widely known. Certainly, everyone at Ops. had heard it. It produced the usual reaction: everybody felt the tragedy of it, but a large proportion ghoulishly relished the sensationalism. It had cast a gloom over the officers, who went about their work with joyless faces and talked in lowered voices.

When Alison heard that Tommy Rowan had gone off with Paul Gretton on what must almost certainly be a one-way flight, she was wryly amused despite the circumstances. Poor Tommy! He had hung around her for nothing, after all: she would be far too weary to contemplate a night in Torquay for at least two or three days.

Morag's devotion to Walford and her loyalty to Paddy Donnelly made her doubly vulnerable. The Cypher Office was too small for more than two people to work in at the same time: Morag wandered between there, the Ops. and Intelligence Rooms and the Signals Traffic Office. In someone usually so stolid, this restlessness betrayed acute anxiety.

Group Captain Laraway was still in Sick Quarters, but he had emerged from the dulling effect of sedatives and his mind was clear. He had ordered a telephone extension to be brought to his bedroom, and set the assistant adjutant up in a temporary office in the adjoining room. Freed of command of the station, Nig Dunford had hastened to the Grettons' cottage.

Cynthia left him alone with Melanie.

Nig avoided his wife's eyes. "Did Cynthia see Paul fly over, a couple of hours ago?"

"Yes. Nig, look at me! What are his chances?"

"About the same as the chaps he's looking for."

"They can't be as good. Surely the Germans will know that

someone's bound to make a search? They'll be waiting for them."

"If Cynthia starts working that out for herself, it's up to you to persuade her she's wrong."

"Do you really think she'd swallow that?" There was a silence. "Darling . . . how . . . how badly was Trevor Walford hurt? And what about . . ."

"Meddings?"

She coloured.

"Yes, Nig; what about Cubie . . . and the rest of them?"

"Unless anything has happened since they ditched, Meddings and one of the air gunners are unhurt."

"I see." She changed the subject quickly. She had often wondered how much Nig knew about her and Cubie; now, she had found out: and, to her surprise, it made her feel cheap. It also, inexplicably, removed all her old concern for Meddings. "Nig, Cynthia and Paul insist that we stay with them until we can find somewhere of our own."

Dunford rose from the table. "Unless my crystal ball is unbelievably murky, Cynthia's going to need someone around."

Melanie looked up sharply, her voice brittle: "Don't sound so callous about it!"

He turned and looked at her, with a wry expression. "I'm only callous about your boy-friends. If Paul doesn't come back . . ." he threw away his habitual noisy, extroverted manner and his voice was harsh, "it'll be questionable whether he's sacrificed himself for anything worth while."

\*          \*          \*

The Me. 109's zoomed over the dinghy and their pilots waved. One of them continued circling tightly at two hundred feet, while the other climbed into cloud.

Stan Glover watched him go. "He's made height so as to give a decent transmission for the Jerry fixer stations to tune in to." He pushed the radio set aside and reached for the fourth paddle.

Brodie groaned as pain gripped his arm anew. "That means they'll send another pair out to replace these, when their fuel runs short."

Duckett said, weakly: "Cloud base is coming down. Looks like a fog rolling over. I think they'll lose us in the next half hour."

\*          \*          \*

It was Tex Latimer who found the dinghy. Suddenly among the

mass of twinkling, fading specks on his screen, one hardened into permanent brightness. He waited a full minute, while the aerial swept four times, before he voiced his contact. Then, with a great lifting of the spirits, he reported: "Captain from radar op. Contact one-two-zero, range two. Looks like the dinghy, sir!"

They were flying south-west and the contact was just south of east. Gretton began to turn at once. Even so, the blip faded.

There were fragments of low cloud scudding about ahead, and as the Wellington nosed out of one of these, Latimer regained his echo. "One-two-zero, range just under two . . ."

All eyes were on the sea, straining for the elusive yellow blob of the rubber boat. Latimer kept giving the range and bearing; until, from Gretton himself, came a quiet: "I've got it! Eleven-o'clock, about three hundred yards."

They looked down on a scene of frantic joy. All six men in the dinghy were waving. One of them was kneeling, gesticulating with both arms. The dinghy rocked.

Pop Shapley scuttled back to the wireless station to report the sighting.

Nobody thought to scan the sky.

A fusillade of bullets from the leading Messerschmitt shattered the cockpit of the Wellington. Gretton and Johnny Rowan died within seconds of each other. The second Me. 109 attacked from the opposite side, riddling Paddy Donnelly at the very instant that his mind was gloating over the success of their mission and their imminent return to base. Tex Latimer leaped to the astrodome, saw the two enemy fighters and shouted to the radio operator: "Me. 109's . . . two of the bastards . . ." and Pop Shapley was still sending out "Emergency air attack" when the Wellington plunged into the sea.

"You asked for it, and you got it," Charles Gillam told himself. He had reached the rear turret and kept firing his guns until one of the fighters made a close pass from high on the port quarter and killed him.

When it hit the surface, the Wellington lost a wing, which snapped off with a report that reverberated clearly to the dinghy half a mile away. The fuselage canted to that side and slid straight under the surface, trapping Tex Latimer and Pop Shapley who were still alive.

Appalled, mute, Walford's crew clung to their tossing boat and viewed the empty sea. Clamant protest tore at their throats, but they were beyond imprecation. Meddings put his paddle over the side and nodded at Snowy. Glover and Duckett swung into action. The four of them, paddling hard, drove the dinghy towards the place were the Wellington had disappeared.

They came to a piece of fabric which floated, waterlogged already, a few inches below the surface; then a big piece from the tail fin, and another which had part of a bullet-holed roundel on it and had clearly belonged to the side of the fuselage. There was no other evidence that a big aircraft and six men had been swallowed here by the sea, and were suspended now fifty or a hundred feet in the black depths immediately beneath the dinghy.

And the fog rolled over them. A cloud bank which came right down to the surface, so that they were hidden from the watching Messerschmitts.

Brodie's voice trembled with venom. He turned on Walford. "So you had to be the big hero and sink a U-boat that didn't give us a chance. That's two Wellingtons lost for it. And we'll die in this boat, too. Nobody'll find us in this . . . this filthy weather. . . ."

Snowy slumped over his paddle. "What's the use? I can't go on. Let the wind and the tide take us where they want . . . I'll be *glad* to see France . . . or a German boat. . . ."

Meddings stopped paddling, defeated. The whistling wind plucked at the dinghy, lifted it, spun it. The cold and the searing wet struck at them with mailed fists, driving spears of pain into their eyes and lungs, tearing at the exposed skin on their faces. In misery they abandoned themselves to despair. Duckett began to sob hoarsely as his leg set up a flaming protest to a sudden jab when Glover shifted position.

Walford fought his way up from the depths of a chasm of insensibility. There was an insane buzzing in his ears, the spinning dinghy made his senses reel, and the rum he had drunk some time before came back sickeningly into his mouth. He felt himself lifted, cradled in an arm, and he forced his eyes open. Stan Glover held him with one arm, with the other hand he offered the rum bottle to his lips. Walford screwed his eyes shut and clamped his teeth and lips together in refusal; but he was too weak to resist and presently Glover forced the neck of the bottle into his mouth and, tilting it, sent a stream of the fiery stuff down his dry, raw throat. At once, coughing and gasping for breath, Walford felt fighting strength, warm and pulsing flow through him.

He opened his eyes, sore, salt-rimmed and dilated. "Y-you've all h-had it? You think this is t-tough? I'll t-t-tell you s-something

. . . there were six Englishmen in that U-boat . . ." he cackled, his laugh climbing a steep pinnacle of hysteria, his voice cracking ". . . survivors . . . from the Sunderland that attacked it this morning. . . ."

Brodie crouched forward, his eyes narrowed. "Y-you knew that? It didn't stop you? You'd rather kill . . . murder . . . prisoners, than lose the U-boat?" His voice was merciless. "What price glory!"

Walford looked round at the sullen, stricken faces. Even Stan Glover, though he still supported him, had moved away from him.

"It was my job to sink the U-boat . . . even though my own brother . . . my kid brother . . . was captain of the Sunderland crew . . . and he was on board U 306 . . ." Walford's voice broke and died away. He turned his head, so that he could hide it in his crooked arm: they watched his body convulse under the deep sobs that racked him.

Brodie stared at him in a terrible awe that was reflected in his hushed: "Jesus!" He took the paddle from Duckett's hand. "Gimme that. Cubie: you and I'll paddle for ten minutes—we've got three arms between us . . ." he looked savage. "Then Snowy and Stan. We'll paddle in ten-minute spells. To hell with France and the ruttin' Jerries. We're going home!"

*    *    *

Pop Shapley's distress signal, repeated several times at high speed, diminishing in strength as the aircraft lost altitude, and finally cut off in the middle of a word, flashed all round the Operations building within one minute. Within five, it had circulated the whole station.

The Wing Commander Flying was in the Ops. Room when the message came. "Two 109's attacking . . . both pilots, rear gunner, nav., killed . . . Mayday . . . Mayday . . . Mayday. . . ."

Squadron Leader Stevenson's face became ghastly. He looked totally bereft of the power to act; he sat, limp and shaking, mumbling over and over again: "Poor Charles . . . poor Charles. . . ."

The message was brutal, but merciful. It at least obviated all false optimism. There was just a chance that Pop Shapley and Tex Latimer were alive and would be picked up; but that was all.

When Dunford had telephoned to the station commander, he sent for Alison Storey and Morag McEwan. They went into the map store, where they could be away from other people.

"There's something I'd like you two girls to do."

Alison flinched. "You're not going to ask us to . . . break it to Cynthia?"

"Of course not. That's my job. But you can both help to make sure that Cynthia doesn't get to hear of this in the wrong way. I'd like you to go down now, and stay with her; but don't let her answer the telephone or speak to anyone. Someone in the village is bound to hear and try to tell her. Don't even tell Melanie: I know it'll be hard for you, but just try to pretend that nothing's happened. Only . . ." he paused, "try to prepare her for the shock. I know I'm asking you almost to do the impossible, but please try. Feed her the idea, as gently as you can, that Paul's gone on a very dicey job and she should start getting used to the idea that he may run into bad trouble."

"When are you going to see her?"

"In an hour or so. Come on, I'll drive you down to the end of the lane."

Ten minutes later he was at the Fleet Air Arm Operational Training Flight's office hut, alternately browbeating and cajoling its Commanding Officer, Lieutenant Webber, D.S.C., R.N.

Webber knew that a refusal to comply with what Nig asked of him would entail no penalty; either from his own conscience or from Dunford's future attitude to him. He could reasonably have refused, for the low cloud and poor visibility alone would have been reason enough.

"Since Wing Commander Gretton thought the effort worth making," he said, "the least we can do is back him up."

"Gretton had an obligation to his squadron. I'm going, to see if there's any sign of two survivors from his crew; primarily. There's also the chance of tangling with a couple of 109's and disposing of them. And there's bound to be a Jerry A.S.R. launch uncomfortably close to Walford's dinghy by now: I'd like to head it off."

"If you think we can do all that in this weather, sir, let's go."

"You're not coming, old boy."

"Oh, yes, I am, sir. That's the only condition on which I can legitimately let you have one of my Seafires. We'll enter this in the book as a weather recce."

Five minutes later, they were airborne; with tanks full and guns loaded: steering by compass directly towards the point that Gretton's wireless operator had given as the position of the dinghy.

Forty miles out to sea, they spotted the air-sea rescue launch that had sailed from Falmouth an hour and a half before. She surged through the choppy water, hull down, with tall bow-waves hissing and creaming, and a long, frothing wake. They dipped over her twice, rocking their wings, and she altered course to follow theirs.

\*     \*     \*

The low cloud drifted past, the dinghy battled through it, and presently the six men were in the clear again with cloud base a thousand feet overhead.

The patrolling Me. 109's found them within a few minutes and resumed their circling. One flew at two hundred feet, to keep the dinghy in sight. The other flew at eight hundred feet: to keep a look out for approaching British aircraft, and to guide the launch which had left from a French port two hours earlier.

Cubie Meddings was resting for ten minutes, while Brodie and Snowy paddled. Automatically, he scanned the sea. Ten yards upwind of them, the waves tossed something aloft and held it balanced on their crests; juggling with it, like circus seals balancing a ball and passing it from one to another.

The ball was about four feet in diameter, painted black and streaked with rust. Its wet, steel skin grew a crop of excrescences each as large as a giant's forefinger.

The cold of six hours' excoriating punishment by icy water and lashing wind. The successive shocks of being shot down and then witnessing the destruction of the Wellington that had come to find them. The enormous physical effort of paddling almost without respite. All these combined had bemused Meddings mentally and impaired him physically; and he knew it. So he doubted his own eyes and brain when they saw and recognized a drifting mine.

He did nothing, while another wave flung it closer to the dinghy. Then his mind and body erupted into swift action. Two more waves, and the mine would be hurled on to them; at least one of its horns would break, and within seconds they would be blown into fragments so small that they could not even be scooped up in a bucket.

Cubie pitched himself head-first into the sea and the violent disturbance of the dinghy's balance brought its other occupants' attention to him. For a second, Snowy and Brodie stopped paddling, gaping. Then their minds registered the situation and

with panic driving them they vigorously tried to shift the boat
from the mine's path.

Meddings thrust out a hand, fending off the mine between its
horns. He kicked his feet away behind him, for fear that his legs
should foul one of the horns that were under water. With his
throat tight with fear, the freezing coldness of the water already
piercing through his clothes, he fumbled with stiff fingers, holding
the mine away. He kept it at arm's length, and let himself sink,
groping for the few links of the broken mooring chain that must
be attached to it. He found them, slimy with seaweed, and held
on with both hands, paying out the chain so that the mine drifted
till it was some two yards distant from him. Then, swimming on
his back, with mighty kicks of his powerful legs, he tried to prevent it from drifting towards the dinghy. He knew he could not
drag it away; but he could, at least, anchor it.

The dinghy had made a good twenty yards, by now; it was well
out of the mine's path. The men in it stopped paddling. The only
two who had enough strength to shout, Brodie and Snowy, who
could hardly raise an audible cry between them, flung their
voices into the teeth of the wind. They waited, hoping to see
Cubie swimming towards them. But he could neither see nor hear
them.

His hands became rigid, locked to the last link of the broken
chain with all his ebbing strength. Long after he died, his grasp
remained unbreakable and the drag of his heavy body and waterlogged clothes held back the mine.

But at last the heaving sea slung his stiff legs hard against the
horns of the mine and from three hundred yards away the occupants of the dinghy heard the thunderclap of its explosion, saw
the upheaval of a mighty waterspout and felt the boat rear and
pitch when widening eddies lifted and tossed it.

*        *        *

The two Seafires, having climbed above cloud to transmit for a
fix, broke through the overcast again at nine hundred feet. To
the north, nearly two miles away, they could see the R.A.F.
launch. Only five hundred yards south of the dinghy, they spotted
the German high-speed boat.

Nig broke into a steep dive. At the same instant, he heard
Webber call a warning: "Two 109's, eight-o'clock, above."

Dunford held his dive till he was just above the water. Tracer
from one of the Messerschmitts streaked past his cockpit canopy.

He levelled off and was met with a long burst from the machine-guns mounted in the bows of the German launch. Jinking sharply, he lost the launch momentarily; then had it in his gunsight again; touched off a short burst; saw his tracer hit the foredeck; and pulled up, half-rolled, pulled through and dived vertically.

His second burst slammed through the boat's wheelhouse and cut down the for'ard machine-gunners. The boat heeled, out of control, and began to run in a ragged circle, losing speed.

The Me. 109 on Dunford's tail sent bullets into the rear fuselage of the Seafire, where they clanged on the armour-plating behind the pilot. Nig swung to one side, half-rolled, climbed inverted, half-rolled out, and caught his opponent with a full deflection shot that tore a massive chunk from one wing and sent the 109 spinning down in flames. Wiping sweat from his forehead, he glanced quickly round. A plume of smoke was drawn across the sky, far above. Nervously he thumbed the transmit switch and called Webber.

"I'm O.K. That's the other 109 you can see, climbing for cloud, on fire. I can't catch him." Webber was pleased!

"You had me worried!"

They flew round the dinghy and watched the R.A.F. launch lift its occupants aboard. They saw the German survivors climb aboard as their own craft settled deep in the water with a heavy list.

They flew as slowly as they could, just below cloud, in wide circles, covering the boat from air attack. Once, two Me. 109's appeared, but the combined fire of the launch's four-gun turret and the two Seafires drove them back above the clouds.

Presently two Beaufighters flew out to take over escort duty and Nig Dunford and his companions turned for home.

\* \* \*

In the Grettons' cottage, the telephone rang. Morag answered it. She heard Stevenson's voice. "I thought you'd all like to know: we've just heard from the A.S.R. launch. They've picked up Trevor's crew; all except Cubie Meddings."

"Are . . . are the others . . . ?"

"All alive and all going to stay alive."

"Thank God." She returned to the drawing-room. "They've rescued the crew."

Melanie asked: "All of them?"

"No. They didn't find Cubie."

"I see." She looked long at the bottle of rye standing on a table in the window bay. There was nothing more to say.

Morag took a mirror from her bag and began to make up her face. She was wearing her best blue, and had spent time on her hair that morning. She said: "I'm going to ring camp and ask for transport to take me to Tawmouth harbour. I want to be there when they come ashore. I'll take Corporal Forrow, too."

Alison smiled kindly. "Trevor will be pleased to see you. You look very pretty, Morag."

Flight Officer McEwan blushed. "Och, well . . . it's the least a body can do. . . ." She fled to the telephone.

They heard the Seafires come in to land and, a few minutes later, the beat of the heavier, twin engines, and Cynthia Gretton, holding her son's hand, ran out to the lawn behind the cottage. She had no way of knowing that the returning Wellington was one which had taken off on a weather reconnaissance an hour before. She and the boy both waved, before turning to run indoors. "Come, I'll put the coffee on . . . daddy'll be home in a few minutes."

But there was a ring at the door almost immediately, and when Cynthia Gretton opened it and saw Wing Commander Dunford standing there, his face haggard, his hands nervously flicking at his hair; when he stood silent, his eyes full of pity, words and courage for once failing him, the redoubtable Nig lost and bewildered, she knew the truth and there was no need for him to tell her what the savage sky had done.

# THE MANTRACKERS
## William Mulvihill

*"The Mantrackers" was published in the
United States by Signet Books*

## The Author

William Mulvihill teaches history in a high
school in Long Island, New York. He is an
authority on Africa and possesses one of the
largest private libraries on the subject in the
United States. His book *The Sands of Kalahari*
won a ten-thousand-dollar award in America
and appeared earlier this year in a volume of
Man's Book. He is thirty-seven.

# CHAPTER ONE

THE column of soldiers moved slowly, for they had come far that day. Overhead, the sun beat down upon the dry African landscape, where, far behind, against the purple mountains, herds of wildebeest and zebra grazed. The slight breeze and the shadows of the wind-twisted thorn trees hinted that the day was ending. It was January, 1910.

Two mounted white men came first. One was blond, handsome, and hard-faced—a man in his early thirties wearing the uniform of the German Imperial Army. This was Captain Pfeffer. Beside him was an older man, a noncom, Sergeant Kalt—short and darker, with a heavy mustache.

Behind them came a column of askaris, native soldiers, twenty in all—uniformed, disciplined, and armed, but barefooted. They were happy now; the patrol was almost over. Tomorrow they would be back in Fort Mabuti and there would be rest and women and kafir beer.

Pfeffer took a soiled handkerchief from his pocket and wiped his face, studying a clump of marula trees far ahead. There was water here, he knew, and water was rare in this part of Tanganyika; they would camp here. The horses would have water and good grass, and they had earned it. One took care of horses in Africa.

Sergeant Kalt could almost read the captain's mind. They would fall out soon and camp beneath the trees ahead. Before they reached the trees, Pfeffer would ride off to hunt. He would come back with meat for the askaris—meat or fowl. Sometimes he came back with nothing, but only in rare cases. He was a natural hunter.

Pfeffer turned to the sergeant. "We'll make camp up ahead there. You'll find water and good grass. I'll be back in an hour. I want to look at those rocks off there on the rise."

"Yes, sir," Kalt said. He watched the big man spur his mount and ride off to their left, toward a rise a mile or so away, a rise topped by an odd arrangement of big rocks—a curious place where perhaps prehistoric men once lived or gathered to appease their gods. Pfeffer was a man of great energy; he could ride all day and then go off to hunt. There was no one quite like him in East Africa—he was the best young officer, the best hunter, the best man. He had been in Africa for a dozen years, in the Kamerun, in Southwest Africa, and now in Tanganyika. He had fought the Herero and the Bushman and the Masai. One day, they said, he would be a general.

Pfeffer galloped toward the rocks, through the high veld grass, free and alone. Fatigue left him; he was alert now, excited. There might be a leopard's den in the rock tangle. He would stalk the leopard and kill it. Leopards were rarely seen and difficult to kill; one could not pass by an opportunity such as this.

The ground got harder and stony; the rise had begun. The grass became thin, and tough bush replaced it. The rocks loomed large and mysterious, like wrecked ships in a quiet lagoon. Pfeffer slowed down to a walk, turned, and glanced back at Sergeant Kalt and the askaris: they were all but invisible now, tiny figures far away.

He rode on, worked his way up the loose shale, past thickets of scrub and clumps of stunted grass. And then he was among the great rocks and it was cool. He left the horse, took his rifle and binoculars, and made his way toward the highest formation, through a yard-wide slit, then up and across a vast flat rock. There were no signs of leopard. He stopped and looked out across the veld. The askaris were almost to the trees and the water hole. He could see them clearly. He would go on, climb as high as he could, and then circle back to the camp, looking for game. It would be a good day.

He crossed the flat rock and started through a jumbled maze of huge boulders. It was cooler here, for the tall rocks cut off the sun and it was high enough to catch the slight breeze. A strange and pleasant place . . .

Later he could never remember all that happened next. He heard the sound, even so slight, of claw on rock, and saw a flash of shadow on the ground ahead. He tried to leap forward and away but the leopard hit his left shoulder and sent him spinning to the ground. There was no pain, for there was no time for pain —only numbness and disgust at his own stupidity. The cat, too, was thrown off balance. In that moment, he fired blindly and the cat rolled backward, a spitting, roaring ball of mottled fur. Then it was up again, and there was no time to reload. He swung his rifle, but the cat was upon him, yellow eyes close to his and the suffocating cat smell. Worst of all, there were the terrible forefeet, too fast for human senses, slapping at him like a boxer, darting at his face, which burned now with a pain worse than anything he had known. He reached for his knife, then vaguely remembered that he had lost it two days ago. Finally, locked with the cat, his rifle somehow held in both hands and forced into the terrible jaws, he rolled in the shale and kicked and fought and screamed and forced the heavy rifle back into the jaws until something broke in the cat's neck and it went limp. He rolled away from it, screaming from the pain, the hot blood in his eyes blinding him. The rifle was still in his hands; he reloaded it and fired again and again until everything went black. . . .

Somehow they got Pfeffer to Fort Mabuti. Sergeant Kalt had heard the shots and came with the askaris trotting behind him. They found Pfeffer a few feet from the dead leopard and were amazed when they touched him and found him alive. Most of his clothes were gone and his whole body was ripped and gouged and bleeding; the ground under him was soaked with blood. And when they saw his face, they turned away in horror and Kalt himself almost vomited. Only shreds of skin remained and in places the bone was visible. Part of an ear was gone and the nose was something that could not be described. The whole face had been torn and slashed, mutilated until it was no longer a face. Only the eyes were intact; somehow they alone were spared from the terrible claws.

When Pfeffer did not die, Sergeant Kalt began to worry, and he started for Fort Mabuti in the total blackness of the night. They carried Pfeffer on a litter, and when dawn came, he was still alive. Kalt left the askaris and almost killed his horse, but he reached the fort in four hours and they sent a fresh platoon out and a runner to Letti Mission to bring the only European doctor in the district. There was an Indian compounder at Mabuti and he was a good one, but Dr. Zimmler had studied at Heidelberg and Zurich and was in Africa to study tropical medicine. He saved Pfeffer. He stayed at Mabuti and for two weeks did nothing but care for him, mend his lacerated body, and combat the infections. He saved Pfeffer but he could do nothing with the face. The face was gone.

## CHAPTER TWO

THE leopard is the most dangerous game. Not all men agree on this for it is like all things: experience shapes opinion. There are those who say that the elephant is the most dangerous, that his giant size and cunning and power make him the most formidable prey. It is true that he is the most intelligent of the big-game animals and it is true that he will sometimes turn and hunt his hunter, but his intelligence makes him wary and he will take great care not to get close to a man armed with a rifle. Only rogues and wounded animals are dangerous; to an experienced hunter armed with a heavy rifle the elephant presents no great problem. When Africa was young, the first of the white hunters found no trouble in approaching a herd and getting a clean shot. Then, as the slaughter increased, the elephant in his great wisdom moved into the bush and the jungle, off the plains, and it became increasingly difficult to get close to a herd.

The water buffalo is dangerous to hunt. Some hunters claim he is the most dangerous. He has size and great power. Unlike the elephant, he possesses good sight and his sense of smell is well developed. And he can hear well. When he charges head on, he is more than a match for a man armed with a light rifle. It takes power to stop him—like the elephant—and a head shot is difficult because of the thick boss between his horns that protects his brain when his head is down in a charge. The water buffalo will also hunt the hunter; it will double back on his spoor and wait beside it for the luckless tracker.

The rhino can be dangerous. He will charge with provocation and there is great power in his rush. But he is stupid and his eyesight is not good. He seldom presses his attack home; he will charge and keep going if he misses his prey. And like the elephant, he will usually turn away from a shot.

The lion's ferocity and courage are legendary. He has a quality that the elephant, buffalo and rhino lack—speed. He comes at his prey in great leaps, as all cats do, and because his size is not excessive he presents a difficult target. He is not turned by the sound of gunfire and, when wounded, he will lie in wait for the hunter to draw close, then he will usually fight on to the death.

But the leopard is the most dangerous game. And he is probably man's oldest enemy. One can imagine prehistoric men building fires in the mouths of their caves to keep the leopard away in the night; or the earlier tree men hunted by the big cat in the very trees they lived in. He is the worst enemy of the baboon, whose cliff habitat is much like that of early man.

A leopard will attack man without warning and with no provocation. His weight is slight compared to that of the buffalo and elephant, but he is large enough to kill a man: his claws are an inch long, his teeth sharp, and his jaws powerful. The forefeet are lightning fast and strike for the eyes, the back feet dig into the stomach and push, the teeth seek the neck. The leopard, when spoored, will sometimes double back, climb a tree over his spoor and wait for the hunter. When the leopard attacks, he is not driven off by fear or by wounds. He fights to the death. Smaller than the lion, he can hide with more ease and he is equally at home in a tree; smarter than the buffalo, he is also faster. He is a shadow gliding through tall grass, a killer waiting in the blackness of a cave, a streak of yellow flying from an overhanging limb. His claws and teeth are always germ-laden from the putrid meat of old kills, and the slightest scratch will cause infection. He is the most dangerous game.

Pfeffer was discharged from the army. He didn't want it, but he did not fight them, for in the end he knew that he stood alone and at that time he really didn't care.

They gave him his papers at Dar es Salaam and his ticket back to Germany. He would get a pension; he had been of great service to the empire; everyone had been proud to serve with him. But he wasn't fit for the army now because he didn't *look* like an officer. They didn't say that, of course, but someone had stamped UNFIT FOR DUTY on his papers and he had been reclassified as disabled on his medical form. *Disabled . . .*

The night before the boat sailed, he sat alone in the bar of a dirty little Portuguese hotel near the waterfront. It would not do to embarrass those he knew by appearing in the more frequented *bistros* and drinking spots. He was unnecessary now, he was not needed, he was unfit for duty—and soon he would be far away, back in Germany, and he would be quickly forgotten. All one had to do was to reclassify and stamp things on a man's records and the whole thing was taken care of, all difficult and embarrassing situations were resolved. A clerk had disposed of him with a rubber stamp.

He took out his travel orders and his steamship ticket. He read

them through and then he tore them up in little pieces and
dropped the pieces into the pocket of the cheap civilian suit
they had given him. He was going to stay in Africa. He was not
going back to Germany and rot in some futile job; he would stay
in Tanganyika and farm. He would take up some good land and
he would farm it and raise fine zebu cattle and have an orchard
and a good well.

He sat at the table and darkness came; the place grew crowded,
yet no one joined him. People feared him; people feared his face.
So he sat alone and drank and thought about the things he would
do on his farm. He would be happy there and in time he would
grow rich and contented and the face wouldn't matter.

A chair scraped somewhere in back of him and it was like the
scratch of the claw on the rock above him; the black shadow
came at him and the savage eyes and the terrible cat smell. His
hand squeezed the thin glass and it shattered; there was blood
running down his wrist again. He shuddered, pushed the table
away, and started for the door, but the drink hit him suddenly.
He lost his balance and fell sprawling to the floor. He lay there
gasping from the pain of his half-healed wounds, and he heard
laughter rising up around him until there was nothing else.

He began pushing himself up and saw his bleeding hand, but
he didn't care. They were laughing at his face, his face—these
drunken cowards mocked him, this swill of humanity found him
funny. He got up slowly, grabbed the man closest to him, and
flung him against the wall. And then he was on the others, forcing
them to the end of the bar. He was a big man who had never been
beaten, and he smashed at them with a fury he had never known.
He would see a face and smash it and it would go down and he
would find another. The bartender came at him with a chair but
Pfeffer took it away from him and hurled him sideways with a
blow that broke something in the man's face. Two big sailors
came at him together. Pfeffer grabbed one by the wrist and threw
him into the other; then he pulled the man back to him, battered
him with his left. The sailor went limp and Pfeffer dropped him.
He hit the remaining man a glancing blow on the neck, and he
slumped to the floor and crawled away.

It was quiet for a time. Pfeffer stood alone in the wrecked
room. Men crawled from him and some still cowered in the corner.
This was something they had never seen—the fury, the madness
of one man attacking a mob, the sudden savagery of it.

Pfeffer moved toward the door and men moved away from him,

urging others in the crowd to leave him alone, not to touch him. He moved through them and into the night; in a little while he was alone. And there was a strange feeling in him, something more than the drink. He was elated now, happy; for the first time in weeks he felt strong and equal to the others.

He walked the streets for a long time and found another dirty little hotel run by a fat Indian. There was nothing empty, the Indian said, but he was lying, and Pfeffer slapped him, took a key from the wall, and found the room himself. The next day he bought three horses and the other things he needed and rode away from the city and the coast, into the interior.

He found the spot that he had been looking for. There was no farm or army post or native village for a hundred miles around. Once he had been here and found the remains of a stone house that had been destroyed long ago. It was in a lush valley, full of springs, and the water ran into a small stream and rushed away noisily. The trees were old and tall, and in back of them a mountain began and ran eastward.

He camped near the ruins and shot an eland. For the next two days he rested and explored the area, and on the third day he began to rebuild the stone house. There were thick vines and small trees to be cut down and burned, rocks to be found and made flat, beams to cut. But he was happy now, for he was alone, creating something with his own hands. The house took shape; it was well proportioned and solid. When the roof was tight, he built a kraal for the three horses. Soon now he would leave the farm and go to the Masai for cattle. He would hunt elephant and sell the ivory like the poachers did and he would buy cattle, good cattle. He would keep them and breed them and in years to come he would be rich. He would find a woman and bring her here.

In time the house and kraal were complete and he left and rode northward to the Masai. On the second day, he came upon a leopard, feeding on its kill. The cat bounded away to a *kopje* covered with thorn tangle. Pfeffer felt the blood rise in him, the old fear, and he shivered. He had wondered about leopards and what he would do when he saw one again. Now he knew. He would kill it. He would kill it if he had to hunt it all day.

He took his rifle and moved toward the hillock and circled it. The leopard was there, crouching in the grass, and for an instant it looked at him and then flashed away. He swung his rifle and fired and heard the bullet hit. The leopard leaped high out of the grass, twisting in the air, and then fell back with a solid thud. He fired again at the swirl of grass, knew that he hit it again. Reloading, he made his way carefully forward. The memory of the other cat came back to him and his hands grew suddenly cold on the rifle stock.

But the leopard was dead. He had killed one now and he was avenged, his face was paid for. He felt strong again. It would be good to shoot one every day. He hated leopards. From now on, every time he came across leopard spoor he would follow it and find the cat and kill it. . . .

On the next day he saw another leopard. It bounded away and he followed. After a time, he left the horses and followed its spoor on foot. He wasn't afraid now, for he knew that he would find it and kill it. And in the end he did. The day passed and the leopard died. He went back to the horses and made camp. In the night, a lion roared close to the camp and he sat up with his rifle. It roared again and he got up and piled more wood on the fire. He went back to his blanket and tried to sleep, but the lion's roar came to him and in the morning he was sullen and angry. He took his .500 Express and went looking for the lion; two hours later he found it under a thorn tree with the remains of an old kill. He killed it with a single shot and went back to camp.

He rode on, vaguely upset, unhappy. His mind was filled no longer with the details of cattle trading, of ivory prices, of his farm and the future of it. Now he thought of leopards—and lions. Lions were like leopards, just as treacherous, just as useless; they, too, had the cat smell about them, the smell he hated.

This was lion country. In the late afternoon, he came upon a big, black-maned male. It stood and watched him and then slowly turned and moved away. He raised his rifle and fired and rode on, not bothering to follow it, to see whether it was wounded or dead. It didn't matter. Two hours later, he came to an outcropping of granite which rose like a wrecked galleon from the level expanse of waving grass. He sensed leopard and dismounted. He fired into the tangle and his suspicions were confirmed—a leopard streaked away for better cover. He followed it, through the thorn and up the loose shale, past sharp spires and gray stone. For an hour he stalked it and he almost wished that it would leap from some- where and attack him. It wouldn't be like the other time: he was a hunter now and he would kill it with a bullet or with his knife or with his bare hands. Now he was a hunter. . . .

After another hour of ruse and backtracking and maneuver, he cornered the cat on one end of the tangle. He was above it, standing on a flat slab of rock, and somewhere below, invisible in the dense growth, was his prey. The leopard had three choices. It could remain crouched in the thorn. It could come out and attack him. It could leave the refuge and try to bound away through the veld grass. He waited for a time and then began to fire into the cat's hiding place.

After the fourth shot, the leopard leaped into view and bounded away in the grass. But he fired and it went down, hit in the hindquarters, thrashing and spitting, rolling over and over. His second shot silenced it.

He was dripping with sweat. He went back to the horse and rode on feeling wonderful and alive. It had been a good day.

Just before noon the following day, he came upon a dozen zebra standing motionless in the grass. Fat, sleek zebra, waiting to grow old and weak for the leopard and lion to pull down—that was the purpose of the zebra: to fill the bellies of the big cats.

He pulled his rifle loose and fired from the saddle, again and again. Three zebra went down and the others ran off. He rode on and made camp an hour later. He was tired of riding, hurrying. The Masai could wait, and the cattle could wait. He was going to do some real hunting.

He got up before dawn, boiled some coffee, and rode off when it grew light. He was excited. It reminded him of the raids against the Herero and Bushmen years ago in Southwest Africa. Only now he was alone and it was better somehow—better to be alone.

He could hear the lions before he came to the carcasses of the dead zebra. He walked his horse forward slowly. There were jackal here, too, and hyena and above, floating in the air like spirits of the dead, were the vultures, the carrion birds.

He sat on the horse, fired at a lion that was dragging part of a zebra through the grass. The lion slumped into the grass and was quiet. A female next, poised and curious—he wounded her and she vanished. He turned his horse and galloped off, swinging wide around the dead zebra. He came near a hyena making off with a heavy piece of meat and he shot it through its evil head. The spoor of the wounded lioness crossed his path but he did not follow it. Sooner or later she would die. He turned and rode toward one of the zebra carcasses. A big vulture tore at it with disgusting ferocity. He raised his rifle and then lowered it: he hated vultures but would spare them, for they fed on the dead, and soon they would be tearing into the dead lions.

He went back to his camp, watered the horses, and made a meal for himself. He slept and when the sun grew weak he rode back to the killing place. He fired and wounded a big young male lion and it came at him, bounding through the high grass. He waited and shot it through the head and wondered at his coolness and his lack of real fear. He rode forward and shot another hyena. There were hundreds of vultures here now, in the sky and on the ground, fighting over the entrails of the things he had killed. They seemed to know that he would not kill them, but they watched him with distrust. . . .

It was morning again. The horses were restless. But he went back to the killing place once more and shot an old, scarred lion and two bold hyena. The vultures feasted. He left them and rode back to camp and packed the horses and went on. Soon a springbok passed in front of him and he killed it without knowing why. And then, later, he came upon more springbok and four of them fell under his gun. He was happy now and he kicked the horse forward, looking for signs of game, looking for things to hunt: leopard, lion, hyena, springbok—anything.

He did not go to the Masai and he did not hunt elephant and sell the ivory and acquire cattle. He remained in the veld. He hunted, shooting from the saddle anything he came upon. When his ammunition was exhausted, he rode to Majubi and bought two thousand rounds of .256 Mannlicher and rode off again.

## CHAPTER THREE

JOHN THRUSHWOOD sat in a chair on the porch of his small house. An old man sitting motionless in the quiet of evening looking out to the far blue mountains, watching the sunset.

He was alone with his friend and servant, Chapupa; they lived here on a farm that someone had abandoned long ago. Chapupa was old, too, perhaps older than John Thrushwood, but he was strong and agile. He had been with Thrushwood for twenty years.

John Thrushwood was one of the great hunters. He was like Selous and Bell and the others; he was the last of them, the last of a few score men who had come to Africa when it was young and had grown old with it. They had come to Africa as boys or young men from all the corners of the earth—from England and America, from Germany, Australia, and France. Africa was young then; Europeans were rare in most of it. The Portuguese were in Mozambique and Angola and the Boers were working northward and there were some missions and plenty of Arabs with forts and roads as far in as the Congo. But they were only a handful in the vastness that was Africa. Most of the old hunters had penetrated unknown country as boys, lived with native tribes who had never seen a white man before them. And most of them had taken wives from the Bechuana and Damara and others whose women are dusky bronze and beautiful. Thrushwood had taken three native wives before he was twenty and had always found white women unsatisfactory. He had been married for a time to a white girl and they had lived in the south near her people, who were Boers of French extraction. But she had died with her second child and he had drifted north with a commando hunting for Zulu and never returned. The first child, a boy, had grown up on the farm of his mother's people; he had been killed by a bull a few days before he became eighteen.

John Thrushwood, like the others of his breed, had been many things. He had tried farming and trading and found them not to his liking. He had spent years looking for gold and diamonds, and he had worked for the Arabs and the stain of slavery was on his hands. He was not a good man in all ways. He had killed men and maimed others in drunken fights; he had taken native women when he wanted them and discarded them when he moved on. He had stolen cattle. He had murdered Bushmen once with a party of Boers, and because he was young and hard he had looked upon it as the Boers did, agreeing that the little men were vermin who had to be exterminated. In the Zulu War he had served with the British Army as a scout and they had given him two medals for his courage and usefulness. He had been in Tanganyika and Mozambique during the Boer War and had stayed there knowing that it was a futile and absurd affair. And he had hunted ivory then among the great herds and grown very rich.

He might have killed, in all the years of his hunting, two thousand elephants. He did not know. When he was young, he had kept count; he remembered his first and his hundredth; he remembered killing number five hundred along the Rovuma. His thousandth kill was within sight of Kilimanjaro. When he had gone over fifteen hundred, he could no longer remember them. He might have been the greatest elephant hunter of all times. He did not know, but now, because he was old, he did not care any longer. Sometimes in the night the elephants came to him and he looked upon them again in the underworld of sleep, in the reality of long dreams.

He had killed other things, and kept no record. He had shot rhino for horn and lion and leopard for hide. He lived by his gun and it fed him and he had shot endless numbers of animals for his own pot. He had shot for the stomachs of others—for natives, for the army, for work gangs and caravans. He had killed many things.

In the old days, forty years ago, the elephants were easy to find and they were not afraid of the sight and smell of man as in the later years. They did not fear men and they did not fear the sound of gunfire. Once in Mashonaland he'd come upon four bulls and two cows standing quietly in the shade of a great tree. He killed all of them from the back of his horse, hardly moving from the position of the first shot.

In 1870, on his first serious hunting venture he'd taken ninety-six elephant in two months. That was in Matabele country. There were few problems in finding elephant and killing them; the real problems revolved around keeping his large crew of boys together and working, getting the tusks cut out and seeing to his wagons.

They used muzzle loaders then and that was the only thing that had saved the elephant from complete extinction. God only knew how many tusks he could have collected had he been armed with a modern breechloader back in those days. He did not like to think about it. It would have been like shooting cattle with a Gatling gun. The antique guns and the few real hunters wielding them had saved the big animals; by the time breechloaders had arrived they had learned to fear men, learned to stampede at the first shot. They became cautious. They became wily. They retreated into the more difficult and isolated areas. They learned a new fear and they survived.

There were rumors now about Pfeffer—stories about him drifting in from remote stations and lonely kraals, of how he rode alone, his beard long, his rifles and horses always in the best condition; rumors of his killing, his strange ways and his distrust of strangers. He did not seek other men; when he saw them, he turned and went in another direction, and when they followed, he raced away or grew angry and threatened them. He was a man who rode alone and wanted to be alone at all times. Now and then he came upon groups of Nandi and Lumbwa herding their cattle, and although they were warriors and hunters and arrogant, they grew uneasy when he came near them; their children hid from the sight of his face and the women felt a strange terror and turned away. And they said of him that he was not a real man but *bwana sitani,* a devil who comes as a man.

Always in his wake were the dead animals he had shot—game of all sorts, shot without discrimination. Where Pfeffer rode there was the spoor of death; when he passed the carrion birds came, the jackals. Now and again natives would hear of him and follow him, feasting on the game he killed, growing bloated and lazy until they could eat no more of his meat or grew sick from its richness; whole villages had followed him for short periods, fighting the lion and hyena for the wealth of meat he left in his spoor. But when he learned of this, when the natives grew overbold and came too close, Pfeffer grew angry and turned his path and vanished.

Rumors arose in Nairobi and Mombasa and Tanga and Dar es Salaam and everywhere, reaching out into Natal and the N.F.D. and remote places in the Katanga. The stories came to John Thrushwood.

He did not doubt them; he believed all the rumors and all the details and more, for he was a hunter and he knew the deep craving for blood that sometimes erupts in men. He had hunted with men like that—butchers, men beset with a kind of blood urge, driven to Africa by a desperate desire to shoot big animals. And even among the natives moderation was rare; they were all forever hungry for meat, but their weapons were slight. The killers among them were not able to do much damage.

Thrushwood listened to the stories and sucked on his pipe and believed them. It was only natural that Africa would produce a Pfeffer. Sooner or later it had to happen: the right kind of man with the right weapons in the right place at the right time. There were no agencies to restrain him. He used modern firearms. He could ride where he liked and kill whatever pleased him in the last stronghold of big game.

Thrushwood found himself asking about the German; he rode into the settlements more often than before, and hung around the shops and transport wagons, asking about Pfeffer, questioning those who told the rumors. Then he went home and sat smoking, thinking of the things he had heard. He sat and rocked on his porch and weeds grew in his small garden; he took long rides into the hills and sometimes he dreamed about the man. And every day the thought came to him that more and more animals lay slaughtered somewhere south of them, somewhere in German East.

He decided to go and find Pfeffer—and stop him.

He would ride south with Chapupa. The Germans knew him and his papers were in order. It had been a long time since he had ridden far. He was an old man and he would die soon; this would be his last ride, his last hunt. He would find Pfeffer. He would stop the killing, then he would come back to the farm. It would be a good thing to have done, to remember when he could no longer mount his horse and fire his elephant gun.

He called to Chapupa and told him. The little man nodded. He knew. John Thrushwood's mind was troubled and he would not sleep well until the German was stopped. They would go south and track this man and it would be like the old days when they rode together after elephant.

Chapupa was glad they were leaving the farm. They had been here too long this time; it had been two years now since the last hunt and then they had been gone only a month. It would be good to move again, to see wild game, to see the faces of strangers.

And they were going after him, the one the rumors spoke of, the killer.

They would be hunters again.

He was old, a small man, almost tiny. There was Bushman in him and other bloods—Masai and perhaps Arab and Somali. He had learned much from Thrushwood, things that few Africans had learned. He could ride a horse and he could handle a rifle; he could understand Arabic and German and English. But these were only minor skills compared to his real value to Thrushwood —his great gifts as a tracker.

One of the many misconceptions concerning the African is related to his prowess as a hunter and tracker and his resourcefulness in the bush. In truth, the average African, like the average tiller of the soil anywhere else in the world, is a poor hunter. He is a farmer, and the jungle and bush are as foreign to him as to most city dwellers. Or he is a warrior and cattle-owner like the Nandi and Masai and has no need to hunt and learn the secrets of spooring and reading the signs of game in the bush; he is wealthy and arrogant.

The real hunters and trackers are few. They are the Bushmen, the Congo pygmies, the Wanderobos of East Africa. They are

Stone Age hunters, not villagers, maize growers, or herders. They live in the veld and desert and jungle, and live from the things they kill. They are true hunters, like the Eskimo and the Australian black. Long ago they lived alone in Africa, roaming the veld unchallenged.

And then the invader came, the great waves of Bantu sweeping southward, great fighting races driving all before them.

The Bushmen retreated, left the lush savanna and veld, found places to survive in the mountain, the deep swamp, the pitiless desert. They learned to survive here, for there was no life for them outside. And even in the badlands they were hunted and exterminated until only the most clever survived; a tiny people who could find water when others died of thirst, who could escape from within a circle of spearmen, who could find nourish- ment from roots and leaves which others spurned. They discovered potent vegetable poisons to use on the tips of their tiny arrows in hunting and in war; they mastered the skills of tracking to follow the game they wounded over veld and desert. And they survived.

Such people were the ancestors of Chapupa.

The next day Thrushwood took a horse and rode off to see Quinell. It was a three-hour ride, and when he came to Quinell's farm, it was so hot that the dogs did not come out from under the shade of the house to bother him. They lay barking at him until he cursed them. They became quiet. He turned his horse to graze and sat on the roofed porch until Quinell woke up. It was a pleas- ant place, Quinell's farm, much like his own—the house of a Swiss missionary who had been murdered long ago. And Quinell was one of the old breed, too. He was drunk most of the time now, and when he was not drunk, he was off shooting to get cash for his liquor. He had been rich and poor many times; he had roamed over Africa for half a century before there were flags and borders and soldiers and foreign sportsmen.

When it was cool and the sun was almost gone, Quinell got up and came out and washed himself in the tub of water he kept on the end of the porch. He saw Thrushwood and grunted; they were old friends and there was no hurry. Talk was unnecessary for the moment; he must first recover from the drunken sleep and boil some coffee.

Thrushwood followed him inside.

"There's a man called Pfeffer," he said after a while. "A German. You've heard about him like the rest of us, I suppose. He's down in German East and he's shooting everything in sight. Some kind of a madman, I take it. Had his face torn off by a leopard when he was in the army. A hell of a good man and all that but he's shooting every goddamn thing he sees."

Quinell had the coffee on. He blew his nose, sat down, and yawned. He smiled to himself, an old, wry smile.

"And you came over here to ask me to go with you and find him," he said. "Am I right?"

"Yes," Thrushwood said. "We could get him, you and I."

"You can go to hell," Quinell said, and he began laughing to himself quietly. He had not shaved in a week and his old face reminded Thrushwood of a hyena.

"A man like that is not good," Thrushwood said. "He should be stopped. He has no right to kill like that."

"Right?" Quinell said. "Right? You need a gun, John, and a little luck and a good horse. That is the right you had and the right I had."

"It's different," Thrushwood said. "You and I hunted. This man exterminates. It isn't right."

"Then let the Germans arrest him or stop him or do whatever needs to be done. He's in their territory."

"When we hunted there were no territories," Thrushwood said. "The Germans do not seem to care about him. They are soldiers and missionaries and there are no laws that he's breaking. We could get him, you and I. They say he is hard to catch, that he never comes near settlements, that he cannot be spoored for too long. You and I and my Chapupa, we could get him."

Quinell was quiet. He stared out the open window, toward the hills.

"I'm going after him," Thrushwood said. "I stopped by to see if you wanted to come. The German is young and strong, but there would be two of us, three; and to Chapupa his spoor would be nothing to follow. It would be good for you. A good ride."

Quinell nodded. A good ride.

"I don't know," he said. "I don't know. How would you stop a man from doing that? If you found him and rode up to his fire —then what would you do?"

"I don't know," Thrushwood said. "I have thought about it and I do not know. But I've got to find him, see him, talk to him."

"We could shoot him, we could do that," Quinell said.

"And he could shoot back," Thrushwood said.

"We do not want trouble," said Quinell. The thought of violence lingered with him. He might go with Thrushwood and he might not go. The German was a queer one and he should be stopped. It was said that he camped near water holes and shot everything that came to them until there were hundreds of dead animals rotting in the sun. A man like that was crazy.

"But we are not afraid of trouble," Thrushwood said. The smell of the boiling coffee was good.

"No," Quinell said. "We're not afraid of a goddamn thing. If he wants trouble, we could bring it to him." There was the vision of himself thirty years before, lean and hard and deadly with the old muzzle loader he'd shot elephants with.

"Then you'll join me," Thrushwood stated.

"Why not?" Quinell asked. "Do I have business here, do I have to work this damn place? And who else would you turn to but Peter Quinell? It's old bastards like us who could find him; we're the only ones that could do it."

"We have the knowledge and the patience and the toughness," Thrushwood said. "And that's what it will take even to locate him, get close to him. He is tough, too, and young; he may be mad and, in any case, he is ruthless; fanatical, as I see it."

Quinell got up, found two cups, and blew the red dust out of them. He poured black coffee and they began to sip it, smoking their pipes.

"It might take time," Thrushwood cautioned.

"We might get a bit of ivory along the way, John," said Quinell. "A tusk or two now and then to pay for things." He meant whisky, and Thrushwood nodded.

"We're bound to see a lot of ivory," Thrushwood said.

Quinell shook his head over the coffee. "How can a man kill like that? How can he do the things that one hears about him? It may be all talk, too; we shouldn't forget that."

"It's all true," Thrushwood said. "I believe it all, for some reason. Maybe it's because of some of the things I've seen, the things I've done myself. I took out parties, too, for some years. An Italian count or something one time. He was like that, a killer. He liked to slaughter. Son of a bitch shot a turtle once, blew his head off at ten feet. Imagine that. A turtle. I was going to quit him but I needed the money to get started again and I stuck with him for two weeks. He went back to Europe then, from Mombasa, because he was a madman for other things, too, food and wine and horse racing. Wouldn't touch a woman. Years later I heard he entered a monastery in Spain. He was something like this Pfeffer."

"I knocked over twenty-one elephants one day," Quinell said as if to himself. "It was slaughter but I got a hell of a pile of ivory. But it was a living with us, John, it was our job."

"We were professionals," Thrushwood said. "It was like that shooting meat for the transports. Game was game and you could always use the meat."

"When do we leave?" Quinell asked. He eyed the interior of the house as if something needed fixing.

"As soon as you want to," Thrushwood said.

"I'll ride back with you."

"Today?" Thrushwood asked.

"Sure. You want to go, don't you? Well, let's get the hell going. I'll go to your place and we can leave from there when you get your horses and gear ready. Finish up the coffee and find your horse. You got anything to drink over your place?"

"Plenty," Thrushwood said. "We can take it all with us." He drained his cup and walked to the doorway. If they left now, they could be at his farm before nightfall and maybe find some fresh meat on the way. He was happy now. Quinell was going with them. It was going to be a great ride.

They left within the hour.

They stayed another day at Thrushwood's place. The few head of cattle that were kept in kraals were turned loose to fend for themselves; they would, in time, drift toward the next farm and mingle with another herd until Thrushwood returned. The dogs would hang around the house for a day or two until they became hungry and then they would go and join Van Rieber's hounds. It was like that when a man lived alone and went on a long ride. Thrushwood locked the door of his house and closed the heavy wooden shutter, and they rode off, Quinell with an extra mount and Chapupa leading two more, packed with supplies. They would pick up more horses when the time came, and bits of equipment they did not have. But they had the essentials—the tins of food and the ammunition and coffee and a small chest of medicine; the matches and rifles and blankets and the personal things that each man needed on a long ride. Thrushwood turned in the saddle and looked for the last time at his farm and then it receded behind them.

"Did I ever tell you about the time I almost blew my silly head off down along the Sweswe river?" Quinell asked.

Thrushwood pulled his horse closer. He hadn't heard the story in some time.

"No," he said. "Not that I recall . . ."

Quinell smiled. "It's funny now but it's the God's truth that it was one of the worst times I'd had. I dream about it now and then and feel that elephant coming at me. It was down in Rhodesia one fine day, near the Sweswe and I came riding up to a fine old bull and gave it to him. Gun missed fire. Cap went but the spark never made it to the powder. Amazing the way we hunted with those muzzle-loaders back then. We must have been trying to get ourselves killed off young. Well, sir, I handed it down to my boy so that he could put on another cap and I pulled out my second gun and put a bullet into the bull, all the time keeping my eyes on the big bastard knowing that he was a mean one. Now can you guess what that boy did with me watching that wounded elephant? Instead of putting on a fresh cap he put in another charge of powder and another ball. Well, sir, the bull decided to charge me about that time and I reached down, took the gun, raised her to my shoulder and pulled the trigger . . .

"Well, you can imagine. There was this terrific explosion which blew me and the horse and the gun in three directions. I landed full on my back and real hard and lay there stunned. I was half blind and figured my back was broken. I could just about draw a breath. I just lay there and cursed that boy and waited for that elephant to come and kneel on top of me and pop me out of my skin. Well, sir, I never saw that beast again. Figgered the goddam cannon-blast scairt him off. Followed him a day or two later but lost the trail. If you ever hand a new boy a gun you better damn sure watch what he does to it. Take my word."

Thrushwood snorted. It was good to be out again and he was glad that Quinell was along this time.

They camped that night in an area so familiar that it seemed as if they were still on the farm. They were not tired and could have ridden all night, but there was no reason to hurry; they and the horses had to settle down to the ride and adjust to it. They ate tinned meat and vegetables from Thrushwood's garden. There was plenty of coffee and they smoked their pipes and traded brands of tobacco. Chapupa sat with them. He was Thrushwood's servant, but he was a friend first and there was no servant-master relationship between them. They were two men, white and black, each with intelligence and skill, dependent on each other. There were white men who resented this relationship; Thrushwood had fought some of them and killed a Boer once in Kuruman, a Boer who took up his rifle and swore to shoot Chapupa. Thrushwood was not a tolerant man—he had fierce hatreds and irrational preferences for people and ideas—but Chapupa was his friend and he would let no man come between them.

"Three old men," Quinell said, sucking on his pipe. "Three old bastards going after a crazy Dutchman. You know, maybe we're the crazy ones. Ever think of that?"

"A perfectly sane man will never catch Pfeffer," Thrushwood said. "You and I, we are a little different; if we had been really and truly sane we would never have come to Africa. We would have stayed home and done something ordinary. I wanted to be a doctor once when I was a boy but something got in the way, as it always does."

"I wanted to be a merchant," Quinell said. "A rich one, you know, with a great house and a few ships in the China trade."

"And Pfeffer," Thrushwood said. "What of him? Perhaps he always wanted to be a soldier and then when they tossed him out of the army maybe he went a bit wild." The man was always in his mind now.

"He is still a soldier," Quinell said, staring into the fire. "But he has gone to war now."

Thrushwood nodded. There was the aspect of war about the German's hunting techniques—there was no selectivity in his killing, no restraint. He struck at water holes and some said he started veld fires.

"He is like an impi of the Zulu," Chapupa said. "He rides forward destroying all in his path. Behind him come the carrion."

Quinell grunted. "I'm going to bed."

"Yes," Thrushwood said. "Tomorrow will get us out of our own area, at any rate. I think we should head for Umzilikuzi; we could make it by nightfall if we rode hard."

The other two men nodded. It was good to be in the open again; good to be with the horses and close to one's gun.

Thrushwood carried only the lightest of rifles. He had no use for the so-called elephant guns of large bore. He killed with small bore weapons, .275 or .303 with bullets of sensible weight, blunt points and moderate velocity. He did not dissuade others who liked heavier guns for he believed that above all a man must have the utmost confidence in his personal weapon.

He reasoned this way: the heaviest bullet striking in the wrong place has no more killing effect than a light bullet. An elephant shot in the brain dies as quickly from a .275 as from a .450 and the brain shot was the only shot he attempted. A light rifle was handy and free from recoil. It was usually more reliable; with any such weapon he could kill quickly and merciful for he had mastered the brain shot long ago.

He had studied elephant skulls and even cut open the heads of fallen beasts to measure and memorize the location of the small brain. Then the long apprenticeship. The first broadside shots had been more difficult than he had believed. Then came the mastery of the frontal shot and all the other basic angles. Always the brain, a tiny almost impossible target in so large a head. After some years he mastered the last skill: he learned to shoot and bring down the giants as they ran *away* from him, waiting as the great head swung to and fro, calculating, guessing and then squeezing the trigger with some uncanny knowing, some age-old instinct of the killer, so that the tiny bullet he released sped after the running elephant, meeting the great head as it swung sideways, finding the bone-sheltered brain, killing instantly. It was a shot that awed those few who had witnessed it, made them quiet in the presence of such murderous matadore artistry.

The land they rode across was an old land.

The first hunters, the first men, had hunted here in bands, waiting in the tall grasses for an unwary animal, circling their prey, waiting for the group-leader to give the signal for their rushing attack.

The land was old. The bones of the first men lay deep in it, the fossil bones of the first hunters and their murderous clubs of antelope bone. The bone was turned to stone now and the skulls and weapons lay lost forever in the darkness of the earth and time.

They hunted in bands and had no fire. They killed what they could kill and ate it raw. In time, long time, they would find fire and improved weapons, they would migrate and discover farming and build villages and invent gods. But they were hunters first; for a long time they were predators, waiting in the tall grass, motionless, tensing for the kill, gripping their bone clubs, waiting for the pack-leader to charge their unsuspecting prey.

Thrushwood had seen the bones of these first men but he had not recognized them or known what they were. Once, riding through a deep and desolate gorge, he had seen the sun glinted on something that the last rain had exposed in the steep side of the cliff wall. He rode close and pulled it loose from the shale. It looked like the top half of a baboon's skull. He turned it over in his hand and then dropped it to the sun-baked ground. It smashed to pieces.

He rode on. A hunter.

They worked southward and westward for several days. They grew accustomed to the saddle, to the routine of the camp, to the taste of the game they occasionally shot.

In Umzilikuzi they lingered for a day listening to the rumors, telling no one that they were looking for the German. They pretended to be on a hunting trip with an eye out for ivory to pay expenses.

And the rumors all said one thing: Pfeffer was west of them and south; some said he was still in Tanganyika, others said he was north of the border, in Kenya now, in the Serengeti. They listened, nodded, pretended not to care, and then rode on.

"If we catch him north of the border," Thrushwood told the others, "we'll turn him over to our own people. It'll make more of a stink that way."

"We can do it anyway," Quinell said. "Who the hell would take his word against yours? We could give him to Hazelton if we were over that way; he's rough on anybody from German East. Always talking about the Germans planning a war in Europe and plotting to take this all away from us when it's over."

They rode easily; they did not hurry. Sooner or later they would find Pfeffer's spoor and when they did they would ride harder. Once Chapupa found a spoor, or even the hint of one, he would follow it until he found his prey. He would never tire or lose interest. He was a tracker.

And then, at last, they came upon natives with their zebu cattle. One of them had seen him, followed his trail for a time and feasted with others on a kudu that Pfeffer had killed. *Ai*, it was *bwana sitani*. This had been twenty or thirty days ago.

They took the herder with them to the place where he had seen Pfeffer. He pointed to the faint tracks of horses in the thin, reddish soil. This was the spoor they sought.

They shot some meat for the herders and camped near them that night. They were on his trail now, they were actually tracking him. They had left Thrushwood's farm six weeks before.

When it was light enough to see, they rode off. Chapupa went first and was soon far ahead, following a spoor which they sometimes could not see. They rode faster now, but it did not tax them, for they and the horses were conditioned to it.

The spoor was straight, because the country was spare; then there were more grass and trees and cover and water, and the trail wandered and sometimes crossed itself. They came to a campsite and then another three hours away; bit by bit they were gaining on him; he was far ahead of them but he was not riding hard. He was hunting.

At the end of the day they found themselves on another campsite, the fifth they had seen in one day's ride. And they had seen other things—the bones and skulls of some of the things he had killed, those that had not been dragged away by lions or hyenas. Once Chapupa had waited for them and when they came to him he pointed to the remains of an elephant skeleton, a pile of dry white bones strewn around the skull, which still held the tusks.

Quinell swore to himself. A pair of fine tusks and Pfeffer had ridden off and left them. Tons of red meat for the ants and vultures and hyenas, and fine ivory rotting in the sun. He looked at Thrushwood.

"We might as well take them," Thrushwood said. "We can trade them off with the first natives we see." He was glad there were only two. It was a sin to let good ivory go to waste.

The natives would be eager to trade for ivory. They knew its value now and hunted elephant themselves with old muzzle loaders and traps and snares. The snares were made with powerful rope, five or six inches thick, made with all sorts of tough hide, giraffe and rhino and buffalo. A noose was made at each end. One end was tied to the end of a heavy log and the other end fixed cleverly in some frequented path to find an elephant's foot and tighten around it. The great animal would fight it and run, dragging the log, growing weaker as the natives gathered and pursued it with their spears. Sometimes the elephant escaped: the log would become jammed between rocks or trees and the rope would snap. But the snares were usually successful even if an unusually powerful animal dragged the log twenty miles. The tormented beast would die within a circle of puny men, dying from a score of spear wounds, sometimes lashing out and crushing one of his killers.

The most deadly way of killing the giant was used by certain tribes who had developed the skill of working iron. The spear trap. A great spearhead was forged by the village blacksmith; the head and long shaft weighing perhaps three or four hundred pounds. A shaft was found, a young sapling twelve feet long and the terrible weapon was ready. A rope was attached to the end and several strong men fixed it above an elephant trail with the deadly point, heavy and sharp, waiting for the unfortunate animal. The rope was taken down to one side of the trail and then across it. It is now camouflaged with vines and jungle leaves and it is sufficiently high for the other game, antelopes and buffalo, to pass under.

An elephant comes. He sees nothing except the usual tangle of vines in his way. He pushes against them, lordly and without effort. The line snaps and the gargantuan spear falls, its heavy point sinks into the vast grey neck or ribs. If the animal is lucky it dies immediately with a shattered spine; if it is not it might linger for days and weeks, dragging its entrails, suffering as only a great beast can suffer until some band of meat-starved natives find it.

Sometimes the wound is not fatal. Thrushwood had shot an old bull along the Rovumba once when he was a mere boy and discovered a yard-long piece of rusting spearpoint in the great wrinkled neck. Now making the great spears was a lost art. Arab firearms had driven such laborious practices out of use. Only a few remote villagers used it nowadays.

The day ended. They stopped, off-saddled and cut grass for the horses before eating. They were bone tired and ravenous. They were getting into the fly country but they had good salted horses, tough animals who should be able to carry on without grain for some time.

Quinell's coffee revived them. Darkness came.

"I got five elephants with only four bullets once," Thrushwood said as they found their pipes. "Did I ever tell you about that?"

Quinell was lighting his pipe and for a long time the question hung in the air. Chapupa got up and went out into the perimeter of darkness to check the horses. Quinell had once heard Thrushwood tell the story to another man, Piet Haas, when they were all shooting in the Lado Enclave, but that was a long time ago and the story hadn't been told directly to him. He was paralysed drunk that night, too drunk to stand up and find a bed and he just lay there near the table and listened. Those were good days in Lado. All good fellows. Piet Haas was dead and LeFebre too and a lot more of them, but somehow he and Thrushwood were still going strong.

"No," he said. "That's one story I never heard. Is it true now or is it . . ."

"It's true, every word," Thrushwood said. "Now this was a hell of a time ago. Long time. I was maybe twenty or so, out with my two wagons along the Chobe. I guess I was the first one to really get up there with wagons and stick it out. It was a good year, that I do remember, five thousand pounds of ivory and I got a good price for it. I took a hundred and seven elephants that season."

Chapupa came back with his ancient cloak, wrapped himself in it and hunched close to the fire.

"I like the Chobe country," Quinell said." I was up there in eighty-eight with Fritzie Uhlan."

"It was a good trip," Thrushwood said. He found his tobacco pouch and began to fill his old pipe. "But one day I came back to the wagons early. A bad day. The horse I had was a rotter and I was just finding it out. Beautiful animal and good for anything but elephant. Later traded her for a good load of ivory. Well, I'd turned back early and headed for the wagons and unsaddled. Just about that time one of the boys came running and said there was a bull half a mile away. I scooped up my gun and ran after him. Sure enough there was a good bull and I knocked him over. When he fell, three cows and another bull broke away from the grove and I took after them, loading on the run. It was about then that I found out that I had only three bullets with me, I'd left my coat in camp. I got one of the cows with a lucky shot a few minutes later. When I came up to her she was real dead. Then I saw something else. There was a small knob on her shoulder. Curious looking thing. I slit it open and sure enough it was my bullet. It had gone completely through her. I got the next cow with this same ball and that accounts for the story. Four bullets and five elephant. You'll go some to beat that, Quinell. You'll go a hell of a piece."

Quinell smiled and handed a burning twig to John Thrushwood.

"It is a good story," he said. "Makes me think about the time me and Jake Aimes went to Ethiopia to buy horses. . . ."


CHAPTER FOUR


PFEFFER watched the elephants for a time, then shot one in the back of the ear and watched it slump into the high grass. The herd trumpeted and broke up, all except two bulls, who searched the air about them. He shot one of them without changing position and by then the other bull had his scent and came charging up the hill. He stood up and shot it through the right eye and it went down, stumbling and falling down the slope, gouging the dry earth with its tusks.

He walked back to the horses and rode on, and in a little while he came upon a lioness and two cubs playing in the shade of a clump of thorn trees. He shot the lioness and one of the cubs from horseback, waited for the other cub to show itself, and then rode on.

Later in the day, he climbed the stony ridge that rose gradually from the flat plain and rode along it. It reminded him of a gigantic wave, erupting from the endless monotony of the veld, a wave that had reached its peak and then, instead of falling back into the sea of grass, had been frozen forever over the lowlands. It became broader and steeper as he rode along its summit; there were no breaks in it, no ravines through this granite spine. It was some freak of geologic time, he reasoned, the remains of some worn-down mountain range or some fold in the once soft earth that had been driven upward by gigantic pressure below.

He worked along the top of it and saw the flow of game below—the patterns of eland and Thomson's gazelle, the herds of zebra, giraffe and wildebeest, all of them feeding and sleeping and waiting for his gun to find them.

After a long time of watching and riding, he realized that there was no way down from the steep ridge, no path or means for him to descend with the horses. But he rode on. The cliffs could not continue forever; somewhere ahead this wall of rocks must end, slope down once more into the veld and vanish; or there would be a break in the steepness and he could scramble down with the horses.

Two hours later, he came to a break in the ridge. A narrow ravine, perhaps fifteen or twenty feet wide, cut through the stone and shale, affording passage from one side to the other. The ridge here was a hundred yards wide and rose sixty or seventy feet above the surrounding country. And on his left, along the ravine edge, the slope grew long and he was able to take the horses down.

No grass grew between the vertical walls of the ravine, and the earth was powdery and fresh with the tracks of game. Beyond it, a mile or two away, there were trees. Pfeffer headed for them and found water, shot an eland that lingered an instant too long. The water was muddy and bitter, but the horses filled themselves and he rode back to the ravine. Three zebra trotted through and he shot two of them. The other turned and fled back the way it had come and he followed it through the ravine to the great veld beyond, shooting it through the body as it stood far off in the grass.

He rode on, close to the ridge now, for there was no way to climb this portion of it. He came upon some baboon and shot a female as she clambered up the shale. The males barked and threatened but they were wily and stayed out of range. The ridge started to fall after the first hour and all at once fell away completely.

That night Pfeffer sat for a long time staring into his fire. And later he had a dream that left him shaking and crying aloud in the darkness.

Dawn came. He got up and rode back to the ridge. When he sighted it, rising like a wall from the flats, he turned and rode far out into the veld until he calculated that he was ten miles or more from the ravine that split the steep ridge. He had passed hundreds of animals, kudu and zebra and wildebeest, but he had not fired on any of them. The sun rose higher and it was very hot. There was no breeze.

He rode on and in a little while he stopped and watered the horses and rested for a while. He switched the saddle and the two animals busied themselves with the moist new grass under the low trees. In his pack there was a watertight bottle filled with matches. He took half of them, stuffed them into the deep pocket of his bush jacket, and mounted the horse. All was ready. He took one of the matches, leaned far down from the saddle, struck it on the edge of his boot, and dropped it carefully into the dry grass. He kicked the horse and rode away from the flames, which came suddenly and with an explosive *whoosh*. He rode hard now, back the way he had come, back to the beginning of the ridge, and every quarter of a mile he slowed down, struck a match, and dropped it into the dry grass until his spoor was a great creeping semi-circle of flame. Once, from a rise, he stopped and watched the game which, terrified by the fire, headed away from it, toward the ridge. A group of springbok took no heed of the lion that trotted near them. Troops of zebra mingled with antelope and even hyena. Water buffalo, driven from their wet thickets, ran with gazelle and rhino to escape the common danger. Everywhere game recoiled from the smell of smoke and the heat of the veld fire.

Now the ridge was in sight and Pfeffer left less of an interval between the fires he started. He would strike a match, drop it and ride on. And there was a breeze now, ever so slight, which pushed the flames toward the cliffs.

He reached the cliff and made his last fire. He rode away from the fire and after a mile or two was able to ride up and over the low ridge. He was in back of it now and he pushed the horse without mercy. There would be rest soon enough, plenty of it.

When he reached the ravine, animals already were trickling through it, gazelle and hartebeest. Here was safety for them; the ridge would stop any bush fire. There was green grass here and water; for ages now it had been a refuge. Pfeffer crossed to the other side and worked his two horses to the top. He mopped his face and studied his work and there was a wild excitement in him. A great scimitar of flame curved from far out in the veld to the ridge miles to his left; a solid wall of flame now, not racing, but advancing, consuming all before it, throwing a great curtain of smoke into the pale-blue sky. And within the great curved buffalo horn of flame were the veld animals, moving, running, leaping, turning now to gaze backward and then bounding madly on. Here were the giraffe and wildebeest and gemsbok, lion, leopard, bushbuk. Pfeffer mopped his face and was very happy.

He tied the horses and took off the packs. He took both rifles and as much ammunition as he could carry and made his way to a flat ledge on the brink of the ravine. He studied the ravine fifty feet below; zebra trotted through now, zebra and waterbuck. Pfeffer could not see the mouth of the ravine from his position because the narrow passageway twisted and turned through the shale and quartz. A hundred feet from him, however, was the narrowest spot; here the ravine was not more than fifteen feet wide. Pfeffer adjusted his hat, mopped his face again, fixed the sights of both rifles for the short range and lay down upon the flat ledge.

A lone springbok came down the ravine, nervous but sure of safety behind the rock cliffs. When it reached the narrow spot he had chosen, Pfeffer shot it through the brain. The animal fell sideways, slumped against the wall, slid down and lay still. Pfeffer felt the blood rise in him: it was his first kill of the day and it was a good omen, for it had been a perfect shot. Three zebra came and only one got past him; the other two fell heavily. And now a lioness approached and paused for an instant when she saw the dead animals; he shot her through the brain. Then a rare animal —a tiny steinbok; then a cow buffalo, which he stopped by a shot in the knee before he pumped three rounds into the head. Kudu came, with twisted horns, and most of them died, too. Twenty zebra shouldered through and panic seized them when he fired; many of them broke through and got away.

Now it was more difficult for the game to move fast in the ravine, for the narrow space that Pfeffer had chosen for a killing area was filled with dead and dying animals, filled with blood and kicking hoofs and thrashing horns. But there was no other place to go, so the animals moved forward and it became a scene that few men have witnessed. First the ground had been littered with the dead beasts, then it became packed; now the narrow space was blocked with a ghastly mound of bleeding meat, a wall of carrion.

The fire was close now and the breeze picked up. Pfeffer could feel the heat of it and the terror and terrible fear that it carried. The smoke came and his eyes wept and smarted; he was constantly thirsty but there was no time to do anything but kill, kill.

He was firing now as fast as he could and every time the rifle cracked something died below and added its bulk to the tons of murdered game. The rifle would burn in his hands and he would lay it aside and take the other, which was less hot, and he would fire and fire and fire. Then the flames reached the cliffs and there was a sound new to Pfeffer; the sound of hundreds of animals being burned alive as they sprang at the rock cliff, throwing themselves in at it headlong or in the last terrible instant turning and running into the fire. For there was no room in the ravine for all the animals, and many hundreds of them died of suffocation and terror and trampling.

The remaining animals, the hundreds or perhaps thousands of living things still packed in the ravine, all went suddenly mad at once. Something gripped them all in one searing instant and they burst through the ravine in a long explosion, wild-eyed and insane from the heat and terror they could no longer endure, pushed on from behind by a similar force and carried along by a movement which even Pfeffer could not stop. The animals he killed now did not fall: they were swept along by the torrent and then ground under it. Fear had left the animals now, for fear is the luxury which precedes terror, and in this moment there was time for neither.

They broke from the ravine and were gone, most of them. Pfeffer did not stop—there were the lame and blind and crippled and those he killed with mechanical sureness. He pulled the trigger and something fell dead. He never missed. After a time it was quiet in the defile; everything was dead. And the fire was gone; it still burned along the cliff but it moved away from the

ravine's mouth. Thousands of animals had escaped Pfeffer's fire
because he had thrown only half of a great semicircle around
them; they had moved away from the ravine or past it and found
safety and lived. But he was satisfied. Had anyone ever killed as
he had killed today? Was there ever such a hunter?

He stood up. Hundreds of shell cases littered the ledge and
hundreds more had spilled off as he fired. He swept them away
with his foot and climbed back to the top of the ridge. He led
the horses down and back to the water he had used the day before.
The remains of the eland were still there. And there were hyena.
He let the horses graze, knee-haltered. He slept in the shade until
the sun was down and the heat gone from the breeze that had
picked up. He moved on as night came, following the wide spoor
of the animals that had escaped the ravine. He came upon a
waterbuck standing alone, watching him as he rode closer. It
didn't move; it looked exhausted, bewildered. He shot it through
the head.

He came upon animals that had been wounded or hurt badly
in the ravine and he did not shoot these, for they would die
anyway, from lion, leopard, hyena and vulture. He had used up
enough ammunition for one day.

Then it was dark and he found a place and built a fire. He took
care of the horses and wrapped himself in a blanket and slept.


## CHAPTER FIVE

ONE night Quinell had a strange dream. He was riding through
the veld and he came upon a spoor and followed it because it was
fresh and he was curious. Soon he came upon a dead kudu,
examined it, and saw that it had been shot through the head.
And he came upon other things—a Thomson's gazelle and some
wildebeest and a beautiful, sleek zebra—all of them dead.

Now elephant—five in one stretch of lowland—great gray hills
rotting in the sun, red with bright blood that still flowed from
them where the tusks had been chopped out and buried. After
that there were only elephant and their numbers grew; soon there
was always a carcass in sight, dead and forgotten except for the
carrion that circled it, ripped it; great bodies of elephants with
their tusks gone.

And in the dream he rode on after Pfeffer. How could the man
ride alone and kill so much and cut the tusks out? Where was he

hiding the tusks? Did he bury them or hang them high in trees as others did, or was there an army of bearers with him? He was taking the tusks now, all the fine ivory, but it had been ripped from all the beautiful elephants that had died, all the mighty and magnificent bulls and the sleek cows.

And now ahead was the figure of the hunter. Quinell dug his heels into his mount and raced on, past dead things, bleeding things, things maggot-filled that Pfeffer had killed.

But the man saw him and raced away and the chase was on, two desperate riders alone in the vast grassland, fighting for space and time as the sun went down and the shadows grew long.

Then the terrible thing happened. He caught up with the rider and they fought and rolled from their mounts; but then he saw the face, the hunter's face close to him, and he began screaming because the face was his own face as it had been long ago.

Chapupa saw the vultures and stopped his horse. Thrushwood followed his gaze and they looked at each other and then without words turned their horses and headed toward the spot where the birds circled, toward a low ridge jutting from the grass.

They came to a rise and halted and saw that there had been a fire here, a week ago perhaps. The blackened veld stretched unbroken to the ridge. They rode on, through the burned area. Chapupa grunted. Something was in the air that he did not like, something that was terrible and unnatural.

And then it came to Thrushwood—a smell. They were miles away and the fire was old and yet there was the smell of flesh, putrid and sickly sweet; a smell that grew and grew and became unbearable. There was a narrow cleft in the granite ridge before them and they headed for it. Vultures, coming from afar, drifted over them and then glided down to vanish behind the ridge.

It seemed that the terrible smell reached out and stopped them, for they pulled back on their reins at the same instant. They sat and looked at the ravine and said nothing. The ridge was a mile away.

They moved forward, trying not to breathe. The horses pulled away—there was something terrible ahead. And then they were close enough to see, but they could not believe.

The entrance to the ravine was blocked. An impassable mound of flesh and bone blocked the way. And before this, a vast canopy of bones and skeleton remains, torn and bare now from the carrion. And everywhere the carrion-eaters: hyenas and jackals and a thousand vultures.

The horses fought and would go no farther. Thrushwood held his stomach and fought the urge to vomit. He let the horse have its way and it turned and streaked away from the sight and the smell of the slaughtered animals. Behind him came Chapupa, leading the slower pack animals. Quinell was last, a cloth over his face.

Pfeffer had trapped them somehow. The fire was his; he had cut off the animals' escape route. All the rumors were true now, all of them. The German was a maniac, a madman. He had to be stopped.

The horses grew tired and slowed down. The air was clean now.

"What do we do now, John?" Quinell asked.

Thrushwood waved him away as if he was occupied with something else. He stopped his horse and got down slowly and walked away from it. He vomited. Quinell and Chapupa rode on very slowly. After a while Thrushwood caught up to them and they stopped and looked at each other.

"We'll circle it and pick up his spoor," Thrushwood said.

"Let's start now," Quinell said. "I'm going to shoot that bastard myself." He took a half-filled bottle of whisky from his roll and drank deeply from it.

"Two or three days," Chapupa said. "He is not far."

"He's a maniac," Thrushwood said. The smell was still in him, in his clothes, on his skin, everywhere. He wanted a bath with strong soap and lots of scrubbing.

"Let's eat first," he told them. "Then we can turn and circle the ravine until we pick up his spoor. We can ride until we can't see any longer. We're close now and we can get him."

"I'll kill him," Quinell said. "I swear I'll kill him with my bare hands." He took another long swig and screwed the cap back on the bottle.

"Water and shade," Chapupa said, pointing backward over his shoulder. He turned his horse and rode off.

The white men followed him. They did not speak until they had finished their black coffee and tinned beef. The sun went down. They found their pipes and filled them with tobacco that was too dry to be good. Then they saddled the horses again and rode off. Chapupa rode ahead and Thrushwood led the pack animals. It was almost dark when Chapupa slipped from his horse and pointed to Pfeffer's spoor in the reddish earth.

They ate a cold meal and slept without a fire. The German

was close by; tomorrow they would take him. The night seemed endless and long before dawn they were all awake, lying in their blankets, waiting for the first streaks of dawn.

At last it came, and Thrushwood got up and made a tiny fire for coffee. Quinell and Chapupa packed the horses and made ready and while the sky was still gray they rode off without speaking, Chapupa in the lead.

The terrain changed slowly: savanna replaced the thin soil and dryness; there were more trees now, and as the sun came up, the grass dried and the insects began their day of noise. The spoor was a ribbon of crushed grass. Two hours passed and they came to the German's camp.

Chapupa slid from his horse and dug into the mound of earth that covered the dead fire. He studied the lumps of horse manure, the crushed grass, the tracks leading away. The man they hunted was only an hour or two ahead of them.

They saw him at last, a tiny figure far ahead in the level veld. The man was not hurrying; he was unaware of them.

Thrushwood had visualized this scene in his mind many times. He had found the German now; soon he would be within rifle range. What should they do?

"Let him know we're here," Quinell said. "Fire a shot. We are hunters and we have come upon him and wish to greet him. He can't know our real purpose. Fire a shot."

Thrushwood did. The figure turned in his saddle and sat studying them. Three riders, white men presumably; an unlikely sight in this part of southern Kenya.

"He's not going to run," Thrushwood said.

"Why the hell should he?" Quinell said. "He's no mind reader. Just act natural until we get up close to him. And remember he's probably out of his head. Keep your eyes on him."

They rode forward. The man waited for them, sitting with his rifle stock on his thigh. They slowed down and approached him at a slow trot. The rifle came down slowly until it pointed at them; then suddenly he held up his left hand, palm out—the gesture to stop, to come no closer. They pulled up their horses a hundred feet from him and for a long minute there was total silence as they studied each other.

It was true. He was a man without a face. He wore a wide-brimmed bush hat and his hair and beard were long and blond; but between the beard and the brim of the hat there were only the eyes, blue eyes, wide and hawkish. The rest of the face was scarred, lumpish and red, mis-shaped and masklike. This was why the natives feared him and called him *bwana sitani*; this was why he had been discharged from the army, why normal men found him impossible to accept and tolerate. In all other men, personality helped shape the face; with Pfeffer, the face had changed and distorted the personality. Chapupa and Quinell and Thrushwood sat and looked at the face, and there was at once pity and fear in them, and disgust for the man who had been at the ravine and filled it with the tons of stinking carrion.

"I'm looking for a man," Thrushwood said, "a man called Pfeffer." His voice sounded strange. Chapupa let his horse drift away from Thrushwood and Quinell did the same. If there was trouble, they would not be bunched together.

"I am Pfeffer"—a hard voice, a voice that challenged all of them. The rifle was a bit lower now, ready.

"My name is John Thrushwood. I want to talk to you."

"There is always time for talk, *mein herr.*"

"I want you to stop killing." It was out now, he had said it. The German knew who he was and what he wanted; it had to be this way before anything else could happen.

"Stop killing?" Pfeffer asked.

"You must stop it," Thrushwood said.

"Are you from the district officer, the police?" Pfeffer asked.

"No," Thrushwood told him. "We have come on our own and we tell you that you must stop this slaughter."

"I am a hunter," Pfeffer said, "a hunter like yourself, the great John Thrushwood. Did you follow me all this way to tell me to stop hunting? You must be mad."

"You've got to stop it," Thrushwood said. *"Now."*

There was a rifle across Quinell's saddle now. Pfeffer saw it, turned and saw that Chapupa had slipped from his mount and stood behind it, a short assagai in his hand.

"Yes, I understand now," Pfeffer said. "This is your domain. I have strayed too far north, over the border, and hunted here. I must go back to Tanganyika."

"You do not understand," Thrushwood said. "You will stop killing animals. You must go back to the coast, to the city, or Europe. You cannot hunt in Africa any more."

Pfeffer stared at him, amazement in the large blue eyes.

"Why?" he asked at last.

"Because it is wrong," Thrushwood said.

"You must be mad," Pfeffer said. "No man will stop me from doing what I wish to do."

"I will," said Thrushwood. Quinell's rifle was on the other man. There was no danger. They would take him.

Pfeffer swung his horse until his left shoulder pointed toward Thrushwood. He was less of a target.

"Then I shall have to shoot you also, *mein herr*," he said. Then Pfeffer did something unexpected. He slid his rifle into the leather sheath by his knee. It was meant to disarm, confuse.

"When we meet again," he said evenly. He swung his horse to move off.

Thrushwood's rifle came up. He had Pfeffer in his sights.

"I'll kill you if you touch the rifle," he said.

Chapupa moved in from the side and held his assagai ready as he took Pfeffer's rifle. He sat quietly. He was disarmed, defeated. The Englishman was no fool; he had seen an opportunity and grasped it. They had come to take him, not to talk or to warn him.

"It was foolish of me to give you this chance," Pfeffer said.

"Yes," Thrushwood said. "It was. A grave mistake."

"What do you want?"

"You," Thrushwood said.

"Why?"

"I've got to stop you. What you're doing is wrong, very wrong. I think you're a sick man, or mad."

"I am a hunter," Pfeffer said.

"You're a murderer," Quinell said.

"I am in good company then, *mein herr*. I have heard of John Thrushwood. We all have. The great hunter. Greater than Selous and Bell and Finaughty and the others. Pretorius, even. We have all heard of you. The elephants alone you have shot. . . . You have killed for fifty years."

"I lived by my gun," Thrushwood said. "I shot to eat, to live. I was a professional."

"Two thousand elephants," Pfeffer said. He said it as if to himself, as if he could not comprehend it.

"I was a hunter," Thrushwood said. "I did not slaughter and maim. The carrion did not follow me. Shooting and hunting were my life, my job. But you—you disgust me; you're a lunatic. You do not hunt; you exterminate. Africa cannot hold you; the world cannot bear you any longer."

"Shoot him now, John," Chapupa said. "Kill him quickly.

The world is too full of talk. Do this for me, John. He will never stop killing."

"Yes," Pfeffer said. "Shoot me. It wouldn't be murder for you. You are John Thrushwood. It would be your job, your duty."

"Shut up," Thrushwood shouted.

"Do it now," Chapupa said. "Or give him to me. Let me have him, John. There will be no pain—a long sleep which never ends."

"No," Thrushwood said. "I'm going to hand him over to the people up in Kericho. Let the English have him first."

"They will talk to him and turn him loose," Chapupa said.

"Perhaps," Thrushwood said.

"I'll come back," Pfeffer said. "In the end I will come back and shoot as I like."

"Then I'll kill you," Thrushwood said. "I'll find you and shoot you."

"No," Pfeffer said. "I don't think so. I don't think so."

They searched Pfeffer's baggage and found another rifle and a service revolver. There was a good campsite ahead and they rode to it and dismounted. Chapupa tied Pfeffer's hands in front of him; the wrists were lashed together a foot apart so that he could eat and manage blankets and take care of himself but yet be captive. Quinell rested in the shade and drank from a new bottle.

"I told them I was going to kill you," he told Pfeffer.

"You cannot murder me," Pfeffer told him, sitting with his back to a thorn tree. "You are a man of honor. You are Quinell the elephant hunter. I saw you once in the streets of Tanga."

"You murdering pig," Quinell said. He spoke quietly and precisely, as if he identified something familiar to him.

"You have killed more."

"Yes," Quinell said. He studied Pfeffer's face. "Now I may kill you, too." Chapupa moved close and stood watching, impassive, ominous. And Thrushwood came closer, thumbs hooked over his belt. They stood over the man and watched fear flicker in his eyes, eyes that were the only normal part of a terrible face.

"The ants would like him," Chapupa said. "We passed an ant-hill just before we caught him."

"He has been good to the ants," Thrushwood said. "He gives them meat and does not destroy them. We could stake him out and camp close to him. I've never seen a man die that way."

Pfeffer spat. "You're wasting time. Africa is not so big that a white man's murder goes unnoticed. There are three of you. You will not murder me because in time the secret would get out and you would hang and you are not willing to do that. Too many people know that you trailed me. Quinell drinks too much. The native here might talk under pressure. No, you will not murder me; not this time."

"He's right," Thrushwood told the others. "We are not murderers." He turned away and went back to the fire, where seasoned meat was cooking. They had actually done it; they had caught Pfeffer. It was hard to believe that it was over, that it had been so simple. And luck had been with them; they had caught him in British East. That was violation enough and it would magnify the incident, give it an international flavour. Pfeffer was an ex-army officer and the British might infer that he was a spy, as the Germans so often did with Englishmen caught below the border. The Germans were getting ready for a war and they would find Pfeffer an unnecessary embarrassment.

They took turns watching during the night. They tied Pfeffer's legs together and put him near the fire where it was light and open. And in the morning they put him on one of the pack animals and began moving toward Kericho.

Thrushwood did not hurry. The horses were thin from the chase and they were all tired. They rode north through the vastness of the Serengeti, day after day through the grass where great herds of game grazed, where the sky was light blue and the blurred mountains always far away. They crossed unknown streams which ran eastward into other streams that would eventually run into Lake Victoria; and they came to great areas of dry veld where the dust was always around them, where water was carefully watched and rationed.

"What makes you do it," Thrushwood asked Pfeffer one night.

"Ask yourself. Ask any hunter."

"They have reasons. I have a reason. I was a professional . . ."

Pfeffer shrugged. "Is that what you call yourself . . . strange. You give it a name and it becomes a good thing. A professional . . ."

"I shot to earn my living."

"You shot because of the urge to hunt, the urge to kill. The ivory was a fortunate byproduct which you could use to finance your trips, the horses and rifles and the vacations in the towns every now and then. You have the killer instinct and I have and there is nothing like it is there? Nothing like bringing now a fine bull with a clean shot. You and I, we are the same you know, except that you have killed more."

"Your killing is slaughter, murder."

"If any killing is bad, all killing is bad. How many elephants have you taken in one day. Twelve, seventeen, twenty-one? It does not matter. They are dead. Was this hunting or butchery? You stole the ivory and I ignore it. You are a hero and I an animal murderer. This, of course, is nonsense. We are all killers. Killers and self-deceivers. And you are worst of all."

"You'll kill no more," Thrushwood said. "Not here, not in Africa."

"You believe this is possible?"

"Yes."

"I might kill you if I get the chance."

"Yes," Thrushwood said. "I know."

Pfeffer tried to escape. Quinell dozed off one night and when he opened his eyes, Pfeffer's hands were almost free: he had rolled over to the fire and held his wrists as close to the glowing coals as he could. Quinell saw him, desperate and alone, crouching over the fire with the redness and the shadows on his torn face; he was like an animal, a wounded hyena. Quinell fired his rifle into the air. Pfeffer had frightened him and he did not want to be alone.

Thrushwood and Chapupa dragged Pfeffer away from the fire just as the burning cord gave way and they felt the great power in his arms and back and heavy legs; without their guns they would be children before him: three old men whom he could sweep away with one smashing blow. They bound his arms again and tied him to a heavy stake which they drove into the ground ten feet from the fire. And when it was all over, they were sweating and tired and no longer sleepy. They looked at Pfeffer and wondered what he would have done if Quinell had not opened his eyes, what he would do with them if they were completely in his power.

They rode on.

The Germans wanted Pfeffer for a number of things. Technically he was still in the army. He had disobeyed orders and not taken the boat from Dar es Salaam. And there was the matter of the slaughter of game. There were no game laws; nobody cared how many lions or buffaloes or elephants a man killed; they were animals and there were millions of them; indeed many of the animals were pests and dangerous to the settlers and natives. The officials did not care about the rumors they heard concerning Pfeffer, they did not care what he shot or did not shoot. They wanted him out of the country. He had been discharged from the army, pensioned off because of an unusual accident. He could no longer inspire and lead troops; his mutilated face made it mandatory that he be separated from the officer corps.

They took Pfeffer to Kericho and handed him over to Captain Hazelton. He was officially charged with illegal entry and that was enough reason to lock him up. Hazelton was happy with the whole thing; it was lucky, he said, that Thrushwood happened to be hunting in the same area. Most other men would have ignored the German.

They told Hazelton about the slaughter. This would be taken up too, the officer promised, when he was turned over to his own people. There should be laws, more laws to protect the game. Already there was talk of it but nothing had been done.

And so they left Kericho and began the long ride back to their farms. They had done all they could within the law.

A detail of askaris crossed the border and picked up Pfeffer at Kericho. He was taken to Mombasa. The details are vague concerning his time there but it is certain he was not court-martialed. His record, up to the time of his accident, was excellent; he was not to be punished severely. But he must leave Africa.

He was put on the boat, this time under guard. The authorities at Zanzibar and Dar es Salaam were alerted and patrols met the ship. He was on his way to Europe. A patrol met the ship at Kilwa but he was not on it; the ship was searched completely three times and he was not found. It was as if he had vanished into thin air. The officials fumed and patrols fanned out over the city looking for him. The natives nodded to one another and stayed away from dark places. *Bwana sitani* was loose again.

Months passed. Nothing was heard of Pfeffer. Rumors started —he had jumped off the boat during the night and committed suicide; he had tried to swim to shore and the sharks had gotten him. Then even the rumors stopped and people no longer talked about him.

## CHAPTER SIX

HALF a year passed.

Then, from far west in Tanganyika, came a strange tale. Two settlers, recently from the homeland, had arrived in Usambasi with a fortune in ivory and they had sold it to Parashi, the Greek there who dealt in all things. The two men were not hunters. One day by chance they had ridden through a high savanna and found it full of the bones of elephants. And among the bones, they had found the ivory. Some of the skulls appeared to have bullet holes in them. They found one place where a white man had camped, where someone had eaten tinned goods and left a whisky bottle in the grass.

It was a strange story but then Africa is full of them. The authorities at Usambasi arrived at a reasonable explanation: Portuguese hunters had crossed the Mozambique border, eluded the patrol and found the elephant herd. They had surrounded it and killed many of them. But then someone had given a false alarm; something had frightened them away; perhaps they thought the patrol was near. And so they had fled and never returned. An amusing story.

And there were others. A planter named Jacob Zimmler had left his shamba in the hands of his best boy and ridden off to the coast. When he came back, he discovered that his storeroom had been broken into and looted. All his standard ammunition was gone, along with an expensive shotgun and two rifles. There was whisky missing also and tinned stuff. Zimmler whipped the boy and threatened to shoot him but he stuck to his story. He had been at the shamba every night; only a ghost could have slipped in and made off with the missing things—a ghost or a devil.

Zimmler found a strange spoor a couple of miles from the shamba and began following it. A squad of askaris joined him at Yuri and they traveled for two or three days, into the Bijuri Plains. The spoor was getting fresh when a veld fire came at them from two directions and they fled before it, losing the spoor and turning back.

Then there were two Swedish botanists who had come upon hundreds of dead animals in the remote and difficult country around Nsuki Gorge—a strange sight, they said, vultures and jackals everywhere. And two hundred miles south, some Nandi herders claimed to have seen *bwana sitani* again.

There were many stories.

In time they came to John Thrushwood. He listened to all of them in all their forms and questioned and nodded; he heard them over sundowners in Nairobi, from travelers who passed his farm, from natives and officials.

He was not surprised. He knew that Pfeffer was alive; that he would go back to the veld again. It was inevitable. And now he must go again and find the German. Now he would deal with him in his own way. There were no laws to stop Pfeffer, so he must be stopped without law.

Thrushwood left Chapupa to get the horses ready for the ride, to close up the house and sell off some of the stock. And he rode away one morning to see Quinell.

The old hunter was drunk and sleeping. Thrushwood found some coffee and boiled it and got him out of bed.

"Yes, goddamnit, I know all about it," he told Thrushwood. "They let him go and he's back there killing again. And now you again. I knew you'd be here today. Well, I'll tell you right now; I'm not going; I'm not going." He reached carefully for the black coffee, drank it, and groaned.

"We can leave in a day or two," Thrushwood said.

"Go to hell, John," Quinell said. It was a flat and cold state-ment and Thrushwood felt the desperation behind it. He said nothing. He sat and watched Quinell weaving over the coffee. After a while the old hunter began talking, staring into the half-empty mug of coffee.

". . . not going to go, never going back there. What's the god-damn use, John? If you do catch him, he'll kill you and they'll turn him loose anyway. No use, no use, no use. And you know something? You'll kill him if you get the chance. I watched you. I saw you. You'd kill him now. I know, I know. You're as bad as he is. You would murder him now, that's what I think, you would shoot him down in cold blood."

"No," Thrushwood said. "Not in cold blood. But I'll fight him. I'll hunt him and let him hunt me. That's a fair way, Peter; it would be fair like that. I want you to come."

"Hell with it," Quinell said. "You're like he is. You think you can wipe something away; you think you can make your mind forget something by killing him. You know why you hunt him, John? I know; Quinell knows, by Jesus. You and me, John, we're the same kind. Up to a point, anyway . . ."

"What are you talking about?"

"About you," Quinell said thickly. "You and your chasing around after the German. You and me, we're the same, you know; you can't fool an old bastard like me."

"You're drunk," Thrushwood said. "Drink the coffee."

"Pfeffer is a part of us," Quinell said slowly. "He's a part of you and me and all the others who came and killed. He's the part we want to forget; the part of us that killed when it wasn't necessary; the part of us that we're ashamed of. You know what I'm talking about? You're goddamned right you do. That's why we hate him, John, that's why we've got to stop him. He'll drive us mad. He's a part of us out there killing again. The others will never know, will they, John? They think we're heroes, big-game hunters and all that rot. But we know, John, we know. We murdered, we're butchers, too. I can hear them at night sometimes, the elephants most of all; they scream and flap their ears and come at me, all of them that I killed, the whole mass that I slaughtered and left for the vultures. I'm a murdering bastard, too, just like you and Pfeffer and the rest of them. Ivory hunters! They ought to hang the lot of us. And Pfeffer—at least he's open about it. He kills every goddamn thing and doesn't make a fuss over it. You and me, we wanted everybody to look up to us. That's why we hate him. He's the real part of us that we can't hide.

"And I don't care about the animals any more. Why should I? I'm hypocrite enough now, for chrissakes. I'm an old drunken bastard who spent his whole life killing and I'm not going to repent now. An old sinner, old sinner—too late, too late. You, John—Jesus, you're trying to make up for it all. It's too late. Let him kill everything, everything, then maybe the things will go away at night—the goddamn trumpeting of the elephants and the thunder of the hoofs and the beautiful things we killed. Let him make them all go away and then it will be quiet and we can sleep at night. Maybe I'll go and help him, help him exterminate the bastards, shoot them all, all of them." He waved his arm and his elbow hit the coffee and it spilled on the table and ran down over his knees. He cursed and staggered and went over and sat on the dirty bed. There was a bottle on the floor and he picked it up with great care and drank deeply from it.

"You can't forget it," he said. "Go home and leave the man alone. He's nothing, really—nothing. Africa's too big for him, too big. You and me, we built him up in our minds, you know. We're scared of him and hate him, but the others don't care, don't understand, never understand. He's the bad part of us that got loose and went back again to make us live through it all again." He put the bottle on the floor and fell back on the bed. He closed his eyes and tried to pull a frayed blanket over his legs. In a few minutes he was asleep.

Thrushwood's hands were shaking. He was speechless, his throat was dry, and his hands shook uncontrollably. He walked to Quinell's bed and took a long drink from the whisky bottle. The whisky cut the dryness from his throat, burned him. He drank more. He looked down at Quinell and cursed him. Quinell talked too much, had too many wild ideas. He shouldn't drink so much. He should keep his dreams and his crazy thoughts to himself. . . .

He finished the bottle and walked out of the house into the bright sunlight. He found his horse and rode off. They would go without Quinell; he and Chapupa would go alone and they would track the man and kill him.

His destiny was entwined with Pfeffer's. Their lives would run together now until one of them was dead. He would never come back to the farm until Pfeffer was dead. The authorities had failed; they tolerated him.

He wouldn't murder. He would give the man an opportunity to stop; he would track him, irritate him, mobilize others against him. And if he made a fight of it, they would fight and one of them would win. Trial by combat—if Pfeffer killed him, then he was wrong and the slaughter would go on. If he killed, then he was right. He and Pfeffer would make their own laws and operate within them. It was a personal thing now, between the two of them.

Thrushwood urged the horse forward. Now he was a man-hunter. His final game was Man, after two thousand elephants and countless lions and buffaloes and bucks and lesser things—from the Cape to Angola, from the Limpopo to northern Kenya; among the Ovampo and Bechuana and Nandi; from Natal to Lake Ngami when the hunting was good there, when it was a lake that only a few white men had seen.

It would be a slow hunt, a dangerous hunt of waiting and guessing and then more waiting. Long ago down in Portuguese East, he'd spent months tracking elephants in an endless forest that seemed to hold some strange attraction for old solitary bulls, old giants with great scarred tusks of one hundred to one hundred and fifty or sixty pounds apiece. Tusks of such weight were rare now; those days were gone. The big lonely bulls roamed free at night, raiding native plantations with impunity, taking what they wanted with great noise and thrashing about. When the night ended they headed for the deep forest, their great bellies filled and rumbling, their hunger appeased.

The forest was dark and cool and free from bothersome insects. The giants moved slowly here, pushing through the heavy-leafed vegetation, passing, letting the green wall close silently behind them. Here the hunter must be at his best for he is in constant mortal danger. All is quiet. There was no trumpeting herd now, only one solitary patriarch, very old and very wise, a noiseless giant playing a deadly game in the mottled gloom. The hunter follows the spoor ever mindful that the elephant might be back-tracking, waiting close to his own trail to smash with heavy trunk and stomp with foot and knee. The silence blocks out all memory. There is the hunter and his prey and the forest and nothing more. Then a swish of a branch, a sense of great feet cushioned with spongy gristle, moving away. The hunter follows. His throat is too dry, his hands slippery on his puny weapon. Within him there is a curious mixture of fear and joy, of approaching victory and imminent death. The stalk continues. The gloom darkens. Somewhere a strange bird calls out. Evening is coming. The hunter stops, turns back. The forest lord will live another day.

Finding Pfeffer and bringing him to earth would be difficult now. It would take all his skill and stamina and nerve and experience. Pfeffer was a rogue now like the clever bad-tempered bulls in Mozambique so long ago.

## CHAPTER SEVEN

Two days later, John Thrushwood and Chapupa rode off again and left the farm behind. They thought of the first time, when Quinell was with them, when they had been unaccustomed to long rides and the horses fought the packs and saddles. Now, without Quinell, they rode faster, the horses responsive and obedient. There was an urgency that had been lacking on the first ride. They were harder, more dangerous; when night came, they were far beyond the spot where they had first camped.

They went south and crossed the border at Rujifi and felt relief. They were in Tanganyika and all the rumors and stories had placed Pfeffer there, in the west and south-west. Twice in the first day they were stopped by patrols, but Thrushwood's permit was still good and they went on.

Thrushwood wished Quinell were with him, Quinell and others. Pfeffer would be ready for him when they met. He would not be taken without a fight. If they could get help, it would be quicker and easier and safer. Another gun or two . . .

They came upon two husky Nandi spearmen far from home. "We are looking for the white man you call *bwana sitani*," Thrushwood said. "Have you heard where he is now?"

"Far away," they said, "in the mountains close to the lands of the Galli Galli."

"We hunt this man," Thrushwood said. "We will find him and stop the slaughter. Come with us. The Nandi are great warriors, greater than the Zulu, greater than the Matabele. Let the songs tell of your bravery."

But the two men would not join them. They were afraid but they did not speak of it. They were busy with other things; their captain had sent them on a mission; they could not go. . . .

They came to Lake Itumbwa, a beautiful place when it was not hot, a place of water and trees and peace. There was a mission here—a white chapel and a school and other buildings.

Thrushwood left Chapupa with the horses and rode to the top of the rise beyond the chapel, past groups of natives who looked somehow different, cleaner perhaps and more humble. He tied his horse under an old mopane tree and walked to the low building which was the house of the German priest, the only white man in the settlement.

A servant greeted him, a black man with Arab features, who wore a white uniform. The father was sleeping. He would tell the father of the visitor.

Thrushwood waited on the wide veranda. It was pleasant here and it reminded him of his own home. Perhaps he was a fool to go after Pfeffer again.

The German priest came, Father Auerbach, a tall man, middle-aged, bald. They talked for a few minutes about the veranda and the mopane tree and the view and the breeze. Then there was a silence.

"I came to you for help, Father," Thrushwood said. "You have heard of a man called Pfeffer, have you not, the hunter? But of course, everyone knows of him. There are rumors concerning him; stories of how he spends all his time hunting, killing game, killing anything and everything."

The priest nodded. He had heard the rumors.

"I did not believe these stories," Thrushwood continued. "When I heard them I did not believe them, for perhaps I did not want to believe them. In any case, it troubled me and I went and looked for Pfeffer's trail and followed it and knew the rumors were mild compared to his real destructiveness. I saw things that I will not tell you because you will think they are mad dreams. He is all that the rumors and stories make him out to be, Father. I came to you for help. Pfeffer must be stopped."

The priest made a gesture of hopelessness. "But if this man is doing wrong, why do not the authorities stop him? Is this not a matter for the field police—the government—the army perhaps?"

"I have been to the police," Thrushwood said. "And they tell me he has broken no laws. There are no laws to stop a man from killing buck and zebra and buffalo. They are not concerned with a man who stays in the mountains and in the veld and shoots game. They are police. They are interested in native boys who run off with their masters' boots."

"Why do you think this man Pfeffer is so evil?" the priest asked. There was genuine interest in his eyes. Thrushwood ignored the question and completed what he had planned to say.

"The police say he is not a felon. He has harmed no man directly. And the government is far away and they do not care anyway. They are concerned with the English and the railroad and matters of national policy. And the army? They do not care, either. You ask about his evilness. He is a butcher, a mass killer, a fanatic of the worst sort. If he shot a native cutthroat in a dark alley, he would be a murderer, a felon. That is the law. But he liquidates whole herds of springbok and shoots down trapped giraffe and the world shrugs and calls him a hunter. Certainly, Father, you see his evilness. You must help me stop him."

The priest shifted in the deep chair. "Perhaps you exaggerate his badness. This man hunts. You admit he has not harmed other men. This Pfeffer is troubled somehow, filled no doubt with some great guilt or fear or something that cannot be measured. No man is all evil. Perhaps he is trying to expiate something deep within him by living close to danger and with great privation. In time he will see the light and return to the world of men, the world he spurned; he will return to his friends, to Mother Church."

"But you could help him now," Thrushwood said. "Perhaps you are right about him and then you might be wrong. He may stay out there killing and murdering for years. I am going after him. I've got to stop him. Come with me and talk to him. He might listen to you, for I understand that he was once devout and God-fearing. Help him now, Father."

Father Auerbach smiled. "It is out of the question. I am in no position to go off on such a chase, even if I thought it was important. And I do not think so. What would the bishop say? What would become of the mission? We are busy here, bringing God to these heathen people. Our church is in need of repair. Our school must be enlarged. The work of Christ must go on."

"I have caught this man once," Thrushwood said. "And I was able to catch him because he thought I was foolish and faint-hearted, like others who had tried to dissuade him. I caught him in British East and handed him over to the authorities. And what did they do with him? They turned him loose, free, let him go. He does his work now and no one stops him. They pretend he is not there."

"God will punish him if He sees fit," said the priest.

"Nonsense," Thrushwood said. "This man is deranged. You might be able to help him. You might save his life. If I go after him alone, I may have to kill him."

"*Kill* him?"

"Yes," Thrushwood said. "I may be forced to shoot him."

"You joke now," Father Auerbach said.

"I do not joke. How else can this terrible thing be stopped? No one seems to see this man as I see him. I do not believe in devils, Father, even your devil with horns and tail and pointed ears. But if I am wrong and there is a devil, then it is Pfeffer. Perhaps you sense this, too, and shrink from him like all the others."

Father Auerbach struggled in the deep chair and got to his feet. He was flushed with anger.

"Go now. I have heard enough of your blasphemy. I have work to do here. I cannot waste time with men who have turned their back on God and then ask the Church to help them in their follies. If this man Pfeffer is evil, he will be punished in the hereafter. Go now, please." He turned and went into the house.

And Thrushwood left and walked out into the bright sunlight across the hard-packed ground to the tree where his horse waited. He was not angry. He had expected nothing and he had received nothing, but he felt better now. He had done all he could do. He and Chapupa would have to stop Pfeffer; two old men where a score of young men would not be too many.

Chapupa was waiting for him. As they rode away, the bell in the whitewashed chapel began ringing.

Time passed. Days went on and became weeks and Pfeffer was always far away somewhere in a different direction than they had thought. It seemed as if the German was aware of them; that he was leaving a difficult trail. And once they did cross an old spoor that looked like his, but it led them to a river. Chapupa tried to pick it up while Thrushwood rode to a village and heard that the German was to the east. A heavy rainstorm cost them another week of aimless circling on a vast plain thick with thorn. And Thrushwood was almost killed there by a rogue water buffalo that came at him from behind. He fired twice, twisting in the saddle, and the animal fell, burying its heavy horns in the earth.

And once they stopped and rested themselves and the horses for two days because they had become limp with exhaustion. They came upon a cool savanna and found a cliff from which a spring flowed. They spent the time eating and sleeping. They must catch the German, but their own strength came first. They had to care for themselves.

They rode on.

"We are old men," Chapupa said to Thrushwood one night, "old men who have seen much and marvelled at the world when it was young. I was a slave once, in Zanzibar, and that was long ago; yet I can remember the bones of the dead in the harbor bottom, white and with a certain beauty; bones of those who died and were thrown overboard to the fishes. It was there that I learned much of the world, of medicine and other secrets of the Arab; I saw the traveler there, Stamlee, a man of great things, quick and with eyes like a lion. And I saw the dhows from Hindustan and Masqat and worked for a time in a great merchant's house. And then I came back, for I had seen too much of the Arab and I grew sick for the sight of my own people."

"Yes," Thrushwood said. The sight of his own people . . . He watched the fire for a time. The day's ride had tired him. Two old men they were, as Chapupa said, two old men on a last great ride, hunting the greatest game of all. It was a last great journey for them into the old Africa of their youth. *The sight of his own people* . . . And who were they? He had tarried too long here to be English, true English. He was something else now and his real land was Africa, not the neat hills and hedges of England. His land was the Zambezi when the tribes had never seen a white man; and the Karroo and the edges of the Kalahari, the Great Thirst; East Africa before they drew the boundaries and brought in soldiers to watch each other. And his people were the good people he had known, most of them black, for he had known only a handful of white men until he was forty. The Bechuana and Masai and the humble people along the Zambezi and Fish River. These were his people.

He was tired. He left the fire and checked his horses and wrapped himself in his blanket. He fell asleep watching the fire play on the dull-gray skin of Chapupa, who sat staring into it.

Pfeffer's trail passed through the country of the Galli Galli, a people much like the Nandi but not as warlike. They owned great herds of cattle and like the Masai and others drank milk and blood. Twenty years before, Thrushwood had spent time with them and hunted lion with their chief, Egon Do.

Thrushwood and Chapupa came upon boys herding cattle.

"We seek *bwana sitani* and follow his spoor. And I seek your kraals. Which way, Lion Killers?"

The boys pretended to be men and told what they knew. Pfeffer had ridden through them but the game was scarce, for the land was tribal grazing land. In one spot he had killed some waterbuck, in another, four wildebeest.

"We shall visit your chief," Thrushwood told them, riding off. "The great Egon Do."

"He is dead," the boys cried. "Egon Do is long dead. Now Manga is our chief. Manga!"

They talked with Manga.

"We hunt a man," Thrushwood said when they sat before him in the big shamba, "a German. Some call him *bwana sitani*, others know him as the Faceless One. His name is Pfeffer. He has passed this way and he is mad. We must catch him, for he kills all things in his path and will one day destroy the world."

"We know of him," Manga said. "My warriors will show you his spoor."

"His spoor is our path," Thrushwood said. "We know it. I have come to seek a favor from the chief of the Galli Galli, from the great Manga whom all know to be virtuous and brave, greater even than Egon Do. I ask for ten warriors to help me catch this man. He is near and it would not be difficult with men of the Galli Galli, men of the spear."

"Why do you hunt this white man?" Manga asked.

"He is a bad man. He shoots all animals that he sees."

"He does not kill cattle," Manga said.

"No. Not cattle. But all else. All but the carrion birds."

"He kills men?" Manga asked.

"No," Thrushwood said. "If he killed men, the police would seek him and take him away and later he would die. Such is our law, as Manga knows. It is much like that of the Galli Galli."

"But what has the Faceless One done then that you hunt him?" Manga asked. He was a young man and had great dignity.

"He kills animals," Thrushwood said.

"All men kill animals."

"But he kills *all* animals."

"He is a white man and a hunter and this is not strange. You, too, are a hunter and have killed much. We know of John Thrushwood. As a boy I heard great tales of your killing."

They talked for an hour more and Thrushwood told him of Pfeffer's past, of the leopard and the loss of his face. And he told of the killing, the terrible day at the ravine, the veld fires, and the relentless slaughter that went on and on. At length Manga agreed that the German was evil. He should be stopped. Thrushwood sat back and rested.

"Then you will help me catch him," he stated.

"No," Manga said. "I can give you no warriors. We are men of the cattle. We do not hunt. We grow strong on the blood and milk of our cattle. The Faceless One would kill my warriors. He would shoot them and my people would grow angry and call me a bad chief."

"No," Thrushwood said. "We would catch him and the people would sing of your wisdom and bravery."

"This is white man's quarrel," Manga said.

"No, this concerns all men," said Thrushwood.

"If I gave you warriors, the police and the army would come to me and ask me why I hunted white men. They might take me away, exile me from my people and my homeland. Or they might tax me more and steal what few cattle the Galli Galli have. All this I see."

"Perhaps you are right," Thrushwood said. "I should not have asked you. I swore once that I would stop this man and already I have wasted too much time seeking others to do what I have set out to do. Once I saw thousands of dead animals choking the mouth of a ravine and it was the work of this faceless man and I swore in my heart to stop him. I shall go now, Manga. His spoor grows cold and his rifle eats lives while I palaver."

"You will catch him," Manga said. "All know you as the greatest of the hunters. If you cannot stop him alone, then you could not do it with a few warriors. In the end it will be your gun against his."

"Yes," Thrushwood said, getting up. "You are young, Manga, but you are a great chief; you do not play with the lives of your people. You are right. In the end it will be my gun against his. The others do not matter. I go now."

They left Manga's kraal and rode off. Soon they were on Pfeffer's trail again and they rode hard until it was too dark to see it. They made camp and another day ended.

Pfeffer, Chapupa estimated, was three days away.


## CHAPTER EIGHT

PFEFFER watched the riders through his army binoculars and nodded to himself. It was the Englishman, John Thrushwood, and his boy. Thrushwood was the only man who had ever tricked him, bested him, and gotten away with it. Thrushwood had cost him six months in the jails and courtrooms and the cities. And the Englishman had said he would come back and stop him, kill him if necessary.

He must not lose his temper; he must not let his hatred for the old hunter run wild, for if it did, the Englishman would win. He must be clever and win; if he lost he would be dead, for Thrushwood had promised that, or he'd be dragged back again to Tanga or Dar es Salaam, and this time they'd deport him in chains.

Thrushwood was a dangerous man. He was old but he was the best marksman in Africa. It would not be wise to get within range of his rifle. And the old man, his boy—he, too, was dangerous, a fair shot with a Mannlicher and with the tracking instincts of a Bushman. It would be best to stay far away from him, too, especially at night, for in the night he was an animal who could move without noise and kill expertly with an arrow or knife or assagai.

But Pfeffer had some advantages. He was younger and stronger. He could choose when and where to fight. He could lead them into traps. He could throw them off his spoor and slip away and wear them down. He could do many things, but he must be very careful, for Thrushwood needed but one clear shot at him; once the Englishman had him in his sights, he was a dead man.

He hurried back to his horses and worked his way down the plateau. He was lucky. Thrushwood was two or three hours away, dangerously close, but it did not worry him, for he *knew*. And the Englishman did not know that he knew.

He came at last to the place where he had swung off and ridden up the plateau. He rode on a few dozen yards and then dismounted and came back. He brushed away the spoor that led upwards to the high plateau and then carefully threw handfuls of pebbles and grass over it. His pursuers, riding fast, might not notice it.

He rode on faster. A gazelle studied him at two hundred yards and he pulled up and killed it. He would lead Thrushwood on, but he was armed with the knowledge that they followed. If he kept moving, he would be safe. Two hours later, he switched horses. The country was featureless, stony, and flat, with little grass, its old ridges worn and shapeless. But ahead the land fell off, became marshy and then merged into a great swamp. Pfeffer kicked the horse. He could lose Thrushwood in the swamp for a time and gain a day or two. He needed time, time to plan how best to kill the two who tracked him.

Two waterbuck appeared to his left. He fired as they sprang away and one of them went down.

Thrushwood and Chapupa followed the trail until darkness came; then they made a fireless camp in the center of a clump of mopane trees. They were close to Pfeffer; too close to have a fire and too close to fire a shot. Tomorrow they would be close enough to leave his spoor and circle it. Then he could be ambushed.

It began to rain.

Pfeffer was awake instantly. He was on the edge of the swamp and Thrushwood was somewhere behind him; close, but not as close as Thrushwood probably figured. He, too, had ridden hard until night came.

And now it was raining. . . .

He rolled up his bed and in the darkness gathered the few things that he unpacked each night, then rode off. He searched his mind for the details of the land through which he had ridden and swung his horse northward. Soon the ground became firmer. He moved away from the swamp and began to circle back in the direction he had come. The rain grew heavier; it fell on the trail he left and washed it away.

The rain had come at the right time. In the early morning

Thrushwood would begin to follow his spoor through the heavy soil of the lowland. The rain would have blurred but not destroyed it. Then, as the land merged into water, as the swamp became dominant, he would be forced to slow down and feel forward slowly, searching for broken reeds, fresh leaves floating in stagnant water, dead branches freshly broken.

But then the trail would leave the swamp, leave the heavy vulnerable growth, the thick underbrush through which two horses couldn't move without leaving a trail. The spoor would lead to drier ground, with little vegetation. Soon it would vanish completely. Thrushwood would stop. He would grow impatient, angry. His tracker would not be able to find the spoor. There would be no spoor.

Pfeffer moved ahead steadily. Rain was rare in Tanganyika. Thrushwood had almost caught him and had been only hours away. Now, with luck, he would be able to put a week's ride between them.

Thrushwood and Chapupa lost five days because of the rain. When Pfeffer's spoor vanished, they halted and camped under a thick baobab. There was nothing to be gained by wearing the horses out in a fruitless search while the ground was still wet and difficult. They slept. They made a small fire and dried more wood and sat around the big fire and ate all the cooked meat they could hold. If Pfeffer was gaining time, they and their animals would gain strength. It rained all day.

When the rain grew too light to wash away his trail, Pfeffer halted and made camp. Thrushwood and the native might have trapped him in the swamp or in the flatland if he had tried to double back.

He ate and slept and rode off at dawn. He must find a place now for his trackers, a place where he could deal with them with little risk to himself.

He rode on. Two days later, he came to a wide river. The current was strong but not overpowering, and he made his way across it slowly, carefully. If he lost his balance here, if the horse slipped or panic gripped it, they might be swept away downstream. He would wait and catch Thrushwood here, in the middle of the swollen river. He saw it in his mind: the two old men with their horses deep in the swirling water. Then, from somewhere unseen, rifle fire. He might be lucky and kill the Englishman with his first shot; in any case, it would be close enough to kill or panic his horse. They would be trapped there in the river, unable to advance or retreat, unable to fight back.

It would be the end of Thrushwood and the old native.

Thrushwood and Chapupa approached the river. Far away, on the other side of it, vultures were circling—five miles away.

Pfeffer's trail vanished into the water.

They sat for a time studying the river, its wideness, the power of its current, and the broken country beyond. They were both uneasy. If Pfeffer was planning an ambush, a showdown, this would be a good place. But they had to cross the river. They could investigate and delay and postpone, but they had to cross.

Thrushwood turned his horse and rode downstream. There wasn't much they could do but choose their own way across it, not follow Pfeffer's spoor. He came to one place and halted; the river was narrower here but the current was swifter. He rode on and some minutes later found a place that looked safe. Chapupa came and they studied it together. They checked the animals and the packs and started across.

The current was stronger than it looked. They each led a pack animal and soon there was only the water and the slippery rocks underfoot and the horses under them, nervous and hard to handle.

A rifle fired somewhere and before the echo of it was gone Thrushwood was underwater, fighting loose from his dying horse, cringing from the thrashing legs. He clawed for the light and the air above and after a time he came to the surface and was swept away downstream.

Chapupa was thrown by his horse as it reared in fright and then struggled to the bank they had left. Pfeffer fired and the horse thrashed in the shallow water. One of the pack animals bolted and slipped and was swept away. The remaining horse quietly made its way to the far bank, shook itself and began to nibble on the new grass.

Pfeffer fired at what he thought was Chapupa's head bobbing in the swirling water but the distance was too great to be sure. He got up from his prone position and hurried to his animals. He rode to the horse that stood nibbling and within a few minutes he rode off again, leading it with his own pack animal. He rode upstream, driving the horse until he was many miles from the place of ambush.

It had been a magnificently executed attack. Thrushwood might be dead; and the native might be dead. If they lived, they had no horses; one, perhaps, if they were lucky. He had smashed them with no risk to himself and even taken one of their pack animals and the goods that it carried. He could have ridden downstream and hunted them but there was the slight possibility that Thrushwood might be there in the thickets somewhere with a rifle, or a revolver, waiting for him—or the native. The old man bragged of his poisons and he might be waiting with an assagai.

It was best to run. Hit and run with no risk to himself or his animals. It had been a fine ambush.

Thrushwood did not struggle in the water; he did not try to swim to either bank. The water took him and swept him along and he did not fight it for it carried him away from danger, from Pfeffer, who might even now be riding downstream to make sure he was dead, to find him sodden and helpless on the bank and shoot him. He floated in the water and after a time caught a small tree trunk and hung on to it.

Pfeffer had outwitted him and he deserved to die. Pfeffer had *known* that he would not cross the river where the trail led into it and he had *known* that his pursuers would cross where they did. He had led them into a beautiful ambush. He and Chapupa deserved to die.

Chapupa—there was no sign of him. He was dead then, with the horses, and everything was lost. And John Thrushwood, the great hunter, was alone in unknown territory without a gun or a horse. He would die now; there was a good chance of it. If he had left the river and struck out across the unknown, he wouldn't have one chance in a hundred of living. There was only one way to travel: with the river. There would be water and small things to eat, things he would kill with a stick or a rock. He could survive that way and hope that the river would carry him to a native village or some settlement.

He hung onto the tree trunk. The river carried him away.

Chapupa came up for air and a bullet hit the water near him. He went under again and let the current take him. Thrushwood was not dead; the first bullet had hit his horse, so he, too, was drifting downstream or swimming underwater to escape Pfeffer.

Chapupa came up again. The water had carried him a long distance. He began to swim for the opposite bank, the bank that they were heading for when Pfeffer struck. He swam and let the current take him and at last he reached shallow water and the bank beyond. Pfeffer might come this way; he might follow the river and hope to find Thrushwood weak and half-drowned.

The old man crawled into the reeds and rested. The growth along this side of the river was thick and afforded good cover: high ferns and reeds and dense swamp bush. He hoped the German would come this way searching. He was old but he could follow close behind the horses, undetected, like a mamba. And then in the night he would slither to the German as he slept and drive a stake into his heart.

He lay flat in the reeds, resting—waiting. . . .

When Thrushwood could no longer trust his strength, he kicked and paddled until the tree trunk that he held touched the bank. He lay in the grass for an hour. He was all alone now and he would die fast if he did not think, if he overtaxed himself.

He slept. The sun burned down on the river and the lush growth that grew along its banks. The river was wider here, the current slower; there was swamp growth along the banks, high reeds and heavy clumps of grass and mangrove. It would be a place of alligators and snakes and perhaps hippos.

Thrushwood opened his eyes and lay for a while listening. At last he got to his feet and walked away from the river. He did not worry about Pfeffer. If the German had planned to hunt him down, he would have found him before this; he had probably ridden off, satisfied with the damage he had inflicted, not sure that the man he had tried to kill was helpless and unarmed.

Thrushwood pushed through the reeds and high grass and in time came out of the undergrowth into flat grassy parks, broken by thorn trees. He went on and came at last to a towering tamboti tree which stood alone on a rise. He found footholds in the trunk and began to climb it. When he could go no farther, he stopped and studied the landscape. There was no sign of life or settlement; the river rolled on and far away the ground seemed lower and the growth thicker. Away from the river the ground rose and became drier and rockier. Far away there were mountains.

He would stay with the river.

He climbed down the big tree and rested for a time in the shade underneath. A slight breeze came from the river, bringing with it the sound of birds and the good smell of water.

He stood up and stretched, and began walking back to the river. If he could find two or three good logs and somehow lash them together, he could make a raft and float down the river in comparative safety. Sooner or later he would come across a native village or a known trail; it was a matter of time and the faster he traveled, the better his chances would be.

He walked along, his mind filled with the details of his situation and the elements of survival.

Then behind him he heard the snort of a buffalo; he whirled and saw a huge water buffalo standing near the tall tree he had climbed; standing with nose in the air tossing its horns, angry that it had come upon the spoor of man.

Thrushwood ran. Behind him the buffalo lowered its great head, shook its scimitar horns and charged. There was just time for him to reach one of the thorn trees which stood alone in the grass. He ran and swung into it, grabbing wildly at the thin branches.

The buffalo stopped and came close to the tree and looked up at him. Then it began circling the tree, pawing the ground and tossing its wide horns, daring him to descend. The sun was high, burning down without mercy, and Thrushwood knew that he would die now, that he would never make it downriver. After all the danger he had been close to, he would die sitting in a tree or under the hoofs of the buffalo. If he stayed in the tree, he would die of thirst and madness; or in a sudden lunge the animal would pull him down like a ripe fruit. One thing was certain: the buffalo would never leave until one of these things had happened. In all Africa there was no animal with the combined intelligence and stamina of the buffalo—the viciousness.

Thrushwood pulled his legs higher in the tree. Without warning, the dead branches cracked and he clutched wildly. With uncanny speed the buffalo lunged and one of the heavy horns brushed his foot, almost pulling him to the ground. In the next instant, he swung himself higher. The buffalo stood, its great chest heaving, staring up at him, its nose wrinkling with his scent. Then it charged the tree head on. The shock almost threw him from his perch, and as the tree swayed from the impact, he cursed bitterly. Backing off a few yards, the buffalo charged again and, as it hit the tree, Thrushwood felt new roots breaking beneath him. The small tree now leaned dangerously, bringing him closer to the ground, closer to the terrible horns. He shifted his weight and the tree leaned back a few inches; if any more roots broke, the tree would most certainly go down, aided by his own weight. The buffalo charged again but he heaved his body toward the onrushing animal so that his weight and that of the tree acted as ballast against the force. The hammerlike blow came, but the tree held. The buffalo backed off and looked up at him and then circled the tree and began to graze on the lush grass. It pretended to forget him.

He relaxed. His head was hot. He was going to die and it really didn't seem to matter. Chapupa was dead and Pfeffer was alive and nobody seemed to care. Pfeffer would go on and destroy Africa and nobody would notice until it was too late.

The buffalo came back and lay in the shade under the tree. Flies gathered on its great black body. It was big—when it stood up, its shoulders were nearly five feet from the ground. Its horn spread was over four feet.

He sat in the tree and began to plot his escape. He was starting to go mad, a part of his mind told him; the sun was getting to him and the thirst and the fear. By night-time he might be raving and in the morning he would be dead.

He thought of running. He had a vision of himself running to the swamp and losing the buffalo in the reeds, escaping into the river. But he knew this was fantasy: before he could take a dozen strides, the bull would be in back of him, running without effort, and it would toss him high in the air and then do terrible things to him with its horns and its hoofs and its knees. It was an awful way to die.

He thought of using his knife. He would leap upon the animal as it lay resting, and in a flurry of stabbing he would blind it and then run to safety. This, too, he knew was suicide. No man anywhere could fight twelve hundred pounds of crazed buffalo with a hunting knife and live. There was no way out.

He shifted his position in the tree. The buffalo was lying in the shade a few yards below him. He knew every wrinkle and seam in the great black body, every expression of the eyes, and he hated it now with fanatical passion. Suddenly he found himself shouting at it.

It was a mistake, he realized too late. The buffalo was on its feet in sudden wrath, pawing the ground and snorting. It scraped the bark of the tree aimlessly with its great horns for some minutes and then suddenly planted its horn-encased forehead against the slim trunk and began to push. The tree began to rock, gently at first, but then, as the animal persisted, digging its hoofs into the soil and raging against the tree, the swaying increased.

Thrushwood shifted his position and swung his body, trying

to break the force, but he realized that the momentum was building up. Now his own weight was pitted against him. Panic seized him as he felt new roots breaking, and now the tree swung each time closer to the ground, within reach of the buffalo. Soon the last of the surface roots would break and the tree would go down. It would be over—the waiting and the terror would be over.

Suddenly the buffalo stopped and walked away to graze. It went to the swamp and drank deeply. Then it returned to the tree and rested in the shade. The day was almost over.

Chapupa saw the vultures and studied them. They circled, gliding in great circles, then fell from view. Something was dying or had died. The carrion birds would swoop down and sit in a circle around a dying animal. They would draw closer. Others would glide down from the sky and flop on the ground and join the circle of death. They would fight among themselves and then, as they grew bolder, they would dart in and attack their prey. And the jackal would come and the hyena and what they left the ants would feed on—the cracked bones, the hide, the heavy skull.

It might be Thrushwood.

Chapupa began trotting towards the vultures. They were miles away but close to the river and on the same bank. It would be night soon, and it was best that he see what the vultures had found. It might be Thrushwood sitting inside a circle of carrion birds fighting them off with a stick or throwing stones at them. And it might be Thrushwood dead and dismembered by the filthy birds.

All day he had followed the river. Now and then he would stop and call out for Thrushwood, listen for an answer and then go on. There was no danger of meeting Pfeffer; he had made sure of that. He had lain for two hours in the reeds waiting for the German. Then he had crawled upstream and found the spot where the surviving horse had stood and grazed. But there were other tracks, showing that the German had come quickly, taken the horse and led it off with his own. He followed the spoor for a time and it led upstream, away from the spot where they had been ambushed. It was a wise thing for the German to do. Chapupa had turned back then and begun searching for Thrushwood, making his way along the bank, calling out, listening for an answer.

But there had been no sign of the white man.

He trotted on. If Thrushwood was alive, they would go to a settlement somewhere and get horses and guns and go after the German again. If Thrushwood was dead, he would go back and follow the spoor, kill the German in his own manner.

He came to open country, savanna and thorn trees. He trotted on along the edge of the river, which was swampy, with high reeds and fern and clumps of grass growing out of the water.

He came upon Thrushwood's spoor.

It came out of the water, out of the reeds and headed away from the river, through the high grass. He followed it and then far away, where the ground was higher, he saw something in a tree. He drew closer and saw that it was John Thrushwood, high in the branches of a small thorn tree, his head slumped forward on his chest, unmoving. Buffalo. There was a buffalo near him, under the tree, a great black beast that kept him in the tiny tree and would never leave it until he was dead.

Chapupa sat down in the grass and rested. He was happy. He had found John Thrushwood. He would kill the buffalo and they would catch the German. But first he would rest; he was old and he would rest, for there was nothing he could do until night came. He got up and moved carefully away; he waded into the swamp along the edge of the river, destroying his spoor. He found a small piece of solid ground covered with tall reeds. There was a tiny blade in one of the leather pouches he wore around his neck. He took it and cut one of the reeds down. He sat down and cut a section from it as long as his arm. He searched for a tiny round pebble and then pushed it through the soft, pulpy center of the reed again and again until the inside was as smooth and clean as the barrel of a rifle. He placed it carefully in the light where it would dry evenly. He got up and wandered through the shallow water and found at last a tiny hardwood seedling, straight and supple. He cut it down carefully and brought it back to the solid ground he had found. He cut a three-inch section from it, peeled off the skinlike bark. He took the long tube and dropped the tiny shaft into the hole. It slid down halfway and stopped. Chapupa put the tube to his mouth and blew into it with sudden force. The shaft came out the other end. He did this several times until he was positive that there were no flaws in the hollow tube.

Now, from the other bag that hung around his neck, he took a tiny needlelike bone. Half of it was dark with a hard, gumlike substance—a poison of great potency made from the sap of a secret tree combined with the natural poisons of spiders and snakes and decayed flesh—a Bushman poison. The other half of the needle was clean and he pushed this end into the center of the seedling and examined it at length. A tiny poisoned assagai; a mortal spear—he would kill the buffalo with it.

He made another dart without a poisoned head, a dart from the same seedling. He practised blowing it through the hollow reed. After a time he was satisfied. The light was fading fast and the night things were growing impatient in the swamp. He fitted the poison dart into the reed and put it aside. He curled up in the reeds and fell asleep in a few moments.

In the dead of night his eyes opened. He got up and removed his cloth, his precious bags, and placed them on the ground. From one of the bags he took a pinch of white powder and sprinkled it on his belongings: it would keep them safe from any animal. He scooped up some swamp muck and rubbed it over his body, over his head, and then he picked up the blowgun and waded into the swamp. He made his way to the bank and followed Thrushwood's spoor for a time. Then he left it and approached the tree down-wind. He came upon fresh buffalo dung in the grass and rubbed it over himself, mixed it in with the swamp muck.

He began to crawl on his hands and knees, the reed between his teeth. When he got within a hundred yards of the tree, he began to slither, moving forward without noise through the grass. He raised his head carefully. Thrushwood hung in the branches of the thorn tree. He had belted himself to one of the branches and he looked unconscious. The buffalo was under the tree, resting with its head up. He rippled his heavy skin and tossed his head to rid himself of the flies, wheezed and flicked his ears to keep them away from the tender spots around his eyes and deep in his ears. Chapupa moved forward like a snake; only an accident could give him away to the great black beast. If the animal decided to get up and walk in his direction, he was a dead man, but otherwise he was safe. He had no scent except that of the buffalo. He would make no noise to startle the animal. He was quite safe in the darkness.

He changed his direction slightly so that he approached the buffalo from the side. The animal snorted again, tossed his head but did not get up. Chapupa slid closer, to the edge of the circle of raw earth that the animal's hoofs had chopped into the veld. He was ten feet from the buffalo. Some of the flies left the buffalo and came to him, clustering on his face, stinging the tender spots they found on his naked, dung-smeared body. But he did not feel the stings, for his mind concentrated wholly on watching the buffalo and aiming his reed. He took it from his teeth and worked it through a clump of grass directly in front of him, put the end in his mouth.

The flies settled again on the buffalo's head. Now Chapupa's body was one rigid extension of the reed and the reed moved ever so slightly, the needlelike dart following each motion of the giant head. Soon now, any instant . . .

The buffalo tossed his head, shook it and twitched his great ears. And for an instant they were open, vulnerable. The tiny dart flew inside like a twig falling from the tree above. It bit into the tender ear and the buffalo grunted and shook his head with added violence. The seedling shaft fell from the ear and tickled no longer. But the shaft of bone remained, the blade of bone daubed with poison.

Chapupa backed away. This was difficult, but his memory was such that he knew the position of each clump of grass, each loose stone, each dry stick. After a long time, he rose to his knees and crawled the rest of the way into the swamp. He washed off the dung and went back to the place where he had left his possessions and fell asleep instantly.

Dawn came quietly—red streaks in the gray-white sky, then the yellow orb of the sun above the jagged horizon. Thrushwood groaned and fought something that troubled him, something that dug into his leg again and again. . . .

He opened his eyes. The buffalo was still there, heavy and black, but now a little black man stood on top of it and poked up at him with the shaft of a spear. He closed his eyes and wondered what he would see next. The prodding was still there. He opened his eyes. The wizened little native was still there, standing on top of the buffalo. It was Chapupa.

"Come down," he said. "The buffalo is dead."

Thrushwood examined the animal and it seemed true. He tried to speak but no words came out of his throat, from his swollen tongue. He tried to undo the belt and after a long while he got it loose. He moved and then slipped and grabbed a branch. It broke and he fell to the ground. It was soft from the sharp hoofs of the buffalo and still cool from the night. Blood tingled strangely in his legs. It was all a dream, a mad dream. . . .

The old native lifted his head and poured some water into his mouth. It was strange and it hurt, but he wanted more of it. He reached for the gourd, but the old man took it away and then poured it over his head. He tried to speak and then gave up. High in the sky above him were vultures. There were always vultures. . . .

He remembered nothing more.

## CHAPTER NINE

PFEFFER rode north for three days, shooting from the saddle; he drifted westward. He spotted a leopard one morning and spent the rest of the day stalking it until it retreated into a narrow cave halfway up a rocky *kopje*. He fired into the cave but the animal did not stir; he threw rocks; he called to it to come forth and it did not. At last, when the sun began to go down, he climbed down and rode off, putting several miles between himself and the animal. He had a fear that it would come to him in the night and he did not sleep soundly. In the morning he returned to the cave. He carried a bag filled with dry veld grass, tightly packed. In the center of the bag was an old shirt, wrapped carefully around twenty shotgun shells.

The leopard was still in the cave. He had shot at it several times and although there was no blood spoor leading into the cave, it was possible that the animal carried a bullet. Pfeffer found a safe position to the side of the cave opening, scratched a match to the rock and set fire to the large bag of grass. He swung it a few times and the flames leaped from it. He tossed it deep into the cave and heard the leopard spit and back away. He held his rifle ready but he did not expect the cat to cross the fire to escape. It probably backed away into the deepest fissure of the cave, hating the fire but not able to get past it.

The fire reached the shells. They began to explode in every direction, pellets everywhere, and then the leopard rolling out of the cave, clawing at the shale, dying from a hundred wounds. Pfeffer shot it through the head. Smoke poured out of the cave and inside shells still exploded as the fire touched them. He backed away and down the slippery slope and rode off. The leopard did not live that he could not track and kill.

He came to Mitati. It was a poor settlement of a few stores and a few officials and a few-score natives. Nothing happened in

Mitati now. Once it had been an Arab settlement, a stopover for the slave caravans that came winding in from the west headed for the coast. It had been an army post for a time when the Germans first came. Now it dozed in the sun, stagnant and without hope.

Pfeffer did not ride into the settlement. He never did. He camped five miles away and when it grew dark he took his rifle and walked to it. He found the main store and in the darkness located the back door and knocked carefully. In time footsteps came. An Indian peered through a crack in the door, which was still held by a chain. And then the muzzle of a great dog came through the crack and it began to growl deep in its throat; it was the growl of a large and dangerous dog. The Indian spoke to it. The growl lost some of its ferocity.

Pfeffer spoke to the store-owner in German.

"I want to buy things from you. I am Pfeffer, the hunter, and I need ammunition and a rifle or two and other necessities. I am in a hurry and do not choose to have others know that I have been here. Let me in."

The Indian hesitated. This was the man they all talked of, the officer who had lost his face to a leopard and had turned to hunt all things. A dangerous man to anger, an armed man who might set fire to his store and vanish into the night if he was not satisfied.

The door opened and Pfeffer entered. The quarters smelled like all Indian shacks and stores and he detested it. The storekeeper spoke to the dog again and it retreated into the corner and lay down, a rumble still in its throat. Pfeffer studied the dog. It was a huge black animal, heavy in the shoulders, big-boned and well muscled. The eyes were yellowish and alert; the teeth sharp and white. The dog did not belong here: it belonged on a farm or in the open, running free.

"The dog is very vicious," said the shopkeeper. "He is always in the store here with me."

"He does not belong here," Pfeffer said. "He is not one to sit and wait and wag his tail. He is a fighter."

"He guards my store," said the Indian. "The store and me."

"I could use a dog such as that," Pfeffer said. "Perhaps I shall buy him from you."

The Indian smiled nervously. "He is not for sale, sir. All else in the store is for buying, but not my dog."

"There is a price for everything," Pfeffer said. "What do you call the dog?"

"There is no name for him. He has none," the Indian said.

"I need ammunition," Pfeffer said, "boxes of it, and it must be brought to my camp, which is five miles from here. I have three pack horses and I want them loaded with ammunition and the other things I shall buy. I need clothing and a heavy rifle, shotgun shells and matches, a good pair of boots. Let us go into the store-room now and I shall show you the things you will bring. I shall pay half of the amount now and the rest when the purchases are brought to my camp. No one must know of my coming and my buying. You will tell no one. Do you understand?"

"I understand," the Indian said. "I shall send mules to you tomorrow night, packed with your goods. A trusted servant shall lead them to your camp. You will draw a map of it before you go."

"And I shall take the dog with me," Pfeffer said.

"He is not for sale, sir," the Indian said. He was nervous.

"I will pay you in ivory," Pfeffer said. "Have a servant follow me when I go. I ride to the west, to the Makorikori Bush, where the great herds are. Let him follow me by one day's ride and he will find in my spoor the ivory of elephants I have shot. When he has the tusks of twenty elephants he will turn and follow me no longer."

"The dog is yours, sir, and you are generous. I need him but the lure of wealth is greater."

"The dog does not like you," Pfeffer said.

"He likes no man," said the merchant. "Let me tell you of him so that you may know his character. He is a sheep-killer and his owner was going to shoot him when I was at his farm. He will attack strangers and kill other dogs. He needs a stout chain and a heavy whip. He is a rogue, a pariah; do not trust him with calves or with black men. He is a killer."

"Yes," Pfeffer said. "He is a killer."

"Do you know a man called Thrushwood?"

"Yes, the hunter," said the Indian.

"Is he mad?"

"No, not mad. A great elephant hunter."

"When did you last see him?"

"Many years ago, sir."

"Here?"

"No, sir, in a village near the coast."

"Do you know my name?"

"Yes, you are Pfeffer. John Thrushwood seeks you."

"How do you know this?"

The Indian shrugged. "It is known."

"What else do you know about John Thrushwood? Is he in these parts?"

"I have heard nothing about him, sir. It is the truth. . . ."

Later, when Pfeffer had chosen all the things he would buy, he went to the dog and talked to it. It growled and bared its teeth and he cuffed it. The Indian drew back in fear; he had never hit it. The animal growled and Pfeffer spoke to it sharply. He took a heavy chain from the wall and fitted it to the dog's collar. The big animal sniffed his boots, his pants, smelled the veld and the horses and the freedom. It stood up and became impatient. Pfeffer studied the merchant's figures and paid half of it with the coin and paper scrip of three governments.

"If soldiers or police come to my camp instead of your servant bearing my goods, I shall be angry," Pfeffer said. "I shall elude them and seek you out."

"I shall tell no one," said the Indian. He looked at Pfeffer's face and knew that it would be in his dreams for a long time. This was not a man to cheat; he was like the dog.

Pfeffer left and went down the dark alley and out into the open country. The dog followed him, light and obedient on the end of the chain. A dog like this would be worth keeping, an extra pair of eyes and a nose for approaching danger. No man or leopard could get him now while he slept; if Thrushwood or his tracker were alive and on his trail, they would have to deal with the dog, too. It would be no trouble. He would train it to hunt.

When he got back to his camp, he tied it to a tree and gave it a rich piece of zebra and a tinful of water. It wolfed down the meat and drank all of the water. He gave it more meat and water and then went to bed. The Indian would not betray him to the police. If anyone came close, the dog would warn him.

## CHAPTER TEN

THRUSHWOOD was feverish for two days and it left him weak; his legs were not strong under him and the sun gave him headaches and made him dizzy. Chapupa would not allow him to leave the camp and the shade of the tree. He set snares and traps and brought in partridge and waterfowl and they ate well and grew strong. But Thrushwood was impatient; each day Pfeffer got farther away and his spoor grew colder; each day there was a new slaughter. In the night he had dreams of Pfeffer, saw him riding relentlessly through the land killing all that he saw. He had to get Pfeffer; he was obsessed with the one thought of stopping him.

When he grew strong, he and Chapupa set to work building a raft. They searched the river bank and located three big logs. They found vine, hundreds of feet of it, and lashed the logs together. They experimented and found that with poles they could keep it under control and choose their own course.

When they were finished, they rested a day, eating and sleeping, and in the early morning they left and began floating downstream, two men, half-naked, squatting on an improvised raft. The river did not change its character; it remained broad and swift. Once they came upon hippo and Thrushwood thought of his gun, for hippo meat was much like beefsteak. They saw some elephants standing in the reeds, drinking from the river and studying them.

When the sun grew too hot, they stopped and pushed the raft into the shallows, into the shade under the limbs of the big trees that grew close to the water. Chapupa went off and came back with two fat ducks and cooked them over a small fire. When the sun weakened, they pushed off again and floated on until evening came. They traveled for three days and reached the country of the Wakamba. They first came upon fishermen tending their weirs, and later in the day they were taken to the chief. He was Sese. He gave them a hut and food and told them of a settlement two days off where they could get horses and guns from a Greek trader who had a location there. He had heard of Pfeffer and he had heard of John Thrushwood the hunter. His grandchildren would tell of how he, Sese, aided in the capture of *bawana sitani*.

Thrushwood did not ask for warriors to help him. The Wakamba were not hunters; they knew nothing of bushcraft. They had gardens and fished and until recently had paid tribute to the greater tribes.

They went to the settlement and Thrushwood, having no money and being unknown to the Greek trader, was prepared to borrow a gun and a horse and shoot some ivory to pay for all the equipment they would need. But it was unnecessary. Chapupa took the white man aside and took from one of the bags around his neck a piece of black gum. He made a tiny fire and the gum melted, revealing a diamond, a beautiful stone of such quality that they were able to buy three fine horses and everything else they needed.

And they rode off again, upstream to the place where Pfeffer had ambushed them. The spoor was growing cold.

Pfeffer came upon a leopard and followed it until it vanished into a ravine choked with thorn. He would hunt it and kill it before he went on, for he hated leopards more than any of the others. He went on foot and took the dog with him. Two days before, they had come upon a buffalo and the dog had charged it before he could call it back. The buffalo had stood, waiting for it, and then lunged with a sweep of its heavy horns. But the great dog swerved away and circled the buffalo, snapping at its legs. The animal was so occupied with the black dog that Pfeffer was able to ride close and shoot it from the saddle. The dog was a true hunter.

Now, as they spoored the leopard, the dog became nervous at his side. He spoke to it curtly, telling it to stay close to him, and the dog obeyed. Then the tension became too much and the great dog bolted away, vanished in the thorn ahead. Pfeffer followed and ten minutes later he came upon the dog and the leopard. The leopard was high in a big acacia and Pfeffer shot it before it decided to jump down and run away. The dog had frightened it, treed it, and led him to it. He patted the animal, talked to it, and then they went back to the horses.

He shot a rhino a few hours later. Game was scarce here, for the land was dry and barren. Soon they would be in elephant country and he would destroy the fabled herd that ranged through the Makorikori Bush. He had an extra .500 Express with him and plenty of ammunition. Elephants were dangerous in bush country; they could smell you before you could see them and two or three sometimes would charge at the same time. He would have to be cautious; this would not be like shooting impala or buck.

Somewhere behind him, following his trail, were the men who worked for the Indian trader. The tusks of twenty elephants, the price of the great black dog—they would cut out the tusks and then go back to Mitati and the merchant would be happy. He needed the merchant's trust, the merchant's credit. In six months he would go back and buy again and then he would pay for everything with ivory. The elephants would pay for all his killing.

Thrushwood and Chapupa came to Mitati. They came upon Pfeffer's camp five miles from the settlement and Chapupa found where he'd had left it and walked into town, returning the same way but with a dog this time, a great dog. Near the town the tracks merged with others and it was impossible to tell where Pfeffer had gone. Thrushwood thought it was to Kuroomi, the Indian merchant.

"Was Pfeffer here?" he asked the Indian.

"Pfeffer? The hunter? The one they talk about?"

"Yes," Thrushwood said. "What did he buy?"

"Sir, he was not in my store," said the merchant. "I have not seen him. Is he in the settlement?"

"He was here and you sold him supplies."

"It is not true."

"You're a liar," Thrushwood said. He looked around the store and turned back to the Indian.

"Where's the dog? I can smell one but I cannot see or hear one. Did he take the dog from you?"

"My dog is missing," Kuroomi said. "He was a wild dog, a sheep-killer, and I kept him locked in the back. Then, some days ago, he vanished. I think he ran away. He was not happy with me and I had no meat to feed him. I am a poor man, as all know."

"You sold him, then," Thrushwood said.

"The dog ran away," Kuroomi said. "Perhaps the German found him and took him with him. I am not sad. The dog did not like living in the back room. There is no place for such an animal. It should be killed."

Thrushwood went to see Schlachtmann, who was all things official in the tiny settlement. The German was sympathetic and he would watch Kuroomi closely. It was true that the Indian had owned a great black dog. Pfeffer had certainly taken it with whatever else he had bought. And some of the merchant's servants had gone off somewhere; he would look into that, too.

"Are the police looking for Pfeffer?" Thrushwood asked.

"The police?" Schlachtmann asked. "Has he done something else now? I know that he hunts like a crazy man, but I know that the police are not after him." He shifted in his chair, sipped his drink. "I am the police, too, you understand. Here in Mitati I am also the Chief of Police. A great job, this." He laughed to himself and poured Thrushwood another drink from a greasy bottle.

"He seems to be trying to exterminate all the game in East Africa," Thrushwood said.

Schlachtmann raised his eyebrows and pursed his lips. "I have heard of him. I have known others like that but they hunted for a few weeks and then went back to the coast or back to Europe and that was that. Pfeffer is different. I think he is mad."

"Someday there will be laws to stop men like him," Thrushwood said. "Laws to stop a man from wholesale slaughter."

"We are making laws for the people now," Schlachtmann said. "When we have them under control, we might turn to other things. The game perhaps, or the resources. Right now we make laws for the natives."

"Someday there will be laws to stop a man from hunting elephants, from shooting females and their young, from slaughtering them for amusement. There is an end for all things and even the game of Africa can vanish unless we have laws."

Schlachtmann nodded. "Why are you on Pfeffer's trail? Are you trying to stop him again? You caught him north of the border, I know, and turned him over to your own people in Kericho, but now why do you track him? This is German territory. Remind me to check your papers later when we have finished the bottle. It is another of my duties, you understand."

Thrushwood smiled. "My papers are in order." He finished his drink. "I'm trying to stop Pfeffer. It is a personal thing, I suppose. I want to catch up with him again and see if I can't get him to stop the slaughter."

"And suppose he tells you to go to hell?" Schlachtmann asked.

"He has already," Thrushwood said. "He has tried to kill me."

"Don't worry, my friend," Schlachtmann said. "If he kills you and we find out about it, the police will go and catch him." He began laughing to himself, deep down in his chest. "There is nothing to worry about. Do not be afraid if he kills you."

"I'm not afraid. I think that soon he might die in the bush. There are many dangers, so many dangers. I sometimes worry that he will die before I have a chance to talk to him again. And if I do find him dead out there in the bush, do not worry, Herr Schlachtmann. I will bring his body to the nearest settlement and see that it gets a full Christian burial."

"Yes," Schlachtmann said. "He should get that. A full Christian burial. I think that would be nice for him."

Thrushwood stood up. "I'm going now. Keep an eye on the Indian. Pfeffer might come back in a few months to get more ammunition. He has a horse of mine. You could arrest him for that."

"Yes," Schlachtmann said. "That is a crime, to steal a horse. But I think I shall be afraid to arrest him. From what I have heard of this man, he is dangerous. I think I will be too afraid of him."

Thrushwood left him and joined Chapupa and the horses at the edge of town. They rode off and by nightfall they were many miles from the settlement. Pfeffer's spoor was easy to follow.

Lions find the great sprawling body of a giraffe that Pfeffer killed and in the darkness they begin tearing at it, two males and three females. The night is filled with their noise.

Other meat eaters hear and smell the excitement and gather around the lions, hyenas first, then jackals. When dawn comes, two of the lions have left the kill but two hundred spotted hyenas have formed a ring around the others and behind the hyenas are an equal number of quick, fox-like jackals. As time passes more ugly, slope-backed hyenas come loping up to join their brothers. More jackals arrive. The three lions do not leave. They feast on the rich red meat and show no concern over the hungry multitude that forms a great circle around them.

The hyenas know the lion. They are the lord. They circle and keep their distance even after long hours of waiting have driven them almost insane with hunger. Behind them the jackals wait, keeping a lane of safety between themselves and their superiors.

The first vulture wheels overhead and glides down behind the ring of jackals. Three others follow, then a dozen, a score. Soon several hundred birds of death form a solid ring behind the jackals.

Another lion leaves, her belly almost scraping the ground as she makes her way through the hyenas and jackals and vultures. The lesser ones back away from the big cat, an aisle opens in each hungry circle to let her pass without incident.

Two lions now. A thousand enemies surround them, pressing in to fill their famished bellies. A bold hyena comes too close and one of the lions turns to defend her meat. The three rings are driven back; the hyena bite each other in mad anger, some of them turn on the jackals who have come too close; a jackal lunges at a carrion bird; the air is rent with the screams and roars of a thousand hungry carnivores.

One of the lions turns and walks towards the pressing horde. They make a path for her as she leaves the kill to join the rest of the pride. The ring closes.

One lion. The army of famished enemies crowd closer, inch by inch. The lord snarls and they shrink back, but they are bolder now and the lion senses the change. Some of the vultures take to the air and swoop close overhead. The lion roars. It has a full belly but is reluctant to leave the meat. It walks around the kill and the hyenas wail and fall away. The lion returns to its feast but there is no peace. There is too much noise; vultures are constantly overhead. Suddenly the lion turns and walks through a lane that opens before her.

The hyenas fall upon the remains in one mad, bone-cracking lunge. The great carcass is rent apart with a ferocity unknown to the leisurely lion. Within a few moments there are only torn scraps. The jackals swarm over these and the vultures are close behind, careful not to get too close. When the jackals leave it will be their turn and they will fight among themselves for the last scrap of hide and clot of bloody sand.

Soon there will be no trace of the giraffe.

In the night Thrushwood awoke and called for Chapupa. He was covered with cold sweat and his teeth chattered. He had the fever. Chapupa threw an armload of wood on the dying fire and covered him with the extra blankets and made coffee. They had some whisky and some quinine tablets; by dawn Thrushwood was no longer shivering but he was weak, unable to eat.

Chapupa got him on his horse and they started back to Mitati. The fever was going to delay them ten days, perhaps more. Schlachtmann had medicine and a bed and plenty of whisky. There would be fodder for the horses. It would be pointless to lie sick in camp when the conveniences of civilization were close at hand.

They reached Schlachtmann's house at sundown. The big German carried Thrushwood inside and put him in one of the extra beds. He fell asleep immediately, feverish and sweating profusely. After a time, Schlachtmann woke him up long enough to make him swallow some pills that he had obtained from the hospital at Tabora.

Chapupa came into the room at dawn and waited for Thrushwood to open his eyes.

"I'm going on," he said. "The spoor grows cold. When the fever leaves you and you are strong again, follow me. I will leave a spoor that nothing will destroy."

Thrushwood nodded. He was sick and he didn't care what Chapupa did—or anyone else. He didn't care about Pfeffer now; when he got well he might go home and rest and forget that there was a Pfeffer. He was sick . . . so sick . . . so thirsty. . . .

He had been close to dying of thirst many times. Once an elephant had saved him. It was up in the N.F.D. east of Lake Rudolf. All of his boys had deserted during the night, afraid to take another step northward, fearing the slave raiders from Abyssinia. They had begged him not to go on, but he was young then and brash and stupid and had refused. He'd buried the ivory and taken after them, knowing that he'd whip the pack of them when he found them. But he never did. He got lost and ran out of water and began to go a little mad with thirst, staggering south-ward through one of the most pitiless parts of Africa. His boots fell apart and one eye closed with infection and the day dawned when he did not even try to stand up. He sat in the shade of a dead anthill and waited to die.

In the evening a line of elephants came towards him and he watched them without believing. But they were real. The dry spell was driving the herds west towards the Turkwell that year and he'd been lucky enough to collapse near one of their ancient trails. He raised his rifle, an old .303 Lee Enfield, and managed to hold it steady enough for one broadside heart shot at the first animal his sights found. He was fortunate. The elephant stag-gered, wandered to one side of the trail and fell forward on tired knees as the others fled in terror. After a long time he got up and went to it. He had just enough strength to cut the heavy hide, bore into the stomach and find the water sac. He drank the clear pure water. It was the reserve all elephants carried. He'd seen some of them bring up the fluid and squirt themselves on the hottest days when they were far from any waterhole.

The intestinal water saved his life. He stayed near the rotting carcase for five days and then struck off to the south and finally reached the settlement at Turka.

Chapupa left and he called for water. Schlachtmann came and he drank deeply and fell into a deep sleep.


A gecko crawls from its crevice and makes its way across the whitewashed wall. Its grey-white body blends with the color beneath it. Flies buzz in the hot motionless air. One grows tired and comes to rest on the wall. The gecko approaches and the fat insect vanishes in a blur of motion. The gecko moves down the wall behind the washstand to the dark places where it seeks other prey. It is a hunter and eater of all things that it can overpower and swallow: spiders and moths, flies and crickets and centipedes and cockroaches. It fears wasps and flies that are colored to resemble wasps; it fears some moths whose great wings contain frightening eye-like spots which remind the gecko of its old enemies.

There is a new black cricket under the bed, half-hidden in an old crack in the corner. The gecko has trapped many crickets here and he moves with assurance. There is a brief moment of conflict. The cricket is powerful and fights with desperation but he is soon crushed and swallowed by the lizard.

The noise has frightened the other insects in the room. The brown millipedes into their narrow cracks; a spider deflates its plump yellow body and shrinks into a deep hole; two other crickets flee in terror to the grass outside of the house: there is greater danger here but it is not quite so immediate.

The gecko crawls up and moves over the window sill to the dark, sun-sheltered wall under the veranda roof. It moves slowly, hoping for another fly. In time it reaches the open window of the storeroom and darts over the sill.

A snake waits in the shadows. The gecko hears a cricket and moves towards the sound. The snake follows.

The gecko feels danger, an aeon-old instinct warns it. The snake lunges. The gecko darts sideways into a dangerous unknown maze of boxes. The snake follows, a few feet behind.

The lizard's tail falls from its body. It wiggles on the floor, a living decoy. The snake lunges for it, swallows.

In this moment the gecko escapes, flees the maze of boxes, darts out of the window and finds refuge in its own crevice. It has dropped its tail but it lives. In another month it will grow a new tail.

Thrushwood sleeps. The afternoon passes.


Chapupa took his horse and rode off. He came to the campsite and rode through it; he pushed the horse hard all day and by nightfall he had made up for the lost day.

He followed Pfeffer for a week, slowly closing the distance between them; the German was not running—he rode one way and then another. He hunted animals and followed them; his spoor was not a straight line and sometimes his fires were close together. Each day Chapupa grew closer and the spoor became fresh, the marks of the horses and the man and the great dog.

And then the spoor suddenly became difficult; it was as if the German had devoted an entire day to obscuring his trail. It led into a muddy river and did not reappear on the opposite bank.

Chapupa sat for a time thinking and then turned and followed
the bank upstream and after some miles found where Pfeffer
had come out of the water on the same side of the river. Later in
the day, the trail led to a low rock plateau and Chapupa had to
lead his horse behind him as he followed a spoor which no white
man could hold for a hundred yards. Now and then he stopped
and scratched an arrow in the rock with a piece of flint. Thrushwood would not be delayed here.

He tracked all day, found where the other man had camped,
and rode on. The trail was easy now, open; there was no indica-
tion that he was trying to hide it. Chapupa reasoned that Pfeffer
had done it to shake off any new trackers who might be following
him.

And he was close to the man. Carrion squatted near the kills,
fighting over half-rotten meat; vultures wheeled overhead and in
the night lions roared. Chapupa did not look at the ground now;
he looked at the far horizon and saw the vultures and rode
toward them.

The kills became fresher. He was a day behind; too close. There
was danger now: the man might swing around and see him by
chance; he might double back on his own spoor and wait beside it
with his rifle. And there was danger from lion and leopard and
hyena; they, too, followed and ate the kills. It might be wiser if
he were to fall back.

But he did not. He compromised. He followed the vultures,
keeping them in sight. He stayed two miles west of the spoor and
was not troubled with the sight of lion and hyena and the fear of
ambush. Pfeffer's spoor was in the air.

And then one night he saw the glow of a fire far ahead of him.
The country had turned flat and dry; there was little game and
it seemed likely that Pfeffer would pass through it quickly to the
lush veld beyond.

Chapupa studied the fire for a long time. Somewhere far behind
him was Thrushwood, moving slowly perhaps, still weak from the
fever. It would be a long while before he reached this spot and
by then he and Pfeffer would be days or weeks away.

He was going to stop the man himself. He would kill the horses,
take away his speed. On foot he would be nothing. Thrushwood
was catching up and when he arrived they could close in on him.

He would go to the camp. The land was flat and it would be
easy to shoot the three horses and get away before the man could
find him. He would not try to kill. That was for Thrushwood to

decide. He would kill the horses and make the man easy to catch. When John Thrushwood came, they would ride him down, encircle him; wait for him to starve or surrender.

Two hours later, Chapupa was close enough to Pfeffer's camp to hear the stomping of the horses and see the faint smoke from the dying fire. He had come on foot with his rifle, an old-fashioned Mannlicher. It was light; Thrushwood had taught him to shoot it. He was a fair shot.

The camp was downwind. The horses stood close to each other; Chapupa knew that his only chance of success was to strike quickly and get away in the darkness before Pfeffer saw him. If Pfeffer did see him, he would be dead, for Pfeffer might well be the best shot in Africa now, better, perhaps, than Thrushwood.

He slid a few yards closer. There was no need to think. He raised the Mannlicher and let the front sight find the horses.

He pulled the trigger and the night exploded. The crack of the rifle was half lost in the scream of horses and the sudden terrible barking of the great dog. Chapupa fired again and again and again. The horses were gone, the horizon was clear of them.

He was up and running, zigzagging in case the German had somehow seen him in the darkness. His back expected the bullet. He would die and Thrushwood would be alone. . . .

He had forgotten the dog. If Pfeffer turned it loose, it would soon be on him and kill him. But it was chained; he could tell by the bark that it was chained to keep it from running into the darkness after a lion or leopard. Some dogs did that; dogs that were without fear, dogs that would attack an elephant if their master ordered them to.

He ran on into the night.

Chapupa did not wait for dawn to break before he rode off. He sensed danger; he knew that he had not succeeded. It had been a mistake to attack Pfeffer. He should have waited for Thrushwood.

He rode off in the dark, heading toward the east. There were mountains here; if the hunter came after him he would have a chance among the cliffs and ravines. On the open veld he was helpless. He kicked his horse and rode on through the night.

When the sun was directly overhead, he heard the dog. It was far away but the distance did not lessen the excitement in its bark. Chapupa started, glanced backward instinctively. He had failed and the mad hunter was coming to kill him. He had put his faith in a white man's rifle and he had failed with it. Pfeffer had one horse and a dog to spoor him. He was going to die now, very soon.

The mountains were still far away; too far. He drove the horse on. The dog was gaining on him, raging; in a few minutes, Pfeffer would be in sight. He would fire once, twice perhaps, and it would be over; his horse would go down and the dog would have him. He would try to kill the dog. He would use his assagai and die with it in his hand. Rifles were for white men. He would spear the dog; that much he could do for John Thrushwood.

The mountains were too far; there was nothing but the level veld and the low thorn trees. But there was a great tree, too, a lone baobab. He swung his horse toward it.

Chapupa rode under the great tree and slipped from the horse. He took his water bag and his short assagai. He whipped the horse and shouted at it and it sprang away, running for the mountains. Pfeffer and his dog were very close now. He had only a few seconds. . . .

He circled the great trunk, found a set of old notches that someone had cut a generation before. He threw his spear upward and it quivered in the soft bark of a high branch. He put the water bag around his neck and climbed carefully into the labyrinth overhead. He found the assagai, moved upward.

He was safe here. He was not going to die now. Pfeffer could not get him, even with the great dog and the rifle. The baobab would save him.

## CHAPTER ELEVEN

THE baobab is the sequoia of Africa. Some of them are thousands of years old—shoots and saplings when Alexander died, when Carthage burned. They live and they survive; they grow and nations die around them.

The big ones attain diameters of a hundred feet; they are not tall as some trees are tall; but they reach up seventy-five feet. When their soft white flowers are in bloom, they are not without beauty.

A baobab is an upright thicket, a tiny forest with networks of branches and thick elephantine trunks twisting and turning, seeking light and air. It is the home of birds and rodents and sometimes a vast treasure house of wild honey; the fat trunk is sometimes hollow and filled with precious water. Bushmen have lived in many of them; people have used them as storehouses for grain and other things. They are a small world, a microcosm of life and time and history. Stone-age people left offerings to their gods under the vast canopy of their branches; slaves died near them and never reached the Arab dhows at old Mombasa. They have lived long and endured. They are close to immortal.

Pfeffer came riding behind the dog, which raged and barked and followed the spoor. It did not race ahead; it stayed a hundred feet in front of the horse. They passed under the tree and rode off. Chapupa saw that his own horse had stopped running. He saw Pfeffer ride up to it a mile from the tree, then turn and ride back over the flat, dry land toward the tree.

It did not matter. He had not expected the old trick to work, and if it had, he would have stayed in the tree anyway. As long as the dog lived, he was not safe. The dog could find him no matter where he hid. He must kill the dog. He climbed high in the tree and found what he had been seeking: a hole in the thick trunk; a cavity large enough for his small body. He stuck his assagai deep into the soft wood where it would be unseen from the ground and worked himself into the hole. He made himself comfortable and closed his eyes. He was very tired; he would try to sleep.

The dog followed the spoor back to the tree and then found where Chapupa had circled and climbed it. He did not bark now, but a deep growl came from him and his fangs ripped at the air in terrible rage.

Pfeffer led Chapupa's horse back and tied it with his own to a thorn bush several hundred feet from the tree; they would be safe here from the Bushman. He was sure that Chapupa did not have a rifle, for the Mannlicher was with his horse. But he would have the short stabbing assagai and the missing waterskin. It would be suicidal to try to climb into the tree and shoot him. The Bushman would spear him or leap upon him with a poisoned stake. He would have to kill him in some other way. . . .

There was the temptation to fire blindly into the tree and try to hit the little man. But it would be unwise. The tree was too vast, the branches too thick. And he did not have the ammunition that he usually had. The two pack horses were dead and the ammunition they carried was buried near them back at the old campsite.

He spoke to the dog, which he called Prinz, told him to lie down and stay under the tree. He went back to the horses, led them to a thorn tree and unpacked them. He built a fire and ate and then sat for a long time looking at the giant baobab.

The Bushman would never leave the tree, and to climb it was out of the question. If he had unlimited ammunition, he could fire into the tree and hope to kill the little man. If he had enough dead wood and unlimited time, he could burn it. But he had to keep moving. Thrushwood could be alive and near; he could not camp here and wait for the Bushman to starve.

He would leave Prinz.

Tomorrow he would ride off and shoot some meat and haul it back on the extra horse. He'd leave it under the tree with tins of water. Prinz could wait for the Bushman to come down or die of thirst. And Pfeffer would ride off. He would hunt and travel in a great circle, returning to the tree. It was a good plan. Chapupa would never come down and fight the dog; even with his spear he was defenseless. It was not likely that he would throw the assagai from the tree, for he would be helpless if he missed and the dog was quick and wary, a difficult target.

It was a good plan. The Bushman would die.

Thrushwood left Mitati leading two well-packed horses. He was strong again; the fever was behind him. And he had not lost his quarry. Chapupa was with him wherever he was. They had an advantage now; their mounts were fresh and they still held his spoor. It was only a matter of time. They would wear Pfeffer down; he would make a mistake and they would get him.

It was good to ride again. Schlachtmann had been generous and it had been pleasant to live again in a house and eat varied meals and sleep in a bed. But always in his mind was the sight of Pfeffer; he would dream of the German and see him riding and killing with the vultures overhead. And Chapupa. He saw the little man on his lone horse riding cautiously day after day in the spoor. He had to get to them. . . .

He rode now upriver following the tracks Chapupa had made.

Chapupa watched Pfeffer ride off, leaving him in the tree with the dog below. The dog would not leave; he would wait under the tree until he died but he would not disobey his master.

There were meat and water for the animal; he would last a long while.

He climbed down to the lower branches. The dog went wild, leaping and barking furiously at him. He squatted ten feet above it and held his spear ready. But he would not throw it: the dog was too quick; should he miss, he would be helpless if Pfeffer came back and came up in the tree after him.

He shouted at the dog and angered it, and the big animal worked itself into a frenzy, leaping into the air and clawing the bark until it grew limp from exhaustion. Chapupa climbed higher into the tree and found a place where he could lie flat. He closed his eyes. When the dog grew quiet, he dropped a dead stick to the ground and the dog was up again, barking and raging.

The German was clever. He had shot a gazelle and left it for the dog to eat, left it in the grass two hundred feet from the base of the tree. There was water next to it, four tins. He had taken two large square tins, cut them in half and filled them with water. There was meat enough and water enough to keep the dog strong and dangerous for a long time.

When the sun went down, Chapupa stood up and hefted his assagai. He would not throw it at the agile dog but there was a target for him: the meat. He removed one of the two small bags from his neck. He rubbed a gummy substance over the blade of the spear, a poison which would contaminate the gazelle. He examined the blade, put the rest of the poison away and the bag back around his thin neck.

He climbed around in the tree for an hour before he found the spot he was satisfied with. It would be a difficult throw. If he failed, it might be best to jump down and let the dog have him.

He stood now far out on the end of a long branch. It swayed under him; the dog was below leaping and snarling. He was tempted to throw the spear at it. His bare toes curled around the smooth bark and his old eyes measured the distance for the hundredth time. He brought the spear back and hefted it and his body began to weave and sway until it was part of the shaking branch. An old war chant came to his lips. He could not miss. . . .

He flung the assagai. It shivered through the air, struggled toward the almost invisible target. It came down to earth again and fell into the center of the carcass of the gazelle. Its wide blade, coated with the deadly gum, sliced through the flesh. In a little while, the meat close to the blade turned dark and the darkness spread. The dog came to drink, sniffed at the meat and drew away. Chapupa watched and grunted. He called to the dog, threw a heavy stick at it, and then sat quietly while the animal wore itself out leaping up at him. Soon now the dog would be ravenous, but it would not eat the poisoned meat.

Two days later, Chapupa climbed down from his hole. He was weak; he had slept and remained quiet for two days, conserving his strength. Every few hours, he would shout or drop a dead branch and the dog would come snarling and leaping up, tiring itself out. And then, after a time, it would trot to the water tins and drink deeply.

There was still plenty of water. The dog would outlast him unless he killed it. He was ready now. He would poison it. He squatted a few yards above the dog and studied it. He knew what he must do. His assagai was gone. If he had it, he could poison the tip and try to stab the animal. It wasn't possible to fashion a bow and arrow from the tree. He had no riem to make a noose with and strangle the dog. He could not make a blowgun as he had with the reed. There were no birds or animals in the tree to poison and feed to the dog. There was nothing.

He found a safe place to sit and took the two bags from his neck. He opened one and took from it a tiny metal blade that was razor sharp.

He severed an ear lobe. Blood from the wound spurted and made a tiny puddle under the tree. The dog came and smelled it and went wild. Chapupa held the severed ear lobe and daubed it with a tasteless poison. He dropped it down to the dog. Prinz smelled it, studied it for a moment, then gulped it down. Chapupa held his bleeding ear. After a long time, the bleeding stopped.

Prinz stretched out under the tree and died. Chapupa waited until he saw flies crawling on the dog's nose. He crawled down and retrieved his spear from the gazelle. He came back under the tree and collected all the dead wood he had thrown at the dog. He built a fire and cut meat from the dog and cooked it. Pfeffer had left the dog to eat him; now he was eating the dog. White men were clever, but sometimes they were not clever enough.

He did not stuff himself. When his hunger was appeased, he picked up his assagai and walked away from the giant tree, following the spoor of two horses.

Thrushwood came to the place where Chapupa had slithered

close to Pfeffer's camp and killed two horses. The bones were white and dry now and the area was scattered with the torn remains of the equipment that Pfeffer had been forced to abandon. Thrushwood studied the scene for several minutes and then followed the tracks of a lone horse away from the campsite, its hoofprints in the hard, dry earth mingled with the footprints of the big dog.

After a time, the tracks joined Chapupa's. Thrushwood frowned and kicked his horse. It appeared now that he was following Chapupa. . . .

He came to the baobab and halted. He walked around for two hours and studied the scene. He crawled into the tree. He came down and saw a small pile of stones on Chapupa's sign. He rode off and found another one where it joined Pfeffer's spoor. Thrushwood did not understand all that had happened but it was obvious that Chapupa was now on foot following the German. The big dog was dead. Pfeffer had two horses; somehow he had taken Chapupa's. . . .

Thrushwood rode on, driving the horses.

Thrushwood overtook Chapupa in the Usambara highlands. The old native had seen him coming from a rise and had built a fire. Thrushwood rode cautiously toward the smoke, saw Chapupa waving from a giant boulder.

"It has been a long time," Thrushwood said.

"*Ai,* but it has been a bad time for the German," Chapupa said. He told Thrushwood of the ambush and the chase and the tree; of how he had destroyed the big dog by feeding it his own poisoned ear lobe.

"And it is my own fault," he continued. "I should have waited for you. I was foolish to attempt such an ambush alone. But I did kill two horses and his dog. He is alone now and we can catch him. The dog was a terrible beast; it was worse than another man."

Thrushwood nodded. There was a time when Chapupa could surprise him, amaze him; now he only accepted the things that the little man did—accepted them and wondered.

Two hours later, they rode off. Chapupa took one of the pack horses. He found it strange to ride again.

Pfeffer discovered that Thrushwood and Chapupa were following him. When he left the baobab, he had swung north and ridden slowly, easily. Thrushwood was probably dead, he thought, and the Bushman would soon die in the tree or in a desperate fight with Prinz. There was nothing to worry about.

Then, a month later, from the top of a high plateau, he had seen them tracking him—two riders and a pack horse. He picked them up with his binoculars and cursed; the two old men were indestructible. And they were close to him now, too close.

He turned and rode off. It was foolish to waste time trying to hide his spoor. The Bushman was a devil. And Prinz must be dead. There would be no rest for him now, no peace, until he killed the two of them.

A week later, Pfeffer came upon four Masai. He rode up to them slowly and they grew tense and held their assagais ready for throwing. They were in open country that was sparse and without cover, and they were at Pfeffer's mercy; if he chose, he could run them down and shoot them. They looked at him and felt his coldness, his danger. His rifle lay across his saddle and he pulled up and sat for a time studying them, just out of range of their spears. There was no danger from the Masai now; they had been broken and held themselves aloof from the white men. The time of the native wars and murders was over. But these four were different. They were not like the others. They were outcasts, criminals; they had been banished from their village. They could be dangerous.

"Where do you go?" he asked them.

They looked at each other and moved a little apart. They were suspicious. All strangers were enemies and this was a white man who might be looking for runaways or thieves; a white man with the look of a hunter in his carriage and a face that struck terror in them.

"Where do you go, Masai?"

"We go with the wind," one of them said. "We are pariahs. We have been cast from our kraals. Now we are like the beasts. We go one way and then another."

"Follow me," Pfeffer said. "In my spoor there will be more meat than you have ever seen, meat for your bellies, rich meat for your hunger. I am Pfeffer, the hunter. When my rifle speaks, something dies."

One of the Masai, the tallest of them, took his assagai and drove its wide blade into the ground. He leaned on it.

"Why does a great hunter befriend outcasts of the Masai?"

"Because I need warriors to guard my rear," Pfeffer told him. "Two men follow me. I want you to catch them. One is an Englishman, a hunter. He is old and jealous like the elders in your tribe. He fears that my reputation as a hunter will be greater than his own and he has sworn to kill me. The other is also old. He is small and foul and knows much of poisons and magic. Bushman blood is in him and he has learned to ride a horse and fire a rifle. These men would murder me while I sleep. If you follow my spoor and guard me, I shall let you join me. My gun will protect you from your enemies and keep your bellies full of meat."

The three other natives drew close to the leader. They talked for a time, looking up at Pfeffer, gesticulating.

Pfeffer watched the natives. If they refused, he would shoot them. Thrushwood and his boy might come upon them and convince them to join and catch *bwana sitani*. Thrushwood was clever with natives and it would not be good to have four more men after him.

The natives stopped talking. The leader came closer to him. He raised his rifle, letting the Masai know that he did not trust anyone.

"We will join you," the leader said. "We will follow in your spoor and feast on the meat you shoot. And we shall catch the two who track you, bring them to you like trussed fowl. Or should we kill them?"

"Kill the *lybon*, the witch doctor," Pfeffer said. "But the white man is mine to kill. Soon we shall make a trap for them and they will ride into it and we shall have them. Then we shall go on together, the five of us. We shall be invincible, an impi that sweeps all before it. Men will fear us and run from the sound of our coming. We will be the greatest of the hunters, the greatest of the warriors!"

"*Ai, ai, ai!*" The Masai were excited now, eager to follow, to serve, hungry for the reward. They were no longer criminals; they were the core of a new tribe. Now their enemies would suffer and the white man would lead them to great glory. For this was the man they had heard of—*bwana sitani*—the man whom all others feared.

"Listen!" Pfeffer told them. "Do not come close to me again unless I seek you. Stay half a day's walk behind me. I do not trust you yet. You must prove your loyalty. Do not come close to my gun. I trust no one. When the grass moves, I shoot. When there is a sound in the night, I also shoot."

"We fear your gun," said the leader. "Do not fear us. We shall follow in your spoor and protect you from those who would stab at your back while you sleep. We are loyal to the great *bwana sitani*. We are his men."

Pfeffer smiled inwardly. He kicked the horse and rode off. He had four assagai to throw against Thrushwood now, four lives to use. He must devise a trap and use them to best advantage.

He came upon rhino tracks and soon found the beast skulking in a patch of dry grass. He fired twice with his .500 and the animal slumped to the ground and died.

He rode on. The Masai would feast tonight on rhino, on rhino too dangerous and powerful for their assagai.

Thrushwood came to the spot where Pfeffer had talked to the four Masai. Chapupa read the signs. The tracks met those of the natives and continued on. The natives were following behind Pfeffer. This was not strange or unusual. Many times before they had come upon the spoor of natives mingled with that of Pfeffer. Natives had little meat and they followed him and stuffed themselves on the kills. They would feast, sleep, and slow down, and in time they would fall too far behind Pfeffer to eat the game he killed. The carrion would get to it first. So Chapupa read the signs but could not know that the four Masai who had joined Pfeffer had sworn to kill him and capture John Thrushwood.

"Soon we shall come upon four men stuffed with meat," he told Thrushwood. "They follow behind and mingle their spoor with his."

They rode on. There was no danger of ambush here. The country was level and mostly bare, arid and laced now and then with the trails of rhino and wart hog. They found no water all day and were forced to use their water bags. Ahead were mountains, high country. If they were lucky, they might catch Pfeffer here; he might attempt another ambush and fail. Or he might succeed. . . .

Chapupa sat in the darkness listening to the insects and the night noises. Thrushwood slept. They had come upon the carcass of a rhino and it was partially eaten. The four men had eaten Pfeffer's kill and then moved on. They had not feasted. They had not rested. They had eaten and then followed the spoor. It was unusual; they had left a wealth of fresh meat for the carrion birds. And if they had left meat behind, they must know that there would be meat ahead. Things had happened that one could not read in the spoor. They must be watchful.

Pfeffer came to the low mountains, crossed them, and found on the other side a vast plain of grass. He sat on his horse and studied the game below. He knew that this would be the scene of his greatest killing. He could use fire here because far to his right the mountains ended not in low hills sinking to the level of the grassland but in abrupt cliffs. He would use fire and it would be like the time long ago when he had trapped the animals in the ravine and blocked their escape with a wall of their own bodies. Only this time it would be ten times larger. He would find a line of unbroken cliff and throw a semicircle of flame around it. He could spend a full day setting fires and, when it was over, there would be dead animals in the tens of thousands.

He kicked his horse and worked his way down to the grassland and camped near a spring which bubbled out of the mountain's heart. Before dawn came, he rode off to where the cliffs began. He rode through the tall grass and studied the granite wall. There were no breaks in it, no ravines; it was sheer gray granite cliff rising from twenty to seventy feet from the plain.

The sun rose and then it began to sink. He came to a ravine; it was twenty or thirty feet wide, the sides steep, the earth packed hard from the countless hoofs of generations of game. He turned his horse and rode into it. It would have to be blocked, for there was no need to end the circle of fire here. He would block it, build a barricade, a wall of thorn trees and brush. He would wait for the four Masai and they would help him build it. And, in the meantime, Thrushwood would come closer and they would trap him.

He rode on through the ravine and it grew broader and then ended as the steep walls fell away and became part of the slope behind the cliffs. Beyond this were rolling parklike hills which merged into the mountains he had just crossed. If the ravine was not blocked, the animals would escape and linger here until the fire died.

He tied his horses in the shade of a large tree and walked back to the ravine. He would sink a line of thick posts across the narrowest part and weave thorn and debris into it. Then, in front of it, he would jam small thorn trees with the branches facing outward and held in place with sharp stakes.

He walked back and waited in the shade near one of the game trails that led out of the ravine. He shot a zebra and cut its throat, so that it would bleed, then rode off. The Masai would come here and feast and he would return to them tomorrow.

He went through the ravine and continued along the cliff and, when evening came, there were still the gray cliffs stretching ahead of him and without a break in them.

Pfeffer rose in the grayness of early dawn and rode back along the cliff, following his own spoor. The grass was still wet, the sky streaked with redness; it was the hour when all things were quiet.

He came to the ravine and rode through it, saw the camp of the Masai and halted. He called to them and they came slowly and sullenly, heavy with the meat they had eaten the night before. It was light now; the sun was drying out the leaves and grass. The sound of insects had started.

Pfeffer led the four men to the narrowest part of the ravine and told them what must be done. First a line of posts or tree trunks must be buried upright in the ground. They nodded and broke the hard ground with their wide-bladed assagais and began digging.

Pfeffer rode back into the low hills beyond the ravine and began cutting posts from the clean-limbed trees that grew there; soon the Masai joined him and began carrying off the logs. They were happy; they enjoyed working, for it had been a long time since they had made kraals and repaired huts, and the instinct of work was strong in them.

In the afternoon they began cutting thorn bushes, whose branches they wove into the stout line of tree trunks. Pfeffer cut a sapling and pounded it into the ground in front of the tangle. He drove it in deeply at an angle, then sharpened the end of it. The Masai nodded and trotted off and began to cut saplings of their own.

The barrier grew. An elephant could break through it but no smaller animal. It was high and thick and strong and everywhere there were sharp thorns and the pointed ends of stakes. Pfeffer began to cut down small thorn trees and drag them to the ravine, using the horses and a heavy rope. These were worked into the barrier. Two of the Masai began to carry heavy rocks and pile them around the base of the posts they had buried in the ground.

When evening came, it was finished. Pfeffer had shot two impala during the day and they made a great fire and feasted. And while they ate, Pfeffer told them what they must do.

The white man and the Bushman were three or four days behind. They would follow his spoor over the mountain; when they crossed it, they would see the fire in the grassland below. He, Pfeffer, would wait until they were starting up the mountain, then he would ride and start his fire so that the timing would be right. Thrushwood would study the fire and know what it was: a trap for thousands of animals. He would think first of the animals, of how he might save them. And he would know that his enemy must sooner or later circle back to the cliffs. So he would ride along behind the cliffs and in time he would see the ravine and he would ride to it and investigate it. The Masai would be waiting; they would surround him. He would not try to fight four spearmen in the bush. The Masai would tie him and hold him. They would kill the Bushman.

The Masai listened to the plan and nodded. *Bwana sitani* was clever. The zareba would trap all his enemies. The white man who followed them would die because he thought first of animals and not of the cleverness of his enemy. They would hide like mambas in the bush and leap upon the old man when he rode by. *Ai*, they were warriors again, *elmoran*, and they would show the Faceless One the skill and courage of the great Masai.


## CHAPTER TWELVE

THRUSHWOOD and Chapupa rode over the last rise, rested on the crest of the mountain, and saw Pfeffer's line of fire far away in the vast sweep of grassland below. The fire ran out from the rocks and cliffs and then turned slightly. It was obvious; Pfeffer was going to throw a semicircle of flame before the cliffs as he had done long ago.

Thrushwood squinted at the fire. It would be useless to race down the miles of mountainside and rolling hills and out into the miles of grass to catch up with Pfeffer. It would be impossible. But it would not be impossible to go down and ride along behind the cliffs and catch the German at the end of his line of fire. He had to return to the cliffs or his mission would fail. He would be tired and his horses spent and they would get him in the smoke and din and confusion of his terrible work.

But was there no way to save the animals? Was there no break in that long line of cliff, no way at all for the trapped game to escape? It seemed impossible. Pfeffer had no doubt blocked a few paths through the rock wall. He and Chapupa could look for such places as they rode along the open country behind the cliffs.

He kicked his horse forward and Chapupa followed; they hurried down the mountainside. From time to time, he explained their mission to Chapupa and the old man nodded in agreement. It was the only choice they had.

The land fell off; the rocky steepness was replaced by soft hills scattered with thorn trees. They approached the reverse side of the cliffs and turned their horses and rode parallel to them. There was the smell of smoke in the air.

Thrushwood rode ahead, his old eyes studying each line and fold in the cliffs. Two long hours passed and then he halted and waited for Chapupa and the other horses.

There was a break in the level line that the ridge made against the sky, a narrow gap which could be a ravine. And if it were a ravine, there would be a barrier across it; a wall of some kind that Pfeffer had built to cut off the escape of the animals he was ringing with fire. The barrier would have to be destroyed; he would have to go down to do it, burn it perhaps, and then go on. There might be other escape routes that Pfeffer had blocked. He turned his horse and rode back to join Chapupa. The old native was resting the horses under a big tree where the grass was lush and green.

"Wait here," Thrushwood told Chapupa. "There's a break, a ravine down there. I can just see it from the rise. I've got to have a look at it, see if he's blocked it. We'll get him this time. He's got to come back to the ridge to make his fire complete. We'll get him when he does. He'll have his back to the fire and his horses will be finished." Chapupa nodded. He would wait with the animals, let them rest and eat the sweet grass.

Thrushwood rode off and came to the rise. The downward slope was stony and at the bottom there was an expanse of sand and then scraggly bushes. The ground leveled off again and it became richer—high bushes now and trees. He came upon a game trail and followed it, walking his horse, for the trail twisted and turned through the high bush. The ravine was ahead of him and he could see that it was twenty yards wide and cut through vertical granite walls. His horse started, jumped, and he cursed it. Then he saw them: four sweating Masai in a semicircle

around him, arms drawn back with long spears ready. Two of
them slipped around in front of him and they closed in. They
had been hiding in the bushes, waiting for him. He had been
trapped. Pfeffer had him.

He knew somehow that they would not kill him unless he
reached for his rifle or tried to escape; their faces told him that
and their stance and the fact that he was still alive to meditate.

The black men closed in around him and pulled him down
from the horse. They were renegade Masai, no doubt, pariahs,
criminals who had been whipped and shamed and cast out of
their tribe. They were doomed to live by themselves and they
could never return to their people. If they came upon other men
of their tribe now, they would be killed without mercy. That
was the law.

They led him through the bushes and came to a lone camel's-
thorn tree. There were riems here, and they sat him down and
tied his wrists together in back of the tree trunk. They tied
his ankles together, then they squatted down and looked at
him.

"Are you afraid to kill me, dogs?" Thrushwood asked. "Does
the jackal slinking in the grass fear the lion even when he is
down? Or is the sun in my eyes and have I come upon women
looking for sticks to burn?"

"You have come upon *bwana sitani*, old fool," said the leader.
"He needs you and he is our master now. He will be pleased with
our work and we shall travel with him and be safe. We are
outcasts and every spear is against us. But now we are with the
greatest hunter."

"Where is the Bushman?" one of them asked.

"He follows the spoor of your master," Thrushwood said. "In
the smoke and excitement he will creep close to the madman
and spear him. Then you will have no protector."

The Masai laughed. Thrushwood realized that he must keep
them here for a while, keep them talking before one of them
thought to follow his spoor back and come upon Chapupa. Before
long the old man would grow restless and come to investigate. . . .

"He will soon be dead, then," said one of the Masai, and the
others nodded. "No one can kill *bwana sitani*. He is too clever."

Thrushwood spat at his side in disgust. "Fools," he said. "Listen
to me if you want to live. You are young and you have done
wrong among your own people and you are pariahs, but you are
men and you wish to live. *Bwana sitani*, as you call the German,

is mad. White doctors say he is mad. His eyes do not see as ours do and terrible things possess his spirit. He is a buffalo mad from the sun and thirst and old wounds, who smashes all before him. He kills everything. Soon there will be nothing in Africa except the white bones of dead things. Believe me, Masai! I have hunted him for many months and his spoor is that of total death. You have caught me, yes; you have me now and you will give me to *bwana sitani* and he will kill me, for among all men he fears me the most. No other man hunts him; they are afraid, they do not know of his true evil. He will murder me and then what will he do? Do you not see, warriors of the Masai? He will shoot you down like hyena who sniff at the body of a lion. You will have no value to him when I am dead, no value. You will die then and he will go on and destroy the world. But you are not ready to die. Go and let me deal with this faceless one or we shall all be dead before the night."

They sat around him, deeply silent. His words held them. Chapupa would not come this way and be caught. He would come on foot and see what had happened and do something. But what?

"Do you know me, soldiers? Do you wonder why I speak your tongue as well as you yourselves? I am John Thrushwood. I am a friend of those who were your people. I hunted lion with your fathers. I have lived among you, know you as only few white men do. I am a friend. Go now and let me burn the zareba that the German has certainly built in the ravine; go and do not wait for him to return. He will shoot you after he shoots me. He does not need you, young warriors of the Masai; he rides alone and wants no man to look upon him. When he has killed me, you will be witnesses. The white police do not hunt him, for he has killed no men, but when he kills me he will be a murderer and he will not let you live to tell his secret. Go now, quickly, great warriors. Do not let his gun find you. Go and let me deal with this man. Then I shall go to the elders of your people and tell them of your great deeds, of your nobility, your wisdom; of how you helped John Thrushwood, friend of the Masai, catch *bwana sitani*, who would destroy all living things. I shall ask them to forgive your mistakes and let you walk once more among your people and look into the faces of your loved ones. I shall speak to the old friends of my youth, to En Do, to M'Bolo of the Leopard Clan, to old Giwi, if he still lives, and his sons Menji and Tamani."

"Quiet, old fool," said the leader. "You cackle like an old crone who fears the coming of the night."

"He will kill all of you," Thrushwood said. "You will be witnesses of the murder of a white man and he will not let you live with his own life in your hands. Go! Quickly!"

"Quiet!" The Leader's assagai was at Thrushwood's chest now. The man was provoked, dangerous. But the words seemed to have had some effect. The faces of the others were sullen and they did not look up. The memory of the warrior was in them and they were shamed. And they were frightened. The leader motioned for them to get up and they did so and moved away silently without looking back.

Chapupa lay motionless on the hot slab of rock. There was nothing he could do for John Thrushwood. The odds were too great; if he showed himself they might kill the white man immediately. They had Thrushwood and treated him as a prisoner. They must be keeping him for Pfeffer—that was the answer. The German had set a trap to catch Thrushwood, and when he was finished with the fire he would return and deal with his prisoner.

But there was something he could do for John Thrushwood. He could kill Pfeffer. Thrushwood was in a hopeless position and the Masai would probably spear him when Pfeffer did not return. And thousands of animals would die, for the barrier would stand now; but when it was all over, Pfeffer would be dead and the terrible killing would at last be over. It was a bad time, a time of great dying. When it was finished, he would follow the spoor of the four Masai and kill them at his leisure, one by one. If Thrushwood had to die, then they would all die; a good man's death would have to buy the death of Pfeffer.

He edged back, slowly and with great care. He slid down the back of the rock and trotted to where he had left the horse. It was bad to leave Thrushwood but he could do nothing here; Thrushwood would want him to get Pfeffer now. And if he killed Pfeffer, the Masai might let Thrushwood go unharmed. The German had some control over them; if he was dead, they might not risk the murder of a white man.

Two hours later, Chapupa was near the end of the cliffs. Somewhere along here Pfeffer would set his last fire. Then he would ride away from it and along the cliffs until he found a way up. He would ride back along the ridge until he came to the ravine

Then he would ride down the reverse slope of the ridge. While thousands of trapped animals died before the barrier, clawing at the granite cliff, he would have one more thing to kill— Thrushwood.

Chapupa sat and studied the horizon. Far away, almost invisible because of the distance, was smoke; thin spires of white against the blue. In time they would grow wide and meet and form an advancing wall of flame that nothing could stop.

Chapupa kicked his horse and rode on along the top of the ridge. Since he had left the gorge there had been no break in the cliff wall, no way to descend, no way for Pfeffer to get up unless he was lucky enough to find a place where he could climb by hand.

He rode faster now, as fast as the rock and brush would allow. Another hour passed and there was still no way down; the cliff was falling off and he was only fifty feet from the grass below, but it was a sharp, vertical drop. And then, ten minutes later, he found a way down: a narrow and dangerous trail that erosion had once started, and enlarged bit by bit over the long years, aided perhaps by gazelle and other animals. Chapupa led the horse, talking to it, feeling the path ahead, and at last they were down.

There was no great hurry now. He rested the horse and let it graze, gave it water from the skin bag. And then he was ready. He took his flint and steel and crouched in the grass. Fire came and spread and the horse grew nervous; flames now in the dry grass marching slowly toward the mouth of the gorge; flames blocking off Pfeffer's only way up the face of the cliff.

Chapupa rode off, directly away from the ridge. He started another fire and noticed the coil of rope hanging from the saddle. He rode away from the flames and halted. There was a piece of wire in the saddlebag, too, he remembered, and he got it out. It was six feet long when he unraveled it, an old piece of bailing wire that Thrushwood had found somewhere. He fastened one end of it to the rope. Then he gathered a great armload of dry grass and crushed it beneath him until it was a solid and compact ball. He wound the wire around it, first in one direction and then in another. He set fire to it and jumped on the horse and whipped it without mercy. The burning ball of grass bounded behind him, spewing fire every few yards; sparks fell from it, igniting the veld grass. A line of fire followed the racing horse, a line which soon became thick and solid and impassable.

Miles later, the burning ball of grass disintegrated completely and fell from the cage of wire that held it. Chapupa stopped and made another ball, but he bound it tighter this time and added other things to hold the fire longer, things from the saddlebag: rags, pieces of blanket, old clothes. And he rode on dragging it behind him, leaving flame in his wake. When he was five miles from the cliff, the second fireball died out and fell away.

He got down and made another ball of grass and rode off, but now he swung to his left, toward Pfeffer. If he was lucky and fast enough, he could trap Pfeffer; join his own flames to the German's and encircle him with fire. If he was unlucky, Pfeffer would escape and shoot him. He whipped the horse now, kicked it, drove it on. There was no turning back now. One of them had to die.

Thrushwood tested the riems that bound his hands. They were very tight; there was no slackness. There was another riem around his boots. This, too, was very tight, but with some effort, he knew, he could pull his feet out of the sweaty boots.

His position was hopeless. He was an old man who was going to die. But the bitterness was not in dying, it was in the defeat, it was in the knowledge that Pfeffer would go on, that Pfeffer had beaten him.

Far away over the cliffs there was smoke. . . .

He struggled against the riems, automatically, irrationally. He cursed himself and his stupidity. He cursed the Masai, called for them.

"Warriors of the Masai! Come! Cut me loose! The veld is burning and a terrible day comes to us all! Quickly, Lion Men, your ancestors call to you to be men as they were, not women who palaver while the world dies before them!"

The four natives came through the bushes. The last one led Thrushwood's horse. He tied it to another tree fifty feet away. Then he joined the others, who came and stood in front of him.

"We have talked," the leader said. "We have talked and thought of your words and we tell you now that we believe you. The German is mad. We know that. And he will kill us, too, as you say, for he does not want men about who could tell the police and the soldiers that he killed you. We were fools not to think of it."

"Cut me loose then," Thrushwood said. "We can go after him. First I want to see the ravine. Is there a barrier across it?"

"Yes, there is a wall of trees and thorn," said one of them. "But it shall stay there. And you will stay here. We are going away. When the German comes he will be angry that we have run away. But he will be glad that you are here and that the zareba is not broken. He will weigh these things and he will not follow us. We will not be witnesses of your murder. We will have done him no harm, only good. We shall be safe from his rancor."

"I am thirsty," Thrushwood said. "Do one thing for me. Take the canteen from my horse and remove the top. Hang it from the branch over my head here so that it hangs in front of my face. Then I can sip from it throughout the day. I am an old man who will die very soon. That is all I ask of you."

The leader motioned to one of the others and he went and got the canteen and hung it on the branch as Thrushwood had asked. It swung before him like the pendulum of a grandfather clock. He held his head forward and stopped it. It swung around and he caught the metal opening in his teeth, tilted it back and swallowed a mouthful of water. The Masai watched like children. In the middle of a life-and-death discussion, Thrushwood had engaged in what appeared to be something inane and silly.

"Let me go, warriors. What you do is good. You will live; you will not die needlessly because you have seen too much. But cut me loose. Let me stop this madman." But now Thrushwood didn't care whether they cut him free or not. He wanted them to go. He had the canteen and he could get loose and burn the barrier and get Pfeffer. He'd been saved, saved by the old battered canteen full of water that swayed before him.

"Hurry," he said to the men. "Cut me loose. Every minute brings the Faceless One nearer with his terrible gun."

Two of the Masai turned automatically and looked behind them, shifting their feet.

"Let us go," one of them said.

"We go now," the leader said. He turned to Thrushwood. "If we cut you loose, he will kill us. If we stay, he will kill us. If we cut you loose and give you back your rifle, you may grow angry and shoot us. We have only one choice. We leave you here." He bent down and tested the riems around Thrushwood's boots and then walked behind the tree and tested those that held his wrists. He grunted in satisfaction. Then he shouted to the others and they were off, trotting, like warriors going to battle. They went through the high grass and the bushes and in a few moments they were gone from sight.

Thrushwood waited. Minutes passed. They would not come

back. He caught the canteen in his teeth and tilted it back. Water poured into his mouth, good, sweet water. But he did not swallow it. He held it in his mouth and then leaned sideways and spit it out on the ground, close to the tree. Then, as quickly as he could, he twisted his body around the tree trunk, throwing his feet around, heaving and straining until he sat on the opposite side of the tree. He felt back with his bound hands and found the scant water that remained and the mud that it had made of the dry earth. He rubbed the riems in the water and mud. He rested for a few moments and then worked himself around the tree trunk again to the spot where the canteen hung. He got another mouthful of water, spit it on the same spot, and then kicked and heaved himself around the tree again. There was more water now, for it did not drain as quickly into the moistened earth. He rubbed the riems into it and then strained against them. The water would soften them, make them expand under pressure. If he had time enough and water enough he could work his hands loose.

Pfeffer scratched another match on the side of his boot, dropped it in the grass, and rode on. He rode on another quarter of a mile and dropped another match. Perhaps he would have Thrushwood when he got back to the gorge; maybe his trap had worked for the Englishman, too, and if it had, he would enjoy himself in the night. He had wondered a long while about Thrushwood, about how he would kill him. There were so many ways to kill, so many ways, and each one good in its own way. He was going to hang Thrushwood.

He rode on and watched eland running away from the fire. He dropped another match but it went out and he swore at it and struck another. He was going to hang John Thrushwood from the big hardekool tree a mile or two from the gorge. He would make a fine hangman's noose with the official thirteen turns and he would fit it on the Englishman's neck with great care. He would not hurry. He would make it last a whole day. He would scrape up a mound of dirt under one of the limbs and Thrushwood would stand on it while the rope was made taut. He would have to stand straight and erect and quiet on the mound of earth and he would stand there all through the day. And when the day was over, Pfeffer would kick away the dirt and watch the Englishman struggle before him, strangle and die for having tried to stop him. He would hang Thrushwood, for hanging is the worst way to die.

He rode on, his mind filled with the vision of Thrushwood with a noose around his neck. Then he became irritated; a vague thought prodded his mind, told him that something was wrong, something was wrong. . . .

He stopped and looked around. What could be wrong? His semicircle of flame was well over half-completed. The cliffs were still far away but visible, and in his wake was a solid wall of flame. He kicked the horse and rode on faster now. And then he realized that the line of fire seemed to run far in back of him. It was an illusion perhaps, or some freak of wind current that had pushed the fire around him. But he was unsettled. He rode on and found a high place, an outcropping of granite. No horse could climb it. He tied the animal and scrambled up.

He rubbed his eyes. He cupped his hands around them and looked in disbelief. A line of fire ran out from the cliffs and circled in back of his own fire. He could not believe it. He looked away, at his horse below, at the stones, but when he looked again it was still the same. It was no mirage, no freak optical illusion. It was real. The fire was there. He was trapped like the gazelles and zebras and giraffes. Thrushwood had set the fire, had watched him from the cliff top and thrown a ring of fire around him.

He slipped and slithered down the rock and ran to his horse. He was gasping, out of breath. He slashed at the horse and they were off at a breakneck pace, heading toward the cliffs. Now they rode into the game, into the herds of springbok and eland, close to a lone buffalo, mad and dangerous to approach. The smell of smoke mixed with the dust now, and once they were almost caught up in a herd of wildebeest. They came upon lions loping along, still dignified and unruffled, and gazelles of all sorts shot past with a speed that blurred their sleek bodies.

It would be madness, Pfeffer knew, to head for the gorge and attempt to crawl over the barricade. By the time he reached it, there would be ten thousand animals with the same thought and he would die with them, squashed between their bodies and ground to bits under their hoofs. There was only one way out: the cliffs. The horse would stay behind and die in the fire but he could find a spot somewhere and crawl to safety.

He rode on, whipping his horse, cursing it.

Then he was at the cliff. He halted. Rested. The cliff was too smooth here but he would find a way up. There was time; the fire was still far away. Which way to go—left or right? He turned the horse and rode to his left, away from the gorge, scanning the cliff. Ten minutes passed and he began to fight a terrible fear that was a knot expanding somewhere in his chest. And then he found a spot that he was sure he could climb; he dismounted and tied the horse to a stunted tree and readied himself for the climb. It would not be too difficult. The cliff here was sixty or perhaps seventy feet high. Once he got above the first ten feet, the climb would be relatively easy; he could inch his way up to where there was a wide V-shaped crack. This would be difficult but he had done it before and knew that he could do it now. He would have to brace himself against both sides of the fissure and work up it, a simple climbing technique. And if he did slip here, he would slide to where the walls of the V were closer together and catch himself.

He mounted the horse and then stood on its back. He found a tiny ledge for his foot and, reaching up, found a knob of rock that seemed solid enough to bear his weight. He began to climb.

It took him twenty minutes to reach the bottom of the split. His hands were slippery and there was sweat in his eyes that he could not rub away. Just as he was about to swing into the fissure, he slipped, his left foot first, and then, as he tried to strike out and find another foothold, his right foot slipped and he hung desperately for a few seconds, grunting and trying to throw himself upward to the safety of the crack.

But he fell, clawing at the cliff, and beneath him the horse bolted, broke loose from the stunted tree and ran off wildly. He hit the ground and the shock jarred every bone in his body. He crawled into the shade under the cliff and rested for a long time. No bones had been broken; he had been lucky. The fire was coming closer, and if he stayed here, he would burn, shrivel up like an insect.

He began climbing again. He had to make it. His fingers were weaker now and his legs trembled under the strain. He reached the place where he had slipped and somehow got past it. Then his hand reached the bottom of the fissure and his foot found a spot that would carry his weight and he was up and in the fissure. He rested for a long time, watching the fire draw closer—his fire.

He began working up the sides of the fissure, one leg braced against each smooth side; and then, as it grew wider, he had both legs on one side and his back against the other. He came to a sturdy root and seized it and knew he was safe. In another few minutes he was up and out of the fissure, standing on top of the ridge.

He began walking and running and trotting toward the gorge, to where the four Masai waited for him. Something had gone wrong. Thrushwood was out on the veld now but it did not matter. There was the extra horse at the ravine, the horse he had taken from the Bushman. And Thrushwood thought he was dead, trapped in the fire. He would take the horse and ride away and hide for a time. Thrushwood would ride away thinking him dead. Only the Masai knew he was alive and when he had his horse and the rifle in his hands, he would kill them.

He hurried along the crest of the ridge. On the veld below him, the great semicircle of fire closed in toward the cliffs, driving great herds of game before it.

## CHAPTER THIRTEEN

THRUSHWOOD'S right hand pulled through the riems that bound it and suddenly he was free. His wrists and hands were numb and bruised from the ordeal; the blood rushed back into the dead fingers and he cried out. He fumbled with the riems that bound his feet, and after a long while they parted. He had lost track of time; there had been the water and the riems and the terrible straining and there was nothing else. Chapupa existed somewhere, but he was far away and forgotten. Only the smoke was there, filling the whole sky. It might be too late. If he fired the barricade, it might send the animals into a mad frenzy and they might stampede back into the veld and die there. He crawled to the horse and mounted it slowly. The ravine was close, a quarter of a mile away. He was halfway there when a rifle cracked and the horse died under him.

He pulled his rifle free as the horse sank down in the high grass. He began to run, zigzagging through the bushes, swerving and sidestepping. Another crack of the rifle: the bullet passed close to him, brassy and angry. The ground fell away and there were large boulders. The horseman followed him. Another bullet bounced off the big rock ahead of him. Pfeffer was gaining on him. He reached the entrance of the ravine, halted and turned. There was time for one shot and he could not miss. He fired and Pfeffer's horse turned sideways, threw him into the air, and staggered away dying.

Thrushwood turned and ran. He could get Pfeffer later. The

barrier now, he must reach it. If he failed, a hundred thousand animals would die in terrible torment.

And then he was before it. He saw heavy posts buried in the ground and thorn tangle before it, high and wide and impassable There was only one way to attack it. But Pfeffer was closing in on him and there was no sign of cover in the narrow ravine. He staggered up to the barrier. There were animals milling behind it, hundreds, thousands. Near one end was an indentation in the smooth granite wall. Thrushwood made for it. He put his rifle against the wall and began gathering sticks and bark and grass. He piled this against the bottom of the barricade near him, where it joined the wall.

A rifle cracked and splinters of granite cut into his cheek. He crawled into the niche, found his rifle. He waited. He could not see Pfeffer. Animal noises were now very close, only yards away, the sounds of trapped animals filled with terror. Minutes went by. There was only one thing to do. He had to get to the debris he'd piled against the end of the barricade. Set fire to it. Perhaps it was enough to do the job. It would mean exposing himself to Pfeffer for another few moments but he had to chance it. He gathered what fuel he could find within hands' reach—dead grass, twigs, dried leaves. He put it all in his hat and shook the powder from three cartridges over it. He turned around, gathering himself like a sprinter. Then, in one motion, he struck a match on the wall of the ravine, dropped it into the hat, saw it catch, and then was up, running for the barricade.

Pfeffer's rifle cracked and Thrushwood's leg buckled under him. But he was close enough. He threw the hat and hit the main pile of debris and spewed fire over it. And in the same motion, he turned back, hopping and falling and squirming, to the cover of the shallow niche. Now Pfeffer was running at him, running desperately to put a bullet in his head and get at the fire.

Thrushwood was tired; blood was pumping from his leg and dizziness was coming on. His hand found the rifle and its familiar stock brought him back to reality. He hefted it almost casually and aimed at Pfeffer. The German was a hundred yards away, ninety, eighty. . . . He pulled the trigger and Pfeffer staggered and went down.

So tired . . . he didn't care about Pfeffer any more. Let Pfeffer kill him. Then he could sleep. He let go of the rifle and it clattered against the rock and lay still. He felt around him; the spot of sand under the overhang was soft and cool. He got his belt off somehow and twisted it around his leg to stop the bleeding. He closed his eyes and everything swerved and went racing down a long spiral. . . .

Pfeffer's knee had been shattered by Thrushwood's shot. He lay in the sand. He tried to crawl forward but the pain was such that he almost fainted. He fired at the niche but the Englishman did not return the fire. He fired again and again. He couldn't wait any longer. Where were the four Masai? If they were here, they could help him up and carry him away. But they had sensed their own death somehow and run away.

The barricade was burning. It was impossible. The great wall that he had labored on was being eaten away. He could not put it out. It was too big and he could barely crawl. But he had to do something! He could not stay here—not here.

He rolled over and began pulling himself forward inch by inch over the sand and stones. Then he fainted.

The barrier burned, heaving and moving like something alive. The bushes and thorn trees turned to hot ash. The posts burned steadily and then fell, one by one. The animals moved closer to it as the heat went away. The push behind moved them toward it. Then a frightened gazelle bounded through the belt of ash and burning sticks and logs; another followed by instinct . . . another . . . another. Now a cow buffalo blinded from the smoke blundered across, then a bold wildebeest. The trickle of animals turned into a rush, then a flood. Some knowledge gripped the great herd instantly. They pushed forward and surged through the embers and ash and smoking debris.

Pfeffer regained consciousness. The ground shook under him. He opened his eyes and saw the sand and the stones in exaggerated size. They shook and quivered; there was a great thunder somewhere, in his ears, in his body now, shaking him. He raised himself on one arm and saw the gray walls of the ravine and the blue sky above filled with smoke. Something ran past him. . . .

He turned his head and looked behind him, down the ravine where Thrushwood was, and the barrier. And, as he looked, the thunder grew and he screamed and tried to crawl away as the first horde of terrorized animals swept down the ravine—a monstrous living tidal wave, pulverizing everything before it.

The great fire burned. It reached the cliffs and it stopped. There was still much smoke, and small fires burned quietly, but the heat was gone and the danger. Chapupa sat on his horse and studied the far-off ridge. He had trapped Pfeffer. The man was dead. But the animals were dead in the ravine. And what of Thrushwood? He might be alive in the hands of the Masai. He must ride and find them and tell them what had happened, tell them to turn Thrushwood free. Or he might wait until night came and crawl close to them and perhaps kill them all while they slept.

He kicked the horse and rode down the fire-blackened hill. He rode for a long time and came at last to the place where he had started his fire, many hours before, where there was a narrow and dangerous way up the cliff face. He dismounted and led the horse. It was easier this time going up.

When he came to the ravine, he sat for a long while looking down into it. It was a wide sward of raw earth. All the bushes were gone and some of the smaller trees had been smashed down, but the hundreds of thousands of animals had somehow broken through the barricade.

He went down the long incline of shale and stone and rode out into the soft earth. He turned his horse and rode into the ravine full of wonder and amazement. Pfeffer was dead in the fire and the animals lived! He must find the spoor of the Masai now and follow and learn of Thrushwood.

He rode on, the raw earth soft under the horse. He came upon Thrushwood, sitting in the niche with his rifle beside him.

"Where have you been, old one? When danger comes you run and hide in the grass like a young maiden."

Chapupa grunted. "I saw you captured by the four boys and so I left you with them to keep you out of the way. Then I trapped Pfeffer in his own fire and destroyed him. Now I have come to bring you home."

But Thrushwood was too tired and weak to talk. Later he would tell Chapupa the full story. He got to his feet and Chapupa brought the horse to him and got him up on it. The leg had bled but Pfeffer's bullet had not hit the bone.

Chapupa led the horse back the way he had come. They would camp here until Thrushwood's leg healed. Soon, this chopped and burned earth would be green once more. The animals would come back. They would breed and multiply and be safe.

# THE CLYDESIDERS

Hugh Munro

*"The Clydesiders"* is published by
*Macdonald & Co. Ltd.*

## The Author

Hugh Munro, the son of a riveter, was born in the Govan district of Glasgow. He left school at fourteen and, like all the men of his family, went to work in the shipyards. The slump of the early thirties cut short his apprenticeship and he worked as a farm labourer and factory hand. Munro is a natural writer, and stirred by the example of a brother who became a star Fleet Street reporter, he freelanced in London and Scotland, contributing widely to press and radio. His tough dockyard detective, Clutha, has featured with great success as the hero of a long series of short stories in the *Glasgow Evening Citizen*. Happily married, he now lives with his wife and three children in the Ayrshire coast town of Saltcoats.

To all the boys and girls who ever sat on a stone stairhead telling stories to while the winter's nights away.

# CHAPTER ONE

THE winch-gear slipped and the pulley drum stopped revolving.

Cursing, Big Mick grabbed at the motor switch-knob, forgetting he had only one cable turn round the drum. Like a ribbon of fire the steel hawser ripped through his fingers.

Yelping, Mick let the cable go. His lift of staging planks leapt in mid-air and cascaded to the bottom of the drydock, the dervish-snaking cable and its free-falling ball-hook bouncing murderously with them.

Under the tumbling load four riggers scattered desperately. The eldest, a stocky man in his forties, only just got clear. As the timber thundered and a plank cart-wheeled across the dock-floor slime to within inches of his ankles he looked up, his frozen, bellicose stance and spiky ginger moustache adding a walrus touch to his fury. His hot brown eyes met the first apprehensive peep of Big Mick edging over the lip of the dock.

"You ham-fisted Irish bastard," exploded the rigger, "who the hell ever told you you could handle a winch?"

Mick's tension eased. He saw the squad was safe and a glance around the wharves discovered no authoritative witness. He spat sideways in relief.

"Not so much of the bastard," he warned. "The winch cut out and there was damn all I could do."

"You're a liar," said the rigger bitterly. "If you'd had a right hitch on the drum the load could never slip. You nearly kilt the four of us."

"Jasus, and it would have been no loss if I'd kilt you, Haig. You've got too bloody much lip."

One of the other riggers side-mouthed to Haig. "Shut yer trap, Collie; the big midden's only looking for a scapegoat."

Haig refused to be placated. His nerves were still jangling and the sneer on the dark face overhead was a taunt his spirit could not bear.

"Shut up?" he echoed deliberately. "Why should I shut up for that?—the big Belfast broth-mouth."

The man on the breast of the dock straightened up. His brows beetled and his underlip pouted. "I'm warning you, boy," he said menacingly. "Wan more word from you and it's the office for you."

"Away and kiss my bonnet," said Haig. "Who ever made you a penny man must've had a farthing head himself. I'll bet your behind's still sore with them kicking you into the job."

Without another word the big man vanished from sight. Forebodingly the three riggers gathered round their mate.

"You've done it now, Collie," said one. "You know what that weed is—and whatever yarn he tells the gaffer'll be right."

"The check boy'll be down the now with your time," agreed another moodily.

"T'hell with them," said Haig. "I've waited to give that one a bellyful for a long time . . . the rotten big soda-heid!"

"Ah, but you've got to swallow these things," frowned the first. Illiterately he stumbled anxiously. "You know, Collie, there's no' a handful of sweeties o' jobs on the whole Clyde just now. Jings, my brother-in-law that's a chargehand in Brown's, was just telling me there's hardly a keel being laid between here and Port Glasgow. Where you gonny get another job?"

"Keel?" marvelled the smallest. "I'll bet this is the only repair job between here and Troon Harbour. We're muckin' lucky to be in out of the rain."

"You're in," said Collie. He nodded up to the rim of the dock where a bespectacled boy, moon-faced from running and the constriction of a three-inch deep rubber collar, had materialized and was waving a pink slip importantly.

"I knew it," mourned the small rigger. "And the big bastard hadn't the guts to come and give you it hisself."

"Colin Haig," yelped the check-boy, "he's to go to the cashier's for his pay."

"See you up the street at dinner-time," said Collie. He swaggered over to the iron ladder set in the dock wall. Silently his mates watched, as hand over hand he pulled himself up its height.

"He's only kidding himself," said one as the boy held out the slip and Haig disappeared.

"Ay, and so are we," said another, making a move. "Big beerbelly'll be back as soon as he sees Collie's away—we'd better square up this lot before he starts to throw his weight around again."

"Lousy big sod!"

They began to pile the scattered planks. Since the General Strike the late '20's was no age for their kind to loiter.

## CHAPTER TWO

FORTRESS-LIKE, the administrative offices dominated the yard. Huge, sprawling, implacable in bulk, even the vaunted dreadnoughts and battleships that grew tall in the tangle of derricks behind never achieved the same impact no matter how high they strained their razor stems. The ships often overtopped the administrative roof-line but never diminished it. They vanished in a night but the office mountain was always there. Despite lip-service and public flattery to their skills, it was the power symbol the inhabitants of Burnford really respected. And often resented.

Haig felt that hate now. Like an ant circling a sandstone boulder he marched round to the cashier's with the gall of injustice sour within him. Impotence and contempt surged so strongly that even his thoughts were incoherent. From childhood the Neptunes and Tritons and great scaly-tailed mermaids splashing in carven splendour along the offices' endless street front had awed him, and, even now, although here and there weather had chipped the prong from a trident or blurred a dolphin's leap, there was something timeless and indestructible about their permanence—like the power and indifference of the fish-faced men around whose austere windows they wreathed.

The building's main doors were of dull brass. Beaten from the barrels of Nelsonian cannon, their triumphant gleam of historical allegory might escape Collie but their day-to-day message did not. Fingering his ragged moustache and sullenly conscious of his greasy moleskins and rusty broken-peaked cap he hesitated before doggedly mounting the six broad granite steps to the cathedral-like porch. Pushing aside the leafs of brass—they swung light as a butterfly's wing despite their weight—he wryly likened himself to the most useless martyr of all, the martyr who inspired no one and whose sacrifice did not even console himself.

Ordinarily, workers never set foot in this managerial holy place. They were issued with their wages on Saturdays at a row of shanty-boxes lining No. 1 launching berth, and the shoddy little tin cups labelled with each man's pay-slip was, in character and design, the perfect industrial alms bowl. The ritual of paying a man in chambers was reserved, by lofty plot or convenience, for the ungrateful who impetuously spurned the cup. The contrast between drenched or dusty queue-shuffling handout and the cathedral calm of oak-panelled corridors was not without its valedictory malice.

Haig squared his shoulders before advancing down the entrance hall. Beneath his feet fat, yellow-brown lino, acre broad, took the stamp out of his iron heel-plates. Great dark doors labelled deeply in gold Manager, Under-Manager, Iron Manager and Yard Manager stolidly ignored his progress. Running the gauntlet of their massive indifference he felt his triviality grow. And his ego shrink.

At its end the hall split into a "T" of branching corridors. From this junction a square, frosted window stencilled CASHIER watched his advance with closed, blind eye.

Haig halted before the window resignedly.

Twice he poised his unwashed fist to knock before finally releasing a quick nervous double rap.

Nothing happened. The grey window stared blankly back at him.

He rapped again.

Beyond the glass a chair scraped, a pen scratched, someone coughed genteelly. It was so quiet in the hall he could hear all these sounds in nerve-sharp focus. But they were only the unsignifying residue of the movements of the gods within. They had nothing to do with him. Instinctively Collie knew his signal had not turned one sleek head. For all practical purposes, like a specimen in alcohol, he could be left drowned and preserved indefinitely in the cloying calm of the outer hall. The window was strictly for pleading, and its echoes warranted no white-collar panic beyond.

Collie pushed the peak of his cap up. Then resettled it farther down. The still moments lengthened. Far away, beyond the brass doors, a tramcar rumbled over points and the iron song of the hammers along the river was reduced to the sleepy murmurous buzz of a distant bee-field. The alien quiet crushed Collie.

In sudden fury he beat on the window with sharper, faster knuckles. The frame rattled under his assault.

He need not have bothered. Nothing happened. Only the silence came back. And, waiting, Haig could hear his own heavy, impotent breathing.

"The bastards," he whispered.

Inside him distrust of sedentary men smouldered to madness. His fists bunched, and behind his rust-bleak eyes an impulse to smash the grey glass throbbed temptingly. In the hinterland of his mind obscene epithets revolved. He'd throw them through the shattered glass at their pasty silly faces. They would be shocked and scurry for the police. One of their own kind, steeped in barbers' lotion and hypocrisy, would sit on the Bench and wag his fat shiny head in horror.

He'd get thirty days and everybody would lick their lips and pretend to be sorry for Julia. And in the Paddy's Arms Big Mick would accept another schooner of stout from one of the creepers and declare: "Ach, shure, I didn't want to pay the poor bugger off but didn't he cry me out of me name? What man that is a man could stand for that, now?"

And all the Tims and Dans around would chorus: "By the holy jaize, Mick, you were very dacent, very dacent indeed. It's a God's blessing you didn't lift a hand and strike him to the ground yourself. . . ."

The window shot up so swiftly and silently it caught him grimacing.

The face that stared out was unimpressed. Nor did it comment.

With a flick Haig tossed across his slip. The clerk picked it off the polished counter and read it. His expression never changed. Middle-aged, he had washed-blue eyes, grey hair bushy above the ears and a completely bald crown that arched from brow to nape. He wore a severe suit of sombre grey and a high-winged collar so prim and tight it propped his long chin at an angle. His name was Meldrum and he was an earnest lay preacher who spent Sunday evenings standing in the centre of a forlorn but resolute little circle of followers advocating the sure spiritual rewards of repentance to embarrassed and unwilling, but tolerant, audiences of tenement corner loungers. Rumour was strong that Meldrum could have been Chief Cashier years ago had his conscience not forbidden him to join in the whisky drinking of managerial conferences. With envious cynicism Haig doubted the truth of this and—at this moment—despised Meldrum's white hands, white collar, douce suit and everything about him with a bitter contempt for all things allied to the trappings of administrative authority. He conveyed his hostility by a brash, unwinking stare.

Meldrum remained unshaken. The tragedy of men being fired or laid off was so much part of his routine that he seemed immune to the passions involved. He glanced over the slip again, glanced back at Haig and moved out of view.

The rigger found himself gazing vacantly at the crowns of two clerks perched on high stools bent over high, sloping desks. They did not look up. He could see their inward-turned toes propped on their spars—one, despite the camouflage of high polish, was distinctly down-at-heel—and he could see the frayed turn-ups of their well-brushed trousers. Yet he felt no kinship. To him they were two sheltered specimens of a soft breed whose activities could hardly be classed as real work and whose semi-indolent existence was supported entirely by the sweat of hard-grafting chaps like himself. The shine on their trousers and the cracks in their boots was not proof of poverty but contemptible brands of their willingness to trade truth for a place at the rich man's table—any place, so long as they sat and were mistaken for hosts.

When, at last, they raised their heads and gazed woodenly at him he read patronage and rebuke in their detached survey. That they were bored or tired never occurred to him. Or that the open window exposed them to a draught relatively more uncomfortable than a hard wind whistling between icy keel-blocks on a frosty morning.

He interpreted their glances as an expression of resentment at his invasion of their tidy, ledger-built castle. Arrogant behind his own dirty face he saw their clean ones as an affront. And automatically hated them.

A door closing in the hall behind him halted the insult trembling on his tongue. He swung round and braced himself as the Yard Manager emerged from his office.

John Ruebent had started his career as a working plater. He had lived that down. A portly little man, resenting his age but still flanking his double chins with the Dundreary wisps of his generation, he wore a sneer as a badge and never looked at a worker without accusation. A North Country Englishman, he had a contempt for Clydeside and its inhabitants but never lost an opportunity to make a sycophantic speech at launching banquets or specially-graced Corporation Burns' Suppers. Now, sheathed in black-coat caste and crowned with his high square bowler, he ignored the very existence of Haig with inviting deliberateness.

As he approached Haig, the rigger braced himself. With subtle instinct he knew the English Manager's indifference was a challenge. And recklessly he accepted.

"Mr. Ruebent!"

The manager walked past three steps before halting.

"Yes?"

The word was thrown over his shoulder like a discarded banana-skin.

"Could I speak to you?"

"You are speaking to me."

Haig swallowed a curse in his throat with difficulty.

"Well, it's like this, Mr. Ruebent—I've just been paid off but I don't think I got a square deal."

Ruebent continued staring. He still did not turn fully round.

Haig stumbled on: "I mean—it was as much the other fellow's fault——"

"What other fellow?"

"The leading hand. See, we're riggers, sir, and——"

Ruebent pouted. He had a conviction often vehemently expressed in the privacy of his own home and in the luxury of his native accent that, "Scotsmen are all a bit daft, real daft. You've got to boss them, lass, you've got to boss them."

Now his contempt showed. "I don't know what you're talking about and I haven't time to find out. But I know I don't want my yard run like a bloody backyard wash-house. If your foreman thinks you should go that's good enough for me."

Haig's chin dropped dourly. "The foreman——" he began. And stopped.

"What about the foreman?"

Haig looked at him. Through the rigger's mind ran the certainty of common knowledge. Big Mick's wife was a dark and generous beauty who shared her husband's ambitions. But maybe it was just a friendly gesture that impelled the foreman to drop in and personally tell her each time Mick had to work late. Maybe. . . .

Maybe nothing. Big Mick sold his wife and as a bargain there was nothing unique about it. And only cowardice, not conscience, would choke the accusation in another man's throat.

Yet Collie hesitated. A principle beyond moral judgments or mercenary malice dammed his spite. There were some things you threw in a man's own teeth or held your tongue on. And anyhow, knowing Ruebent, he had a fair idea that the Englishman would not welcome an abrupt challenge levelled against his subordinate's integrity. It takes more lubricants than tallow grease to launch a record number of ships, and a little light corruption is a smooth agent in any big business.

"Well?" the manager urged impatiently.

Collie took a deep breath. "I think the foreman might've spoken to me himself," he said lamely.

Ruebent's button nose lifted an inch and his scorn of Haig was complete. "My God," he stormed, "is that all your complaint? Taking up my time bleating there like a bloody sheep! Get out, man, and get your money. And stay out."

The rigger nodded resignedly and almost chuckled. "You're another."

"Another what?"

"Another bastard like Big Mick and the foreman."

He wheeled and found the lean clerk back at the window. Behind him the manager fumed: "Give this man his money. And see that his name is never put on our payroll again."

Fumbling, the clerk splayed coins on the counter. When he was certain Ruebent was gone he said: "I've made it up to dinner-time—don't forget to give the gate-keeper your check going out."

Haig picked up the treasury note and florins. His face was ugly with anger. Forgetting the gratuitous hour's wages he saw only the mask of authority on the long, impassive face drooping behind the service window. And something in its remoteness, its air of calm but dispassionate reproval, and especially the high white collar that was both badge and support of its apparent disdain exploded a trigger to his torment.

Clutching the money in his left hand the rigger plunged the other to his hip. Dragging the traditional shipyard brass identity disc from his pocket he hurled it past the clerk's head. "Give him the bloody thing yourself," he snarled.

The ping of the check hitting the far wall jerked the two ledger boys upright.

But Meldrum did not blink. Unmoved he watched the rigger swagger down the corridor. He did not even turn his head in response to his indignant juniors' queries. And only when the big brass doors stopped swinging behind Haig did he gently pull down the grey glass shutter of his window.

## CHAPTER THREE

"SPECKY CARTER" led the Third Standard out to the sunken concrete playground in good order. The ten-year-old boys bottled their anticipation well. "Physical Exercise" was the highlight of their school week. But a year in the Third had taught them not to rejoice too soon.

Specky was unpredictable. His pince-nez, knock-knees and wee Charlie Chaplin moustache were not comedy characterictics or sign-posts to weakness. At least not for his pupils. In the back-courts and stairheads of Burnford tales of Specky's discipline were legendary. In class his strut before the desks was constantly accompanied by the parabolic whirling of a two-tongued tawse. He swung that menacing black strap round his wrist until its winding ended with a flat leathery slap. Then he reversed his wrist rhythm and spun it back again.

Invariably Specky kept that strap swinging through every lesson. And in his quiet classroom the pistol-shot crack of its punctuation was never a bluff. A double-hander from Specky was real punishment. Two was cruelty. And four—his usual reprisal, two on each hand—crippled the toughest fingers for hours. And Specky made no secret of his personal enjoyment in punishing malefactors.

There was never roystering in the ranks of the Third Standard.

On his command the twin lines halted instantly in the centre of the square formed by the three tall barrack-blocks of stone classrooms and the low, grey railing-topped wall dividing the playground from the street. On the score that patience is good for the other fellow's soul—especially if he has no choice but to wait your pleasure—Specky let the class stand rigidly at attention for a long two minutes.

He sauntered all round them, savouring their suspense and apprehension of his intention. Mr. Carter had often been described by members of the local school board as "a good strong teacher".

On the street passing housewives rested their shopping baskets on the wall and gazed sentimentally through the railings. The thirty little boys in grey Norfolk jackets or homely knitted blue and red jerseys inspired nostalgic memories of their own sons, or even the distant days when a penny a week had paid for their own dear-bought education. The younger women, arming tartan-shawl wrapped babies, had more vivid esoteric memories of enlightening happenings, witnessed or experienced behind the red brick lavatory annexes. Their childhood was still recent enough to sharpen their view of the tableaux with a reserve of private cynicism.

Carter enjoyed their audience. Puffed with his own social superiority he was as contemptuous of them as he was of their children, but not enough to neglect the opportunity of parading his professional status. Tucking his hands under his coat-tails he took up a commanding position. He rocked on his toes a little and squared his castor-oil bottle shoulders.

"Well, boys," he invited, lifting his soft chin. "What is it to be today—handball, rounders or what?"

His class was not fooled. Specky's speech was always mild before witnesses. It was his characteristic to be ingratiating, logical, even matey as a preliminary to inflicting something subtly vicious on his victims. He knew perfectly well, if the choice was really theirs, no debate was needed. And knowing him, the sickening thought was in all their hearts that this grandstand pose was just a tantalizing forerunner to another sugar-coated denial.

Carter knew what they were thinking. And with what passed with him as whimsy, and for their future confusion, decided to prove their forebodings wrong.

"Come now, boys," he urged sweetly, "shout out someone—surely you know what game you want?"

The boys sideglanced at each other. They had been through this hoop before.

"Well?"

"Fitba'," a dour boy in the second row, with the fatalistic conviction that denial might better come soon than late, dared to breathe.

"What was that?" Carter's small black eyes mocked their watchful faces. He lip-read rather than heard the boy, but it was part of the game to keep them on edge.

A barefoot ragamuffin with a toothless lisp plucked up courage. "Football, sir," he sprayed, and jerked back in the shadows of his neighbour.

"Football?" The teacher's tone was pitched on the exact note of mild surprise that invited the women ranged along the railings to appreciate his jolliness. They chuckled accordingly and admired his nice suburban suit and well-bred accent. Roused by their tolerance the class had to respond to their own single passion's lure.

"Yes, sir."

"Football!"

"Football!"

"Please, sir!"

The pleas gathered courage and volume. The two ranks began to bend and surge. High-held fingers snapped eagerly, and faces glowed with sudden hope.

Still Carter tantalized them. "Not Rugby?" he suggested, lips twitching beneath his little moustache in sardonic foreknowledge.

"Aww!"

The groan in concert was heartfelt. To escape from their desks the boys were prepared to play anything from skipping ropes to hopscotch, but even to pretend interest in Rugby was beyond their powers of hypocrisy.

In their world a ball was sacred to kicking, and people who debased its holy purpose by running with it in their arms were not only beyond the pale and beneath the salt, they were probably handicapped both mentally and physically. One could pity them but to be forced to practise their abuses was a misery only one degree removed from the serfdom of sums and spelling. Apathetically they glowered at Specky.

"All right," Carter simulated generosity. "Football it is then. . . ."

The cheer and joyous jumping that greeted his concession was instinctive and could not have been smothered by the most oval-headed autocrat.

"Keep the ball low and watch the windows," ordered Carter. "All boys wearing boots or shoes take them off. And no tripping!"

As he spoke jackets and caps were being tossed into four heaps against the opposite walls of the surrounding buildings to form two goals. Chattering like robins they pranced expectantly, the better clad boys tearing off footwear at record speed to put themselves on level terms with half their classmates who habitually, from necessity, went barefoot.

"Oho!" they chanted, trotting with high knees in tight little circles like their heroes at near-by Ibrox Park, "the old baries. Who's got the ba'?"

A red rubber ball twice the size of a cricket ball bounced mysteriously from somewhere. Eagerly they scrambled and mulled round it, heading it with professional side-flicks and well-timed forehead accuracy. In these preliminaries they all looked miniature world-beaters, and in their dreams, because it was a Protestant school, each was sheathed in the light blue jersey of the Rangers Football Club.

The playground was only forty yards square. But for them it was wonderful. Their two sides, each twenty strong, made light of the negligible area of manoeuvre. For them, cramped conditions were natural. The only time most of them trod grass or kicked a real football was on the annual day trip with a Sunday School. Their daily arenas were between street lamp-posts or even the narrow black earth of tenement-trapped backcourts. The rare experience of having the whole playground to themselves—small as it was—was a luxury.

And most of them were masters of the ball. Turning handicaps to advantages they had raised close control to an art. Any stretch of wall was a practice net, and to keep a ball bouncing between it and a bobbing forehead for a thousand times or more without a fall was too common an exercise to be considered a feat. And since most of them ran every errand through crowded streets and winding pends and closes always with a rubber ball bouncing at their feet, intricate feints, swerves and dummies were an instinctive pattern of their dribbling. Only the clumsy player was unusual.

Physically the boys did not rate. Undersized and undernourished, many of them had ugly bone defects—crooked backs, buckled shins, splay feet, hen toes—all the variations of rickets mockingly characterized throughout the rest of Scotland as "Glasgow legs". Many of them, too, had broken skins and sore faces and two had violent eye squints.

But they were gay in spirit. And no Eton wall game exacted more hard knocks or saw bruise and tumbles endured with less complaint. In the pursuit of that red ball they displayed all the qualities that ever graced the noblest green field hymned in poetry.

Yet Carter had no affection for them. And he made no effort to win theirs. The son of a Saltmarket fruiterer's assistant, who had tamed and penned a wandering packman into matrimonial stability and small shop prosperity, he resented his origins and his indebtedness to his parents for his education. A first generation snob with no real talent, his soul was so small he could not even wear the mask of culture without it shrinking into a sneer.

At heart he was still so near to the pavements that the crude accents of his class was a daily reminder how narrowly he had missed the gutter. And he took his revenge by dipping his small whip of authority in acid and hoped its constant flick would brand them with a consciousness of his superiority. It only burned hate into their judgments.

Taking the ball he moved into the centre and viewed their divisions coldly. He cocked his prim Homburg for a moment to the mnemonic chant of an infant class in a corner room reciting C-A-T spells CAT, D-O-G spells DOG, before warning: "Now don't yell your silly heads off or I'll take you all inside again. Understand?"

Forty pairs of eyes made dumb oath. He tossed the ball up.

They played with the concentrated determination of dedicated individualists. Their pack movement towards the bouncing ball was illusory, any tactic of teamwork was really a penalty of frustration. The single idea spurring each boy was to get that ball between his feet and wriggle and twist close enough to the opposing goal to smash a dramatic counter that would single him out as a hero. Only when cornered in the unyielding angles of the playground's granite walls, and the sheer mass of the bodies of pursuing friends and foes made extrication impossible, would they willingly venture a pass, and then they heralded their self-sacrifice with hypocritical grunts of "Right, Boab," or "It's yours, Sammy."

But they played hard. Their bare feet flailed and swung and slithered across the concrete without hesitation. A concave sunken drain running across the whole breadth of the playground added dangers to their struggles, but they stubbornly ignored it, stubbing toes in its trough with a mere yelped annoyance or temporary hop that put shame on the injured dramatics of the professionals whose cantrips they admired every time some elder Samaritan lifted them over the turnstiles of the city's soccer arenas.

From the dungeon shadows of a pillared alcove thrust under the school's main block Carter watched their gyrations.

Unathletic himself, he could never extend gesture to the generosity of refereeing their contests. And always in such moments of spectatorship his frustration at qualifying only for a parish school board post seethed in quiet bitterness. Unlike the housewives by the railings he neither forgave the boys' rowdy faults nor feared for their future. He was not interested enough to speculate on their destinies, and he regarded his own part in their education as a personal martyrdom. He loathed each day of it, but the inescapable knowledge that it was the only comfortable way he could earn a living without measuring himself against other men only put an edge on his malevolence. Defiantly he lit a cigarette, but, mindful of the Headmaster's disapproval, carefully kept a pillar between himself and the school's main door.

The game surged frantically. An eel of a boy in unwashed shirt and trousers so torn his skinny stern showed with every stride was making a wonderful run. Three opponents in succession he tricked by flicking the ball sideways off the wall and running round them to catch it on the rebound. It was a trusty street dodge but no less difficult to counter because the victims expected it—the wily boy timed the trick always as they lunged to tackle and had their wrong foot forward.

"In at him," yelled the goalie. "Don't let'm shoot!"

At the last moment, as the goalkeeper crouched and the raider spread balancing arms to speed his drive, a Horatio in red jersey and sweat-straggled hair swooped in at an angle and smacked the ball clean off his toe.

"Jook, Specky!" yelled a boy in sudden fear.

Carter did not duck quickly enough. The ball hit his hat like a bullet and ricocheted unheeded under the low bench seat circling the shelter. As the hat spun off the more common women round the railings reacted with high-pitched skirls of delight. But over the playground only a few nervous juvenile laughs cracked the sudden silence.

Picking up his hat the teacher crooked a slow finger at the boy who had shouted warning.

The lad came forward reluctantly. He was a small, slim youngster with a pale, narrow face. His blue jersey was darned at the elbows but his rough grey trousers were unpatched. He had a cowlick, and an old cut on one bony knee had healed into a dry scab. He watched Carter with very wary, apprehensive blue eyes.

"Jook!" mimicked the schoolteacher. "What is a duke, Haig?"

The boy licked his lips nervously. Somewhere behind him a sycophantic titter was cut short by the stab of a neighbouring elbow.

"Come now," coaxed Carter. "You used the word—surely you know what it means. What is a duke?"

"A kind of nobleman, sir. I meant dodge."

"Ah—I see." Carter smiled thinly. "Very kind of you, Colin. Very thoughtful. And what was the epithet you used in association with this generous warning?"

The boy was silent. The rest of the class stood scattered where each had halted. They watched the duel uneasily.

"You have forgotten?" mocked the man. "Just as you forgot my warnings about impertinence. You know it is an impertinence to call your teachers nicknames?"

The boy bit his lip and looked down at his twisting toes.

"Don't you?"

"Yes, sir."

Carter's bumptiousness could not relent. Although he knew

veiled sarcasm only intimidated without enlightening his pupils, he took pleasure in adding: "In gratitude for your generous concern about my safety I must cure your poor memory. Remind me when we get indoors, Haig. Will you?"

Haig said nothing.

"You heard me, Colin. You will remind me, won't you?"

"Yes, sir," young Haig mumbled.

"Good." Carter threw away his cigarette and picked up the ball. "All right, boys. Form up. I think we've all had enough game for the moment, eh?"

As the two sullen lines filed back on the doorway arch a squat boy with an ape-like face sidemouthed harshly: "That's your fault, Haig. You wait till after twelve."

Colin hardly heard him. Puzzled but foreboding, he was trying to visualize what Mr. Carter's cure for ill memory might be.


CHAPTER FOUR


AT lunch-time Colin ran from school purposefully. His dart across the playground to the street gate was silent. Usually, like the boys around him, he celebrated release from the classroom with a wild formless yell. In that first gallop to freedom he vaguely lived the part of one of the Light Brigade charging Russian guns or as a victorious cowboy pounding after murderous Redskins. He generally gave colour to the daydream by smacking his hip and holding imaginary reins chest-high in his left hand.

Today reality was more stern. He trotted with fingers loose— Mr. Carter's memory course had left him with a blister on each palm—and there was no cantering lollop to his strides.

He knew most of the class had forgiven his part in the disastrous abbreviation of the games hour. But nods and scowls across two notorious desks had added point to the atavistic whisper.

As he ran he watched for them. And as he swept round the first corner they were waiting for him.

Casually they blocked the pavement but their eyes were cruel. Colin pulled up. He felt a flutter of fear at his heart. He wished he had run home another way. These two came from Burnford's grimmest slums and mercy was not in them.

"Just the very man," said "Monkey" Neil ominously. "What'd you go and ca' Specky 'Specky' for? It's a punch on the nose you need."

"That's right," agreed Tod Watson, his buck-toothed hench-mate. "Give 'im it, Monk."

"Gaun and gettin' the bloomin' game stopped just because of you——" Monkey worked hard on the grievance and on his own passions. Normally he never gave Haig much thought, but now the sight of Colin's almost tidy appearance moved him to hate. Any boy, in Monk's opinion, whose hair looked remotely barbered or whose dress and demeanour did not suggest recent acquaint-ance with a sewer was an instinctive enemy, a milksop to be abused, robbed and humiliated to the very limit of Monk's stunted but horrible ingenuity. Lacking reactions to the normal tolera-tions of society, torture and terror were his chosen pastimes. And he welcomed any excuse to practise them.

Without hope Colin tried to placate him. He declared: "I didn't mean to shout 'Specky'—it just came out. You know it got me four of the strap, too." He displayed his swollen hands. His tormentors viewed the weals with momentary satisfaction.

"You were near greetin'," jeered Tod. "I was watching your eyes."

"It was sore," admitted Colin. "Twice I got it on the wrist."

"Now you're going to get it on the chin," promised Monk relentlessly. "It was your ain fault for getting the strap but it wasnae our fault for having to go back into the class."

"That's right." Tod edged in. He read the fear in Colin's face and a new leer, horrible on one so young, crept into his. "What d'you say, Monk, we make him take down his trousers?"

Monk responded instantly. He glanced round the busy street and his warped little imagination lighted. "Ay, go on," he threatened. His fists bunched menacingly. "Slip the strides."

"No." Panic put a squeak in Colin's voice. "You leave me alone or else——"

"Or else what?" gritted Monk.

"Rake his pockets first," urged Tod.

The thought halted Monk. With fists poised he considered the desperation in his victim's face. All around the great, grey stone tenements looked down unheeding. In little window boxes, whose hand-carved trellis work echoed in miniature inarticulate dreams of fields and fences, the first flowers bloomed. Behind them in dim rooms half-screened by short dusty curtains frilly-bloused women with heavy, high-piled hair moved spasmodically to and fro from their black iron sinks to their sooty, cavern-like cooking ranges girded in brass and steel. Over the square, flat cobbles great jingling horses pulled the metal-shod carts in an unnoticeable, because it was never-ending, thunder of sparking hoofs and rumbling wheels. Occasionally a square-nosed motor van lurched past trailing a tail of harsh vapour. Across the street placards fronting a dingy newsagent's shop screamed RED CLYDESIDERS SHOCK WESTMINSTER. And over everything, arching the racket of horses and tramcars and hooting horns, in a staccato blanket of brittle pride, the long-shafted hammers of the riveters threw their iron tattoos from yard to yard across the steaming sky. Monk drew a bully's confidence from the anonymity of noise.

"Let's see what you've got," he commanded.

"No."

Tod moved in with Monk. An endless tide of cloth-capped men and shawl-wrapped women streamed past arguing, laughing, chiding; some hurrying, some dragging their feet, some searching the shop windows eagerly for predetermined prizes, others with the resentful, puckered eyes of poverty or indecision. None looked twice at Colin's fear.

"Give us what you've got and we'll no' take your strides down," promised Monk.

Terror and the hot shame of certain ignominy paralysed Colin. In his tablets of memory there was no past and no future, no family and no friends. No succour. Only the vivid horror of stumbling along a crowded pavement in his shirt-tail and all the world jeering at him. His boy-brain had no doubt it would jeer. And Monk and Tod twirling his trousers in triumph would scamper round a corner laughing back at his misery.

Colin had no doubt it would be like that. Yet he made no martyred inventory of his marbles, his ha'penny, his set of twenty-five football cards or even his great wee double-sided knife with the tartan sheath. He only faced with bleak hopelessness the unrelenting determination in the cruel eyes of his enemies. And as they closed in he remembered, suddenly, the time when he was only seven and a big boy had deliberately punched him twice on the face and once on the stomach. The pain of that beating surged back vividly and he curled his toes to prevent his knees quivering again. "No," he sobbed, more to himself than to anyone else. And lashed out.

The blow was so unexpected it took Monk by surprise. Landing high on his cheek it flooded his eyes with tears and stopped him in his track. "Oh, you——" he yelped.

Tod punched in and hit Colin's ear. Colin swung back blindly, and by good fortune his knuckles smashed sideways across the ferret-faced boy's prominent nose. Whining high with the pain and shocked with the unusual sight of his own blood staining his clasping hand Watson temporarily lost interest in the battle.

But Monk bored back and in panic Colin grabbed him. Suddenly they were hemmed in by a dozen other kids appearing from nowhere. "Gawn, Monk," the gallery chanted delightedly, and with the toadying instinct of the herd anxious to ingratiate itself with the known champion. "Go on, Monk, give 'im it!"

Monk was no taller than Colin, but slum breeding had instilled an iron strain of remorselessness in him that was terrifying. He fought like an animal, with a lust to really hurt that was a guarantee of victory against gentler boys.

In the clinch he clawed at Colin's neck. Colin crouched to prevent his face being pulled round to take a blow. Monk brought his knee up fast. By luck Colin grabbed it before his nose was fattened. He held on and tugged. The fluke unbalanced Monk and he fell, pulling Colin on top of him.

"Is that no' terrible?" a woman with a whining baby sharing a basket pram with an overload of groceries paused to ask the world at large. The world, represented by a dirty slater with a ladder on his shoulder, two boozy old street corner loafers, a carter and a growing circle of wildly clamouring children, paid her no attention.

"Just wait," panted Monk through ferociously clenched teeth.

Colin did not wait. In quiet desperation he kept punching on. Dimly he was aware that Monk's fists were thudding about his chest and shoulders. Twice in quick succession he felt the impact of his own knuckles bounce on flesh. He felt very tired and his mouth kept gaping in the effort to feed his straining lungs. He forgot Monk's threat and his horror of defeat's consequence and only kept fighting automatically. And then, suddenly, through a haze of sweat and weariness he saw a fresh bead of tears glint across Monk's eyelashes. With a shock he realized, too, that he was—unbelievably—sitting astride Monk. And that Tod Watson, with jackal instinct, had shirked rejoining in the kill but had shrank to the safer sadism of spectating. Amid the growing exasperation of their first urgings he heard the shrill fickle ring add the sweet incredible saving-line, "C'mon, Colin boy, wire in; you've got 'im now!"

With a sudden burst of energy he hoisted himself farther up Monk's chest and swung a fist high. Monk's head twisted instinctively and naked fear flattened his cheek hard against the dusty pavement. Before he could pound the fist down a big hand clamped on the back of his jersey and yanked him clear.

"That'll be enough, sojer," the carter said. "Never hit a man when he's down."

"He hit me first," Colin claimed inaccurately.

"Never mind, you've had the best of him." The man reminded Colin of his father. His hand had the same solid grip and there was the same dependable smell of sweat and hard work off him. He dismissed the incident with a typical off-hand nod: "Shake and forget it."

Monk got to his feet. His eyes were dull and cold again. "I'll get you, Haig," he said, and pushed his way through the jeering ring. Tod Watson fell in at his side, only looking back to mouth, sullenly, "Just you wait."

The carter shrugged and went back to his lorry. Colin drew the back of his hand across his nose and looked at the blood. Three very small boys kept dancing round him shouting, "Good old Colin!" He shook them off and trudged home, but always looking back over his shoulder.

## CHAPTER FIVE

LEANING on a handle of the smoke-board Julia Haig stopped stirring the big black pot of soup to listen. Behind her the kitchen table, sheathed in pink oilcloth and with its folding leaf up, was set for four. Julia prided herself that her family's dinner was always ready and waiting.

As the first steam siren blasted its signal from amid the tangle of cranes and derricks visible from her three-storey window she glanced at the brass clock wagging on the room's widest wall. The clock responded with a throat-clearing whirr of springs and obediently clanged out twelve grudging chimes.

Julia smiled faintly. Every time she heard the shipyard hooters she remembered The Clincher, a Glasgow street-character's classic rejoinder to a departing rivet-heater. "Maybe that, Mac," bawled The Clincher to the figure disappearing in the big gates, "but daft or no' daft nobody needs to blaw a whistle to tell me when I'm hungry and when I'm full. Only a bloody Black Squad man's as daft as that!"

Julia was the kind of woman who understood that kind of wit.

Easing the smoke-board up a few inches she brought each plate over separately and ladled the soup out of the iron pot. It was good soup made of carrot, turnip, leeks, parsley, barley and peas and thickened with the juices and marrow of a big meaty ham-bone. The steam and smell of it filled the kitchen with a cloying fug.

Julia did not notice the fug. She did not feel hungry for the soup either. Constant cooking four times a day over the heat and smoke of the wide, black iron fire-range had left the finer edge of her appetite permanently dulled.

Julia's own idea of delight was a solitary cup of tea at midnight and a wee soda scone garnished by the knowledge that her man was working, that everyone was safely in bed and that her room and kitchen was as tidy as brush and shovel and floorcloth could make it. If she had wider ambitions she never confessed them.

But she had other standards for her family. And as a clatter in the little lobby that led to the stairhead heralded someone's entry she returned to the pots flanking the rib-boxed fireplace, and with a fork vigorously mashed a cooked mixture of potatoes and carrot. Without turning her head she said: "Wash your hands, Ella—and put on a pinny before you sit down to that soup."

"Och—soup again, Maw!" Ella's little doll face wrinkled and the blue bows at the end of her two fair plaits bounced with a petulant wriggle. "I don't want soup."

Julia continued stooping before her sooty cavern. She did not look round. Giving the mash a final stir she shifted her pots around the hob to the best advantage. She gave a sausage and mince stew a shake and lifting a square tin tea-caddy decorated with pictures of King George V and Queen Mary from the mantelpiece swiftly measured out three teaspoonfuls into a big brown enamel teapot. Filling the teapot from a boiling kettle she laid it before the fire-ribs on a highly polished steel slider-ledge.

Still frowning with an eight-year-old's temper Ella tugged open a brown cupboard door beside the iron sink and dried her hands on the towel hanging inside. As she dried them she irritably pushed aside the dishcloth hanging from the same nail and put out a rebellious tongue at the cups and plates and spare pots stacked on the three shelves inside. The edges of the shelves were decorated with crinkly pink paper attached by drawing-pins.

"Some day," said her mother, "you'll stick that tongue so far out you'll not get it back in again."

Ella twitched her nose quick like a rabbit and stalked sullenly to the table. Sitting on the near-side chair she clasped her hands determinedly in her lap. Without turning away from her watch on the fireplace her mother said, "You sup that soup, my lady, and no more of your nonsense."

"Well, you *know* I don't like soup!" whined Ella.

"You don't like a lot of things," said Julia briefly. "Was Colin not in front of you?"

The child flicked her spoon peevishly. "I don't know where he is—I never seen him."

Unhurriedly Julia turned with the stirring fork in her hand. Without heat she said: "I'll take my hand off your jaw if you speak to me like that. You eat up that soup and if you dribble any of it on that good frock I'll warm your behind for you. . . . I'm not your father, y'know."

Resignedly Ella dipped her spoon. After two mouthfuls rancour faded from her face and she asked normally, "Is my daddy not late?"

"I'm just thinking that. He's generally in as quick as you."

A sound in the lobby turned both their heads.

"It's Colin," Ella decided as a scuffle and thud signalled the quick closing of the house's dark little lavatory. "He always goes to the closet as soon as he comes in."

"Ay, and here's Jenny." Julia distinguished the quick light entry of her elder daughter and awaited the inner swish of the kitchen door with mild curiosity. As the girl swept in she asked: "D'you not see your father coming up that street?"

"What's for the dinner?" demanded Jenny breathlessly.

"I asked you a question."

"No, I never seen him, Maw." The auburn-haired girl's attention was still directed to the table.

"Him and Colin are both late."

"I'm famished." Jenny tossed hat and coat into the box-bed that flanked the door and filled most of the kitchen's far wall. Fifteen years old with bobbed and fringed hair, her lively pale face emphasized every statement with exaggerated grimaces and her wide dark eyes habitually head-lamped trivialities. Her shoulders heaved now as clattering a chair and plumping down she declaimed: "Y'know, mother, some day I'll murder our foreman. D'you know what he did the day, maw?"

"I know he didn't fling that coat and hat across my bed," said Julia evenly. As she placed Jenny's soup before her she insisted:

"Now you go and hang your clothes up in the lobby where they should be—my house is no' a jumble sale."

"Och, mother, I'm starving!" But the girl rose and removed the coat and hat. As she fumbled at the hooks in the lobby the lavatory door opened and they heard her scold: "Are you just in? What kept you?—the school's been out ages ago."

"Mind your own business," Colin snapped.

"I'll ring your ears for you, you cheeky wee ned," and the boy shot into the middle of the kitchen propelled by her push. Instantly he swung round with hand lifted.

"Here!" said his mother. The note she put into the single word quelled his gesture. "You keep your hands down too," Julia reproved Jenny. "I'll do any shoving that's to be done in this house. . . . What kept you, Colin?"

"Nothing."

"And did 'nothing' put that bump on your brow?" she asked dryly.

"He got the strap the day," Ella chimed in suddenly. Her lips set in a prime line and her little chin lifted accusingly. "He got the boys' Physical Exercise stopped for calling the teacher names."

"You did not?" Jenny squealed, her eyes expanding in scandalized delight.

"He did! He did!" Ella relished her rôle of sensation-monger. "All the girls in his class were talking about it and Nancy Muir says her big brother was sent to the Training Ship for the very same thing."

"You sit round and finish your dinner," Julia ordered, quietly dividing out the stew. "And get the plait tied right or you'll be losing the ribbon."

"Wee bitch!" breathed Colin, gingerly rinsing his bruised hands at the tall swan-necked tap.

"Oho!" goaded Jenny.

"Mother—he's swearing!" accused Ella instantly. "He called me a B-I-C-H, so he did!"

"I'm not telling you to sit round again," said Julia patiently but with menace. With a look she halted her son's passage from the sink to the table. "What kind of way's that to speak to your wee sister? Where are you hearing that kind of talk?"

Sullenly Colin let his chin and eyes droop.

"Answer me. When did ever you hear expressions like that in this house?"

"You're a wee clipe-clash." Suddenly Jenny glared across the table at her sister. "You're aye getting folk into trouble. Why can you no' shut your mouth and let things be?"

"Ya!" Swift as a lizard's tongue Ella's small pink tip flashed out and in again. Her nose concertinaed and smoothed with equal speed. Jenny half-lifted her hand to swipe.

"That'll do now," their mother quelled them with a glance. Yet without anger she asked: "Anybody wanting more potatoes? —I'll need to keep some for your father."

"He's awful late, isn't he?"

Nodding, Julia filled her elder daughter's plate. "Maybe he's working the meal-hour," she said. Jenny's eyes dropped but the query in them was not satisfied.

Going on to serve Colin, Julia turned over one of the boy's palms. He winced at her touch.

"Specky didn't miss you anyway," she commented on the weals running up under his jersey sleeve. "What did he strap you like that for?"

"Because he called him 'Specky'," Ella emphasized with taunting smugness.

"You're a right wee eejit. What did you let him hear you at that for?"

"I didnae mean to, Maw," protested Colin. "It come out when the ball flew past his napper. I was only telling him to jook."

"Hmph—he's thin-skinned!" Julia looked mildly annoyed. "And did he skelp you on the face, too?"

"He was fighting with another boy." Ella could not contain herself.

"Looks like you got the worst of that, too." Julia dismissed the dramatics of her son's day to their proper place in the importance of things and voiced the uppermost problem of her own thoughts: "I wonder what's keeping him?—unless they're docking a boat?"

"Tammy Watt across the street would've shouted up," Jenny decided shrewdly.

"Sometimes he's no' working near Watt," Julia strove to convince herself. "It could be something that cropped up. . . ."

Colin gulped his last forkful and pushed back his chair. "I'm away, Maw."

"Not wanting some pudding?"

"I'll just take another jeely piece." He hurriedly plastered a thick slice of white bread with two or three heaped spoonfuls of factory jam from the big rorrily labelled brown earthenware pot dominating the centre of the table. In deference to his mother's last-minute scrutiny he gave a token-tug at the blue and white hose-top stockings drooping round his ankles and hustled out. As the outer door banged behind him Ella slid her helping of bright yellow cornflower pudding away, barely touched. "Any ice-cakes, Maw?" she suggested ingratiatingly.

"Ay, when you sup your pudding," Julia said. "You're one that would just live all her life on sniceters."

"Should see the lovely blouse Sarah Gracie's got for the wedding," mused Jenny. "It's got kinda beaded braid round the collar and you know yon pearl buttons, Maw—the kind my Auntie Lizzie fae Barrhead had on the black bombazine frock she wore at grandfather's funeral? Well, like yon, only bigger."

"Is the wedding to be in a hall?"

"No; they're having it in his mother's big room—they stay up Toff's Brae in one o' them big houses in the red building. They say it's magnificent, a three-room and kitchen and they've got a piano."

As they gossiped Ella poked at her pudding without noticeably diminishing it. "Can't I get a cake now?" she finally demanded.

Julia looked at the messy plate. "What a slutter!" she frowned. "If I was your granny I'd make you eat every bit of that up. Take a German biscuit if you like but leave the fruit cake for your faither—he's fond of flies' graveyard."

"You aye say 'German' biscuit," Jenny marvelled, watching Ella grab the iced disc with its red gelatine blob on top. "They're Empire biscuits."

Her mother's calm, pale face verged on a smile. She put her hand up to the half circle of comb that clamped her thick black hair in position. "Ay," she agreed, "the lassie in the Co's aye given me into a row for calling them that—it wasn't 'til the war they christened them Empire biscuits. Of course we were all awful patriotic then."

"Well," sighed her daughter, dismissing with a chuckle the holocaust she barely remembered, "just to keep it international I'm putting a couple of Paris buns in my pocket—I get that empty round about four o'clock. Sometimes I think it would be great if we could just get a wee fly cup in the afternoon like you."

Julia pulled a face of droll protest. "By God, by the time I wash up after you lot run down for a message or two there's not many cups of tea I get." Helping Ella on with her coat and whisking the child's plaits clear of the collar, she went on:

"Anyway you're not in the hosiery to drink tea—you're in there to mind your machine. And see and stick in and make a pay and no' have the boss getting on to you."

"The boss?" Jenny sniffed. "Nobody worries about him—it's yon snidey forewoman. . . ."

"I'm away, Maw." Ella swung on the kitchen door. "Will I get another German biscuit at four o'clock?"

"Great Scott!" Julia clicked her tongue. "Are you thinking on your stomach that far ahead?"

"Gutsy wee besom," commented Jenny, blandly ignoring her own foresight.

Ella put out her tongue and vanished: "Mind the horses!" her mother called after her.

"I'm away too, Maw." Jenny popped her buns into a paper bag and slung on her coat. She hesitated on the doorstep and suddenly, guiltily, without looking directly at her mother asked: "My da's got no money has he, Mother?"

"Not that I know of."

Their glances crossed and then the girl smiled too forcedly. "He'll be working right enough."

"Likely."

With the sound of Jenny's running feet still echoing back up the sounding stairway Julia crossed to the window. Bending across the narrow sink she threw the lower sash up and leaned out. A window box across the sill kept her elbows tucked in and its clump of green fragrant mint brushed her firm round chin. The little damp pocket of earth beneath the mint sent its own virgin fragrance up to dilute and sweeten the heavy plant aroma.

She could see right down the straight street to the farthest corner where the Dock Road tramcars grumbled past at regular intervals.

She watched Ella chum up with another little girl who emerged from a neighbouring close. She watched the two little figures until they turned out of sight. Jenny half-running and with her snack poke swinging, was overtaking them fast, but before she turned the corner that hid them she spun backwards on her heels and waved with the certainty of cheerful ritual to her mother.

Julia stretched out her arm in answering salute. And then she resumed her searching gaze of the long street as it grew quiet and almost empty after the receding ebb of returning workers and trotting school-children. Soon there was only the spaced lamp-posts, a hawker's barrow and a scatter of crawling infants on the sun-drenched pavements to hold her attention.

## CHAPTER SIX

HAIG did not come home until midnight. Julia and Jenny heard his voice drooling in company all along the dark street and up the mocking close. They recognized the partner in his duet.

For hours they had known it would end like this. But facing each other across the steel and black front of the gaslit fireplace they ignored the certainty.

About ten o'clock Julia said: "You away to bed, Jenny, you've to rise to your work in the morning: I'll let your faither in."

For the first time in life the girl tacitly defied her mother. Rising she poured another cup of tea for each of them. Squatting back down on the fender-stool she asked, guilelessly: "Maw, where did you first meet my da?"

The high planes of Julia's pale face remained placid. Gravely and gently she touched the top of a long poker between the vertical ribs of the grate to clear grey ash from its bottom bar. A half-burned cinder toppled out, bounced on the slider, missed the ashpan underneath and rolled, spluttering and fuming, across the hearthstone directly under Jenny's seat. The girl fished it out with long-handled tongs and dropped it back into the fire.

"That's a visitor," prophesied her mother.

"Were you introduced?" persisted Jenny.

"I met Haig at a Volunteers' Ball," Julia said eventually. "Your Uncle Erchie had taken me there as his partner—in them days no lassie or fellow could go to a dance alone. And the fellow had to hire a cab. Our Erchie never had the price of a tram ticket, far less a cab. He couldn't take a strange girl. Fine I mind I even had to pay for the cab as well as the ball tickets. But—my—the lassies in the mill were jealous. A ball was a great thing in them days."

"The Volunteers were a kind of Territorials?" Clasping her ankles, Jenny hoisted her feet on to the long stool and chin-rested her head on her knees. Her big eyes widened still and attentive.

"Ay, but——" Julia hesitated for the right word. "The Volunteers had a kind of swank about them—maybe it was the red tunics. And, of course, the officers were all real gentlemen, most of them lived in big houses out by Ibrox or the Pollockshaws; business men and kind of landed gentry. A Volunteers' Ball wasn't just a dance like a glorified jigging. It was the greatest thing in the year."

"Did you go to a lot of dances, Maw?"

"Not a lot, Jenny. We hadn't the money, and you weren't considered decent if you were aye running to dances. In those days—before the War—there weren't so many picture halls. If you got a day down the Clyde to Largs in the summer and a couple of Sunday school soirees in the winter you thought you were doing wonderful."

"We don't get many days down the watter ourselves, Maw. . . . D'you think we'll get a holiday this Fair?"

Julia stared into the fire. "It's hard to say, hen," she confessed. "Your nine bob out o' the hosiery makes a wee difference. If we could count on him getting a spell without idle-set I'd maybe go down to Saltcoats and look for a place. We'll see."

"It'd be rare. I like Saltcoats."

"I'd like to get my feet in the watter mysel'."

Jenny heaved an anticipatory sigh. "And did you get danced a lot at the balls?" she persisted.

Julia almost smiled. In the depths of her calm eyes a light kindled and was quickly veiled.

"I got danced," she said with quiet composure. Vividly Jenny had a picture of her mother, as young and slim as she herself was now, hair high and a-glitter in the old-fashioned way and strangely innocent in a great flurry of rustling petticoats and twinkling sequins, curtseying and gliding through quaint ranks of whiskered men in red uniforms and Boys' Brigade pill-box caps. A pang of fear touched the girl as she studied and sensed the memories buried in the patience of the familiar face across the fireplace, and she cringed from the thought that ever the years would mask her own laughter in resignation.

The lost light in Julia's eyes flickered. "Poor Erchie," she mourned mischievously. "I was awarded the Belle o' the Ball that night. He nearly fainted!"

Jenny's eyes widened. "Why?"

"Because it meant he had to stand drinks to every fellow in the boofie."

"And had my Uncle Erchie nae money?"

"I'm tellin' ye, your Uncle Erchie never had money. He had to borrow a half sovereign from Haig—that was when he gave me a knock down to your da."

Jenny shook with delighted laughter. Julia nodded reminiscently: "From that day I got no peace. Every time I went doon the street Haig was standing at the corner. He kept at me till finally I had to go out with him."

"How—did you not . . ." the girl hesitated before finishing daringly, "did you not love him?"

For a moment the faraway look in Julia's eyes deepened. Then her half-smile surfaced. "I don't know about love," she confessed, "but, after that, your faither never rested till he got me to the minister anyway." As a private afterthought she added: "And here I am."

"I'll need to be awful much in love before ever I get married," Jenny said firmly. "In fact I don't think I could ever go out with a fellow I wasn't daft about."

Julia looked at her daughter with a shrewd sadness that was almost hostile. "You're young yet. When your time comes you'll be like the rest of us."

"I'll certainly never have a man that takes drink."

The prophecy came out impulsively. And the girl immediately regretted saying it. She looked away and looked back from under repentant eyelashes. But her mother took no offence. "I said that, too," she mused. "What you marry and what you get are not always the same. If everybody could see into the future I doubt there'd be a lot less weddings and a lot more old maids."

"Still," Jenny qualified hesitantly, "there must be some good men?"

Julia put her cup and saucer on the hob. She chuckled. "My granny used to say the angels paired everybody with their true mate—the trouble was God gathered the weans up in armfuls and tumbled them over the side of Heaven and it was on the road down most of us got separated. You've just got to take your chance in meeting up with the one that was meant for you."

Except for the metronome tick of the old wall clock the kitchen was a cube of silence. Half an hour had passed since any stairhead door had slammed. And outside, in the dark, even the dockland noises drifting across the tenement roofs had softened to a murmurous midnight tempo.

"Better put another penny in the gas," said Julia. The girl took a coin from the mantelpiece and, lifting a chair, went out into the lobby. Even on the chair she had to stand on tiptoes to reach the meter on its shelf. The ratchet whirr of gears and the clank of the penny dropping into the tin box was magnified in the surrounding quiet. Stepping off the chair Jenny put her head in the room door facing the lavatory. "They're both sleeping," she assured her mother as she put the chair back in its place. "A good job," said Julia cryptically. The girl curled herself back on the footstool and they both resumed listening.

"Mother," said Jenny suddenly, as the first notes of song crystallized far down the silent street outside, "Mother—you've had one hell of a life."

Her mother's head lifted almost comically. Never before had any of her children deliberately used such language in her hearing. Automatically her features stiffened. Then the measured solemnity of Jenny's delivery touched the chord of her own quiet humour.

"You'd better not let your father hear you at that kind of language," she tempered her rebuke. "He'll scalp you."

"We'll hear his language in a minute or two," said the girl bitterly. "As our mechanic in the hosiery says, when the drink's in, the truth'll oot. . . . I've heard my faither spelling too often in my lifetime now to bother what he thinks."

"You'd better watch yourself just the same."

They listened to the singing come nearer. "Maw—he's awful drunk."

Julia rose and put the stew-pot on the gas-ring.

"And he's got that rat-faced wee Irish parasite with him," Jenny added venomously.

The song reverberated in discordant volume into the funnel of the close. It was punctuated by the winding pattern of the stairway. The singers droned in uneven rapture up each separate flight of steps, their words and harmony staggering as slovenly and with as little real grace or mission as their stupidly interlocked arms mocked fellowship and support of each other. At each landing they paused to chuckle and congratulate themselves and threw their heads back and moaned out long dragging high notes, their eyes closed in an alcoholic ecstacy of sentiment and imagined virtuosity.

It took them ten minutes to ascend the building's three upper floors. There were three doors on each landing, two fronting each other and one right-angled between. Except for the Smiths in the close and the Elliots two up—both notoriously sloven families—all the doors were trimly grained, the wooden doorstep scrubbed white and every bell-pull, door-handle and nameplate polished in a ritualistic display of domestic pride.

The blank solid rigidity of the doors at the revellers' noisy passing was criticism more humbling than any wideflung protest.

It was a criticism that stabbed home in the upper kitchen. In mutual misery Julia and Jenny interpreted the sounds and the silence. And only their heads turned when the house shook to the shock of a blundering boot stumbling against the outside door.

They watched as the lock rattled stupidly. The door swung open with a crash. There was a wheezy moment of tittering remonstrances and the creaking impact of loose swaying bodies. Then an ingratiating voice remonstrating: "Easy, boy, easy now. For Jaisus' sake, Collie, you'd think ye were drunk. Hould it a minute till I get ye berthed."

Haig was home.


## CHAPTER SEVEN

THE scuffling awakened Colin. The room he shared with his sisters opened directly on to the little lobby. For a moment the boy thought the men were stumbling in on him.

He blinked away the dregs of sleep and listened. Light from the kitchen bent round the lobby angles and flattened itself across half the width of the wall opposite him. Lying near the floor on an extended iron bed-chair he could trace dark blobs on the wallpaper. He knew they really were great vivid bunches of red and green roses nestling in symmetrical haloes of blue and yellow leaves—at least they had been vivid when the paper was new, but that was before he could remember; now even in daylight they were faded and in the shadows of nightfall their colours were neutral. Always, in such moments, his imagination traced the flowers' outlines into grinning skulls and pools of blood.

He opened his eyes wider. Like Jenny and his mother, experience had taught him to interpret sounds photographically. Automatically he knew his father would be swaying stupidly on the kitchen threshold, challenging his mother's censure with the silly smile beer and whisky always stamped across his face.

It was a smile Colin feared. Behind its inanity lay cruelty. It was an unholy thing. With childish truth the boy always linked that smile on his father's face with the possessive Devils in the Bible. Colin knew that behind the mask of drivelling daftness an Evil Thing watched and plotted an excuse to foam and go berserk. And buried deep in his fear the boy nursed hate. And plotted revenge for the years ahead.

Taut, with blankets clutched to his chin, he waited.

"Well?" he heard his father challenge. "I'm hame."

"So I see." His mother's voice was quiet and controlled.

"And it's me you've got to thank for that, Julie." Recognizing the brogue, the boy's form shrank with dismay. Whatever misery was in store the presence of Terry Flanagan ensured its prolongation. While there was a copper in a purse or a drop in a bottle there was no end to a spree including Terry.

"And have I you to thank for the state he's in?" Julia's quiet voice asked.

"What d'you mean 'state'? Who's in a state?" Colin could see his father bracing himself in boozy indignation. "D'you see me in a state, Jenny?"

"My mother's been sitting here all night waiting on you." The bite of Jenny's anger was accusative. In the dark of the room Colin's teeth clenched in a new fear. Never before had Jenny waited up, and suddenly the boy realized he had missed her comforting whispers from behind the concealed bed's curtains. And with the realization came fear for her. "Dear Father," he found himself mumbling into the blankets, "make my Daddy no touch Jenny. . . . Make him go to bed soon. . . . Make Terry Flanagan go home to his own house. . . . Make my Daddy no' shout at my Maw. . . ."

The jumbled phrases hardly reached beyond the back of the boy's throat. "Oh, Jesus, please don't let there be any fights." Mechanically and without much faith his lips framed the thoughts while all his active senses strained and searched each echo from the kitchen. From the recessed bed he heard Ella mutter in her sleep.

"Oho!" Flanagan's exclamation was slyly provoking. "You're the lucky man, Collie—sure and it's two fine women you've got waiting up for you tonight."

"B' god, so I see." Jenny's presence suddenly registered with Haig. "Why are you no' in bed, my lady?" In his mind's eye his son could see him swaying, his muddy eye aggressive in drunken dignity.

"She's just keeping me company—what d'you think she's doing?" In its casual control Julia's tone was evocative of a hundred similar placatory humblings. "Sit down and I'll put Terry and you out some stew, I've been keeping it warm all night."

"Never mind the bloody stew—I want to know what she's doing up at this time o' night?"

"I'm telling you—she was just keeping me company." Colin heard the rattle of a spoon on plates as his mother served. He wondered where Jenny was standing and trembled for her despite the warmth of the blankets. "Come on, Terry," Julia went on, "draw in a chair. You aye like a drop of my stew."

"I do that, Julie. I was just telling Collie tonight that you make the best stew of any woman I know outside of Ireland—and for God's sake, I says, don't ever tell Bridget I said it."

"Bridget'll be wondering where you are."

"I want to know what this one's doing up at this time?"

"My mother told you—I've been keeping her company waiting on you."

"And why do you need to keep her company?"

"Is that right, Collie boy—if God should strike me dead tonight did I not say that?"

"Because somebody has to keep her company," the girl's voice was desperate with unshed tears and reckless hysteria. "Sitting in here and not knowing where you are or what's happened to you. I don't know how you can do it——"

"Jenny, you be quiet. Collie—sit down and take a bite while its warm."

"I know what'll be warm in a minute."

"Sure now, as the auld hen cackles the young wan learns."

Colin swung his bare legs from under the covers. The worn waxcloth was ice-cold on his feet. As the voices rose he padded across to the door and crouched. His limbs quaked and his heart was a pounding pulse that burst at the walls of his chest. "Oh, God," he breathed, "make me a man quick and I'll go in and kill them!" The voices in the kitchen rose in a babble.

"Jenny, away you ben to your bed."

"Aw, for Jaisus' sake, Collie."

"Dictate to your faither, would ye?"

"I don't care, I don't care! You're always drunk."

"Now I'm warning you, Collie—don't you dare!"

Then Jenny screamed. And Julia screamed. And Colin suddenly found himself sobbing inside the kitchen door and the world was a frenzy of oaths and cracking furniture. He had a memory of Jenny rushing past him. Vaguely he saw Flanagan and his father wrestling on the floor with bed draperies fluttering grotesquely and intertwining with their threshing legs. As from a great distance he could hear Ella wailing in the bedroom. But he had no clear recollection of his mother tugging his hand or their flight downstairs. That only came back to him later in awful dreams out of which his brain awoke first and his body remained paralysed in a death-grip from which there was no voluntary release until nature reacted mercifully and he could roll in an anticlimax of relief and cold sweat. . . .

When terror dimmed he was sitting in a big chair in front of the Wilsons' fireplace. The Wilsons lived in the house immediately underneath their own. He had never been in it before but he knew it was the Wilsons' kitchen all right because Mattie Wilson, who was in his class at school, was peering sleepily and scared at him round the curtain of the box-bed.

She had fair hair and her curls were all tied up in little cloth rags for the night. Because she was looking at him he strove to control the quivering of his jaw and squeeze back the tears that kept rolling down his cheeks and dropping on to his bare knees. He clasped his hands tighter and pushed them harder down in his lap. . . .

On the stairhead the voices were still babbling but not angry any more.

"No," Julia was saying, "I don't want to do that. It's an awful showing up in front o' the neighbours but he just had a drink too much and him and the lassie had words."

"It's up to you, missus," the eldest policeman said. "If you don't charge him there's nothing we can do—he's in his own house."

"No, just leave it at that—he's had a fright. I'll manage him all right now he's kind of sobered up."

Mrs. Wilson came back into the kitchen. She was a big stout woman and the coat she had thrown over her nightgown made her look enormous. She went to the cupboard on the dresser and took out a sugar bun. Handing it to Colin she patted his head and said, "Your mammy'll be down for you in a minute, son."

Shyly he took the bun, aware for the first time that he was still in his shirt-tail. It was difficult to bite the bun with sobs still forcing their way up his throat. He sank his teeth in until the big sugar crystals it was dusted with rasped on his nose. Over the top of the bun his gaze met Mattie's again. Fright had gone from her eyes but they were now abnormally wide with curiosity and puzzled surprise. In hasty embarrassment he tried to swallow the bite too soon and choked. The pain in his throat brought new tears to his eyes, but in a confused fashion he was glad of the watery mist they threw over the world.

When his vision cleared he steadfastly looked into the red

embers dying amid the grey ashes of the Wilsons' grate. He shivered a little as a draught from the open front door swirled in round his legs. The voices on the stairhead were reduced to a gossiping mumble. He knew Mattie was still watching him but he listened determinedly for the sound of his own folk. He wondered what had happened to Jenny and strove to catch her voice but could only hear Mrs. Wilson confiding to someone: "Y'see I got such a fright wi' my man being on the nightshift—but maybe it's just as well for he might've got involved. . . . Ay, y'know . . ."

And then she was saying sympathetically: "Is he in bed, Mrs. Haig? Och ay, he'll be all right—he's such a quiet man when he's sober, you can hardly believe it. . . . Oh, that's true—company! company!—that and that cursed drink! They can a' say what they like but it was the happiest day o' my life when John Wilson joined the Brethren."

Colin could not hear what his mother said, but although her voice dropped to an even more confidential note he heard Mrs. Wilson agree: "Of course, of course—and it's just round the corner. When you know where she is too—och ay, she's just as well wi' your sister for the night. It'll a' blaw by. . . ."

The voices drifted on. Out of the corner of his eye Colin saw Mattie had dozed into sleep again. Suddenly he felt very tired himself. His teeth were chattering and he tugged his shirt tighter round his thighs. A stray memory of Monk Neil jerked his drowsiness. He wondered if Monk and Tod were in their beds. Slowly he relaxed and lay back in the Wilsons' big chair. The tug of his mother trying to get her hands under his knees and shoulders started him into tense wakefulness again. "I'll carry ye, son," she whispered.

"Naw, Maw." He struggled up instantly. "I'm no' sleeping. I'll walk."

As they crossed to the door together he glanced swiftly at the long draped curtains shielding the recess. They never stirred. Five minutes later he himself was fast asleep.


## CHAPTER EIGHT

Near the end of the long summer holidays Stuart McQuade showed Colin his football jersey. They were playing banker on the halfway landing of the second storey—for cigarette cards. Stuart had just turned up a jack for Colin's trey when a door on the first landing opened. With frank curiosity the great dough-faced woman who appeared lumbered up a few stairs to see what held their attention. Squatting guiltily in the recess of the stairway window the boys watched her inquisitive eyes draw level with their position. Stuart held the half packs in upturned display. At sight of the miniature gaming cards the woman's huge breasts swelled and she gave them what she afterwards described as "the edge of her tongue".

"A rerr sunny day," she stormed, "and youse two sitting playing Devil's Cards all over a landing that's just new pipe-clayed! My God, what are your mothers thinking about?"

Neither of the boys spoke. Her glare rested particularly on Colin. "I'll let yours know the minute she comes back her messages. My God, it's bad enough we canny get sleeping at night for drunk men without having the close turned into a gambling school through the day."

Stuart closed the pack and gently stood up. Rising with him, Colin said: "It was only a wee game in funny, Mrs. Beath—we weren't playing for keeps."

"Don't give me any of your lip. You've nae right to be playing cards at all." Her malevolence shifted swiftly, taking in Colin's chum. "Anyhow, I never met a left-footer yet who didn't play for keeps—even if their mothers do teach pianos."

Stuart's pointed chin lifted. He was a pale little boy whose fine skin and sandy hair lent an air of deceptive delicacy to a wiry frame. He was generally admitted the quietest and least obtrusive boy in the building. But now he said, firmly: "My mother minds her own business."

"You cheeky whelp!" Surprise only temporarily stifled Mrs. Beath. She bent a bare arm like a bleached ham across her vast bosom threateningly. "If I come up there I'll take my hand off your jaw, you impident wee toe-rag."

Colin nudged Stuart. Silently, with their solemn eyes never leaving her face, they slid round the central wall and backed farther up the stairway.

She called after them: "Ay, youse had better get out my sight. And—mind—Colin Haig, I'll let your mother know the company you're keeping. And what you're up to. For there'll be no Father O'Flynns to sell you pardons, or burn candles or keep you floating aboot in Purgatory. You'll go straight to the Bad Fire—and Hell mend ye!"

"Auld bitch," said Colin, when they squatted in sanctuary

underneath the top landing window. "What right has she got
to tell my maw?"

Stuart shrugged thin shoulders. "Mine doesn't speak to her.
She went to the factor about our piano. Tried to get us put out."

"We're going to get a piano——" said Colin firmly, then added
conscience-stricken, "some day."

Without emotion Stuart remarked, "Before my father got killed
in the War we had an organ as well."

Frowning, Colin tried to imagine the glory of having a father
killed in battle before you were born.

For him the fact was an enviable essence to counter-balance the
defect in Stuart's religious background. His own father's short
period of military service before being recalled to work in the
shipyards always seemed such a disappointing gambit in stairhead
romancing. He did not really wish that his father had died a
hero's death. But he did regret, secretly, that Collie had not
earned a medal, wound or even hair-breadth front-line escape.
The only battles ex-Private Haig could boast of were bar-room
brawls, and even they were short of estaminet colour. Collie's
martial travels had taken him no farther than six weeks on Salis-
bury Plain, a fact he resented as deeply as his son and which, in
drink, he betrayed by bitter and self-apologetic outbursts against
the authorities who dictatorially robbed a fellow of the chance to
prove he was as game a man with a rifle as the next one. A plea
Colin never doubted but—like Collie himself—knew lacked conviction when matched against the sagas of more active warriors.
In the long winter nights, when the boys of Bulwark Street
crouched under the stairhead gas-lamps and re-told the highly
prejudiced terms of their fathers' reminiscences, he stoutly fell
back on the colourful exploits of uncles and cousins, dead, dying,
or surviving of whom—like all the boys—he could boast a formidable host. Yet the nearest blood relationship was still short of
paternal prestige. And with characteristic generosity he honoured
the orphan accordingly.

"Does the factor no' know your faither was a Petty Officer?
They'll not can put you out if the Government knows about
that?"

"My mother was greetin' anyway."

"I'll bet your mother could play the piano all night if she likes.
I'll bet they canny do nothing to a war widow. They tried to put
oot my Auntie Bella in Partick but she got Pat Dollan—the
Labour town councillor—by jings, he sorted them!"

"My mother's trying to get another house."

"Does it take long to learn the piano?"

"I don't know." Stuart lost interest in his mother's struggles. "I'm playing for the school this year."

"No you're not?"

"I am so."

"The big team?"

"No—well—the kind of third eleven. Like to see my gensay?"

"You havnae got a jersey?"

For answer Stuart flashed up the final half-flight of stairs two at a time. The McQuades' door fronted the Haigs' with old Mrs. Martin's in the middle facing the head of the stairway.

Leaning back on his elbows against the sill of the stairhead window Colin waited enviously. Idly he wondered why the top landing in a tenement close was always the cleanest. The pipe-clayed borders were always fresher, the white-washed upper walls always less scribbled and even the chocolate-brown paint on the walls' lower reaches had always a more lasting shine. Maybe the big skylight window in the high ceiling prevented shadows or maybe the extra light goaded the landing's housewives to more strenuous efforts. Or maybe it was just the best housewives always gravitated to top landings.

Craning his head back he studied the skylight. Some day—when all the big folk were out—he must climb up there.

Once he had tried to get up the man's ladder when the chimney-sweep was on the slates. It had not been a successful venture. The sweep had thrown a soot bag at him. It nearly knocked his head off, blinded him with soot, and almost knocked him off the top of the ladder. And just to round things off his mother had practically burst his eardrum with the wallop she served him later for getting his best Norfolk jacket all soot. Still, some day he would get on that roof even if he had to go up outside the rhone-pipe. . .

His gaze and attention wandered again. The wall that both supported and divided the tenement's stairway from ground level ended at the flat he stood on. The last half-flight of stairway was fenced and garnished by a wrought-iron balustrade. As surely as the gates to a mansion Colin accepted that railing as the top-drawer trimming that finally stamped the superiority of all upper flat dwellers. And its last six feet guarding the approach to the McQuades' door was the supreme symbol of aloof dignity. And mystery.

Although they had grown up together he had only been inside

Stuart's home once. Memory of the experience still unnerved him.
And left him feeling guilty.

Crucifixes and holy pictures on the walls. A statue of the Virgin
Mary on top of the coal bunker. A queer dumpy little Bible with
a cross stamped on its covers lying sinisterly on the lid of Mrs.
McQuade's sewing machine. Her offer of a piece of bread and jam
—at first hastily refused—did nothing to reassure him. Neither
did her unconcern for the safety of her piano when Stuart took
him through the room, ostensibly to show off a full set of Fifty
Famous Flags of the World. And though a glance convinced Colin
that his own cigarette card collection, especially his Dreadnoughts
of Britannia set, was in better condition he still did not enjoy his
close-up of the famous piano for casting fearful side-glances at a
huge coloured picture of a Pope above the mantelpiece.

The whole atmosphere of the house disturbed and intimidated
him. His Presbyterian soul shrank before the sinful display of
religious tokens—graven images his parents called them—and
their very existence confirmed inherent suspicion. In this house
anything could happen to him.

At any moment a priest might walk in or, worse, maybe one of
those great bat-like nuns. Colin's imagination boggled at the
horrors that could befall him in such event. Every good Protestant
child knew kidnapping was only the least he could expect. And
certainly his mother and father would never learn what happened
to him. Even yet, two years later and a little bolder, Colin could
still remember the relief he felt when at last he had got back out
to the safety and freedom of the stairhead. . . .

McQuades' door flung open and Stuart reappeared. He held a
jersey, white pants, green-topped stockings and a pair of new
football boots. Colin's eyes widened.

"Holy smoke!" He breathed current slang's supreme epithet of
approval reverently. "Hey, Stue, they're raji!"

He took the jersey in his hands. It was bright emerald green
blazoned with a bold white V. He laid it against his chest for size.
It was the first real football jersey he had ever handled.

"Jings, that's all right," he admired, generously smothering an
instilled aversion to the Glasgow Celtic colours. "D'your maw
buy it?"

Stuart shook his head. "Belongs to the school. Got to hand it
back if you're not in the team."

Without comment, Colin examined the crest on the jersey. It
was a funny little bald-headed man in a nightgown surrounded

by the name St. Bede. With puzzled wonder he realized all Roman Catholic schools seemed to be called Saint Something or other.

But he only said: "Right enough, it's a rare gensay." Then, born of mingled regret and resentment adding to a vague sense of inferiority because the Burnford Parish School had no organized teams, he added: "I'm going into the team at the High."

"You're no' at the High," objected Stuart.

"No—but when I pass my quali."

Stuart nodded. Neither of them understood the economics of education. Because Mrs. McQuade taught music obviously she was "comfortable". Had she been poor her son would have gone to St. Michael's, the local Catholic equivalent of Burnford Parish. By the same standards had Collie Haig been a foreman, a draughtsman or even a constantly employed tradesman Colin might have gone directly to the fee-paying Burnford High. The courage and sacrifice behind Mrs. McQuade's single-handed ambition to give her son an education struck no conscious chord in their juvenile breasts. Nor did the Haigs' inability to do the same for Colin strike them as culpable or even socially unjust. Such differences were and tenement children accepted them philosophically.

But at teatime Colin startled his family by repeating, "I'm going to the High."

"Are you, son?" said Julia whimsically.

From under puzzled brows Collie Haig stared at his son. "You're going to the High?" he marvelled. "Have you passed your exams yet?"

"No. But I will."

Ella let out a skirl of derisive laughter that choked on a hastily swallowed crust. "Greedy besom!" pronounced Jenny, thumping her back without sympathy.

"Well," gasped Ella, tears of pain and laughter dropping to her plate. "Imagine our Colin winning a bursary—he canny even do his counts."

"I'll learn them," vowed Colin.

"I'm sure you can, son," agreed Julia good-humouredly. "But who's going to pay to keep you at the High. A bursary only pays you in. There's books and pencil cases and school bags to be thought about. And you can't run along to the High in patched trousers and darned jerseys, y'know. You've got to look the part as well."

Collie's frown deepened. He rounded on his wife. "Don't put

the boy off," he growled. "If he wants to study let him study. There's be nobody better pleased than his daddy if he turned out a scholar." He nodded encouragingly at his son. "You stick it, lad. You get to the High and we'll get you rigged out somehow."

Julia said quietly, "Ay, son, if we had some of the money that's been poured out of this house into the publicans' tills it would be nae bother."

Her husband's head lifted. "For God's sake, Julia—I've been teetotal for months!"

"You've been idle for months, too."

Their glances met in a flash of intimacy that excluded sight and sound of the children round the table. "Are you blaming me for that, too?" he challenged with a sneer she instantly knew camouflaged inner miseries of grief and conscience. And her heart filled with reciprocal remorse. But she merely said, "Hardly—no' when half Glasgow's idle at the same time. Still, if you had watched yourself, Collie——"

"Och ay," the fire died out of him. "But that was your mistake for no' marrying a fly man."

"I never asked for a fly man." With a quick little headshake she repudiated regret. "But when I think on some of the ones who are walking about in hard hats in their five-pound-a-week jobs——"

"I know," he forestalled her remonstrances with a shrug.

"You could've been a foreman before any of them. Your pal Terry Flanagan has telt me you've forgot more about rigging than half o' them'll ever learn. Why, even that big Irish weed that got ye the bag out o' Burnford Yard—I mind Terry telling me the man didnae know how to tie up a clothes-line 'til you very kindly took him in hand. A dirty big tattie-howker! And lookit 'im now! And look what he did to you!"

Collie nodded without rancour. "I know all these things better than you, Julia. There's nothing new about them. The chances I've had and the chances I've flung away come the road o' a thousand men. But maybe it's one of God's blessings that only one in a hunner can bring himself to take them. I know I never could."

"Mean to tell us, Faither, you could've been a foreman?"

Collie shifted uneasily in his chair. It was not his custom to bring his work home as fireside gossip. And he had contempt for men who did so. It was seldom Julia or the children heard more than the comic incidents of his outside life. The feuds and treacheries inevitable among the sellers hawking their semi-skills in a buyers' market were memories he preferred to leave outside his own door. And with them the resultant bitterness that demeaned a man and soured his family. Now he parried Jenny's curiosity with a half-laugh, "Foreman! Och, I could've been a manager."

"You could not?"

"Ay, he could've been a foreman." With unusual sharpness Julia defeated Haig's effort to blunt their daughter's interest. "Whether he could ever have been a manager or not I'll no' say, but there was nothing but pride between him and a bowler hat two or three times. It's us that could have been well off the day if you faither had only been like lots of other men."

Jenny's eyes and mouth opened wider. But before she could get in her bleat of exasperation Colin said quietly: "Are foremen bad men, Daddy?"

Haig looked at his son. For long—since the night of his last wild drunk—he had been aware of a restraint in the boy's relationship with him. It was something deep and secret and its nature eluded him. Jenny, who had come home from her refuge in her aunt's two days after his return to sobriety and contrition, had vented her emotions by threatening to leave for good next time, and then just as swiftly resumed the trends and exchanges of everyday life. But Colin. Haig knew he had not forgotten. And the fear was with him that the boy had not forgiven. So now he answered him carefully. "Not always bad men, Colin—at least no' after they're made foremen. It's the depths they have to sink to to get the job that I could never stomach."

"What have they got to do?"

Haig half-laughed. And took a deep breath. "Well, you'll never get any of them to admit it but every other man who ever dropped a time-check at a works' gate knows it's true—the only way to become a foreman, or even just a chargehand, is to break something inside you, something that makes you feel you're still your own man even when you're skint or on the Buroo or havnae got a friend to your name. Maybe you're too young to follow me or maybe I'm too ignorant to make mysel' clear, but it's a kinda price the Masters demand—a kind of Shylock's pun' o' flesh, if you know what I mean?"

Colin nodded gravely.

Collie went on: "For working men polite rules don't apply. I believe myself—if you've got the right background and start high enough—a clever chap'll no' be held back. But if you're only a labourer or a riveter or a rattle-headed rigger like your daddy, it doesn't matter how good a fellow is at his job it goes for nothing —you've either got to kiss somebody's behind or cut your own mate's throat. There's no other way."

"Do you really believe that?" Julia challenged. "There must surely be some men promoted on their merit? They canny a' be rascals."

"All the ones I know are rascals," her husband said flatly. "They don't all admit it. Most of them don't even know it themselves. But somewhere along the line, at the right time and in the right company, they gave the sign that registered. Don't ever think, Julia, that gaffers and penny-men and all these other steady-job lance-corporals and sergeants that you and all the other women in the Co-operative grocers admire, don't ever think that their names are picked out o' the hat like sweeties oot a lucky-bag—they're there because the bosses know they'll always toe the mark when required."

Jenny let out a gurgling laugh. "To hear you, Daddy, you'd think you were one o' they Bolsheviks. D'you mean to say if I become the best machinist in Hoetup's Hosiery they wouldn't make me a forewoman?"

"And lose your output as a machinist?" Her father looked at her pityingly. "D'you think auld Hoetup's daft? You'd likely be the last one he'd dream of making forewoman."

"But if I know the work?" Jenny swelled in indignation. "If I was there long enough and the chance turned up I'd think it wasn't fair if I wasnae made forewoman."

"You wouldn't be the first that thought that way. And not be the first that broke their heart aboot it," Collie grinned wryly. "But by that time you'll likely be too old or set in your job to do much about it." He shook his head. "I'm only trying to tell you that Bosses don't promote workers for the reasons you might think. In a world where there's three workers for every two jobs, anybody with half an idea of the work to be done can be a foreman. When you have your pick o' workers the doing of a job's nothing. They'll see it through. But it takes a special kind of conscience to play the one man against the other, to laugh wi' the one side of your face and girn wi' the other, to pat one fellow on the back and kick the other fellow in the teeth—and do it all according to rule and regulation." Collie laughed shortly again. "Sooner or later the best gaffer that ever lived knows he'll have to balance his own job against humanity to some wee nonentity. He knew that before he put on the hard hat. As your maw says, I just didn't happen to be one of lots of men that can take that decision."

A half-sad, half-guilty expression spread over Haig's blunt, ruddy features. "For your mother's sake I sometimes wish I had but, if I had, I doubt I'd've been drunk even oftener than I am noo."

"You'd've had more money, Daddy," broke in Ella gaily. "Sure you would?"

The air of gravity in the kitchen broke. Haig laughed, "No' half, hen. And you'd've had cream cookies to school every day."

"And I'd've went to the High?" exclaimed Colin.

His father's face sobered. "That's right, son. And that's why, even yet, I'd like to see you goin' under your own steam. No' for any glory for me, but because a man should aye try to make himself something better than his faither. I wish I had."

"What was your faither?"

Collie exchanged a swift secret glance with his wife. And chuckled: "A traveller—only he didnae travel far enough."

Jenny sighed, "I'd love to travel."

Her mother rose from the table saying, "All right—when you've helped me do the dishes maybe you'll travel up the street to your Aunt Sue's and ask her for the loan of a shilling for me?"

Jenny's face instantly lost its dreamy look. "Me?" she choked. "Again! I'm fed up going to my Aunt Sue's for the loan of money. Can she no' go?"

Ella's fair plaits bounced as her head spun round. "I went the last time," she declared indignantly.

Julia shrugged wearily. "Please yourselves. If some of you don't go you'll all go out hungry in the morning. I can't chap that woman next door again and kid on I've run out of bread. I owe her two loaves already."

As they wrangled Colin slipped quietly out of the house. Crossing the backcourt to join the gang playing marbles he glanced up the face of the tenement fearful lest the room window be thrown up and a recalling summons signal a sisterly solution by delegating him as envoy to Aunt Sue. Relieved to see the curtains undisturbed, a twitch of those shielding McQuade's room attracted him. With a wave of the school-book in his hand Stuart saluted wistfully. Colin waved back up. As he turned to mingle with the "moshie" players he realized, with a vague consolation, that the fee to a place in a school team was even higher than his mother computed.

## CHAPTER NINE

BLAIR, the newsagent, looked at Colin dispassionately. He was a drab, colourless little man in a brown Homburg with a Woodbine forever welded to his lower lip. He never smiled and he never took off his hat in the shop. He had no faith in his customers and less in small boys. His haphazard shelves probably reflected his patternless mind. If he had anything special to live for it never showed.

"When did Robbie break his leg?" he demanded in a drawl that was too tired to rate as a sneer. "He was all right this morning."

"Ay. He broke it coming home from school."

"Fae school! How did he manage that?"

"We were taking the short cut through the Loan and Robbie fell off Marshall's dyke. I helped to carry his bag into the ambulance."

"They took him away in an ambulance?"

"Ay, the polis did. His maw's away to the Infirmary now."

"Hmph!" More from habit than doubt Blair remained suspicious. "And you want his job, do you?"

"Well, I thought——"

"Oh, I'll need somebody. Whad'd'you say your name was?"

"Haig—Colin Haig. I stay roon' the corner in Bulwark Street."

"Bulwark Street—um!" Blair digested this piece of geographical information as if it had some profound bearing on Colin's qualifications as a newsboy. "Ever worked before?"

"In Pearson's Dairy. Wi' the milk."

"D'ye chuck it?" He flung the query accusatively.

"Naw." Colin shook his head with the earnest solemnity the implication demanded. "She said her nephew was auld enough to go wi' the milk noo and she didnae need me."

"Hmm. D'you know Robbie's run?"

"Most of it, Mr. Blair. I often went wi' him when I had nothing else to do."

Blair's scrutiny was incurious. Actually he was not particular who delivered his papers, he was really debating whether he could save a copper or two on the changeover. Robbie had cost him three shillings a week and he had always grudged it.

"Well," he pondered, "I was actually thinkin' on getting a bigger boy—one that could sell as well as deliver——"

"I know," Colin's eagerness could not be contained. "Robbie thought that. Well, see, Mr. Blair, I'm fourteen now, I'll no' be back at school after this week. I could sell papers after I finished the delivery run."

"I see. . . . But can ye shout?"

"Oh, ay. Oh, I can shout all right, Mr. Blair. Want to hear me?"

"Well, naw—no' the noo." The newsagent's wedge-narrow face remained humourless and inscrutable. With great deliberation he lit a new Woodbine off the last, dropping the last-gasp stub to the bare boards and grinding it carefully underfoot. The narrow passage behind the counter was starred with the unswept tobacco and ash spludges of a thousand butts.

"I'll give you a trial," he said finally, in a tone that lent near criminal implications to the phrase. "Two shillings a week to do the run and a penny a dozen when you start selling. Fair enough?"

Colin knew Robbie had got three shillings. But he showed no disappointment. A boy could not haggle in an age when grown men were allotted—if they were lucky—fifteen and threepence a week Dole money.

"Ay, Mr. Blair," he said gratefully. "D'ye want me to take Robbie's evening papers now?"

"Well, you've got the job," grumbled his new employer. "Who else would take them? And mind—nae keehoy or acting the goat till the customers are a' served. I like my boys dependable."

When Colin got home Julia heard his reason for being so late quietly. But his father glowered. "Two bob! You go back and tell wee Blair to stick 'is job up 'is——"

"No ye'll not," Julia said flatly. "I've a road for all the two shillings ye can bring into this house, son. It's a fine thing being independent when ye've something to be independent with. If the one that's laying down the law hadnae been so ready to tell other folk what to do you wouldnae need to sell papers."

Collie looked at her sickly. He was sitting at the fire with his stockinged feet crossed on the hearthstool. But there was no peace of leisure on his face. Long idleness had aged him. His red hair had dulled and the ruddy bronze of his cheeks had died, leaving the little bloodshot veins stark. He had temporarily shaved his moustache in a vain effort to look younger, but its absence only emphasized the bitter lines round his mouth.

"I say he'll not take the job," he repeated. "No son o' mine'll work at a cut-rate for anybody. If Blair wants his papers delivered for nothing then he can deliver them 'imself. Colin's not doing it."

"But I've to get commission, Faither," Colin urged. "Jings, they say Fergie at the Subway makes a fortune wi' his papers!"

Collie's mouth twisted. "You're not classing yourself wi' Fergie, I hope? A gutter-rat if ever there was, the scum o' the town! Anyway, Fergie's a man and has sold papers all his life. There's just no comparison."

Pausing in her hair-brushing before the mirror propped on the coal-bunker-cum-dresser Jenny turned her head. "If Colin wants to do it what difference does the pay make—so long as he's happy? It's him that'll be losing."

Collie swung on her irritably. "You be quiet, you don't know what you're talking about. It's no' a matter of Colin's pay. Or your pay. Or anybody else's pay. It's a matter o' principle—I'm no' rearin' weans to provide cheap labour for wee Blair to get fat on——"

"By Goad, he's no' very fat!" commented Julia.

"Naw—but his bank balance'll be." All the frustrations of forced idleness and consciousness of failure added poison to the comment.

With unwitting cruelty Jenny turned the knife. Shrugging her indifference, she said, "I just think any pay's better than no pay."

"That's what I say." Julia's agreement with her daughter was impulsive. But having committed herself she plunged on recklessly. "I wish to God I could count on a pay, even it was only a pound a week, so long as it was steady." She looked hotly at her husband, an undercurrent of guilty realization at the nature of the wound she was inflicting only goading her on. "If it comes to the bit, what right have you got to lay down the law when half the time you're no even getting Buroo money? We never know where we are wi' you. The one week they take money off you because she's working and other time some Board disallows you or sends you to the Parish for a grub line!" Her voice rose in a turmoil of emotion. "You know the struggle I have to keep the roof over our head yet you can sit there acting the big man. Have ye any idea what two shillings means to me?"

She stopped for lack of breath. The silence that filled the kitchen was a thing that could be felt. For a moment Collie's face turned ugly. Then, hopelessly, its angry angles smoothed into a grey mask. The chair creaked as he drew his stockinged feet under it. All the weary weeks and hours standing at street corners, the endless miles tramped along the Clyde, the thousand angry questions flung at soap-box orators and the off-hand finality of a legion of foremen's headshakes was quietly arched by his bowed shoulders. He put his elbows on the chair-arms and said, softly, "I wondered how long it would be before we got round to that."

His lack of rancour shocked them all to instant wordless contrition. Even Ella, engrossed in a corner, was distracted enough by the mood of the moment to raise her head from the wonder-world pictures of a comic-paper. Big-eyed, she gazed round and absorbed the atmosphere of guilt and embarrassment. Then since no one spoke—since sensitive apology was beyond their ready range of expression—she bent her head to *Comic Cuts* again. Collie kept on staring into the fire. . . .

Next morning at a quarter to six, with grey wool shawl over the shoulders of her flannel nightgown, Julia awakened Colin.

She was the family alarm-clock. Sometimes their tin timepiece worked and sometimes it did not, but Julia never overslept. Since the first week of her marriage she had developed a sixth sense that never failed, and if over-worried or distraught she felt dangerously weary she solved the fear of oversleeping by simply staying up until it was time to put whoever was working out. Then, as she phrased it, she could go back to bed with an easy mind.

"An easy mind," was all Julia Haig asked of life. She seldom had one. Apart from near-poverty there was the ever-present fear of Collie's bouts of drunkenness. And her one consolation in the long periods of unemployment that were his destiny as a shipyard worker was the knowledge that while he was idle there was little money to drink.

Yet as she stooped to rouse her son, a quirk of association brought back memory of her first domestic wakening.

Collie's pride had rebelled at her continuing her job in the mill after their marriage. She had insisted. Vividly she conjured the image of those Spartan mornings when shipyards started at five and mills at six. Married on the Friday night, with Saturday and Sunday their honeymoon holiday, she still blushed and lingered over the passion of that far-off week-end. And shivered at the chill of its dark winter Monday.

In that first single-end house there had been no gas-ring, but Collie, with youthful enthusiasm and ingenuity, had fashioned her a wire hook to suspend a tea-can over their gas-mantel. Even yet she recalled her pride and wonder at this device which saved her re-kindling their fire to boil water as she hurried on their first working breakfast. No time then for love-making. She had stuffed Collie's mid-morning sandwich into his dungaree pocket and pushed him out of the door, shyly confused but pleased at his last-minute fondlings.

And then she had hurried on her own meal. She could still recapture the shocked surprise as, a boiled egg decapitated and the spoon halfway to her mouth, she heard the key turn in the lock and saw Collie re-enter the kitchen.

He merely answered her startled look with a shrug. Her heart failed her. All bridal fears and trepidations returned and coalesced into one innocent and dreadful conclusion: she had married a lazy man!

"Are you not going to work?" she finally whispered.

"Ach, I don't feel like it," his casual repetition of the shrug confirmed suspicion—Collie had "a touch of the weaver". She fought down panic but could not smother the note of anger and challenge in her swift: "Well, I'm going to mine."

She snatched hat and coat from the hook behind the door and stuffed a newspaper-wrapped snack into a crocheted hold-all. She was so agitated she actually dropped the teaspoon and her unfinished portion of boiled egg in as well.

Collie watched her with an amusement she interpreted as wholly conscienceless and first proof of his feet of clay.

"I'll have supper ready when you come back," he called as she practically fell out of the house. Her answer was to slam the door with a bang that rattled every other door in the building.

Stumbling down the dark stairway, tears of disillusionment had burned her eyes. No greater tragedy could befall a girl than to be tied to a shiftless husband. But to reveal his true character so soon!

She was still stunned when she reached the close. So confused were her emotions that, not until she was halfway along its narrow passage, did it strike her as odd that at this hour two middle-aged neighbour women should be framed in its street opening.

Silently they watched her approach. And silently they moved aside to let her pass.

She saw the lighted street. She saw the shop windows glaring and the bustle behind their counters. She saw the lorries passing and the children playing on the pavements opposite. Then she saw the sly delight on the women's faces.

"Oh!" she gasped.

"Ay—'Oh!'" chuckled the women.

"It's not——?"

"Haha!" they leered. "It's six o'clock all right—six o'clock at night, hen!"

"Oh!" she could only parrot feebly. Knowledge that she and Collie had slept on through a full day overwhelmed her. And the humiliation of having the knowledge shared by these smirking women soiled the wonder of her wedded privacy. As she scuttled back upstairs, their merriment followed her. "Tell him to lie off the tail of your nightgown the morrow morning," was the least of their witticisms.

Nor did it help to find Collie anticipating her return with a grin as wide as the mantelpiece. Or that he regarded his own part in her closemouth discomfiture as no more than a joke.

"Well," he chuckled, "they got the laugh on me—I didnae see why you should dodge it, too."

"I'll never forgive you," she wept. A vow soon broken. But she never slept in again. . . .

Her son turned over before her hand touched his shoulder.

"I'm wakened, Maw," he said. His eyes were bright. She knew he had been awaiting her coming.

"I hope," she smiled soft and wise, "you'll aye get up so easy. And that you'll aye have something to get up for."

He bounded through to the kitchen in his shirt-tail and pulled his trousers on before the cold ash-grey grate.

"It's funny, Maw," he chatted, "how, even tho' the fire's oot, ye like to put on your clothes in front of it. Why is that?"

"Because ye generally feel warmest there, I suppose."

"D'you think the Prince o' Wales pulls on 'is strides in front o' the fire?"

She paused with the porridge pan poised over his plate. Watching his excited fingers tug as he fought with a twist in his braces, she felt a wave of sentiment unnerve her. But nothing showed on her broad calm face as, with a jerk of her head that tossed the thick single plait she always slept in over her shoulder, she said: "Aw, he'll likely get his breakfast in bed. He'll no' get up till the fires are a' lit."

Colin chuckled. "I'm glad I'm no' a toff. They a' wear pyjamas, Maw. Crikky, imagine havin' to take off a' ye're clothes in the mornin' and put on a cauld shirt. D'you no' think that's daft.

"It's just the way you're brought up. C'mon—get your face

washed and eat your porridge while it's warm. I'll have to be gettin' Jenny up in a minute or two."

As the water sang from the swan-necked tap and the boy puffed and blew at its icy touch, his father stirred in the wall bed. Hunching his shoulders against the kitchen sounds Collie pulled the blankets higher over his ears. And turned his face to the wall.

## CHAPTER TEN

COLIN met Tug Henderson at the corner of Glenhill Terrace. The sun shone on the Terrace's little front gardens and, after six months' freedom from the toils of education, warmed Colin's appreciation of the wider life with the still vivid zests of truancy. Shouldering his canvas bag of newspapers with a swagger he rejoiced in the forenoon quiet of the back streets and exulted in a mental picture of all the servile heads still bowed over school desks. It was great to be "left". With a twinge of regret, quickly smothered, he wondered about the unknown boys and years whose touch would age and mellow the initials he had carved on so many of those desks. And would they wonder about him? Throwing the thought off, he faced Tug's pouting stare with jaunty interest.

"Near done?" Tug demanded.

Colin nodded up the steep Terrace. "I've Swanks' Brae to deliver. Then I've some to sell."

Tug shook his head. "You shouldn't be sellin' around here. Big Fergie'll eat ye.

"Who telt ye that?" Colin's scorn was derisory. But inside he felt a tick of fear. "Fergie's pitch is at the Subway."

"All right." Tug's shrug was neutral and as symbolic as Pilate's hand-washing. At sixteen he had acquired a talent for street-corner fringemanship that qualified him as an authority on every feud without the pain of committal. He had also a talent for over-looking age differentials in an economic pursuit of entertainment. His shrewd, worldly-wise face puckered now as he considered Colin. "For a game in Sam's after?"

"No. I'm gonny pick up some Noon Records."

"I'll gie ye twenty up."

The younger boy crooked his mouth scornfully. "Think I'm your uncle?"

"All right." Tug's eyebrows knotted in reckless calculation. "Make it twenty-five?"

"Hundred up?"

"Aw, have a heart, Haig. You want jam on it? The half hour?"

The discovery of billiards was too recent for Colin to resist its lure and possible prize of a free game. "Okay," he nodded manfully; "see ye in Sam's." With a feeling of terrific sophistication he hitched his news-bag higher and jogged on up Swanks' Brae.

The obvious thing about Glenhill Terrace was its class. That was why the children of grimier tenements gave it the Swanks' Brae soubriquet. It was not only the little garden pinafore flanking each closemouth or the absence of chalked pavement games on its sidewalks, it was the tangible atmosphere of conscious superiority that wrapped and almost embalmed the whole street. Along its whole length not one woman in fat bare arms leaned from an upper window and no gossip group cluttered its ubiquitous twin pinked steps or blocked a single entry. Although nearly every window had its aspidistra monumentally sheathed in its china bowl, they were discreetly framed between lace curtains of impenetrable length, width and secrecy. No window-boxes flaunted mint or rorily trailed Tom Thumbs across the Terrace's austerely naked sills. Sober and sure, in red sandstone facings, gentility and refinement were the crowned gods here. Not even King Billie or the Pope could claim a rival slogan.

That Swanks' Brae inhabitants were superior people was accepted by Colin. He tugged its well-polished bells and tapped its doorknockers with an instinctive deference that was absent from his assaults elsewhere. And in the Terrace the speed and answer to his summons was in equal character. Doors were not flung wide here, as they were in Dock Road or Harbour Street or even in his own aspiring Bulwark Street, nor did the householder greet him with homely or robust familiarity that embraced threat, plea, or promise as the situation warranted. Up Swanks' Brae— even when they owed him money, as many did with a regularity that at first astonished him—they never let him forget that he was only the paper-boy. Today his first greeting was typical.

"You didn't leave my *Journal* yesterday," remonstrated the customer. A snow-haired lady, she peered round her half-open door as if grudging him even limited glimpse of the grandeurs within. Actually she was fifty-two and a slut, but because of her white hair Colin was convinced she was an ancient aristocrat living on borrowed time. On account of this great age he was genuinely tolerant.

"I left it behind your flower-pot, missus," he indicated the painted drainpipe supporting the aspidistra that was Swanks' Brae's favourite threshold sentinel. Looking across the landing at the forbidding sheen of her neighbour's darkly grained mahogany door he asked, "Did you no' get it along with your *Herald*?"

"There was no *Herald* either," she snapped. "You didn't come at all yesterday."

"Oh ay," he assured her with boyish earnestness. "I chapped and chapped and got nae answer. I was gonny leave it wi' the woman next door only her man's on the nightshift and they don't like being rapped up."

"If you had left it behind the flowerpot it would be there," said the grand dame primly and firmly. "I was not over my door all day yesterday and I certainly have no intention of paying for newspapers I did not receive."

"I left it," Colin pled, but hopelessly. He knew what was coming. He could see the commission on three dozen sales go whistling down the wind. His plea was not for payment but an oath on his own honesty. Such was his respect for the inhabitants of Swanks' Brae that he never doubted the scowling lady's own integrity. The aspidistras, the polished linoleum on the common landing, the solid doors and the dark shine of unscratched varnish—all were the hallmarks of a world of undeniable wealth in which there obviously was no need to stoop to the shifts and evasions of more desperate circles. He knew the lady's husband worked in an office —he actually went to work in a tailor-made suit and played golf at Bellahouston on Saturday afternoons instead of going to watch the Rangers at Ibrox Park—so there could be no doubt that it was a genuine mistake. Unfortunately it was a mistake from which he was foredoomed to be the loser. Looking at her he could only repeat, pathetically, "I left your papers, missus. Are ye sure ye didnae take them in?"

"Indeed I did not." She thrust the coppers for the day's delivery into his hand with an emphasis that left the coins' imprint on his palm. "Likely you sold them to someone else."

"No, right enough, missus——" He found himself addressing a firmly closed door. The inhabitants of Glenhill Terrace were not given to prolonged doorstep discussions with scrub-haired newsboys.

Puzzled, he trudged on up the Terrace. Maybe a hawker or a beggar had nicked the papers off her doorstep. But that was hard to imagine. Swanks' Brae did not attract beggars or hawkers. Boys who could sniff rebuff in the drape of a street's curtains or the clip of its hedges and would not waste time or talent that could be gathering guaranteed ha'pennies in the heartier warrens of Bulwark Street and its offshoots.

It was all very mystifying. And Colin could only naïvely marvel that it was a mystery that repeated itself with unfailing regularity in places like Glenhill Terrace. Not for a long time was his innocence to yield to the cynical recognition that these little economic mishaps invariably involved the same customers. And it took even longer before he got round to wondering why he and the rest of the world supinely connived at maintaining and shielding such maggots in their cosy wormholes. And even then he dismissed the problem with the conclusion that deinfestation would condemn too much timber behind the veneers of Swanks' Brae's shining mahogany.

When he completed his deliveries Colin trotted back to Anchor Road, Burnford's main traffic artery. Bawling *"Herald, Record* and the *Bullet-een!"* he waylaid likely looking customers and flourished his newspapers beneath their noses. At this hour most customers were salesmen or clerks rushing for trams or Subway and who grudged the time lost in stepping into a newsagent's shop. In a short space he disposed of his remaining papers and, with his canvas bag flapping on his hip like a banner, hared back to Blair's.

"You're not finished yet!" his employer greeted him censoriously. "Great Scot, it's hardly ten o'clock!"

"But I'm selled oot!" declared Colin. Over the months of their association it had become apparent to him that the demands of the newsagent fed greedily on his enthusiasm. At first Blair had admitted grudging approval when Colin raised sales a little beyond normal. Then he accepted the unusual as customary. And latterly demanded that every copy be disposed of, though the selling of a last solitary newspaper might add another hour's hawking to a morning's work. And, like every piecework employer, at every boost in Colin's effort he sought excuse to cut the boy's commission.

"Selt oot!" he echoed. "Already? Jeeze, you'll be makin' more money out o' this shop than I am."

"Some hopes!" chuckled Colin.

"Naw, but I'm no' kiddin'," Blair continued aggrievedly. "D'you know that's about nineteen dozen papers you've selt the day?"

"Ah know."

"Well. Count for yourself. That's one and sevenpence for aboot three hoors' work! And then two bob a week on top o' that! Jings, there's men on the Buroo no' getting that money!"

Colin's face sobered and grew wary. He knew what all this was leading to, and the lure of the green tables and the clicking clues was strong on him. With boyish, earnest logic he answered, "Ay, but, Mr. Blair, you get another tuppence dizzen on the papers. It's to your profit, too, if I sell a lot."

"Oh, you think so," Blair glowered mysteriously. "And who d'you think pays the rent on this shop? Who has all the worry o' facin' travellers and chasin' tick customers, eh?"

"Ah, I know," agreed the boy, confused but conscious of the justice of his stand. "But you agreed to pay me a penny a dizzen."

"Ah'm no' saying ye'll no' get your penny a dozen," Blair braced himself against the far shelf that displayed his cigarette stock. He spoke with the air of a sorely tried man striving to be both patient and lucid. "But you admit that's a lot of money for me to pay a boy?"

Colin frowned. He felt he was being harried into a false position. It was a favourite trick of Blair's to emerge from his morose silences and tie the simplest issues up in a parcel of words until Colin lost track of the original argument and found himself conceding an advantage unwittingly. "All the newspaper shops pay a penny a dizzen," he ventured at last.

"Do they?" said Blair cynically. Suddenly his head shot forward with a speed that almost dislodged his Homburg. "But do they a' pay two bob a week for delivery as well?"

"Oh, ay," said Colin. In sudden inspiration he added: "Some o' them pay more."

With shrewd cunning Blair changed the subject. "Are ye wantin' any 'Noons'?" he demanded abruptly. He turned away indifferently and made pretence of arranging the magazine racks. Nonplussed, Colin shifted from one foot to the other. Looking at the tired fringe of black scruffy hair straggling lengthily from under the back of Blair's hat he was timidly conscious again of his dependance on the little newsagent's goodwill. In a flash of fear he remembered how much his earnings meant to his mother. And his voice almost cracked as he blurted: "Oh, ay, Mister Blair—I just want to do a wee message then I'll be back for them."

"Huh." Blair shrugged without turning round.

Colin hesitated. The thought of Tug Henderson and the smooth roll of the red and white balls into the pockets overwhelmed him.

"I'll only be half an hour, Mr. Blair. The big race is on the day an' I'll soon get rid o' them." He was edging out of the door as he spoke.

"Ay, okay." Blair turned to serve a woman customer, whose convenient arrival reduced the affairs of his newsboy to their proper insignificance. But he did not miss the shade of doubt that troubled Colin's parting glance. And as he served the housewife her tin of boot polish and packet of safety pins his devious little mind was already plotting the next stage in his campaign to prise the paltry florin from his delivery boy's earnings—a mental exercise, ironically enough, he might well have saved himself.

For his part Colin only worried about the threat to his income for as long as it took him to run along to the drab, obscure back stairway leading to his current heaven. A narrow cobbled pend between two gables led to the stairway which was signposted on the gables by two weather-beaten boards, one advertising SHOP PREMISES TO LET, and in small, almost indecipherable print: Apply Finnon & Dickett, Solicitors. The other board proclaimed in bold but drunken red letters, CLUB BILLIARD ROOMS.

Colin went up the wooden steps, worn concave by age and traffic, two at a time. If ever the door at the top had been painted it bore no traces now. Carved, initialled and hacked by countless penknife sculptors, the top left-hand panel was brutally cracked but still solid with the indomitable weight of Victorian carpentry. Across the centre board where, anciently, a horizontal letter-box had hung, a patchwork board was nailed on the inside and the slot on the outer side left to gape on the world, raw and uncamouflaged. Oddly enough some of the finest decorative craftsmen in shipbuilding, painters and woodworkers, were patrons of The Club, yet, as in their pubs and homes, it never occurred to them to demand or exercise in these leisure surroundings the same critical standards they automatically applied at work. Like them, Colin, with his hand on the shabby door's crude, big cast-iron knob, saw, smelt and heard nothing but the magnetic click of the balls inside. Turning the handle he stepped into the hall.

The Club had eight tables arranged in two rows of four. They filled almost the whole area of the big rectangular room. A wall bench ran right round the place for the convenience of spectators. It was generally well occupied, especially at this hour, by muffled optimists studying racing papers and hoping to pin-point the day's horse winners rather than expecting to witness the rise of future Inmans and Lindrums. To reward the results of their

research, and in cynical denial of the NO GAMBLING notice
prominently displayed, the bookie's runner had the nook of
honour at the far corner. In a niche near the door a partitioned
cubby-hole sheltered Sam, the proprietor. Sam was a wizened little
man with no hair and bad teeth and a vocabulary no worse than
most of his clients, but which by sheer repetitive foulness won him
the almost impossible distinction, in The Club, of having a dirty
tongue. Although he was oftener circling the tables than in his
den, and carried all the takings in his pocket, he preserved his air
of management by ritually returning to the cubby-hole and
accepting table charges only through the pigeon-hole cut in its
wall. No one was issued cues or balls until they had pre-paid the
table charge of sixpence a half-hour.

When Colin entered only three tables were in use. But his
arrival was the signal for Tug Henderson to detach himself from
a group of form students and shrill: "I thought ye had crapped
it?"

"Crap it against you?" scorned Colin. "Don't be silly. You're
meat."

Henderson's answer was to mark twenty-five on the marking
board opposite number four table. "Get the balls," he invited
briskly.

"After you put down your tanner," objected Colin. "I know
you, Tug." Grinning, Tug handed a sixpence to the nearest
onlooker. Colin went with Sam to the office to pay the required
sixpence for the table and be issued with a set of billiard balls.
Returning he chose a cue from a row hung on the wall. Tug was
already, with professional nonchalance, chalking his cue with a
cube fished from his own pocket. Colin used the chalk chained
to the side of the table.

"You break," invited Tug.

"We'll toss for it."

"Aw, have a heart, you're gettin' the start."

Reluctantly, Colin played the first stroke of the game. Leaning
forward into the fierce cone of light the low square shades directed
on the table, his pale young face took on an expression of dedicated concentration.

From the shadows that always draped the hall's circumference
the obscenities, challenges, and derision that were simply the
normal conversational exchanges of the club's patrons merged
with the perpetual mist of tobacco smoke to create an incense of
excitement that temporarily appeased the boy's emotional rest-

lessness. Adrift from better prize or ambition, his urge to prove himself was magnetized by the glamour of the green baize tables. Without any other standard of comparison he accepted the stale atmosphere and tawdry accoutrements as an apex in manly social experience, and the will to excel consumed nearly all his imagination. Carefully, but with the tactile misjudgment of the tyro, he tried to bring both balls safely into balk. He failed. The red cannoned off three cushions and came to rest within easy distance of a middle pocket. His cue ball fared little better, rolling back over the balk line to provide his opponent with the choice of several scoring strokes.

Tug stepped up to the table with an off-hand air that barely concealed his smirking certainty of a free game. With the small competence of longer experience, he went on to make a break of sixteen, leaving Colin a difficult shot to play.

At the end of twenty minutes Tug had wiped out Colin's start and the board showed their score as 93-76.

"Come on, young Haig," a benevolent well-wisher in a cap and criss-crossed muffler urged. "Don't try these fancy cannons—get in off the red all the time."

"That's right," approved another beery-whiskered expert. "An' then pot 'is white and scunner him. Ye've got to play these wide boys at their own game."

Tug smiled. It pleased him to be accounted smart. He was still smiling when he said to Colin, confidentially, "Look who's in."

Following his glance, Colin swallowed nervously. The newcomer let his gaze rove round the tables and then saw Colin. He stalked up the passage between the wall-bench and the tables grinning unpleasantly, "I knew I'd get ye here."

And as Colin backed away uncertainly from Big Fergie's outstretched hand he realized Tug Henderson had drifted back into the ranks of the puzzled but curious onlookers.


## CHAPTER ELEVEN

EXCEPT on the days when he signed the Labour Exchange register Collie Haig seldom ventured far from his own fireside. Without money and without hope, he preferred the escapism of novel reading to the monotony of standing at a street corner exchanging gossip with men as despairing as himself. In the years of idleness he had read every book in the local free library and had a better informed mind on general subjects than most professional men.

But he carried literacy secretly, and was even unaware of it. Sober he was not extrovert enough to become articulate, and his choice in serious literature tended to confirm the cynicism with which he viewed life. For him reading was merely a substitute for reality and had no positive end. Gradually, because they only sharpened the pangs of personal experience, he deserted the declamations of the reformers and drowned himself in fiction.

Although he heard Colin come into the house he did not lift his head. These days the coming and goings of his family were mere periphery accompaniment to the dream consolations of the printed page. As unemployment lengthened and the dramas of his drunks and their aftermath ceased, his importance in the pattern of household activity had quietly declined. The very length of his idleness had reduced it from tragedy to commonplace. His children neither pitied him nor patronized him, but their acceptance of his status as a permanent fireside ornament was the most destructive agent in the crumbling of his personality.

The succession of little noises complementary to his son's return —the draught from the opened front door, the flat bump of the toilet seat, the long liquid rush from the flushed pan, the creak of the opening kitchen door—all these things were only perimeter intrusions on his concentration on a jungle safari with Rider Haggard's Zulus. Disjointed exclamations from Julia a yard behind his shoulder added up to no more than a usual taut-temper scolding over the economics of a torn jacket and the stair-head prestige of a dirty face. Not until his wife's exasperation tailed into sympathetic query did he lift his head in interest.

"Never mind who I was fighting," Colin snapped irritably. "It's all by now anyway."

"Jings, he's gave you a right keeker!" Julia's concern took on a retaliatory note.

Collie watched his son splash his face at the sink tap. The bruise round the damaged eye extended in fast blueing tracery down the length of a cheekbone. The boy's lips were swollen, too, and a cut on his chin started to bleed again. Collie also noticed a tremor along the thin bare arms that experience told him ran down probably to the lad's knees. "What's the matter," he asked conversationally, "did somebody hit you with a billiard table?"

Julia's face hardened instantly. "That's it," she stormed. "That billiard hall—I've warned him time and again not to go near it. It's nothing but a den o' iniquity. He'll finish up wi' gettin' the jail there. There's nothing but a bunch of rascals hang about that place!"

"Aw, it wasn't the billiards."

"What was it then?" Collie's curiosity remained academic.

"Just an argument, Faither. You know how it is."

"Hmph!" Collie turned back to his book. "He made a right mess of you anyway, whoever he was."

"Ay, that's a' you've got to say about it." Julia directed her annoyance on Collie. "The polis are never away from that place and I live in the nerves. He'll finish up getting us a' a showin' up an' you're sitting there no' saying a word. . . ."

As she ranted on, Ella came in from school and giggled and pointed. Colin ignored her taunts and munched steadily on at the dinner his mother continued serving as an accompaniment to her complaints. But when Jenny arrived she walked straight across the kitchen and, with a hand on his shoulder, spun him round.

Half-turned in his chair and masking his annoyance with a look of long-suffering patience he returned her wide-eyed scrutiny calmly.

"The dirty big bully!" Jenny said bitterly.

"Aw, forget it." Her brother shook her hand off and swung to his meal again.

"Somebody should give him a battering," Jenny raved on. "What right has he got to lay down the law?"

"Who are you talking about anyway?" Julia paused with a pot in her hand. "Do you know who he was fighting?"

"I told you to shut up!" Suddenly Colin's faced screwed in an effort of ferocity. But the drag of his brows was more appealing than savage. His elder sister completely ignored the underlying plea.

"Yon bletherin' brother of Annie Scott's stopped me on my road up the street," she explained to Julia. " 'Oho,' he yaps, 'your Colin got a right beetlin' fae Big Fergie. I'll bet he'll no' cut Fergie oot o' any more customers!' See—I could've took my hand off wee Scott's jaw," Jenny added bitterly.

Collie's head lifted slightly from the back of the armchair. Across his shoulder he studied his son. Julia's concern took on an outraged note. "I thought it was another boy ye were fightin'? D'you mean to say that big rascal at the Subway did that to you?"

The boy chewed on morosely. "You should shut your mouth," he admonished Jenny.

"Shut her mouth!" Julia was galvanized into sudden fury. She swept a hat and coat from a hook behind the kitchen door. "No, I'm sure she shouldn't! By God, I'm going down to charge that big midden now—I'll take good care he doesn't get away with this."

"You'll only get yourself into a lot of bother, Maw," Jenny turned calm and cynical. "Don't forget, Big Fergie's brother-in-law's a baillie. Even if you charge him he'll not even get fined. Big Fergie's one o' the folk who can get away wi' murder."

"But it's no' right." Julia paused. "He bashes my boy and then there's not a word to be said about it?"

"Maw, will you give me the rest of my dinner." Colin sighed. "There's nothing wrong with me. It was only a couple o' punches because I was nabbling his customers before they got to the Subway. I'll get my own back some day."

Jenny nodded. "Ay, you've got to play these folk at their own game. Charging them's no good. Sure you know, Maw, all the free clothes and lines for groceries and tickets for sails doon the Clyde go to a' these twisters with the pull. If you're connected to an official or have an uncle wi' the gift o' the gab on committees the world's your oyster, as Uncle Erchie aye says. Decent folk have nae chance. If you went doon and got the polis to Big Fergie all that would happen would be his brother-in-law would be on the Bench or speak to whoever was on the Bench that morning, and before they were by it would be oor Colin that had punched the big fellow. Either that or they'd make a laughing stock out o' you making a song and dance because your son got a slap on the ear." Jenny's face twisted cynically. "You can't beat them. They'll get the better of you every time."

Julia hesitated. Colin's bruised face stirred a strain of vengeful motherhood that had been dormant since the days when her children were very young. Years of want and penny-scraping had overlain her natural spirit with stratas of practical wisdom until honest impulse was too powerfully geared to caution. It made a sickness inside her but she knew Jenny was right. Working-class folk were impotent in the face of "influence". That society was corrupt was not, for Julia, a speculative theory. She and Jenny and Collie and all their kind knew and accepted it as a fact.

"All the same it goes against the grain to let 'im off wi' it," she rebelled, but putting back her coat. "Had it been the other way about the polis would've been up at this door by now. I hope the big sod falls in the Clyde some night when he's drunk and his pockets are too full o' pennies to let him float. Him and his rotten political relatives I could——"

"Any more soup, Maw?"

Still breathing balefully, she served Colin his second helping. Her son grinned up at her. From his pocket he pulled a handful of coppers. "That's my commission the day. Away an' buy yourself a fur coat."

Julia gazed at him. "It's a godsend," she said simply. "I don't know what I'd do without your paper money."

"Aw, have a heart," objected Jenny. "Don't forget your big smasher of a daughter's working, too! Or does my pay no' count?"

"It a' counts—every penny o' it," Julia emphasized, hastening to correct the hint of favouritism. But she looked at her son anxiously. "You'll not sell so many papers now though?"

The boy shrugged. "I'll manage. There's other roads. Big Fergie was just beefin' because I cut off his business men. I'll just have to swing wider and chin the blokes goin' for tramcars. Fergie's got no shout on them."

"Watch what you're doing anyway." She turned to Collie. "What are you wanting, Faither? I've got a herrin' I got off o' Haddie Bob—he had nothing else on his cart the day. Will I fry you that?"

Her husband rested his book. Always he left household arrangements to Julia. Insurance, rent, budgeting, menus were the province of a wife. He looked at her drolly now. Even when he was working he dictated on nothing. He handed over the whole of his wages and was content with a minimum of pocket money. Often, sitting reading by the fireside, they chuckled over some newspaper paragraph illustrating the Englishman's habit of allotting a wife a household allowance.

"That's how I should work," he would declare. "Give you a quid a week and demand to see the Co-operative checks every Sunday. Maybe I could save a few wallies then?"

"Very good." Julia would nod benignly. "Whit are ye waiting for? Just you keep your pay and get on with it. You'll get the rent book and the insurance cards all in the wee chest. And I wish you luck—I've been waiting twenty years on you taking an interest in things. You'll maybe get a shock."

"Ah, but I'd go about it systematic like. Y'know—ten bob for the butcher, ten bob for the baker, ten bob for the grocer——"

"Ay, go on," Julia's eyes would narrow in mockery. "You're doin' fine. You've spent thirty bob. I hope you're minding ye only have thirty-eight bob a week—and after you pay your union and your wee sweepstake and have a bucket on the road home there's only thirty-five in the poke by the time you reach here. Is the odd five bob to cover the milkman the coalman the gas-man and buy clothes and—of course—gie you your tobacco and pocket money?"

Collie would pucker judiciously, "Of course, I'd have to work it out on paper. Sorta give priority to the main items one week and something else another."

"Uhuh." Julia's nod would be sly. "You mean we'll a' starve one week and run about wi' ice cream wafers the next?"

"Aw, it would sort itself out."

"Not half. Well, you can take the purse this week and sort it out. I'll sit back and be educated."

At which point Collie would wag his head and laugh at the paragraph again. "Imagine any man wanting to know what his wife spends on the hoose! God struth, they must be a right bunch o' Jessies!"

"Naebody'll ever accuse you o' that."

"No bloody likely." Collie would shake out the paper in disgust. "I wouldn't know what to ask for in a shop, far less argue about its price. What the hell do they marry a woman for anyway if they canny trust her to lay out their pay? They might as well hire a housekeeper."

"The English are different." Julia was an authority although she had never been over the Border. "They think we're a' daft—just a bunch o' comics in kilts eating haggis and porridge."

"Ay, and that's whit's wrang," Collie would answer all the vague criticism implicit in such apologetic references to national tradition. "The trouble is we don't eat enough porridge and tatties and saut herrin'."

Today, however, he made a little grimace of indifference. "Ach, not just now, Julia—put it aside and I'll maybe get it for my tea." He glanced at the herring lying on a plate on the sink draining-board. "Better still, give it to Colin—he's chestin' into it there like as if he could eat for a week."

Julia met her son's innocent glance. "Would you like it?"

The boy halted a last spoonful of stew on its way to his mouth. "Ay, well——" He hesitated. "If nobody else wants it?"

Jenny's lips immediately set in a tight line. "Away you gusty wee rascal!" she scolded. "That's my faither's dinner!"

Colin's mouth dropped in dismayed appeal. "I didnae ask for it!" he protested.

Collie met Julia's glance of hesitation with a quick head jerk. "Give him it."

She unhooked the frying-pan from under the draining-board. Even with Jenny's and Colin's earnings housekeeping on Dole money was a feat. That Collie would not start a meal until certain that all his family was fully fed was characteristic. Julia accepted it, but deep inside she hugged the knowledge with a fierce quiet pride that belied her outward armour of taciturnity. She also ignored the fact that half a slice of toast had been her own only food that day.

"I havenae felt like eating much myself," she said casually. "I think it's this heat. We'll have a cup of tea when they're by."

"Oh ay," joked Colin innocently. "Saving the Paris buns and sugar cookies till we're all out. Oh, dead leerie!"

Ella's eyes widened instantly. She looked at her brother. "Is that right?" and then swung round on her mother. "Maw, I want a cookie!"

"I'll cookie ye," frowned Julia, but with a glint dancing in her eye. "Where would I get cookies the day before the Buroo?"

"Well, he says it." Ella was always willing to be convinced that the household was conspiring to trick her of treats. "What is he saying it for if it's not true?"

"Away you silly wee besom," scorned Jenny. "He's only kidding you on."

"Naw, I'm no'." Having got his younger sister roused, Colin played the joke to its limit. "Once Jenny and I are oot and you're back at school they have a real picnic every day. They get peace then, see!"

Half convinced, Ella's glance travelled suspiciously between her brother and her mother. Jenny snorted over the rim of her cup: "You shut up—ye'll have her believing it!"

Colin chuckled delightedly. The aroma of frying herring filled the kitchen. As his mother put the fish before him he still nodded and winked meaningfully at the bemused schoolgirl. Behind his back Julia opened the little cupboard that sat on top of the coal-bunker-cum-dresser and withdrew a biscuit.

"There," she said, "that's an Abernethy I was keeping in case anybody dropped in for a cup of tea. Maybe ye'll be satisfied now?"

Jenny's dark brows clamped into a hard bar across her sparking eyes. "You little tinker!" she spat. "Don't think God doesn't see you, ye selfish wee beast!"

Ella's face crumpled. "I didn't do anything," she sniffed. "What are you getting on to me for?"

"Nobody's getting on to you," Julia interrupted. "You leave her alone, Jenny, and let her eat the biscuit. I gave her it. She's as well having it as a stranger."

"Ach!" Words failed her eldest daughter. "That one couldn't see green cheese but her mouth would water. And it's you and my faither to blame, Maw: ye'se jist spoil her!"

Julia turned her head and looked at her husband. As they wrangled he had crossed into the lobby and was putting on his cap and jacket. "Where are you going?" she asked, surprised. "I've just filled up the teapot again!"

"Ach, I'll get it when I come back." Something in his manner held her. "I'm just going down to the corner to stretch my legs."

"But your tea's ready—sure you never go out without a cup o' tea!"

"I'll no' be two minutes I tell you." There was an odd finality in his tone. He went out of the doorway saying, "Just put it on the hob, I'll get it when I come back."

With the teapot still in her hand Julia stood looking at the closed door. Jenny forgot her tirade and suddenly watched her mother. Colin's attention followed his elder sister's.

"Any of you give him any money?" Julia asked at last.

Jenny shook her head. "I gave him tuppence for Woodbine last night, that was all I had."

"You got all mine, Maw," Colin confessed. "Bar a tanner for a game at billiards, I kept nothing."

"He's been T.T. for so long. . . ." mused Julia. Her glance slid back to Colin. "It was in the billiards room that fellow hit you?"

Colin shrugged irritably.

"When does the afternoon papers come out?" Julia pursued her secret thoughts.

"Round about now," the boy glanced at the clock. "But you know I don't run wi' the early editions——" He stopped abruptly.

"Does Big Fergie?"

Without answering the question the boy suddenly spun in his chair and was out of the front door before they could stir. Julia and her daughters remained silently looking at each other.

## CHAPTER TWELVE

BURNFORD Subway Station entrance occupied most of one side of a small paved square set off the busy Anchor Road. A glass

roof extending over half the pavement gave arcade cover and
made it a traditional gathering place for local characters and
idlers. Directly opposite the Subway, on a large traffic island, an
iron canopy as big as a small bandstand sheltered a marble and
bronze fountain gifted sixty years before by one of the founder
magnates of the Burgh's shipbuilding industry. Known locally as
The Well, wind and weather and lack of paint had taken toll of
this massive marvel until its Victorian whorls and castings were
distinguished more by flaking red rust and cracks than its original
green and gold glory. Nor, owing to a lack of plumbing service
or a secret official economy on the water rate, did the fountain
play any more. Yet, even dry as it was, tradition still invested
The Well with an aura of splendour in Burnford eyes that could
be understood and sympathized with only by born natives. In a
practical fashion, too, the seats round The Well were a boon to
countless centenarians and three street bookies' runners. Here, in
sunshine or snow, citizens could dream over fortunes lost or wealth
still to come in the pleasant knowledge that the rest of the world,
including the Law, would diplomatically stream along the Anchor
Road minding its own business.

In the old days when the Clyde at this point had only been a
burn, the site of the Subway Station and The Well had been the
crest of a cattle brae leading down to the ford that gave the
original clachan its name. Now, with tenements walling it in on
three sides and the uprights of seven shipyards reared on the
fourth like a Goliath hedgerow and screening the blink of the
river even from casual view, the place still retained its ancient,
gregarious pull. It was said if you stood long enough in Burnford
Subway Square you would surely meet everyone in the Burgh.
And if you were a forceful newsvendor the Subway was the
obvious place to make a pitch.

At thirty-five, Big Fergie had been Burnford's leading newsboy
for fifteen years. Barring accident, disease or murder he was likely
to reign in the rôle for another fifteen.

For Fergie was a rugged individual of the type secretly admired
and openly privileged by Burnford. An ex-rivet-heater, he had
been black-listed in the local yards before he was nineteen for the
casual use of tongs, rivets and bolts as persuasive aids in the
settling of minor arguments with workmates. Shipyard workers
are rarely critical of robust debate, but hand-riveting is team work
and it is uneconomical in time and attendance to incorporate a
"boy" in the squad who habitually emphasizes disagreement with

his technical superiors by tossing a white-hot rivet into the holder-up's lap or tries to bend a screw key over the left-hander's skull. As a youth Fergie was prone to express his personality by such practices. Eventually, more in sorrow than in anger, not even the most uninhibited squads would employ him. His morning visits to the various shipyard "markets" where pairs of riveters teamed with a holder-up and enlisted a rivet-heater and a putter-in—the small catch-boy who caught the hot rivet from the heater and ran or crawled through manholes and tunnels and thrust it in the seam the holder-up crouched by—such visits became so abortive that Fergie drifted into newsvending. Being ambitious he soon inherited the Subway stance from an old man who wilted under the constant threat of assault and battery every time some aspect of his competition irked Fergie.

Years and prosperity had rubbed impetuosity off Fergie but, like a champion who can afford to choose his opponents, his prestige as a fighting man remained constant. He laid his papers on the Subway pavement secure in his monopoly. Even during the noon hours, when racing tipster editions formed the bulk of his stock, the most reckless horse-punter from The Well would not dare lift a paper without dropping the necessary copper. Dark and swarthy, in dirty white sand-shoes and an equally dirty white sweater that looked as if it had been knitted straight from raw fleece, Fergie ruled the Subway Square. Standing five foot nine and barrel-chested he was, by every slum-stunted standard of the majority of shipbuilding workers, a real big man—in the back streets of Burnford anyone who shot beyond five foot six became legendary in their family as "a fine big fellah".

Fergie was arranging batches of the first afternoon editions of the evening papers when Collie Haig came round the corner. Stooped to the pavement the newsboy's first view of his caller was his trouser legs. Expecting the request of a customer he glanced up.

"I'd like a word wi' you," said Haig.

Looking over his shoulder Fergie remained crouched. His expression reflected the mildest curiosity.

"Up the Bing," Haig added casually.

The question on Fergie's face dissolved instantly. His eyes went flat and cold. To the nearest loafer he said, "Keep your eye on the pitch, Danny?"

"Don't be long," agreed the corner-boy. "I've to sign the Buroo at two o'clock." Something in the watchfulness of Haig's waiting kindled his interest. "How'ye, Collie?" he said carefully. "Don't see you often these days—still idle?"

Haig barely nodded. Silently he walked off at Fergie's side. Danny watched them go. As they took the first turning into the little street leading to the ash wasteland behind a huge engineering factory, he hailed the rest of the corner loafers: "Hey, that's Collie Haig away round the Bing wi' Big Fergie!"

On the way to Burnford's traditional site of pitched battle—and pitch and toss—Fergie and Collie exchanged no words. Fergie only knew Haig by sight, as a local face—generally dirty—among hundreds that streamed daily past the Subway corner on their way to the yards and docks or down and up the Subway stairs themselves. If Danny had not mentioned his name Fergie would not even have had that to identify him. Now, walking along with their shoulders a careful foot apart, he idly wondered what he had done to cross the old fool. Not that it mattered. His name struck no spark of notorious familiarity and he had obviously passed his physical prime. He was giving away height and weight as well as years. Pleasantly Fergie felt the stirrings of animal anticipation.

They turned on to the grey ash and rubbish wasteland stretching for several hundred yards between a distant row of lurching tenements and the high wire-barbed rear wall of the engineering plant. An open sewage burn trickled its way across the area, and on its near bank a flattened depression between hillocks of kitchen refuse and the discards of every rag-store and smithy in the neighbourhood formed a dusty amphitheatre.

As they approached Death Valley, as the gully was ironically christened by local wits, two clusters of cloth-capped men occupied its opposite ends. The nearest and largest, the pitch and toss "school", was intent on the frequent rise and fall of a pair of pennies spun by the tosser. They bet on the chance of the pennies together falling heads or tails, and they bet with the tosser's mate or they laid private bets with each other.

Because it was a week-day and most of the gamblers were unemployed, the stake money was mostly coppers, but on Sundays the school would number hundreds and scores of pounds would change hands. The tossing coins would be half-crowns and there would be a strong-arm man with a swinging studded belt or a revolver to keep the circle. Every approach to the ring would be covered by watchers who could sense a disguised plain-clothes detective five steps after he stepped off the cobbles of the nearest road-end.

The dozen men in the smaller group crouching round a dirty deck of cards were playing banker.

Because they had been well scrutinized crossing the coup the gamblers hardly looked up at the approach of Haig and Fergie. Then, out of the corner of his eye, the tosser saw the newcomers peel off their shirts. His arm shot out instantly and cut a swathe in the air beneath the falling pennies. "Bar them!" he called, signifying that the toss was cancelled and no bets would be paid on its result. At the same moment the man in bank at the card game halted laying out a fresh board, saying: "Wait—two jokers got an argument."

Without fuss the gamblers and their onlookers formed a quiet circle round the antagonists. All of them recognized Fergie but Haig, by virtue of his greater respectability, was not so well known.

"Big Fergie'll murder him," said someone dispassionately.

"Ay."

"I'll give two to one Fergie," offered the man who had been tossing the pennies.

The card school dealer looked over. "I'll have a dollar's worth."

The tosser's nod of agreement was as discreet as an auctioneer at Christie's. "You're on."

"You've been doing all right?" someone joked. The dealer, an ageless little man with a muffler round his scrawny neck, merely said: "I've another dollar if anybody likes?"

From opposite sides of the ring Haig and Fergie turned to face each other. As they closed warily Fergie called: "What is it to be, mac—a fair fight?"

"Any way you like," Collie said.

"All right—you said it."

With the exchange of their first punches Colin, panting and breathless after a search and run that had finally brought him here, wriggled his way through to the inner edge of the ring. Stunned he watched his father stagger and grunt under the impact of Fergie's first blows. With a strange embarrassed shyness he saw how pale his father's body was. He felt angry pity as he measured its naked white frailty against Big Fergie's hairy torso. In an instant his concept of the world was shaken. It was as if a familiar picture had been lifted from the wall and the contents of its immemorial landscape jerked across the floor. For the first time he saw his father, not as a colossus, nor even as a giant whose drunken tread shook the world. With a queer little stab of shame —guiltily smothered—he suddenly saw his father as just a rather small red-haired man with a bald patch and made even more punily ridiculous by near indecent exposure. The realization of his father's true insignificance filled the boy with horror. Taut, silent, and without faith, he watched the fight in a numb agony of private remorse and dreadful apprehension.

It was a tough fight, even for Death Valley. It lasted nearly five minutes. Before the end both men were streaked with each other's blood and sweat. In the beginning Fergie was very confident. He advanced straight in to slog Collie senseless. Collie took everything and kept on punching back. Two of his counterblows actually hurt Fergie and the big man decided to use his extra weight. He tried to throw Collie. Haig avoided the big grasping hands with surprising speed. Fergie circled after him in a wrestler's crouch. The dust rose between their shuffling feet. Breathless and gasping, his heaving belly advertising the fact, Haig knew he could not spar much longer. His calf muscles were giving out and his thighs were trembling. The pith was going from his arms. He feinted clumsily and drove straight between Fergie's arms. As bodies clashed he tried to bring a knee up. Fergie's iron thigh foiled him. Deliberately he double-rapped his forehead at the bigger man's face. Fergie grunted and tripped him.

They went down in a swirl of dust, the brittle ashes rasping blood-flecked scores on their flesh as they rolled over and over. All the time they kept punching. Among the spectators no one shouted. The smack of the blows rang out as flat and vivid and impersonal on the watching air as the slap of a dairyman's trowels shaping butter. When, finally, Fergie came uppermost the boy on the edge of the ring stooped and groped for a half-brick at his feet.

But in a last convulsive heave Haig tossed Fergie off. As he sprawled Collie's will-power forced himself upright. Before Fergie could do more than kneel Haig hauled a full-blooded punch from some unsuspected reserve and smashed his face.

Fergie keeled over backwards. Following up Collie lifted his foot. Flat on his back Fergie shook his head. "That'll do," he said wearily.

Mouth gasping, chest heaving, Haig looked down on him. He said: "Don't ever lay hands on my boy again—he'll sell his papers wherever he bloody well likes. Mind that."

Understanding dawned on Fergie. Lying still he said nothing. Collie stood long enough over him to mark his victory. Then, drawing a hand across his bleeding lips, he turned away.

The card player held out his hand. As he paid ten shillings the tosser remarked with mild wonder, "I thought Big Fergie'd've ate him."

"Ach," the little man spat his disgust. "I knew the Haigs before ever Fergie's faither stepped off the Irish boat. I've seen the day Collie wouldna need to've taken off his jaiket to that bloke."

Shrugging himself into his shirt Collie noticed his son. His face darkened. "When did you get here?" he demanded roughly. And added: "What's that for?"

Remembering the brick, Colin dropped it quickly. He mumbled: "I thought for a minute he had you."

His father's expression did not change. "And you were going to use that?"

The boy looked embarrassed. Collie stooped and shoved his face close to his. "Well, let me tell you, son—don't ever let me catch you at any of these tricks. If you canny beat a man wi' your hands don't ever fight at all."

Colin hung his head. By the time Haig dressed the gambling was restarted. Across the ash patch Fergie was still stiffly putting on his clothes. He paid no attention as they moved away. Not until they were halfway home did Collie speak again. And then his tone was painfully self-conscious and apologetic. "I know what you're thinking, son. And it's hard for me to explain it. God knows, I've no room to talk but—ach—fighting on a midden-heap's nothing to brag about. I know I havenae gi'en ye much of a kick-off but I'd like to hope you'll win your battles on better places than that."

Turning into Bulwark Street they saw Julia leaning from the window. At sight of them she hesitated long enough to study them well before disappearing. Collie laughed down at his son. "An awful woman, your mother."

The boy felt his heart swell. A tremendous surge of loyalty and love robbed him of speech. The fear-filled nights, the shouting, the drinking—all vanished in a humbling wave of pride in the man beside him. And for the first time he dimly sensed the bond between his parents. Going up the stairs the lump in his throat nearly choked him.


## CHAPTER THIRTEEN

"You've gave me five bob too much, Mr. Blair!"

Counting again, Colin spread his wages across the counter. The blinds were down and the heavy street door of the shop locked up for the night. They had just finished checking his sales commission and adding on his weekly delivery florin. As always on Saturday evenings there was a special air of mingled accomplishment and celebration about their final proceedings. Colin was never quite sure whether it was because it was the last day of the week and the public were locked out for a full day and Blair himself rejoiced in the fact or whether it was simply a personal reaction to the prospect of a Sunday; anyhow, Saturday closing was different. Always at this hour, when the street view was shut off and he and Blair moved freely about bundling up returns and stacking portable billboards into their backroom niche, the little shop seemed to grow smaller and in its cosier privacy Blair's usual martinet pose relaxed. If business had been especially good the Homburg hat would go a little farther back and the normally dry little newsagent might even crack a joke about Colin's Sunday dates with imaginary girl friends. Tonight, however, he had not suggested that Colin was rushing away to meet "a bit stuff" and the boy was rather relieved. Not being glib or cocksure he always felt it a bit of a strain when middle-aged authority forced decorative banter on him. Generally he found adult ideas of humour, if not completely baffling, often embarrassing and mostly ponderous. He was quite prepared to find that the inclusion of the two extra half crowns in his money was some droll and indefinable leg-pull of Blair's.

The newsagent paused with a carton of cigarette packets in his hand. He did not look at the money and he did not look at Colin. His attention was fixed on a rack of gaudy periodicals suspended from the end wall.

"No," he coughed with a half-choked little laugh. "That's just a wee bit extra." He squeezed the laugh out again. "The thing is, Colin, you're gettin' a bit auld to be a paper boy."

"Eh?"

Blair fiddled with the box. He knew this was the lamest excuse. Good newsboys were never too old—or too young—and both of them knew Colin was a good boy. He ploughed on: "Well, you know what I mean—you're comin' on sixteen now. Surely ye don't want to be a paper boy all your life?"

"No, but——"

"Does your faither no' think it's time you were at a trade, or something?"

Colin kept looking at him blankly. In a confused fashion he still thought the man was trying to put over a joke. Blair grew angry

at his own ineptitude. "The truth is," he blurted, "I'd rather have
a younger boy. I don't want you to come back on Monday. That's
why I put in the bit extra."

"But——!" Colin was stunned. He could not find words to
argue. Or express his dismay. He remembered his first pay-night
and the thrill of receiving money he had actually earned himself.
He remembered how huge and heavy the coins felt in his hand,
more solid and wonderful than any treasure he had ever possessed.
His finger-tips had stroked the milled edges, and an intoxication
of wealth and power and confidence had seized and remained with
him until this moment. Now that confidence was shattered. It was
unbelievable. That first night he had trotted home along the
streets oblivious of tramcars and pavement crowds and hooting
horns and the drunks who staggered out of every pub—and yet,
sensitively and superbly aware of them all. This was the city and
it was all his. Before him stretched a wonderful future sign-posted
into infinity by a weekly Eldorado of never-ending pay-days.
Ecstasy reached its pinnacle when he burst home into the kitchen.
Putting the money into his mother's hand he had simply said,
"There!"

Julia had looked long at the little clutch of silver and coppers.
"Your first pay, son?"

"Ay—two bob for delivery and one an' eleven commission for
sellin'. S'all right, Maw, i'nt it?"

"It's just great, Colin. Your daddy got nae Buroo money this
week and I was just wondering how in heaven's name I was gonny
manage on Jenny's ten bob. This'll see us by for a couple of days
at the Co anyway."

He had swelled in importance. "Mr. Blair says maybe 'e'll can
make it more once I know the runs a bit better—you've got to get
fly, y'know."

"Don't get too fly, son." But her glance had been proud. "And
how much pocket-money have I to give you back?"

"Och, I get tips," he had been magnificently off-hand. "Wan
woman gave me a penny this morning and auld Mr. Stirrat, the
cobbler, gave me three ha'pence for running back to the shop for
his tobacco. I can do without pocket-money, Maw."

With a little smile she lifted her purse off the dresser. Except for
a yellow Co-operative receipt check in its back compartment it
seemed empty, flat and hungry-looking. Its leather was shiny and
smooth with years of clutching. Its seams were good because they
were never strained. Flicking back the little clasp that sealed its

middle division she picked out her last solitary threepenny bit. "Here," she said, "you've got to have pocket-money. Anybody that works deserves their share o' what they earn. Only misers and millionaires expect folk to work for nothing. See and don't waste it on a lot of rubbish."

He had taken it because she insisted. He would, secretly, have been disappointed had she not. With his fivepence ha'penny he went out feeling like Croesus.

And now it was all ended. And for no good reason. The boy could only gape at Blair stupidly.

When he got home he laid the money on the table silently. Jenny's sharp instinct was instantly alive to his dejection. "S'matter with you?" she demanded with sisterly suspicion. Her voice turned Julia's attention from her dish-washing. Anger rose in the boy and an insulting retort trembled on his lips. Instead, to no one in particular, he said: "I've no' to go back. Blair says he wants a younger boy."

"What!" Jenny's disbelief was comment enough for everyone. From the other end of the table Ella accused pertly: "You been short in your money, eh?"

"No, I wasnae short in my money." Misery and bewilderment exploded in Colin's swift denial. His face screwed and he glared hate at his young sister.

"Well—what did he pay you off for?"

"You shut up." Jenny's glance was still on Colin. Julia came from the sink, the plate in her dish-cloth dropping water spots on the frayed carpet. "When did he tell you this?"

"Just the noo, Maw." His grief over what the loss meant to her suddenly overwhelmed him. Dismay, hurt pride and disappointment tossed his inarticulate emotions into a hangdog mask of guilt. With a clutch of fear at her heart his mother studied him narrowly. Inconsequently she noticed he was growing too old for short trousers and a detached portion of her mind wondered where the money was to come from to buy his first real suit.

"You mean to say he never gave you any hint afore today?"

"I'm telling you—he just gave me an extra five shillings and said, don't come back. . . . I dunno why."

"There must be some reason," Jenny persisted.

Julia looked at the surplus half-crowns. "Wee Blair's no' one of the giving kind . . ." she mused. With a quick gesture she flicked off her apron. "You finish drying these dishes," she ordered Ella.

"And there's a sausage in the pan for Colin," she told Jenny. "I'll not be long."

"Where you going?"

"Never mind." Her glance included them all. "But if your faither comes in before I get back don't say a word to him."

In speculation they watched her throw on her hat and coat. In alarm Colin asked: "You're not going down to Blair's, are you? Anyway he's shut now."

"Never mind where I'm going," she repeated. The door closed behind her with admonitory firmness. . . .

Julia Haig took her philosophy from the Bible. Each of her days was, of necessity, sufficient for itself. Her horizon was filled by the small vital things—how to pay the rent, how to keep out of debt, how to govern her family for their good and not for her glory. Inheriting no grandiloquent traditions, her standards were plain but rigid. After over twenty years of marriage she endured her husband's drinking bouts with regret but compassion. Behind a veneer of homely satire she concealed an intelligence that matched the aggressive rebellions of his. Hurrying down the street she summarized in hasty, abstract fashion all she knew of their son.

Colin had been a good boy. Not brilliant, not notable for anything. He had gone through school without distinction but also without trouble. His outside escapades had never been serious enough to bring the police to her door and his feuds with his sisters had been brief and normal enough to create no more than a kitchen flurry. If he had never overwhelmed anyone with displays of sentiment, she was content that his casual acceptance of his home life was grounded in affection.

But she was also aware that his world was growing with him. The billiard halls, the backcourt banker schools, the sniggering girls in dark closes—she had no illusions about their attractions—and what they could do to a boy of limited interests. The mystery of his sudden dismissal from Blair's alerted all her subconscious fears.

She did not go to the shop. Blair lived in a single-apartment house in a side street. She went straight there. A bachelor, the newsagent himself answered her knock. He carried a steaming teapot he evidently had been about to pour. Her call brought him no pleasure, for he gave no sign of recognition or welcome.

"You know me, Mr. Blair," Julia stated bluntly. "I ran up to find out why you paid Colin off?"

Keeping his free hand on the edge of the door and without

opening it more than half his own breadth of shoulder, Blair looked more dyspeptic than ever. Behind him, in the lobby shadows, an inevitable array of jumbled coats and jackets hung from a row of upreared double wall-hooks. Somehow the stale mustiness of such garments, most of them never moved or worn from year to year, always characterized entrance to the poorer tenement houses. But Julia shrewdly guessed the interior of this one would be especially depressing, despite kerbside legend of its tenant's supposed wealth.

"I told Colin why I laid him off," Blair said wearily. "I'm sorry, Mrs. Haig, but I don't think it's fair to keep a boy selling papers when he should be getting himself a real job."

"Getting it where?"

"I mean—starting his time or something."

Julia remained dispassionate, but her challenge did not falter. "You know as well as I do, Mr. Blair, that there's no jobs for boys nowadays. It's just those and such as those can get their sons a trade. And we don't happen to be among the lucky ones."

"But you wouldn't want him to be a paper-boy all his life?"

"Why not? There's a lot of grown men selling papers in Glesca the day. After all, except you're standing behind a counter, what are you?"

Blair's mouth dragged. "If you've come to be insultin'——!" The door began to close.

"I'm not insulting anybody." The flat calm of her tone held him. "I just want to know the truth. No shopkeeper gets rid of a good boy for nothing—and certainly no' because they're interested in his welfare. Was my boy stealing?"

"Oh—no!" The door jerked wider. "Oh no, Mrs. Haig, nothing like that. Whatever made you imagine it?"

"What else would anybody think?"

He looked at her dumbly, his habitual expression of private misery only a little more pronounced. She sensed his indecision was not altruistic. His unease was selfish. Whatever secret motives actuated him, only a personal consideration would cause Blair to reveal them.

She said quietly, "Much as we need the few shillings you paid him I'm no' asking my boy's job back. But I'm his mother and it's for my peace of mind I've got to know. And I shouldnae need to tell you if I don't get a satisfactory answer his faither'll want one. I'd rather he had nothing to do with it at all."

Blair's hesitation stretched only another moment. He twitched the door wider and swayed rather than stepped back. "Better come in a minute," he said without enthusiasm.

Except that it faced south instead of north the kitchen was a replica of her own—black grate, window sink, coal-bunker dresser, hole-in-the-wall bed, the usual huddled fittings. Sometimes, in moods of rare revelation, Julia felt Victorian landlords must have resurrected dungeon architects to design Glasgow's workers' warrens. And then, acknowledging the boon of running water, slot-meter gas and wax-cloth on her floor, she would register mental thanksgiving for skipping her grandmother's generation.

Absorbing the details of Blair's home she felt she had stepped back forty years. His dim brown wallpaper had yielded its pattern long since to the overlaying stains and dust of a lifetime. Any whitewash adhering to the ceiling was so flaked and pock-marked it had ceased being decorative and was as offensive as a scabrous skin. A hardwood chair and another huge one of high-lugged pattern, with the horse-hair oozing from its seams, were the only leisure furnishings. The scarred table had no cloth to hide its unwashed, unvarnished surface. The naked boards of the floors were unscrubbed, and the dirty yard of ragged carpet tossed down before the unlit fireplace only heightened the nightmare of decay and neglect. On the table the messy jampot, the encrusted tins of condensed milk, the flies crawling over the sugar still in its torn blue paper bag, the single half-filled teacup with the stains of other meals scarcely rinsed off—all signposted the dreary indifference of the housekeeper.

"I've not had time to make my bed yet." Blair matched her glance into the undraped cavern's shabby upheaval. "Not that it matters, 'cos I'm the only one who's ever in it."

She looked at him swiftly. But the tired lassitude with which he sank against the big chair's arm guaranteed the innocence of the remark.

"You've got to get up so early for the papers. I've no time to tidy up in the morning." Picking up his tea he sipped it and went on with wry but unapologetic honesty. "Nor the notion at night as you'll notice." He looked up and saw she was still standing awkwardly at the end of the dresser. "Can you not sit down—or are you frightened you'll no get out again?"

"I'll get out all right," she said, without moving.

"You know how we're fixed in Burnford," he said abruptly. "Govan, Partick, Anderston—all the old Burghs have been taken over by the Corporation long ago. Some folk even want the city to take over Renfrew and Paisley and Barrhead and God knows where else." He shrugged. "But we're still on our own. Some folk think it's a good thing, some don't——"

"It makes us independent?"

Blair coughed out a laugh. "Glesca tramcars. Glesca Subway, Glesca lighting—where would we be without them? We're only kidding ourselves."

"What's all this got to do wi' my boy's job?"

Steadily he looked at her. "The wee building my shop's in happens to be Council property—and I've only got a year-to-year lease on it."

"Well?"

"D'you know what Tam Fixx was tellin' me no later than yesterday?"

"Fixx—yon dirty wee man that aye wears a red open-neck shirt? Him that's on the Council?"

"The very same. Him that's Big Fergie at the Subway's brother-in-law."

Julia stiffened. "No," she said. "What was he telling you?"

"He was telling me that some of the Council were beginning to think it's time my building was knocked down to make way for a big new lavatory—or something. What he called improving the amenities of the Burgh."

"And what about your shop?"

Blair's shoulders lifted. "It would come down along with the building of course."

"I see." She looked at him reflectively. She mused how the absence of uniform diminished a man. Behind his counter Blair's air of detachment, even condescension, had always stirred vague criticism. Although his responses were civil, their perfunctoriness when handing over change after a purchase had a take-it-or-leave-it tang that invested every transaction with a reverse quality. In his shoddy framework of trivial shelves and cheap magazine racks it was if he was actually doing the customer a favour and—more aggravating still—that at the expense of his better judgment. This aura of contrary values was irritably intensified by the unvarying affection of the Homburg hat and complete suit in contrast to the nondescript raiment of most of his regular customers. It had built up a variety of local legends ranging from those of his miserly wealth to one of his tragic fall from grace as the embittered son of a rich and refined family. Whatever their theme, popular fancy always arrived at the conclusion that the insular little

newsagent did not really need to work and that his shop was only
a time-filler in a disinterested life.

Now, in raw kitchen intimacy, Julia saw the puny hunger of
the thin white arms, the hidden poverty of the ill-patched shirt.
They were of a piece with the half-hearted sandwiches cut from
the wilting loaf, the stained cup without a saucer. Tragic in his
bachelor loneliness, she felt her anger fade.

"But surely they're not pulling down the building right away?"

His dead eyes watched her across the rim of his cup. "Fixx was
letting me know they're only thinking about it—it's the kind of
thing that could be talked one way or another . . . in the meetings
the Party have before the Council meetings, I mean."

"Oh!" she knew the answer before she asked. "And what does
Fixx think about it himself?"

Blair put down his cup. He spread himself butter from a pat
still in paper. Spacing his words with the glide of his knife across
the bread he said evenly: "He hasn't quite made up his mind.
Like a good conscientious councillor—public servant, was how he
put it—he comes to see me as an interested party, to talk about
it. You know?"

Slowly Julia nodded. "I know. He would mention who you had
working for you?"

"Casually."

In silence they looked at each other. Everything was clear now.
Julia said, "Oh, well, I'm pleased to know it was nothing you
had against Colin."

Blair wagged his head in solemn assurance. "Nothing like that,
Mrs. Haig. I'm more than sorry to have to let the boy go."

Colin's mother nodded. With the outside door opened she
looked back. "I hope ye keep your wee shop, Mr. Blair. You've
been there a long time."

She got her wish. Twenty-seven years later the new lavatory
was built on waste ground opposite the little newsagent's. By
that time the shop had a new tenant. Blair had died four years
previously during Thomas Fixx, M.B.E.'s, seventh term as Burnford's Provost.


## CHAPTER FOURTEEN

WHEN she was twelve Ella got "converted". A chum coaxed her
away from the Tin Church Sunday-school to a Brethren meeting.

Under the spell of hearty singing, hell-fire preaching and the personal interest of its leaders she acquired quick fervour. After occasional preliminary warming-up criticisms of the rest of the family's religious shortcomings, she stunned them all at tea-time one night by bowing her near albino head and lip-mumbling a thanksgiving grace.

At sight of his daughter's closed eyes Haig's jaw fell open and he halted his fork midway between plate and mouth. After one glance he quickly avoided Jenny or Colin's gaze. Equally embarrassed, they could only register their feelings in mime—Colin clasped his brow and Jenny rolled expressive eyes upwards in anything but pious appeal.

But they respected Ella's gesture. Their quiet turned Julia from her cooking. The self-conscious misery on three faces was so comic the frying-pan in her hand quivered in sympathy with her effort of self-control. Choking back an instinctive quip, she studied Ella briefly before resuming her fireplace activities without comment. And later, when the girl had gone out and Jenny referred impatiently to the incident, she reproved her eldest daughter sharply.

"Leave your wee sister alone," she warned. "If Ella wants to pray let her pray. We could all pray oftener. A good dose of religion does nobody any harm."

"Oh, she can be as religious as she likes for me," disclaimed Jenny. "She can join the Salvation Army if she likes! But I just hope she's not going to start ramming it down my throat. When I come home from Hoetup's at night all I want's my supper—I'm in no mood for tea-meeting. I get enough preaching at work without coming back here to it."

"Who preaches to you at Hoetup's?" Julia unsnibbed the drop-front of the coal bunker but paused, stooping, with the shovel in her hand. She preferred to tend the fire herself because the others, hasty in their shovelling, filled the kitchen with the fine dust that accumulated at the bottom of the bunker. Even when the coalman called only Julia herself had the knack of clearing the dresser-top swiftly while still humouring the impatient, sack-laden, stair-weary man to heave his burden in gently enough to keep the inevitable cloud of grit to a minimum. As she tartly explained, "It's me that has the washing of the bed-slips and curtains in this house—standing another minute'll no' kill the coalman but someday youse'll maybe have to pick me up off the wash-house floor." But now, as she invited a chief joy of her day—

her daughter's recital of hosiery events—her pale but still attractive face was calmly patient and the usual hint of mischief was subdued in her eye.

"Oh, we have all kinds." Jenny shook her head at memory of her workmates. "Holy Rollers and Hail Marys—it's hard to know which is the worst. I wouldnae mind if they'd live up to what they preach but half o' them, the holier they are the hellier they are. D'you know our boss is an elder in a big kirk, yet he said he'd shut the place down first afore he'd put a penny on our rates. Said he was running at a loss as it is!"

"Maybe so he is."

"Away for goodness' sake, Mother!" Jenny's black eyes sparkled in indignation. "Have you ever seen his house out at Langside? A mansion, that's what it is. And his wife!—she's drippin' in diamonds! Miss Tait, oor forewoman, says they go to the Channel Islands ever year for their holidays and everything's of the best." Jenny's head tossed. "No, no, Maw, don't tell me auld Hoetup's hard up—when he says he's losing money he means he's only making a hunner pound a week instead of two hunner." The girl's mouth set in a bitter line. "When I look in yon shop windows along Argyle Street and see the cardigans at nine and twelve shillings that he pays us fourpence ha'penny for running up on the machine I could chuckle the auld rascal—hangin's too good for him."

Julia emptied the shovel into the grate and brushed away the ash that filmed the bright of her steels. "He canny be that auld," she said remininscently. "I mind fine when he started." She looked over at her husband. "How old will Mattha Hoetup be?"

From the depths of his armchair Collie looked over his book. "Mattha Hoetup?—och—be getting on for sixty. Maybe aboot ten years aulder than us?"

"Ay," Julia nodded. "Canny be much more. They hadnae an awful lot then. Grace Hoetup had to come down herself and help. And many a time I've seen him goin' away wi' a suitcase o' samples to do his own peddlin' because they couldna afford a packman. There was nae fancy holidays then and they just stayed in a single-end in Whitedyke Street above your Aunt Bella. No doubt if you were askin' they'd tell you they've had their struggles."

"And now they're going to keep everybody else struggling." Her mother's tolerance irritated Jenny. Vivid in her eye was the picture of the low-raftered loft where she and a dozen other girls nhaled a diet of wool fibre and oil fumes while operating a battery of machines cramped into an area originally spanning two bedrooms. She thought of the black iron sink in the corner, with its single drunken faucet and the chipped enamel mug that served them all as a drinking vessel. Her stomach turned as she thought of the scabrous big rats Lachie, the mechanic, trapped regularly. And she remembered the dirty scribbled whitewash of the halfwall that divided the two scummy toilets and the token to privacy their cracked lop-sided doors afforded. Sourly she thought of the weekly haggling over pay-lines and the abrupt arbitrariness with which most disputes were settled. Her literal mind baulked at equating the daily facts of her employment with the public face of her employer. "If that's Christianity," she said venomously, "we'd be better off under Zulus. And our Ella needn't think she's going to impress me."

"I don't suppose Ella's trying to impress anybody but God," said Julia mildly. "Only the well-to-do and the hungry put on religion as a camouflage. Your wee sister's trying her best to do what she thinks right."

"And buy herself a place into heaven," sneered Jenny.

"And what's wrong wi' that?" Collie looked up unexpectedly. "If the price is as cheap as the corner Bible-thumpers make out, she's as well to put her name down early—it's about the only thing the bunch that run this country leave a wee soul a chance to bid for." In sudden irritation he stood up and strode through to the room. Julia looked after him and smiled. "The funny thing is," she said, "likely when the novelty wears off our Ella'll turn out a bigger heathen than any of you." Her tone hardened admonishingly. "But one thing's certain, she'll never say she was put off in her own house. I'll see to that."

Pausing in the dish-washing she had started, Jenny swung round from the sink. "Jings, Maw, you don't think much of us. Are you disappointed 'cos Colin and I plunk the kirk. We don't have the notion for that kind o' thing but that's not to say we're a pair o' hooligans. After all my da nor you don't go about the church."

Julia nodded. "Neither we do," she admitted honestly. "We did at first but he fell off and then I wouldn't go unless I had the clothes. I used to take you and Colin when you were wee, but you were such an idiot jumping about the pew trying to imitate the organist you only gave us a showing up."

Jenny threw back her head and laughed without contrition.

"I mind of that," she rejoiced. "It was the way yon woman used to dive across the keyboard grabbing at the plugs they pull out and in—I thought it was marvellous."

"The baldy auld man in the seat in front didn't think it was marvellous the night you nearly skited the last three hairs off him."

Leaning limply against the sink, Jenny laughed louder. "I know," she confessed. "It was terrible. And you were that affronted!"

"No wonder. I thought the minister was going to speak down to you from the pulpit—he was always lookin' across."

"Even our Colin kept digging me in the ribs—oh, I must've been daft!"

"Daft or wise I never risked taking you again."

"Well, Mother, it really wasnae a place for weans! Them sermons—oh, I thought they were never going to stop! I was glad when you stopped taking us."

"If you'd had my mother to deal with you wouldn't have got off so easy. By jings she had us all at the kirk mornin', noon and night. And you darenae say no!"

"Och ay, Mother," interrupted her own daughter, "but things were different in your days. You were right behind the times. And know what I sometimes think, Mother?"

"What?"

"My Grannie Graham must've been a right auld tinker. I mean, she didn't give any of you much of a life, did she?"

Sitting sideways on one of the kitchen chairs Julia folded her hands in her lap and smiled. In such moments of repose, with her print apron a little soiled and the lines of middle age beginning to show round the corners of her firm mouth, Jenny always imagined her mother looked rather like a figure from one of the brown old Dutch paintings they had over in Kelvingrove Art Galleries. With a far-away note in her voice she sighed: "Maybe we hadnae much of a life. Many a time I wished I could run away, your granny was that strict. And, of course, whatever she said was law by my father—he just took the big leather belt off his waist and rattled you across the legs wi' it. Ay, and ye could greet as much as you liked, there was nae sympathy for you. But there was nae favourites. And we had our good laughs, too. Maybe we hadnae sc many picture halls and things like that but we knew how to amuse ourselves. . . . There was only one thing——"

"What was that?"

Julia's nod was severely certain. "None of us would ever've dreamed o' contradicting my faither and mother the way you do your daddy and me. Ay, to the day and hour she died—and I was merrit and had two weans by then—I wouldnae daur have argued wi' my mother."

"Why not?"

Mrs. Haig looked at her daughter pityingly. "Because she'd just've drawn me a look and asked who I thought I was talking to. And don't laugh—whatever it was she and her kind were born with, she could make you feel the size o' tuppence. Even your faither—and nobody could say he was a meek man—always gave her her place." The little smile crooked Julia's mouth again. "Funny enough, they got on champion. He would do anything for her, and even when he was on the batter she would make excuses for him. She aye said he was the best son-in-law she had and the only real man in the family. She thought a lot of your faither."

Jenny's head tilted. "Funny I never hear my da talking much about his folk. Why is that?"

"Och, the Haigs were a queer lot," Julia frowned and wrinkled her nose. "Families are a' different y'know. Whatever else we were we always kept close to each other but not the Haigs—bar your faither, none o' them seemed to have any real feelings at all. They could pass each other in the street without blinking an eye and when auld Sam'l died your faither was the only one that went up to see his mother before the day o' the funeral."

"That's terrible!"

"You don't mind of auld Sam'l—you were still in my arms when he died—but he was an auld rascal. He gave Barbara an awful life."

"My daddy's mother?"

"Your other granny, ay. She was a wee, delicate cratur, but awful proud. I never liked her much but my heart used to be sore for her."

"Was he the boss?"

Julia looked at her daughter frankly. Since the night of Collie's wildest outburst the girl had increasingly assumed the prerogatives of confidant. Where before her efforts to assert herself had swung between the hesitant and truculent, now she eschewed the apologies and challenges of adolescence and quietly assumed the rights and dignities of a person. Although their temperaments sometimes still clashed and although she never yielded final dominance, Julia found herself gradually becoming dependent and appreciative of their growing mature relationship. In moments of crisis it was comforting to find another woman at her elbow. Now she said bluntly, "Sam Haig was a ladies' man. And if you think your faither's got faults let me tell you, that's worse nor drink. A gambler, a boozer, a loafer—any of them can break your heart. But the man that runs after other women, he tears it right out of your body. A man that's no' faithful to the mate he picks for himself is faithful to nothing and nobody. Although he was lousy with money—he had a good job in a bonded store—auld Sam'l wouldn't have given any of his family a drink of water."

"Maybe he gave them whisky?" Jenny quipped.

"Nor whisky either. The minute they left the house that was them finished. When your da merrit me, both him and Barbara were blazing. They always maintained Collie married beneath himself although God knows why, for they had neither given your faither a right trade nor done anything to encourage him to make something of himself. Your da aye said his faither was that busy chasing lady-loves and your grandmother was that busy chasing him that neither o' the two of them had time to notice they had a family of their own at all."

"I never mind meeting any of my faither's folks."

"They used to come up occasionally. But then Ella, his sister—that's who our Ella's called after—married a sergeant-major in the Army and went to live down in England. She wrote to me a couple of times but, oh, it's years now since we last heard from her. . . . The two brothers didn't stay long in the house either after they got up a bit. Robert, the eldest, went to Australia, I think, and James—I liked James, he was an awful quiet chap—he went to sea and the last we heard of him was during the War. Maybe he got drowned, poor fellow."

Jenny looked thoughtful. Her efforts to clothe in flesh and blood figures in her mother's reminiscences were always defeated by the time barrier. Rarely, even with aid from the stiff, frumpy figures postured in the family album, could she visualize her parents young and smooth-skinned. Although they must only have been bordering thirty when she first became aware of them as people, she still retained an infant fixation of their great age. Even now, though Collie was barely fifty and her mother was several years younger, she grieved for them as being frighteningly near the grave. Yet when she met their living contemporaries she always experienced a cheated sense of disappointment. They

seldom matched their histories. They were such solid, ordinary
people not yet dissolving into the shadows of senile mystery but
with the gloss of vigour blurred into the uniformity of undramatic
midde age. Somehow they always shrunk from the conception
founded on the pictures her mother painted. As they came and
sat prosaically by the fireside and gossiped of work and idleness,
births and deaths, Jenny found it indecent and certainly grotesque
to imagine them ever hot with passion or bitter with despair.
Their philosophies were so resigned and desiccated and their
enthusiasms so stunted that in their presence she was for ever
consumed with a secret irritation that only ingrained good
manners and loyalty to family pride in hospitality curbed.

"Why," she suddenly yearned aloud, "why had I no wonderful
relations?"

"What do you mean—wonderful?" Julia looked up sharply.

"I mean, folk that are important." Jenny sighed in her effort
to express herself. "Folk like gentry—lords and ladies or even
rich uncles that went to America and made fortunes. Why is it
we've got nobody like that?" She looked round the little kitchen
in sudden distaste. "Everybody connected to us are that bloomin'
ordinary. I'm no' even like Lizzie Barr in the work, who's aye
braggin' about her great-grandmother who's supposed to have
been a Heilan' laird's daughter. I'm no' even like Nora O'Brien,
whose whole family have a' got farms in Ireland. Nobody
knows who we are or who we come fae! And all the kin we
do know are no better than ourselves. We're just a bunch of
nobodies!"

"And what's wrong wi' that?" bridled Julia. "All these Irish
farms turn out to be six hens, a pig and a peat cottage in the
middle of a bog. What d'you think they're over here labouring for
if they've got estates in Ireland? Use your heid, lassie! As for the
gentry!" Contempt carved Julia's face like a physical pain.
"When I left school first I was in service for a while, and if I told
ye some of the things I know ye wouldnae need curlin' pins the
night. Don't think because some folk have big houses and turned-
up noses that they're always the clean potato. Often enough the
biggest swanks have the most to hide."

"That wouldn't worry me," Jenny vowed. "And I just wish my
faither was getting wheeled home to a castle instead of staggering
back to this—at least in a castle we'd all have room to keep out
of his road."

Her mother smiled thinly. "You'll live and learn. And, give 'im his due, your faither's no been bad this long while. But if it's ancestors you're after it's auld Suzie in Paisley you'll have to visit—she's the one that knows the family history."

"Who is she?"

"Aw, my mother's cousin. She must be about ninety now and looks as if she'll live to a thousand. Suzie's never looked a day older all the years I've known her—I think a diet of gossip and pan bread must've given her the secret of eternal life."

"Is she married?"

"No, Suzie was never married. She was aye too busy attending other folk's weddings and funerals to think about getting a man for herself. But she's the one to see—she can talk for a week just layin' it off about relatives I never even heard of. Actually she's a great old case and can go away back to the days when your great-grandfaithers wore tall hats and brought their wabs into the town market once a week."

"Wabs?"

"Their webs. The cloth they made in their houses. A lot of the folk you've sprung fae were weavers. And according to auld Suzie gey well-doing bodies at that. You'll no' catch Suzie letting anybody put airs over her. She aye maintains that the Grahams come off o' good stock and that her grandfaither flung himself away marrying a farm lassie." Julia shrugged. "But, och, every family in Glesca has these kind of yarns. My ain mother's mother was supposed to be a naval captain's daughter who ran away wi' the coachman. I don't mind of her myself but by all reports she was a real lady and wouldn't stop in her step to speak to a neighbour in the street or even go to her own door without her mutch on."

Jenny shook her head. "That's what I mean. We are only the scrapings of the pot. Likely if we knew the truth of it the naval captain would turn out to be a Hielan' deckhand and the coachman would be a Broomielaw carter. Now, if that brother o' my faither's would only turn up from Australia loaded wi' sheep ranches that would be something. At least if we have no past it might give us a future."

"I'm telling you that's the trouble wi' the the world, there's too many folk wi' pasts. As for the future," Julia looked at her daughter, "well, at your age you've got as big a share o' the future as anybody. See and don't waste it."

## CHAPTER FIFTEEN

COLIN stood in the Pawn Close watching the snow drift down. It turned the cobbles wet and set the dray horses skidding, but in the window corners of the houses opposite it piled in little white triangles, making the dark face of the tenement look picturesque. He hoped it would fall thicker and heavier. Although it was six years since last he hung a stocking up beside the mantelpiece, he was still young enough to associate snowfalls with Christmas and its expectant excitements. He felt he could do with some excitement. In reality snowfalls generally added up to no more than wet, cold feet and maybe a bust ear from a stone in a snowball. But the legend overlaid experience. And the thrill of the great year when Santa had afforded a *Chatterbox Annual* and the other when his stockings had stretched with the wonderful weight of an air rifle plus all the usual treasure of coppers, oranges and boxes of crayons still left their magic. With satisfaction, he watched the snow pile more solidly along the angles of the gutters.

"Christ, this is a do!"

Surprised he spun round as Binger Maxwell arrived and slapped his cap against the Close wall. Binger whistled amazed at the crust of snow that fell.

"Why the panting?" kidded Colin. "Think it was cauld to hear you!"

"Bluidy right it's cauld," insisted Binger. Of an age with Colin he was an inch or two shorter, but his hollow-jawed face was more cynically mature. Binger prided himself on not only being a man of the world but claimed he knew his way around in the underworld as well. "By Christ," he emphasized, "I'll be over the wall into McCready's coal-ree the night, you bet! Would you believe my mother hasnae got a shovel o' dross left in the bunker? And none o' them buggers that come up our street would give her a bag on tick either—the bastards!"

"My auld lady would take a canary fit if I took anything into the house that was pinched."

Binger shrugged. "Who said anything about pinching? I'm just lucky at finding things. T'hell, you canny see them sitting without a fire!"

"I wouldn't either," Colin agreed defensively. "We've never

been stuck yet, though. The auld lady's pretty good at spinning things out."

The thickening snow drifted into the close.

"Funny," said Binger, "how everything gets quiet."

"Dark, too." Colin looked upwards. The tramway power cables were almost lost from sight in the whirling flakes. The sky was an abyss of impenetrable grey pressed right down to the rooftops. "Wonder what it would be like up in an aeroplane just now?"

"Could do," muttered Binger out of the side of his mouth. "Here's a couple of slops—big Fairy Feet and his mate."

"They'll chib us." Colin made to go.

"Stand still," dared Binger. "Maybe they'll pass."

"Like hell."

The official figures, huge in their domed helmets and with the snow on their capes ballooning their breadth into enormity, paced closer. Their well-shod feet squelched in the thickening slush. Drawing level with the Pawn Close the inside constable, his waxed moustache silvered with snow, halted as ponderously as a tug-tethered liner heaving to. His companion moved half a step round with the same heavy inevitability.

"C'mon," said Fairy Feet. "D'you not see that notice?" Without taking his contemptuous glance off them the twitch of his helmet indicated the bold NO LOITERING notice freshly stencilled on the Close's gaunt wall.

"We're just in oot the snaw," Binger mumbled apologetically. "We didnae think——"

"Are you moving—or d'you want a boot in the arse?"

They edged out of the Close. The policemen watched them go before resuming their beat. At the echo of their fat chuckles, Binger gritted, "Big blue bastards."

"I told you," shrugged Colin. "You can't argue wi' a polisman—they're always right."

"They'd get you hung."

They drifted into the shuttered porch of an empty shop. Its opaque whitened windows and dirty, chalk-scribbled door lent poignancy to the dereliction of their days. Binger blew into his hands to warm them. "Wish I had a dout," he mourned, "the old bloke went through my pockets this morning and pinched my last Woodbine."

Colin laughed. "Away for God's sake, Binger—when had you ever a whole Woodbine?"

Binger laughed, too. "I made a thru'penny bit yesterday carrying an auld toff's bag from the station. I bought fags with the tuppence and gave the auld wife the odd penny for the gas. You shoulda heard the auld man—you'd a thought I'd robbed the Bank o' England 'cos I didnae give him halfers. He was gonny take the fags off me!"

"My auld man doesnae know I smoke."

"The less they know the better."

"Jeeze, it's no' half lying!" Critically they studied the spread of snow creeping up from the gutters and defying the onslaught of traffic wheels and churning hoofs. The passing lorry nags snorted and blew like warhorses, and the flakes lay on their manes like sugar icing. Pedestrians hugging the lee of the tenements barged on with stooped heads and reddened cheeks. The warmest-looking women were the shawlie women from the slums who pulled their tartan wraps closer round their straggly hair and scliffed by in leaking boots and ragged-edged skirts.

"I wouldn't mind a big shawl myself the noo," Colin admitted, turning up the collar of his jacket. "Mind auld Home-Rule Simpson and the stories he use to tell us at the history? Mind he telt us how, in the auld days, they used to wrap the plaid right round them—didnae need any coats nor jaikets nor nothing! Jings, that wouldna suited my maw, she'd a helluva job getting me this suit o' long yins. I think she's still paying it up."

"Ah, but Home-Rule was a good auld scout," Binger nodded approvingly. "It was a bluidy sin, we took a right rise oot him."

"Ay," Colin smiled back down the immense vista of two years. "Then there was yon other one, Specky Carter. Mind him?"

"Dae I no'!" Binger's lips tightened. "I always meant to find out where the runt stayed so I could go along and break his windows. Yon *was* a bastard."

Two figures darted in out of the weather. The tallest aimed a playful punch at Binger's middle and Colin made room in the doorway for the other.

"Where you heading for?" he asked, when the pair had settled. "I thought youse were getting a jump on an Allan Line boat?"

"Jump!" Binger sneered. "Tip nor Francie couldnae get a jump on the Govan Ferry. Who the hell telt ye that?"

"Aw, it was right enough," the tall youth was indignant. "I got the wire that this chief steward was needing a couple o' pantry boys."

"An' then did he discover how much you could eat?"

"We were just unlucky. Before we got there somebody'd tipped off those Plantation blokes——"

Tip stopped suddenly. Colin and Binger had removed their caps and solemnly replaced them on their heads upside down. "Aw, if you don't believe me," he exploded, "ask Francie here. . . . Sure I spoke to the steward, Francie?"

"Ay, right enough," agreed Francie loyally. "We were all set."

"Away for Christ sake—ye canny buy a jump on a boat the noo," derided Binger. Arranging his cap he changed the subject, asking challengingly, "Do you think you've got any chance on Saturday?"

Smiles faded instantly. A wary look settled on all their faces. "Certainly," decided Tip. "Why no'? The Celts'll go through them like a dose of salts."

"For God's sake!" Binger spat his disgust out into the snow now mantling half the pavement's breadth.

"I'm telling you." Tip was emphatic. "D'you see them in the Glesca Cup?"

"I saw them in the Glesca Cup," Binger's head nodded forward in emphasis.

"Then—holy Jesus?" Tip spread his hand appealingly.

"Thon referee should've got his throat cut," suggested Colin.

"Away and take a run at——" Francie stirred derisively. "If ever a referee wore blue specs yon yin did. D'you see the way he let Meek boot McGrory? Then was a bluidy liberty!"

"I hope he puts him right over the grandstand on Saturday," Binger yearned viciously.

"Meek'll no' do that," judged Colin. "Davy's too good a half-back, he doesn't need to lay in the leather. If he gets a fair do he'll play the whole Celtic himself."

"Away for Jesus' sake." In his overpowering contempt Tip took half a dozen steps out in the snow to the pavement edge and back again. Through clenched teeth he said, "I'm offering any Bluenose 2-1 the Bhoys trim you on Saturday anyway."

"You're on," Binger said instantly. "A draw in my favour?"

"Ay, a draw in your favour—certainly."

"I'll have a tanner's worth on that. The Rangers are a cert.'

"We'll see. Where's your tanner?"

"Where's your bob?"

"You put doon your tanner and I'll cover it."

"Nutt at all. You're offering the bet, let's see your money."

They argued pointlessly, their voices rising, until Colin said

"Shurrup, you pair of chancers, none of the two of you have a maik?"

Francie grinned agreement. "Tip and I are just after trying to bum auld Granny Spence for a packet o' Woodbine on the slate. Auld bitch wouldnae give us it."

"She's stacked too," Tip was emphatic. "I got the wink she keeps a biscuit-tin full o' money in her back kitchen. Some night I'm gonny do that wee shop."

"That's an idea!" Binger was eager. "We could go through the Ham Close and over McGregor's wash-house——"

"An' into Barlinnie." Colin's scorn was sarcastic but serious. "What d'you think youse are—a couple o' Scotch Jimmies? Auld Granny never leaves the house. D'you think she's gonny lie still and let you rake the place?"

"Aw, well, somebody'll do it," Tip said dourly. "She's asking for it."

" 'Cos she wouldnae give you tick? I'll bet you owe her a bluidy fortune?"

Tip shrugged.

"Who doesn't?" mourned Binger.

"Here's Fairy Feet and his mate coming back." Colin peered up the street through snow now falling in alternate spasms of gentle perpendicular calm and furious whirling eddies. He had to narrow his eyes against the flakes' sting. On his warning, Tip immediately said, "Christ, I'm off. That big bastard's got his knife in me already." Francie slipped out of the doorway with him and in a moment the blizzard hid them.

"We'd better skite, too."

"Sure." Flipping up his collar Binger fell into step. "C'mon, we'll go along to the Rally Rooms and see if there's any I.L.P. meetings on—sometimes they're good for a laugh."

As they trudged through the snow he went on. "See how these Papish bastards got off their mark? That's what I aye say about the Fenians, you canny trust them. My faither aye says the same."

"Och, I don't know." Suddenly Colin felt perverse. The boredom of mulling over the same arguments, tramping round the same haunts, seeing the same faces hit him with unusual force. In the eighteen months since he had lost his paper round with Blair he had been unable to secure another steady job. Sometimes he earned coppers running tradesmen's errands or washing windows up streets like Swanks' Brae but, generally, life was a

succession of back-court football games or cop-watching for the
tossing schools. Because it was a common enough existence and
he had no lack of fellows, he now accepted it as normal. The welter
of adult political argument and flaring newspaper headlines on
unemployment with which he had grown up had long since
ceased to have even the little personal relevance it ever had. The
future had no positive goal for him. And, without even being
aware of it, he had lost the impulse to expect any different kind
of life. His acceptance was so complete he had almost forgotten
how to be unhappy. Or to rebel. Malice rather than conviction
impelled him to suggest: "There must be some good Catholics.
Jings, there's one next door to us would give me anything."

"Who's that?"

"Stuart McQuade. Stue's all right. His mother, too. When I
was a kid she'd gie me a piece on jam any time mine was oot.
Nae bother either."

"Ach," Binger was contemptuous. "That's only to get you on.
Never be kidded by that stuff. I'll bet you if ever the Papishes got
to the heid o' things in this country its no' jeely pieces they'd gi'e
ye."

"What would they give us?"

Indignation nearly choked Binger. "Well," he gestured widely.
"Ye know what they did the last time!"

Colin felt ignorant. In spite of himself he felt caught up in his
own argument. He frowned partly in thought and partly in
defence against the driving snow. "The last time?" he stalled.
"Well, what did they do the last time?"

"What did they dae?" Binger grappled around in his own
mind. "Sure they kilt a' the martyrs—tortured them and burnt
them an' God knows what all!"

They were walking aimlessly on with the suggested I.L.P.
rendezvous forgotten. As they passed beyond Burnford's last line
of tenements the trees of the Memorial Park on their right and
the shrub-shrouded hill of the local cemetery on their left added a
sense of elemental nature to the exhilaration of the storm. Underfoot the snow was now deep enough to cushion their footfalls,
and Colin absently kicked his toes in as he objected: "Is that
what auld Home-Rule used to tell us? If I mind right did he
no' say it was that English mob—what d'ye call them?—Cromwell
and his tinribs——"

"Christ, you're worse than me, Colin," Binger exploded in
laughter. "Ye mean the Ironsides?"

"Ay, well, whatever they called them. It doesn't matter—but are you sure they were Papishes?"

"Naw, they were English Kirk—what dae ye call them?—Episcopalians. I get mixed up wi' a' their names." Binger grew serious and emphatic again. "But it doesnae matter. It was the Fenians that started it all. Sure, bi'Christ, the Pope was at the back o' it. Anybody'll tell you that. And no' till King Billie gave them laldy at Boyne Watter did we get the open Bible." Binger shook his head sadly. "No' kiddin', Haig, you're like a' the rest —you want to learn your country's history. You want to learn what ye come off o'."

Colin's jaw set dourly. "Aw, I don't know," he objected. "My auld lady used to be a great church hand and she aye made us go to the Sunday School. I'll bet you I'm as good a Protestant as you are."

"Then why are ye no' in the Order?" demanded Binger triumphantly. "If you're feart to wear the colours you're not True Blue."

"Ah, my shirt!" Colin was openly contemptuous. "Don't let anybody hear you say that. Jesus Christ, when it comes to marryin' a Pape there's more Orangemen turn their coats than any other kind."

"Who the hell telt ye that?" Binger stopped and swung round aggressively. As second triangle player in the Burnford Bravest Junior Flute Band he felt his honour touched. "You canny tell me one member o' the Burnford Lodge that ever turned their coat?"

Colin faced him resolutely. But cunningly he switched his attack. "Maybe no'," he admitted, "but how many of you go to church as often as the Papes?"

"Aw, there you go!" Binger resumed walking doggedly. "You half-and-half blokes are a' the same—never a straight answer. Everybody knows the tarriers have to turn up at the pineapple for Mass or else——! That's the difference wi' us. If a minister came to our door, maybe wi' a walking-stick, too, threatening us wi' hell and damnation if we didn't go to church, my faither would kick him down the stairs. We got liberty of conscience, see."

"If a minister turned up at oor door the shock would likely kill my faither," said Colin dryly. "At least the priest visits the Papes. The only time you ever see a minister in any of our houses is at a wedding or a funeral. Ministers have no time for ye if you're no running about their church."

"That's a bluidy lie."

"Is it? Then when do you last mind of a minister up your close?"

"Oh, they come."

"Ay, like hell." Binger's confusion was obvious. Colin pressed home his advantage. "If you ask me, being a minister's dawdle. You only need to stand up in the pulpit and get it off your chest about Jesus feeding the five thousand or Noah building the Ark —all the old stuff anybody can read for themself——"

"That's just it!" Binger got excited again. "Can the Papes read it for thirselves? Naw, they've got to take what the old Father tells them. That's why we carry the Open Bible at the heid o' the Walk. No bloody Pope can kid us what God says. We can read it for oorsels an' make up our ain mind. That's why the Protestants are a' Presbyterians an' Baptists an' Wee Frees an' Christian Volunteers——"

Colin shook his head weariedly. The snow had mantled on their shoulders and both their frowning faces were turning bluish with the bite of the wind. They had circled the Park boundaries and were trudging back into Burnford.

"You seem to know all about it," he said. "But if you ask me our minds are made up when we're born. If you're born a Catholic you are a Catholic and if you're born a Protestant you are a Protestant. It's your auld folk makes you what you are. And that's all about it. What about Tootle Tait?"

Binger looked wary. "Tootle Tait?" he hedged.

"Ay," Colin was scornful. "Tootle Tait. You know who I mean. Mind he was at our school and used to play the cornet in the Salvation Army?"

"Aw, I know who you mean all right." Binger was defensive. "Stays down the Old Cut. His mother was a Catholic."

"That's right." Colin was triumphantly off-hand. "And what happened to Tootle, eh? The minute his faither died his auld lady whipped him oot the Parish an' into St. Serf's. They tell me she burned his Salvation Army jersey the day after the funeral."

"Somebody should've burnt her," said Binger. "Papish bitch!"

"Maybe that," scoffed Colin. "But look at Tootle now—never without a green muffler on and plays the bugle for the Celtic Brake Club. I even heard she's trying to get a grant to make him a priest. What good did it do for him being a Protestant?"

"I dunno," confessed Binger. "But I'd rather him than me. They tell me once they get you into these monastries they don't hal

ladle into you—it's worse than a reformatory. Maybe after a wee
while Tootle'll be wishing he was back wi' the Hallelujahs even
if his dog's collar does get him a stand seat in Paradise and a nod
fae Willie Maley, the Celtic manager."

Colin laughed spontaneously. "You're a helluva case, Binger."
He screwed his eyes and looked up at the darkening sky and down
at his feet. "If this lies it'll put a' Saturday's games off."

Binger nodded. Ecclesiastical argument was forgotten in the
realization of impending disaster. "Jings ay," he agreed pessimis-
tically, viewing the passing tramcars unrelenting snow had converted into great lumbering ice-cubes. Anxiously he looked
upwards. Through the tumbling snow rows of gas-lit tenement
windows emphasized the speed of night-fall. A lamp-lighter passed
them, the snowflakes hissing and spitting at the tongue of flame
flickering from the end of his pole. "A bloody carry-on," he
decided, "if Ibrox's unplayable. Oor Elkie's on one of the gates
at the Broomloan Road and I was a certainty to get in for nothing.
I hope they get the park cleared in time."

"Me, too," Colin's natural instincts reasserted themselves. "If
the ground's heavy it'll suit the Rangers. I want to see them take
about six off this bunch."

"It's in the bag," Binger stated confidently. And moved by
sudden wild enthusiasm threw back his head and chanted:

"Follow, follow, we will follow Rangers.
    Everywhere, anywhere, we will follow on...."

Inspired Colin took up the refrain,

        "Follow, follow, we will follow Rangers.
            Everywhere the Rangers goes we'll follow on...."

Through the enveloping silence of the snow their voices
shrilled in disembodied arrogance that faded into a near pathos
as distance and the night swallowed them.


## CHAPTER SIXTEEN

ELLA missed the Morning Meeting because Jenny had worn her
best underskirt to a dance the night before and torn the hem.
When the young sister saw the tattered rip she burst into tears,
and the storm of her anger echoed through to the kitchen.
Stirred from the drowsy half-world of his Sunday "long lie"—

although in unemployment one morning had no more character than another—Collie lifted his head off the pillow and peered round the heavy lace curtains draping the front of the box-bed. "In the name——?" his appeal trailed.

Julia turned from the range and the porridge pot she was stirring. Workmanlike, in flowered bib apron over blouse and skirt, only the uncoiled plait of her heavy black hair advertised that less than twenty minutes had passed since she had climbed over Collie and hopped from a bedside chair to the cold waxcloth. In that time she had washed, dressed, lit the fire and set the table for breakfast. Out of a thin blue sky streaked with long ribbons of white cloud a watery sun was shining and someone's dovecote-bred homing pigeons fluttered in the lee of the long squat tenement chimneys opposite. No hammers rang along the river, and the calm of Sabbath was a tangible thing over Glasgow although the peal of the first church bell was still an hour distant.

"Ay," she agreed briskly, "is that not a fine carry on for a Sunday morning. Every neighbour in the building'll hear it!"

"If I throw my leg over this bed I'll give them something to yell about."

"Ay, you would," Julia sniffed cynically. With the passage of time Collie's disinclination to assert his parental authority became more marked. Without status in the outside world he felt correspondingly reduced at home. Julia poured the porridge into separate plates saying: "That one Ella, especially, she just twists you round her wee finger. Sometimes you'd think she was God in this house."

"Hmph!" For lack of a better rejoinder Collie sank back into the hole-in-the-wall's shadows. "Listen to who's talking! But she's certainly getting it off her chest just now like she's His Avenging Angel. You'd better see what's biting her before they call out the mounted polis."

"I'll angel her," said Julia. She put down the pot and went through to the room.

Dressed only in knickers and vest, Ella was standing in the middle of the floor with the underskirt in her hand. Her crumpled face was tear-stained, and the moment her mother appeared a torrent of accusation and appeal flowed from her quivering lips.

"Mother!" the plea, savage and restrained, came from the room's recess bed. "Will you tell her to shut her mouth? I'll buy her a new underskirt!"

"Look at it!" sobbed Ella, unappeased, and holding out the

rent garment. "And I telt that big lump not to put it on. She's *always* wearing my clothes."

"Will you be quiet the both of you," ordered Julia.

"Ay, maw, and for pity's sake get the pair o' them out of here," from the folding bed under the window Colin's tone was martyred. His spiky bush of hair was just visible above the hunched bedclothes. "I might as well be sleeping in a menagerie," he complained.

"It's the only underskirt I've got," lamented Ella, "and I promised Mr. Meldrum I'd be at the breaking of bread this morning——"

"I know what I'll break if you don't stop that whinin'," warned Julia. Her glance ran up and down the girl in withering contempt. "Have you no shame in you—standing in front of your brother in your knickers? A big lassie your age! Get ben the house before I take my hand off your jaw."

With a moan of sheer heartbreak Ella fled. Over her shoulder she sobbed, "You always take that big yin's part! Just because she's working."

As the kitchen door slammed with a violence that shook the house Julia stepped farther into the room and looked into the girls' bed. In contrast to her recent fury her voice dropped suddenly low.

"You didn't need to put on her underskirt—you've two of your own."

Jenny sat up in bed. Her dark eyes were eloquent. She leaned forward, supporting herself on knuckled fists, and the droop of her loose flannel nightgown showed the cleft of her breasts. "I had to put it on, Mother," she pleaded. "Mind I burned my black one ironing it? And my white one's still below the bed to get washed."

"Then why did you no' wash it? You knew you were going to that dance."

"I know, Maw. But Annie Cruickshanks promised me the lend of one of hers and then I didnae see her. I'd nae time to wash one."

Julia's face darkened. "Since when did you start borrowing clothes off o' strangers?"

Jenny's face twisted. "Och, it was only a wee lend. Many a thing Annie gets off me."

"No matter. Don't you bring other folks' clothes into this house. . . . My God, if your faither heard that he'd kill you." She shook a finger. "What you haven't got, my lady, just you learn to do without. We might be hard up but we're not going begging."

The girl's bosom heaved in exasperation. "Och, Mother, don't be daft. A' the lassies in the work lend each other things."

Her mother nodded. "I know all about it. I worked in a public work before ye were born. . . . And then when youse fall out you all talk about each other. Well, I don't want anybody talking about my family. Keep yourself to yourself and then you'll no' get into any bother."

Her daughter's face settled into an expression of long-suffering patience. "Mother," she declared, "we're not living in the Victorian age."

"That's well enough seen." Julia nodded grimly. "If my mother had caught me lying half-naked in bed like that she'd've dragged me out on to the floor by the hair o' my head. D'you forget you're a young woman now?"

"Oh!" With a flounce of despair Jenny flopped down and pulled the blankets up to her chin.

"And it *was* a dirty trick," her mother went on evenly. "You know that wee soul's got little enough clothes. You might at least've taken care of it."

"It was just an accident." To hide her contrition Jenny snapped her answer into the muffling folds of the bedclothes.

"Who were you with, anyway?"

Something subtle in the query—its pitch rather than its content—brought the girl's head up. On the other side of the room Colin's bed creaked uneasily. Shocked and furious, Jenny stared straight into her mother's eyes. "I was with Peggy Black, Agnes Reid, Isa McIlroy"—the names came tumbling out—"and two or three other lassies. And we all came home together. And if you want to know any more, my heel caught in the underskirt while I was doing the Charleston." As the rush of words ended the girl bounced back down and pulled the clothes right over her head.

Julia continued to look down at her for a moment. Then, smothering a quick smile, she poked the humped shoulder with a strong finger. "Your porridge's ready—are you getting up for it or are you wanting me to bring it ben?"

The heaped blankets made her daughter's reply unintelligible.

Julia said: "Don't get on your high horse. If I wasn't worried about your company who would be? Are ye getting up or are ye no'?"

Reluctantly the mop of red-brown hair reappeared. The girl sighed and compressed her lips. "What is there to get up for?" she asked herself aloud.

"What is there to get up for?" her mother echoed. "A lovely day wi' the sun melting the tar in the streets and you want to know what to get up for! Get up and go to church the same as a lot of other lassies in the street."

Jenny smiled wryly. "Are you kiddin', Mother? Go to church with the same coat I've had for two years now! No fear! Anyhow, I always fa' asleep in church—and I've telt you before, I'm not cut out for the religious stuff."

"Well—go a walk round the park. Take the ferry over to the Art Galleries. Or take the caur oot to Possilpark and see your Aunt Lizzie—but do something!"

The girl yawned and stretched. She craned and peeped past her mother at her brother still lying. "Hmph!" she said, and chuckled. "Tell you what, Maw—you bring ben my breakfast and then I'll see what I'll do."

"I know what you'll do," prophesied Julia. "You'll lie back doon and sleep to dinner-time and then get up moaning about a sore head. And it's me that's got a sin to answer for for encouraging you." She turned and looked at Colin's back. "And what about you? You don't need to lie in bed all day Sunday. At least she's working and has some kind of excuse. But you——!"

The youth turned over slowly. Through half-shut eyes he smiled lazily. "Did my faither get the *Post* or the *Mail*?" he asked.

"No, your faither didn't get the *Post* or the *Mail*," Julia snapped swiftly. "Even if there had been anybody up to go for it I've nae money for a Sunday paper these days." She shook her head. "Sometimes I think the whole world's gone mad. Youse do nothing but live and talk fitba' a' week, then when it comes to the week-end youse want to do nothing but lie in bed and read about it." Her voice sharpened. "Get up out of there when I tell ye and get out and get some fresh air into your lungs. That's no way to live."

Her son looked up at her. The smile did not leave his lips but his sleepy eyes suddenly acquired a blue-black depth that was cynically mocking. "Who's livin', Maw?" he asked gently.

Julia hesitated and then answered staunchly: "Well, you're no' deid yet. As my mother always said, beds are for dying in and nobody should bide longer in them than they have to. You get up out of there and don't have your porridge lyin' till it's too cold to eat."

Through in the kitchen Ella was sitting on the fireside chair with the underskirt on her knees. Between dramatically emphasized sniffs she was stitching the torn hem.

"Good God," said Julia, "don't tell me you're using a black thread?"

"It was the only one I could get." Ella swallowed another sob.

"If anybody sees that they'll wonder what kind of mother ye've got!" Impatiently Julia snatched the skirt and rumaged in a flat oval tin on the dresser whose lid portrayed a gracious crinoline lady and whose contents had once been mixed chocolate biscuits. Unearthing a white bobbin of cotton from the tin's present treasure store of buttons, hair-pins, bits of string and carded wool she bit off a length and threaded it into a needle with a competence that was devastating. "You hand your faither over his porridge and take a plate ben to Jenny. I'll have this done while you're eating your own."

With her father served, Ella whirled in sudden realization. She still wore only her knickers and bodice and her bare arms and legs had a pathetic look of scrawny immaturity.

"I'm taking nothing ben to that one," she declared. "If she wants any porridge she can get up for it—I'm no' being her slavey."

"Do what I tell you."

"I will not. It's her fault I missed the Morning Meeting." Ella's lips trembled in self-pity. "I'd smash the plate in her face first."

Without looking up from her sewing Julia said: "Is that what they learn you at the Brethren?" Letting the rebuke sink in, she added: "And pull on a frock and don't be running about the house like a Red Indian."

When Ella had gone, still smothering sobs, Collie looked out of the bed. "Right enough," he protested, "that's a bluidy sin. That wee soul's away ben there breaking her heart. Why d'you no' make the big yin get up and get her own breakfast?"

Before Julia could reply Ella reappeared and sat down with a thump that shook the table. Following on her heels Colin came, shouldering his braces over the shirt he slept in. He tickled the back of her neck teasingly. She shook his hand off with vicious vigour. "Yah!" he grimaced. "Bad temper!"

"Leave her alone," said Julia.

The boy shrugged. "Maw's pet lamb." On his way to the sink he peered in the small wooden-framed mirror propped on the dresser. Rubbing his fingers reflectively along his pale jaw he said, suddenly hesitant, "Hey, Faither, mind if I use your razor?"

Leaning out to place his empty plate on the bedside chair

Collie paused, stooping. From under ruddy eyebrows his glance met Julia's swift humorous exchange. "My razor!" he echoed in stressed astonishment. "In heaven's name what do you want a razor for?"

"To cut his throat, I hope," Ella mumbled low and instantly into her plate. From her fireside seat Julia frowned half in real horror and half in amusement. "You have less of it, my lady."

As they quipped, Colin crossed briskly to the sink and started washing himself in a great rush and fury of water. Through the gush of the tap turned full on and his own exaggerated splashings and blowings he gasped, "Och, I just thought it was time I was getting some o' this hair off my chin."

His mother rested her sewing on her lap. Ignoring Ella's explosive—and expressive—splutter, she turned her head and studied her son's back. Her face mirrored a change of mind on something she was going to say. After a moment she merely said, "Mind where you're throwing that water, Colin—we don't want the whole house flooded."

"Ay, it's splashing right on to my plate," agreed Ella, remembering her martyr rôle. Grabbing a towel from the knob of the inset window shutters, Colin pulled a face through its fold at her. "No' as many splashes as you dribble over your plate, Bubbly," he jeered.

Collie waited until the boy was seated at the table before he screwed his eyes and peered with pantomime difficulty. "I must be needing specs right enough," he marvelled. "D'you see anything on his chin, Ella?"

"Ay, blackheads!" she snapped waspishly.

"Oh, you can laugh!" Having got over the introduction Colin strove to infuse a proper gravity into the subject. Angling his firm but still softly rounded chin he stroked his jawbone with tender fingertips. "Look—I can feel it right along there. Bet I'm gonny have an awful heavy growth, Faither."

Without a smile Collie nodded. "D'you think the one razor'll do?"

"Och, ay——" Belatedly the boy recognized the hidden chuckle. "Awful funny," he huffed. Over his shoulder he asked: "Tea no' made, Maw?"

"There's the tea on the hob," said Julia. "And there's a bit bacon in the pan you and the lassies'll just have to divide."

"Good-o!" He whisked the frying-pan from off the warm range-top. Whirling round to the table he stopped with serving knife poised. "What are you an' my daddy getting?" he demanded. "Have youse had yours?"

"Long ago."

He looked from her to his father and saw Collie's empty plate on the chair. "Away!" he scoffed. "Ye don't eat ham before your porridge. Mean to say youse are no' getting any kitchen?"

"Ye know fine I can never eat a fry in the mornin'," Julia claimed irritably. "And your father didnae want any. Just you do what I'm telling you."

The boy looked at the pan's contents. Its savour teased his ready appetite. "You're sure?" He hesitated manfully.

"What do you think I'd be telling you for?" Julia flared. "Get your breakfast out and no more old buck—I never seen such weans for arguin' as my family."

Colin exchanged glances with Ella. Both guessed the truth. Both knew their parents were sacrificing breakfast that they might face the day fed. And, as always, Colin wanted desperately to protest against the sacrifice. But, as always, emotion choked him. And, anyway, he knew his mother and father would simply overwhelm his objections in a flood of splendid raillery. Swallowing shame and bottling resentment at all the circumstances that created such situations, he quickly lifted a large piece of bacon on to Ella's plate and, as a gesture to his conscience, made his own portion a streak of rind fat.

"Mind and leave some for Jenny," warned his mother offhanded and smoothing out the sewing on her knees. "There, Ella—that should tide ye over the day. I'll see if the wee second-hand shop has anything in the window tomorrow and try and get you another one off your daddy's next Buroo money." Sharply she looked round at the bed and added as an afterthought, "I hope you're getting Buroo money this week?"

Collie turned restlessly in the blankets. "Well—my claim should be through all right. It's more than a fortnight since that last Board."

"Them and their Boards," said Julia bitterly. "I know who should stand the Boards."

Pushing aside her plate, Ella hunched her shoulders with a sigh of content. "Any cakes, Mother?" she asked hopefully.

"Cakes after porridge and ham!" Colin was virtuous in momentary consciousness of the economies of life. "You're a gutsy wee besom! D'you want jam on it?"

"You'll get a plain cookie in the wee press," said Julia tolerantly.

"Your Aunt Mima brought up six last night, and her and I had only one each to a cup o' tea."

Beaming, Ella secured her tit-bit. "If I hurry up I'll be in time for the Open Air," she decided suddenly. "We're having it at our corner this morning."

"That'll be nice," nodded Julia. "Pity you couldn't get your brother to go along with you."

"Mother! Mother!" the plaint stabbed piercingly from the bedroom. "When am I getting the rest of my breakfast? I'm starving!"

Julia glowered in the direction of the sound. "You've just all got me for a proper soft mark," she commented conversationally. But when she went through, bearing the meal on a tin tray chipped with use but still gaudily depicting a Highlander in a bearskin defiant above the slogan, Scotland for Ever, Jenny warded off further remonstrance by beaming, "You're a champion, Mother, a right wee gem. Dear knows what we'd do without you!"

"You'd have to get up and make your own breakfast for one thing."

Chuckling, her elder daughter reached under the pillow and withdrew a small purse. Fumbling among the few coppers it held she said: "Send Colin down for a paper for my da."

Julia took the money slowly, thoughtfully. Then she said, "Ay —it's a long Sunday for him if he doesn't get a glance at a paper."

"And Maw——" Julia waited. "Tell that wee tinker she can get a lend of my lilac hat—but she's no' to squash it."

Julia frowned. "Your lilac—the one wi' the half veil?"

Munching steadily, her daughter nodded.

"But that's your good one!"

Twitching her nose recklessly Jenny shrugged.

"D'you think it's too old for Ella?"

"She'll think she's marvellous. She's aye got her eye on it."

Julia's expression softened. In defence against sentiment she almost snapped, "If some of your clicks could see ye now they'd get a shock."

Wiping her nose upwards with the back of her wrist the girl in the bed twitched a bare shoulder and mumbled through a full mouth, "Are you kiddin'? So would I." Before Julia reached the bedroom door she called again, "Maw!"

"Och, here, I'm in a hurry. What is it now?"

"This is rare ham!"

## CHAPTER SEVENTEEN

MELDRUM made his visit on a foggy night. The two girls had gone out after washing and drying the tea dishes and Julia was sitting darning socks. She frowned as a loose flake clinging to a puncture in the gas-mantel caused the light to flicker. Suddenly her attention was diverted by a sound other than the guttering gas.

"Is that a knock at the door?"

Collie, enthralled but not astounded by the revelations of his latest public library capture, a Sinclair Lewis novel, glanced across the fireplace. "I'm getting that bloomin' deaf these days," he complained. "I never heard."

Julia's own black hair showed its first stray white threads as she tilted her head to listen. "So it is," she decided, as the sound repeated itself. "An awful kinda genteel rap—can hardly hear it wi' that lobby door shut!"

Her mild irritation vanished when she recognized their caller standing on the stairhead. "Mr. Meldrum!" she marvelled. "I know you by sight," she felt constrained to add. Her face puckered in sympathetic dismay. "And is that not a spite—Ella's not ten minutes away down the stairs."

Meldrum, dark-coated and gaunt as an undertaker and with his high white collar the hallmark of sartorial exactitude, seeming to tower almost to the glass-boxed gas jet that palely lit the landing, coughed diffidently. "It's not really Ella I've come to see, Mrs. Haig——"

"Oh!" Julia was bewildered. "I thought it was something about the Meeting?"

The tall cashier shook his head. "It is really about the boy, your son."

"Colin!" Controlling her surprise Julia pulled the door open wider. "I'm sorry, what am I keeping you standing here for," she apologized. "Won't you come in a minute, Mr. Meldrum?"

Inclining his head the visitor, black Homburg hat in hand, followed her through to the kitchen.

"It's Mr. Meldrum—you know, from Ella's Meeting." She glanced back and forth hesitantly from each of the men. "But, of course, maybe you've met Ella's father?"

The intrusion startled Collie. He had not spoken to the cashier since the long-gone day he had thrown the time-check. He had not even been inside the gates of Burnford Shipyard since. Now the aura of Meldrum and his prosperous clothes seemed to fill the kitchen. Suddenly, vividly, the stock yards of Chicago did not seem so far away. In a flash Collie was aware of his own worn waxcloth and the line of washing hanging from the ceiling pulley ropes. Hostility surged within him, hostility to all he considered Meldrum represented, yet he stood up with formal courtesy and only allowed his stiff face to betray his independence, saying, "Oh, ay, Meldrum and I have met before now."

The tall man nodded, details of their last meeting diplomatically locked beneath the grave surface of his smile. "Yes, we have, Mrs. Haig—rather a long time ago tho', I'm afraid."

"Sit down." Haig pulled a chair from beneath the table. He sat down himself, his attitude casual but wary. "Foggy outside tonight?"

"Well, of course it's November."

"Ay, the year's wearin' on—soon be Hogmanay."

Meldrum cleared his throat. "I was rather hoping your boy would be in—Ella was saying he was unemployed?"

Collie's coughed chuckle was cynical. "Unemployed? I suppose ye could call it that. Hasn't worked since he left school."

"Oh, he's ran with papers," Julia protested. "But——"

"Oh, I'm no' blaming the boy!" her husband disclaimed touchily. "God, ye canny blame weans for being the same as yoursel'."

Meldrum nodded in a movement that was non-committal but sympathetic. He looked at Haig with delicacy. "Have you never worked yourself since . . . ?" His voice trailed.

Haig took him up with aggressive speed. "Since auld Ruebent threw me out? Dampt little, I can tell you—not but I wouldnae do the same again."

Meldrum said nothing.

Half-ashamed, Collie went on: "I had a wee spell in Fairfields . . . a couple of months in Harland and Wolff's and then I was in the Linthouse for a while." He looked at Julia. "How long was I over in Clydebank?"

She looked into the fire reflectively. "You had a good wee while there—four or five months, I think."

Collie laughed without mirth. "Taking it all in, I don't suppose I've worked two years since I got the bag out of the Burnford." He grew savage. "I wouldn't mind so much but ye've to stand these bloody Boards at the Buroo. . . ."

"But you do get benefit?"

Collie looked at him. With an effort he said civilly: "Oh ay, ye get benefit—if they've no' lost your claim or decide to investigate how much your lassie's earning at a hosiery." Suddenly the bonds of his restraint burst. "Imagine me having to stand in front of a lot of pot-bellied shopkeepers and overfed schoolmasters proving whether I'm looking for work or no'! Men that a day's hard graft would kill! Talk about your Stanley Baldwins and Ramsay MacDonalds—nae wonder the Russians shot them a'! Christ—and excuse the expression, Meldrum—but it would drive ye bloody well mad. 'Are you looking for work? Are you sure you're looking for work?'" he mimicked savagely. He put an exaggerated effeminate cadence on the echo of his tormentors. "'Where did you look on Monday morning? And Tuesday? And you're sure you were at that yard on Wednesday? And where will you go tomorrow morning?'" Bitterly he reverted to his own tone. "And not a dampt boat being built between here and Troon!" His eyes glittered as he challenged Meldrum. "D'ye know who asked me all that no later than this week? Yon parasite that plays the big kirk organ."

"Oh!" Meldrum's brows raised in genuine interest. "Mr. Welkent, the elocutionist? I didn't realize he was on the Means Test Board——"

"Elocutionist?" Collie's wrath was not to be side-tracked by polite biography. "A leech and imposter like all the res o' the weeds that have the gall to sit in judgment on working men. I know the kind of elecutionin' he's done. Lived off his mother and her Trongate hat-shop all his days, never done a stroke of real work in his life. Oh, I know he gives poetry lessons to two or three wee lassies and is always to the fore when some swanky Bible class or Kelvinside dramatic team are giving a show. He can talk all right. He's walked about in plus-fours and heather suits for years talking himself into elderships and money-for-nothing deputations. In a fancy way he's just on a level wi' paid Trade Union officials and so-called Socialist politicians. He's on the make, a born bum. He's the kind o' twister this country falls for, the no-user Governments and Upper Classes always put behind counters to do their dirty work," Haig finished sourly. "Nae wonder they've to pay two big polismen to stand at the door every time there's a Board on."

If he was embarrassed Meldrum did not show it. "We're living in difficult times," he suggested. "It's all quite a problem. Even professional people are feeling the pinch."

"They'll get by." Haig was relentless. With the unyielding hatred of the unwilling dole-drawer he conceded nothing to the black-coat world. "We hear all these yarns about hard-up business folk and struggling financiers but you never meet any o' them on the Parish. The lawyers, the doctors, the ministers—all that bunch—the newspapers make a great song about their hardships, how their stocks and shares are hardly payin' enough dividends to keep them in servants and how their poor sons can hardly get a salaried job after they leave the University. Ha, it's a terrible disaster if the wind blows on them! You'd think the whole world had come to an end if *they* find they've only two or three thousand left in the bank." Haig threw back his head and laughed satirically. Years of soured emotion found a target in the presence of this well-clad image of all the people he blamed for his misfortunes. He forgot why Meldrum was there, or, if he remembered, did not care. Nothing was important but that, for his pride's sake, he voiced his protest with scorn and a defiance untinged by servility.

The force of Collie's tirade stirred Julia. "Yes," she agreed quietly, "they can spend millions on this and that wi' the stroke of a pen but let anybody suggest an extra shilling or two would be a God-send to the unemployed and they nearly lift the roof off. I'm only a working man's wife and I don't envy anybody and I don't wish anybody any harm, but when I think on all these folk wi' their mansions and their motor-cars, I don't know how their conscience lets them sleep at night: if there's a God in heaven He must have a real hot-spot reserved for our ruling classes for, since the War, they've certainly made life a hell on earth for us."

"Well," said Meldrum gently, "you know what the Bible says."

Julia returned his glance steadily. "The Bible says a lot of things," she observed. "And the people who make it their business to quote the Bible generally manage to twist what it says to suit themselves. But I know this much, if a hand-to-mouth existence is the best two thousand years of Christianity can do for decent folk we might just as well a' have stayed heathen."

"You don't really believe that, Mrs. Haig?"

"Why shouldn't she?" demanded Collie. "She's had nae life. Work and worry and wonder where the next pay's gonny come from. That's been her existence. Why should she be religious?"

"Come along to the Hall on Sunday and learn," smiled Meldrum. "You know what the Good Book says: 'Come unto Me all ye that labour and are heavy laden . . .' "

"Aw ay." Haig nodded his head disparagingly. "We know all these texts too, Mr. Meldrum. We were brought up on them. And our fathers before us. But times are changing—and folk are changing. I just can't believe God meant me and my weans to live in poverty while the rest of the world have a dampt good time. If He really meant to keep us in misery then—God or no God—He'd'a been better never to've brought us into the world at all."

"That's what I think," agreed Julia. Her tone was touched with regret. She watched Meldrum without offence and yet with a judgment in the depths of her calm, grey eyes. As she often did in moments of real emotion she departed from the dialect and spoke with a simple clarity that was effortless and devastatingly effective. "Nobody needs to learn me to be religious. I was reared to believe in my Bible and I've reared my own family the same way. Maybe I've not went to church as often as I should—or even as often as I'd've liked to—but I never forget God. I've thanked Him every night for giving me healthy weans and a man that was willing to work for them." She inclined her head in gentle drollery. "True enough, whiles he takes a dram too much and he's sitting there—and he'll not deny we'd have been better off if he didn't—he knows he never got any cause in this house to go out and drink. But he's a funny man that's got no faults and I didn't expect an angel when I married mine."

Collie stirred uneasily. Reassuring him his wife relapsed into the Doric. "Calm yourself, I'm no gonny preach." Her glance returned to Meldrum. "We can't all be perfect. And if I blame him for liking the pubs too much I don't forget to blame the folk who plant one at every street corner in Glasgow to tempt him. But, even with that, he never neglected his work. And although —like the rest of the world—we had our own wee rows he never neglected his home either." Julia took a deep breath. "But putting all that to the one side, Mr. Meldrum—and if you'll excuse me— the bit I can't understand is why God or the authorities or who-ever you like to name can have the heart to let him, and millions of good men like him, sit and rot! I know folk like me are not supposed to have many brains, Mr. Meldrum, but I think if God had wanted to drive men to Hell he couldn't have chosen a better way to do it. And if the great men at the head of affairs wanted to show how little we mean to them and the country they're always shouting about, then, by God, they've succeeded."

Meldrum sat quite still. His long face was a little more deeply lined but as inscrutable as on the day he had accepted Collie's pay-off line through the cashier's grill. In his life as an evangelist he was used to being the medium for attack and argument. He knew the Haigs were not attacking him maliciously or personally. Neither did they expect answer to this distress of mind. Secure in his own faith and insulated by the certainty of celestial reward, he could only grieve with them and for them. And avoid the error of patronizing them with holiness.

Very quietly, almost humbly, he said: "As you know, in our Meeting we don't believe in the permanence of this world or anything in it—that's why we take no part in politics."

"Oh, I know you're very strict." Collie shared a smile with Julia. "That's what beats us wi' our Ella—what kinna fascination have youse put on her? The wife and I just can't fathom it at all!"

Welcoming the change of subject Meldrum's gravity eased but did not relax into levity. "Ella's a very good girl," he approved. "She's been a wonderful asset to us. Have none of you heard her singing at the Open Air?"

"D'you know, I got the shock of my life one Sunday." Some of the strain went from Julia and her pale face lit with pleased animation. "I heard the Meeting at our corner and I threw up the window—I like to hear the hymns and I like that lassie Murdoch's playing on the harmonium——"

"Alice is faithful, I don't believe she's missed a Gospel meeting in—oh—five years."

"Ay." Julia nodded her approval. "And I always like to hear Gavin Allison giving his Testimony—to be only a coalman I think he's a rare speaker."

"Oh, Gavin can preach," agreed Collie. "It's hard to believe his auld granny was a bitter Catholic."

"Was she?" Their visitor's surprise had the lift of real interest. "I never knew that."

"Och ay." Collie was authoritative. "She was a Riley. Straight from Connemara and as Irish as they make them. Never missed a Mass in her life. When Bridgit—that's Gavin's mother—started to wench Jock Allison they were gonny tear Jock fae limb to limb. The whole family had a go at him."

The cashier shook his head in sad wonder.

"They might as well 'ave tried to shift the Tron steeple."

Collie's satisfaction was partisan and complete. "None of the Allisons were what ye'd call soft marks and Jock was just about the hardiest o' the bunch. He gave as good as he got. At last they left him alone and tried to break Bridgit's heart."

Meldrum's nod was knowing. "That's how it usually goes, isn't it?"

"They had the priest at her as well." Julia's tone and expression hinted at every horror of the Inquisition. "Dear knows what the poor soul come through!"

"But she defied them?"

"It was a funny case. It had its funny side, too." Collie turned whimsically judicious. Julia, frowning at him, said hurriedly, "You'll take a cup of tea, Mr. Meldrum? I'd've had it masked by this time but with us blethering . . ."

She rose in haste, but Meldrum stretched out a restraining hand. "Not for me, Mrs. Haig, not for me. I'm just after a meal."

"Are ye sure?"

"Certain, Mrs. Haig. Absolutely certain. I really only dropped in to talk about the boy."

"Oh ay." Remembering, Julia sat down, her expression again warily anxious. "You'd pass him at the corner—the young fellows are never away from there nowadays."

"No. . . . Well——" Meldrum hesitated awkwardly. "What age is he?"

"Colin?" Mrs. Haig looked at her husband, not so much for advice or confirmation as in an effort to steal time in the effort to guess at the outcome of their visitor's interest. "Jenny's nearly twenty-two now. Colin'll be seventeen his next birthday."

Meldrum nodded in satisfaction. "Just the right age. Do you think he would like to serve his time?"

"Serve his time?" The query surprised Collie. "What at?"

"The plating." Meldrum cleared his throat. "I was talking to Adam Raisdeck this morning—y'know Adam?"

"Oh, I ken Raisdeck fine. Is he starting boys?"

"Just one or two. You'll know we've got an order for a small cattle boat?"

"I heard talk that way." Collie interest quickened. "But, och, we've been hearing yarns for years now. Even Kirkwood canny get a hope out them. The way I see it, there's that many idle boats lyin' up the Gareloch the shipowners'll no' need to lay down any new keels for the next twenty years. No' but the half of them should've been scrapped long ago," he added bitterly.

"Some o' them it's only the paint that's holding them together. Jings, the last repair I was on——"

"And you think Colin has the chance of a start?" Julia's interruption was eager but unbelieving. Having been accustomed to an existence in which paid employment was one of the remoter possibilities, like winning an Irish Sweep, she found herself afraid even to hope.

Meldrum nodded. "Well, when Adam Raisdeck mentioned his intention I remembered Ella saying some time ago her young brother was idle. The thought crossed my mind that it might be a chance for him—that's if he'd any notion of being a plater?"

"It's no' what you've a notion of," Collie said. He cleared his throat self-consciously and in secret apologia to any dreams his son might have. "He's dampt lucky to get the chance."

"Colin'll not worry what it is. He'd take a job at anything," emphasized Julia. "It would take an awful load off my mind if I just see him started—started at anything."

"The plating's quite a good trade." Meldrum's assurance had just the faintest trace of condescension.

"Jings, ay," agreed Collie, with a semi-skilled man's ready acceptance of a clerk's right to be superior towards craftsmanship. "I've known platers that made big money—the likes o' a shell squad plater getting a run o' two or three boats on contract can be better off than many a gaffer. Oh ay," he breathed in envy of the piecework giants of shipbuilding, "even a good jobbing plater's all right."

"Then do you think Colin could come down to the platers' shed tomorrow morning? Tell him to ask for Mr. Raisdeck and explain who sent him."

"He'll do that," said Julia quietly. "And it's been very good of you to put yourself to the bother, Mr. Meldrum."

Meldrum shook his head in genuine self depreciation. "It's nothing at all. I hope the boy gets started." Standing up to go he asked Collie: "Do you never take a walk down to the yard these days yourself, Mr. Haig? I have a feeling things are beginning to pick up."

Collie's headshake combined sheepishness and mockery. "I never go near the Burnford. You know how I stand down there." A shadow of apprehension chased resentment from his expression. "I just hope being my son doesn't bar Colin?"

"No, no,' the cashier was reassuringly confident. Delicately he added, "You know Mr. Ruebent died about two years ago? I don't imagine anyone remembers your—well, your little disagreement."

Collie grunted, "I know Ruebent's away. My stomach turned when I read yon tripe they put in the papers about him." He almost belched in a repeat of scorn. "By jings and Ruebent was some benefactor. If he'd had his way he wouldn't have let the light o' day shine on the Clyde. As for being a naturalized Scotsman!—he hated our guts. He was like nearly all the promoted Englishmen ever I knew that came here to work—he despised us and grudged every minute he had to stay in the country. Their own idea is to pile up as much as they can while they qualify for a good pension and then beat it back down South. Ruebent was just unlucky—God dropped his check before he had time to get away wi' the loot."

Meldrum laughed. "Well, true enough, maybe Mr. Ruebent had no great love for us, but I think he was rather the exception —most Englishmen, I find, are pretty fair and decent chaps."

He glanced at Julia for support. She shook her head. Not even to safeguard her son's prospects could she play hypocrite. "They're too plausible for my liking," she said. "I've no doubt there's good ones among them but I never can understand why they should get the best of everything. You've only got to read the papers to see that if there's anything going in the line of work the bulk of it has to go to England. We're only an afterthought. Even at this very minute, when the country's supposed to be in such a state, there's not a tenth of the unemployed in England that there is here. Nobody can tell that that's a fair thing."

"Ah—I hardly think your figures are correct, Mrs. Haig."

Collie looked up sharply. "Man for man o' the population? Of course they're correct. I'll bet you there's as many idle here in Glesca as there is in London and we're no' a quarter the size o' it. It's a bluidy scandal!"

"Of course." Meldrum swayed on his toes and gazed upwards judicially. He averted his eyes downwards swiftly when his glance rested on a pair of blue flannel knickers drooping from the pulley. "Of course, we must remember that there are so many more people in England that the opportunities for employers are greater there."

"Naw, that'll no' wash." Collie shook his head stubbornly. "It's just because it's England. I'll bet if the Cockneys and the rest of them had been even hauf as hard-pushed as we've been there'd been a revolution in that country years ago. It's just a case of every dog looks after its own, and Parliament takes dampt good care things never get out of hand round its own doorstep."

"But we have members in Parliament."

"Look." Collie swivelled in his chair, his face pursed in disgust. "Don't talk to me about Scotsmen in England—especially blokes in Parliament and the House o' Lords and all the other high-falutin places they like to get into down there. They are worse than real Englishmen. They stink. By God, Mr. Meldrum, I'm no' very fond of the Irishmen but at least ye've got to give their boys credit, they stick up for Ireland—but our lot!" Collie stared at his visitor as if he was accusing in his inoffensive countenance the false face of every traitorous Scottish Anglophile. "They are the world's lowest. They're great guys when they're up here bummin' their chat, lookin' for votes and scroungin' preference. Let me get at them, they say, and I'll go right down there and clear the half o' England; I'll tell these so-and-so's down in Whitehall they can't put it on to poor auld Scotland. Ha!" Collie shook his head in slow contempt. "The Red Clydesiders! The Wild Men o' Glesca! The Blue-Blooded Hielan' Chieftains! It's all one what side they're on—they all end up the same way. They yap for about five minutes after they get over the Border, just long enough to get their name in the papers a couple o' times, and then the Government or somebody makes them an Under-Secretary or an Assistant Director and that's them by. They're fixed. T'hell wi' Scotland—bar when they've the brass neck to stand up in a hired kilt at some swanky London Bonny Prince Rabbie Burns Dinner and spout a lot of stuff about the heather and Bannockburn and how their chest swells when they hear the bagpipes. That always gets them another wee notice and a photo in the papers for the benefit of the mugs back here, and keeps their reputation warm wi' their English bosses as genuine hairy-kneed but house-tamed tartan characters." Collie shook his head again. "No, Mr. Meldrum, on the Buroo I've had time to read a bit and had time to size them a' up and it's my opinion what we produce as spokesmen would make a dog vomit. It's no' blood they've got in their veins it's pease-brose. They're everything first and Scotsmen last. They're the yes-men o' the British Empire and they're no better than we deserve because we put them there."

"Well, as you know," temporized Meldrum, "in our Meeting we take no part in politics——"

"Politics?" growled Collie. "I'm talkin' about the life and death o' a nation. But if you must bring religion in, can you

picture what John Knox would say if he was walking past the
street corners o' Glesca the day? Don't forget he was the fellah
who wanted every wean in Scotland educated. D'you think if he
saw Scotland the way it is he'd stand up in St. Giles' and preach
patience? And don't forget he was yin o' the fellahs that won
you the right to have a Meeting."

"Oh, yes, we are all indebted to Knox. But as the Good Book
says, 'Render unto Caesar the things that are Caesar's and unto
God the things that are God's'. We at the Gospel Hall are content
to occupy ourselves solely with God's affairs, so I'm afraid I'm
not much of an authority on these other matters." Meldrum
smiled solemnly but with disarming effect. "Will you not think
about having a turn in at the Yard, Mr. Haig?"

Julia looked hopefully at Collie. But her husband shook his
head. "Naw—there's nae use kidding myself. Big Mick's the
head gaffer rigger now, and as long as he's there I haven't got a
snowball's chance. If jobs were teeming down on Burnford Yard
like raindrops that big Papish midden wouldn't let me cross the
gate to wet my lips. He's like all the rest of the Fenian crew, he
never forgives and he never forgets."

"Like Gavin Allison's grandmother?"

"Ay," Collie responded to the humour in the cashier's tone.
"And I'm a good bit like his faither—I don't bend easy either."

Meldrum could not restrain his curiosity. "Exactly what did
happen—did Mrs. Allison defy her people?"

Julia frowned again but Collie was reckless. His estimate of
the sensitivities of the strictly religious was more robust than
hers. "You could call it that," he chuckled. "The truth is they'd
finally got poor Bridgit coaxed to give Jock up when, here, she
discovered she was—well—you know what I mean——?"

Meldrum's wag of the head compassed every aspect of com-
passionate yet sorrowing condemnation of human frailty.

"So the fun started all over again," nodded Collie. "Y'know
what like they are—they promised Jock every mortal thing if
only he'd get married in the chapel and swear to bring the wean
up a Catholic. But no' Jock." Collie's satisfaction was reflected
in an indefinable fashion even on Meldrum's long, circumspect
countenance. Only Julia said, with wistful sympathy, "It was an
awful carry on."

"Jock Allison just telt them flat," relished Collie, "if Bridgit
wants me she can marry me in the kirk—my kirk. I don't turn
my coat for anybody. As for any weans o' mine—let there be no

mistake, they'll go to the Protestant school and like it. Nae priests nor Jesuits are comin' between me and my family."

Meldrum shook his head mournfully. "That's the tragedy of mixed marriages. The children always suffer. It just doesn't do."

"Oddly enough," said Julia, "it turned out all right with the Allisons. Whatever heartbreak it caused her, Bridgit stuck to her Jock and never looked back. Right enough, after the wedding she never entered a church again, but then neither did Jock. But he made sure a' the weans went to Sunday School."

"And a right nice family they turned out," admired Collie. "Gavin's no' the only one that's well doing."

"And Mrs. Allison's family had nothing more to do with her?"

"Och no," Julia denied soberly. "For long enough there was bad feeling with most of them but gradually they came round. Bridgit's brothers and sisters were out and in her house regularly. Only the auld mother never relented. To her last day on earth if she met Bridgit in the street she'd turn her head. It must've given poor Bridgit many a sore heart."

"Ah well, Gavin's a fine chap," Meldrum said, turning to leave. "He certainly is a great pillar in our Meeting and it just shows again the wonders of God's purpose with His servants. . . . Well!" He spun his hat with nervous finality. "I hope Colin gets on all right."

"It was good of you to think of him." Julia held open the outside door, her tone of gratitude as near deference as her proud, unservile character would allow. "We'll not forget it, Mr. Meldrum."

From the middle of the kitchen, Collie, wordlessly, nodded farewell agreement. Almost stumbling in embarrassment, Meldrum gave a last self-conscious salute as he disappeared round the turn of the stairs.

# CHAPTER EIGHTEEN

As she did most nights except Friday—they washed their hair on Friday nights—Jenny met Flora Denvars at the corner of Bulwark Street. They had no particular aim in view. Arm-in-arm they strolled window-gazing by the light of the street standards. In the main shopping centre branches of the great multiple stores were brightening Burnford by leaving their own display lights on all night. The trend was welcomed by girls whose hours of work left only Saturday afternoons for bargain hunting.

"Oh, here!" exclaimed Flora, dragging on Jenny's elbow. "there's that skirt I was telling you about—only 7/11 and I saw one the very same up the town at 15/-. Sure it would go smashin' with thon pink blouse o' mine, the one that's full in the front?"

"The town" or "the city" for Flora and Jenny meant that centre of Glasgow bounded by the glittering arteries of Sauchie-hall Street, Renfield Street, Argyle Street and Buchanan Street. Like all natives of suburbs whose independent village and burgh histories were still recent enough to be valued as a personal heritage, they instinctively thought of Glasgow as a separate entity. For them, although it was only a very short tram, bus or subway ride distant, a visit to "the city" was as gay an expedition as a fringe Londoner's excursion to the West End. Even more because, proud as they were of local separateness, they were more closely conscious of proprietary interest in the grandeur of their metropolitan heart than any London suburbanite ever achieves.

Peering at the skirt, Jenny tilted her head bird-like to examine its price-tag. "It's nice," she agreed doubtfully, "but—oh look! There's the hat I've always wanted."

As they stumbled excitedly into the open porch to view the hat to better advantage two young men in snap brim hats and over-wide trousers paused on the pavement. The newcomers' sartorial glamour was heightened by a pearly glint from the buttons of their double breasted waistcoats, and the short man of the two had allowed his sideburns to race magnificently down to ear-lobe level. Matching this Rabbie Burns affectation with another of the poet's failings—if not his technique—he said ingratiatingly, "Hello, girls—anything we could buy?"

Without turning her head, Flora said instantly, "Ay, buy yourself a pair of skates."

"A real wee comic, Andy," chuckled the cavalier, unabashed.

"I like a girl with a sense of humour," Andy approved generously.

Ignoring them, the girls continued their wistful window-shopping. The hunters were not discouraged. Propping an elbow against the side-window Andy smirked, "Awful good taste, haven't they, Alec?"

"Oh rah-ther." Alec mimicked the accent-abortion popularly attributed to middle-class Kelvinside. "You're so right, Gorgeous —thet het's just you."

Brushing past them, Jenny and Flora stalked out on to the pavement. But Andy and Alec were persistent. Falling in on either side they abandoned laboured witticism and resorted to direct cajolery. "Come on, sugar," Alec bumped shoulders with Jenny, "it's a rare night; what about you and I hitting it off for a wee walk?"

"Sure," seconded Andy closing in on Flora. "I'm certain I've seen you at the dancing. D'you go to the Plaza?"

Flora stopped abruptly and Jenny halted with her. "If you pair don't get off your mark I know who'll be getting hit off!"

"Ah now, baby, don't get tough."

"I'm warning you. I'll call the police."

"Aw, you wouldn't do that, would you? A nice girl like you!"

For a full minute the girls stood stock still. They had no fear. They were in no danger. With no more than casual glances Burnford's strolling population jostled past them, but one serious appeal would have roused a host of champions. Despite the exaggerations of dramatic fiction, weak magistracy had not yet loosed the menace of broken bottle, concealed knife and unrevenged thuggery on Glasgow's ordinary citizens. Not fear of the men but horror of a scene restrained Jenny and Flora. "You're only wasting your time," Jenny said finally, "we're not pick-ups."

"Nobody said you were," flattered the tall, gangling Andy. "We're only bein' sociable—trying to keep you company."

"We don't want your company," declared Flora flatly. "Now, beat it."

But like hound-dogs the Lotharios would not be shaken off. Tossing stale banter they escorted the girls determinedly. Arms linked tighter, Jenny and Flora strolled on, their faces stony and their gossip silenced. They paused at no more shop fronts but continued on out of Anchor Road's main shopping glitter until, gradually, plate glass displays were replaced by little dim-fronted newsagent-tobacconists, and the swinging doors of pubs threw their foetid beery exhausts across the pavements between the ground-floor windows of cheaper tenements. Above the opposite roofs crane and gantry lights from riverside shipyards threw a star-quenching glare across the sky, but at street level shadow patches were deep and innocent pedestrians were invested with cloaks of possible menace. As Jenny and Flora sauntered on their two unwelcome followers' confidence grew.

"Come on," urged the small side-whiskered one. "We're surely

not going to walk along like the front row of a band? Break it
up and give us your patter."

"Sure," applauded his partner. "What about you telling me the
tale of your life, Brown Eyes?"

Jenny's and Flora's only reaction was to lean closer on each
other and stare woodenly ahead. Approaching the corner of
Bulwark Street their aura of hostility was a thing that could be
sensed yards away. It impinged on the consciousness of a green-
shirted lounger framed dimly in the half-dark entry of a tenement
close. As they came within a yard or two the glint in Jenny's eye
stirred him. Easing his shoulder off the wall he asked, diffidently
but cheerfully: "Are you all right, hen?"

Jenny's glance swung. "We'd be better if these pair of cuddy-
faced sheiks would gallop back to their tents and give us
peace."

"Oh!" The exclamation was mild and low. But the green shirt
moved half a step forward. Both lady-killers swung wide and
stopped. Nastily the tall one invited. "Were you saying something,
pal?"

"Not me," said the lounger. "But it looks like you've been
saying too much."

"You think so——" began short Alec of the sideburns, and
suddenly stopped.

Inconspicuously three figures arguing football at the pavement's edge twenty yards farther on had drifted back. With an
air of quiet, polite enquiry—in shattering contrast to their
previous loud and aggressive tones, habitual and unconscious
characteristic of men used to day-long bawling above the rattle
of hammers on steel—they grouped themselves around. They said
nothing. They just stood. After a long pause, during which the
amorous Alex's and Andy's darting eyes betrayed more than
unease, one of the three, who wore a bright blue scarf, asked,
"Any trouble, Danny?"

"Pesterin' the lassies," Green-shirt said succinctly.

"Oh?"

"Now, just a minute!" appealed Sideburn Alec hastily.

Unhurriedly Jenny and Flora continued their walk. As they
moved away another of the three who favoured a tie as green as
Danny's shirt, said, without emphasis, "This looks like your cause
comin', pals—if you've tuppence."

Without a word Alec and Andy swung on their heels and raced
for the approaching tramcar. As they fled the last of the three

who also wore a blue muffler, called after them, "Next time it'll be an ambulance."

"Who's the judies?" asked one of the blue scarfs.

"Dunno," said Danny. "They stay up the street somewhere."

"No' bad bits o' stuff," approved the lad in the green tie. "Wouldnae mind a walk wi' any of them myself."

"The blondie's a Denvars," explained the blue scarf knowingly. "Her faither's a craneman over in Dalmuir."

"Och ay—I know who you're at now. Auld Sanny Denvars wi' the game leg? Used to keep a whippet?"

"Ay. The gingery one stays up 98—Haig's her name."

"Och, that'll be Collie Haig's lassie! Got a wee sister sings in the Meetings? S'that no' her brother that's playin' wi' the Welfare?"

"The very same. Turnin' out no' a bad half-back, young Colin. They tell me the Bens are after him."

"I know the Ants are watching him. They could fairly do wi' a good half-back."

"The Ants, Danny! D'you see yon on Saturday up by? Is thon no' pathetic playing in a blue jersey?"

"Christ, Jackie, don't talk! You want to have been at Parkhead. The Rangers have got nothing worse than yon . . . I mean, McGrory's standing waitin' on the ba', nothing to do but nod it hame—and does big soda-heid no' go and blooter it away to the wing. . . ."

Jenny and Flora walked on into Bulwark Street. Flora glanced back only once with the comment, "It's a good job our Davy wasn't at the corner!"

"Is Davy working yet?"

"Did I not tell you? He got sent by the Buroo a fortnight ago— I think I heard him say he's working over beside your father."

Jenny nodded contentedly. "It's been great this while back since my da got a start. I only hope it lasts."

"Then Colin workin' too'll make a difference? How's Ella getting on at the nursing?"

"Och, you know our Ella!" Jenny's grimace was a sisterly amalgam of tolerance and vague criticism. "She comes home once a month and my mother hardly sees her—between her Saturday night Tea Meeting, the Early Morning Meeting, her Open Air Meeting and then the Gospel Meeting after dinner she's never in the house a' day Sunday. Then at night, if she's no' on a Deputation to somewhere they're welcoming a Deputation from somewhere else. By God, if our Ella doesn't get to Heaven it's not for the want of trying."

Flora choked a giggle. "Och well, Jenny, if that's what she wants to do it's nobody's business. At least your mother'll know she's all right."

Jenny nodded. "That's what my maw says—better a Bible thumper than a street-walker. Sometimes I think she wishes I was a wee bit more like Ella. Y'know, she worries if I'm late at the dancing and that——"

"Mine's the same." Flora shrugged. "But I always tell her— Maw, times are changed fae your day: I'm not going to sit at home wi' my knitting when I can be out enjoying myself. . . . As I say, there'll be time enough to settle down when I'm married."

Jenny sighed. "I doubt they'll need to raffle the pair of us. I was just thinking, Flora, d'you know, I'm nearly twenty-four now? And you're a year older."

"I know—you don't need to rub it in."

"They'll be lining us up for our pension soon."

Flora laughed outright, the fair fringe above her brow dancing. "I can just see us—you in your mutch and me in my Shetland shawl toddlin' around to the Parish Office. Likely they'll take one look at us and say, Right, the Grubber for you pair."

"More likely give us a pill," said Jenny. "I heard my da say that's what Hitler's doing wi' the old folk in Germany. By the time you and I are wearing elastic-sided boots and long combinations they'll be doing it here, too. They say it's cheaper that way."

"By God and if it's any cheaper than starving you to death I don't know." Flora leaned across her chum confidentially, her lively face a mirror of scorn and condemnation for all officialdom. "D'you know my maw went in to auld Granny Park up-the-stairs and the auld soul hadn't had a maskin' of tea in the house. She's sittin' there without a fire and not one of her family goes near her! Do you know, Jenny, if it wasn't for the folk up our close that auld woman would've been dead years ago! It's a crying shame the way they treat the old folk."

"You should hear my faither!" Jenny's mouth and chin squared in approving memory. "He'd get the jail if anybody heard him. He says we've got the worst rottenest country in the world— always the big shots, always layin' down the law to everybody else and never tidyin' up our own midden. He says a' the murderers and thieves and blaggards gets sympathy fae us. But if you're poor!—that's the biggest crime in the British Empire."

Flora nodded sagely. "My faither says it's the rich folk theirselves who make Communists—they're that damp stupid they don't know when they're puttin' their finger in their own eye. They think we're all half-wits and—my daddy says—they're going to get the shock o' their life some morning when they waken up and discover the ba's burst!"

"No." Jenny disavowed the suggestion firmly. "We'll never have a revolution in this country. We're too soft. And we're too easy kidded. Look at—what'ye call them?—Ramsay MacDonald and J. H. Thomas and all these kind of gasbags. Great men! Gonny do wonders! And then what happens? I'll tell you, Flora. Nothing. Absolutely nothing. Once they get down to London the only battles our leaders ever mix in is the one to get on the Honours List or have their names entered for the next free World Tour. One thing certain none of them ever die o' wounds or heading a Buroo queue. And that's how it's always been in this country and that's how it always will be."

Flora sighed. "My da says Jimmy Maxton is the best man among them. No nonsense with Jimmy."

"Ah, well, he's about the only one," said Jenny grudgingly. "For most of the rest, I would trust them no farther than I could throw the Tron Steeple."

"Here," said Flora, wearying of half-digested politics. "Come on over and we'll get a chip in Toni's."

Longingly Jenny looked across the street where a double shopfront was crowned with the faded gold gilt legend, Toni's Famous Scotch Fish Restaurant. The window to one side of the door was filled with soaring pyramids of dummy popular cigarette cartons. The other, lined with a multi-coloured background of cinema playbills, had as centre-piece a huge china swan with a drooping aspidistra growing from between its wings. Through the half-open door a battery of roll-top stoves and polished racks glittered invitingly. Even from across the road the sizzle of frying fat, with its accompanying appetite-teasing odour, sounded a siren-song only the snob palate could resist.

"What'll we use for money?" Jenny hesitated.

Flora dug into a little ornamental purse. "I've got one and thru'pence left—mind I told you I knocked two bob of my bonus?"

Guiltily, but mesmerized by Toni's lure, Jenny fell into step only protesting, "Och but, Flora, I don't know how you've the nerve to skin off your pay—my conscience'll not let me."

"It doesn't worry me," derided Flora. "See if I give my mother more than she's in the habit of getting—she just goes out and buys our Davy a new shirt. Or goes and hands it over to my Aunt Nellie to get something for the weans." Flora snorted scorn at her mother's reckless philanthropy. "No, I wouldn't keep it off my maw if she was desperate but to see it handed away! Huh! After me horsing all week to earn it!"

Inside Toni's the atmosphere was warm and heavy. Two rows of little tables marched along each side under great steam-dimmed mirrors lining the upper walls. Projecting from the wall each table was supported by a single iron leg and provided scarce enough space for four customers to prop confidential elbows. Until recently the tables had been separated by solid partitions and the floor sawdusted, but in a burst of modernity Toni had swept away the partitions with the sawdust, and the resultant triumph for space—and overseeing—had been underscored by sheathing the floor in the very latest linoleum of sea-green and ivory terrazo tile effect. Toni's patrons agreed it was all a wonderful step forward—second only to the installation of the hearty mechanical pianola occupying a corner of the long rectangular room and whose selections could be enjoyed by inserting a penny in its slot.

Toni himself was a squat, loquacious man with a large moustache and a complexion like dusty pigskin. Despite the large framed picture of himself conscripted into a 1914 Gordon Highlander's kilt that dominated the space above the cooking ranges, Toni's English was still as broken as it had been on the day of his naturalization thirty-five years before. Rosa, his huge black-haired wife, who industriously supervised the serving of the fish and chips Toni endlessly shovelled from the cooking caverns, was even less bi-lingual than her husband, except in the language of currency, when her addition and demand for the exact price of every bill of fare was precise and distinct to a farthing. Her black eyes flashing in constant ward over every table in the café, Rosa ruled Toni and their two young imported fellow-countrywomen with a machine-gun barrage of Neapolitan commands that provided their uncouth Glasgow clientele with a constant fund of amusement and good-natured conjecture. It was the only free bonus anyone ever got in Toni's.

"You wanting a fish?" Flora asked generously as she and Jenny slid into wall chairs opposite each other. On winter nights they always chose this table nearest the counter because it was farthes from the ever-swinging front door draught. At this mid-evening hour the place was still quiet, not until the cinemas emptied and the drunks staggered homewards would the carrying-out trade and the late-snack diners fill it up.

"No," a combination of thoughtful economy and tempered independence prompted Jenny's choice. "No—just a chip and I'll get a wee bit off your fish."

"A fourpenny chip and a fish supper," Flora smiled familiarly on the youngest of the waitresses who, except in girth, was a dark-eyed replica of her mistress. "And, Maria, bring two American Cream Sodas, too."

"Och, you shouldn't bother," remonstrated Jenny guiltily.

Flora shrugged. "Might as well be skint as left with thru'pence. I want a drink anyway."

Toni's big head rolled and he glanced over his shoulder. "You two lassies no' oota wi' the boy-friends tonight?" His sweat-beaded face wreathed in steam and the wire-meshed potato scoop that was almost part of him twirling as dexterously as a drum-major's staff, he leered with the cheerful insolence of long acquaintance. They returned his gaze happily. Toni's endless manipulation of the tools of his trade and his mysterious endless alternations of opening and shutting the damper lids and roll-top covers enclosing his long shining frying range was one of the fascinations of his patrons.

"No boy-friends," disclaimed Flora. "Jenny and I are waiting till Rosa goes that holiday back to Italy, then the both of us are coming round to keep house for you."

Toni threw back his head and his huge belly heaved under its white apron. "Very dam' good!" he roared. "Very dam' good!"

From the other end of the counter Rosa glowered expressive contradiction of lingual disability. "By Godda!" she exclaimed, "you be fond!" She glared with great contempt at her chuckling husband. "He's no dam' good."

"Oh, Rosa, I wouldn't say that," remonstrated Flora. "I'll bet when the pair of you are together you're just a couple of real wee passion flowers."

"Passion flowers!" Rosa clutched her brow while Toni rolled in another crescendo of mirth. "Mia, mia, mia! Sant——"

"Never mind Santa Claus," teased Jenny. "If you're not going to part with Toni, could you not put us on to a couple of his rich cousins from up the City?"

"My richa cousins!" The broad little Italian quietened

instantly. He spread his bare hairy arms in a wide Latin posture of amaze. "Where you thinka I get any rich friends? My gooda God!"

"It's all right, Toni," Flora nodded knowingly. "What about giving us a knockdown to a couple of yon handsome sheiks you gang up with at the big Italian dances—thon kind that's got fancy big ice-cream shops all over the place and a bank roll that would choke an elephant?"

"Ay, somebody as well stacked as yourself," agreed Jenny.

"Me! Stacked? Oh my Godda!" Toni chuckled and delved vigorously into his cauldrons of bubbling grease.

"No' my God at all," kidded Flora. "You've got the stuff all right. Look at all the money you take off us poor soft Scotch folk. No wonder Rosa's dripping in diamonds."

"Eh?" Rosa spun round again like a pivoting tank. Eyes flashing and hands waving, she exploded in a broadside of crackling Italian that set Toni's shoulders bouncing again. She finished by tapering into outraged Glasgow and plucking at the great scintillating brooch clipping the black blouse across her mountainous bosom. "Dam' Woolworth's," she wailed. "I have to buy mysel'. Him? Ach!" She conveyed her opinion of her husband's generosity by a rolling flash of her shoe-black eyes and a vulgar full-lip combination of razzberry and spit. "If he be the ghosta he no' gie ye the fright!"

"That's all right, Rosa," scorned Flora. "You're not letting him go, anyway. . . . Never mind, Toni, whenever Rosa snuffs it I'll be round to hang up my hat with you. Is that a bet?"

"By God no!" Toni shovelled another scoop of gleaming white chip potatoes from a side-partition into the boiling, crackling fat. "One-a women enought. If I get oota this lot I never be caught again. By God, yes!"

His wife's swift rejoinder was lost in the crash of the pianola as someone put a penny in its slot. Under cover of the opening bars of the Stein Song Flora kicked Jenny's ankle. Leaning across the table she whispered urgently: "Look who's arrived—yon chap you gave the dizzy to last Friday night."

"Oh, no!" Jenny shot a swift glance towards the opposite tables and stooped low over her plate. "Don't let him see me."

"He's looking across."

"I hope he doesn't come over."

"I thought you and him were getting on all right? He didn't——?"

"Oh, no," Jenny's grimace was graphic. The flash of eye and toss of head betokened the fate of any man who misjudged her virtue while the frown and wrinkled nose gave chivalry its clearance certificate. "No, nothing like that. But, och, he was such a gasbag. Got a big hit for himself, too. I only made the date to get rid of him."

"He's that well-spoken." Flora's glance was sidelong but searching. "He's got a pal tonight—thon chap that used to run with Mary Bryan. Mind she was aye bummin' about him?"

"Hmph!" The throaty rasp was enigmatic. "Mary Bryan would brag about anything in trousers. Her clicks are always wonderful."

"Oh, here! They're coming over!" Flora's head drooped lower. "Don't you be saying anything now!"

The young man who sauntered to their table was about twenty-five, neatly dressed in navy blue suit, white shirt and maroon-coloured tie. His bare sandy hair was creamed firmly back. His smile was as firmly in place and his parted lips, rather long across his narrow face, discreetly bared a gold tooth in his right upper jaw. "Fancy meeting you here," he said brightly but with sarcastic undertones.

The girls' start of surprise was a dual masterpiece of hypocrisy. "Oh!" they both said, and swayed backwards elegantly. Jenny added with minute malice, "No, but fancy meeting you here!"

"Why?"

"I don't know—I just didn't imagine you came into fish-supper shops."

"What makes you think that?" Without invitation he sat on the empty chair next hers. Glancing up he commanded his companion—who was hanging back diffidently, "Sit down, Ian." To the girls he said: "I hope you don't mind Ian and me sitting beside you?"

"It's a free country, Arthur," said Jenny. As she said it she shot a resigned glance at Flora and was inwardly humiliated to realize it was also intercepted by Ian. A dark, stocky man also in his middle twenties his grey eyes remained cool but slid back to study his friend enigmatically.

"I heard you were dead." Arthur gave his full attention to Jenny. Before he could continue she exclaimed in hurried apology but also with an impulse to impress Ian more favourably, "I'm dreadfully sorry about Friday night, Arthur. I know what you must think. But, honestly, I couldn't help it."

Arthur's expression was a mixture of disbelief and self-pity. "I

waited outside Dennistoun Palais for about an hour. I wouldn't
have done it for everybody, but I never thought, Jenny, you were
the kind of girl who would stand a fellow up."

"But I didn't—honest, I didn't." Jenny's face flushed with
secret guilt and public embarrassment. "Isn't that true, Flora—
sure I simply couldn't get out on Friday?"

Loyally Flora lied, "Definitely, Arthur. Jenny's mother took
an awful bad turn—they had to send for the doctor."

"We were up all night putting poultices on her," elaborated
Jenny with an instant glibness that would have startled Julia into
her first physical set-back in years.

Arthur smiled bravely across at Ian who remained impassive.
"We never doubt the ladies—do we?"

"Your friend's very quiet?" cut in Flora shrewdly. "Maybe he
would rather sit elsewhere?"

Looking her full in the face Ian said unsmilingly, "No. I
don't care where I sit. I'm just keeping Arthur company."

"Oh!" Flora bridled instantly. "Then please don't let us keep
you back. Jenny and I are quite happy with our own company."

For answer Arthur hailed Maria and ordered four drinks.
"Not for me, thanks," Jenny refused quickly. "Nor me," added
Flora. "We were just leaving."

"You can drink another lemonade," Arthur pleaded. "Don't
let me down. I've been telling Ian what great girls you are."

For the first time Ian half-smiled. "So he has," he admitted. He
looked at Jenny. "Are you a sister of Colin Haig's?"

"Do you know him?"

"He sometimes comes up to the drawing office for blueprints."

"Here we go!" Arthur rolled his eyes in mock martyrdom at
Flora. "We're going to build boats again."

Her fair head nodded sympathetically. "You're well out of it
now."

Jenny ignored the sallies. Her tension relaxed a little and she
asked, "You work in Burnford's? What do you do?"

"Draughtsman."

"That's quite a good job. D'you like it?"

Ian nodded.

"Why?" lamented Arthur. "Why does everyone in this city
think draughtsmen and engineers are wonderful? Why does
nobody ever get excited about insurance men?"

"Oh, I think an insurance man's a great job!" Flora leaned
her chin on her hand and studied him through narrowed eye-

lashes. "No dirty overalls or starting whistles to bother about! And practically your own boss! And look at all the different kinds of folk you meet! And it's steady too!"

"Yes, but it's not all honey. . . ."

Suddenly Jenny and Ian were not hearing them. Facing each other diagonally across the narrow table Ian was earnestly explaining how if he passed one more examination he meant really to go after a better position.

"That's what I would do if I were a man," and somehow her solemn approval pleased him immensely. "Once you have the qualifications, my daddy says, you can choose your job—you're not tied down to whatever they like to offer you on the Clyde. . . ."

When at last they left Toni's, Arthur walked on ahead explaining to a flatteringly attentive Flora why the manager in his office was so jealous of him. Ian and Jenny followed at a slower pace. Afterwards, lying in bed in the dark, looking up at the ceiling, Ian realized he could not remember where or when they had lost sight of the other two. Jenny kept Colin awake for an hour throwing questions across their room about this awful nice draughtsman, Ian Angus.

# CHAPTER NINETEEN

EIGHTY feet above the ground on a three-plank staging Colin Haig put his back against the stem of the half-built ship and looked down. The air around him and the planks under his feet vibrated with the Clyde's iron anthem, but as a seasoned member of the Black Squad he accepted the mutilating assault on his ear-drums as a natural phenomenon and was literally unconscious of it. The same could not be said of his mental reactions towards a tiny figure, dwarfed by perspective, chatting unconcernedly with another miniature on the ground. To take his mind off his mate's dilatoriness Colin let his attention wander. The view was familiar but never ceased to give him a queer sensation of personal pride.

Immediately beneath him, spilled like the contents of a child's toy box, the V-roofed sheds of Burnford Shipyard and its tangle of railway shunting sidings fringed the half-dozen launching ways. Two of the ways were empty, even from this height were visible the even march of their keel-blocks to the water's edge scarred by the weed-grown lurches of neglect that spells poverty to the shipbuilder. But the others bloomed better. In addition to the

hull Colin was working on one bore the first centre-line plates of
a new keel, another sprouted floorings and transom frame and
the fourth had a ten thousand tonner red-leaded and ready for
its sheen of launching paint. Beyond all that, to the east and
south, stretched the roofs of Burnford. Idly Colin singled out the
church spires, the Congregational, the Burnford Memorial, the
Old Parish and the soaring arrow of the English. With satisfaction he compared them with the squat insignificance of the
unbelled tower of St. Teresa's. Beside the mellow stone dignity
of the Protestant churches, its newer red brick economies was a
tawdry intrusion.

His survey lifted and took in the distant speckle of crosses and
angels peppering the hillside shrubbery marking the sprawl of
the municipal cemetery. Beyond the cemetery the streets straggled
and thinned into the open green fields. He tried to pinpoint the
route he had followed on his last cycle run up through Renfrew-
shire to the Ayrshire Coast.

A solid bounce on the staging distracted him. Turning his head
he recognized the skinny stooping figure appearing round the
bow from the starboard side of the ship. Mildly surprised, he
nodded. "Hullo, Terry."

Wide-legged on the still quivering planks Flanagan halted.
"It's yourself, Colin." He spat into the unfenced void beside them.
"B'Christ I've wasted half the afternoon chasing our gaffer. Ye
haven't seen him, have you?"

Colin looked back. From their forward vantage point they
could see right down the main deck declivity, still rust-raw and
bare of superstructures. Air hoses and rivet fires cluttered the
area. Half a dozen hand and pneumatic riveters added their
drummings to the staccato solos of three or four machine caulkers.
At shoulder level, within a few yards of them, a hole-borer reaming
deck holes struggled and fought with his kicking machine. Amid-
ship two bowler-hatted carpenter foremen stroked their chins and
peered pensively at some problem buried in the chasm of the
open hold they brooded over. But nowhere was the familiar bow-
legged figure of the labourers' chargehand Flanagan sought.

"No," Colin confessed, "I haven't seen wee Screwtop up here
the day." His attention fixed on a squad of deck platers. Heads
tilted they were watching the jib of a great travelling crane
swing their next plate inboard. The plate, about half the size of
a small dance floor, spun in the breeze blowing off the river. Men
scattered. The platers' leading hanger-up blasted a warning signal

on his whistle and his leather-lunged helpers told the craneman what they thought of him and his judgment in a stream of short traditional Anglo-Saxon words. The craneman leaned forward out of his observation window and spread his fingers to his nose.

Terry glanced up contemptuously. The crane cabin, rotating dizzily on its stilt legs, towered another forty feet above them. "That's Deef Baxter," he recognized. "He'll kill some bugger yet."

"Funny how he's got away with it so long," marvelled Colin. "I was putting in a breast plate the other day and he nearly dropped it on my head."

"Well, sure now, you know he does his spare-time gardener to the Manager," Terry laughed shortly. "But it's the God's truth, boy, more men are kilt by favour and bloody stupidity than by hate and gunpowder. How's your faither getting on?"

"He's down in Dalmuir, Terry. He'd a wee labouring job in the Linwood for a while but, ach, he chucked it. No money in it."

Flanagan nodded understandingly. "Is he makin' anything of it down the watter?"

"Well, he gets the odd night late. And he had a Sunday a couple of weeks back. It always helps."

"Sure, boy. We've got to take our coppers how and where we find them."

Colin suddenly realized Flanagan was growing old. Since the night, years ago, when Jenny had run out of the house he had rarely visited them. Although they had made up after that night's brawl he and Haig had gradually met less often and drank less deeply. The youth realized the resignation in his tone and the heaviness in his stance was new. For the first time, too, it occurred to him he had grown bigger than the once detested Irishman. And, oddly enough, the fact brought him no exhilaration. Looking at Terry's sharp-lined little face he suddenly felt touched by a strange regret—and panic. The sadness of witnessing the giants and even the ogres of the older generation shrink and grow passive overwhelmed him. It implied a shift and necessary acceptance of responsibility he did not covet. Vaguely he yearned for a permanency that was subtly being denied him. As if Terry read his thoughts he asked, "How much of your time've you got in now, Colin?"

"Nearly four years. I start my last year in November."

"Good boy. You'll soon be getting married?"

Colin laughed derisively. "Are you kiddin'?"

Terry's smile broadened. "Jaisus, boy, don't tell me you niver go out with girls?"

"Aw, I'll not say that." The manner was boyishly offhand. "I don't mind an odd date: it always passes the time. But steady —aha—nothin' doin'!"

"Now, didn't we all say that," Terry chuckled. "I hear you're quite the fitba' player, too?"

"Ach!" Colin's headshake was deprecating and modest.

"Ah, but it's a good thing, boy. You make the most of it. I hear the Celtic have been lookin' at ye?"

"First I've heard of it."

"Could be. But I got it from a good source." Terry looked at his friend's son quizzically. "Would ye not fancy going to Parkhead?"

A sense of delicacy kept Colin's expression impartial. "Never even thought about it." He did not deceive Flanagan.

"Look, boy," the older man emphasized seriously. "Don't you be a head case like the most of them." His gesture covered half the city spread out beneath. "Maybe ye dream of playing for the Rangers? Well, sure now, there's nothing wrong with that. Ye might even fancy the Thistle? Or the Clyde? But if the Celts came along and asked ye first I hope to God, boy—and for your own sake—it wouldn't be the colour of their jerseys would hold ye back?"

Colin laughed embarrassedly. "I'm only a juvenile yet!"

"Juvenile or junior, Willie Maley, Celtic's manager'll decide whether you're good enough. And if he did, ye'll remember ye'd not be the first Protestant to play in the green and white."

"But I don't think there's any Protestant directors at Parkhead?" The retort was out before Colin could control it.

Terry shook his head. "Ye've a lot to learn, boy. Did your ould man niver tell ye of the time I played in the Orange Walk?"

"You?" Colin's smile was broad.

"Ye don't believe me?" Terry stepped back to the stem and looked down along the stagings on the far side. Satisfied that Screwtop, his foreman, was not yet in sight he came back and lit a broken clay pipe. "Ye can ask yer ould man when ye get home." He shook his head in reverie. "It was wan day about seven or eight years after the War. Jaisus, but things were bad! Him and I were on what they called 'The Gap'—a kind of blind spell when they gave you no Dole money at all but if you were starvin' they'd give your wife a line for a few shillings of groceries. Anyhow,

Collie and I are standing round from the Subway with Nippy Tait and—it's the Christ's truth I'm tellin' ye, boy—we hadn't a smoke between the three of us. Says Nippy, sorrowful like, 'It's a bloody pity, Terry, you're a Papish—I could've put you in the way of pickin' up a pound note this Saturday.' "

Terry spat between the shell of the boat and the staging. Wiping the dribble from his underlip with the back of his wrist he went on: "I don't need to tell ye, Colin, your father and I looked at him. 'And where in the hell could I get a pound note if I wasn't Papish?' I asked right away. 'Och,' says Nippy, 'it's the Royal Finnieston Pipe Band—they're booked to play in the Walk on Saturday with a Southside Lodge and here, bigod, their big drummer's went and took the flu. Drummond, the pipe-major, is about off his head wondering who he'll get to take his place.' 'Drummond,' says I, 'nutt Chanter Drummond that was pipey with the ould Hairy Battalion?' 'The very same,' says Nippy. 'D'ye know him?' 'Know him,' says I, and I tips your father the wink. 'By God, and if the Chanter needs a drummer he's got one!' "

"And did you go?" marvelled Colin.

"Did I go! For a dry pound note I'd've played tambourine for a tribe of South Sea cannibals. But, Jaisus, boy," he emphasized, "it was hard-earned money."

"I can picture that. Every tune must've tore your heart?"

"Hell, boy," Flanagan was contemptuous. "The tunes didn't bother me at all. I can beat time to 'No Surrender' and 'Dollies Braes' as aisy as to the 'Boys of Wexford'. That would niver put Flanagan off his step. No—it was the bloody marching. From the minute we set futt in this town that was entertaining the Walk that year we had to play up hill and down dale. I marched past more chapels in that wan day than in all the years of me life as a born Roman Catholic. And play! Let the Chanter but give me the nod to beat the double-tap so the boys could have a breather and, by all the holy saints, the pipes were nutt down off their shoulders but the divils behind us were yelling, 'Whut's wrang wi' oor baun? Play up, kilties; give us Boyne Watter again!' "

Terry looked rueful. "To this day I tip me cap to the bandsmen in an Orange Walk—they earn their washers. But I was glad of the money then, just as I was glad of the pie and chip supper the Orangemen gave us at the end of the day—it was a feed and a half! I'm telling you, boy, I was only sorry they didn't have a 12th of July every week." He looked hard at the youth. "But ye see me point, Colin? If any team comes along and offers you fower or five pounds a week for kickin' a ball around a park don't you worry about the colour of their jerseys. Let the lunatics round the railings worry about that. You think of your ould mother, boy, and how many grey hairs an extra wage would save her."

Colin's grin was old-fashioned but conciliatory. "That's what I am thinking about. Me in a Celtic jersey would turn both her and my da grey. . . . Naw, Terry, no offence, but I don't think I could do it. These feelings are just something you're born wi'."

Flanagan shook his head in slow regret and looked down the ship's length. So close that she seemed to brush their stern-counter, a big Anchor liner was being shepherded downstream by fussy, deep-baying tugs. As she slid smoothly past their berth, majestically blotting out the width of the river, their informed admiration took in her every detail from masthead to boot-top and from fore-peak to stern post. In a silent communion of worship they feasted their eyes on her white tier of decks and enjoyed an unreasonable unnameable sense of proprietary pride in her parade of lifeboats and gracefully arched davits. When she passed, leaving a dying churn of creamy waters, they still stood momentarily inarticulate. At that moment the sun came out gilding the distant spires and domes of the Art Gallery and University in an almost translucent haze of fairy beauty. Farther, amid a tangle of rooftops and hillside streets, the green trees of Kelvingrove and the Botanic Gardens bloomed like velvet banners set in granite frames.

Abruptly, argumentatively, Colin said: "No' a bad city, Glesca, when ye see it right. What are they a' greetin' about?"

"Sure, boy, it's a great city. Damn the word did ever I say about it." And then Terry laughed more than a little self-consciously. "Well, you'll tell your faither I was askin' for him won't ye now? And your mother, too—Bridget's always wondering when she's going to take a run up?"

"Och, you know our house, Terry. It's never empty. If it's no' our own ones our Jenny's aye got some of her chums up. My mother never gets out a night." On a generous inspiration Colin added, "Why do you and Mrs. Flanagan not come up yourselves? I'm sure there's nothing to hinder you?"

Terry's smile was wise and wistful. "Ach, ye know how it is, boy —the women are niver aisy when Collie and I get together. Nutt but maybe they've reason."

The youth's appraisal softened with a sympathy he would once have believed impossible. "You're a couple of hard cases," he commented. "How long've ye known my faither now, Terry?"

"Thirty years or more, boy. I came across to work in the ship-yards when times were bad back home and niver went back. And, bigod, they've been bad enough here at times. Anyhow your faither and I got to know each other and, Jaisus, we've argued the bit out one way and another ever since."

"Funny—I never heard him say you were a drummer?"

The Irishman laughed. "Ye know now, son, that's one of the things Collie could niver forgive me for. I learned to play the big drum wearin' the kilt."

"The Irish kilt?"

"Hell scud the Irish kilt, boy. I learned it in rale tartan—during the war, in the good old H.L.I. And yer faither niver got over me goin' through that and him gettin' sent home." The roguish light faded from Terry's twinkle. "But d'ye know what, boy—and ye'll forgive an illiterate auld fool for mentioning it again—when ye're lyin' out in a shell-hole and your dead mates are hangin' on the barbed wire before ye you niver ask the fellah beside ye in the muck whether he's church or chapel, Rangers or Celtic. You're too damned glad he's there at all and that ye're both livin'."

"I suppose not," Colin admitted awkwardly. To change a delicate subject he pointed to the dwarfed figures below, singling out the one with a long length of slender white wood arched across his shoulder. "See my mate," he said inconsequently. "I sent him down for that template to lift some shell-chock moulds and he's stood there for ten solid minutes with Hammy Dodds. And wait till you see—on Saturday he'll be moanin' because we've no pay! I could make two pays in the time he wastes for us every week."

Terry peered between narrowed eyelids. "Is that nutt Big Mick the Rigger's boy?"

"Ay. I keep telling him—don't think because your old man's a gaffer you can get away wi' murder. Especially on piecework. But, och, you might as well talk to a wall."

"How do you get on with him?"

"Who—Andy? That's the aggravatin' bit—ye canny help getting on wi' Andy. He's a pure comedian. He just laughs at everything you say."

Flanagan's thoughts chased a half-smile across his narrow wizened face. But he did not voice them. He merely said: "He's not like his faither—a more unhumorous big sod of a man niver drew the holy breath of God. . . ." He stopped and ejaculated, "Christ, there's Screwtop now—I'd better away down and grup him before he slips out the gate and up the road for his mornin'—— Now mind, boy, and tell yer faither . . . ?"

"Ay, sure, Terry."

Colin watched Flanagan dive for the nearest upright and scramble down its trellis-work like a bemufflered, ageing—but still agile—monkey. When he saw his haste was still not going to achieve its purpose he curled his tongue under his strong young teeth and whistled a single piercing blast that cut through the iron din around like a rapier and pricked the hurrying labourer foreman's consciousness. Glancing guiltily over his shoulder he halted in resignation at sight of his gesticulating pursuer. Up on the staging Colin chuckled to himself. "Don't worry, Screwtop, you'll still make it—they don't shut for hours yet!" Then he saw his whistle had also turned young Andy's face upwards. Lifting his foot he put his forefinger with unmistakeable threat on the toe of his boot. Even at that distance he could see his mate's mobile features cheekily mouthing a string of obscenities. But having thus satisfied his spirit of independence Andy threw a last laugh at his confidant and, turning, hustled across and up the long slope of the main gangway. Satisfied he was really on his way at last Colin lifted his gaze again and looked down river across the smoky miles to the vague misty hills that hid Loch Lomond. He found himself wishing he had not promised to play football on Saturday. He had a daft notion he might enjoy a run on the bike better.

## CHAPTER TWENTY

JULIA lifted the smoothing iron away from before the fire-ribs. Dusting its black iron surface with a corner of her apron, she clipped on a polished tin shield and turned again to the blanket-covered table. Seated in Collie's big chair her sister Mary watched with professional interest as she chose another garment from the shallow, big wicker-basket on the floor.

"Is that one of Colin's shirts?"

"Ay; and he wants it for the dancing tonight." Julia held it up for inspection. "You know what the young yins are—everything's got to be dead right. That's one I paid eight and six for up the town."

"It's a nice shirt—I like the semi-silk fronts. Our Archie'll wear nothing else. And they're that hard to keep clean!"

"I saw Archie jumpin' on a caur the other day but I don't think he saw me—my, but he's getting such a big fellow!"

"Och, he can wear his faither's suits now, nae bother. I'm about driven off my head wi' the pair o' them. . . . Is Colin's time no near out yet?"

"A month ago." Julia turned and gazed with quiet pride at the new adornment on her dresser. "His first journeyman's pay helped to buy that."

Mary nodded. She was a small greyer edition of Julia but her shoe-button eyes tended to spark with a meaner fire than ever the older woman betrayed. "I'm just looking at it," she nodded. "My, it's a lovely wireless set. Has it no' got a loudspeaker?"

"No, that's one of the very latest. I don't understand them but they're a' kinda self-contained. Loudspeakers are well out-of-date nowadays."

"Is it no' great what they can do!" Mary shook her head in a fashion that could be interpreted either as admiration or disapproval. She rose and touched the highly varnished surface of the cabinet. "It's bonny right enough," she admitted grudgingly. "Our Archie's aye at me to get one but I just tell him, Who'll pay the instalments if either you or your faither get knocked idle?"

Julia thumped vigorously with her ironing. "That's it," she agreed. "The lassies were at me to get one long ago—especially our Jenny, she's Henry Hall mad. And then, of course, that fellow McQuade next door has been making crystal sets ever since he was at school."

"That's the Catholics for ye—you couldnae be up to them. Get the best o' education, too—at our expense."

"Ay, of course, but Stuart's a nice enough boy. And, of course, he often had our yins in to hear his sets. But I just telt Jenny, you'll get a wireless when ye can pay for it." She looked over her shoulder at the radio again with a longer, critical look. "So there it is—paid and signed for. Nae bob-down-and-tanner-when-you-catch-me strings about that one. Her and Colin had been saving up and the minute he got his first big pay the two of them away down to that new fancy shop in Anchor Road and ordered it. Cost seven or eight pounds, but as I said to their faither, it's their money and they could've spent it on worse things."

"Well, that's one way to look at it," Mary admitted, but

warned, "You'll need to watch your dresser mats with these electric bottles, though. A neighbour o' mine spilled one and it just ruined the top of her sewing-machine cover."

"Oh, I don't touch it." Julia screwed her face in disownment. "It's up to them. Right enough, me and Collie enjoy the bands and I fairly like when they sometimes give you a programme of good Scotch songs but——" Compelled by her sister's fascinated interest and in direct contradiction to her own vow, she laid her hot iron across an upturned saucer at the corner of the table and turned towards the dresser. Nervously she reached to the control knobs.

"Oh, don't put it on for me!" Mary protested.

"I'm no' sure," Julia hesitated conspiratorially. "It's either the one with the green spot or the red one you turn. Now, let me think, is it to the left or the right?"

"For God's sake, Julia, don't break it!" Appalled, Mary stood back nervously as a crackle of whistles and whines leapt from the set. "I'd get the blame if it——"

With satisfying suddenness the devil's cacophony smoothed and dissolved and a clear flow of horn and violin music filled the kitchen. They listened intently, Julia with a relieved air of accomplishment and her sister with an expression of strained but genuine admiration.

"Some of the high-class stuff they give you doesn't appeal to me," Julia apologized honestly as a ultra-refined announcer introduced another quartet piece in A minor. "I can never make head nor tail of it."

"Nor me," Mary laughed. "That's because we're no educated."

Toning the volume of the music down, Julia resumed ironing. "Just leave them," she urged as Mary carried their afternoon tea dishes to the sink. "I'll get them in a minute."

Ignoring her, Mary rinsed the crockery. "Is Jenny still wench-in'?" she asked. "We haven't had her up for a while."

"Oh ay. She's been going steady now for months." Julia gazed reflectively into space. "I'm just hoping they don't decide to get married before I've time to get the room done up."

"They'll surely not want to come and stay here! Where would Colin sleep?"

"No!" Julia's scorn was amused. "It's the loss of her pay I'm thinking about. I'm getting one of these divans for Colin—y'know, the kind you can fold up swanky through the day?—and I'll do away wi' the old iron bed. And I'd like a nice new wardrobe—

their clothes get all crushed in that lobby press. And the lassies have that many!"

Mary looked round the kitchen. Evidence of growing prosperity was not confined to the new radio. The former scrubbed and scarred plain wood table was gone. Julia was ironing on a polished drop-leaf variety that, when folded, pushed unobtrusively against the wall. The old iron range was gone, too, and a compact, tiled-front fireplace added a new spaciousness to the hearth. "My, that wallpaper's made a difference here too," she sighed. "I wish I could coax my fellow to do our place. I'm always at him."

"Ho!" Julia laughed, looked round. "Don't think it was the auld yin that did that! The paper could fall off the wall for all he cares. Young Colin did the papering. I picked it and Jenny did the trimming and then the two of them got stuck into it. Away ben and see the room—they done it, too."

Returning, Mary nodded her head approvingly, "Ay, they've made a good job of it. Ella'll see a difference next time she's home. How's she getting on in her new hospital?"

"Champion. I just wish it was a wee bit nearer hame but she seems to like it. . . . Says they're a' nice nurses and the Sister seems to've taken a notion to her. Of course, Ella's a Staff Nurse now. I think she had a good lot to do wi' the operations and that."

"I mind ye telling me. Oh, dear, I doubt nursing's one job I'd never do for! As for operations—one look inside yon theatres, as they call them, is enough for me!"

"Somebody has to do it."

Mary hung up the dish-towel she had carried through to the room. "Ay," she agreed; "somebody has to do them. But when I think on the wee tinker your Ella used to be. . . ." Mary paused in wondering recollection and shook her head. "Mind the rows she caused? She'd just screw up thon wee face of hers. I used to be heart sorry for your Colin. She never gave'm a minute's peace. And she'd let nothing go by her—she had to get every-thing!"

"She was a warmer when she was wee," Julia admitted, but grudgingly.

"And I used to get that mad at you—the way you flew at the other two and half the time it was Ella to blame."

Her sister shook her head. "Oh, I wouldn't say that. The faither and I tried to treat them all alike. But, of course, Ella was the youngest and she could aye get to the soft side o' Collie."

"You were both soft wi' her," Mary declared with sisterly

bluntness. "And it's a God's blessing she turned out as well as she did. I must say for ord'nar' I'm no' awful stuck on Christians but—to give her her due—Ella's certainly one that's lived up to her preaching."

"They're both good lassies." Julia folded her last piece and pushed the empty basket underneath the bed where the drape hid it. Lifting the iron clothing from a chair beside the table she separated it and stored the items in the chest of drawers standing beneath the clock. With one hand on the open top drawer, she said, "And Colin's a good boy, too. I just hope to God he doesn't get tied up wi' some trollop out the dancing."

"That's it!" Mary nodded vigorously. "You never know what they'll do. You rear them and try to advise them the best you can but you know what young yins are nowadays—they know everything. You canny tell them anything. If we speak to our Archie he just looks at us as if we were daft."

"Oh, I know——" Glancing at the clock, Julia took an embroidered cloth from the dresser and spread it over the table. "They'll start coming in," she voiced her uppermost thoughts. "I'd better get the table set. I've got a tin o' awful nice salmon —I think I'll just give them that the night and save me cooking anything."

"Ay, and I'd better away round myself," sighed Mary, but without making any move. "He's working to nine and the young yin's goin' straight to a fitba' match but I like to be there in case——"

"Och, just wait and get a bite wi' us," Julia insisted warmly. "What's the sense in going hame to sit in a house yourself?"

"Och, well——"

"By the way, how is Archie getting on—Colin was saying he'd chucked his job?"

Her sister's mouth set in a tight regretful line. "Ay, the silly fool—didn't like working in an office. Oh, his faither was blazin' —after all the trouble he'd went to get him in! I thought he was goin' to murder him that night!"

"And what's he doing now? On the Buroo?"

"Naw, nutt him. Got started in the fruit market the next day —goin' wi' a lorry. Likes it fine, he says."

"Och, well."

"Oh, he'll have to stick it now. But, as his faither says, it's not now he'll regret it, it's in ten years' time when he realizes what he threw away——"

"Collie always says that's the first mistake any man makes—takin' his jacket off."

"The faither telt him that. He says, 'You start off like a white coolie and ye'll finish up like one. Don't let them kid ye,' he says, 'only mugs lift anything heavier than a pen.' Oh, the auld yin warned him. . . ."

Julia nodded. "Still," she offered consolingly, "there's good money to be made in fruit. Maybe if he sticks in and gets a wee float of his ain——"

"Our Archie!" Mary laughed in candid scorn at thought of her son in business. "He's too soft in the head. He couldnae run a message far less a fruit cart! It's my fault, just the same," she added regretfully. "With him being the only one I was too soft with him. I know that now but—och!—as I often say to the faither, God help the lassie that ever marries our Archie; she'll have her hands full."

"Ah, he'll maybe surprise you," Julia comforted. "Sometimes I think there's a Providence looks after the ones that are no' supposed to have any brains. They often go farther and finish up better than the smart ones. D'you no' mind yon Sammy Rogers that stayed up our close—mind we always thought he was that glaikit? Mind how he got on?"

"Was that no' the one that married thon awful bonny lassie from Mulguy?"

"The very same. Well, he——" The sound of the front door opening turned both their heads. "My God, that's Jenny and I've no' got the tea masked!" Julia forgot her reminiscence in a sudden burst of activity. Jenny pushed open the kitchen door while still removing her coat in the lobby. "Hullo, Aunt Mary," she called warmly, "I thought I heard your voice."

"This is me up to pinch your tea," her aunt joked.

"Know what I'm going to tell you, Auntie—this is the only time I get a decent tea, when there's a visitor."

"Away, you cheeky tinker, you've got me eaten out of house and home." Julia smiled at her sister. "I'm not kiddin', Mary, that one could eat her way through a mountain o' black puddin's. Her faither says it's no' an appetite she's got, it's a bottomless pit."

"Oh, mother!" Jenny whirled in appeal. "Auntie Mary—do you not think I'm getting thinner? I'm on a diet."

"Oh, my God, on a diet!" Julia's eyes rolled upwards. "Two eggs and ham and four slice o' bread going out in the morning, not counting her porridge and the bag of chocolate biscuits she takes with her. And if ye saw what she faces at dinner-time—it would frighten an Irish navvy."

Jenny laughed herself but protested. "Now, mother, I only took one plate of soup today. And I very nearly never took the chocolate biscuits this morning."

"I like your skirt," Mary remarked.

"Do you?" Pleased with the compliment, the girl spun and smoothed it. "My mother's not very keen on it."

"Oh, yes, I think it's quite nice."

"Far too tight," Julia frowned. "Makes her behind stick out too much."

"Mother! Don't be vulgar!"

"Of course that's the style," Mary soothed diplomatically. "And you know what they say, Julia, as well out the world as out too much."

As they talked, Collie came in. Hanging up his rusty cap and jacket he walked straight from the lobby to the sink where Julia had a basin of hot water poured for him. As he rolled up his sleeves and tucked the neck of his shirt in Mary said, "You'll be glad that's by?"

He nodded in subdued acknowledgment of her sympathy. "Ay, Mary, it doesnae get any easier. How's Bob getting on these days?"

"Oh, just like yourself, Collie, battling away. There's not much else for it, is there?"

"No," he answered her, through a splash and flurry of soapy water as he rinsed the shipyard grime from arms and face. "We greet when we're idle and we greet when we're working—in fact, we're like Christmas Cards, we're aye greetin'."

"Ay." Mary glanced roguishly at her niece. "Talking about cards—when's the invitations coming out?"

Jenny looked startled and then slowly blushed. "Invitations, Aunt Mary! What do you mean?"

"That'll do ye now," her aunt wagged a finger. "We've heard all about it. When are ye bringing him up to see us."

Jenny laughed, but her blush deepened. "Don't be silly, Aunt Mary—it's only friendship."

"Friendship?" Mary's chuckle was teasing. "D'you hear that, Collie?"

"Ay," Collie laughed between the fold of a towel. "It must be me he's friendly with then for I canny get to my bed at night. He sits here for hours until I don't know what to talk about next...."

"Och, away, Daddy!" Jenny cried. "Mother! Sure Ian hardly ever opens his mouth. My daddy keeps building boats on the carpet there until I'm fair affronted——"

"Ay, and you sitting burstin' waiting to get Ian out to the stairhead?" Her aunt nodded with slow, wise emphasis.

"Oh, no." Julia shook her head in brisk negative. "The room fire's got to be lit two and three nights a week now. No stairhead."

"Oh, has it reached that stage?"

"Ay. And you should hear our Colin when he comes in and can't get to *his* bed. And I'm always wondering what that fellow thinks of that room."

"Well," Jenny's head inclined emphatically, "if he doesn't like our house he knows what to do. I'm not chasing him——"

"Quite right, Jenny," her aunt applauded. "Always keep a good conceit of yourself. And if he's the right fellow for you his eyes'll no' see anything else but you. Your maw's furniture'll be the least of his bother."

"Come on," interrupted Julia, "draw your chair over, Mary, and we'll get by before Colin comes in. He's aye in such a splutter —if he's no' rushing to the fitba' he's fleein' to the dancing. . . ."

## CHAPTER TWENTY-ONE

Jimmy McBride and Colin stood beside the band dais in Burnford Public Hall watching the dancers glide past. McBride was one of Colin's regular friends and frequent dance companion. "Who's the thing in the black ankle-length?" he asked now. "That red-haired one dancing with Beanie West?"

Singling out the couple Colin shook his head. "Stranger to me," he confessed. "Be something Beanie's got in tow with up the city."

"Nope." McBride was positive. "I've had my eye on her. Her and a black-headed thing came in together."

"Her dancing with Snakehips Smith?"

"Oh, gee ay," McBride nodded his head comically. He was a fair-haired, snub-nosed youth of nervous energy and twinkling eye. "Might've known. That's the pair o' them stating their case already."

Together they chuckled at the alertness of the two local Lotharios.

McBride looked over his shoulder as the band-leader, without taking his trumpet from his lips, reversed the Fox-trot placard on its tripod. "They've made it a Novelty," he enthused; "what about cuttin-in on Beanie and Snakehips?"

Colin shook his head. "No, I see Mattie Wilson in the night and it's a long time since her and I had a birl."

He stepped into the crush of dancers and tapped a youth on the shoulder. "Right, Sparrow."

The energetic dancer he addressed relinquished his partner with a cheerful, "Hoi, Colin. How's it going?"

"Not bad, Sparrow. Doin' all right yourself?"

Mattie Wilson had grown into a plain but pleasant girl who combined inborn dancing skill with a talent for good fellowship. The straw-coloured plaits that had peeped round the bed-curtain at Colin so long ago had darkened to an undistinguished brown; when he thought of it at all he always hoped her memory of that night had faded too. If it had not, she certainly never betrayed it. All the boys dated Mattie but, so far, no one had courted her. If she had any regrets on this she never betrayed them either. She slipped into Colin's arms with a characteristic jerk of her head. "I was just wondering," she chided, "when you were going to give me a dance."

"Darling," he ogled, "I come here specially tonight to give you a dance. I was just saying to McBride, if I don't get a dance wi' wee Mattie the night's wasted."

"You liar," she scoffed. "But, right enough, I haven't seen you for a while, Colin—you'll be too busy hittin' about the Locarno and the Plaza these days, likely?"

"Off and on." He grinned rakishly. "Got to give the other girls a break, too, y'know."

"Oh ay." Mattie leaned back in the crook of his arm and narrowed her blue eyes. "The old Burnford P.H. isn't good enough for you now, eh? Turning into a city slicker? You'll be dodging up the town in your dinner-jacket and bow-tie next?"

Wisecracking with the familiar latitude of old acquaintance, they circled in the effortless glide that was the heritage of their city's passion for ballroom dancing. Like most Glasgow girls Mattie's response to her partner's turns and twists and sudden little intricate foot patterns verged on telepathy rather than on physical communication, for he held her lightly and made no effort to impose his body on hers. During the dance they forgot each other's sex and seldom was Colin consciously aware of any partner's feminine contours.

When they reached the arched doorway leading to the ballroom's refreshment annexe he steered Mattie purposefully through. "Oho," she cheered softly. "Standing on our hands tonight? The plating must be looking up?"

"I swindled the tally sheet," he winked.

Like the main hall, the ante-room was not elaborately decorated —its plain walls were washed down in biscuit colour and the narrow friezes limmed in gold and pink. However, as a concession to its rôle, the plain bench seating bordering the dance floor was substituted in the buffet by real cane chairs set round little circular tables. At the far end a long trestle table covered by a white cloth was presided over by two matronly attendants. Their brisk service of soft drinks and chocolate biscuits was punctuated by a quick-fire barrage of innocuous repartee with their better-known patrons.

"For an ice-drink?" Colin suggested.

"No, I'd rather have a McCallum."

Leaving her to choose their table he elbowed his way through the crowd and finally secured his drink and the small dish of ice-cream with its blood-red synthetic raspberry topping Mattie preferred.

"Pure murder," he commented, returning to the corner table she had secured. "I was nearly putting the hammer on a bloke for the way he was pushing. A proper ned!"

"Oh, some of them could learn you a thing or two," Mattie agreed knowledgeably. Sitting opposite each other they surveyed the comings and goings of their fellow dancers with the contentment and sophisticated bonhomie of Paris boulevarders sipping aperitifs in the sun.

"It's quite good the night," Mattie approved. "I always think the P.H. band's as good as any in the city—I mean, for a wee hall."

"Ay, it's not bad." Colin's nod was that of authority. "I don't like their tangos, though. Kinda dragging."

"Oh, you should've been here last week." Mattie portrayed restrained ecstasy. "They had Tony Argentina—y'know, his mother's got yon wee chip shop along Rivet Street—and can that boy play an accordion! Stickin' out!"

"McBride and I were up the Palais—Philip and Scutts were demonstrating."

"Great dancers." Mattie's tribute to the leading ballroom professionals of the day was spontaneous, and inspired as much by real artistic and technical appreciation as by native patriotism. "The best in the world. Cathie McLaren and I saw them one night at Barrowlands and, no kidding, they wouldn't let them off the floor. And—oh!—what a dress Miss Scutts had on! Magnificent! Y'know, Colin, I could just've stood and watched them forever."

Colin nodded. "Makes you realize you don't know nothing about dancing."

"How'ye, Colin!" A smack on the shoulder turned him round. "Hear ye got beat the day?"

"Hullo, Tommy—Johnny!"

"Hi, Mattie! Howzzit goin', sweetheart?"

Acknowledging the newcomers' greetings they invited them to sit down.

"No, no," the cheerful pair were adamant. "Don't want to break up a good thing."

"Who are you kidding?" Mattie was contemptuous but blushed her secret pleasure.

"Where was the Welfare playin' anyway?" Tommy pursued his main interest. "Were you away fae hame?"

Colin grinned wryly. "Out in the country—an Ayrshire bunch, Mossbride St. Saints."

"Oho! We played that lot in the Shield last year. I'll bet they ploughed in?"

"You're tellin' me!"

"Was yon curly-heided big-centre-half still wi' them?"

For answer Colin stretched out a leg and pulled his trouser up to the knee. A blue-black bruise flecked with congealed blood extended the length of his shin.

"Here, here!" Mattie feigned shocked modesty. "Remember there's a lady present!"

Jimmy admired the wound and chuckled. "Well, pal, you know what to do next time."

Colin grinned non-committally.

"Sure," agreed Johnny. "What's good to give's good to take. You lay in the clug when you get them at Burnford." He added aggrievedly, "Some of these country blokes think because a team comes from the city it's there for the kickin'. Talk about the Billy Boys! They're waitin' on ye wi' everything but the kitchen sink. It's a pure liberty!"

"Never mind, Colin," insisted his friend, "give us the wire when the Saints come to the Welfare and we'll be there too. After what they done to us I wouldn't mind leading a break-in—especially if that centre-half's playin'."

As they drifted away Mattie's attention was drawn by hilarious laughter to another table. "Beanie's in form tonight," Colin noted. "Who are the dames?"

Mattie shook her head. "Their faces are familiar, but if they like Beanie's jokes I'd rather not know any more about them."

"Bad as that?" Colin looked at his partner quizzically. He put his elbows on the table and leaned closer. "Funny, Mattie, how you can know people a long time and still be a stranger."

"How?"

"Well—take you and I? We've lived up the same close for years and yet, what do you know about me?"

"I know plenty," Mattie joked and then corrected herself hastily. "At least I think I do?"

The youth nodded wisely. "Ay, you think you do. What you mean is we've passed each other in the close, danced together, even been to the same parties. But, just think, this is the first time we've ever really talked together."

Mattie smiled into his eyes, but behind the smile was a shy timidity. "I never thought about it," she lied.

"Well, for instance——" Colin toyed with his tumbler, "somehow or another I always thought you rather enjoyed a joke——?"

She was quick. "You mean—blue jokes?"

"Well, I mean, I didn't think you were—well—jane?"

"Neither I am." Mattie's denial was neither indignant nor provocative. But she stirred her spoon in her glass uneasily, and avoided his gaze. "Only you've got to draw the line somewhere. Beanie's one of those kind of fellows who goes over the score."

Colin looked across at the other table. He had sometimes wondered at the success of men like Beanie with women. He could never understand why girls were attracted to gigolo types. But most of them were. And, despite her protest, he sensed Mattie was, too. He wondered how much of her contempt was due to secret pique. Innocently daring he asked: "Did he go over the score with you?"

"No fear. He never got the chance." Her denial was too ready. It brought the ghost of a smile to his face. And she resented that too. Hurriedly she added, "No, but I'll tell you, Colin. Know what he had the cheek to say to me one night?"

The youth shook his head.

" 'I'll see you home, Mattie, if it's all right?' Now, what do you think, Colin, of a chap that would say that to a lassie? Was that not an insult?"

Suddenly, shrewdly, Colin realized the secret truth of Mattie's aversion. He also realized she did not understand it herself. But with misjudged humour he said, "Well, he wasn't going to waste anybody's time, was he?"

Mattie's plain face chilled. Poignantly direct she challenged: "How? D'you think it's a waste of time to see a lassie home and not—not?"

Colin looked away and felt guiltily uncomfortable. This was not his usual line of conversation. Sex and morals were things to joke about with other chaps, but never with women. And you certainly never admitted personal involvement. His standards, like those of his friends, amounted to a dedicated inhibition. His mother had taken care of that. Although he had shared a room all his life with sisters, a woman's body still retained its mystery. Jenny and Ella might strew the house with intimate garments and wash their hair in the sink but, ever since childhood, the mere discipline of a temporarily forbidden door or a backward turned chair had preserved their inviolate sanctities. It was a close-order drill that had built an innocence and continence into his make-up that was reflex and automatic. And now there were no halfway apologetics in his philosophy. Seduction was sin, and even its secret contemplation inexorable mental shame. This iron Calvinism was so inbred that puberty had been a lonely hell unredeemed by the involuntary nature of its erotic dreams and uncontrollable physical reaction. Memory and recurrence of them still had the power to fill him with disgust and personal repugnance. His great secret bewilderment was the failure of prayer to dam the torrent of youthful virility. It was one of the things he never quite forgave God.

"I never said it was a waste of time," he fenced haltingly. "What I mean is—if you are only after one thing you're as well being honest about it. Likely that's what Beanie meant? I mean, it saves everybody disappointment?"

"Is that how you look at it?"

"Aw, hey, Mattie," he squirmed irritably. "I wasn't talking about me. You started on about Beanie and I was only giving you my opinion. Sure you don't need anybody to tell you what he is? As far as I'm concerned any dame that encourages the likes of Beanie or Snakehips asks for all she gets."

"Meaning I encouraged him?"

"Och!" He pushed his chair back. "Come on—we'll get this rhumba?"

"No thanks—on you go." A half-smile covered her heart-sickness within. "I'd rather sit and smoke another fag."

Colin looked down at her, confused and half-angry. "You're not taking the needle are you?"

"Not at all!" Her disclaimer was too polite. "I just want to watch and rest the bones for a wee while."

Unconvinced, he studied her. Then, baffled, he swung and strode away. Her smile remained. She did not turn her head. Her stare was bright and dry. But as she withdrew the cheap cigarette packet from her handbag her fingers trembled.

Haig returned to the edge of the dance floor feeling both injured and guilty. McBride hailed him with an accusing: "Where the hell've you been? At the pub?"

"I'd've been as well there."

McBride chuckled. "Mattie no' playin'?"

"Jeez, are you another one?"

The return was so bitter, McBride's eyebrows jumped. "What's biting you?"

"Never mind."

McBride shrugged and returned his attention to the dance floor. Nothing ever destroyed his enjoyment of a Saturday night dance. It was all he lived for. As the band stopped and the floor cleared, most of the girls streaked unescorted to one side of the hall, their partners strolling back to form a complete masculine congregation on the other. Ebulliently McBride nodded towards the feminine mob. "Fancy the pair in the yellow?—they're always looking over here."

Colin followed his glance. "Are you seeing right?" he said briefly. "Want us taken up for baby-snatching?"

"D'you think so?"

"Sure—they're only about sixteen. Dunno what they're letting kids like that in here for at all."

"They don't look that young to me."

**"For God's sake, Jimmy!** That's why I'd rather not come to the Public at all. Nothing but a bunch of school-kids hanging about it now."

"Right enough." McBride was glad to be agreeable. "It was better two or three year back. Don't seem to be so many of the old crowd about——"

"Hey." Haig nudged him confidentially. "Pipe the argument."

A slow grin crinkled the other's chubby features. He stared across at the group by the buffet door with puckish interest.

"Huh," he divined. "Snakehips's pick-up's had her ice-cream and now she doesn't want to dance any more."

"Her mate's mad at her, too. Look at Ginger getting it off her chest!"

"Snakehips's not half stating his case. Jings, if he's spent any real money on that thing and now there's nothing doin' he'll cut her throat."

"And look at Beanie! Watch the hands going. Crikey, if you handcuffed Beanie he'd be struck dumb!"

"They've got her coaxed. She's going to go on the floor after all."

"Ay, but judging by her face I wouldn't take even money on Snakey seeing her home. Whatever's happened, he's rubbed her the wrong way."

"Game to split them now?" McBride rejoiced in such situations.

Colin looked at the band-number card. It proclaimed the dance a DOUBLE NOVELTY. The resentment stirred by Mattie Wilson had simmered into a craving for devilment. "Wait till they come round," he said. "You take Beanie, I'll cut in on Snakehips."

Round the floor bystanders of both sexes—the definition DOUBLE gave the girls equal opportunity to profit by the dance's NOVELTY tag—were stepping into the stream of dancers and exerting the privilege of stealing a partner. A NOVELTY dance was the opportunity for the shy and unconfident; it gave them scope to try out their nerve and skill, often almost apologetically. But it was also the dance for banditry and guerilla conquest. Colin waited until Snakehips and the black-haired girl glided within yards of him and then reached out and touched the tall, sinuous youth's shoulder.

Keeping his back turned Smith ignored the touch. It was a manoeuvre that sometimes discouraged raw or self-conscious interrupters. Colin was neither. Over the hunched shoulder he saw the girl lean away in an effort to release herself. Deliberately holding her fast, Snakehips danced on. Walking smoothly behind, Colin tapped again, but with a jab in his fingertips. "Right, Snakey," he said.

The lean fellow's quick glance of surprise was practised but fooled no one and he knew it. "Hullo, Colin," he said, obviously grudging the civility.

Without a word, Haig thrust his left arm between him and the girl and took her hand firmly. The push of his shoulder completed her separation from Smith.

She was a wonderful partner, perfect in every movement, instinctive and effortless in anticipation. They danced in silence until, abruptly, Colin asked, "Come here often?"

Equally cryptic she said, "No."

They covered half the length of the hall with a couple of reverse turns before he said, "Where d'you usually go?"

"Paisley Town Hall."

"Come from Paisley?"

"No."

"Where do you come from?"

"Burnford."

He stepped back from her and cocked his head. She had pale, boyish features and neat black eyebrows. Her straight jet hair was cut in a bob so close and smooth it seemed to have fitted round rather than grown on her well-shaped head. He had an impression of a white slender neck disappearing into a high-bodiced, simple red frock. "I don't know your face," he confessed.

"I've had it for years."

"Oh—wise girl!" and they both laughed.

"What's the attraction in Paisley?" he quizzed as the band resumed after the first of the two customary encores.

"My pal likes it there."

He looked to where the red-head was gliding along but talking animatedly in the arms of McBride. "Is she giving the home town a break tonight?"

"Oh, that's not my pal," the brunette followed his glance. "My regular chum couldn't manage to the dancing tonight and Lily asked me to come here with her."

"Funny I don't know you. What did you say your name was?"

"I didn't say."

They laughed again. But by the end of the encore he knew her name was Ann White. She and her friend were assistants in a multiple store. Lily knew Beanie and Snakehips and it was on the strength of that acquaintanceship the two had monopolized them.

"I'm not awfully struck on one chap hanging round me all night," she confessed casually. "I like to dance different fellows."

"Was that what you were arguing about?"

"You must've been watching?" her head tilted quickly.

"My mate drew my attention. We'd seen you in the buffet."

She nodded. "That one you cut in on thinks if he buys you a lemonade he's taken a lease of your life. I let him know different. I didn't ask him to take me into the buffet. I told him, when I come to the dancing I'm quite prepared to buy anything I want for myself. Don't need anybody's help."

"Independent, eh?"

"Why not?"

"Sure."

They danced on in pleasant silence. No one divided their partnership because Colin carefully steered their steps well wide of any possible rival. He saw Snakehips watching morosely from the fringe of the floor, but knew the tall fellow could not quite screw up his courage to defy the niceties of convention and cut back in again. As the music swelled into the last crescendoing bars marking the end of the number he asked, "I still can't get over never seeing you before—what school did you go to, Ann?"

"St. Michael's."

"Oh, ay."

She caught the control in his voice. Blue eyes cool and direct, she countered instantly. "Where did you go?" He told her. The music stopped and he smiled, "Thanks, Ann." She returned his smile. They both walked off the floor in opposite directions.

McBride was waiting for him. "Well, how d'you get on? Okay?"

"All right. Not a bad dancer."

Jimmy was enthusiastic. "The other one's okay, too. And can she come the patter! What d'you say we try to cut Beanie and Snake right out? For a laugh, eh?"

Colin looked across the ballroom to where, already, the two glamour boys had closed in on the girls again. "Not me," he said indifferently, "they're left-footers."

"No!"

"The wee one went to St. Michael's."

"Is that right? Jings, I can generally pick a tarrier a mile away. Still . . ." His nudge dared Colin. "No harm in seeing them up the road. I always say, once you're in the back of the close it's all one whether they're Hindoos——"

"Not for me." Haig's disdain was definite. "That's how you get landed, boy."

Behind them the band flowed into a slow-foxtrot. One by one, long-striding couples drifted out across the polished floor. The music was sentimental and cigarette smoke and perfume hung in the air like incense. Here and there a couple laughed into each other's eyes but mostly the dancers glided past seemingly oblivious of each other, solemnly happy in an individual ecstasy of rhythm for the enjoyment of which a partner was mechanically necessary but not romantically important. In like communion Colin looked round for a partner. As if she had willed it, he found himself looking across the hall into the pensive gaze of Mattie Wilson. He hesitated and then, with a mental shrug and without a word to McBride, strode towards her.

Mattie came the last three steps to meet him. Halfway round the floor and without looking at her face he said, abruptly, "Anybody seeing you home?"

"Not yet."

They rocked through a dreamy turn, floated diagonally across the main stream of dancers, went into a long, slow, perfectly balanced spin technically known as a "Belgian birl" before he added, "How about it then?"

"If you like," she said, equally off-handed.

Coming out of the spin they pulled off the floor in the corner nearest the exit. Passing, his glance rested on a solitary girl standing in the shadows. Even in the gloom the girl's hair shone like ebony and the oval of her face had a soft magnetism of ethereal mystery. Her blue eyes remained cool. She watched them separate to collect their coats from their different cloakrooms with knowledgeable but casual disinterest. Yet, suddenly, inexplicably, Colin found himself wishing it was her and not with Mattie Wilson he was going to walk home along the long lamplit streets.

## CHAPTER TWENTY-TWO

Scud Ralston drove like a lunatic. He always did. True or false, the legend that in his youth he had worked for Detroit bootleggers had to be maintained. To preserve his own composure Collie Haig asked the third man jammed with them in the lorry cab, "Where did Robby say this puffer's beached?"

Billy Frew clutched the side-door as they lurched round a bend. A square, fat little man, Billy at that moment would have given all the ships on the Clyde for one tipple of methylated spirit. Without taking his bloodshot eyes off the rocketing road he said, "Somewhere by Bowlin'—if we live to get there."

Delighted, Ralston leaned across the wheel to get a better look at Billy's distress. "Watch the bloody road," yelped Frew. "You bugger, you'll kill us all!"

Scud laughed louder and winked at Haig. "I know where it is.

I was down last night. You'll have one goddam job—she's lying right on her beam-ends."

"Robby said she was high and dry?"

"She's high enough—twenty yards from the water's edge; but as for dry—she's gunnel deep in mud."

"Then we'll need to see about dirty money." Frew took his eye off the road long enough to make his protest. "By the sound of it I don't think its a rigger's job at all anyway. What are we supposed to do?"

Collie looked back through the cab window. Three younger men hunkered down amid lifting gear piled on the lorry's open floorboards, their penetrating, glottal accents bawling in carefree ribald song. For them any expedition away from ordinary dock-yard routine was their nearest approach to a paid holiday.

"You heard what the gaffer said," he answered Frew. "She dragged her moorings in last week's gale and very nearly finished up on the Dumbarton Road. If we can unship the funnel and engines we'll maybe manage to haul her back into the water. Failing that she'll be a dead loss and they'll have to break her up."

"From what I saw," opined Ralston, "you'll have to break the tub up to get the goddam engine out. I'm telling you she's lying right on a mudflat!"

Without warning, he swung them into a full left-handed turn. Tyres screeched. Frew and Haig, slewing helplessly across the seat, almost tore his hands from the wheel. From their three mates outside a volley of obscenity exploded.

"Hell's bells!" cursed Frew, his left hand waving wildly for support, the other sandwiched uselessly against Collie. On the cab-window a fair-haired youth hammered and screamed with contorted face at the pitch of his voice. "You bastard, Scud, you nearly cowped the windlass on top of us!"

Ralston laughed at them all. Haig took a slow breath and said quietly, "You bugger, if you don't slow down I'll break your neck when we do stop."

"Oh yeah!" Lean-muscled and wiry, Ralston was still on the right side of forty. The grin on his angular face remained a friendly taunt.

"Ay but 'oh yeah'," Frew reacted almost hysterically. "And I'll give him a hand. You're a bloody menace!"

Their driver kept it good-humoured. Steering with one hand, he poked a cigarette into the corner of his lips and nail-flicked a match to flame. "You guys panic too easy," he puffed. "Gee, I remember coming down out of St. Catherine's one night with a waggon-load of harness bulls on my tail——"

"Bulls!" Frew snorted. "Don't give us that. The only bulls that ever tailed you were ones out the Glesca Cattle Market." Disinterested, he and Haig gave their attention to the scenery. They had left the Dumbarton and Balloch bound traffic stream and were heading down a narrow side road leading directly to the banks of the Clyde. Flat pasture fields, still sodden by the recent storm, lay on either side. At irregular intervals the long succession of thorn hedges and drystone dykes flashing past was broken by the appearance of one or two isolated cottages. Approaching the last of these hamlets, Collie was roused to see a few hundred yards beyond its street end the unmistakable hulk of a small, stranded collier. He had just got Ralston's nod of agreement when Frew, squirming and peering backwards at a squat white-washed gable-end, let out a hoarse grunt of real interest. "Hey, there's a wee boozer—what about it?"

Ralston looked at Haig hopefully. Collie shook his head. "We'll get the gear off first. We don't want Robby coming along and getting us parked at a pub."

"Aw, Robby'll no' be here till after dinner now," moaned Billy. "We'd be as well to nip in while we've got the chance."

"We'll get the job first," said Collie flatly. "I know who's neck Robby'd jump on if he got us a' sitting in a boozer."

The metalled road had deteriorated into an earthen track, and they were bumping across a field flooding had nearly reduced to marshland. Frew forgot his disappointment long enough to bleat, "For Jesus sake, Scud, don't run us into a bog—I canny swim."

"Don't worry," chuckled Ralston, "you wouldn't sink."

"How would I no' sink?"

"You're too well pickled in Red Biddy, bud; you'd float on top like a goddam oil-patch."

"Very funny. There's one thing anyway, wise guy."

"Yeah?"

"I'll no' float far on anything a bum Yankee give me to drink."

Haig and Ralston were still laughing when they jolted to a halt in the lee of the grounded ship. It was only a small coaster of about 500 tons, but in that odd landward setting of rough grass and soggy hillocks it towered like a leviathan. Half a dozen drenched and dismal cows grazing near by added the final incongruity.

"By God, it's been high water all right," marvelled Collie

noting the distance to the now placid river bank with curiosity. "It's maybe a good job there was nobody on her when she struck."

"How? Where were they?" asked Billy reprovingly.

"Where you'd've been on a dark night far from home," grinned Scud, opening his door, "up the road for a wet."

They all jumped out and cursed the moment they hit the grass. Water seeped round the welts of their footwear. Even Collie, the only one wearing a reasonably heavy pair of boots, knew he would have wet socks long before knocking-off time. The others, shod in typical shipyard labourer's subs, were sodden-footed before they started.

"Christ, Collie," one of the three young fellows complained, splashing around, "who the hell sent us here?—it's no' riggers they want, it's divers."

"Ay, and burners too," grumbled Billy, looking resentfully at the ship. "They'll need to strip shell-plates and frames before we can lift anything out. They might as well scrap the lot."

They walked round the wreck magnifying, as was their custom, the problems of their task. The younger men sided with Frew and concluded the ship a loss. Only Collie delayed his opinion until they had scrambled all over her. Finally he asked Ralston, "You're sure Robby had a good look at this?"

The driver shrugged, "We were on the road back last night from that job at Helensburgh and he just took a squint at it from the road-end there. He never got out of the lorry. But he says they're desperate to refloat her if they can."

Haig shook his head doubtfully. "It'll take more gear than we've brought. From what he said to me in the shop I thought we migh light her boiler and get a winch going. But we'll need to jack he up first. And that's going to take some doing."

The blond youth stamped his foot on the sodden turf. "Aw Collie, shores and jacks'll sink into this."

"No' if we've timber under them. That's only flood water o top." He pointed to the curve of the ship's bottom resting on th ground. "She's been lying there a week now and hasn't settled an Still, as you say, it'll be a job."

"I still think it'd be cheaper to buy a new boat," scoffed Bill "Must be the insurance folk that's trying to salvage it."

Haig grimaced contemptuously. "After brilliantly scrappin half the best shipyards on the Clyde, likely somebody no figures this country's gonny need all the boats she can get soo

I wouldn't be surprised if the like o' this is worth its weight in gold before you or I are much older."

"Ay, hey," agreed the smallest of the youths. "D'you see yon bloke Mussolini in the pictures this week? Oh, ye want to've see him! Talk about doin' the goose-step! He jumps off this platform like a loony and struts it out in front of this Tally regiment. Christ, the girl and I nearly slid below our seats laughing. Imagine you see auld Chamberlain doin' yon!"

"Ay, wi' his umbrella!" The other two young fellows started to mimic the dictator's prancings.

Frew, impatient and edgy, could contain himself no longer. "When are we goin' back up the road?" he blurted. "That wee shop'll be shut while we're a' standing here blethering."

"You got any money?" Scud asked pertinently.

"Certainly I've got money."

"Good enough. You'll be on the bell then." Ralston winked at Collie. Their fat little mate's panic grew as the other three gathered round with joyful anticipation. "Good auld Billy," they cheered. "Standing on his hands at last. Must've had a double up, eh? Gonny bring back a dozen wee dumps for the afternoon too, sure you are, Billy?"

"Hey, now, just a minute." Billy drew back indignantly, too agitated in his anxiety about the approach of closing time to appreciate their foolery. "Who said I was on the bell? What the hell d'you think I am—Carnegie?"

"Don't be a crapper now, Billy," goaded the blond young fellow slyly. "Don't go back on your word. You invited us all up to the boozer. You hear him, Collie?"

"Well, that's what I took out of it."

"Away to hell!" Without waiting to hear more, Billy's short legs galvanized into a near gallop as he set off across the flat in a fever of urgency. "Think I'm a Gilbert! Buy your ain bloody drinks."

Rejoicing in the success of their leg-pulling they watched his departure. "But we can't all go up at once," Collie reasoned. "It's not likely Robby'll show up now before dinner-time but there's always the chance. Some of us had better unload the lorry. Scud, how about you and Joe going now? Me and the other two can slip up after dinner—that's if Robby doesn't hang on all afternoon."

"Oh, you know Robby," Joe's blond quiff bounced beneath his up-thrust cap-peak in vehement derision. "He'll want a drink himself. No, on you go wi' Scud, Collie, the boys and I'll make a start on the lorry. We'd rather all go up together anyway."

Haig nodded. He accepted as reasonable that the younger men should prefer their own company. He had a personal moral scruple, too, about lending his presence to youthful drinking. Actually, except for his age and experience, he had no real authority to organize any of the squad's activities. Yet he enjoyed enough prestige to add warningly, "Okay, but mind—it's only a drink we're going for. When you do go don't turn it into a party."

"Want to know something?" the aggressive lift of Joe's chin was nullified by the affection in his regard. "You worry too much, Collie. You're worse'n Robby. At least he gets paid for worrying."

"That's right," chuckled his shortest companion. "And the laugh is, Robby's never on a job half the time—certainly never when the real graft's getting done."

"Sure—that's the way it always is," drawled Scud. "Same in the States, same here, same wherever you like to go—the guys who pull down real folding money only show up when the nigger work's over."

"Never take a tumble to that, Collie?" asked the third of the young fellows—a youth with shrewd eyes and perpetually hunched shoulders. "That's where Robby and all the boys above him, right up to the top, are smart. It's one of the tricks that put them there." He jerked a head towards the stranded ship. "Just watch—we'll do all the horsing here, hauling and pulling and up to the arse in muck—rigging up tackle and God knows what all. You'll just about go off your head, 'cos you're built that way, plotting sheer-leg angles and working out ways to get the job done right."

"Ay," agreed Joe, "there's a Collie in every squad. And we'll be lucky if we see Robby half-a-dozen times till this thing's back in the watter."

"And when we do see him," taunted the cunning youth, "he'll be wrapped in Company's oilskins and wearing rubber boots up to his big fat belly. He'll stand back and howl and bawl for about half-an-hour then nip away in the wee car again."

"And you know what'll happen when we're nearly finished," Joe cut in again. "He'll show up with two or three ya-ya blokes from the Head Office. And they'll walk round about in the fifty bob suits and their chase-me-Charlie hats lookin' helluva technical and bummin' their load and lookin' down their noses at r

'Get those ropes coiled, my man' they'll whine, and 'Can't you cover that windlass? Costs money, y'know!' Then they'll whip back into the cars again and scoot back to the city for a couple o' quick ones before they write reports and make speeches about how they handled that tricky salvage job down the river. . . . We'll still be splashin' about in the muck clearin' up!"

Haig laughed, "You've got it all weighed up, Joe?"

"Ay, bloody likely, Collie. And I'll tell you something else —if this war they're all talking about breaks out these are the buggers that'll all be officers or admirals or generals before the rest of the world even knows what army they're fighting for or why they're fighting. You can't beat these guys, they've got it to a fine art, so why moan when we've got a chance to knock them for an hour or two?"

"I'm not moaning," Collie said quickly. "When I've got anything to moan about I get it off my chest to the people concerned, not in the middle of a park where nobody but my mates and the seagulls hear me. If I hadn't been like that I wouldn't have been here today. Understand?"

"Aw, I'm not meaning anything personal, Collie," the young fellow hedged.

"No. You'd better not. 'Cos now I'll tell you something—I don't need you nor Scud nor any other wide men to tell me about the different impostors we carry on our backs. I was fightin'— and losin'—all these kinds of battles before you and Curly and Wee Nicky there were born. But that's no' the point. It's no' the matter of knockin' the firm for an hour or two, it's a matter of keeping ourselves in a job. I've had a bellyful of the Buroo in my time and I'm not risking any more just to keep you blokes company in a booze-up. Either we go for one drink and finish— or we don't go at all!"

Ralston blew his nose into the grass. "You can count me in on that," he said, wiping his hands down his hips. "Come on, Collie, if we don't get up there quick Frew'll be in below the table."

"He will like hell!" Joe gladly seized the excuse to break the tension. "If I know Billy he'll be still standing waiting on youse arriving to put one up for him—Billy never has the price o' a wine after Saturday."

They all laughed except Haig. Little Nicky answered the challenge still dour on his ruddy, weather-beaten features. "On ye go, Collie," he placated. "When it's our turn one'll do us, too. That's a promise."

"All right. Don't forget you said it."

But when he and Ralston had gone twenty yards Joe could not resist calling after them, "Ay but I still say it—ye auld bugger, ye're worse than Robby!"

Collie halted in his stride. Then his glance caught Ralston's eye. They laughed together. And without looking back continued plodding towards the little white-washed gable at the road-end.

## CHAPTER TWENTY-THREE

Laughing and jostling their way down the terracing they argued about the best transport home. The argument was traditional tail-piece to their attendance at Ibrox. As always, it was settled by whim. McBride insisted: "We'll run for a car—jeez, they're lined up in the Paisley Road waitin' on us."

"No, we'd be as quick walking it," claimed Colin. "If one jumps the points somewhere you're stuck in Govan for an hour."

Watson settled it by turning towards the nearest Subway queue. Looking down at his feet, he said, "These new pointers are killing me—I'm shufflin' along in this lot to give my dogs a rest."

The other three let out a howl of derision but stayed with him. Edging towards the underground entrance in ten-yard spurts, they joined in the babble of football talk of fellow fans around them. The inevitable exchanges between a typical dwarf-sized Glasgow wit and the huge helmeted police shepherding the queue provided characteristic colour. Throughout their ten-minute progress a blind accordion player retailed a background of lively folk music whose rustic origin struck a strong but illogical chord of sentiment in their breasts. The musician's partner passed along, thrusting a collection cap under everybody's nose in a business-like fashion chanting acknowledgement of their equally automatic contributions with a brisk staccato, "Thanks, Mac," that established the proper democratic dignity of Glasgow's busking.

Getting their tickets and bursting through the turnstile they completed the descent to the underground platform with a wild drumbeat of flying feet that skimmed the iron-shod stairway three and four steps at a time. Like their descent from the Ibrox terracing, their passage was completed through a running commentary of crude threats and vivid vilification from the older, slower men they barged and swept aside in their hurry.

Halfway down McBride bumped into a stout, grey-moustached man and sent him stumbling. Only a clutch at the handrail and the swift support of those around kept the man from falling. But he was obviously the victim of middle-age's susceptibility to shock. And showed it.

"You stupid young bastard!" was the mildest of the instant barrage of protests that followed them. "Put yer foot in that fair-haired one!" was another plea.

They kept on running. "Christ, you might've watched," panted Watson.

"I didnae mean it!" McBride pled, but chuckling, unable to visualize his victim's broken night's sleep and the elderly wife's hours of anxiety and toilsome effort at massaging pain out of ageing and unresilient back muscles. "Hell, he stepped right in front of me and I only touched'm wi' my shoulder."

"We'd better get lost or that mob'll murder us anyway," Campbell, the fourth of them, declared. "You always do the stupid things, McBride."

They reached the bottom of the stairway still wrangling and laughing. The long platform between the twin tracks was crowded. At two-minute intervals blasts of cold air whistling through the tunnels and a diabolic humming crescendo heralded the arrival of the stubby squat trains shuttling the football crowds around half the city's area. They were just in time to crowd their way into a departing carriage before the automatic gates clanged shut. They rode the first stage on the observation platform, but at the next station they surged up the passage between the fore and aft seats as passengers left and fresh arrivals pushed their way aboard.

As usual McBride made the move in an impetus of high-spirited energy. Talking and gesticulating about the game, he ignored the jolt of the train gathering way and allowed himself to cannon into Colin's back. In an effort to recover his balance Colin grabbed at a strap and missed. To the great joy of McBride, Watson and Campbell, he half-sprawled into the lap of a seated girl in a green coat. McBride instantly guffawed, "Hold on to your coat, Sweetheart, he's a Rangers' supporter!"

"Ay, green sends him daft," abetted Campbell.

Most onlookers, irrespective of prejudice, smiled. Side issues of Green and Blue rivalry were accepted with surface tolerance. And because it was always safer. But here and there a face frowned. Colin himself felt anger and guilt at the clumsiness of the incident.

He pushed himself free of a tangle of brown paper parcels with mumbled embarrassment. It helped little to find his own red face within inches of Ann White's.

"Oh, hullo," he stuttered. "I didn't notice it was you."

"Would it have made any difference?" she asked icily.

"No, but I'm really sorry," he apologized desperately. "What I mean is—I really am sorry."

"It's quite all right."

"Are your parcels all right?" Honestly concerned, he hurriedly moulded the dents out of a wrapped shoe-box. "I hope I haven't broken anything?"

The sandwiching crowd in the passage kept him swaying above her. There was no room to assess damage to the parcels. But the earnest anxiety in his face and voice touched and soothed her. Swiftly, shyly, she smiled, "Don't worry yourself—there's nothing really breakable."

He became aware of his companions' unending flow of laboured jokes. "Shut up," he spat over his shoulder with a force that jerked them silent. "That's the second time you've done that the day, McBride. The next time I'll chin you."

"Oho!" drawled Campbell, sarcastically humorous.

"I'll chin you, too." And suddenly they realized he was in earnest. "Now, lay off."

"Have a heart. We're only jokin', Colin," McBride temporized. "No need to lose the head. I mean, I didn't mean to bump you."

Haig's anger died as swiftly as it flared. "Okay, but you might've made me hurt this lassie."

McBride recognized Ann for the first time. Instantly his ebullience exploded disarmingly. "Hullo, china," he hailed with all the good-nature typical of him. "I didn't spot you there. Jings, if it wasnae for the colour o' your coat you're lookin' smashin'. Been up shop-liftin', eh?"

In spite of herself, Ann smiled and everyone around smiled, too. The car growled importantly into a stop, and half a dozen rose to leave. Smoothly McBride slipped into the vacated seat beside her. "Haven't seen you at the Public since yon night," he chattered on. "Don't tell me you've chucked the dancin'? How's you and Snakehips gettin' on?"

"Snakehips?"

"Ah, now, that'll do—don't kid you don't know him. You and him were dead thick that night."

"You mean—the tall, skinny fellow?"

Her indignation was swamped in the stir of a general exodus as they pulled into Burnford. Least interested in her reaction was McBride and the other two, who instantly propelled themselves with vigour and impatience towards the head of the exiting queue. Haig, hesitant and still guilty over his stumble, lagged apologetically.

"You manage these parcels?"

"Fine. I'll manage."

Having satisfied his conscience with the gesture he yearned to hurry on. But the press of people closed in on them at the stairway and hemmed him. Automatically he put an arm round her to fend off the bull-rush of just another irresponsible like McBride.

"Who are you shovin'?" the impatient fellow called over his shoulder.

"I'm shovin' you," Colin reacted instantly. "You nearly knocked this lassie down!"

"Sorry, hen ... but you watch yourself, Mac."

"Who? Me! Come back here I'll shove your face in."

The solid confidence of the challenge convinced the fellow that speed was still the better part of valour. He kept on going.

"Right enough, some of them would walk over the top of you," Ann commented with apparent unconcern. But she was pleased. And, somehow, Colin knew it. Reaching the long street-level tunnel the crowd thinned and they walked side by side.

"I shouldn't be finished yet," she explained, "but the manager asked me to leave these in our Burnford branch. He sometimes does that and it always lets me home a wee bit early. That's the worst of being up in the City shop, you're often late."

"D'you like in a shop?"

"Yes," she spoke with a cool, quiet enthusiasm he found attractive. "It's cheerful—and I like serving people. I've always worked in shops."

On the pavement they halted. Colin said, jokingly, "I'll need to look in the first time I'm up the City to see if you've any bargains."

"So you should," she agreed, with a twinkle that intrigued him. Ignoring the impatient waves of McBride and the others waiting along the street, he said, "That's a promise. What counter do you serve?"

Her smile broadened. "Ladies Lingerie."

Her French pronunciation only half puzzled him. "Ladies what?" he frowned.

Casting a mischievous look around at the jostling passers-by she leaned a little forward and breathed with exaggerated mouth movement: "Underwear!"

"Oh, jings!" He spun a complete circle in real confusion. Just as quickly their laughter died. To cover the silent moment she glanced at her wrist-watch, saying, "I'll need to away or I'll not get these in before the shop shuts."

He nodded. As she was moving away an inexplicable impulse made him exclaim, "Oh—Ann!"

She paused, and read his intention before he spoke. Her glance was both a dare and a warning.

"Fancy going to Barrowlands dancing tonight?"

Her hesitation was without guile. He saw the reflection of his own deepest prejudice in her appraisal. And as recklessly as he had done, she thrust it aside. "I wouldn't mind."

"Meet you here at half-seven?"

Her nod was unexpectedly shy. Fearful of something in each other's eyes, they turned and walked quickly in opposite directions. Neither looked back. And in his turmoil Colin did not miss the absence of his friends who, weary of waiting, had disappeared ahead.

His preoccupation lasted through tea-time. Twice his father asked about the game without getting an answer. The last time Collie growled, "I'm beginning to wonder if you were at the match at all! I'm saying, how did Walker play?"

Colin jerked out of his reverie. "Oh, great stuff, faither. Lovely ball player. If Hearts had another one like him they'd've beat the Rangers."

"I said he was a good yin the first time I saw him," Collie nodded, with the satisfaction of a man vindicated before hosts of critics. "He's not got Big Bob McPhail's drive but he'll go far enough."

"He'll go farther than you anyway," said Julia, fussing with the teapot. "You're getting that lazy you'll not even change yourself nowadays to go and see a match."

"It's old age creeping on," declared Jenny. "Mind, Mother, when wild horses wouldn't have held him back from Ibrox on a Saturday?"

"Ay, and it took the wilder ones to drag him home again after it."

"Och, it's just I wasn't in the mood today." Collie's resentment at the age inference brought a concerted laughing jeer from his family. He smiled himself. "Anyhow," he said, "if youse were anything like the thing you'd club together and buy me a season ticket for the stand. It's this hanging about on the terracing my legs'll not stand up to nowadays."

"God help ye," Julia sympathized drily. "We'll buy you a wheelchair as well then you'll no' even have to walk to the Subway."

"Yes, Daddy," chuckled Jenny, "and we'll all take Saturday about pushing you up the Broomloan Road."

"Maybe that," sniffed Collie nettled, "but I was never that tired when I was a young fellow that I chucked playing the game because I couldn't be bothered training."

"That's not true," Colin said quickly. "I packed up football because I knew I wasn't good enough. Anybody that's still playing juvenile at my age has reached their limit."

"Great Scot!" Collie spun exasperatedly in his chair. "You got the offer to go to three or four junior teams and wouldn't go!"

"Ach, d'you think I'm a head case?" his son waved downward derisively. "Go and get kicked up and down a park every Saturday for a half-a-crown and a hot-pie? Nutt likely! I'd rather be at the dancing."

"You mind how you're waving that jam over my white table-cloth." Cunningly Julie broke up discussion on a sore subject. "Ella'll be in in a wee while and I don't want it all marked. You know how she'll just look down her nose at the least spot."

Jenny and Colin exchanged amused glances. The monthly week-end homecoming of their young sister was now the highlight of their mother's calendar. Always houseproud she excelled herself on these red-letter Saturdays. The whole tiny place sparkled with her exertions. Although she seldom spoke other than in droll off-taking fashion of Ella's professional status and sharpening standards, they knew that pride in her youngest daughter was an emotion special and beyond words. It was not something that could be listed in a league of family merit. Like her separate love for each it was a sacred thing, not for boasting, and could only be expressed contrarily.

"It's a great carry on when the nurse comes home," Jenny said airily. "How is it, Julia, you don't put out white table-cloths for us? Are we not worth the fatted calf?"

"We don't have the glamour," Colin sighed to the ceiling. "It's the uniform that does it."

"If this bloke Hitler carries on the way he's goin' you might get a uniform soon enough," said Julia. "And not so much of the 'Julia' from you—I'm still your mother, don't forget."

"Oho?" Colin rocked his shoulders tightly in pantomime swagger of a Glasgow tough. "Right on her tottie tonight."

"I'm telling you," Jenny nodded.

"I'll 'tottie' you!" threatened Julia. "Come on, are you wanting another bit ham or black pudding before I put the pan away?"

"Trying to butter us up now," Colin winked at his sister; "this is so's we'll not say anything when she whips out the chicken and gammon for her wee ewe lamb."

"Of course," Jenny nodded. "Anything does for us—we only live here."

"What do you mean—anything does? Sure you've had a lovely tea—ham and black pudding and Waddell's best pork sausages! What more do you want?" Although she knew they were only teasing, Julia could not endure reflection on her catering. The years of bread-line budgeting had left her oddly sensitive on the subject. The unstinted furnishing of her table was a fetish. Frugal in appetite herself, she delighted in providing a board kings might envy. She interpreted as personal slight the least hint that anyone was rising from her table dissatisfied. "By jing," she lectured her grinning son and daughter, "I hope none of the two of you ever sit down to anything worse! The very best sausages! And the ham!—Have you any idea how much it was?"

"Ah, don't give us that stuff," provoked Colin in mock disbelief. "The old frozen meat racket!" Because he knew it infuriated her he reached across to the heaped cake plates and stuffed a cookie whole into his mouth. With bulging jaws he appealed to Jenny: "See—plain tea-bread for us, the workers. But when Florence Nightingale arrives—oho!—out will come the meringues and cream cookies."

"You better believe it," Jenny agreed solemnly.

"You lying devil!" Julia's good nature surfaced in a smile. "How much more do you want? There's a whole plate of fruit-cakes not touched. And there's shortbread. And——"

"I wish you'd all shut up a minute," said Collie testily. Throughout the meal he had kept the radio switched on and now, as the sports results were being read, he rose and turned it louder. With head cocked and attention concentrated he let the by-play of banter surge round while he leaned an elbow on the dresser. As the day's football scores came booming through he nodded in confirmatory satisfaction at the Rangers victory announcement. Next moment he looked sharply across at his son with an expression of equal delight. "Hear that, Colin—Celts beat 2-1!"

Colin's face lit with similar exultation. "2-1? At home, too! The stuff to give them!"

"That'll shake the Vatican." Collie recrossed to his chair. "I wish it had been 10-1."

"Is that the Celtic beat?" Julia reflected her men's pleasure.

"Wait till I get into the hosiery on Monday," Jenny rubbed her hands in glee. "I'll not miss thon Katie Boyle and Nora Shevlin—they've got plenty to say when Rangers lose."

"There's Ella now!" Julia watched the kitchen door. It flung wide and Ella, not unconscious of the dramatic effect her billowing blue and white nurse's coif and cape achieved in humble kitchen frame, paused in a moment of all-round greeting.

"Home again," Julia smiled contentedly.

From his fireside seat Collie camouflaged emotion with a nodded, "You're back, lass." Jenny and Colin's "Hullo" was deliberately restrained.

But Ella was not fooled. With the new and generous effervescence that contact with a less insular world was nurturing, she swooped across the kitchen, cape streaming and headdress fluttering, and threw her arms around Julia. "Oh, it's nice to see you again, Mother," she hugged. "How are you getting on? Are you looking after yourself?"

"I'm all right. How about yourself?" Julia's heart was so full she could hardly speak. Sentimental expression was completely foreign to her nature. She just did not know how to respond to it. Yet she was so happy she thought she was going to choke.

With another wise quick hug of understanding the girl turned to her father. He was sitting petrified. Like his wife he viewed such exhibitionism as Anglican and unmanning. Horror seized him as Ella flung her arms around his neck and laid a wonderfully soft cheek against his and almost crooned, "And how's my dear old daddy getting on? Oh, but it's wonderful to see you again!"

Collie cleared his throat hurriedly. "Ay, lass; ay, ay," he growled. "Did ye come in the train?" He was vividly conscious of the rest of the family witnessing this almost indecent exposure of feeling. Yet, in the midst of his embarrassment, he suddenly experienced an uplift of spirit. He felt like a man who has unexpectedly recovered a treasure long lost but always within hand reach. In a flash he remembered all their babyhood days

when he had nursed each of them on his knee. He remembered
how the firelight had played on their trusting faces as he told
them the age-old stories of childhood. With a strange ache he
realized how the years had overlain the memory of their hero-
worship of him. And suddenly, he felt both humble and proud.

With inspired tact Colin bridged the moment. Appealing to
Jenny in martyred tones, he said: "Well, that's the ba' burst now
all right. You and I'll be lucky if we get the tail-end of a haddie
for supper the night!"

Jenny responded instantly. "You're telling me! I don't think
I'll bother coming home tonight. I think I'll just stay the week-
end at my Auntie Mary's—at least, I'll be sure of a visitor's share
there."

As her brother sauntered out of the room, Ella's glance darted
around questioningly. "Och, these idiots say I plank all the
sniceters for you coming home," Julia derided apologetically.
"They say I starve them for your benefit."

Laughing gaily, her youngest daughter tossed her coifs and
cape across the bed. Divested of official trapping the simplicity of
white blouse and blue skirt made her look even more youthful.
"That's one thing, Mother," she praised. "No one will ever say
you starved us. I was just saying to some of the girls the other
night I've gone oftener to bed hungry in the hospitals than ever
I did at home. How did you manage it, Mother?"

Her father glanced round. "The same as she managed a lot of
things, Ella—by thinking on everybody but herself."

The young nurse nodded knowingly. She surveyed both her
parents with grave affection. Suddenly her hand shot out and
she seized Jenny's wrist. "No!" she exclaimed. "And you never
told me?"

Proud and pleased, Jenny let the ring sparkling on her engage-
ment finger be examined.

"Oh, but it's lovely!" Accusingly, Ella looked at her mother.
"And you never said a word in your letters?"

Julia's head shook in disavowal of fault. "I could hardly tell
you what I didn't know? She only came with it last night."

"Can I try it on?" Gurgling in ecstasy Ella flourished her hand
at arm's length in rapturous admiration. "And when's the
wedding?"

While they were discussing the ring and its number of stones
Colin drifted back and forth from the room to the kitchen,
washing and sprucing himself. As he shrugged on a trim-belted

raincoat and adjusted his tie for the last time Jenny looked up knowingly. "We're very pernicketty tonight, surely? A heavy date?"

"Don't be daft!" He smiled in contemptuous scorn. "D'you think my head's as soft as Ian Angus's?"

"Oh, it's soft all right," Ella lifted her chin with roguish insight. "The tougher they are the harder they fall." Even as she mocked him her sisterly scrutiny took pride in the masculine and modestly handsome picture he presented. She felt quiet gratitude that none of her family were people she need ever be ashamed of. "Are you not putting on a hat?" she asked inquisitively.

"He never wears a hat," Julia explained.

Frisking his father's bald patch in the passing, Colin grinned, "You only wear a lid when you've a fine head of skin."

"I'll skin you!" Collie growled.

"Are you going to the dancing?" Julia called as, after a couple of playful boxing feints at his sisters, her son waved back from the lobby.

"Might," he shrugged. "Might take a run out to the Barrow-lands. Be seeing you."

"Ta-ta. Don't be late."

"Bring in a fitba' paper," his father called after him.

"Is he going with a girl?" Ella asked, as the door slammed.

Jenny looked doubtful. "I don't think so. I think Colin has a different one every week. Is that not right, Mother?"

"Don't ask me!" Julia spoke from a cloud of steam as she poured a kettle of boiling water into the basin in the sink for the inevitable washing-up. "Sure I never know what any of you are doing nowadays."

Collie looked up from his book. "Bar me," he said firmly.

The three women laughed together.


# CHAPTER TWENTY-FOUR

PUTTING her basin, chamois cloth and drying duster conveniently on the sink draining-board, Julia pushed up the kitchen window. It was a grey day and would rain soon but the soot specks on the glass had annoyed her all morning. Of late the men scolded her when they learned she had washed the windows herself, but even if she could no longer deny that increasing weight reduced her agility she would never admit that their vigorous performance could match the crystal-clear perfection of her own efforts.

"You don't dry them right," she complained. "You're always in such a hurry to get by you'll not take time to polish them off with the duster. I'd far rather do them myself than be annoyed lookin' at a lot of streaky marks for the rest of the week."

"That's pure swank." Colin always accompanied the accusation by poking his admonishing finger under her nose. "You just won't admit anybody can wash windows as good as you."

And when she slapped her son's wrist down his father would agree. "That's a woman all over, Colin. Some day she'll maybe learn, better a black streak on the windy than a red streak on the pavement."

"Don't you be so cheerful!" she would shudder. "I've washed my own windows all my life."

What she did not tell them was that she really enjoyed sitting out on the sill. Although she could hardly climb a chair without feeling dizzy, sitting backwards on a narrow ledge with a sixty-foot fall beneath her, and with only the nominal support of a window sash clamped across her thighs, gave her all the confidence of a steeplejack. In a way it was like borrowing a privilege of God. Isolated high above the street she captured a strange sense of tranquillity, even of omnipotence. From beyond the window pane her familiar kitchen acquired its true diminutive proportions. Always, with a never-failing pang of discovery, she realized how tiny, dim and box-like her domain really was. Looking in, with typical wry humour, she would mentally observe: "Just like a rabbit-hutch—I've seen bigger cages in a zoo."

Yet these days she also took pride in her oblique inventory of household treasures. For long moments she sat itemizing in quiet love fulfilments that had overtaken her almost unaware. Looking through the newly-polished glass, the patterns and colours on the big carpet that now covered most of the floor regained the glamour and luxury that had caught Jenny's and her own admiring notice when they were first attracted to it spread under the display lights of the city showroom. Although the shadows in a tenement apartment did nothing to point it so cunningly she could still hear Jenny's ecstatic, "Mother! That would just set your kitchen off!"

At first she had resisted the eager tug on her arm. Too many Dole years of poverty still left a curb on her impulses. But young Jenny, girded by prosperous marriage, was gaily outgrowing skeleton life. Determinedly, she had pulled Julia closer to the big store's window.

"I like the crimson," she enthused, "it's bright and warm and would cheer your whole place up, Mother. And those daffodil whirligigs round the border would just go with your new fireplace. Can you not just see it?"

"I can see it all right," Julia had admitted drolly. "What I canny see is me payin' that price for a kitchen carpet."

"Don't be silly, Mother—it's a dead bargain! Four pounds ten! And it would cover your whole floor!"

They had both studied the sales card shriek: SLASHED FROM £7! WONDERFUL VALUE!

"You'll certainly not get a carpet like that anywhere else in town. I can assure you of that!" Jenny had insisted. Since courtship and marriage her speech had aspired to refinement. The result irked the inverted snobberies of class-conscious friends and undeniably aped the hybrids beloved of Glasgow's tame satirists of radio, but in its strivings it reflected a brave and simple desire to be worthy of her husband's draughtsman status. "Oh, I really wish you would buy it, Mother—it would *transform* your living-room."

"Living-room!" Julia's head had wagged wonderingly as she remembered the iron sink and the coal in the dresser-bunker. "That's a new one on me." She chuckled on: "What I'm thinkin' about is me running all day wi' a shovel in my hand brushing crumbs off a fancy carpet. You forget your maw hasn't got a wee semi-detached bungalow out in Mosspark yet."

Jenny had given her arm a shake. "Don't be silly, Mother. A carpet's not any harder to keep clean than waxcloth—when I think of us all hopping over spread newspapers every time our floor was washed. . . !" Words had failed Jenny at the familiar memory. She went on firmly, "Anyhow, you've got to move with the times. I'll tell you what, Mother—you buy the carpet and I'll treat you to that little carpet-sweeper in the corner. Now, is that fair enough?"

Sitting on the window-sill with a steadying hand tucked under the lowered sash and the cries of the children drifting up from the street beneath, Julia could still vividly recall that shopping moment's pulse of emotion. It was not acquisitiveness for a free thirty shillings' worth of technical gadgetry that had stirred her. But as the shopping crowds surged past and her daughter inexorably propelled her through the portals of the glittering shop the lump in her throat was occasioned by more than pride and gratitude. It was inspired by the sudden quiet realization that the family Collie and she had raised were all good people.

Squeezing the wet cloth in the basin she leisurely washed all the glass before her. Shaking out her duster she dried the pane before pushing the lower sash up and pulling the upper one down. In the intervals of wetting and rinsing her chamois leather she reviewed the panorama below with critical interest. The coalman's lorry was making its slow progress down the middle of the street. Leading his big brown horse and shouting, the man hopefully turned his black face up in her direction. She looked at the square price-board with its chalked announcement sticking up from the end of the cart.

"Three shillings a bag!" she called down. "That's an awful price! Is that the cheapest you've got?"

"Aw but it's good coal, Mrs. Haig," he bawled up. "The best brown ash. Burns away to nothing."

She frowned and swiftly considered the inconvenience of scrambling in and out the window to open the door for him. "Och no, Donald," she decided. "I've a good rough bunker. If you're round the morrow I'll get two bags."

"Oh, I might no' be round tomorrow," he warned.

"Ah, well," she said, dryly-sweet, "in that case I'll get them off somebody else."

Defeated, he tugged the old horse's bridle and plodded on, baying his melancholy single-vowel sales-cry which sounded like a deep long-drawn moan of pain but which all his customers recognized as the name of his wares.

Glancing casually from side to side she continued her inventory of street activities. The little hardware shop at the opposite corner was getting its sign repainted at last—it must be thirty years since its faded gold-leaf lettering was touched up. And the MacIntoshes in the low door directly opposite were white-washing their ceiling—she'd always wondered what kind of house the MacIntoshes had and now, with the window curtains down, she could see it was just bare enough. Of course they could have shifted most of the furniture into the room for the cleaning but, even so, the wallpaper looked pretty shabby. Maybe it was just the way she was looking down on it. . . . And there's big Fairy Feet and his mate making their rounds. That seems a new young fellow Fairy has with him—ah, the big fellow's getting old too! Must be near retiring age, the Fairy? Still, when all's said and done, there's worse jobs than a policeman—paid for walking round about most of the time. . . .

The acrobatics of children playing on the kerb took her eye off the constables passing from sight immediately beneath her. Her face puckered in disapproval as two girl toddlers, smudged faces grubby and sticky and their uncombed tangles of hair likely-looking nests for lice, scampered into the road after a bouncing ball. My God, they'll get killed! There's that many of these motors on the streets now a wean hasn't a chance. And their lazy bitches of mothers'll be standing round the backcourt blethering away without a care in the world. I know what I'd do with some of these young women nowadays. . . .

Her reveries were broken by a subconscious distraction. She listened. Muffled by the window the sound repeated itself. Huh! Sounds like my door right enough. . . . She looked along the almost deserted street. Even the police had vanished. The knocking drummed again, insistent. . . . Funny, I never noticed any of our ones coming up the road. By jings, if I've to scramble in this window for a hawker. . . .

But now there was no denying the determination of the summons. As she pushed the sash up off her knees the rapping on the door beat loud and urgently through the house. "All right, all right," she answered irritably, although the caller on the stair landing would not hear her. "Take your time, I'm coming."

Sighing heavily she levered herself in on to the floor. Her annoyance swelled as the tattoo repeated itself yet again. Muttering exasperations, she hurried to the lobby pausing only to wipe her damp hands on her apron before turning the handle and swinging the outside door wide. Sight of the blue uniforms stopped not only her protest, it stopped a heartbeat.

"Ay?" she faintly squeezed. It did not sound nor feel like her own voice.

Big Fairy Feet and his mate seemed to fill most of the landing. Fairy Feet himself hesitated. Until this moment she had never looked closely at him but now she saw that either his face was different or her previous impressions had never been exact. It was not quite the mask of a monster. It was really only that of a tired and ageing big man. By comparison, the solemn, fresh-faced young constable with him was only a boy in uniform.

"Is this where Colin Haig lives?" Fairy Feet asked quietly.

"Ay."

From habit she held the door half-open by its edge. Fairy Feet never took his washed-blue eyes off her. "Are you Mrs. Haig?"

"Ay."

Suddenly something would not let her ask any questions. She just watched the big policeman with a queer, numb terror.

"Could we come in a minute?"

His civility paralysed her. She could not speak. She thought she inclined her head. She did not even remember walking the half dozen steps back into the kitchen. She only knew she was there—waiting—and Fairy Feet, tremendous by size and implication, was there with her. She believed the young constable followed them but that did not register. She had a vague memory of Fairy Feet asking her if she was in the house alone. When she nodded she thought he glanced at his mate, but that was another thing she could not clearly remember. The one vivid thing was Fairy Feet's watchful gaze as he said, "I'm sorry to bring you bad news, Mrs. Haig, but there's been a bit of an accident."

"Oh, no!"

She was sure it was someone else whispered the exclamation. Her brain was engaged with the picture of Colin going out that morning and putting his head back round the door to shout, "And mind, Maw—have my suit laid out for I'll be in a hurry tonight. And if my shirt's no' well ironed I'll be lookin' for other digs."

"Good enough," she had cried, "the sooner the better. Just you see how long a strange landlady would put up wi' you and your wants."

And now. . . .

"Is it bad?" she heard herself ask.

"Never you worry about that," Fairy Feet said illogically but kindly. "Just you sit down a minute."

"Is it bad?" she repeated, anguish resisting his gentle effort to seat her in the big chair.

His eyes were stolidly calm. "I doubt it is, Mrs. Haig."

"My God! My boy!"

Power drained then from her limbs and she was sitting in the chair. She did not see the frown cross Fairy Feet's face. But after an age she became aware of his stooped solicitude. She had to force herself to understand his words. "This is an elderly chap, Mrs. Haig. Is your man's name not Colin?"

"Collie!"

"Is he a rigger?"

And then, remarkably, her brain was very clear. She saw the

young policeman hovering with Mrs. Wilson in the background. Fairy Feet was pressing a glass of water into her hand.

"Where have they taken him?" she asked harshly.

"The Southern General."

Without another word she rose and plucked her coat from its hook. Mrs. Wilson said, "I'll come with you, Mrs. Haig; we'll get a car at the foot of the street."

"You're sure you'll be all right?" Fairy Feet asked.

"Will anybody have told my boy?"

"Where does your son work?"

"He's a plater in Burnford's," Mrs. Wilson said.

"We'll get word to him."

Dry-eyed, Julia looked at Fairy Feet. He was watching her with the cool, steady sympathy of experience. "I'll be all right," she said firmly. And then added with a calmness that won his silent admiration, "And thank you—you've done all you could. . . ."

Going down the stairs she startled Mrs. Wilson even more by remarking in a casual but faraway voice, "Right enough—the police get some rotten jobs."


# CHAPTER TWENTY-FIVE

The undertaker assured Colin it was a genuine oak coffin. Colin knew it was not. But no one is ever in the mood to argue with undertakers. The main thing was that it was decently brown and polished and had brass handles that glittered as it lay on the room table. It had tassels too and a little shield-shaped name-plate on its lid which gave Collie's age.

"Your father'll be insured?" the undertaker asked. He was a fat, healthy little man with sharp eyes and a repertoire of solicitude that fooled no one but was accepted as part of his service. "Yes, yes—about forty pounds," he drooled knowledgeably as Colin hazarded a brain-weary estimation of the life-long weekly pennies' total his mother contributed to three frayed account books; the covers of the books carried pictures of office buildings as imposing as those of Burnford Shipyard. When he was little Colin used to marvel that such grand insurance companies could be bothered with his mother's coppers. His father's funeral helped to educate him in the realities of pennies by the million.

"Now don't you worry," the undertaker finally assured him, "I'll take care of everything; it'll all be done just the way your

mother will want it. As I always say, son—in cases like this—
there's no sense in going in for an expensive ebony casket. It's
not a matter of being disrespectful to the departed. Don't think
that. Don't you let that worry you at all. But you see, son, we
must think on the living—we must try and leave your mother with
a pound or two to tide her over her wee bad spell. You understand
that?"

Colin only understood he wished the man would stop clapping
him unctuously on the shoulder. The economics of death did not
interest him at all. He was still too stunned by the finality of
intimate tragedy to worry about anything else. Floating through
everything he kept seeing his mother's face of grief. Dully he said
to the little man, "Just you tell me what to do. And don't worry
—everything'll be paid for."

"I know, oh I know that fine. Now, let me see, first we'll have
to go the Registrars—to get the certificates, like. And then—
how many cars d'you think you'll need. . . ?"

His bill eventually came to thirty-eight pounds. But, as Collie
himself would have said, as a funeral it was a great success. Next-
door neighbours with Samaritan authority spirited away Julia's
bulkiest furniture and substituted their own plush and horse-
hair-filled chairs to line the room walls. They knew exactly the
decencies that death demanded and ensured to the limit of their
resources that they were not lacking. As the Haigs and their kin
gathered, some singly and some in family groups, every curtain
in the building was drawn and no children played on the stairway.
And no other door in the close opened or slammed until the
hearse was gone.

Colin greeted the arriving mourners in the little lobby. Dressed
in his best blue suit and white shirt, only his black tie and the
solemnity of his features distinguished his regalia from that for
a dance. And devilishly, sacrilegiously, a tick in his brain registered the fact. Desperately he put the thought from him. . . .

As he opened the door to each apologetic, almost furtive knock,
young relatives avoided his glance with a shame-faced silent nod
and squeezed their way timidly into the kitchen. The older
generations stopped and looked hard into his face whispering
anxiously: "How's your mother?"

Because he could not really guess he gave stock answers to that
one. Since the moment the police had called him from the yard
he could not tell how he himself felt. There had been the confused drama of the dash to the hospital. Then there had been

the emotion-blurred return home with all his energies striving to find the key to comfort his mother. That had been a hopeless task because both of them knew there was no key. Words were only gibberish before the memory of his father's dead face. And in the stunned silence of her grief his mother showed that, too.

Later there had been Jenny's semi-hysterical arrival, the more frightening because she was pregnant. There had been a procession of other people whispering their way in and out of the kitchen but welcome because they provided a contrast to the discovered dead-end of his own philosophies. Mouthing and nodding responses to their mumbled condolences all he really heard was the questions his own brain kept tossing round about a vacuum inside his head. "Where's this great God now?" it kept jeering. "What about this Resurrection thing? Where's all the old wives' ghosts and signs and omens of this hereafter they all talk about? Your father's dead and nobody can do a damn thing about it. And you can't say your mother looks as if she thinks she'll ever see him again!"

Unbidden and unwelcome, the questions bounced behind the false calm of his eyes. They circled and repeated and interchanged themselves like little demons in rubber shoes. They exploded endlessly like rotating peas rattling round an insulated lining in his skull. And all the time he kept watching his mother's face of stone.

In some ways the second day was worse. Sleepless they had sat all night before the fire. The mechanics of why a block and tackle had broken and a jib tumbled had no real significance beside the awful emptiness of the house. The utter finality of their loss and regrets was heartbreakingly encompassed by Julia's periodically reiterated, "Collie didnae deserve that."

He had welcomed Ella's early morning arrival as a professional reinforcement. Nor did his young sister fail him. With a taut-faced discipline he knew was valiantly donned to buttress them better, she took control. Only when they brought the coffin home and manoeuvred it round the lobby into the room she broke for one moment and clung to him sobbing, "Oh, Colin! My daddy!"

The rest of the day was a macabre nightmare of writing relatives and inserting obituary notices in newspapers and satisfying every casually met acquaintance's lust for Death's last detail.

But now it was the third day and his brain reasserted its clarity. At last he saw the edges of grief begin to eat into the marble of his mother's solitude. Forlorn and strangely round-shouldered in

her unfamiliar dress of black and black wool cardigan, her
punctuation of each newcomer's sympathy with, "You'll be
wanting to see Collie?" acquired added pathos with repetition.
Whatever their private preference—and his newfound per-
spicacity recognized many a shudder nobly concealed—all
responded generously to Julia's simple disregard of even the
thought of decay and corruption in association with her Collie.
With a love and tenderness that seemed new only because it was
so unashamed she led each of them into the room and walked to
the bier with a pride and soft step that was strangely reminiscent
of a young mother about to display her new baby. The undertaker had left the coffin lid pivoted just open enough to allow the
face cloth to be lifted. Each time Julia revealed the waxen features
beneath—and Death's ironic contrast of pale, bloodless flesh and
the continuing vigour of Collie's red moustache invested the
corpse with a near patrician beauty that was shattering even to
his family—Julia said gently, "Isn't he lovely—like he was just
sleeping?" and stroked the cold brow with an unafraid hand of
lingering affection.

Most of the mourners could only nod. Whatever their initial
aversion to the moment, her example humbled and strengthened
them. They glanced round the rows of wreaths and almost forgot
the heavy smell of death as she, forgetting them, continued to look
down on the face of her man. "Yes," they whispered at last, "he's
awful natural. You can see he never suffered. That'll be a comfort
to you."

Still watching Collie, she never answered that. And her son
wondered if her enigmatic calm was a sign of reborn faith or
resigned fatalism.

When the minister arrived Colin received him with embarrassment and the mumbled thanks of conscious obligation. He did
not even know to which denomination the man belonged. Ella
had, by virtue of her religious connections, arranged his services.
She had suggested calling in one of the Brethren's lay preachers
but their mother, with her sole demonstration of authority
throughout the mourning, had said, "No, although he was nae
Holy Willie your faither was a good Protestant and'll be buried
wi' a right minister. We're no' Papishes, our Kirk'll no' refuse
its last full blessing to anybody."

The minister was a slight, pale man with wise, inoffensive eyes.
Handing over his umbrella and top hat to be laid on the kitchen
bed amid the pile of overcoats and handbags already accumulated

there, he assumed his rôle among the mourners without affectation or false humility and yet with a certainty of mission that won their approval. After Colin introduced him to Julia he stayed beside her a moment before taking her hand again and saying to the company, "Now, if you are all ready will you please just come through to the room with us?"

They sat Julia on a chair by the empty fireplace with Jenny and Ella on either side of her. Jenny was swollen with child and they had tried to persuade her not to attend the funeral but she had angrily insisted, "My daddy'll not go away for the last time without me being there. He would expect me there and I never let him down yet." Now she sat sobbing quietly but continuously and, standing beside her, Ian Angus's anxious hand comforted her shoulder. Ella's eyes were red with private weeping and her face seemed pinched and drawn, but her gaze never left her mother. Julia, shrunken and suddenly old, sat with a handkerchief to her face and an arm across her bosom supporting the bent elbow, occasionally her bowed shoulders shook in a muffled sob. From his stance inside the doorway Colin watched the three of them. Even in the midst of the short service and prayer his strange mood of detached observation stayed with him. Desperately he concentrated on the solemn phrases, "The Lord giveth and the Lord taketh away—Blessed be the Lord. . . ." but could derive no comfort from them. Instead he saw only the grief of his mother and sisters. With guilt he found his glance roving round the room resenting its claustrophobic scene—the minister crushed against the head of the bier, the uncles, aunts, cousins, nephews, nieces —even good old Terry Flanagan—huddled and cramped and perched on borrowed chairs, their conscientious expressions of woe perverted into masks of hypocrisy by the very homely familiarity of their background. Rebelliously he found himself picking sentiments from the half-heard oration and jeering back silently. "If this is just a beginning surely a man—even a common wee rigger—deserves a better launching than this? Talk till you're blue in the face, mister, you could never sum up all that was good about my daddy. . . ." And then, suddenly, his throat was full and something was expanding and bursting in his chest. His gulp for breath ended in a shuddering effort to control a sob. To his dismay he was blind with tears that would not be blinked away.

He was still fighting for composure when the service ended. He stepped back into the lobby to allow everyone to shuffle past him. As Ella, her arm tight around her mother, passed, the outer door half-opened and the undertaker pushed his head in expectantly. Without waiting Colin's acknowledgement of his conspiratorial nod he beckoned his men in with subdued but unconcealed urgency. Not even professional etiquette could camouflage the fact that in death, as in life, time means money.

"Have you given out the cord cards?"

Startled, Colin turned to find his Aunt Mary gazing at him anxiously. Fumbling in his waistcoat he found the eight visiting-size pasteboards with their macabre sketch of a coffin lid. His aunt shook her head in reproof. "They should've been distributed before this," she hissed. "D'you know who to give them to?"

Wearily Colin shook his head. "Can I give Terry one—he was my faither's chum, y'know."

"No, no, no!" Aunt Mary was scandalized. She almost tore the cards from his fingers in agitation. "Terry's not a relative. Look —you take No. 1, you're his son and must go to the head of the coffin. Your faither's got no brothers here so give No. 2 to your Uncle Erchie seein' he's your mother's auld brother. And then, I think, No. 3 should go to Cousin Malcolm frae Barrhead, he's the auldest o' that side of the family. . . ."

She apportioned the cards according to a jealously calculated merit of blood or marital tie. Bemused but cynical, Colin listened patiently. His own roster of those who loved his father best and were present out of affection and not formality veered so widely from hers that for a moment he was seized by a mad and horrifying impulse to burst out laughing in her face. He controlled himself, but, insinuating himself through the still solemn groups crammed with incredible patience in the kitchen, he suffered a humiliating sense of guilt in the furtive ritual of passing the cards to their chosen recipients. Like fellow conspirators each accepted his card and instantly concealed it with such deliberate lack of expression that he felt party to a rather discreditable plot against all the other male members of the family. He was glad when, on a signal from the undertaker that the coffin was safely down in the hearse, it was time for him to escort the minister to the first carriage.

On the street he was surprised to find more than a score of working-clad dockers and riggers lined up unevenly behind the last of the four taxis he had ordered. When the big wreath labelled, "In Deepest Sympathy—From Fellow Workers," had been delivered he had accepted it as an ordinary traditional token. The business of being badgered to contribute a shilling for such a purpose was so much a weekly incidence in his own working life that he would only have been surprised had it not arrived. But to see so many of his father's mates present in person, and knowing that their attendance entailed sacrificing two or three hours' pay from their already criminally low wages, moved him. Looking at their brown, dirty faces, ragged jackets and broken-peaked caps he knew this was the guard of honour that would have pleased his father. Stumbling behind the minister into the car he felt that unmanning wave of emotion well up in his chest again but he also felt fiercely proud.

It was a strange journey to the cemetery. For economy, to leave room in the other three cars for all of the remaining male mourners, Uncle Erchie and Cousin Malcolm shared the first car with the minister and himself. A gaunt man, with great pouches under his eyes and exuding no air of prosperity even in his best blue suit—Colin knowledgeably guessed this funeral had probably necessitated the suit's hasty redemption from a Partick pawn-shop—Uncle Erchie maintained his social end by confining his exchanges with the minister to nods and headshakes. A great gambler, Uncle Erchie knew the form of every racehorse and greyhound listed in the columns of the *Noon Record* or the *Sporting Chronicle*. Often, by an intricate system of doubling, trebling and even quadrupling an initial stake of shillings on a day's racing card, he had been known to win hundreds of pounds. Such passing fortunes made no enduring or material difference to his ramshackle way of living. He and his fat, near-slatternly but happy-go-lucky wife occupied a tumbledown room and kitchen whose bare minimum of furniture remained exactly the same as it had on their wedding thirty years before. Occasionally Uncle Erchie was known to accept a job around the docks—generally under pressure from some influential and over-conscientious relative—but he never let the habit master him. Ironically enough when, in hard times, most of the more admirable members of the family were patiently half-starving on Dole or Public Assistance pittances it was nearly always Uncle Erchie, hungrier looking than any, who would circle round the family's outposts distributing quids and half quids with the reckless generosity of a man confident of his tomorrows. "Ach," he would brush aside their protests of repayment, "I'll get more where it come from. The bookies have plenty." Accepting it they salved their conscience with the small justification that Erchie would only waste it gambling anyway. The measure of Uncle

Erchie's greatness was that when, in his more frequent periods
of poverty, the family waxed virtuously over his sloth and
improvidence he never reminded anyone of these gratuities. In
Colin's eyes he was a great man and as a family asset worth a
regiment of Cousin Malcolms.

Cousin Malcolm lived in a terraced cottage in Barrhead and
looked it. He was an elder in the kirk, a superintendent of a
Sunday School and held a post vaguely defined but reputed to
carry fabulous authority in a cotton mill. While admittedly not
ranking with, possibly, the Coats, he did go to work "dressed"
and it was known for a fact that his subordinates feared and
fawned on him. The millgirls all called him Mister. He was a
small man with high, ruddy cheekbones and sharp, dark-browed
eyes. He had arrived late for the funeral service but took care
to claim no deference from Julia or those other Burnford relatives
whose age put them on terms of childhood familiarity. For the
younger members of his kin he reserved a studied courtesy that
held them at their distance. To them he was only a name and a
boast in their parents' gossip that while faithfully materializing
at every funeral never appeared at a wedding. Now, exactly
correct in sombre suit and with black hat poised expertly on his
knee, he chatted easily, intimately with the minister. With slight
amazement Colin found himself half-listening with gratitude.
After all there was nothing in this for Cousin Malcolm. He was
not even coming back for supper. His life and interests had long
since drawn him miles apart from the loyalties of Bulwark Street.
Yet here he was, as he never failed to do, carrying the banner
of gentility for them in their crisis. As their cab trundled wearily
at the tail of the flower-decked hearse Colin, without loving or
admiring him, found himself honouring Cousin Malcolm from
Barrhead. . . .

It was a long drive. Not in distance but in time. Gazing blank-
faced out of their car, but sensitive to its grinding progress, Colin
guessed the little undertaker would be cursing the foot mourners
whose pace geared their own. He could visualize him sitting up
there in front of the wreath-filled hearse, a straight-backed figure
of appropriate rectitude in his top-hat and frock-coat, while side-
mouthing lurid professional irritation to the driver. Colin had
no illusion about the façades trades-people wore to face their
customers. It was a cynicism newspaper selling had first planted
in him. Since then, in strikes, lock-outs and pay-offs, he had
witnessed the same public plausibility even among millionaire

shipping magnates and measured it against the miserable immoralities camouflaged beneath the launching buntings. He thought of the apprentices tossed out on the street the week their five years' cheap labour was completed. He thought of the piece-work agreements ruthlessly disavowed the moment competent men ran up decent wages. Already he knew the official hatchet-men were haggling with his widowed mother over the degree of liability and terms of compensation for his father's death. And he knew, with a certainty sprung from the apologetic asides punctuating their preliminaries, that however funereal he looked the little jobbing ghoul fronting the bier had only one thought ticking through the adding machine he called a conscience—the time of his afternoon's next funeral. . . .

People along the pavements stopped to watch them pass. Because it was Glasgow few of the men lifted their caps. And Colin thought no less of them for that. Only exhibitionists made an excuse of strangers' sorrows for personal dramatics. The women in the shopdoors and close entries stilled their gossip and stared silently. At street corners and pavement edges chaps stopped arguing and gazed with self-conscious solemnity, the flat calm of their eyes and the immobility of their features guarantee enough that they appreciated and were aware of all the significance of this last passing panoply of a man's mortality. Colin knew that when the last car passed they would relax, the women saying, "Mrs. Haig's man—from Bulwark Street. Oh, an awful thing . . . !" And the men would agree, "Helluva hard cheese—bloody pulley-block went. A straight wee fellow too, Collie. . . ."

The graveside ceremony was short to the point of haste. From the moment they arrived the chief grave-digger took command. A wiry, crow-faced man with leathery, weatherbeaten skin and corduroy trousers caught under the knee he hopped among the grave-planks as athletic as a dervish. Indestructible looking himself, he gave the impression that he enjoyed his work and the speed with which he hustled the ceremony on was proof that more than his hands were calloused. From the moment his three helpers laid the coffin on the planks bridging the open grave he never wasted a minute. With a barely concealed impatience that nearly drew a snarl from Colin he mustered the cord-holders, almost thrusting them up on to the parapets of soft red loam lining the grave. While he and his men took the real strain on their ropes he gaffered the lowering of the coffin with a string of

commands as crisp and unreverent as a furniture-remover man-
handling a piano down a staircase. When the casket hit the
bottom he gave the token-bearers the order to drop their cords
and whipped away his own ropes with an alacrity sharp as the
ring of a cash register. "Right—gather round now, gentlemen,
please, gather round!" he adjured the mourners, watching the
minister take his place at the head of the grave with the exact
expression of a time-pressed chairman reluctantly permitting
one more speaker. His automatic preparatory clutch at a handful
of earth for the "Ashes to ashes, dust to dust," rite was so
mechanical it was blasphemous. Even during the prayer the back
of his cap barely levered grudgingly clear of his skull, its peak
remaining firmly clamped close down on his narrow forehead.
And the instant "Amen" was pronounced its echo was overlain
by his abrupt, "That's all now, gentlemen—just stand back,
please, will you. . . ."

For the hell of it Colin stood still. Looking down into the
damp narrow slot in the ground, with the scars and slices of the
spades etched horribly in its precisely manicured walls, he strove
to achieve some significant spiritual experience, some holy, tear-
laden reaction to quiet the guilt of his too objective lucidity.
Instead he was aware of the grey arch of sky above, the same kind
of sky as any other day. The cranes, and jibs, and stagings, the
ships' masts and tenement rooftops were fretted around the
horizon as ordinarily as always. People were walking and hurrying
up and down Anchor Road and Argyle Street and Buchanan
Street and all the other streets arguing and looking in shop
windows and undressing each other with their imagination and
planning their Fair holidays just as if Collie Haig had never
lived at all. At hand the marble angels with their folded wings
and demurely bowed heads competed for awe with the obelisks
and the huge purse-proud Victorian arches. And lurching in the
grass and creeping among the ivy and toppled lily vases the prim
slabs and headstones matched in motionless competition their
frozen sanctimony with the glass-encased affections and granite
scrolls and stone Holy Bibles.

Woodenly Colin tried to relate it all to his father lying down
there in that box under that stupid brown mattress thing. What
was that blasted quilt for anyway?—was it supposed to keep
the dead warm? Or keep the worms off them? From the corner
of his eye he saw the crowd of riggers drift away down the straight-
ruled pathway towards the main gate. The family mourners were

climbing back into the taxis with discreetly ostentatious slamming of doors. Under his nose the gravediggers began shovelling the first sods back into the hole. At his elbow he could feel their foreman's impatience swell to the point of compulsive interruption. Stepping down off the clay parapet he just beat the man to it.

"You'll see all our wreaths go on the grave?" he challenged.

Swallowing irritation, the fellow instantly moulded his face in a mask of unctuous sympathy. "Of course—that's one thing we're very careful about."

"My mother'll be up tomorrow and she'll look for every card," Colin said quietly. He looked over his shoulder at the flailing spades. A bitter impulse to ask if they were on piecework seized him. Instead he thrust a ten-shilling note into the chargehand's greedily expectant hand and trudged across to the car. . . .

The minister asked to be dropped off at a busy corner and Cousin Malcolm, making the excuse of a connection to catch, left with him. When they got back to Bulwark Street the women had transformed the house. The curtains were thrown wide, two tables were covered with dazzling white cloths set end to end in the room and every aspect of mourning had been banished. Ella had even put on a cheerful overall to supervise the laying of the supper. Jenny, because of her condition, remained seated near her mother, but conversation throughout the house was general and both were drawn into and took part in it with a resilience that was remarkable. Talk ranged over everything from the price of sausages in Bridgeton to the luck of Aunt Belle Paterson's lassie from Townhead moving into a new Corporation house before she was a year married. They discussed, praised, criticized and reminisced on the health, characteristics and fortunes of absent relatives strewn from the Gorbals to New Zealand from Govan Cross to California. Looking at the variety of their faces, his mother's kin and his father's, his own cousins, nieces, nephews, uncles, aunts and blood connections so tenuous he was baffled by their real relationship, he marvelled, despite the surface evidences of differing temperaments, at their common quality. They were kind. And loyal to each other. Even their criticisms were regretful. They genuinely rejoiced in news of each other's success and their envies were open and unmalicious. As the reason for their congregation was more deliberately ignored, anecdotes took a lighter turn and their laughter broke freely. Latterly Colin saw Jenny's eyes sparkle as she dug a reproving elbow into wee Uncle Lachie from Bellshill over something he said in the fashion only

he could say it. By the time Ella summoned them all into the
room the atmosphere was more of a celebration than a funeral
feast.

The tables were laden with boiled bacon, tongue, cheese,
salads, biscuits, fancy cakes, brown bread and plain bread. Pickles
and tomato sauces and brown sauces were spaced at regular
intervals in their makers' bottles. But the cutlery gleamed and
the three-tiered cake salvers shone with a silver magnificence
impressive as anything a Buchanan Street hostelry could present.
As they squeezed shoulder to shoulder into their seats, joking
about each other's girth and accusing the least assertive of
manoeuvring with a strategic eye on special delicacies, Colin
wondered again at the elastic magic of a room and kitchen.
These two apartments, which latterly had seemed cramped
housing five, had at times this afternoon held fifty people; even
now it was fantastic to realize thirty people were dining over the
floor space normally occupied by the unfolding of his divan
bed. . . .

"You can wait a minute for yours?" Ella muttered confidentially
as, steaming teapot held high, she crushed between his chair and
the wall. "I want to get the older people served first." Conscious
of the family's responsibility, he nodded in eager co-operation.
But a moment later Mattie Wilson, who was helping Ella serve,
swooped along and filled his cup.

"Ay, that's right, Mattie," approved Aunt Mary, with a
knowing turn of her head, "you take care of Colin, he's worth
looking after."

Mattie laughed but moved away flushing. Across the table
Terry Flanagan looked from under shrewd eyebrows. "That's
the women for ye, boy," he sympathized. "Ye're nivver safe when
they're around—if it's nor theirself wants ye, they're tryin' to
hang ye on to someone else."

"Away, you auld devil," scolded Aunt Mary. "I'm sure if
Bridget was here she'd tell a different story about how you got
her. . . ."

While they bantered Colin rose and fetched a specially pur-
chased bottle of whisky from the kitchen. Except when Collie
had been drinking and brought it in, alcohol was something Julia
never permitted in the house. But today was different. Unobtrusively he went round the table filling the glasses. Only about
half the guests accepted. He filled Terry's glass so full the Irishman protested, "For Jaisus' sake, boy——!"

"Knock it back," muttered Colin, "it's on my daddy."

Their glances met. Terry's slid to Julia's and found a strangely sad but warm wisp of a smile. He raised his glass. Colin went back into the kitchen and, hands spread on the sink sill, stood a long time alone looking down into the street. . . .

## CHAPTER TWENTY-SIX

A NEWSBOY ran past bawling about a pocket-battleship shelling a Baltic port. Colin let him run. He had his own crisis to worry about.

Lighting a fresh cigarette from the butt of the last he dropped the discard between his polished shoe-caps into the gutter. Standing on the edge of the pavement he was safe from the risk of being moved on by any officious policeman exercising obstruction authority.

Three friends passing nodded. One cracked, "Is she keeping you waiting?"

She was not. He was early. It only seemed long. It was an impatience many trysts had quickened rather than soothed. But tonight was different. Tonight he was consumed by more than ordinary emotion. Even thinking of his intention made him sweat. But he knew it was tonight or never.

To kill time he considered crossing to the confectioners opposite and buying a box of Black Magic. The occasion called for supernatural support. However, he decided against it. There was a charm about watching her choose her own sweets—the way she clung to his arm swaying and peering across a window-range, rejecting this brand or that while appealing for advice; and then the warm, finger-touching intimacy as he unobtrusively slipped her money, disclaiming, "Just you go in and get what you like; you know fine I don't bother."

And the uncoquettish honesty of her half-rueful smile as she shook his arm chidingly, "But I want to get ones you like too. Something special. . . ."

He looked up the dark street again. Beyond the third lamp-post her close was a black rectangle on the perimeter of the lamp-light. Just opposite it a woman with a shopping basket over her arm was shaking her head to the pleading of a cloth-capped man in an unbuttoned overcoat. The man's hands were spread wide in oath-taking sincerity. Finally, reluctantly, the woman reached to the bottom of her basket and taking up her purse gave the man something from it; as he took it her head jabbed forward in last-minute remonstrance. From his eager speed of retreat and throw-away husbandly assurance, Colin would have given even money that the words of farewell were: "Only one drink. I'll not be ten minutes. . . ." Fatalistically the woman vanished into the shadows.

Colin's glance travelled up the face of the tenement. Above the close all the front windows were lit. He singled out hers, two storeys up. She should just be about ready now, probably touching her hair and taking a last look at herself in a mirror. . . . His gaze rose higher to the black void beyond the rooftops. Somewhere in the darkness above the city's glow an aeroplane throbbed. Idly he tried to catch a glimpse of the machine's lights but failed. He wondered if it was one of these Bristol biplane fighters Stuart McQuade was bragging about recently. Great how old Stue could recognize any aeroplane in the sky—of course that was because of this Auxilliary Air Force training he and all the other brainy boys were going daft about these days.

Cynically he shrugged at his thoughts. He grinned at the memory of Campbell and Watson and a lot of other hard-pressed blokes who, falling for the £5 bounty and a fortnight camping down at Gailles, had enlisted in the Terriers. A bunch of mugs. Time enough to grab a uniform when they came for you. . . .

He looked back along the street. And she was there—tugging at her gloves and pausing hesitantly in the black frame of the close. Seeing him waiting, she swung eagerly out on to the pavement and the rhythm of her walk and the cut of her figure was something he would single out in any crowd in any street. A million women had legs as lovely and bosoms as firm and, maybe, faces as pretty but only this girl had something beyond beauty that, forever, could hold him. And, suddenly, the ache inside him was beyond bearing.

She came up to him smiling. "Been waiting long?"

"Another five minutes and I was coming to knock you up."

"So you should." The dare had implications that made both smile.

Slipping her hand under his elbow she fell into step with him. They walked along the pavement savouring the moment of reunion. Turning into busy Anchor Road he nodded towards a glittering window. "Better get some sweeties."

She resisted his impulse towards the shop. "I've some in m'

bag, Colin. You don't need to be always buying me sweeties."

"Watching the figure, eh?"

"How? D'you think I'm getting fat?" The instant anxiety in her tone set him chuckling. They walked on exchanging pleasantries until he said casually, "D'you mind, Ann, if we don't go to the pictures tonight?"

She caught the sober undercurrent in his voice at once. "No," she said, watching him steadily, "I don't care, Colin. Where do you want to go?"

"I thought we might go a wee walk instead?"

"Whatever you like. Will you go back the way?"

Turning they sauntered away from the lights. A gravity descended on both. Silently they strolled on, leaving shops and tenements behind until the bushes and boundary trees of the cemetery arched deep rustic shadows overhead. Instinctively their steps took them farther on to a favourite nook of privacy, a small public park set off from the main road. A hundred yards along the path leading from its ever-open ornamental gates they were fortunate to find unoccupied a secluded bench behind a statue to Burnford's first Provost. In the blackness cast by his guardian circle of tall ash and beech trees, the great frock-coated figure of the Victorian Provost in his concertina-wrinkled trousers, and holding his stone scroll out to the unheeding stars, loomed mysteriously monolithic. Alive to the more sordid menace of Peeping Toms Colin circled the statue's plinth before seating Ann.

"It's a lovely night," she said with studied inconsequence as he sat down beside her.

"Ay, so it is," he agreed, bringing a packet of cigarettes from his jacket pocket. Giving her one they sat and smoked while their eyes became accustomed to the surrounding gloom. With his elbow resting on the back of the bench he pulled her shoulder close to his. "Are you cold?" he asked.

"No, Colin," her face was a pale oval, breathing sweet invitation. Even through the thickness of her dark woollen coat the warmth of her body against the curve of his hand was exciting. Restlessly he tweaked the droop of her little red beret. She said, unsmiling, "What's worrying you, Colin?"

He stirred and flicked his cigarette away. It streaked high in the darkness and fell, a small red star, to lose itself in the tangle of rhododendron bushes across the path. For a silent moment he watched where the glow had fallen, then, half-turning on the narrow seat, drew her closer. With every nerve and sense taut and quickened he was instantly conscious of the silken rub of her knee against the coarser serge of his trousers. Instinctively he drew his foot away to preserve her precious stockings.

"Ann——" he said, and stopped. His fingers tightened on her shoulder. She said nothing. "I don't know how to say it," he began again. "But it's got to be said—and I'd rather say it to your face."

Easing herself up a little from his embrace she dropped her cigarette on the ground and put her foot on it. As she relaxed backwards he slid his free hand between the buttons of her coat and round her waist. She was wearing a blouse and slyly his fingers insinuated under its elastic hem.

"I know what you are going to say," she whispered. Her voice was only a breath on his cheek but every word rang clear to his heart. Black night wrapped them like a cloak. Beyond the park's ragged, inky line of treetops the trams dragged their long moanings like the muffled agonies of another world and in the sky the glow of the city was the last halo of dying Time. Tenderly his hold pressed on the fragile sheath of her underslip, and for a half-pleading moment his fingertips drummed gently in the naked hollow of her soft shoulder-blades. "You want to finish up?" her statement was matter-of-fact and devoid of accusation.

His expression remained as stolidly controlled as her own. Dimly she saw the straight dark line of his brow and the brooding honesty of his gaze.

"I don't *want* to," his emphasis was mild but bitter. "You should know that. But what else can we do?"

"You mean—religion?"

He drew her against his cheek and murmured in quiet anguish. "I've thought and thought about it. It's for both our sakes. I think we'd better pack it up before it's too late."

A sad shade of a smile touched only her lips. "That's being sensible," she confided almost to herself.

"No!" and she could feel the curt grinding of his teeth. "It's hellish. But there'd be no peace for you or I any other way. We're not the kind that can turn."

"We've never talked about it, have we?"

"No. Neither we have, Ann." Fondly he rubbed his cheek against hers. The caress displaced her beret and it fell unheeded to the ground behind the seat. She moved her encircling arm and with shy fingers stroked the hair at the nape of his neck. He continued in jerks, blunderingly. "I'm not much good explaining these things."

"I know what you mean, Colin."

"None of my people have said anything. Of course they've been tipped off I'm going with a Catholic—there's always somebody ready to put in the poison."

"My father only said he'd rather see me dead than married to a Protestant."

"You never told me!"

"Oh, it was only one night he had a drink in him. But I know my mother's heartbroken."

"Mine, too. I've been told she says my old man would turn in his grave if he knew."

Ann turned her lips against his cheek. "Oh, Colin!" she breathed. "Why did you have to be a Protestant!"

Bitterly he said, "Why did any of us have to be anything? Sometimes I wonder . . . !"

"But you'll stick to your religion?"

His voice was low but uncompromising. "Yes, Ann, I'll stick to my religion. God knows why, for I haven't been inside a church since I left the Boy's Brigade. But I'll no' tell you a lie, Ann—an' I know I'm not expert—but I just feel that we're right." He hesitated. She said nothing. He plunged on pleadingly, "Not just because I support the Rangers or anything like that. . . . And I'm not saying that your folks are wrong. It's just I could never believe the things you've been brought up to believe. It would go against my grain!" He paused. Then said firmly, "In their hearts I don't think anybody can ever really change what they've been born with. If you've been born a Catholic, you die a Catholic; if you've been born a Protestant, you die a Protestant. I know that's how I'll be."

"And nothing'll change you?"

"Nothing." He drew back a little and looked at her squarely. "But I'm going to tell you this, Ann—you were the right girl for me."

She just looked at him. He read all he needed to know in her tearless grief. Desperately he pulled her to him. "You see," he stumbled softly, "I'm no' good wi' the words. But that first night at the dancing——"

"You went home with someone else."

"I know. But passing you at the door. . . ." She felt his head shake in wondrous amaze at his own perversity. "I just knew I was going home with the wrong one."

"So did I," she breathed.

His head drew back in mild accusation. "You hardly looked at us."

"Ah . . ." Her smile was melancholy roguish. "Ah, but whiles a lassie has to hide her feelings. You had made your choice."

He caught her close again. They clung silently. Then he said, "They'll never be anybody else like you. When I'm wi' you, Ann, I feel right. Know what I mean?"

She squeezed him tenderly. Under her blouse the palm of his hand was hot and restless against her spine. For a moment as he kissed her fiercely, urgently, it moved round towards her side dragging her underslip down against the shoulderstraps. The soft pressure of her fingertips on his arm was plea rather than denial. Only a moment he hesitated, then his lips lifted and his embrace regained its kindness. "Ann, Ann," he whispered, with his cheek against the side of her mouth. "I wouldn't hurt you for worlds. I've wanted you from the first moment I saw you but never had a wrong thought towards you. . . . You'll mind that?"

"I'll always mind it, Colin."

Gently he withdrew his hand and tucked the back of her blouse into the hem of her skirt. Taking his arm from under her coat he hugged her tight again. Putting a hand on each of his cheeks she turned his face to hers and looked into his eyes. Then laying her lips on his she kissed him with a long, desperate intensity. As he crushed her to him all the ache in their souls seemed to merge in the straining despair of their yearning bodies. Abruptly he pulled her to her feet, saying, "Come on, I'd better take you home."

They had gone ten yards when she clapped her fingers to her mouth, "I've forgot my beret!"

She waited while he retrieved it from behind the seat. And stood patiently while he insisted on arranging it to his idea of a proper angle on her sleek black hair. Then, silently, only taking their arms from each other's waists when they reached the park gates, they strolled on.

He left her where they had always met, three lamp-posts from her close. In the little moment that they stood her lips suddenly trembled. The pallor of her face frightened him. "Oh, Ann," he said huskily.

Her chin lifted and she tried to smile. "Maybe," she said, and her eyes had the astonishing brightness of supreme sacrifices, "maybe I could turn?"

He looked at her. And his chest felt as tight and torn as it had the day he buried his father. "No," he said harshly. "No, Ann, you couldnae turn, you know that."

She kept her smile. He watched her until she reached her close. Only in the last two steps did her head droop. Then she ran. Colin stood and stared long at the black rectangle that had swallowed her before he turned away.

## CHAPTER TWENTY-SEVEN

THE moment she heard the front door open Julia knew who it was. She had waited a year for the sound. Now she found she could not rise from the chair.

He came only a step in from the lobby and halted. The naval uniform made him look different—the blue coat and wide trousers magnified his breadth and solidity. Beneath the rake of the flat cap his face was older and harder, like that of a stranger. Then he grinned and it was as if he had been away no farther than the street corner. "Hullo, Maw," he said. "What's in the pan?"

"Colin!" was all she could say. He held her tight and all the waiting was worth while.

"Talk about walking into it!" he laughed at last. "The yards were coming out just as I came off the Subway—I think I bashed into nearly everybody I knew coming up the road. Even met McBride—I couldn't get away from him!"

"If I had known you were coming I'd have had everything all ready." She was bustling back and forth using the activity of preparing a meal to cloak her joy and hero-worship. "Put your things in the room and get a pair o' house-shoes on—you must be dead-beat travelling all day!"

"The trains are murder," he agreed. "I sat on my bag all the road to Crewe."

"Where is your bag?" She paused. "D'you leave it in the room?"

His smile was apologetic, evasive. "No, I left it in the station —I'll pick it up tonight on the road back."

"The road back?" Premonition took the sparkle from her tone. "You're no' goin' back the night, surely?"

"Not to Chatham." For her sake the laugh was extra casual. "I'm going on up to Scapa—joining a new ship up there."

"The night?" She still refused to relinquish the conviction that he was on leave. "But you haven't been home since you 'listed!"

"I shouldn't be here just now," he chuckled, determined to preserve her spirits. "I had to wangle to get a connection to St. Enoch's—I'm really supposed to be travelling up through Edinburgh but I knew if I could hit Glasgow I could pinch a couple of hours changing trains."

"And when are you going back?"

"I'll get my connection about eleven."

She looked at the clock. It was after six already. Disappointment had put the lines of age and loneliness back on her face again. "They might've given you a right leave seein' you were this length," she said sadly.

"Are you kiddin'?" he rallied her. "D'you think the Admiralty's got nothing else to worry about but a matelot's leave? Jings, Maw, if you only knew how lucky I am——" He stopped suddenly and decided not to tell her how lucky he was. For an instant he heard the JU's roar again and felt the icy grip of the sea. He saw his dead mates float past. . . .

"What do you mean—lucky?" She was anxiously quick. His laugh was as swift. "Lucky in this posting I mean. They tell me it's a dawdle."

"Another minesweeper?"

"No, no!" His denial was stressed for her reassurance. "This is a swanky berth."

She shook her head. "I'm no carin' about the swankies—I just wish I seen you hame. I keep worryin' about you on these minesweepers, they always seem to be gettin' sunk——"

"Ah well, lash out the grub and don't worry any more—I'll be safer than you are."

"How that? And you in the Navy and a war on?" Her natural good sense rejected groundless comfort. But still she looked at him hopefully. "As many folk have told me you were a right fool, you could've been reserved like a lot more in the yards. I've never got to the bottom yet o' how you managed to get called up——"

"Never mind that, Maw," he laughed. "I'd've looked a right Gilbert hittin' up and down Bulwark Street and Stuart McQuade and a' the rest of the boys away fightin' for me. Don't make me laugh!" To distract her he went on, "Anyhow, the buzz is this boat I'm going to now is the biggest one there is. My daddy would know a' about it if he was here."

"Ay, he knew a' the boats." Julia's reminiscence was proud.

"That's right. I'm no' tellin' you its name because that's what they call an Official Secret. But he would know it all right. And if it does turn out to be that one he would tell you the whole German Navy couldnae sink it—so you neednae worry about me, I'll be safer than you down here among the bombs."

"We're no' getting it anything like they are down in England." Anxiety clouded her face again. "I canny sleep at nights for thinking about Ella and our Jenny and the wean. Sometimes I think the world's gone mad."

"Jenny's man down there for good now?"

"Ay, the firm's got him a house as well. They even paid for a' the flitting. Jenny went away down last week wi' the wee one—I wanted her to stay because of the bombing but she wanted to be beside Ian."

"Ian's no' daft—he wouldn't let her go down if he didn't think it safe enough."

As he enjoyed his meal they talked of homely family affairs, but always, she kept watching the clock.

"When I was at Skegness I tried to get across to see Ella but something always cropped up. How is she liking it down South?"

"Och, well, you know our Ella. I think she'd get on wi' anybody. At first, right enough, she wasnae awful taken on wi' the hospitals down there. And she said some of the English were funny."

Colin laughed shortly. "So are some of the Scotch, Maw."

"Maybe that." His mother's expression betrayed that, privately, she preferred to remain loyally prejudiced. "Anyhow, Ella soon let them see they weren't taking a rise out of her. She seems to like it fine now."

"That's champion."

"I think one of the young doctors has a notion of her. He's had her out a few times and wants her to go some week-end and visit his people. From what she says he seems a very nice chap."

"He can't be too nice for our Ella."

Julia smiled. With shy but shrewd curiosity she glanced at her son. "What about yourself? None of these smart English dames caught your fancy yet?"

"No fear!" The denial was emphatic enough to carry conviction. "It's bad enough suffering all that English patter from the lads aboard without being married to it. Imagine wakening up every morning to hear somebody yelping, 'Camm ahn nah, Cowlin, yir brykefast is oun the tyble!' Jings, Maw, I'd leave the country first."

Julia laughed at his mimicry. "They don't all speak like that!"

"One way or another they all speak like that," he declared dogmatically. "Even some o' the best B.B.C. announcers can't say words like India without putting an 'r' on to the end of it. And they're the kinda folk that generally try to take their water off the likes of us!"

Not ill-pleased she smiled. "I doubt, Colin, the Navy hasnae changed you much—you're still a real Glesca keelie."

"And why not? Glasgow's a great city." He drew his chair over to the fire beside hers. "Let me tell you, Maw, I've been in a few places since I went out that door—London an' Liverpool an' all the rest of them—and when all the shouting's over none of them are any better and most of them are a dashed sight worse than good auld Glesca. It's got them all skinned."

"We're supposed to be a lot of hooligans."

"Don't believe all you read." His derision was contemptuous. "Were you a hooligan? Was my daddy a hooligan? How many hooligans do you know in Bulwark Street?" He sighed in heavy disgust. "Maw, there's more real neds in some streets in England than there is in the whole of Burnford. When I think on some of the characters I've met down there I know it's a proper liberty the way they knock Glasgow."

A twinkle appeared in his mother's eye. "You stick up for us, Colin."

"Too true." His declaration was quietly earnest. "Whenever anyone tries to take a fiver out of me because I come from Glasgow I just put one on them. You get peace then."

"And they'll believe all they ever heard about us?"

He laughed with her. "Maybe that. Some of the English are that ignorant they think we're still running about in kilts. But as long as you kid them on a bit you get on all right."

"And you're liking it fine?"

He understood all her concealed emotion—fear for his comfort and safety and moral well-being and the dread of losing him for-ever to new ways and experiences. With the insight of his own war-tempered maturity the complete loneliness of her widowhood struck him with new poignancy. The quiet, uncluttered tidiness of the kitchen was itself a barb to memory. He could guess at her solitary vigils listening to the clock tick, striving to read a book, hearing the radio—except for the news—with only half her atten-tion. Knowing with a sick finality that not any more could a long evening end with an echo on the stairhead, the turn of a doorknob and cheerful footsteps in the lobby. He knew she was aching with hungry pride to share in his accounts of active service but dreaded them, too. So he simply said, "Ach, the Navy's all right. You have some great times, too. Did I no' tell you in a letter about Alf, a wee Cockney mate o' mine, going into this pub and drinking Jimmy the One's beer?"

She shook her head. He talked on making Service life sound like a cross between a night at a pantomime and a sail down the Clyde on a Glasgow Fair Saturday. By his account war in the North Sea and the Channel was only a half-daft interlude of recuperating cruises between skylarking excursions at Government expense. Before he was finished he had the satisfaction of making her wipe tears of laughter away with the corner of her apron.

"It's a wonder you don't all get the jail," she chuckled, only half believing him. "Wait till I tell your Uncle Erchie about youse selling the man his own oary-boat—by jings, that beats shifting the steeple clock to swindle the bookie. He'll get a laugh at that, I know."

"How is Uncle Erchie?"

"Oh, battling away yet. He had a coupon up the other week and he was up first thing to know if I needed any money."

"You get my allowance all right?"

"Och, ay, and you know I've hardly touched the three hundred they gave me for your faither."

A bitter smile touched Colin's lips but he nodded his head in a signal of content. The delays and the denials, the downright roguery and the miserly cheese-paring of industrial compensation as it affected worker victims was too raw a thing for his comment. He felt there was no kind purpose in elaborating to his mother his true feelings on the official evaluation of a rigger's life and, say, the honorarium gifted to an overfed brandy-filled director at the end of a cosseted career. Such things burned in decent men's souls and could only be expressed in the language of the stoke-hold. To change the subject he said, "And how's everybody else? No excitement or scandals or anything?"

"Not a thing." Julia laughed. "Not a riot even. Everybody just minding their own business. You'd hardly think we lived in Glesca at a'. But you'll know one of your old sweethearts has got married?"

"No!" he exclaimed with more interest than he really felt. "No, you never mentioned it in your letters. What one?"

"Mattie Wilson."

"Get away! Didn't even know she was wenchin'. Who'd she marry?"

"Some fellow from the Water Cut—Neil, they call him. Works about the docks."

"Not 'Monk' Neil?"

"That's right—that's his nickname." Julia looked at her son's shocked face. "You know him?"

"Jings, ay. We were in the same class at school together. What made Mattie take up with the likes of him for?"

Julia's denial was sadly speculative. "I don't know—I don't know anything about the fellow. I only know Mrs. Wilson wasnae very pleased. She thinks Mattie threw herself away."

"Of course we all change." Colin strove to be just. "I mean it's years since I knew Monk. The fellow might be quite all right." He hesitated, doubtfully. "Only——"

Julia's sidelong assessment concealed more than mere curiosity. "I think Mrs. Wilson always hoped that you and Mattie might . . . ?"

She did not fool Colin. He looked straight back at her. "So did you, Maw. You'd've liked it fine if I'd taken up wi' Mattie!"

His mother did not trouble to deny the challenge. "Well," she admitted gravely, "Mattie was a nice lassie. I always liked her. She'd have made you a good wife."

Colin nodded. He was remembering hot kisses and breathless whispers at the dark end of the close. He felt again the idolizing clutch of arms and saw again the pleading yearning of eyes pretending to smile. But he said, "Mattie and I were always good pals. We got on well together. But there was never any question of a serious love affair. I've told you that before, Mother."

Julia nodded wisely. "I know, son, I know you did—but Mattie never. She was in love with you all right."

"Ach, you're daft." He tried to make it sound casual. "Mattie had a hundred boy friends. Still——" His frown was genuine. "I hope it's working out all right for her—I'd hate to think she'd pulled a boner."

Julia's sigh was fatalistic. "God drops us down in pairs—it's just we don't all catch up with each other."

"You always said that." He smiled quick and reminiscent. To his own horror he found himself adding, "D'you miss my faither a lot, Maw?"

Her gaze remained fixed on the fire. Neither grief nor embarrassment marred the calm of her expression. Instead a little smile softened it. Quietly she said, "Ay, Colin, I miss your daddy; maybe more than you can imagine. . . ."

When the time came she rose to put on her coat and hat. Colin tried to dissuade her. "I don't want you coming to the station," he protested. "It's silly for you to trail out in the blackout. And I'll worry about you getting back yourself from the city! I'd far rather just leave you sitting here where I can mind you the way you always were."

"How?" she reacted instantly. "D'you think you'll no' see me again?"

"For the love o'——!" He clutched his hair in consternation. "Where d'you get the ideas? No, I don't think anything of the kind. Cricky, you certainly dig up the cheerful notions!" He laughed in assurance. "Ay, by jings, Maw, I'll see you again. Don't think you're getting rid of me as easy as that—I'll be back to torment the life out of you until you'll be yapping you wish I was back in the Navy again!"

"Like enough," she nodded, wishing for the day but returning his smile gallantly, "only I don't want to be left in an empty kitchen the now. Let me at least see you to the Subway?"

Her loneliness stabbed him again. He hid his emotion with a saluting foolery of surrender. "Okay, okay, okay—have it your own way. But no farther than the Subway. Mind . . . !"

They walked through the war-darkened streets almost in silence, their snatches of over-casual conversation spasmodic frothings puffed across the surface of their real thoughts. The little torch Julia had fumbled from the recesses of her handbag proved a great help as a cover to their self-consciousness. "Great Scot, Maw!" joked Colin, "if you turn that thing up to the sky you'll blind a' the German pilots that ever was. Talk about the Pladda Lighthouse—they'll see the glow of that in Berlin!"

Clutching his arm in exasperation, Julia flicked the ray to the pavement at their feet. "To think I should live to see the day I'd have to walk through Burnford wi' a leerie in my hand!"

Around them the blank heights of the blinded tenements shut out the stars. Tramcars rumbling past with their irrepressibly defiant splutter of blue-green trolley sparks only seemed to emphasize the Stygian nightmare of science at war. Motor-cars had hooded eyes. Even the sudden blinks and flashes of other pedestrians' torches stabbing out of the intimidating darkness carried the menace of the unexpected rather than the consolation of company.

"If they wouldnae wait till they got right up again you before they flashed them in your face," Julia complained, "I could see the sense of it!"

Colin laughed. "It's your fatal beauty, Maw, they just can't let it go by without a wee keek. They're all dead jealous of me."

"Och!" She gave his arm a shake. He remembered when he used to clutch her hand, trotting to keep up with her. She had towered over him then and the pavements had stretched endlessly . . . now she was bowed a little, stout and not up to his shoulder. But already they were turning the Subway corner.

"Late Final! Last Race Special!"

Big Fergie was not so big now either. Huddled into the shuttered door of a closed pub, with his papers bunched at his feet. Colin had to stoop slightly to make sure it was him. As he paused, Julia tugged in sudden alarm. He patted her fingers reassuringly.

"Paper, Jack?"

Studying the square blob of face in the shadows Colin let the proffered newspaper hang between them. He smiled as Fergie hesitated, nonplussed at his delay. He let the newsvendor's bewilderment stretch a little longer before accepting the paper. Pressing a coin into the ready hand he said, "Sure, Fergie—for auld lang syne."

Feeling the milled edge his old enemy started in sudden interest and peered upward. "Do I know you, Jack?"

Walking on, Colin chuckled back, "No, Fergie—but you knew my faither."

"'S'that right? Hey!—Okay, Jack, and the best o' luck, sir."

"And the best of luck to you, Fergie. . . ."

One low-watt bulb threw a blue radiance around the Subway entrance. Tucked high under the porch canopy, its sickly glow barely illumined the pay turnstiles. In the quiet of the near-deserted streets it was the black-out's final furtive touch, the ghastly phosphorescence from the decaying corpse of a murdered era.

"Reminds me of the yarns I used to read as a boy," Colin grinned; "y'know, where the good ones come to the secret dunny in Chinatown leading to the opium den. . . . Mind how you used to shoot out your neck when you got them under my pillow?"

"You and your Penny Dreadfuls! I was aye feart you'd set fire to the blankets wi' yon candles."

"Ay, and you egged our Jenny on to play the watchdog and she was worse than I was—she was lying waiting to get the book after me. . . ."

Gallantly he sought to divert her. The yards from farewell to the other side of the turnstile stretched emotional leagues away. When the slender figure of a girl materialized hesitantly from the pavement's farther darkness he welcomed the little distraction.

Then he recognized the girl.

"I ran into Jimmy McBride on the road home tonight," she said, oddly breathless, nerves adding thrust to her words and pitching her voice a tone harsher than its true nature. She held out a box of cigarettes. "He told me you were going straight back so—so I waited to give you these." The last phrase came in a rush. As he hesitated, dumbfounded, she added almost defiantly, "I hope you don't mind?"

"You waited—you've been waiting here all that time? But—Jings!—we get cheap cig——"

He stopped. He was aware of his mother beside him, watching. But he saw only the anxious cameo-pale face of the girl. Beneath their bright sheen of pent courage he saw the soft, wide depth of love. The echo of his babbling trailed and drifted into the darkness unimportantly. Conscious of his gawkiness he fumbled and clasped the cardboard casket. "That was good of you." Without turning his head he said, "This is Ann White, Maw. I don't think you've met her?"

"No," said Julia.

"I just wanted to wish Colin luck," said Ann.

"Of course."

Colin stirred. "Well, thanks for the fags, Ann." He looked at Julia. "I'll need to go, Maw."

Julia nodded. He put his arms round her. "You'll look after yourself?" she whispered. Choking a sob, he nodded tight against her cheek. Her hold on him was fierce, achingly possessive. Suddenly, unexpectedly, it loosed and she called across his shoulder, "Here!"

He looked round to see Ann hesitate beyond the edge of light.

"Come back!" His mother's command was as clear and imperious as ever he remembered it. Still hesitant, timidly even, Ann obeyed. Julia waited until she was quite close and then said with a queer, quick little laugh, "Some sweetheart you! What kind of way's that to leave your lad?"

The girl's lips trembled. Two great tears glistened down her cheeks. In one movement Colin swept her into his arms and his mouth was covering hers with a hunger all time could not appease. After a long long moment he reached out with his left arm and pulled Julia into his double embrace. "You'll watch my girl, Maw?" he said huskily.

"Ay, Colin—like she was my ain."

"And you—Ann?"

"You know I will, Colin—always.'"

And then the turnstile cranked and he was down the first stairway and the clear light of the landing was full on him. He turned and lifted his hand in cheerful salute, then disappeared down the second bend of the stairs.

Walking slowly into the darkness and speaking from the lore of a dockside lifetime, Julia said resignedly, "I think he'll be all right. He didnae say but I think he's away on the *Hood*. . . ."

From somewhere by the river an unguarded welder's arc flashed. In a brief bright moment the chipped Neptunes and gargoyles prancing on the shipyard walls were thrown into stark relief. As darkness clamped down and shut them off again Julia reached and linked her arm in Ann's. "This cursed black-out!" she said, adding anxiously, "You'll have time to come up for a cup of tea?"

"You'll never get rid of me," said Ann. Together they groped their way home.

# INCIDENT
# AT PROJECT FOUR

Michael Barrett

## The Author

Michael Barrett's novels *Stranger in Galah* and *Appointment in Zahrain* have both appeared in previous volumes of Man's Book. In addition to novel and short-story writing he is closely interested in the cinema and its techniques, since he considers the screen probably the most powerful of all media for expression.

# CHAPTER ONE

ALREADY the landslip was beginning, high up over the dam site and unseen. Above the spot where the toe of the slope had been excavated to form the new channel, the slide was under way: gobbets of clay, stones, small boulders, the cracking and subsidence of the whole face: slowly, slowly downwards to the working floor, and no one was aware. . . .

The time was ten-thirty in the morning of Tuesday, the second of February. Across the Kadiri dam site work had been going on since the day-shift had started, with restless energy amid the clashing of steel and the hissing of air compressors: men's shouts and whistles blowing, the grinding, chattering racket of a battery of drills, thud of hammers, the blasting echo of dynamite shots which sounded back over the gorge from the rock walls.

Three men stood on the lip of the gorge, high on the nearside bank, watching the workmen labour far beneath them. These men were Alex Machin and Jerrold Karnow of the B.A.C. construction group, and Husain Iqbal, Pakistan Government chief safety inspection officer for the site. They were raised high above the working floor, over this scene of attack and confusion, and the whole panorama was spread beneath them as the noise and dust and fumes of excavation, scaffold-erection and shot-firing drifted up from the river bed. The winter weather was cold here on the exposed summits of rock, and a bleak wind blew over the hills to tug at their clothing. They wore heavy jackets and strong boots, kept their collars upturned.

Machin raised his head once, staring about him. In this place, here on the edge of the hills, the Punjab met the North Western Frontier Province. Down from the north on their right, from the distant snow-covered mountains of the Himalayas, down through Kashmir plunged the mighty river to sweep this gorge: through ravine and fissure, swelled by other waters, on through the rocky valley. And then, south of this place, out into the open steppes of the Punjab where it would lose its energy and impetus, broadening into wide basins and being sapped into meandering irrigation canals. Finally, far out of sight, it ran towards the lower barrages and the ultimate sea. Here at Kadiri while the river was still lithe, the new gravity overflow dam would strike across, providing water reservoir and added hydro-electric power for West Pakistan.

Machin saw the quiet, remote northern peaks in their white caps of snow, the ragged and dark cliffs amid clefts and long falls, then to the other side the empty brown plains where the river flowed cold and gleaming and endless.

But now in this dry winter season the river was tamed and sunk low; in its enfeebled state it had allowed the engineers to work their will upon it. Now a part of its flow had been led off through diversion tunnels bored through the far-side bank, to rejoin the main stream below the working area. On the dried-up river bed a new channel had been dug, the near-side coffer dam was in course of erection to enclose the working area against the floods of spring which would come in March when the snows on those far mountains would melt.

And towards this place below, the unseen, swelling and murderous slide of rock wall continued, dark and slow like malice. . . .

The three men stood beside their jeep, near the road which had been laid across the shoulder to connect the dam site with the small towns newly built for office staffs and for accommodation of the workers. The mushroom growths were cultivated in ordered rows just behind on the hillside, prefabricated shacks and made-up roads geometrically intersected, self-contained units complete with main services and street lighting. Two towns had been erected, almost alike, side by side: one for the employees of the Anglo-American B.A.C. construction group, the other town for the workers and staff of the Russian main contractors.

B.A.C. were to carry out the earth-moving, excavation and certain other preliminary jobs; the Russian group had been given the contract for building the dam itself. This was an uncertain, uneasy example of East-West co-operation over a neutral state. Project Four. . . .

Jerrold Karnow was the American local boss of B.A.C., and Machin was his British deputy. Karnow looked up at the grey sky. "Wonder just how long we've got before the big flood?"

Machin pulled a grimace. "Barely long enough."

Husain Iqbal looked thoughtful and serious.

Karnow jerked out, "Brother—we're going to do it." He spat forcefully over the side of the gorge; the spray drifted into nothingness on the wind. He was a short, burly man in his forties, square-headed and tough, with a rocky, weatherbeaten face and a thickened voice. He was uncultured and vigorous, a driving and obstinate leader, a qualified engineer who had started out as roustabout on an oil-rig. Beneath the leather jacket he wore a workman's tartan shirt, and his big hands were scarred and seamed. He had no frills about him; but he carried authority and responsibility, and he got the biggest jobs done within schedule. He had never yet been beaten.

Machin was taller and thinner beside him, a sparser, more cynical Englishman. He could never show Karnow's driving vigour because he always found both sides to a problem: so usually he squatted on the fence and considered. He was a skilled engineer and an intelligent man; but because he saw no clear path ahead he lost himself in doubt and negation. He found mostly futility, with a dry, sardonic humour. He too was in his early forties; he had acute blue eyes, a wry and disinterested mouth.

Husain Iqbal was a Punjabi, pale-skinned and quick to smile, pleasant-faced. He was sensible and cheerful, staunchly patriotic towards the interests of his young country. His soft voice came fluently in educated English or Urdu, Punjabi dialects or Pushtu. He was slender and gentle-seeming, and he had fine, tapering fingers.

Karnow gestured downwards. "Let's say, five weeks. There's a helluva lot still to come——"

They gazed below. The broad containing arc of the coffer dam was expanding slowly, a protective shield. Multi-hammer pile-drivers thrust down heavily on the sheet steel piles in their frames; a dull thud-thudding rose across the windy air as the interlocking piles drove on, on, down through seventy feet of clay towards bed-rock. And the river flowed torpid or a dormant snake beyond, awaiting its transmogrification into a rushing tiger of March.

Karnow repeated, "Five weeks. And if we *should* fail——"

"I know."

Iqbal said softly, "Perhaps the thaw may come late this year. . . ."

Karnow grunted. Then he cursed again in congested anger. "Those craphead surveyors. Why didn't they spot it?" They stared at the deep, destructive chasm in the river bed.

"Just the way it goes," Alex Machin said. "No use blaming them——"

"I know, I know." Karnow stared back at him. "One dam' thing after another—that's what's caused it. Too many holdups these last couple of weeks."

Iqbal suggested, "Your record has been very good so far. And the fall last week was unpredictable." He too glanced at Machin.

Machin stared away.

"So I know this," Karnow said gruffly. "So I'm not getting at you, Alex. And I'm sorry as all hell for that guy who got crushed. But another twenty-four hours chucked away on the schedule—this takes some catching up. Jees, we gotter do it though." He stumped a few paces away.

Machin muttered uneasily, to his own conscience, "I should have told Radford to start a retaining wall before. Time, time, all this bloody race against time. . . ."

Husain Iqbal rested a friendly hand on his arm. "Not your fault, Mr. Machin. No. . . ."

Machin was still peering down, at the chasm which split the river bed. They followed his gaze. "Bastard," Karnow said. "Sonofabitch bastard."

The chasm. The chasm, the root cause of all their trouble, their failure to keep to schedule. A hundred yards wide at the top, a fault in the rock of the river bed deep enough to bury a church and its spire, and choked with silt and clay. When they had excavated to bedrock they had discovered what the surveyors had missed or underestimated, the fissure running across the site of the dam, over the spot where the coffer dam would meet the rock slope.

Now it was almost cleaned out, ready to be filled and sealed. A couple of drag-shovels were still working in the gulley, way below the normal level of the bed; a dirt ramp had been built down inside the chasm and haulage trucks were bringing out the last loads of material. Tiny figures moved, far down among that mass of rock and clay.

Karnow was still cursing. He was nearer to being licked than he had ever been yet, and he hated it. Night and day the shifts were operating: five weeks, and if the coffer dam and site were not ready by then the river would flood the area, and there would be no more working until September. Christ almighty, and the Russkis breathing down their necks. . . .

He stared back at Alex Machin, and Machin looked at him with that same knowledge of tension, and then they gazed again at the dam site.

Husain Iqbal said consolingly, "We must wait and see."

Karnow grunted once more, controlling his exasperated scorn. A relay of dynamite shots sounded from the site below, booming loud, and his shaggy eyebrows lifted. "He's——"

Then at this moment the rock-face finally disintegrated, down to their left, and a thundering load of rock and rubble tumbled down the slope; noisy as a thousand steers in stampede, grinding, scraping, dropping headlong into the site, over the useless retaining wall which was still going up, into the river bed by the coffer dam: and then sliding over the edge into the cleared chasm, falling like an avalanche over the men and machinery working down below.

Karnow cried high, and Machin groaned. A cloud of dust founted skyward, and upon it rose the sound of tumult and the far-away yelling of men.

Karnow turned to rush for the jeep and Machin followed him. Husain Iqbal scrambled into the rear seat and the vehicle rocketed forward, tyres scrabbling on the verge, picking up on the road surface and hurtling down towards the site.

\*　　\*　　\*

On the river floor work had ceased; now the cloud of dust was settling. The chattering of drills and scrape of shovels had found an abrupt stop: there was just the hiss of escaping compressed air and a hushed stillness. The workers stood around in groups, Punjabis and Europeans, their faces shocked. The working area was a chaos of hoses and cables, ladders and scaffolding, trestles and fall-lines, rope and wire and machines and the smell of stone-dust and wet cement. From the overhead cabins of the cranes, men's faces were peering down. Above loomed the cliffs of the gorge; the same wind blew through the thin clothes of the labourers, blew over the silence.

Karnow, Machin and Iqbal ran heavily across to the scene of the fall. The slope was gashed open above them, a huge mass of rock and rubble sprawling over the foot of the wall; they peered over the edge of the chasm and the nearside end was choked high by the landslide, a great heap of piled stone. From it, on the floor of the chasm, protruded the twisted boom of a shovel. Men were down in the chasm, probing uselessly at the steep mound of rock.

The crowd of workers pressed around Karnow and Machin, still watching. Machin turned to the site engineer who had taken charge. "Anyone under it?" His voice was low.

"About ten men."

Machin sucked in his dismayed breath.

Karnow stood rigid, staring down; for a moment his face was black and stricken with bitterness and violence, then he swung on the engineer. "Who?"

Radford pointed an arm which trembled slightly; he was still young, taut and shaken. "There's a time-keeper's hut under that lot. And two shovels. . . . A clerk, two men off the shovels, the others are labourers. . . . The rest of them got away up the ramp in time."

"Punjabis?"

"All of them."

Karnow was still, struggling with it. Iqbal gazed at the site with dazed incredulity, then up at the towering rock-face.

Machin asked tightly, "Many others hurt?"

Radford gestured across the site to the first-aid post. Groups of men crowded the doors or sat around outside, bandaged and quiet.

The working area was full, engineers, artisans and labourers, Pakistani safety men, all clustering around the lip of the chasm, and waiting. . . .

Radford said at last, desperately, "What d'you want me to do, Mr. Karnow? Start digging?"

Karnow looked at Machin. At last he said heavily, "Nobody could be alive under that lot."

A whisper passed around the crowd, a sigh of fear. Machin stared up at the broken retaining wall where the slide had poured over. He was sick. Below in the chasm all now was stillness. Machin repeated, "Nobody. . . ." The wind was suddenly colder, piercing and cruel, down below the air lay unstirred as in the tomb. A last stone slithered down the slope and fell among the boulders piled on the river bed; all was over.

Then behind them somewhere, a telephone was stridently ringing in that stillness. Machin heard an outburst of high, hysteric voices in quick Punjabi, howls of fright. The crowd split apart; a Punjabi clerk stumbled through to Karnow and Machin, his eyes wild, his lips parted in terror. "O sirs, O sirs!" He quivered in panic.

Karnow spun round. "What in hell——?" His own thick voice was higher and faster than normal. "What is it?"

The Punjabi pointed an arm. "O sir! The office—the telephone!" He gestured to one of the foremen's shacks which stood in the working area a few yards away.

Machin said sharply, "What about it?"

"O sir. It makes me very frightened. It is the telephone which goes—down there." And he gestured wildly again, towards the chasm.

Machin stared blankly. Then he remembered: the time-keeper's shack in the chasm had a phone link to the upper office. His eyes widened. Karnow exclaimed, comprehending in his turn.

The Punjabi wailed hysterically, "I think it is the dead, sir. . . ."

A moan of horror passed through the crowd. Karnow turned on them. "Don't be fools!" Then he ran for the office, and Machin went with him.

They crowded into the foremen's wooden office. Shrilly the telephone on the desk began pealing again, urgent and frantic. They stared at the grey metal box, superstitiously shocked and rooted despite themselves. Outside the construction gangs swarmed round to stare blank-eyed. At last Machin moved forward, lifting the handset. His voice choked; then he said fearfully, "Yes?"

A rapid gabble of Punjabi burst into the room, squeaking desperately from the earpiece. Machin pulled himself together. "All right. . . . All right. Speak English if you can. Who are you?"

The voice changed into accented English, struggling for control. "O sir, O sir. . . . I am Rafiq Hayat, timekeeper's clerk. . . . O sir, we are trapped——"

Machin's eyes lifted to the others in the office; they watched him fixedly, suspended in tension. Karnow took a step forward. "Find out——"

Machin spoke into the microphone, searching for assurance in his own voice. "Listen, Hayat. This is Machin speaking. . . . You are going to be all right, we shall dig you out——"

"O sir——" the distant voice gulped, found itself. "O sir, it is to be hoped you can. We are very dark in here, and it is bad. . . ." The man was calmer now, finding bravery.

Machin said, "You're inside the hut?"

"Yes, sir. There are rocks all around us, we cannot get out. We are completely imprisoned, sir."

"Don't worry about that. Now we know you're all right, we'll soon reach you. . . . You say there are others in there beside yourself?"

"O yes, sir. Five of us. The others ran in when they saw the rocks coming down——"

"Five. Nobody else?"

"No, sir. All the rest is rocks. They are piled outside the hut window—we are very lucky they did not knock the whole place to pieces——"

"Yes," Machin said. "Wait just a moment, Hayat. I'll come back to you in a minute." He took the handset from his mouth and covered the microphone with his hand, straightening up. The others watched him expectantly.

He said to Karnow, "There are five of them in the hut. It's completely covered in by the rock fall—as we know."

Karnow chewed a lip. "Terrible. . . . All right. Find out the names of the others down there, tell them we'll keep a man on the phone. Then we'll see how we stand."

Machin nodded. He spoke again into the microphone. "Hayat?"

"Yes, sir, yes, sir?" The voice showed a desperate eagerness for renewed contact with the outside world, for the sound of living voices.

"Give me the names of the other men with you. Then Mr. Karnow and I are going to start making plans for getting you all out. We'll leave someone on the phone the whole time so you'll have someone to talk to."

"Sir, that is very kind of you. . . . Wait one moment. . . . These are construction workers, I see no faces in the darkness. . . ." Machin heard low muttering and then the voice again. "Sir, here is Manzur Qureshi and Abdul Quadr. Mohamad Mashriqi and Ahmad Siddiqi. . . . And myself, sir. . . ."

"Right." Machin scribbled down the names. "Now listen, Hayat. . . . As you probably know, the rock face has collapsed on you and we've got a lot of digging out to do. I'm going to put somebody else on the phone to keep in touch with you while we make arrangements. I'll come back again soon."

"Yes, sir. I am very grateful." And Hayat's voice was still steady, quick but valiant.

Machin stepped back. He held out the handset to one of the Pakistani foremen; the foreman took it gingerly, staring at the metal handpiece with horrified attraction. "Keep them cheerful," Machin said impatiently. Then he followed Karnow into the inner office. Karnow beckoned to Husain Iqbal. "You better be in on this."

He closed the inner door against the others, and the three of them stood in the empty office, gazing out through the windows over the site to the rim of the chasm, to the pile of rock which rose in the depths. They could see right down, to the cleared floor and the abandoned excavation equipment, to the tangled metal of the shovel boom which protruded from the wreckage, to the scattered fallen stones.

Karnow looked up, towards the rock face and the vanished slope, the crumbled wall. There was no danger of anything else coming down: nothing was left to come. Suddenly he clenched his ham fists, beat them against the side of his head. *"Christ almighty!"*

Machin said hollowly, "If only we'd finished that retaining wall. . . . Nobody thought it necessary, *nobody*. . . . All the experts —that'll never shift, solid as iron. Oh, damn——"

Karnow swung on him. "*Sod* your 'if only'. It's down, it's crapping well down. That's it, that's all." His face was red with passion and despair.

Husain Iqbal said worriedly, "When are you going to start digging?"

Karnow's fury died into ashes, into emptiness. "We'll start right away." His voice died low. "It'll do no good. We'll never get them out alive."

Iqbal looked aghast.

Karnow gazed through the window again. "Take a look at what's on top of them—one of two things will happen. Probably when we excavate we'll cause a settling and they'll die in the ruins of the hut—it's a miracle it's still standing anyway. And even if that doesn't happen—they can't be getting any air through that pile. They'll suffocate long before we can reach them. They're dead and in their grave, friend." And he winced, as in fearful pain.

The same pain shot through Machin, and then a sweeping nausea. Karnow opened the door and they went back to the main office; Karnow said to Radford: "We're gonna start shovelling."

Machin picked up the handset of the telephone. "Hayat?"

"Yes, sir?"

"We're just beginning the digging. Hold tight and be patient. You've got a long wait, but we'll get you out." And the false promise choked him.

"Thank you, sir. Oh, thank you."

They walked out, to the cleared bedrock. Machin said to Radford: "Get it moving. Put every bloody piece of equipment on the site into the job. Every pair of hands that won't get in the way. Draglines and dragshovels above, get the bulldozers and scrapers clearing the ramp down below and then begin there. We've got no more than a day to do it, and then their air will run

out. And if we go at it too roughly—there'll be a fall-in and they'll
be finished anyway. Good luck to you."

Radford pressed his lips together, and then he nodded and
turned aside, shouting. The crowd of men broke apart, running
for the power equipment, clearing a way. Diesel and electric
motors burst into life. All was urgency and desperation, the
running of feet, the scrambling of caterpillar tracks and giant
tyres over rocky, slippery ground.

Karnow stood on the edge of the chasm, watching the first great
metal teeth approach and bite into the mass of rock and stone.
The boom shuddered, the cables creaked. Slowly the vast jaws
closed; dripping, they rose and withdrew, dumping their load,
returning voracious for more. . . .

Karnow stared fixedly at the pile of rock, seeking down into
its depths for the trapped five men, and for the other bodies which
were already still. He pulled from his pocket the progress schedule
summary, and studied it with grim, fierce face.

Husain Ibqal said softly, "Tonight I shall be forced to despatch
a report. . . ."

Karnow gazed across the dam site to the entry road which ran
down from the hill. A harsh exclamation broke from him, and
the others looked up. He muttered, "I was expecting that."

They watched, and a large black car was descending the road,
moving towards the working site and the scene of the accident.
The automobile was a Zis, and it was the car of the Russian
Project Manager.

## CHAPTER TWO

THE Russian limousine pulled up at the end of the road. Four
men climbed out and began walking bulkily across the river bed
towards the edge of the chasm, toward Karnow and Machin.
They were swathed in weighty black coats and they came dark and
bunched together, striding out.

Leading them was the Project Manager; Nicolai Vasnetsov was
short and broad, swaddled and bearlike, thickly clothed as though
the temperature were well below freezing-point. He was of heavy
and fleshy peasant stock, cast from almost the same external
mould as Jerrold Karnow himself and yet colder-faced, and sallow;
his eyes were darker and bagged, and more severe. He stared
fixedly at Karnow and Machin as he stepped forward.

Beside him came his assistant, Sasha Bucar. And if Vasnetsov and Karnow shared a physical similarity. Bucar and Machin too seemed allied; Bucar was lean and skinny, with angular bones to his face. He had about him an air of brooding, a melancholic humour like something out of an old, dead Russia. He walked carefully besides Vasnetsov.

And the other two Russians walked with them, sturdy and empty-faced.

They came up to the group beside the chasm. To one side, the excavators continued their urgent gouging into the pile of rock. Vasnetsov said evenly in English, "Good morning, gentlemen." The other Russians nodded.

Karnow's voice was wary. "Good morning."

Vasnetsov turned to glance over the chasm. His black eyes absorbed the scene. "We heard you had trouble. . . ."

"You heard right."

"There are some men beneath this?"

"Ten, so far as we can check," Karnow said. "Five dead, five still alive."

The heavy stare lifted. "How do you know?"

"Five of them are caught in a hut down under the fall. There's a telephone line still going through."

"Ah. . . ." Vasnetsov declared, "I'm very sorry." Using English, his voice was barren and incongruous in its lack of intonation. He glanced round the site again. "So what are you doing?"

Machin said, "Digging them out, of course."

Vasnetsov turned to regard him. Again his stare quested. "You think you'll succeed?"

"Why not?"

Vasnetsov addressed Bucar. "What do you think, Sasha?" He was still using his stiff English.

Bucar hesitated, and then shrugged his shoulders.

Vasnetsov spoke to Karnow again. "I don't think you'll be successful, Mr. Karnow. Much though I regret it, I think you'll fail."

"We'll succeed." Karnow's tone sharpened with obstinacy.

"That is to be hoped." Vasnetsov was still for a while, examining the chasm. Then he declared again, "Yes, I'm very sorry. Personally I should have suggested a higher retaining wall would have been advisable. . . . But that's not directly my business, of course."

"You're dam' right it isn't." Karnow's voice went sharper yet.

Vasnetsov's tone remained flat. "I must leave it to you. I can only wish you good results, and I hope the men will be released safely. . . . Of what nationality are they, by the way?"

"Pakistanis, if that makes any difference." Karnow watched the draglines bring up and spew out another mass of stone and clay from the chasm.

"There is any help we can offer?"

"None."

"Yes. . . . So I leave you to it." Vasnetsov turned aside. Then he looked back. "It would be tasteless of me to remind you at this moment of how urgent the whole matter is becoming. For you know already what will happen if the site isn't completed before the spring thaw——"

"You don't tell me? Believe it or not, *I* know. . . ." Karnow snapped exasperatedly, "Right now, these lives are most important to me——"

"Naturally." Vasnetsov said, "I dislike to have mentioned it. But of course you're aware the penalty will operate if you are not finished by next month. And that this will mean a hold-up until September, and by then the compensation will be, yes, rather more than considerable. And of course you know I want this no more than you——"

"All right, all right." Karnow was struggling to keep temper and control, his face flushing with wrath. "You needn't bother yourself, Mr. Vasnetsov, I'm fully conscious of the way things are. . . . Now I've work to do. You'll excuse me——" And he spun on his heel and strode away.

Vasnetsov said in his toneless voice, "Good morning, Mr. Machin." And he jerked his head; the other Russians nodded formally again to Machin, and then they moved away. At the edge of the working area they stopped and glanced back, talking among themselves, then they got back into the black Zis. The car rolled forward, climbing up the road out.

\* \* \*

Husain Iqbal came over to join Machin on the edge of the chasm. "What did they want, Alex?"

"Just to remind us about the crippling penalty clause."

"If this tragic accident caused failure to complete, it would of course cost your firm a great deal."

"By September, I should think B.A.C. would be dead broke. I'd say this contract looks like being a gamble which won't come off."

Iqbal nodded slowly.

Machin said, "Not that I'm blaming the Russians. They're waiting to get on with their part of the job—they want to have it done on time for their own reasons. Prestige counts for a lot— the best excuses for failure don't take its bad smell away."

Iqbal smiled with brief, wry understanding. "I think you have more sympathy for the Russians than Mr. Karnow has."

"Ah, that's my trouble." Machin said gloomily, "I'm too bloody good at seeing the other fellow's point of view, Husain. It gets you nowhere, it destroys you. . . . For example, just now I can see the five of them alive under the fall down there. . . . Dark and cold and claustrophobia and fear, the roof pressing down, silence. . . ." He shivered, and the same quiver ran through Iqbal, the quiet expression turning to apprehension. They gazed into the pit once more.

Iqbal asked seriously, "You think the chance is small?"

"I think honestly it's infinitesmal."

And they stared over the chasm, where all the machines were now in operation. The mound of debris was going down slowly, almost negligibly. Below, the bulldozers were slamming into the fall across the service ramp, shovelling the waste to one side; men worked with spades and bare hands, digging and clearing. The remainder of the site was empty and deserted, all progress abandoned.

Husain Iqbal looked up at the sky. "It seems incredible——"

"I'll guess it's real enough if you're down under it."

Jerrold Karnow came back to join them. "This is slow, much too slow. We'll never do it. . . ." The expectation of defeat sat like a new, strange thing on his broad face, troubling it. He brushed a sweaty forehead with a rough hand. He was big and powerful and disturbed.

Iqbal suggested, "If only we could tunnel——"

"Through this goddam mixture of rock and clay? Not a hope, not a hope. We got no time——" And with anxious irrelevance, Karnow stared at his watch.

Machin said, "We didn't get much comfort from the Russians. Not that I expected any."

"Vasnetsov would see his old mother burn to get the job done on schedule. . . . What'd he have to say when I'd gone?"

"Nothing. He went right away."

Karnow nodded briefly. "He knows we're wasting our time. But what else can we do? Christ almighty, what else can we do?"

He asked uneasily, "Have you been on the phone recently to the poor bastards down there?"

"No. I'll see how things are." Machin was reluctant.

"Nothing else you can do up here. Bill Radford's got the work well under way." Karnow scrubbed a hand over his unshaven chin, pulling a face. "Me, I'm going up to main office to ring Golding in Lahore. The big boys will be just too pleased to hear about this latest little incident, just too pleased." And restively he paced away.

Machin said cynically to Iqbal, "And it won't be the unlucky blighters down below they'll be thinking of. Like the Russians, our B.A.C. overlords will be driving themselves crazy over completion dates, over the looming ghost of the Schedule. . . ."

"Against men's lives?"

"Five men weigh little on the balance scale against several million rupees." Machin and Husain Iqbal were close enough friends for him to talk freely.

"Because they're humble Punjabis?"

"Any five men, Husain."

Iqbal nodded gravely. "But that depends on who may be doing the weighing. . . ."

They went into the foreman's office. Machin took the phone from the Pakistani who was holding it. "How are they?"

He nodded. "They are not too badly."

Machin said, "Rafiq Hayat? This is Machin again. . . ." He kept his voice level, but within he was queasy and anxious.

"Ah, Mr. Machin. Thank you for coming again, sir." The distant voice sounded tinny and high-pitched down the wire, and small and fragile.

"Don't thank me," Machin said roughly. "How are you getting along, Hayat?"

"We are all right. We are waiting patiently, sir. . . ."

"We've got every machine and man in the place working to get you out. Just hang on." But he was convinced he was talking to a dead man, and his fingers trembled.

"We shall hang on, Mr. Machin."

Machin stared through the hut windows, to the pile of rock where the gangs laboured. It was difficult to connect this small voice with the depths of that rock, it came from nowhere, already from some limbo of darkness. . . .

He asked, "What's it like down there? You've no light at all?"

"There is one electric torch. We have had a look around and now we are saving it."

"Is the hut undamaged?"

"It leans slightly. The window has been broken—but a large boulder blocks it, and nothing has come in."

"Is it all rock around you, or clay?"

"Sir, it seems they are rocks."

Machin asked, "Is the air fresh?"

"At the moment it is all right." The voice said, "But I do not think there is any path through."

"We'll have you out," Machin repeated loudly. "But I'll tell you, you'll have a while to wait, Hayat."

"We are patiently waiting."

Beside Machin, Iqbal stretched out a hand. "May I talk with them?"

Machin passed over the handset, and Husain Iqbal began a conversation in Punjabi with the men below. At last he finished; he held out the handset enquiringly to Machin. Machin shook his head hastily, and Iqbal passed back the telephone to the other Pakistani who had been maintaining contact.

Machin repeated, "Make sure someone's on the line the whole time. Never leave them alone."

"But of course, sir."

Machin and Iqbal went out of the hut, standing on the edge of the chasm once more to stare fixedly at that mass of rock and dirt which the excavators tore; while above the old, still cliffs of the gorge remained.

Machin asked, "What were you talking to them about?"

Iqbal shrugged. "Nothing very much. Mostly repeating what you had said, and telling them how matters stood."

Machin glanced at him sharply. "You didn't say it was hopeless?"

"Naturally not. At the moment they are quite confident we shall get them out. . . . When one can speak directly with those in safety, the gap seems so little, a prospect of death seems so impossible."

"I know. Hell, it makes it almost worse."

"For us. Not for them."

Machin nodded slowly. At last he said impatiently, "I can't wait here doing nothing. Let's take a check around."

"Very well. Later I'll have to make a complete inspection for my Government's report."

"Come on, Husain." And Machin strode restlessly over the river-bed. They walked down the ramp to the floor of the chasm and examined the fall from there. Then they climbed up to the slope and stood on the edge of the fall, where the rock and dirt had broken away and tumbled: down, to the heap where the men and machinery toiled. Machin stared at the shattered foundations of the retaining wall and a deep, unreasonable sickness of guilt upset him. He muttered to himself.

Then they returned to the working-area. Braziers were burning on the dried river-bed, warming the men who crouched around them in thin clothing while awaiting a turn on the rescue gangs.

And then there was nothing to do indeed but wait; Machin and Iqbal squatted down on a couple of empty drums, near the heat of the fire.

It was meal-time, and hot food in metal containers had been sent down from the commissariat for the rescue workers; they ate in brief shifts snatched from the job, while the work and clashing of metal, the scraping of rock and the rumble of wheels went on.

Iqbal suggested, "Get some lunch, Alex. There is nothing we can do at this moment——"

Machin shook his head. At last he said raggedly, "I've a feeling of responsibility. I should have made sure of that slope."

Iqbal leaned forward, his eyes warm. "That's so ridiculous. You ordered all precautions, all possible tests were made——"

"Perhaps."

"Listen—it is *our* job too to see all is done satisfactorily, Alex. I tell you, if any risks had been taken, *we* would have spoken with you of them, *we* would have demanded action——"

Machin heaved his shoulders, sitting silent. He was conscious of the vastness of the gorge and the sky, the smallness of the men struggling like ants over the pile. . . . At last he said wryly, "Thank you, Husain. You're a nice fellow. You're surely the nicest Government Inspector I ever met, anywhere."

Iqbal smiled back, shy and likeable and transparently honest; he was a rare character in a world where Machin saw so often deception, following as he did so often after chicanery and political-financial machinations, the corruption of profit-hungry consortiums and the bribe-seeking hypocrisy of local officialdom, in so many parts of the world.

And then again they sat silent, gazing at the slow, blue shifting of the flames within the brazier, and listening to the rough clatter of metal against stone, beside them.

During the afternoon Jerrold Karnow came back to the site. He stood with the younger, slighter figure of Bill Radford, watching direction of the digging operations, and then he joined Machin.

His square and tough face was still worried. "Like I thought, Alex—we're in the doghouse. When headquarters heard the news about this goddam latest, they went right up the wall. We gotter work fast to save our own necks."

"We're doing all we can." Machin's own face was drawn and weary.

"So I know, so I know." Karnow stood stocky and aggressive, staring at the chasm with his jaw thrust out. "To hell with those sonofabitches in Lahore anyhow. We got enough to handle right now." He glanced up at the rock-face. "I'd say it was the blasting brought this down on us. Working too near, curse them——"

Machin said, "I'm taking the blame, Jerrold. I slipped up——"

"Jees, be quiet." Karnow turned on him. "We'll waste no time right now on an inquest anyway. What's done is . . . Say, is the line still through from the hut?"

"Yes."

"They're still all right?"

"Yes."

Karnow watched the steel traps dig into the debris. "It's a settle-down I'm most afraid of. . . . But we can't tell them to take it slow or we'll be too crapping late anyway."

"Yes."

"We just got to risk it."

"Yes."

"Can't you say any stupid dam' thing except 'yes'?" He was abruptly irritable and edgy.

"Let's not get worked up."

"All right, all right." Karnow turned away. It was a rare thing for them to jag each other's nerves.

Karnow spoke again over his shoulder after a while. "Families been informed?"

"I don't know. I'll find out." Machin was glad for something to do. He went over to the foreman's office where a Pakistani was still at the telephone. The crowd of watchers had dispersed and the office was almost empty: for now there was nothing new to say to the men below, and only the waiting, and it was upsetting to stand there by the telephone: speechless and helpless in the face of disaster, speechless as one might stand at a long-drawn-out deathbed. . . . Machin rang through on the other line to the employee records office and obtained the address and next of kin of the trapped men. The four workers from the labour force lived in one of the Punjabi villages on the other side of the hill; Rafiq Hayat had a prefab bungalow on the new estate. Nothing had yet been done to inform the relatives.

Machin hesitated, the slip of paper with the addresses in his hand. Then he asked for the other phone, and spoke to Hayat. "I'm just going to let your families know what has happened. We shan't get you out now before normal finishing time tonight."

The soft, quick voice came unchanged. "That is good of you, Mr. Machin."

"Just check these addresses, will you?" He read them out.

"Yes, they are correct."

Machin said, "Do the wives speak English?"

Hayat addressed the other invisible, inaudible men in the buried hut. Then his voice returned. "No, sir, the wives of the other four men know no English. My own wife, Nurjehan, she speaks English very well." A touch of pride was in his voice.

"Right." Machin said, "I shall go myself, but I'll take one of your countrymen with me when I see the other wives, Rafiq. Goodbye for now. . . ."

"Goodbye, Mr. Machin."

Machin gave back the handset. Outside the hut he met Husain Iqbal again; Iqbal suggested, "I shall come with you to interpret, if you wish."

"I'd be very glad of your help, if you can get away."

"Of course I can, Alex."

They got in a jeep and drove up the service road, away from the scene of the accident where machines dug endlessly, out over the hill in the late, cold February afternoon. The wind slashed at them under the canvas roof.

Machin said flatly, "This is a job I don't enjoy."

"At least you're not bringing news of certain death, as someone will to the others."

"Wouldn't that be better?" Machin turned aside to the road ahead. . . . The tar-sealed track ended abruptly and they were on the old dirt way to the Punjabi village. The vehicle pulled into the narrow street: a winter-stripped pipal tree, a few mud-walled huts and a well. Iqbal said, "I'll tell the *lambardar*." He jumped from the jeep and went to the headman's hut to explain the position; then he returned to Machin, beckoning.

They walked with the headman down the deserted street, calling at the four huts in turn. Iqbal told of what had happened, to each one of the robed, black-haired women with gaunt cheekbones who listened; and Machin watched uneasily as their cautious faces reacted, flickering into fear, and the wide lips broke into words he could not understand.

Then they drove away. The jeep bucketed over the rough road in the bleak day; Machin said uneasily, "I hope they don't come down to the site to watch. God, that's one thing I couldn't stand —the women weeping——"

"No." Iqbal shook his head. "They'll not do that. It's not the custom around here. They will—just wait."

They reached the new B.A.C. town where the other wife, of Rafiq Hayat, was living. The sharp contrast came to them, of sudden Western pseudo-civilization after the old ways; paved streets and plastic-built bungalows, electric light and sewerage and curtains at the windows. Machin pulled up the vehicle at Husain Iqbal's main office. "No need for your help with the other one—she speaks English."

"You don't mind breaking the news alone?"

Machin exclaimed shortly, "I don't mind."

Iqbal climbed out of the jeep and walked up the concrete path to the Pakistan Government safety inspection office. Machin set the vehicle moving and drove a few blocks to the street where Mrs. Hayat lived; he glanced at the slip of paper, and then pulled up outside the numbered bungalow door.

As he walked up the pathway he caught a fleeting glimpse of her face at the window, and then sickly he remembered this girl.

## CHAPTER THREE

MACHIN hesitated; but it was too late, and he had to knock on the door. The girl opened it, a young brown face with brilliant eyes, a body wrapped in swathe of green robe. Her eyes gave a flash of recognition, but she said calmly, "Yes?"

His tone was startled. "Are you Mrs. Hayat?"

"Yes?"

"Wife to Rafiq Hayat?"

"Yes, Mr. Machin."

Machin said slowly, "I have to talk to you for a moment about your husband." Then he remembered that time about three months before, the same words in a different setting; and still he was taken aback, and shocked.

"Come in." She showed no concern.

He hesitated again. "You're alone?"

"Yes. But that does not matter." She smiled with fine teeth. "My husband Rafiq is very Western, very modern. He does not have the old ideas, as you may know. . . ." She opened wider the front door. "We cannot talk here." She seemed completely at ease.

At last Machin followed her inside, walking carefully. The living-room of the small cabin was barely furnished with the standard B.A.C.-supplied pieces, and without individuality. The young woman stood in the middle of the room, waiting for him.

Machin struggled for words. He found himself completely confounded, and depthlessly afraid. Finally he said, "You have moved. . . ."

"It's much nicer here." She spoke very fair English, with a low voice.

He remembered how he had discovered that she spoke English, on the first time; he had gone to the drab hut in the village with one of the Pakistani staff, and on a similar errand. "Your husband has been taken ill at the dam site." The moment was clear and sharp, and still puzzling, and still shocking. "A heart attack. I am very sorry—he is dead ."And he remembered his sense of disquiet then: this ripe and nubile young woman, less than twenty, against the white-haired, emaciated and prematurely-old boneheap of a man in his fifties who lay stiff on the hospital bunk. . . . And the girl had appeared desolate; yet before they had left she had lifted her head and looked up at Machin, and there had been such suggestion and such invitation in her dark, flecked eyes that he had trembled.

Because cynically withdrawn and world-sceptical he might be, yet in flesh the world had its chains upon him, in fierce desire like a scourge of red iron, a torment for this wilderness. . . . And a couple of afternoons later he had returned to the hut alone, uneasily informing himself it was to discover how the bereaved young widow might be. And after that he remembered a dirty *charpoy* in the stuffy back room, and darkness and the nausea of his shame and contempt.

Now he said stumblingly, "I'm afraid I don't—quite understand. The last time——"

She appreciated his confusion and bewilderment, with a small secret grin. She explained, "Before—it was when Mubarak was taken ill. You understand—he was my other husband, Rafik's elder brother. They bought me between the two of them, I was wife to both. . . . After Mubarak's death, when Rafiq got the work in the office, the two of us moved here."

"I see. I didn't connect—I didn't expect to find you. . . ." Machin spoke raggedly. He could not think what to say next.

She asked, "It is about Rafiq you come, Mr. Machin?"

"Yes." And still he was struggling with dismay. At last he said, "You're very unlucky, Mrs. Hayat. I'm sorry to tell you Rafiq has also met with trouble at work. . . . No, he isn't dead." And he told her what had happened.

She stood thinking about it. She seemed upset, and yet she was calm, a secretive creature who was more complex than her sisters, than the sapped village women whom Machin had only recently left.

But she was younger than these others, and not yet dried to gauntness and bone; she had softer contours, flesh and light-brown skin and darkened, bolder eyes which demanded equality and not inferiority; eyes which might offer or sell but which would never give submissively. And setting her apart from her tired sisters was this quality of the aloof, the provocative; the green robe adorned her slight body like that of an houri from Eastern courts. And she stood on the cheap Western rug among the cheap Western furniture; and noticing all this, Machin remembered too the smell of the airless village hut, and lice and dirt and sticky sweat. And God, above all the shame.

Finally he said, "We shall let you know immediately we have some news, Mrs. Hayat." He sought refuge in impersonal anonymity. "We shall do our very best to get your husband and the other men out. . . . And now I must go." He turned for the door, and then he looked back. "You'll be all right?"

The girl was still standing on the rug. She said slowly, "I am —very fond of my husband Rafiq. I shall be unhappy if anything happens to him."

"I know you will," Machin replied awkwardly. "I'll do all I can."

"Now I shall go to my bed."

"You've had a shock. It will do you good." He spoke stupid conventialities.

The girl walked across the room to the bedroom. At the door she turned and stared back at him. Suddenly her face had changed. The slow sorrow had gone from her and her expression was as he had seen it once before, at the same moment indifferent and suggestive. "You can come with me again, Mr. Machin, if you like." And then she smiled.

Machin recoiled and retreated. And then the blind despair got him, and he was back where he had been before, with only a terrible ache in his loins and anguish through his brain. And stiffly he began to walk towards her, across the quiet room.

When he came out of the bungalow later he was shocked and destroyed. He caught himself peering cautiously at the windows of the neighbouring buildings as he hurried down the path, an illicit and furtive lover. . . . He scrambled into the seat of the jeep and drove wildly away from the place and from the smooth brown body, away to where his burden of responsibility lay. To the chasm and the fall, the rock-pile and the betrayed, doomed husband.

He squatted dazed and nauseated beside the glowing brazier on the river bed. *God,* he repeated to himself, *Why, why?* Early darkness had fallen over the dam site and the yellow arc-lights were blazing down, garish and violent upon the confusion where the noisy excavators still laboured.

Machin moaned slightly to himself in his self-disgust, writhing. Behind him was the shuttered lamp of the foremen's hut, the telephone link: and before him the pit, and the grunting, struggling sound of conflict in the night. And he was sick, sick.

Harsh voices, the clashing of metal and the heavy cascading of stone. Men passed, gazing at him curiously, but he did not move. He shivered, with the cold at his back and fire in his face. Later, he felt someone squat down beside him. The quiet voice said, "Hullo, Mr. Machin." He looked up at Husain Iqbal.

Machin nodded, staring away into the coals of the fire.

Iqbal watched him. "You mustn't take it so hard." The light and dark shadowed the earnest, fine-boned face.

Machin closed his eyes.

"Everything that can be done, is going ahead. . . ."

At last Machin opened his eyes again, and sat back. "I know."

Iqbal said, "What is it, Alex?"

"For heaven's sake, drop it."

"I'm sorry." Iqbal began to get up.

Machin seized his arm. "It's for me to say sorry."

Then they sat still for a while, as the job went on around them.

Husain Iqbal declared seriously at last, "So much work, so much trouble—to save five men. Who we know will probably die anyway. And there are five others lying down there dead near them, and these are already forgotten. . . . I have been thinking on the value of human life, Alex."

"Well?"

"Sometimes it's placed so high, and sometimes so low. You know? In different places and different times, it's so cheap or so dear. I remember your words. . . . Five lives weigh little against millions of rupees. . . . You know?"

"I know," Machin said tightly.

"I think the West has always had a different understanding of life's worth, compared to the East. In the East it has always been obvious, life is short and often brutal, and death is at every dawn. Western ideas have usually rated the individual more highly, and so his life has been held more precious. . . . And yet——"

"Well?"

"I am never sure how much this higher estimation of the value of life is genuine, and how much is a mere—abstraction. I mean, something which is a fine conception, but which makes no difference to the way people treat a situation. . . . I'm expressing myself badly, because my own thoughts are not clear."

"There's little difference." Machin spoke emptily, out of the depths of his own despair.

"What I mean—take a tragic position such as this. When we have five lives to set against this vast financial loss, and the great holdup of time—I wonder if there is truly any difference in approach to this—by, say, you or me, or a Russian or an American or a Chinese. . . . Often I think about these things." And his expression brooded.

"Leave me out of it," Machin said. "I don't get you."

"No. . . . I mean——" And then he frowned. "I think I don't know what I mean."

Machine stated, "There's no difference, Husain. Not by race or religion—only by individual character. Either you're a man of compassion who lives with his fellow-creatures, or you're a cold man and calculating, who lives against them."

"I'm not completely sure. Alex, I think you over-simplify."

Machin shrugged. "Just now I don't feel like comparing humanity. I merely feel like jumping over the edge into that heap of muck to join the others down there." He stood up, and walked slowly to the foremen's office.

He picked up the telephone with the dark load of guilt and foreboding upon him. The soft voice answered and he tried to fix a face around it, the face of the man he had cuckolded: a face he must have seen many times before, on the dam site, but now he could not recall it. Just a worried voice in his ears, at his conscience.

"We are still very well, sir."

"Good. I just wanted to reassure you everyone is still working full out, Hayat." He spoke with difficulty.

"Is there much still to be moved?"

"Quite a lot."

Hayat asked, "You told my wife, Mr. Machin?"

Machin's tongue touched dry lips. "Yes, I told her."

"She speaks very good English, does she not?" Again he sounded proud of her.

"Very good indeed, Hayat."

"You would call her beautiful, Nurjehan, sir?"

Machin said, "Yes."

"I will think about her." Suddenly there was a note of pathos in that small, distant voice. "Then the time will go more quickly. . . . I am lucky to have such a fine young wife awaiting me."

Machin licked his lips again. "Yes." He suggested, "Now it's evening. You'd do best get some sleep, to keep your strength up."

"We have each been dozing, Mr. Machin. But it is difficult to sleep, you know."

"Yes," Machin repeated.

"We have been telling each other stories in the dark. But time goes very slowly, and it seems so much more than nine hours."

"You'll be all right." Machin spoke raggedly.

When he came out of the hut, he walked away by himself into the dark, into the night.

The morning light was chill and grey over the site. Now the lamps burned dull and then died out; but the great machines still toiled unceasingly at the pile of rock, and now the heap was diminishing visibly; the ramp leading down into the chasm had been cleared and from top and bottom the earth-moving equip-ment was driving into the debris, advancing steadily. But still the place where the hut lay, near the side of the chasm, was buried under many feet of the fall, too many feet. And only that one, fragile cable of telephone wire led down into the middle of the heap. They dug around it, taking infinite care not to snap this one tenuous thread which bound them to the trapped men.

Rescue gangs with drawn faces worked over the site without a break. The booms of the cranes swung side to side. A wind stirred, giving a sharp, urgent bite to the morning. The area had been cleared of those employees who were not needed at the excavation, and the ground lay derelict with its abandoned, neglected apparatus. Amid all the noise the silence of the pile-drivers seemed freakish, a vacuum of sound in the absence of that endless thudding, as though some great beating clock had ceased and a spring had unwound.

Machin stood on the edge of the chasm, rooted still, bleary-eyed to watch the debris rise up; and then he saw Jerrold Karnow come pacing rapidly across from the service road, and he knew from Karnow's face as he came that something else bad had happened.

Karnow walked up to him, broad and massive, panting for breath, and his tough expression was twisted into fury and bitterness. "Alex," he snapped. "Alex, come over here."

They turned aside to the foremen's hut, went through the outer office past the telephone, to the inner room. Karnow slammed the door and turned to peer through the window. He beat his fists against his forehead, and his face was stricken.

"What is it?" Machin jerked his arm.

"The Russians. The lousy, inhuman swine——"

"What?"

Karnow stared round the office. At last he spoke, and his voice was still congested with fury and violence. "Vasnetsov's just been down to see me. Walks in and calmly tells me we got no sweet hope of digging out in time. So he says to maintain schedule we got to fill in the chasm right away and seal off. Cement the poor bastards down there into their tomb——"

He broke off, and they looked at one another with horrified eyes.

*      *      *

Machin found his voice at last, through the fear which had paralysed him. "He's mad——"

Karnow shook his blunt, cropped head. "No. Nothing like it —he's just too goddam sane and realistic. He's inhuman, he's got no soul——" But now Karnow was getting a grip on himself; the hot flush was dying from his cheeks and he was harder, grimmer.

Machin muttered shakily, "Murder—just murder." And he turned to look out at the fall of rock where the men lay, and the nausea in his stomach rose sour into his mouth.

"I know the way he's thinking. Too dam' well, I know." And now, Karnow's control had become greater than that of Machin. His full lips were set straight, and his guttural voice was fierce and sombre. "He's no cursed fool. Vasnetsov knows we don't stand a cat in hell's chance of getting them out alive—we're just deludin' ourselves, putting on a show. He says there's no time for that, we got to write-off and get on with the job. Jees, he's got no heart, he's pitiless—and he don't mind admitting it." There was reluctant, shocked understanding in his tone. "And he makes me want to spew."

Machin turned his head away, swallowing his own choked sickness. "We're not going to do it?"

"You bet we're not. I've got a call booked to Golding right now——"

"Vasnetsov can't make us——"

"Don't fool yourself about that—according to contract he can. You know it, Alex—as Project Manager he's got overriding authority." Fresh anger spurted up in Karnow. "This is one time we don't accept it. I'm going back to pick up that Lahore call now—thought I better let you know right away." And Karnow too stared through the window, over the scene of the accident. "Lousy, dirty luck." He spat the words, his face grey. "Not a cat in hell's chance. . . . They're done and they don't know it. And we know it, but we got to go on. . . . But it's them I'm thinking about, Alex. God almighty, to do that to them. . . ." He turned for the door. "Let you know, soon as I've spoken to Lahore. I'm going to get authority to tell Vasnetsov what he can do with his orders. Just where he can put 'em. . . . I'll say now, he'd never dare to make a case of it anyway—if the news got around, the Russkis would be something more than unpopular with the natives, heh?" He pulled a tight, bitter grimace and went out.

Machin stood alone in the office; then he could not stand this aloneness among the quiet with its echoes of voices, and quickly he strode out. In the other office he passed by the telephone. He walked rapidly to the outer door and then, drawn by his cruel sense of responsibility, he came back.

He said to the foreman in charge, "How are they?" The man held out the handset, wordlessly. Machin repeated, "Hayat?" And then again, "Hayat?"

When the voice came it shocked him afresh by its slowness, its painful concentration. "Yes, Mr. Machin?"

"Is everything still all right?"

"Yes. . . ." He was remoter than ever, down a long, echoing tunnel. "We are still here. . . . But naturally we're still here. . . . But we are growing very tired. . . ."

"What's the matter, Hayat?" Machin spoke urgently.

"Sir, I think it is the air." Hayat struggled into wakefulness. "I believe the air is running lower, that is why we are so tired. It is—very stuffy, we are developing headaches."

"You're imagining it, Hayat." He was harsh and desperate. "Not for a long time yet, and by then we'll be down to you. We're well on the way, you must keep yourselves lively and alert. Don't let yourselves give up. You hear me?"

"Yes, Mr. Machin. And we shall try, we are doing our best. But it's so dark, and there's dust in our mouths, and we have nothing to drink——"

"You're men, Hayat, you must wait bravely like men." And again Machin was sickened by the falseness of his own authority. "It's morning—by evening we shall be down to you."

"Sir, are you sure of this?"

"Yes." He promised recklessly, "Just wait until evening."

"Then we'll endure, indeed we'll endure."

Machin heard a quick chattering in Punjabi, and in the background, away below, the throaty exclamation of relieved voices. Hayat repeated, "Sir, now we'll be better. For we were beginning to lose hope. . . ."

"You'll be all right. You're going to be all right." Machin came out into the open air, still hearing the words of his own frantic promise, and he was unsteady and more deeply afraid.

He went over to stare once more into the chasm, irresistibly drawn towards the sight, and powerless, while the engineers and workers laboured about him. Now the wrecked shovels had been uncovered, their holed cabs, the broken doors; the mound of debris was being eaten away by the steady jaws of the machines, too slowly, too slowly. And carefully as the men worked, every instant there was the risk that their operations would start another slide of the fallen rock, and a packing-down which would crush the buried hut as the crumpling of a matchbox, into silence and end. From below came an outburst of noises, and then quiet, the excavators temporarily stilled: Machin peered below, and the broken body of one of the men who had been caught in the open, was uncovered. Carefully the body was carried up out of the chasm, and borne away. Men's faces turned to glance, and then were averted. Then the diesel and electric motors whined into action again, and once more the heavy steel traps dug in. . . .

Karnow's jeep came back down the service road from the office, pulling on to the river bed. Machin waited as Karnow climbed out and walked slowly across the dried ground to him. When Karnow was close, Machin could not read the meaning of the look on his face, and its stiff rigidity puzzled him.

Karnow said, "Any developments?"

"They've discovered one of the other bodies—down there."

Karnow nodded. "And the fellers in the hut?"

"I spoke to them a while back. The air's beginning to run out."

Karnow's gaze lowered. There was a long silence. Then Karnow said, "Let's go back in that office, Alex. I got something to tell you." His voice was heavy.

Machin glanced at him, and then followed him to the shed. Karnow called out to one of the engineers. "You seen Mr. Iqbal?"

The engineer pointed across the site.

"Send someone to fetch him, will ya? I want to talk to him."

They stepped inside the office. Karnow glanced at the grey telephone box with its patient attendant as he went by, then quickly he stared away. Machin came behind him, and he was suddenly made uneasy by Karnow's manner.

They leaned against the bench in the inner office, their eyes still drawn automatically to the rescue operations beyond. Then Karnow dragged his stare away; he pulled out a pack of cigarettes, and his bearing sagged as though he were tired. The fleshy, sturdy frame drooped slightly. "Cigarette?"

"Thanks." They smoked rapidly.

Karnow said, "We better wait till Iqbal gets here. It'll save going through this twice."

Machin frowned. He inhaled, then coughed.

Karnow was restless. He chewed the end of his cigarette, spat fragments. Then he said, "These crapping accidents. Every blasted job you work on, you get these fatalities. I call myself tough, I guess I should be used to it by now. But I'm not, God knows I'm not. . . . Still, that's the way it goes. Like a goddam war, you want to win, you got to lose some lives. . . ." He seemed to be trying to justify himself, to console himself.

Machin waited, feeling a slow, apprehensive tension beginning to rise.

A knock came at the door. Husain Iqbal entered, glancing curiously from one to the other.

Karnow nodded. "Ah." He held out the cigarette pack; Iqbal

shook his head. Karnow fiddled the pack between his fingers, and then roughly he stuck it in his pocket and straightened up. His face set firm, in some hard decision. "I asked you to join us, Mr. Iqbal, because this concerns you too. . . . I've just been speaking with our Lahore office about this—this unfortunate tragedy." Now his voice came louder and he spoke harshly, driving his words on roughshod to their end. "We've come to a decision— that's to say, headquarters and myself both—and you must be the first to hear. I'll say it's difficult, I'll say it's even terrible, but it's inevitable. *Inevitable.* . . . We're going to abandon our rescue attempts down below. We're going to fill in, and seal the chasm the way it is now." And then he watched their faces.

## CHAPTER FOUR

HE was prepared for a wild, recriminatory outburst, but at first instead came frozen and incredulous stillness. Machin's mind threw sudden, fearful images: wet and slurping cement, a tortured face, then the smile on the lips of Nurjehan Hayat, and then the crumbling and breaking of the half-finished retaining wall: the load of cement and rock upon his own shoulders, so he too was gasping for life and air. . . . And he choked.

And Husain Iqbal's expression was as stricken; he stared disbelievingly at Karnow.

Machin said at last, "You know you can't do this, Jerry."

Iqbal began to speak. "No. . . . No, you must not, Mr. Karnow. How could you—to bury living men. Indeed, it would be murder, the vilest murder——"

Karnow said harshly, "Listen to me. Now give me a chance to explain." He trembled slightly, passing a hand across beads of sweat on his brow; such small signs alone indicated the stress that was within him. His face remained fixed and sure. "I never expected you to praise me—let's just get it clear the way things are."

Again they stared at one another in locked horror. Iqbal was shaking his head violently; Machin remained transfixed in fear.

Karnow spoke hoarsely. "I tell you, they're done. At the rate we're going we'll never possibly reach them alive—and before we get down much farther it's a practical certainty there'll be a cave-in. I tell you, they're dead men. . . . There's nothing we can do to save them. And a major job like this you've got to treat like a war campaign—individual sentiment don't count, you've got to go for the main objective——"

Iqbal stepped forward suddenly and slapped Karnow's bristled cheek. His eyes were burning; Karnow put a hand silently to his cheek. Iqbal said in a low, passionate voice, "And you'd bury alive my countrymen, Mr. Karnow."

"No." Karnow burst out in one frenzied bellow at last, like a stuck boar. "No. *Will* you listen to me. . . ." He was breathing hard, quivering now. "I didn't say that. You think I'm the lousiest bastard under the sun? I tell you, I'm just facing realities, the way you're not. . . ."

Then he stopped, and again they faced one another, wild-eyed. Outside the window the work went on, within was silence.

Karnow said in a desperate, throaty tone, "At the moment we've got all the gangs, every machine, working all out on the fall. We can't go on like this any longer, on this futile attempt. We've stopped the pile-drivers in case they cause any further settling. . . . We just can't do it, time's too precious. . . . So we got to start work again on the site, we got to beat the deadline. . . . We'll have to draw much of the power equipment away from the fall, to use it on other work. Then we'll start filling in the chasm from the other end. Any of the labour force we've got over—sure, we'll leave them on the job and we'll let them do all they can until it's time to pour. They'll never reach those guys, I'll tell you, and the men inside will be dead long before we're ready to seal over. . . . But I'm sorry, believe me I'm sorry as hell. Listen, if my own boy was down there I couldn't feel worse about it. . . . I only know I got a job to do." And now a rough, tormented agony showed upon him.

Iqbal repeated hopelessly, "You mustn't do it, Mr. Karnow."

Machin said, "So what changed your mind, Jerry?"

Karnow faced him. "We thrashed it out over the phone. I tell you, this is the only way——"

"Seems to me you've been brainwashed. . . . Now you're on the side of the Russkies, eh? Communists and capitalists, lying down together. And to hell with the poor fools underneath——"

Karnow said, "Shut your goddam mouth, Alex——"

"No, thanks. . . . It's the money, isn't it? Back in Lahore, they're thinking of the penalty clause. Not about Hayat and his friends——"

Karnow said tightly, "We've got to get that coffer dam completed. There's no other choice."

"You think one day's going to make any difference?"

"Even a few hours might settle it one way or the other. You know that as well as I do. . . ."

"Call in Radford. He'll tell you how long he reckons to be——"

"I'm not interested. It's too late. I'm sorry, we got to go ahead——"

Machin demanded, "Do the Russians know what you've agreed?"

Karnow hesitated. "Yes. I rang Vasnetsov after I spoke to Golding."

"Before you told us, eh?"

"I was up in the main office," Karnow said roughly. "Blast it, Alex, I'm boss of this——"

"It's on your head."

Husain Iqbal repeated, "You mustn't do this, Mr. Karnow." His pale brown face was obstinate and shocked.

Karnow said flatly, "I'm sorry."

Machin felt the unstable, sick fright in him, and the burden of his guilt; he found time to ask himself fleetingly if the depth of his revulsion came from his sense of common humanity, and if he would have been so wildly horrorstruck but for that deep, overriding sense of guilt. Surely he would; but he did not wait for the confirming answer. He said loudly, "Those men have a chance, Karnow. Remote it may be, but there's a chance and you know it. And while there's that smallest possible chance, we have to concentrate all out upon saving them. That's all that matters."

"Such is the position." Iqbal nodded.

Karnow shook his head. "I told you we've thought this thing out, and we've decided——"

"You, you're just thinking of your own skin, Karnow. Afraid you'll be chucked out of your job. I never knew you were chicken-livered as all that."

Karnow took a pace towards Machin. "I told you to shut your blasted mouth."

Anger licked up afresh like flames into the room. Machin said hotly, "You and the bloody Russians. You're in fine company, you bunch of assassins."

Karnow's gaze flickered, but still he watched Machin narrowly. "Just why are you getting so goddam worked up? Never known you blow off like this before. . . . Got something on your mind, eh? Too late now, boy, too late——"

Machin's consuming fire of despair broke out, and then they

were struggling with one another, their faces contorted. Husain Iqbal pushed his lean frame between them, tugging them apart. He spat out words. "Men are dying—and you lose your tempers and fight like children. You should be ashamed——"

They stood apart, shaking and panting, recovering themselves. Beyond the window, the machines still brought up great gobs of clay and rock; the work went on. Karnow mopped his face. Machin turned aside. Iqbal gazed stilly at the two of them.

Karnow opened the door to the other room. The Pakistani foreman remained crouching over the telephone; he looked up curiously. And from the inner office they stared out at the metal telephone box. Then Karnow closed the door.

He went over to the window and gazed out, his broad, square back to Machin and Iqbal. At last he said, "Vasnetsov's car is just arriving. I arranged for him to come down again to see the way things stand. I'll fetch him in here and we'll get this thing settled." He turned and strode out of the office; from the window they watched him walk slowly over the site to meet Vasnetsov and Bucar, who stepped from the Russian car.

Machin and Iqbal stood facing one another; Machin's eyes fled away from Iqbal's glittering stare, and his skin burned feverishly as though disgusted by its own colour.

At last he said unsteadily, "I'm ashamed all right, Husain. I'm ashamed. . . ."

Iqbal spoke now in a dead tone. "So now I see. Things are made clear to me. . . . No more talk, no more lies and arguments. Politics, catchwords, democracy and communism and freedom and equality. . . . I spit in all their faces. . . . Talk, they talk, they're all the same under the mask. Men without pity, without compassion, with only selfishness and self-interest. . . . There's no honour."

They were silent. Machin remembered dully the lust which had betrayed him, the soft quiet voice of the man down below, and he was choked by the same swill of disgust.

Finally he said, "What are we going to do?"

Iqbal's dark brown eyes were on him again. "We?" And his voice renounced their friendship, setting Machin among the others, these invaders who came to a country without respect like any colonial power of old, bringing only opportunism and seeking only profit, of money or influence.

Machin jerked a restless hand. "We can stop this. You know we can—whatever they intend, they daren't go ahead with it against public opinion. If we threaten to spread the news around —to your government, to the unions—they'll have to give in. Hell, their names would stink through all this corner of the world. They could never risk it—neither the Russians, nor our own people. They'd sooner let the dam go hang than face that——"

Iqbal was watching him uncertainly. "I think you're right. And I shall make this clear to them. . . . But I can't trust you either. Now, I shall not trust you, Alex." He was unhappy.

Machin turned aside. "No," he said slowly. "And I don't want your trust, Husain. . . ." Then he straightened up. "They're coming."

He opened the office door as Karnow came back into the hut with Vasnetsov and Bucar. The burly figures tramped across the wooden floor; then Karnow spoke to the Pakistani at the telephone. "You can go now, thanks. We'll take over the line for a time." Vasnetsov's stare covered the metal box, expressionlessly. Then he moved on with the others, to the inner office.

Karnow shut the door and they stood facing one another around the room. It was warm and heated; Vasnetsov unbuttoned his overcoat, glancing carefully from Machin to Iqbal as he did so. "Good morning, gentlemen."

Iqbal nodded. Machin made no reply. Karnow said with harsh, ragged urgency, "All right. Let's get this thing done."

Beside Vasnetsov, Bucar's lean frame was stiff and cadaverous; his expression showed a certain disquiet. Vasnetsov's heavy-browed, rounded face remained prepared but unemotional. Machin waited, frowning, and Husain Iqbal stood isolate beside the wall. Karnow hawked roughly and uneasily from his throat.

And in the outer room, the telephone lay quiet and deserted. Through the steamed windows, the rescue gangs still toiled at the fall.

Karnow said, "This is a tragic business, gentlemen, and nobody feels worse about it than I do. . . ." He was speaking slowly now. "We all know the facts, so I'll only repeat the essential ones. Mr. Iqbal is here, being a representative of the Pakistan Government, the rest of us speak for our own groups. We have to make the decision right here between us, before we let the rest of them in on it. All right——"

Iqbal interrupted quietly. "If this is an official meeting, Mr. Karnow, it should be reported. And I have no authority——"

Karnow said, "It's an emergency meeting. Let's not get formal with each other—this is one time to talk freely."

"I agree." Nicolai Vasnetsov waved an impatient hand, his heavy body still. Despite his impassiveness there was about him nevertheless a suggestion of positive drive, a banked energy. The small close-cropped head was set alertly on his shoulders.

"All right," Karnow said again. "So we've got five men down here. And no chance of getting them out alive——"

"There's a small chance," Machin said.

"No chance. No goddam chance at all." Karnow's voice rose.

"None," Vasnetsov agreed.

Machin said, "Just what do you know about it, Mr. Vasnetsov?"

"No chance," Vasnetsov repeated, ignoring his words. "None at all, I tell you."

Iqbal said, "But these men are still alive——"

"For how much longer?" Vasnetsov answered in the thick, unstressed accent. "I'm told the air is going. . . . Very little longer, I am sorry."

Jerrold Karnow dropped a clenched fist on the bench, the noise resounding. "No chance. . . ." His voice died, came back to fierce vigour. "So we've two alternatives—to continue the shutdown and this wasted struggle, till we get down there and find them stone-cold, fetch up the bodies just to bury them again. . . . Or else we cut our losses and get some of the men back to work on the coffer dam. That way we still stand a lousy hope of completing in time. The first way, we still lose those guys down there and we lose the dam as well. . . . So we got to make a tough decision, and I feel bad about this—bad as it comes. But I know we're right."

Machin said, "If the decision's already made, why this conference about it?"

"Just to let everyone get it clear."

Machin said with cold, bitter malice, "Who's going to tell the men down below, Jerry? Tell them that we're abandoning them, leaving them to their own bloody bad luck? Are you?" He paced to the door, jerked it open and pointed at the grey, silent telephone box. "Tell them. Go on and tell them. . . ."

Karnow wiped the back of his hand across his mouth. Then he said heavily, "I know how you feel, Alex. Jees, I tell you I feel the same way. But it's no good. No dam' good at all. There's nothing else we can do."

Machin stabbed a hard, desperate finger. "Tell them!"

Vasnetsov lifted a hand as though to interrupt. Then he glanced at Bucar and was silent. Iqbal's pale brown face was stricken.

At last Karnow moved forward. He pulled his big body like a deadweight across the office, towards the telephone in the other room. Then he turned back to them, and his expression was grim. His hand reached out: but he did not pick up the handset. Horny fingers grabbed for the flex which led to the cable connection. He jerked, and the broken ends dropped to the floor. "They're dead men," he said hollowly. Then slowly he came back to the other room.

Machin stood away from him. "Jerrold——"

Vasnetsov spoke seriously. "It's done, Mr. Machin." He explained: "Everyone would not understand. So we shall have it given out on the site, before we recommence work, that the men are already dead. . . . Yes, I know it is cruel, but once again it must be repeated, there is no other choice."

Bucar added in a low, set tone, "It's true, there's no other hope." The long frame relaxed, in some sense of decision completed.

Machin turned to Iqbal.

And Husain Iqbal thrust himself forward suddenly; he stood upright and severe and his eyes glittered once more. "No, it isn't done." His speech trembled in his intensity. "The decision isn't done, Mr. Karnow. I will not let it be made. If you try to carry out this monstrous thing, I shall inform my Government the truth of what you are doing. And I'll make the same truth known to the trades union representatives, and to the press. There'll be an inquiry, you will be labelled as murderers throughout Pakistan and far beyond, your names and your countries will be reviled in the streets——"

He stopped, breathing wildly, and there was silence. Machin added, his voice dragging behind: "And I'll support Iqbal. I'll swear you away into hell if you take one single man or machine off the rescue work." But there was no conviction of righteousness behind his words, and only fresh sickness.

Karnow was still and moody like a hewn rock figure, squat and fierce, thinking it over. Then the broad shoulders heaved in a great shrug. He sat down carefully on the bench, and stared at Vasnetsov, then at Husain Iqbal.

After a long time he said, "You're judging us too harshly and unfairly, Mr. Iqbal. We didn't have to let you in on this, y'know.

We could've kept it quiet, given out word they were now dead, and I guess nobody would have known better. . . . But I'm no goddam murderer though you seem to think I am. I tell you, knowing all the circumstances and judging all the chances, and thinking of those poor bastards below as much as though they were my own flesh and blood, I tell you I'm still sure we got to do what I've said." His gaze moved across to Machin. "And that goes for you too, Alex."

Machin closed his eyes. He heard Vasnetsov speak. "You must surely understand, Mr. Iqbal, how much is at stake in this moment, in this Project Four. For if this stage of the work is not completed in a few weeks you know it means a hold-up of several months, perhaps a whole year. And you know how urgently the district is awaiting the benefits which the dam will bring. Water and power, greater development of the land—we bring new life itself. Who knows, the waste of one year might lose many more lives than these five below. We have to think of these things, and we do so. I promise you, we are well-meaning men who work for the good of all people. . . ." He spoke stiffly, but he seemed sincere.

Husain Iqbal's voice came slowly out of the silence, hesitant and strained. "I am sorry if I misjudge your motives, Mr. Karnow, and you too, Mr. Vasnetsov. Sincerely I apologize. . . . But still I insist, I cannot possibly agree to what you say."

Machin kept his eyes closed. There was a further silence. At last Karnow spoke again, and he was gruff and abrupt. "All right. If that's the way you feel. Obviously you force me out of it— we'll carry on just the way we are. One more day—and you'll see if I was right, by the end of that time."

Machin opened his eyes at last, and lifted his head. "You could never possibly be right, Jerrold."

Jerrold eyed him bitterly without speaking. His face was clotted with resentment. There was a gathering of the same dark temper on Vasnetsov's brow; then he shrugged. "It will be seen, certainly." He turned to Karnow. "Then if this is so, I wish to remain down here, Mr. Karnow, to watch the operations. You've no objections?"

"Suit yourself." Karnow swung round and strode rapidly from the room. Vasnetsov jerked at Bucar's arm, and the two Russians followed.

Machin and Iqbal were left. Then Iqbal too walked out, silently, and Machin was left alone. He gazed through the window over the chasm once more; then he went back to the other office.

The telephone cord still dangled to the floor. He fetched a pair of pliers and squatted down to the terminal box, rewiring the joints. He finished the job and stood in the empty office for a while, staring at the silent instrument. Then slowly he lifted the handset and made the connection.

\*    \*    \*

The voice came through high and eager, the words tumbling. "Yes, yes, Oh yes? Who is it?"

Machin struggled for speech, over a breathless gap. Then he said, "Machin here. We had a break in the line. . . . You still all right?"

"Sir, we're so relieved to hear you. We wondered what had happened. . . . We thought we were cut off."

"You're still all right?" He repeated it.

"Yes, sir, we still endure, all of us. But the atmosphere grows heavier, we are finding it difficult." Hayat's voice had dropped from its high initial fervour to a breathless sigh, as though exhausted by its outburst.

"We're getting closer to you. Can you hear anything?" Machin spoke quickly over the silences in his mind.

"Yes, Mr. Machin, now we hear the noise through the rock. Of grinding, and striking——"

"There's been no settling down?"

"No, I don't think so. . . . You promised us by evening, Mr. Machin? It will be so?"

Machin hesitated and then he said blindly, "Yes."

"Ah. . . ." The voice was quiet for a moment and Machin heard only heavy, deliberate breathing over the distorting phone. "That will not be too soon." Hayat said with hazy concentration, "It has not been so very long, but it seems an age. It is—it is only eleven by the clock. Is that right?"

"Yes." Machin was disturbed by the dazed, incoherent quality which had come into the voice. "Don't speak too much, Hayat. You'll waste the air."

"My mind has been working fast, much faster than I could ever speak. Only—yesterday morning—that I left my home, and my wife Nurjehan, to come to work. I think that is very far away, so far."

Machin said desperately, "It won't be long now."

"Sir, I have a terrible headache. Terrible. . . . Yet through it I see pictures. . . . Mr. Machin, what if you should fail and we die?"

"No." He heard his own word crackle into the microphone. "We'll not fail. You've only got a few more hours to wait, Rafiq."

"Sir, I think you are right. Only a few more hours." Hayat whispered, "God is great and wise and merciful. So there's no sorrow, whatever comes. . . . But I would like to live, I am not yet eager to die. . . ." And then he had dropped from English into Punjabi, and was muttering something Machin could not understand.

Machin said sharply, "Wake up, Hayat. Come on——"

"Of course, I am sorry." Hayat's voice returned towards normality. He spoke calmly. "I am very grateful to you, Mr. Machin. It has made a great difference, to know what you are doing for us——"

"You owe me no gratitude," Machin interrupted. "Now save your strength. Take it carefully with what air you've got left— you'll last it out." His mind was split, each half listening to his words and putting its own meaning into them: one half accepting them at their face value, clinging frantically to that ghost of a chance he had argued with Karnow, that these men would still come out alive and his own sin would be assuaged: and the other half of his mind knowing these words for easy promises to calm the last hours of the doomed, and to calm himself, the whole ridden I.

Hayat said from far away, "Until evening. Goodbye, Mr. Machin." And the line clicked dead.

Machin sat listening, but nothing else came. Then he put down the receiver and walked outside slowly, on unsteady legs. It was cold across the dam site, but his brow was clustered with sweat.

He stared with empty eyes across the chasm. Two more bodies had been brought up from the floor of the pit, and they lay shrouded nearby, awaiting removal. Machin looked at them, and then again into the heap of rock where the thin telephone cable sneaked downward. The metal traps of the machines continued the endless gouging into the fall. Vasnetsov was watching on the lip of the chasm with Radford; he appeared to be supplying orders or suggestions, his hands gesturing, his face resolved. He had thrown off his overcoat and donned a dirty overall, and he seemed energetic and purposeful as any of the men on the gangs, one among them with his short, broad figure and blunt worker's head.

Bucar stood with him. Jerrold Karnow was on the other side of the pit.

Machin's eyes lifted to the rim of the canyon, to the shelf where the cement mixing plants were built and prepared ready for the pour, for sealing-off the chasm. . . . And then he thought again of the clotting of wet cement over agonized faces, and then again of the face of Nurjehan Hayat.

Suddenly he turned and walked from the dam site; he took a jeep and drove to the woman's bungalow.

He knocked at the door and she opened. She wore the same robe and her figure was as nubile, but her eyes were afraid when she discovered him.

"Don't worry," he said. "I just want to talk to you for two minutes."

She inclined her head, and he followed her into the living-room, her small bare feet padding the floors. Then she stared at him carefully, and she saw only the ashes and desolation of the lust which had been on him before. Again she inclined her head.

Looking back at her, Machin knew he would never understand her, even if he understood too well himself. But he had neither time nor wish to understand. He was conscious only of that black ash of defeat and desolation inside him, a black stain on all beauty. He said flatly, "I have come here to apologize, Mrs. Hayat."

She waited a while, her head turned away. Then she said, "But it is for me to apologize, Mr. Machin."

They were silent. At last Machin said, "I wanted to apologize to your husband. But of course I cannot——"

She lifted her head and stared at him. "He is——?"

"He's still trapped under the fall. We're working nonstop to get them out."

She murmured under her breath. "You will?"

"I can't be sure. But we'll try."

"I may come to watch?"

"I think you will be better at home. We'll let you know immediately there is news——"

Then the young, lush face was stark and bare as a primitive's in grief, with high cheekbones and long, falling hair.

"I'm sorry." Machin was clinically cold in his despair. He moved for the door. "You forgive me?" He was seeking through her to the man whose forgiveness he would never get.

"Yes." But he did not think she would understand. She said,

"I do not want Rafiq to die." And her lips were unsteady as a child's.

"I know." Then Machin came away, and drove back to the dam site.

\* \* \*

He was down in the chasm, waiting while from above and below the earth-clearing machinery dug into the pile; Husain Iqbal walked down the dirt ramp and crossed over to him. "Alex?"

"Yes." Machin's collar was upturned and his head was sunk on his chest as he watched. He did not look up.

Iqbal said, "I have been speaking with the Ministry in Lahore. They are sending up a Commission to enquire into the disaster."

"Yes?" His tone was indifferent.

"I know. . . . Who cares what comes after? This is all that matters. . . ." And Iqbal's narrow, keen head turned to the fall where machines and men struggled. Above, from the river bed faces peered down; and higher still rose the old rock of the gorge, to the rim where the bitter midday wind swept by.

"*You're* all right." Machin muttered it.

"What do you mean by that?"

Machin drew himself up, shivering. "Nothing. . . . Just that you've nothing to reproach yourself over. I have. . . ."

"Why?"

"That's my worry, not yours." He felt a need to confide or confess, but he had no confessor. . . . He grunted, "Oh, forget it."

Iqbal turned to him. "I have been thinking over what I said to you this morning—about not trusting you. I'm sorry, Alex. I was upset—will you let me take it back?"

"There's nothing to take back. Never trust anyone—that's the safest outlook on this bloody world."

Iqbal's dark eyes regarded him. "You feel this thing very badly. Fate is fate—some men run into catastrophe and destruction, some are spared. Such is life, such is God's way. We have to accept and understand it as it comes. So long as we do all in our power to assist others——"

"Platitudes. . . . You talk about aid—myself I find more often helping hands ready with another push over the cliff edge."

"These?" Husain Iqbal nodded gently to the rescue gangs which battled unceasingly against the stubborn rock.

"Oh, men are comradely enough when they've nothing much to lose by it. But when it cuts right across their own interests——"

"Ah. You're thinking of Mr. Karnow and Mr. Vasnetsov?" Iqbal's tone had changed.

"Among others. Among others nauseatingly well known to me, whom I could name." And he was conscious of weak self-pity mixed with self-disgust in his voice, and despising it.

Iqbal said, "I have been thinking too of these men. I wish I knew——"

"What?"

"When they spoke this morning Mr. Karnow and Mr. Vasnetsov seemed sincere—that the course they recommended was the best, from a reasoned point of view. And I prevented that course, and I am sure *I* was right, but still I wonder. . . ."

Machin watched another load of excavated material pour from the opening jaws of a shovel, to the dump above. He said slowly, "Jerrold Karnow has never before fallen down on a contract. He's got a job and a reputation to lose. Vasnetsov is in the same position, and working to the greater glory of the U.S.S.R. . . . Maybe they *think* they're being objective and clear-sighted—" He shrugged. "I don't know. I don't know. I can't fool myself *I'm* unbiased. I've got a load of guilt on my back and I can't shrug that off."

"You're crazy, Alex." Concern came back to Iqbal's expression. "So many times I've said, the landslip was unforeseen, incredible. You're *not* to blame——"

"We were working against time. Everything was cut too fine. . . . Anyway, I've got other reasons." And again he stared away.

Iqbal shook his head slowly from side to side, several times.

Machin said wildly, "We're all guilty men, Husain. Because we live for our own lousy affairs, our own desire and our own pride and our own fear, and to hell with the rest of them. And the devil takes his victims. *We* put them down below, friend—nobody else."

"I wonder if Karnow and the Russians would have had the same intention, if the men trapped had been Europeans?" Iqbal's tone was intense.

Machin grunted. "See that—it's the same in yourself, friend, don't deceive yourself. You're not so damned interested in the fate of those men just as men the way you believe, out of warm humanity. No, it's because they're of your race and you identify yourself with them, against the foreigners. It's yourself you're thinking about really, it's race consciousness that drives you——'

Iqbal paled. Then he cried softly, "No, No!" He swung round and walked off quickly, in some state of high agitation.

Machin called out. "Husain!"

But Iqbal did not heed; his long legs carried him away fast, and he was almost running.

Machin cursed. "God," he said at last. "I've destroyed enough. It's time to *do* something. . . ." He stared up at the wintry sky, where once he had seen blue empyrean worlds.


## CHAPTER FIVE


HE climbed up the ramp and tramped across to where Karnow stood with the site engineer, Radford. The restless, neurotic tension which had been building up in Machin spilled out wildly. "Listen," he said. "I can't stand hanging around any longer. What can *I* do to help for God's sake——?"

They stared at him. Radford said slowly, "Nothing, Alex. Nothing at all. We just have to wait. . . ." His young, unshaven face was curious.

"I can't wait. . . . Let me take over an excavator. Or anything. I just need to do something with my hands——"

Karnow snapped, "Be your age, Alex. Just get a grip."

"Maybe I've got more conscience than you——"

"Shuttup," Karnow said savagely. "Shuttup."

Radford gazed at the violence upon them. Then he shrugged awkwardly and moved away. Karnow and Machin stood together, glaring.

At last Machin dropped his eyes. "All right," he said. "All right. I deserved that."

Karnow stood with his short booted legs set apart, on the edge of the chasm and looking out over the scene of the disaster, and he was still and wrapped in concentration. When he spoke his voice was different. "I got conscience too, Alex. Yeah, I got more than you believe, more than I ever thought." He was quiet, words breaking thickly from his throat and caught on the slow wind. The tough, scarred head moved, seeking. "You know I've never fallen down on a job yet, never lost out on a schedule?"

"Yes, I know that."

"This means something to a guy like me. Pride in a job, building up a reputation—that's goddam life to me, that's most all there is. . . . Y'know, no family . . . too late to do anything about that now. . . ."

Machin said suddenly, "What is it, Jerry?"

Karnow was caught in some thought. Then he said, "I just realized a man don't know where his own decisions come from. He thinks he makes them clearly in his mind, out of the known facts —but now I'm not so sure. I guess there's something in what these psychiatrists say—there's one helluva lot down below the surface. Sonofabitch iceberg men, that's us."

"So?"

Karnow pulled his fur collar about his neck. "When I agreed to write off these poor guys down under, I believed it was the right thing to do, knowing the whole circumstances and thinking it all over, just a clear and reasonable decision which only fool sentimentalists would condemn. . . . Now I guess I couldn't see clearly at all, I'm beginning to change my mind. . . . I'm no religious man, not been to church for twenty years, but I'll say pride's a stinkin' sin, sure enough. . . ."

"There are worse ones. I've got my share." Machin watched him with no more anger, with only emptiness. Below and beside them the chunks of rock clattered and tumbled to the dumps, a brittle, slithering noise with its associations of falling, of destruction.

Karnow stepped back from the edge, turning to Machin. "You reckon we'll get to them in time?"

"No," Machin said. He added slowly, "But at least we'll have done all we could."

"Not in the mind," Karnow said harshly. "Not in the mind." And again he turned away.

Machin gazed at him, seeing within the hard, stocky frame a degree of sensitivity he had not met before in ten years of acquaintance.

Karnow's tone changed. "Here comes Vasnetsov."

The Russian walked across the site to join them. He wore still the suit of overalls, and his broad face was dirty with clay and grease. He said, "It seems we are getting down close to the hut. Mr. Radford wishes to stop the machine excavation and continue by manual labour only."

Karnow nodded carefully. "We'll have to. Otherwise there'll be a fall-in, that's ten million to one."

Vasnetsov suggested, "I would think the odds would be the same in either case. For if we go on by hand labour, it will take so long that the men will be dead for sure."

Karnow breathed out heavily, like a giant expiring. He seemed to deflate with the sigh, his barrel chest contracting. He stared down into the chasm. Much of the ground was clear: the one great pile of fallen rock remained over the site of the timekeeper's hut, against one wall of the fissure. And still the frail thread of telephone cable led through. "We'll stop the machines," he said finally.

Machin glanced at Vasnetsov, expecting him to protest: for with the continued use of the mechanical excavators, at least all would be over quickly and filling-in of the chasm could be carried out: whereas use of manual labour would only prolong the slow death and futility. But Vasnetsov merely shrugged.

Radford came across, lean and made haggard by the choice confronting them. "What's it to be?"

"You reckon you've gone down as far as you dare?" Karnow questioned him grimly.

"Sure thing. Already we've got signs of a shift. I don't like it——"

"How much further d'you guess?"

"I'd say about forty feet to the roof of the hut."

Karnow sucked in his breath. "All rock?"

"Seems so. Mostly big stuff now—it's getting a tricky job with the shovels anyway. Lousy great boulders, the way you can see——" He gestured to the drag-lines.

Karnow spread his hand low. "Cut them. Get the gangs on the job—and Jees, tell them to take it careful."

"Right." Radford strode away. The booms of the machines came up; crawling, the excavators began to retreat from the pile, dark ugly monsters, the last stones dripping from their jaws. The noise of their motors died into silence. The pile of rock lay deserted and still unbreached, offering no hint of the men who lay buried within. It was quiet after the racket of engines; then the working gangs went forward, and the clash of pick and the judder of the drills echoed up from the resounding walls.

Karnow, Vasnetsov and Machin stood in a small group, gazing down. Karnow gripped Machin's arm. "I went back to repair that phone connection, but found you'd beaten me to it. . . . Any more news over the wire?"

"I haven't heard."

"Find out, will you?"

"Yes." Machin tramped through the mess of the river bed to the office. There was a man attending the phone again; he raised a worried dark face to Machin. "No answer, sir."

Machin grabbed the receiver. The line was still open. "Hayat," he said. There was no reply. He called out again, and then shouted. But still there was no reply.

Then he thought he heard some exclamation, or a moan. He shouted into the microphone again, pressing his hand against his other ear to close off all other sounds. Then faintly, he heard tired breathing coming over the line, dragged-out breathing like that of an old man. . . . Again he spoke loudly into the microphone, but again there was no answer.

Machin swallowed. Finally he gave back the handset to the Punjabi, without meeting his eyes. "Keep listening."

"Yes, Mr. Machin." He agreed uneasily.

Machin walked outside and stood in the chill evening air.

The sky faded to darkness as he stood there, and the arc-lamps burned up into angry light once more, garish brilliance over the area. The walls of the gorge, the sky and land about, all were gone; just this one lighted spot, the heap of rock with the antlike, struggling figures; and all around the hush, and the dark.

And so it was through all the night, the muffled sound of the striking tools, the occasional bursts of drilling, the tumbling stones. Men came off shift, warmed themselves at the braziers and took hot drinks, dark and white faces gleaming in the night, in the firelight; and the invisible heights of rock beyond, and silence beyond.

Every few hours Machin went back to the telephone, and shouted down into the moist diaphragm, shouted loudly enough even to reach the men below without need for wires. . . . But there was never any reply, and now he could no longer hear that slow breathing. And finally he went back to the site, and waited for the tardy dawn to come up in the sky, and for the lights which glared over the rock to pale. . . .

At last the morning came. He stood helplessly waiting as the day grew brighter. Thursday. . . . He had promised Hayat that rescue would come by the previous evening. And rescue had not arrived; but had release. . . ?

Sasha Bucar approached him. "Mr. Machin?"

"What?"

Bucar pointed with a long, thin arm. "A woman is causing trouble—over by the entrance to the site. She says she's the wife of one of the men down there, she wishes to come across and see what is happening, but they are keeping her away. A Mrs. Hayat. . . ."

Machin stirred painfully. "What's that to do with me?"

"I wondered if you might wish to talk to her." Bucar spoke with the same toneless, stiff English of Vasnetsov.

"Why the hell should I?"

Bucar spread his hands. "You're right. There is nothing we can do—she must wait."

They stood together for a while. Machin glanced restively across to the service road entry. Among the overalled men who were grouped around, he thought he could distinguish the brighter dress of a woman. But indeed there was nothing he could do for her, and he could not face another encounter.

He said uneasily to Bucar, "Time is going, going. . . . I think there's no chance now."

Bucar nodded. "I know, Mr. Machin. . . . You still want to continue?"

"Until we're sure——"

"They're not now answering?"

"I'm afraid they're unconscious. The end's not certain yet. At least we shall have tried. . . . I suppose you support your boss in the line he took. But naturally, you have to. . . ."

Bucar's gloomy face showed more melancholy. "A construction work like this is a campaign, planned like a battle in wartime. It is not possible to escape losses—one regrets them sincerely." He touched his heart. "But one cannot let them destroy the overall plan."

"That's the way Karnow spoke." Machin said bitterly. "Myself, I wish I could accept that argument. I can't—it's not a war, and life is more important than money." But his voice was empty and without fire. He was still hearing that choked, dying breathing over the line, now silent. "Ah, hell," he said violently again. "So long as it's not themselves. That's all anybody cares. Look after number one——"

"I would not say that, Mr. Machin." Bucar was careful.

"That's *just* what I'd say."

Bucar broke away, gesturing suddenly. Over at the excavation site something was happening: the men were collected together, staring down at the fall. The drills and picks had ceased work: there came a chatter of voices.

Machin ran forward, Bucar beside him. They joined Karnow and Vasnetsov.

Below, the working gang had dug deeper into the pile, penetrating lower into the stone and rock. Now they were staring at the spot where the telephone cable dropped sloping downwards to the hut: the surrounding material had been cleared and a crack was revealed, a black gap among the yellow and drab lumps of rock, like a hole. . . .

A man came running down the ramp into the chasm, bringing a battery hand-lamp. Radford grabbed it; he clambered over the rock and stuck his head and shoulders into the cranny where the cable led through. The lamp gleamed inside.

Karnow shouted out. "Everybody stay back—that's an order." Then he ran for the road below, and Vasnetsov, Machin and Bucar followed him. They reached the base of the fall. Karnow shouted again. "Everybody off!"

The workgangs withdrew to the floor of the chasm. Karnow picked his way like a great agile ape up the side of the fall, and the others came after him. They reached the summit, the telephone cable and the hole. Radford pulled himself out, grimy-faced; he switched off the lamp.

Karnow demanded, "Well? What is it?"

Radford said slowly, "I don't know. Some kind of a gap, a shaft almost, right where the line goes through. You can see several feet down. It goes quite a way——"

Karnow grabbed the lamp. "Gimme." He flicked on the beam and stuck his own broad shoulders into the hole. The others crowded round; the light of the lamp waved and moved, down inside. At last Karnow pulled himself out. He passed the lamp to Machin.

Vasnetsov snapped, "I wish to see——"

"My turn first." Machin lowered himself into the gap. The lamp probed the darkness, and then he exclaimed while the blood rushed to his head; because this was more than some small airgap in the rocks caused by the loose piling of the boulders: the beam darted down, and the rock walls lined its path along the curve of the telephone cable, and this was a narrow crevice, almost some kind of a freak tunnel, formed through the natural heaping of the boulders. And it led ten or eleven feet down, and then the line deviated around a projection of rock, and the beam would penetrate no farther.

Machin heaved himself out. Vasnetsov took the lamp and peered down, and Bucar followed him.

They sprawled on the top of the rock while the working gang watched from above them, from the edge of the chasm. Karnow said finally, "Well?"

Vasnetsov spread his hands. "A chance irregularity in the fall. The hut is—how far below us?"

Radford said, "About thirty-odd feet."

Vasnetsov pulled down his mouth. "We can hardly hope for any passage through, to continue that far. It's quite impossible——"

"No doubt," Karnow snapped. "All the same, somebody could go in and take a look. . . ." He swung on Machin. "What's the latest?"

"Still no reply on the line. No good deceiving anyone—they're either unconscious or dead." He glanced at Vasnetsov, but saw only a suspended uncertainty.

"You agree it's worth a chance, Alex?"

"Yes—while we're going on. Though now it's a lost hope."

Karnow said expressionlessly, "We're going on."

"Yes." Surprisingly, Vasnetsov nodded. "We shall go on. . . ."

Karnow turned to Radford. "What's your opinion, Bill?"

Radford pushed forward. "I'll go down. I'll find out how far it travels."

"No," Machin interrupted. "It's for me. I'll try." At last there was something he could drive himself into, vain the chance. . . . "I want to."

"You can both forget it." Karnow said roughly, "*I'm* going."

"You?" Machin said. "You're too damned fat—you couldn't even get inside, Jerry."

Karnow glared at him. Vasnetsov spoke quickly. "There is no need for discussion. *I* shall see what lies below."

Karnow swore. "This is no time for cheap political gestures. We've no time for playing to the crowd." He pointed up to the swarm of Pakistanis who watched.

The first, flaring anger burned on Vasnetsov's pale face.

"That is most unworthy of you. It's my personal wish to go. I have been accused of the intention to murder—at least I shall do all I can."

"We've no time for individual satisfactions or vanities either." Machin repeated, "I'll do it. For God's sake let's stop arguing." He reached for the lamp.

Karnow knocked his hand aside. "Keep out of this, Alex. And you too, Bill. We'll leave it between Vasnetsov and myself——"

Radford said again, quickly, "You're both too broad-shouldered, Mr. Karnow.

"Not enough to make any difference." Karnow eyed Vasnetsov. "I'm going."

"*I* am Project Manager."

"Then you're too goddam big a noise to go crawling in dirty rat-holes——"

They stared at one another. Then Vasnetsov said, "Very well, Mr. Karnow. If it means so much to you, go and see what you can do. I'm afraid you risk yourself without hope." But now his anger had gone, and there was something like understanding between them.

Radford yelled for a coil of light rope. Karnow tied one end around his waist; he took the lamp in one hand and fixed a pick head to the rope. Then he crawled over the edge of the hole and lowered himself in headfirst. His thick body squeezed through the aperture; his heels waved and slowly he disappeared into the darkness, along the line of the cable.

Another lamp had been brought up, and they flooded the crevice with light, watching him go. The rope paid out gradually, foot by foot; the gap was so narrow that Karnow was jammed against the sides like a cork through a bottleneck, and the telephone cable and rope were pressed tightly against the rock faces.

Radford muttered, "He's crazy. He'll get stuck." He was unsteady with apprehension. Vasnetsov stared down, his dark, acute eyes unflickering into the depths.

Bucar said, "It cannot go any farther. There's no chance, no chance at all. . . . How is he going to crawl back? We'll not be able to pull. . . . Yes, he is crazy."

The same fear seized Machin and he trembled. And despite it all he would sooner have been down there, doing something in expiation, than here restlessly and jaggedly waiting. . . . God, they all felt guilt, and they all wanted release. . . .

The paying-out of the line ceased. Karnow's large, metal-tipped boots were all that showed, unmoving at the end of the tunnel.

Machin whispered stupidly, "His shoes alone are big enough to trap him." Then they heard the chink of steel against stone.

Radford cursed. "Useless, useless. . . . He's only got a toothpick, against this stuff." And savagely he thumped the cold rock.

Then the line began moving again. The body down below wriggled forward; the feet strained, and then it drew itself out of sight, around a protruding shoulder, following the bend of the cable. The beam of the lamp showed only the empty crack in the rocks where the great fallen boulders bulged out.

Now they were sure he was done. There would be no room for him to turn, no way for him to crawl backwards up to the day.

He was lost in a dark, tight chimney of rock. Radford gripped the rope desperately, and then released it. "Fool," he said. "Fool. . . ."

Vasnetsov and Bucar talked quickly together. Vasnetsov pressed his lips, munching at them. Machin squatted dully still, waiting. He lifted his eyes to the men on the edge of the chasm, and they too were waiting, locked in the suspense.

A voice called out softly to him. "May I come?" It was Husain Iqbal. Machin beckoned, and Iqbal ran down the slope and climbed to join them.

He asked anxiously, "It's Mr. Karnow?"

"Yes."

"He'll be trapped himself. . . . He'll be dead." Iqbal stared worriedly at the narrow hole.

"I know."

"This is terrible."

"He wanted to try," Machin said.

Iqbal's eyes fell away from him. "This is a horrible affair all round. So shocking, so disastrous. I wish it were over——"

"Don't we all?"

Vasnetsov demanded, "Quiet."

They listened, and again dimly from the depths they heard the chinking of metal against stone. And then again slowly, the rope began to slide down.

Bucar gasped. "The gap must go farther. Unbelievable, the most freakish fall. . . ."

Radford said grimly, "It's got to go a long way yet." Then they sat still again, and waited.

The morning continued as grey clouds scudded the sky high above. Inch by inch the rope was drawn down. Machin said harshly, "It's no good. No bloody good at all. He'll never get back again. . . . Even if he chewed a way down with his own teeth, we'd never get the others through. . . . But he won't, he'll get stuck and pass out, it's just a bloody, useless waste." And he clenched his hands, and shivered. "*I* should have tried, the job would go on without me——"

Vasnetsov said, "Keep quiet, Mr. Machin."

And again they waited. All was still over the site, with no movement, just the occasional, anxious shifting of men.

Machin asked, "How much rope has he had?"

Radford checked, and his eyes widened. "Over twenty feet."

"That's a long way down."

"You're telling me, it is."

Machin glanced at his watch. "They'll be dead anyway. Five dead men, waiting for him. . . . God, it's mad, mad."

"Keep quiet," Vasnetsov said again.

Machin pulled himself together at last. There was no more fear, because he had spent it all. Just this slow waiting.

And still the rope drew itself down, inch by inch, winding incredibly into that hard, solid-looking mound of rock, over smooth plane and sharp edge, into darkness, into airlessness, down, down. . . .

Bucar repeated, "He'll be done."

Husain Iqbal was solemn. "If he succeeds, it will be the work of God——"

"To die down there among the others? Where's God's purpose in that?" Machin choked derision.

Radford said astoundedly, "Thirty feet. . . ."

Vasnetsov shook a bewildered head. "I would not have believed it possible. Such a rare, unexpected formation. . . ."

Machin said desperately, "Karnow's a tough guy. He's probably carving his own way through, the way I told you."

The telephone cable twitched, drew taut, then relaxed. The rope drew out a further inch.

Machin raised his eyes briefly and looked up once more, at the rock sides of the chasm which rose above them, at the silent, peering watchers on the rim, against the murky sky. Then he stared back helplessly into the hole.

And then they heard it, and felt it beneath them: a quiver, a fragile shifting in the pile, the faint noise of grating stone which drifted up the tunnel. A puff of air and dust founted over them. And then silence settled again.

They stared at one another with shocked faces. Nobody spoke. At last, fearfully, Radford reached out for the lines. He pulled gently at the telephone cable and it still held firm. But when he tugged at the rope it slid back easily, loosely and without weight on its far end. . . .

Machin swallowed. He said slowly, "We'd better get the gangs back on the job—fast. But they'll never find him alive."

Radford brushed dirty sweat from his face. "Why didn't he let me go. . . ." His voice shook.

Vasnetsov put a hand on Radford's shoulder. He climbed carefully to his feet, and he too was stricken. "I——"

His words were swamped by an outburst of noise from the rim of the fissure above: they gazed upwards, and the Pakistani from the office stood on the edge, rolling-eyed, arms waving. "The telephone," he shouted. "The telephone. . . . It is ringing again."

Machin scrambled down the rock heap for the exit ramp, and the others came after him. He rushed for the office, yelling at the Pakistani. "Didn't you answer?"

"Sir, I was too frightened." The man trotted beside him.

Machin plunged inside the office. At the phone he hesitated for an instant, and then he grabbed for the receiver, fumbled, lifted it to his ear. The others clustered around him. He struggled for speech. Something broke out. "Yes. . . . Yes. . . . Who is it?"

The voice which answered croaked like his own. "Alex? . . . I guess I made it. . . ."

## CHAPTER SIX

MACHIN stared up wildly from the phone. "Karnow———"

Vasnetsov demanded urgently, "He's through?" He gabbled in Russian, dumbfounded. Bucar's shaggy eyebrows shot high. Iqbal's face was petrified.

Radford muttered dazedly, "How could he get in?"

Machin choked. "Hell—how did you manage———"

"Just the way it went. . . ." Karnow spoke with difficulty, panting. "Structures full of holes—luck, I got through, one to the other. Jees, how this telephone cable stood up to it———" He broke off, coughing.

Machin said, "We heard the fall———"

"Yeah. Came on me just as I reached. . . . I knocked out the window a bit more and crawled in. . . ." Karnow's constricted voice dropped lower. "They're all dead. Not a spark of life in any of them. It's goddam thick down here———"

Machin sucked in his breath. "Hell, Jerry———" He looked up at the others. "They're all dead." A wave of great anguish swept him. "Dead. After all this———"

"I knew it." But Vasnetsov spoke with only despair. Husain Iqbal groaned and Radford swore loosely. For a moment they stood, still caught in the shock.

Machin said, "How long can you last, Jerry?"

"Not long. Not long at all, boy. . . ."

"We'll get you out———"

Karnow muttered, "No use. . . . It's packed down now, there's no climb back. That's the way it is."

Machin turned to the others again. "He's done. The gap's fallen in."

Vasnetsov said softly, "There may still be a path through from the top. I shall try." He was calm and serious.

"If anyone goes again, I do." Machin spoke rapidly into the telephone. "It's your turn to hang on, Jerry. We're going to have another try down your tunnel——"

"No." Karnow's voice burst out from the receiver loud enough for the other men in the room to hear. "Don't waste your time. There's no way through, I tell you. Just forget it——"

"Are you insane? Listen, Jerry, we'll get you out——"

"I tell you, no." Karnow ground out the words from the blackness below, from the dead foetid hut. "Jees, I won't have it. Listen, Alex, you know what I said before. I was gonna leave these unlucky bastards to the worms because the job needed it, because they were done. Listen, that goes for me too. I ain't got a chance, you're gonna lose no time on me either. Just you call it off and get on with the job, the way I said. I mean that, I'm telling you——" He gasped out the words, wheezing.

Machin shouted, "Leave out the heroics, Jerry. No self-sacrifice stuff——"

"Jees, will you do as I say. I'm telling you again, I'll never get out of here alive. So get on with it and to moses with the rest. Listen, I still got my pride——"

"Pride? God, you'd die for that. . . ? Jerry, you changed your mind about Hayat and the others. You know you did—you realized they were worth more than the job after all. . . ."

"If there was a chance. Here, there's no crappin' chance. . . ." Karnow croaked, "Get on with the job. Cement us in. I guess if we got souls after all, they'll get away through seventy feet of concrete. . . ." And he tried to chuckle. "Now leave me alone, Alex."

Machin shouted again, "We're coming down to find you, Jerry. We're coming." Then he rammed the handset back on the rest. He stared grimly at the others. "He told us to leave him down there. But I'm going in to try——"

Vasnetsov stated, "*I* wish to go, Mr. Machin."

"He's my boss. This is *my* job."

"We argued before. Please—I ask it."

"Why?"

Vasnetsov said quietly, "Not for personal justification after all, Mr. Machin. But because I think it is owed, the fitting thing."

Machin looked at him. Then he spoke rapidly. "All right. Then we'll both go——" He turned to Radford. "Ring him again when we're on our way. Tell him to hang on——"

He brushed past Radford's dubious face, and ran for the doorway with Vasnetsov lumbering after him.

Vasnetsov said, "We'll take an air drill."

Machin stopped, aghast. "God, no. . . . Even if we could get it down. . . . We'd bring the whole bloody lot in on us."

"It's hazardous. But there's no other possibility of clearing a passage——"

Machin stared, quickened by abrupt fear despite himself. Then he nodded sharply. They went on towards the fall, and he yelled for drill and compressor to be brought up. They stood above the entrance to the crevice; again the handlamp beam illuminated the nearer depths.

Machin stripped off his coat; they stood in the cold air. Iqbal said anxiously, "Be very careful."

Machin shrugged. Vasnetsov took up the drill with its cumbersome coil of tubing. Machin said, "I'm going first."

Vasnetsov shook his head. "Please."

Machin hesitated, and then he waved Vasnetsov to the hole. Vasnetsov climbed bulkily over the edge, lowering the drill in front of him; Machin followed with the rope around him, easing the rubber tubing over the rock. Each had a lamp; the beams shifted over the hard surfaces of stone, seeking down.

Slowly they began to crawl ahead. The last glow of daylight died behind them. Vasnetsov's big, sweaty body dragged itself down the sloping gap in front of Machin. There was the scraping of the drill over the rock, the puffing of Vasnetsov's breath, the tearing of jagged rock against their clothing and against their bodies. The air grew heavy and starved. For a few feet the crevice ran direct, along the line of the cable; and then they reached the bend, the gap between two boulders where Karnow had chipped himself a narrow entry. Vasnetsov struggled, and then his broad body eased itself through. Machin came after.

The cleft dropped vertical; Vasnetsov lowered the drill and then swung himself down. Again they went on, where the thin sheathed telephone cable penetrated into the dark. Machin muttered, "All right?"

"Yes," Vasnetsov replied. "This is incredible. . . ." The devious path through the fallen rock went on, down and down, between sharp, flaking surfaces of stone. The airline stretched out behind them; at any moment Machin expected it or the rope to snare at some twist in their route. The fear in him grew deeper, a claustrophobic dread of these tight, encompassing walls, fear of the death to which they went in the dark, in the dusty, trapped air. And then the thought of Karnow, below.

Vasnetsov seemed less beset by the imagination; his stocky form drew itself on, squeezing betwen packed boulders which might settle down at each moment and crush him into a bloody mess, slowly onward as the torchbeam flared ahead. Down, down. . . . Machin examined the illuminated dial of his watch, and the time was one-thirty. They had been inside for an hour: surely it could not last much longer. . . .

Vasnetsov exclaimed. For a while he lay still.

"What is it?"

Vasnetsov said, "We've reached the blockage."

Machin drew himself up, across Vasnetsov's legs. He peered over his shoulder and saw the end of the crevice, the fall which had trapped Karnow down below. There was no way through.

Vasnetsov wriggled on for a few inches. He shone the lamp through a small gap in the rock: and the light gleamed on broken white wood and felting, the roof of the hut. . . .

Vasnetsov was silent. Then slowly, he pushed forward the air drill. He said over his shoulder, "Well?"

Machin stared around them, at the unstable mass of rocks which might shift and move at any noise or vibration. . . . At last he said steadily, "All right then. Get it over——"

Vasnetsov muttered something, and whether it was a prayer or a curse Machin did not know.

Then the stuttering, violent noise of the drill broke loose, the breaking of the rock, splintering of chips, stone-dust and choking air and a booming, resounding echo down the tunnel; tight, deafening pressure on the shrinking ear-drums.

Silence. Vasnetsov moved forward a little. Then the strident noise and disturbance, the onslaught started again. Then again came silence.

Vasnetsov let go of the drill; at last they dare breathe again, could acknowledge they still lived. The beam of the lamp struggled through the gritty air and the dust. Vasnetsov pulled himself forward again. Then he spoke thickly to Machin. "We're through." A throaty, almost animal voice called out beneath them. They kicked out the broken wood of the roof and lowered themselves through into the hut.

A beam of light covered them. Karnow said, "Jees . . . Jees . . ." He stepped uncertainly towards them. The air was foul, and at the other end of the twisted hut lay the five still bodies in attitudes like sleeping men.

Karnow hung on their arms, wordlessly. Vasnetsov said, "Now we must get back." Lungs strained at the lifeless air. He glanced at the bodies. "You're sure they're dead?"

Karnow nodded. "Another hour and I'd have been among them." He gulped.

Vasnetsov said, "I'll let them know above." He stepped through the darkness to the phone, listened, then dropped the receiver. "The line is dead. We must have broken it on the way down."

Karnow struggled to speak. "You reckon we can get back?"

"Come on."

Machin stared for a while at the dead men on the floor. His torchbeam flickered over them: the one in the shirt and trousers would be Rafiq Hayat, the soft-voiced, the wronged. He could not see the face; he did not want to see it. For a moment, amid all the darkness and faintness and the headache which struck him like fists at his temples, amid his own urgent fear, remorse struck him more cruelly than these. Then he turned away.

They pulled themselves up to the roof and entered the crevice again. Vasnetsov went first, Karnow next and Machin followed last. The climb upwards was more difficult than the descent had been; the air was thicker and Karnow was a weak man, only semi-conscious; between them they had to pull and push him through the gaps in the rock.

Halfway up, Karnow slipped and his feet struck the side of the passage; a loose boulder fell out and bounced lower. Something shifted behind it, and again they felt it tremble in the pile. Grit and dust swarmed up to them and they lay motionless. Machin flashed the lamp behind and beneath them, and a new fall had closed off the passage once more. Ahead, the way was still clear. Slowly they dragged themselves upward.

At last they crawled between the jags of rock, and they were in the uppermost pocket. The air was fresher, and there was a grey gleam of day. For a while they could not stir. Karnow was muttering dazedly.

Then a shout came from above; lights shone down into the hole, finding them. Radford swung himself inside to help. Gradually they dragged themselves up the rest of the way, their heads poking like blind moles' skulls into the harsh glare, into air, into a vast, wild roar of relief which went up from the waiting crowd.

Then the cheering died into silence as Vasnetsov staggered to his feet; he pointed downwards into the hole from which they had crawled and spread his hands wide in a gesture indicating finish, indicating death and the dead who lay below.

\* \* \*

A pallid yellow morning sun broke the dull overcast, and the same chill wind roamed the dam site. Down from the cement mixing-plant sped the rail trucks, down to the bay where the cranes grabbed the buckets and swung them over the site; downward again to the chasm. Most of the fissure had been sealed, the cement grouted in. Now here where the wreckage of the hut lay, the last loads were falling. . . .

The dam site was quiet again, the men still waiting. The pile-driving hammers were ready, the drills and excavators. As soon as this last job was done the rush to work, the frantic effort to complete the coffer dam and beat this tide of falling days towards the spring and thaw, would be under way. But in this moment, silence as at the entombment of the dead. . . .

Men spoke in hushed voices; they coughed, shuffled their feet. All were watching, Pakistanis, Europeans, with fixed faces. The buckets came down, swaying gently on the fall-lines.

Vasnetsov and Bucar, Karnow and Machin, these stood in a group on the edge of the chasm, a small way distant from the others, gazing down. Husain Iqbal was with them. They were close together and yet each one was set apart, sunk in his own thoughts. They looked downward, faces deep in upturned collars, heads bare.

From the far side of the site came a wailing, shrieking lamentation. A woman burst from the waiting crowd and ran wildly, barefooted over the rocky bed, towards the chasm. Machin gazed across, and she was Nurjehan Hayat. . . . She came frantic and screaming, hands waving and long black hair loose, the robe billowing out behind her; her face was contorted and she rushed for the edge of the fissure in some hysterical bid for destruction within the pit. The look on her face was like madness. . . . A few yards from the edge a Pakistani foreman caught her and she was dragged back to the roadway, still screaming. . . .

A shudder struck through Machin, and the others stirred with him. Again they turned to the chasm, and watched the buckets approach. The slow wind moved against their faces, blowing down from the bleak rim of the gorge. Each man had his own thoughts whispering within his brain, sounding in his throat and then breaking harshly as words from his mouth: words which were audible and yet heard only by the speaker, because each had ears only for his own confession. . . .

It was over and done, the end had arrived, the finish which could never have been avoided since the landslip had taken place. Write it off as fate or act of God for the unlucky, as experience for the alive. . . . Experience? They had learned something, these last few days had altered them? No. . . . They were still ordinary men, incomplete, variable, swayed by impulses they did not understand and weaknesses they could not control, flaws and fractures. Indoctrinated, prejudiced, confused. . . . If a similar thing happened again they would react similarly, out of evil and out of good, compulsively. Nothing had been learned, nothing gained from defeat. There was no moral, no benefit, only waste and loss. And yet even so——

Vasnetsov said dully, "I am guilty. . . . I was not truly thinking of the majority good, but of my own prestige. The bosses may acclaim, but a man is responsible primarily to his *own* conscience. . . . I must remember that."

Karnow said, "Lucky it's not *me* under that lot. Jees, I deserved it. I'll never talk of expediency again. I'll trade one life for every lousy dam in the world. I'll never fool myself again. . . ."

Machin said, "I'm guilty. I'll remember this moment all my life. I'll drive myself day and night until I'm clean, until I've returned good for bad. . . ."

Husain Iqbal said, "All men are much the same, wherever they come from, and they have mixed qualities and tendencies within them. It's up to the individual man, which may prevail. *God be with you who are dead.* . . . I shall judge no man unless I know him like a brother. . . ."

The wind carried away the low whisper of their voices as they stood in a line along the edge of the chasm, swirling away their promises into the skies. Then the buckets tilted: the cement went down below, thick and wet, slurping over the rock and the stones.